Lost Histories

ISBN: 9798991779319
Ebook: 9798991779302

This book is a work of fiction, inspired by people, events, and locations of real history. However the people, events, and locations have been fictionalized to suit the world and story. Other characters, events, and locations are products of the author's imagination. The views within this story do not necessarily reflect the views of the author, their LLC, their editor, or artists.

Cover Art by Aspen Garner
Map Art by Kyle Cavazos
Internal Design by Victoria Bryan

To Dad, wish you could've seen this

A Word From the Author

Let me start with my uttermost gratitude to you, dear reader, for picking up this copy of *Lost Histories*. This book has been the culmination of many years of writing, rewriting, more rewriting, study, and research.

I wanted to share with you some of that research and the inspiration for the book before you begin. Initially, *Lost Histories* was meant to be an "alternate history-high fantasy" heavily based on our world with fantastical elements. This idea remained in effect for a good portion of the rewriting process. Because of this, both the physical and political geography of the world is similar to our own, albeit in the 17th century. The history is also similar with certain events taking place around the same time as they did in our world. However as the scope of the story grew, calling it an alternate history became less and less feasible, as the divergent point for where real history starts and alternate history begins, would go back to before recorded history. It would have gone back to before mammals even evolved.

So, do not think of this as an alternate history, but an alternate world. An earth much like ours, but different in its own way. I am a firm believer in the importance of history and that many times, history is more fantastic than fiction, so I have kept the inspirations and some of the geography from the early drafts, while also changing it to suit the needs and world of the story. So in reading, you will encounter characters and events similar to real world history, such as Karalthergroz and Ziurin Ludher, and while they occupy a role similar to their real-world counterparts, how they got there and what they did, is different.

Continuing from this is an important note; I am neither a linguist nor a philologist, but I find both subjects utterly fascinating. Though this fascination is halted by English being the *only* language I can fluently and clearly speak and write. Because of this shortfall, I must use real-world languages in place of fictional ones. I would like to make one important distinction; the languages the characters speak are *not* real-world languages but are represented by real-world languages. For example, the main ecclesiastic, proper, upper-class language of this world is known as High Rinnish, which is represented, often in italics, with German. In-universe, High Rinnish would not bear any resemblance to modern or even early modern German but is instead more of a mix of Old Frisian and Old Norse.

Likewise, this world is also one not graced by the Roman Empire and where Latin is nearly non-existent (to a certain degree as you'll find out). This is a problem, as English has heavy Latin influences; everything from vegetable to soldier to coin all has Latin roots. This presented quite the conundrum as why would characters who speak a Germanic-esque language have so many Latin-inspired words in their speech? To get around this, I researched and borrowed from scholars and enthusiasts who have worked on something called 'Anglish,' which is English using few to almost no Latin or non-Germanic words. Though, in using Anglish, I had to find a good balance of worldbuilding and easy readability. So, in the course of our characters travels, they will come across many new words, words recombined into new uses, and other words reused in place of Latinate ones. For example, churchgoers "beseech" instead of pray. The dead are burned on "deadheaps" rather than pyres. And kings are "helmed" rather than crowned. A glossary will be provided in the back of the book, and footnotes are included in sections where an explanation may be needed, but the characters are unable to provide one without halting the story. I do ask for forgiveness in areas where I had to use words that crossed a cultural divide. Sometimes in English, certain words are, as the French would say, *Le mot juste*.

That's all for now! I hope you enjoy the book!

Thank You,

Calvin Lionel Edwards

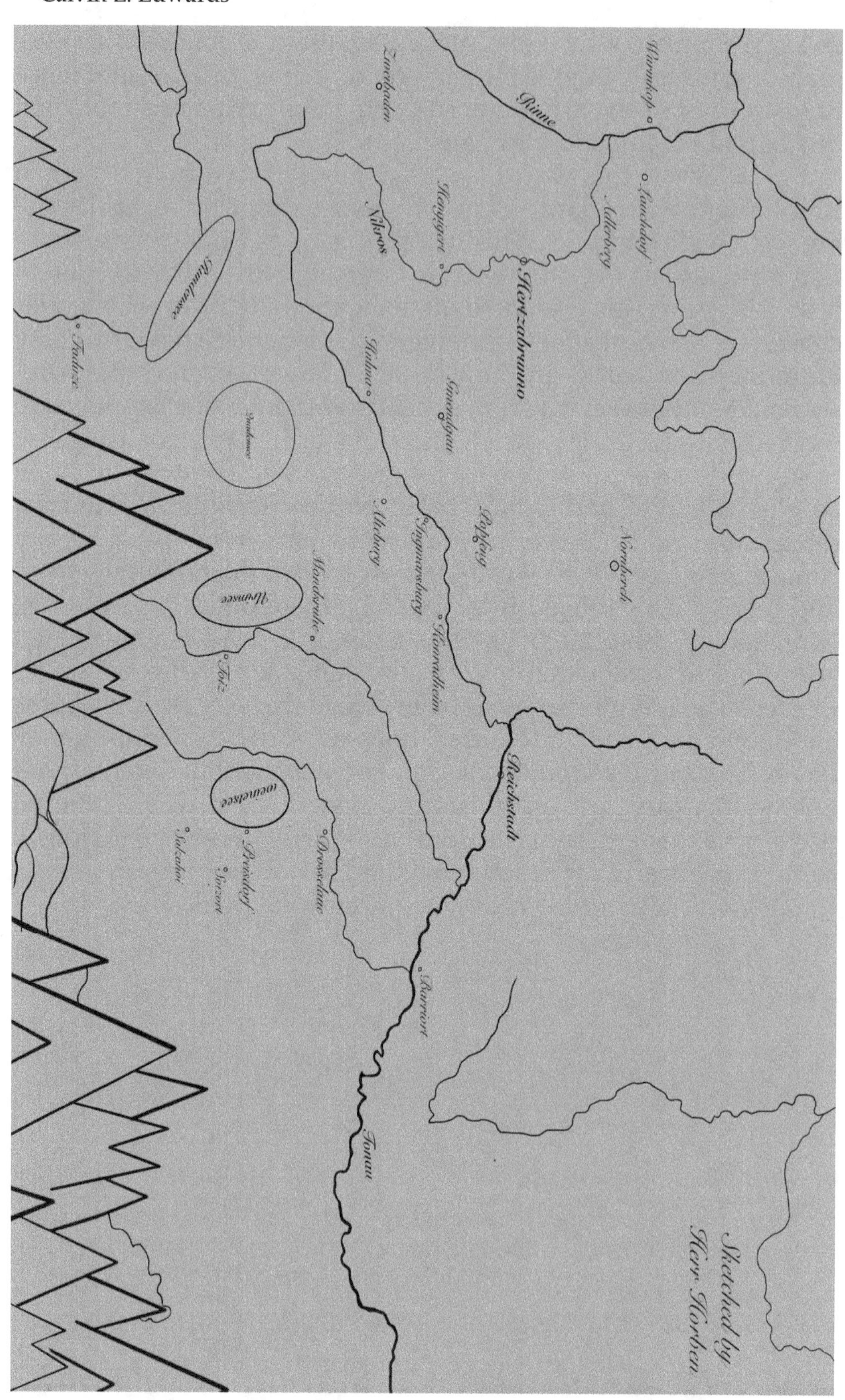
Rinne
Zweibaden
Adlerberg
Hertzabrunno
Nikros
Kulme
Alteburg
Konradheim
Mondsruhe
Reichstadt
Preisdorf
Tonau
Sketched by
Herr Horben

Part 1:

As Below

1

"Alright Friedrich, up and at 'em. The caves wait for no man." Herr Bergmann kicked his fellow who was still curled up in his sleeping bag. "I've got bacon and potatoes frying on the fire. Get your fill; we won't have time for a proper mid-meal."

Friedrich Bauer rubbed his eyes and crawled out of his sleeping bag. He lumbered over to a nearby log and put on his boots, double-checking to make sure they were on the correct feet. Herr Bergmann passed him a tin plate with food, Friedrich struggling to stay awake as he ate. Sunlight was barely breaking through the tops of the trees surrounding them, lighting the nearby mountains like a stained-glass window. The crisp air was fresh and sharp; the scent of pine and fir mixed with the smoke of their campfire. *This was the life,* both silently agreed.

"The Weiße Hügel always look their best in the summer I always say," Herr Bergmann commented between bites. "It always amazes me how the tallest ones still have snow on them." Friedrich muttered some kind of affirmation as he shoveled food into his mouth. They had camped in the midst of a forest just at the foot of the mountains. This range, properly called the Weiße Hügel, or White Hills, was the mightiest range in Erebus, striking upwards as they graced the clouds. Herr Bergmann stared at their peaks wistfully as Friedrich began stabbing at his food with a dagger. "Friedrich!" he chided. "Use a fork like a tame man."

"I'm just trying to use the birthday gift *you* gave me," he defended. Bergmann rolled his eyes. The dagger in question had been a gift Friedrich received over a year ago. It was an exquisite piece of equipment, imported from the finest craftsmen of Viteliú (though the design was Bythoner in origin) with a flawless, gleaming blade almost two fingers long and a handle composed of one part deer antler and one part beech wood. As evident by his eating habit, Friedrich always had it in his hand. "I'll eat like a tame man when you eat like one." He laughed.

Bergmann had a peculiar way of eating. He would lean forward, tucking his chin towards his chest so grease or crumbs wouldn't fall into his carefully maintained, greying beard. It was the last bit of hair he could grow, and he was proud of it. "I am eating like a tame man. A gentleman takes care not to spill on himself," Bergmann shot back.

"Aside from when he drinks." Friedrich grinned. Bergmann rolled his eyes again. Friedrich would never let him hear the end of their misadventure in Karlstadt several years ago.

"Hurry up and wash your plate off. We've still got a bit of a hike before we get to the Toller Mund." Friedrich wiped his dagger off on his trousers before returning it to the sheathe. He wolfed down the last of his food, then jogged over to a small stream to clean off his dishes. Bergmann stamped out the fire before he began rolling up his bedroll. Friedrich followed suit, securing his bedroll and bringing it over to their pack mule. He affectionately scratched the creature between the ears before offering it a carrot.

"Do you want to lead Greatness?" Bergmann asked as he secured his bag to the mule's load.

Friedrich added his own belongings to the load. "Are you sure you don't want to? It is your last time with him."

Herr Bergmann snorted. "Ha! This old ass is more trouble than he's worth! I'll be glad to be rid of him." He rubbed the mule's nose. "Lot of memories with this fellow. I wonder if he'll miss me."

"Are you talking about me or the donkey?"

"Why'd you mention yourself twice?" Bergmann grinned. Friedrich rolled his eyes, his mind going to work thinking of a retort as he grabbed the guiding rope and followed his master.

Friedrich and Herr Bergmann were free toilers, not tied to any land or lord, and so made their living with caverneering. For their current outing, they had come to the Landgrafschaft of Waldiestein,[1] a small land nestled comfortably in the center of the Weiße Hügel range. Here, they were free, away from all the hustle and bustle of regular life, surrounded by the allure of verdant nature.

As they hiked eastward, Friedrich studied their surroundings. To his right were the Weiße Hügel, tall, lifeless, and grey, capped with permanent white peaks. To his left was the lush green forests of the foothills, where bugs buzzed and birds chirped, leaves rustling in the wind. The trail they were walking was rocky and uneven, and

1. Landgraviate, a type of border territory march.

whenever he was closer to the mountains, all Friedrich heard was silence, not even a breeze. But when he walked closer to the forest, he heard all the animal life and felt the gentle caress of the wind. It was rather fun, straddling a thin line that separated two vastly different worlds.

"Pfennig for your thoughts, Friedrich?" Herr Bergmann broke his caravan of thought.

"Huh?"

"Just keeping you on your toes. Don't get so caught up looking around; remember what ground we're on. Watch your footing."

"I know, I know." He tugged the rope, forcing Greatness to keep pace with him. "If you're paying me for my thoughts however, I'm still curious as to what you think we'll find in the Toller Mund."

"Oh, what won't we find? The place is a true hoard. There's all kinds of tunnels and caves yet untouched by man. We're bound to find something. We always do."

"How many times have you been there?"

"About five times. I went there twice with my master and then thrice on my own. Each time, I always found something good. Though one time, I did get lost. I won't be forgetting that anytime soon. Living off crickets and spring water and cave mushrooms."

Friedrich laughed. "What do cave mushrooms taste like?"

He sucked his teeth. "Boiled, unsalted beef. It has the feeling of wet clay as well, hard to chew."

"How'd you know they weren't fouled?" They began climbing up a steep incline, walking sideways to keep their footing. Friedrich had to yank the rope for Greatness to follow.

"I didn't," Bergmann confessed. "I waited a few stounds after trying them to see what would happen. Of course, I did pose myself to give whoever found my body an awful fright. They didn't kill me, though the taste made me wish they did."

"Wait, was that the time you got lost and only found your way out because you followed the bats?"

"No," Bergmann corrected as he stabilized himself. "That was further west, over in Helvensland. This was the time I thought about eating my shoes and only found my way out because of those smugglers I met. Really nice folks, we still keep in touch."

The ground leveled into a serpentine trail crossing its way up further into the mountains. *The difficulty of the hike is not a jest,* Friedrich thought as he wiped his brow. He looked over at the trees.

They were just below the tops of the tallest ones, the air already getting thin. They pressed on.

"Did you find anything while you were lost at least? Was it worth it?"

"Oh, it was very much worth it, the greatest find of my life: a small chest, full of gems and old chips. I gave the smugglers some of the booty then took the rest to a learnedman at the High Learnhouse in Zoltalgart. He said they were really old, several thousand years old. Paid me a handsome sum for them."

"Several thousand years? How could he tell? Can't cut it open and see the rings like a tree."

"Oh, the delvers have their ways. Way he explained it, they had found chips like that before and used zahlken to backdate. You know, thinker stuff. Doesn't matter how old they were. What mattered is that he paid for them, and I got to eat. And, all that thinking aside, who's going to bury freshly made chips in a cave in the middle of nowhere?"

He had to concede to that, though he had his gripes about delvers. "Ugh," Friedrich scoffed, "I can't imagine a life like that. Surrounded by nothing but dusty books, spending all day in a cramped burgh, always having to smell someone else."

"Yes, it really makes the odds of dying in a cave-in and being trapped behind a rock for the rest of your life sound much better." Bergmann grinned.

"I would take this life over a learnedman or churchman's life any day. The fresh air, the view, the finds. I still can't fathom that you're giving all this up to retire to a town, and a coastal town at that." The coast always had the worst smells and the coldest winters.

"I'm getting too old for this. You need to be spry and agile to be a caverneer. One bad slip or one loose rock, and I'd break my hip! As fitting as it is, I'd rather not wind up something another caverneer finds. Besides, I've passed on all I learned to the youngsters. That is if you've actually remembered anything I taught you."

"I have. I'm remembering that bit about mushrooms."

"Have you ever thought about learning to write? Being able to write all of this down could come in handy when you're teaching a fellow of your own, if you ever do. Not to mention, when you retire, you could sell the book, have yourself a steady source of income. And you know Burghers would love a good tale like ours. They'll always pay top thaler for it."

Friedrich laughed. "Writing? You don't know me at all Herr Bergmann. I know, maybe I'll travel to the New World. I heard even lowborn, dirty toilers like ourselves can make a good living in the settlements."

"If you want a free life and to make good gold, why don't you become a trader, come join me on the coast?"

"Or instead, I could just woo some homely lady scion and become a lord by wedding."

"And break poor Clotilde's heart?" Friedrich shot him a dirty look; Bergmann snickered and shook his head. "I can see it now. The unread and uncouth Graf[2] Bauer mingling with the most well-bred and oldest families in the Realm. I'm sure you'd be invited straight to the Kommandant's hall in Grenzburg. As a jester," he muttered under his breath.

"I heard that."

"I'm sure you did."

The trail flattened out again after a few hundred feet. They were now over the treetops and could see the morning fog and dew begin to whisp away. At last, they had reached their destination: The Toller Mund.

Friedrich stared up at the Toller Mund, this being his first time here. The cave was wide enough an entire troop could have marched through it in formation. It was as tall as a church steeple with stalactites the height of a man hanging down from the roof. The name, which roughly meant 'Great Mouth' was an especially apt description; the whole structure looked like the maw of something from the darkest depths of hell. The mountain it belonged to was a rich grey color, marbled with bands of black and tan, with speckles of quartz and other gemstones shining in the morning sun. It seemed to scrape the clouds, dividing them like the fork of a stream as they floated by.

"Awe-inspiring, isn't it?" Bergmann asked.

"It's huge! It makes every cave we've dug so far look like, like, like a piss ditch!"

"It's even better on the inside." Bergmann grinned.

Friedrich found a rock just to the right of the cave entrance and tied up Greatness. Since the ground was barren, he left a small bowl full of potatoes and carrots out for the donkey to eat. With the donkey-of-burden content, he began helping Bergmann unload their

---

2. Analogous to a count, one of the lower ranks on the hierarchy of nobility.

supplies. He loaded his haversack with rope, stakes, and climbing axes. Then, he tied a bag of travel food to his waist. A small amount of dried saltmeat and bread would be their meal. He smacked the flat side of a pickaxe against the soles of his shoes to clean them off. He grimaced at how smooth his boots were. He'd have to get them resoled when they got home. He should have gotten them resoled before they left, but the night he could, his friend Kurt's cousin was getting wedded, and he had been invited. Who could give up free and flowing beer to take care of some boots?

Bergmann slapped his own boots with the pickaxe before tucking it into his belt. He lit a lantern and passed it to Friedrich then lit his own and led the way. He staked a small red flag at the entrance to mark their path. His liver-spotted hand shook slightly as he set it in place. A ball of twine, hanging from a custom holster on his hip, was wrapped around the flag and followed the two like a loyal dog into the darkness. As they climbed down further into the cavern, the sun behind them continued to slip away until all they could see was a simple pinhole of light. They were headed deep into the heart of the mountain. All they could hear was the running of water and the occasional screech of a bat. Their lanterns, illuminated by a wick dipped in animal grease, could only show a few feet ahead of them.

Through intuition, Friedrich knew they were in a chamber, larger than a stronghold's great hall, where many different tunnels and caverns would converge. No doubt this area had been dug through dozens of times over. They paused as Bergmann shone the lantern around, looking for their next route. "This way." Bergmann staked down another flag, wrapping the twine around it. He shone the lantern at a passage on the far right of the chamber. "I haven't gone down this way before." They climbed over stalagmites for several hundred feet, scraping their hands on sharp outcroppings of rock.

"It's warm down here," Friedrich commented. "A lot more humid than the other caves we've gone down."

"This cave is so large, sometimes it will rain in here."

"Rain? Inside the mountain? You lie."

"Honest to God, Friedrich. Come back during the rainy time. You'll see for yourself."

Friedrich didn't know enough to refute him and changed topics. "How did something like this happen anyway? Think God poked the mountain like he did the Rundensee?"

"Maybe. One of my friends thinks that lava is what carves the rock, melts it away like metal in a forge."

"Lava?"

"You know fire mountains? Like the Hellmouth down in Viteliú? They're full of it. According to my friend, lava is this red-hot orange rock that spews out of fire mountains, comes from deep, deep inside the world, like there's some kind of furnace or smithy just melting all the rocks and warming the surface."

"The Lightless are making weapons out of stone now?"

"Either that or Helheim isn't as cold as the churchmen say."

They paused before coming to the entrance of a tunnel. Bergmann took a drink from his waterskin before pouring some on his shaking hands.

Friedrich smirked as he wiped his hands off on his shirt, purposefully and noisily rubbing his callouses. "Hands getting soft already? You aren't retired yet, old man," he joked.

Bergmann shot him a scowl. "Watch your tongue boy. My hands are thicker than cowhide. Just stabbed myself on a rock is all." He dried his hands off on his trousers and staked another flag. They both set their lanterns down and began clearing rocks from the entrance. The tunnel was narrow at the opening—they would have to crawl in—but widened out a few feet in. Bergmann took his haversack off and began to crawl in, shining the lantern to signal for Friedrich to follow.

This tunnel descended at a steeper grade than the other chambers. Friedrich passed the lantern over the walls once he could stand. The tunnel was almost rectangular in shape, similar to a mine shaft, barely tall enough for them to stand fully upright. The floor, similar to a staircase, was smooth, eroded by water. The roof and upper walls still had knobs and outcroppings of rock jutting out, causing the men to duck. The whole tunnel was a beige limestone with streaks of white and grey permeating throughout. They continued on, steadying themselves by holding onto outcroppings or holes in the wall. They paused after walking several hundred more feet, resting to take another drink of water. "It just keeps going," Bergmann muttered. "Whatever is at the bottom better be worth it." He staked another flag into the wall and pressed on. The tunnel just continued, occasionally snaking to the left or right in a linear path like a river or a road.

Bergmann stopped again. He leaned forward, dropping a rock ahead of him. It hit the ground quickly. Confident, Bergmann sat down and lowered himself into the next room. Friedrich followed suit, landing just behind his master. This chamber was much colder than the previous one and much smaller. It was also drier and rockier with more stalagmites and stalactites. Coming from an unknown source but echoing and bouncing off the cave walls was a solitary, slow dripping noise. "We must be at least two hundred, maybe three hundred klafters[3] below the surface," Bergmann guessed. "If we were outside, we'd be just below the tree roots." He shone the lantern around. "Well, I don't see any broken rocks. We must be the first to ever step foot in here. Here, I'll take the left side, you take the right. Make sure we can always see each other's lanterns."

"Right, boss man." Friedrich walked over to the right side of the cave, carefully scanning the path ahead of him, so he wouldn't trip. Most of the rocks were normal limestone, bumpy from years of water buildup. The whole room was a mix of limestone and schist, same as the mountains above. He knelt down, carefully scanning loose rock with the lantern, looking for telltale specks of gold or other minerals. "Nothing over here!" Friedrich called out.

"I'm finding some amethyst. Just pebbles though. Keep going!"

Friedrich took out a rock hammer and began striking at the stalagmites, seeing if any deposits were hidden underneath. "Just useless limestone," he grumbled. They could start a quarry in here and supply half of Erebus with stone. Holding the lantern in one hand, and using the other to feel Friedrich fumbled his way forward, looking for the cavern wall, a good landmark to orient himself. A glint in the darkness caught his eye. Kneeling, he found a small hole in the wall like a rat burrow. He reached in; his hand pricked against the familiar shape of a gemstone. With a tug, he pulled it out, holding it up to the lantern. "Amethyst." He grinned. "Good sized chunk too." He turned to tell Herr Bergmann, but he couldn't see his lantern. "Herr Bergmann?" he called out.

No response.

Friedrich put the amethyst in his bag and began to walk back. "Herr Bergmann?" he called out again. He moved his hand to his dagger sheath. He suddenly dropped his lantern as an unseen assailant grabbed him, covering his mouth.

3. A unit of measurement equal to 4 feet US or 1.21 Meters.

"Be quiet." It was Herr Bergmann. He reached down and covered the light. "I saw something crawling. Coming up from a tunnel," he whispered, relaxing his hold.

Friedrich reached up, scratching his own cheeks. "What was it?"

"I don't know. I only caught a glimpse, but it didn't look like a man."

Friedrich took deep breaths, his chest tightening as he began to shiver. His teeth chattered.

"We're going to back up to the tunnel we came in and blocking the entrance. Then, we'll just go down a different cave. Pick up the lantern, and tie it to your belt, keep it dimmed." He let Friedrich go but kept a hand on his shoulder.

Bergmann led the way, holding onto Friedrich's shoulder as they made their way to the exit. They didn't talk. All they could hear was the dripping sound and their own breathing. The air seemed to grow stale, like the entire cave was holding its breath.

In the course of their travels, Friedrich and Herr Bergmann had seen their fair share of weirdness; sometimes they'd find skeletons of men or wildlife, packs of feral cats and dogs, and even a wintering bear. Sometimes they would come across rocks that would form weird shapes, looking vaguely fiendish, but Bergmann always kept a cool head. *Nothing* had ever spooked him like this before.

Friedrich bumped into the back of Bergmann; he had stopped. "Are we at the exit?"

"Quiet."

They listened, holding their breath. All they could hear was the dripping. Then a new sound started, scraping of rock on rock. Friedrich tightened the grip on his dagger while Herr Bergmann untied a pickaxe from his belt. They backed themselves up against a wall, slowly following it. The scraping sound continued, echoing off the walls, getting louder. Friedrich was still shaking. He sheathed his dagger, balling one hand into a fist, the other scratching his face again, all while biting his tongue to stop himself from whimpering. The scraping stopped, but they knew there was another presence, another being in the cave with them. They could hear a low growl, a guttural, animal-like panting.

Bergmann grabbed Friedrich and pushed him towards the exit. "It has our scent. Start climbing. Don't look back." Friedrich pulled himself up. He looked over his shoulder where Bergmann would be. He saw a small light appear as Bergmann uncovered his lantern, tightly gripping his pickaxe and taking a fighting stance. "Go!" he hissed without looking at him. Friedrich, crawling on all fours, started heading up the stairs. He heard Bergmann give a battle cry, only to be answered with an inhuman scream. Friedrich froze at the sound of metal on flesh. More animalistic, high-pitched screams followed. Bergmann gave a scream as well, almost drowning out the sounds of tearing fabric and scraping metal as his assailant struck back.

He needed to help. Friedrich drew his dagger, flipped on his back, and slid down, catching a glance of whatever it was they were both now fighting. The creature was red, and the arm that Friedrich could see was sinewy and thin. Friedrich screamed as he plunged his dagger into the arm, and the beast let out another howl and swung at him. Friedrich pulled the dagger out and ducked.

"What are you doing!?" Bergmann yelled. "I told you to get out of here!"

Friedrich didn't respond. He slashed again at the beast, hitting the bone in its legs. Friedrich pulled out the dagger again and hopped to his left. Bergmann raised the lantern as he swung the pickaxe again, coming down onto the creature's chest. As the creature stumbled backwards, Friedrich got his best look at this *thing*. It was tall, taller than either of them, standing on bird-like feet with a large, curved talon on each foot and knees bent backwards. It swung at the two of them with clawed hands, sporting a thumb like a tent stake. It was colored blood-red with hints of black, a horn or frill coming off of the back of its horse-like head, with four clear eyes set in the skull, eyes full of hate and fury.

Friedrich's mind raced through the various beasts and monsters in the many tales he knew, searching for a name of whatever this thing was. He had never seen anything like it in a woodcut, nor in a church-play, nor heard any taleteller or master singer ever describe an unholy thing such as this. They were facing a new enemy, one he could only describe with a broad and inexact name—a fiend.

Friedrich cried out, slashing again with his dagger. He missed, grazing the calf of the beast. A clawed hand reached down and grabbed Friedrich, throwing him easily across the room. Bergmann let out another cry and struck the beast again with his pickaxe. The fiend roared back. Friedrich could hear the primal evil in its call. Bergmann dropped the lantern and his pickaxe and cried in fear.

He grunted and kicked, yelling for Friedrich to leave. Then the creature let out one final roar, and Herr Bergmann was silenced.

Friedrich groaned as he tried standing up. The fiend had thrown him against several stalagmites, breaking them into pieces. He saw the lantern laying on the ground and could only hear the labored growls of the fiend. Friedrich began feeling around, looking for his dagger, swearing when he could only feel broken rocks. The fiend began to move, sniffing the air, searching for Friedrich. With the dagger nowhere close by, Friedrich began to grab whatever chunks of rock he could find. As the fiend stomped closer, Friedrich crawled backwards, holding his breath as it paused. He flinched as it roared. It found him, staring at him with those malicious, pupilless, blank, white eyes. The image was seared into Friedrich's mind as the eyes stared right at him, coming closer.

Friedrich began throwing rocks with all his might, breaking off more chunks when he ran low. The fiend began swiping at the air. Friedrich kept crawling backwards, praying he wouldn't run into the wall. The fiend was faster, its roar and foul breath only finger-lengths from Friedrich's face. He reached for a rock, thinking it might be his last, when he found the familiar grip of his dagger. The fiend's claw scratched his chest, tearing the straps on his haversack. Friedrich grabbed the fiend's forearm and brought his dagger down. The fiend howled again, slashing with its other arm. The claws stung as they slashed across his chest, warm blood oozed from the wound and poured down his torso. Friedrich screamed as he slashed again, cutting off some of the fiend's fingers. The fiend lunged forward while the desperate Friedrich, with the last of his strength, stabbed with his dagger. The blade struck home, hitting the fiend in the lower jaw, the blade jutting up into the skull. The blank eyes went dark, and the fiend collapsed onto him.

He laid there, feeling either piss, his blood, or the fiend's blood pooling around him. The water drip had stopped; all he could hear was his own heavy breathing. Adrenaline had since evaporated, leaving him exhausted and devoid of thought. He did not know if his eyes were open or closed, if he was alive or dead. His head felt heavy and light, his body sore but numb. His left hand grabbed at the floor; he only felt rock. Vitriolic bolts of pain shot through his body from his shoulder. He was still alive. But he wouldn't be unless he did something. Common sense and instinct resumed control; he pushed the fiend off and pulled the dagger out, wiping it off on his trousers. He winced as he felt his chest and shoulder. They were slick with blood. He leaned forward, cutting off the hems of his trousers in spirals.

Once done with this, Friedrich fumbled around for his haversack. When he found what was left of it, he searched around for his flint and steel then looked around further, finding a half-broken candle. He lit it, tucking it into a rock as he tied the ersatz trouser bandage to his chest and shoulder, wincing. At least the bleeding had stopped. He waved the candle over the fiend, double checking that it was dead with another stab through the brain. Friedrich caught his breath, wiping off his dagger again, then pulled himself up, struggling to gain his balance. His lantern was smashed to pieces, and his haversack was torn to shreds; its contents were sprawled out around the area where he had landed.

He limped over to where Herr Bergmann lay and saw the damage the fiend had done. It had torn his belly open and spilled his guts, blood and viscera pooling around his corpse. Friedrich knelt and lifted Herr Bergmann's head, the life gone out of his eyes and his chest still. Friedrich felt like he should cry or scream, but he was numb, cold to any stimuli. He knelt there, holding his master's head, his mouth agape as he processed what had happened. This must be a dream or some sort of hellish nightmare! They had just met a fiend, a creature of myth and legend! There had to be some explanation! He must have eaten a bad potato or drank poor water or found a pocket of gas! None of this should be real! Yet when he reached down and saw his hand coated in blood, he knew it was real. He slammed his fist on the ground, cursing and screaming that it wasn't fair. How could a good man like Herr Bergmann go? How could God or anyone else so benevolent allow this to happen? Friedrich sat by his master's corpse, pounding the ground in frustration, muttering 'why?' over and over to himself, breathing heavily.

As he mourned in anger, a realization hit Friedrich, and he was humbled. In his last moment, Herr Bergmann had done what he had always done before, looked out for Friedrich. "Guess I'll always owe you one, old man." He laughed weakly as he closed his master's, his friend's, eyes. "I'll be sure to give you a good burning," he promised. He picked up the dented but still shining lantern and surveyed the cave, grabbing a stalagmite to steady himself. "Better find where this thing had come from, stop anymore from coming," he muttered to himself. Orienting himself from the entrance, he limped over to the left side of the cave, looking over where Bergmann had been. He found it, a small entrance emerging from the floor. It was no bigger than a person; the fiend would barely have fit. The air from the entrance was warm, as if it was a chimney for the hellish lava forges Bergmann had teased.

Friedrich set the lantern down and looked for a large rock to cover the hole with. He paused, realizing he couldn't just prop a rock in front of the entrance. He'd have to force it in, like a cork in a wine bottle. He leaned in, trying to estimate the dimension of the hole to find the right rock. He leaned in deeper, shining the lantern to see how far the tunnel went. The tunnel was deep, much deeper and much darker than any tunnel he'd seen before. It was foreboding and menacing, like he was looking down the throat of some monstrous beast. Nothing good was down there.

As he pulled himself out, time seemed to stop. All at once, his shoulder gave out, his arm slipped out from under him, his boots lost their grip, and his life flashed before his eyes. He dropped, falling forward, as the lantern fell from his hand and tumbled into the darkness. Friedrich screamed as he fell onto his stomach, sliding down into the tunnel, sliding into the unknown, watching as the lantern bounced ahead of him until it either fell out of view or was extinguished. Friedrich desperately reached for something to grab onto. He found something, an outcropping of rock. He jammed his left arm to stop himself, slamming his face against the rock, breaking his nose. His arm went numb, pins and needles shooting up and down the limb.

After catching his breath, he reoriented himself, pressing his back against one wall and his feet against the other. It was a precarious position. The pull of the darkness was strong, threatening to drag him further downward. He didn't know how far he had fallen. It was pitch black, even darker, if possible, than the previous chamber. Both his arms were useless, his chest began to bleed again, and sharp, white-hot pain ran through his torso. Was he going to die? He felt like he was going to die. How long had he been down here? It felt like a day, but it couldn't have been more than a few stounds. Whenever he and Herr Bergmann caverneered, they would often only go down for eight or more stounds, usually from sunrise to just before sunset. Herr Bergmann has an almost sixth sense for time management. *Had*, Friedrich corrected himself, his poor master having passed. If his arms didn't get better, he would very well be joining him.

As he readjusted himself, he slipped on the stone, falling on his back, and sliding deeper into the tunnel. Friedrich went limp, only screaming as gravity took full control, dragging him ever downward. For what felt like many wegstundes,[4] he slid down. He felt his clothes disintegrating through friction, and the heels of his shoes nearly burst into flames as he tried to stop himself. His skin was peeling; sharp outcroppings of rock tore at his back like hooks. He would probably die of blood loss before he hit the bottom.

Then, the sliding tunnel gave out to a cliff edge. Friedrich slammed onto the ground, rolling until he fell into a river. He heard a rib crack. He regained control of his body, struggling against the current as the river carried him. The sound of roaring water was unwelcomed. Life shot back into his arms, and strength filled his veins as he fought to survive, swimming and screaming and gasping and inhaling frigid cave water as he tried to reach the shore. His muscles ached. His entire being was panicking. It was futile, the end of the water came, and Friedrich plummeted over the edge, following the cascade as it fed into a massive underground lake. He dove up from the water, coughing and hacking as he struggled to stay afloat. The current carried him to the shoreline. He floated on his back, drifting in and out of consciousness. He was exhausted, and every part of him ached. He didn't know where he was. He didn't know how he was still alive. Had he died? Was this the afterlife that the Church had taught? He didn't move, he didn't speak, he didn't even think, for however long, drifting in and out of sleep.

Friedrich felt himself jolt to life after feeling a touch. Someone, something, had touched his chest. He lifted his head, trying to look at whoever it was. It was a cloaked figure, their hand running over his wound on his chest, pausing over his heart. Through the tears in his shirt, he could feel their hands were cold and clammy. He couldn't see them fully, his vision a blur, all his senses numbed. He laid his head back; the world was spinning around him. Through the haze in his eyes, he saw light. No, he saw lights, dark blue and faint. He had no time to register them, to react to whatever had pulled him from the water. A small voice told him to stay awake, perhaps his survival instinct working overtime, but he ignored it. His eyelids weighed several tons; he had neither the strength nor

4. Way of tracking distance, roughly how long an average man can travel in an hour. Usually equates to 2.5 miles.

willpower to keep them open. Not the worst way to die, he presumed, finally letting his eyes close.

2

The figure observed the one they had rescued, giving them another examination to check for wounds, praying they would wake up soon. They had been found near death, covered in bruises and lacerations, half-drowned, concussed, and with more sprains and dislocations than seemed physically possible. And yet, they were still breathing and their heart still beating. It was miraculous, especially given that the wounds they had received did not seem to be healing on their own; the bones only reset and the skin restitched after intervention. How curious. Even stranger was their rejection of rations, spitting them out unconsciously. All they took was water. Curiouser and curiouser.

That was only the beginning of the strangeness of this being. The rescuer, content they had treated all the wounds, took the time to now properly examine their charge. Whatever this person was, they were tall, only a fingerbreadth shorter than themselves. Their muscle mass and callouses made them out to be some sort of laborer or artisan, a miner perhaps, given their surroundings? Their skin was a strange, pink-white color with dark brown blemishes, most no bigger than a pinhead, splattered on their arms and face. The face was most peculiar of all. Starting with the teeth, which they had checked for damages, were straight, but oddly, naturally dull and starting to yellow. This, the rescuer found extremely odd and added to the continuously growing list of questions they had. Another oddity was that their cheeks were pockmarked with scars, as if someone had rubbed pebbles into their face. They were old scars, existing long before the other injuries, so they were left untouched. As was the scar on their right shoulder made by some kind of blade. The same went for the decolorized blemishes and scars across their chin. The final curiosity was the hair, both in color and location. They have never seen this color before, it was colored like brown ashes.

The rescuer again prayed fervently that they may wake up soon. They sat by the fire they had made, breaking the lid off their own rations, nursing the contents as they watched their charge breathe. They were absolutely bubbling over with questions. Who was this being? Where had they come from? Why did they look like that? What new knowledge and ideas did they have to share?

Consciousness rushed back into Friedrich, snapping him out of his exhausted slumber. "Herr Bergmann!" he cried as he awoke. His muscles ached, and he was sweating. And his mouth had a strange . . . iron-copper taste? He stayed motionless on his back, glancing around. He was still in a cave, the same one he had fallen into. A few feet away was the lake and waterfall where he'd fallen. The waterfall was pouring out of the rock from a hole no larger than a horse cart. No wonder he couldn't get to the shoreline; there was no shore to get to. The lake, or more accurately pond, was small, resting in a crater with small streams pouring over the rim, crisscrossing the cave in a spiderweb-like fashion. Brightly colored, dare he say glowing, mushrooms dotted the walls and floor. At first glance, this cave was like any cave he'd been in before with one noticeable exception. He could see in it. Somehow, despite being god only knew how far underground, there was light. The source was a collection of gemstones, jutting out from the roof in irregular patterns. The light was a faint, dark blue but brightened the cave better than any lantern or candle. This somehow felt so familiar but unique, almost a different world.

Nearby, to his left, a fire crackled and popped. Friedrich looked over and saw the hooded figure from before walking over to him, a cloak obscuring their face. The fire was also unnatural; there were flames, but most of the light and heat came from a large, translucent, orange gemstone set in the middle. It was large, roughly the size of a man's head, and glowed like a torch. Gemstones didn't burn, no matter how hot a fire got. He must be in another world.

The figure knelt and examined him. He struggled to sit up, groaning as he shifted around, but every fiber in his being fought back, forcing him to lay back down. He felt petrified like a statue. All he could see of his mysterious rescuer was their hands, their pale, silver-colored hands, whose touch felt like a midwinter's snowstorm. Friedrich leaned his head forward and watched as the figure felt around his chest, poking for any more broken ribs or cuts. That's when he realized the ersatz trouser bandages he had made were gone as were the wounds from the fiend. Thinking about it, he realized his ribs didn't hurt either. He even reached up and felt his nose. It was back in place, perfectly aligned.

The figure looked directly at him, placing both hands on Friedrich's temple. The hands, though cold, were smooth and thin, delicate and ladylike, with well-calloused figure-tips. "Wha-wha-what? What are you doing?" He froze up, his deep knowledge of tales had nothing like this. This was a wholly new experience. The figured took one hand off his face, gesturing to continue, before putting it back. "T-t-talking? Is that what you want? Please, I don't mean any trouble."

The figure pulled their hands away and took off their hood, still looking at him. Friedrich let out a squeak of surprise. His rescuer was a woman! She was magnificent, the most alluring and winsome woman Friedrich had ever laid eyes on. And she was young, no older than himself. He was instantly smitten. Something overcame him, and he just stared, mouth agape, up at her. She possessed a beauty unlike any he had seen before or even heard of. Her face was flat and ovaloid with a petite nose. Her hair was stark white, white as the snows of the Weiße Hügel, while her entire body was a brilliant silver color. Her lips, the inner parts of her eye, and visible muscles, all of which were normally red, were instead a deep violet color, which struck Friedrich as odd and slightly unsettling. Despite all of this, her most alluring feature was her eyes. They were a master craftwork, the best way Friedrich could describe them. They were large, round, and a piercing golden color, more golden than a pure, refined ingot. It reminded him of an owl's. There was a magnetism about her, an almost innate and unspoken charisma. Friedrich couldn't describe it; he didn't understand it. He just wanted to listen, to follow her.

Which is what he must be meant to do. He must be dead now, he decided, and this was some sort of staging area before his judgment. This woman must be a Valkyrie, a heavenly being sent to guide him. Or, barring that, his guiding Norn. "Who are you?" Friedrich slurred. "Are you a val-val-valk-jorie?" His tongue felt heavy. As he stared at her, she stared back, watching as he struggled to form a sentence.

"Are you alright? Where else are you hurt?"

Friedrich nearly choked on his own amazement. She could talk! She spoke his tongue! How? Her accent was crisp and learned, almost purified from his own. "I-I-I." He was still speechless, transfixed on her eyes. How did she know Teutonish? How was he able to recover so fast? Who was she? "I am well," he finally blurted out. He shifted his body and sat up, resting on his elbows.

His back was cold. His shirt and trousers, even his shoes, were in tatters. What was left was ragged and stained black. He assumed that he was alive since no woodcuts or drawings he'd seen of the great beyond had people in raggedy clothes.

"Do you need anything?" the woman asked.

Friedrich puckered his dry lips, smacking them to get rid of the metallic taste. "I could use some water." The woman nodded and stretched out her hand towards the pond. A small glob of water rose out and came towards them then was gently guided into Friedrich's mouth. His eyes widened. This woman knew witchcraft! Worry began to set in. What was she going to do to him?

"Are you sure nothing else hurts? I have healed your external injuries as best I could. It is fortunate we have similar anatomies."

What was she talking about? Friedrich's mind raced through all the tales, churchy or otherwise, he had been told or had heard. Who was she? Was she some kind of pixie? No, they were always malevolent. A draugr? No, she was not dressed as a warrior or rotting. Maybe she was Frau Berchta. That was a well-told tale in this land. But didn't she only come out during the holiday times? And why would any of those things talk with such a refined tone?

She waved her hand in front of his face. "Are you sure you are well? You seem distracted. How is your head? Your concussion may be worse than I thought." She held up three fingers, though in an odd manner, holding up her pointer, middle, and ring, rather than the first two with her thumb as was the norm. How did she know his tongue but not how to hold up her fingers? "How many fingers am I holding up?" she asked. "Can you see properly?"

"Three," Friedrich told her. He shifted again, moving every joint to check for pain. He felt good. There was soreness but no cuts or even a headache. "I'm, I'm well, just . . . just bewildered." She knew witchcraft. Witches were the one evil agreed upon by everyone in Erebus. Nothing short of sickness or death were feared more. His stomach growled; he would have to worry about this later. For now, he had to survive. "Do you have anything to eat?" he asked. Something about her was calming, uncomfortably so. But, food would need to come first.

"What do you eat?"

Friedrich gave her an odd look. What did he eat? What did *she* eat would be the better question. Was she the kind of witch from Bouya who ate children? Fortunately, Friedrich was in his 20s. Unless she had some kind of age-reversing witchcraft. He knew tales like that. "Uh. I eat about anything. Saltmeat, bread, cheese. I'll even take roots if you have some."

The woman furrowed her brow. "I do not have anything like that." She looked around the cave. "Those fungi are not toxic. Would those suffice?" Friedrich gagged internally but swallowed his pride and nodded. The woman stood up and plucked some of the growing mushrooms off of a rock and brought them over to Friedrich. He cleaned off the cap and bit into it. It was just as described, like bland, over-boiled meat. He finished off the mushrooms just as the woman brought over another glob of water.

"How-how are you able to do that?" he asked, pointing to the floating glob.

She gave him a curious look, as if he caught her off guard. "Through years of diligent study and observation. Can you not do thaumas like that?"

Friedrich blinked several times, dumbfounded. Every action she did only bred a new question. "Uh, no. I . . ." He squeezed his eyes shut and shook his head then pinched the loose skin between his thumbs and pointer finger. He had to be dreaming. "Where am I? Who are you?"

"I would ask you the same question. To my knowledge, these tunnels are mostly unexplored and uninhabited. Where did you come from?"

Well, she wasn't a Valkyrie. They were supposed to have an intimate knowledge of men and their dealings. As did fairies, at least as some tales go. "I'm from . . ." Should he tell her where he really came from? Didn't witches use that to curse folk? He looked at her eyes, his fear almost melting away. "I'm from the Free-Stead of Hertzabrunno," he explained.

She gave him another curious look, furrowing her brow again. "The what? I have never heard of that place. Are you an independent colony? Some kind of rogue settlement?"

What was she going on about? "No, we, we're true to the Kommandant, mostly. I, I don't care."

"Kommandant? That is a Strixan word! Or, at least derived from one."

"I, uh. I don't think we're on the same page." He cleared his throat. "I'm from Erebus, up, up there. Way up there." He pointed up towards the waterfall. "I fell through a hole, slid down in the darkness and wound up here."

Her eyes widened; joy crept across her face. "You mean, you are from up there? There is life above us? On the surface?!" She was smiling but her teeth were hidden, almost purposefully. It was an unnatural and unsettling smile, almost inhuman. A chill went down Friedrich's spine. "Oh! This, this is wonderful news! You must tell me everything!"

Friedrich leaned back away from her. "I uh, er, um." He did not feel safe at this moment. Something about her was . . . off. She must be some kind of witch, sealed down here by a priest or a Holy for some reason. Though, every time he looked at her, his worries seemed less founded. "What, what do you want to know?"

"What is the surface like?"

"Green?" Friedrich blinked several times trying to clear his head. He felt like he'd just been hit by a coach. "There's, there's a lot up there. A lot of beings, a lot of water, wildlife, bugs."

"Your people, who are they? What is your state like?"

"Well we . . ." He went to touch his waist where he always had girded the dagger and a small wooden shield, his altersschild, his age-shield. They were marks of both his manhood, age, and his culture. Color drained from his face and his eyes went wide, breath choking in his throat, as he felt his waist. *His dagger and age-shield were gone.*

"No!" he screamed. Life and movement shot into all his limbs. He scrambled up from the ground and ran to the edge of the pond, much to the bewilderment of his caretaker. "No! No! Where are they! *Gott im Himmel* not those! I can't lose those!"

The girl was at his side then stepped away as he climbed into the water, diving below. "What is it you are looking for?!" She was equal parts appalled and curious.

Friedrich ignored her, diving back down into the water after catching a deep breath. He was down there for several seconds, alarming his rescuer, until he resurfaced, panting on the shoreline. In his hand was half a belt, a sheathed dagger on one end and a small wooden shield on the other.

All that trouble and excitement for this? the rescuer wondered. She reached out to touch the belt, especially the small wooden shield. It was circular, one half painted an orange-gold and the other a dull red.

"Don't, don't touch that." He pushed her hand away. He had pulled himself out of the water and lay on the dry part of the shore. "God in heaven be thanked," he whispered, shaking his hair dry.

"Apologies, it is a unique adornment. I have never seen anything like it before."

How? Friedrich asked himself. If she spoke his tongue, she would know what this is.

"Please, allow me." She raised a hand over Friedrich. All of the water soaking what remained of his clothes was stripped away, forming a globule that hovered over him before being tossed back into the pond. Friedrich thanked her and sat up, holding the belt like it was a child. "May I ask why all the concern over these?"

"This is my Altersschild." She stared at him blankly. "The age-shield? Given to every boy when they become a man?" Still blank stares. "It shows my stem, which cut of Teudish I come from. The Scyts have their cloaks, and the Tujue their onion-hats. And we have this."

The lady studied the shield closely. "Fascinating. Is the pugio a sign of maturity as well?"

"Yes. But it was also a gift."

The lady furrowed her brow in thought and sat down. "You wear peculiar garments, speak a strange language, and your teeth and skin . . . . You are not a Strixan, are you?"

"No? I'm, I'm a man."

"Is that your tribal name?"

"No, man is . . . man is . . . our race?"

"So, it is your people . . ." She nodded, understanding. "A different race of beings, so similar and dissimilar to us. Incredible. Can you tell me more about your people? How are you organized? What is your life like? Are you in tribes, city-states, empires?"

Friedrich stammered to answer. "Huh, well, everyone belongs to a stem, and then a sippe within the stem. Well, no, that's not right . . . er, hmmmm." He had to pause and collect his thoughts. How did he explain life on the surface? It was like explaining the taste of salt! "Everyone lives in either a hamlet or a town, which are always under a Graf or Burgermeister or Aufseher.[5] And above everyone is the Kommandant. At least, in the Realm." A questioning on the Realm's politics was not what he would've expected after falling below the surface.

The woman beamed with amazement. "This is all so incredible! I always dreamed that there was *something* above us! But to find out there are such complex and organized beings! Oh! This is

5. Clerical rank analogous to a Bishop.

remarkable! Prayers have been answered! Tell me, what gods do you worship? What is your culture like?"

"Culture?" She was throwing so many strange words at him.

"Culture! Your art, habits, costume, maxims, your religions! Tell me about it!"

He furrowed his brow. Did she mean folkcraft? That had to be what she was talking about. "Well . . . to start. No Gods, just one, just . . . God. Well, one full God, a lot of half gods." What was she expecting as an answer? Again, it was like describing salt. He gave up. "Well, I . . . I don't know how to answer the rest of your question."

"What do your people do for amusement? What is your art like, your plays, food, dress, poetry?" she clarified.

"Art?" She mimed dipping a brush and painting on a canvas. "Oh! You mean crafts. We . . . uh, well it depends on the craft. The church has a lot, Holy-plays, woodcuts of tales from the Sagas, things like that. We eat a lot of meat and bread, drink a lot. We're . . . we're hard-working, best builders and workmen in the world. And warriors, I've heard us called a warrior folk, but I don't like that." He started to breathe heavily and scratched at his cheeks.

"Are you not a warrior?"

"No, no, I . . . I hate war."

"But you are armed?"

"Everyone is. Doesn't make me a fighter. This may be a dagger, but it's a tool as much as it is a weapon. I can whittle, chop food, clear weeds, butcher hogs. Only thing I've killed that wasn't livestock was a fiend. I don't see it as a weapon."

She stroked her chin as if she had a beard, nodding along. "I see." She made a mental note of asking about that later. A warrior from a martial culture who abhorred fighting? How peculiar! "I must say I find this all fascinating! I never thought such a thing could exist outside of Strixan culture. How long has there been life on the surface? What other life is there? And what kind of wonders can they work?"

"Life? For, forever, I guess. Since God made everything, all the wildlife, the tamelife, and . . . us." He gestured to himself. "I, I don't, what do you mean by wonders?"

"Wonder-working." She pulled another glob of water out of the pond. "Like this."

"Oh . . ." He accepted the water but still kept his distance. "That is witchcraft. It is outlawed. They'll hang you or burn you at the stake for that." Shouldn't she know that? Is she assuming the times have changed? Unless, was she from . . . before? And what did she call herself? Stricken?

"They do what?"

"They kill them. Witchcraft is a hateful thing. It's evil." He watched her carefully. "You're some kind of witch, aren't you? A wild woman?"

She stared at him, dumbfounded. "You mean your people cannot do things like this?" She snapped her fingers; fire illuminated her fingertips. Friedrich shook his head, nervously gulping as he watched the fire flicker and dance. "That is preposterous! How could you survive without this?" She saw his unease.

"I uh. What do you want from me?" he asked. "Are you planning on using me for some sort of blackmeeting? Do you want my soul, my blood?" She tensed up slightly. "Look if you want gold, I know how to find it. Gemstones, gold, silver, I can help you find them. Just, just don't kill me." The terrifying thought that he had been called down crossed his mind. Afterall, he was a virgin, and for whatever reason, virgin blood was prized by witches, though he always heard they preferred girls.

"Kill you? What? Of course not, I would never dream of doing anything so barbaric."

"Then, what are you? Some kind of nice witch?" His hand slowly went to his dagger.

"I am not a "witch." I do not mean you any harm." She extinguished the flames. "I believe proper introductions are in order; I do not even know your name. Mine is . . ." She seemed hesitant before saying her name, or more likely, she was trying to translate it. "I am Vytilia Quintia. I am a Strixan." Saying her own name in his language seemed odd to her, but Friedrich felt the same way when called "Frederick."

He relaxed. He didn't know what a Strixan was, but at least he knew her name. "I am . . ." He bit his lip. Should he tell her his name? She had told him hers, but how did he know it was her real name? He'd never heard of anyone named "Vytilia" before. It sounded made up. Maybe he should give her a fake name. "What are you going to do with my name?" She frowned and stood up, straightening her clothes. Friedrich noticed what she was wearing, an odd set of otherwise fine and well-cut garments, a loose, dark colored dress and sandals, along with her cloak and a veil around her shoulders. He'd never seen such manner of dress. It almost looked archaic.

"I am not going to do anything with your name except use it to talk to you." There was a definite, subtle hint of annoyance in her voice. Friedrich decided not to push his luck.

"My name is Friedrich Bauer."

Her frown disappeared. "Friedrich? That is an interesting name. Is it a common name on the surface?"

"Yes? I've met many other Friedrichs in my life. I think the Kommandant is one. I even met a Frederick from Merkya."

"Now that we know each other's names, I was wondering if I could ask you more questions."

Now she asked for permission, he mused. "Only if I can ask some as well," he insisted.

She nodded. "First, how did you end up down here? It has been a dream of mine to find some kind of fissure or tunnel to the surface but never could."

"Well . . . I fell." She didn't look amused. He pointed to the waterfall. "I was exploring the Toller Mund with my master when something attacked us. After I killed it, I tried blocking the hole it came from, in case there were more, but I lost my footing and just started sliding down. I must've fallen a few thousand feet. Then I landed in the water."

Her eyes widened. "You were attacked? What attacked you?"

"A-a-a . . ." A chill went down his spine, as he remembered those lifeless white eyes. His tongue felt heavy. "A fiend," he blurted out, shaking his head to clear his mind. "I'd never seen anything like it. I don't know what it was."

She knelt next to him, grabbing his shoulders and staring him in the eyes. "Describe it," she demanded.

Friedrich's teeth chattered. Her breath had an iron smell, and he felt her cold touch through his tattered shirt. "It was red and tall. Long skinny arms, a weird, horse-shaped skull, and four eyes. Ugh . . ." Another shiver went down his spine. His chest felt heavy. "I can still see the eyes."

"And this devil, you killed it?"

"Yes, just barely, the forsaken thing nearly tore out my ribs. Killed my master first then tried to get me."

She stood back up, staring at the waterfall. "Have you seen anything like this before?" she asked.

"Never. We don't tell tales about fiends. It's a word you use for anything evil. They're campfire tales. I thought witchcraft was a tall tale too, but here we are."

She turned around and stroked her chin, pacing back and forth, her brow furrowed again. She was muttering to herself in some unknown language. After a minute, she stopped and turned back toward Friedrich. "Are you capable of walking?" Given the context of her question on food, he didn't know whether that was an inquiry on his wounds or if she legitimately didn't know if he was capable of moving without fear to move him. He could swim but walk? Friedrich stood up, steadying himself on a rock. He walked over to Vytilia with a slight limp, standing before her. He could see that she was a few zolls[6] taller than him; his eyesight just reached her upper lip. She was a tall woman, with long legs and strong arms, but was slender and feminine without a hint of weakness.

She looked Friedrich up and down, stifling a laugh at his clothes. He really was only wearing the front half of his shirt and . . . a strange garment with two legs. His strength was more apparent as he stood up. She had to admit to herself. There was a sort of plebeian charm about him, though she did not know if it was because of his foreignism.

"Well, I can walk," he announced. He tried wrapping the belt around his waist but it was too short. He slung it around his neck like a scarf.

She nodded. "That is good. We need to get to Nidus." She turned around and headed towards the fire then clapped, extinguishing the flames. She knelt and grabbed the orange gemstone in one hand, placing it in a leather knapsack. Friedrich only stared, amazed that she not only lifted the stone with one hand (he estimated something that size would have been very heavy and not something anyone could easily pick up), but she touched it immediately after it had been on fire all, without complaint or even a grunt of effort. This Vytilia, though mysterious, was incredible.

He shook himself out of his amazement and walked over to her, discarding what remained of his shoes and throwing them into the pond. All he had on were a pair of thin, holey socks. He could feel the cold, rough surface of the cave floor. "Where did you say we were going? Nidus? What is that?"

6. Friedrich's people's equivalent of an inch.

"It is the capital of my people, our main refuge here underground. It is safe there."

"Safe? Safe from—hey, wait, people? Who are your people? More witches?"

She looked at him, annoyed. "I told you. I am not a witch; I am simply a thaumaturgist. And, I also told you, I am a Strixan. That is my people."

"That, that doesn't tell me anything. What are Strixans? Where, where are we?"

She paused, looking Friedrich up and down, lingering on his dagger. She moved her head strangely, tilting it to the side or moving her head forward and back. It reminded Friedrich of a bird. "I will explain everything when we get to Nidus. It will be safer to explain there. *We* will be safer, and it will be easier for you to understand. Follow me and stay close. I cannot risk letting my guard down."

Friedrich stayed put and watched as she headed for a tunnel opposite of the waterfall. He didn't particularly want to follow Vytilia, and her lack of detail or explanation of this Nidus place was unnerving, but he also didn't have many other options. Her witchcraft didn't seem malicious, at least what she'd shown him, and she did rescue and heal him, but the innate fear of witchcraft and the unnatural, instilled since childhood, made him want to keep his feet rooted to this cave. He watched as she turned around and urged him to follow, his mind still debating what to do.

Vytilia noticed that Friedrich was not following her. She looked back, waving at him to follow. He stayed where he was, watching her. He wore his superstitions on his sleeve, and she felt that that could be a problem when they got to Nidus. His fear, and his people's apparent fear of thaumaturgy and its practitioners, would also be an obstacle. She would have to work with him carefully. In her heart, she knew that this was a once-in-a-lifetime opportunity, a blessing straight from the gods to aid her and her people, and if she let it slip through her hands, she would live the rest of her days with regret. Though he would not have any inclinations, she needed him; his knowledge of the surface and its workings could mean the difference between mere survival and actual living for her people. There was a certain irony that the Strixan's survival depending on this graceless plebian and his barbaric-sounding language.

"You can trust me Friedrich!" she called out to him. "I promise, I do not mean you any harm! When we get to Nidus, I can provide you a better meal than fungus!"

What reason do I have not to trust her? he thought. She had rescued him and healed his wounds. Granted, she practiced witchcraft, which was unnerving, but she seemed to have good intentions. He ran through the huntbook of fairytale beings he knew; she didn't have a tail or hollowed-out back, which ruled out a huldra. She certainly wasn't a Valkyrie, come to whisk him to the afterlife. She wasn't a fairy, or niss, or any of their ilk. Perhaps 'Strixans' were some unwritten kind of being that hadn't entered most folklores. And, just maybe, his guardian Norn had guided him here, intertwining his orlay with her lot. And if not, they may at least have a way back to the surface, along with a hot meal and a change of clothes. He moved his hand away from his dagger and followed her. And in the end, he could at least get a chance to travel with an exquisite woman.

They walked down the tunnel. Glowing silverfish crawled over the walls and floor, skittering whenever one of them stepped too close. The tunnel was illuminated by those same star-shaped gemstones from the previous cave. Friedrich ran his finger along them. They were smooth, finer cuts than any jeweler could make, a perfect geometric shape, yet none seemed alike. Some were triangular, some rectangular or circular. Some shapes he knew no name for.

Friedrich knew he was awake, but he could not shake the feeling that this was all some kind of dream, a fantasy land he would've played in as a child. None of it seemed natural, from the stones and plants that glowed without fire to his companion who could light fires and levitate water with just a flick of her wrist. But the rock, the familiar, commonplace living rock, mere schist, granite, and limestone, brought him back. It was an anchor, letting him know he was still in the real world, surrounded by the familiar while facing the unfamiliar. He was . . . comfortable being surrounded by rock.

They hiked in silence for a long time, time was merely a word without clocks or sunlight, the tunnel twisting and turning, raising and lowering in elevation. Every so often, Vytilia would look back, her neck twisting to an almost impossible degree as she watched him. Friedrich had no sense of bearing or direction, but Vytilia seemed to have an innate sense of where they were going, almost like a dog. He followed her as she navigated the labyrinthine tunnel, keeping a distance behind her. There was still something off about her. He didn't fully trust her, and he kept racking his mind for some sort of folktale that explained who or what she was. She had to be some kind of fairy or niss, though given the accounts of their tendency for mischief, she must be the exception to the rule.

He could tell that she was still bubbling over with curiosity and questions. She kept glancing back at him every other klafter to make sure he was real. She would fidget and mutter to herself in her own language, counting or making lists on her hands. His landlady was the same every time he'd come home from a trip. She'd be abuzz with excitement, asking what he saw, what he found, who he met, had he been in any danger. The fact that she had to navigate was probably killing her, forcing her to focus on where they were going rather than asking Friedrich all about the surface.

Both of their focuses shifted towards a purple-hued light glowing from the tunnel in front of them. They walked towards it and came to a large, uphill chamber, filled to the brim with the most exquisite and lustrous gemstones. Friedrich almost fell to his knees in awe. Every nook and cranny, every crevice and surface of the room was covered in large clusters of rich, violet amethysts and banded, blue-green fluorspar. The clusters were larger than Friedrich's hand with some of the gemstones reaching lengths longer than his arm. He wanted to cry. The mineral wealth of this room alone could pay for an entire dynasty's worth of King's ransoms.

"Can we . . . can we take a slice? Get some rest?" Friedrich asked as he examined a clump of fluorspar.

"A rest? We have not even gone that far!" They both gave each other odd looks. To Friedrich, it felt as if they must have traveled several wegstundes, some of which was uphill on rocky ground. Even an experienced traveler would have found that a *far* distance.

"I, I just need a quick breather," he explained as he sat down, leaning against a rock. He didn't want to leave. If he could just bring even a fraction of this cave with him to the surface, he could live in luxury the rest of his days. This was a caverneer's dream. "Are there other caves like this?" he asked.

Vytilia nodded. "Dozens upon dozens upon dozens. Deposits like this are quite common. Though we do not have much use for them."

"No use? Wha-what?! These are the most brilliant gemstones I've ever seen! How can you just ignore them!"

"Jewels cannot aid in our war effort. They are more of a nuisance than anything, making construction and exploration difficult." She looked at him, her head tilted again. "You mentioned a master earlier. Are you a jewel fabricator's apprentice?" He shook his head. "Some kind of gold smelter or metallurgist? Or perhaps an artisan?" He shook his head again.

"I'm a caverneer," he announced as he stood up.

"A what?"

"A caverneer. I'm a freeman who spends his days exploring caves in search of treasure."

Vytilia frowned, and the bubbliness Friedrich noticed quickly dissipated. "You mean you are nothing more than a scavenger?"

"Er. In one sense of the word, I suppose. We mostly focus on raw ores, though we have found old stuff before that is worth quite a bit."

Her mood turned downward. "All you are is a scrounger?! Digging through caves!" She shut her eyes and bit her lip, the veins in her neck bulged. She let out a growl and slammed her hand into a cluster of amethyst, shattering it into a thousand glistening pieces. "Godsdamn it!" she swore through clenched teeth. She was not fazed by what she had just done. Her hand showed no signs of injury.

Friedrich leaned back further, watching her wide-eyed.

She let out a deep, guttural sigh then opened her eyes. Friedrich could see the disappointment written all over her face. She slumped her shoulders in defeat. "I do not know what I expected," she muttered to herself. "Millennia of isolation, and you are what we found?"

Millennia? Isolation? What?

She took another deep breath. "I am mistaken. This can be beneficial; I can work with this. This, this is still a boon," she told herself, taking another deep breath. She turned back toward Friedrich. "Allow me to be straight: you are not what I was hoping for or expecting. If I had it my way, you would have been a fellow scholar or someone of higher birth, but you are what you are and what the gods have given me."

"And . . . what, what is it you want from me?"

She sighed tucked loose strands of white hair back into place. "My people, the Strixans, are a shadow of what we once were. I have dedicated my life to helping us get back to where we were. We were oblivious to the possibility of other beings or life existing, let alone living above us. My hope is that you can tell us about the surface, maybe even how to make contact with your people, to help us rebuild."

Well, he could still be of use, do whatever he could to at least get back to the surface. "I can still be of help," he announced. "I might not know much, but I'm well-traveled. I've seen more of the Realm than most toilers ever will. I can be of use."

She smirked, perhaps in admiration but most likely doubt.

He was still wary of Vytilia. The fact that she had destroyed several groups of gemstones with her bare hands, something that normally required a hammer or something even stronger, was distressing. But, yet again, he didn't have much of a choice. He could stay here, here in this beautiful room where money was literally growing from the rocks, but he would eventually starve or die of exposure. Vytilia may be frightening, but she knew the path. And if what she said was true, about them needing his help, there might be a reward in it for him, maybe enough to get his own land and retire. And there's sure to be a motherlode of tales to bring home.

Vytilia led the way out of the gemstone filled cave. Both nearly had to crawl on all fours up a steep incline to reach the next tunnel. Traveling was awkward for both of them. Friedrich wanted to remain quiet to both not set Vytilia off and to conserve his energy. These caverns were cool to the touch, and the air was almost seeping energy out of him. His hands and feet were covered with scratches and cuts from the rocks. Worse was how tired he was, even with how long he had slept when he landed down here. How long had he been down here? Without the sun, his sense of time was nonexistent.

As the ground leveled out to another tunnel, again illuminated by the star gemstones, Friedrich paused to catch his breath. "Hey Vyti, how long will it take us to reach Nidus?"

She froze, her head turning around, again to an impossible degree. "What did you just call me?"

"Vyti."

Her eyes narrowed like a predator's. "My name is Vytilia, and you will only refer to me as such. Do you understand?" Friedrich nodded. She turned her head back around, muttering under her breath.

"But, how, how far is it to Nidus?"

"It is a two-day journey from here. Though at our current pace, since you keep insisting on pausing and wasting time, it might be three." She started up again, heading down the tunnel. Friedrich groaned and started following after her.

"Don't you get tired?" he asked. "You didn't even break a sweat when you shattered those gemstones. How did you not destroy your hand?"

Vytilia sighed. "Is it going to be like this the entire journey?"

"I've never done anything like this before! I've been all over the Realm. I've seen some feats of strength but nothing like that! And why're you getting mad at me? You were nothing but questions when I woke up. How come I can't ask some?" He cleared his throat to keep fear from creeping into his voice.

"Our situation has changed," she explained. "After you told me that you encountered a devil, I realized these tunnels are not safe. We need to get to Nidus and the safety of the Arx before asking anymore questions. We cannot afford to let our guard down." She shook her head. "I fear what attention my . . . outburst may have drawn."

"So, we're just going to stay mute while hiking for the next few days? That'll be very boring." He thought witchcrafty folk were supposed to be . . . fun. "Don't you know any sort of spell that makes us quiet? Or blocks anyone from listening?"

"It is better to be silent and alive than vocal and dead," she countered. "And stop calling it witchcraft. That is such juvenile thinking. It is called wonder working or thaumaturgy. And along with the proper terminology, there are not any wonders that would render our speech mute to anyone else. Keep walking."

Vytilia quietly fumed as she led the way through the tunnel system. She could have easily answered any questions Friedrich had and kept a lookout for devils, but the frustration of what he was not was too overwhelming. He could have been anyone else, a legionary from a lost colony, another scholar exploring the caverns and tunnels, even just a runaway tiercel from a yet unknown outpost, but instead, he was some lowbrow scavenging plebeian. Her people's first contact with another civilization, and it was *him*, a barbarian who looked as imbecilic as his manner of dress.

But she had to keep reminding herself that he was all she had. For better or worse, they were saddled together for the sake of her people. Maybe it was a blessing from the gods, or maybe it was pure chance. Perhaps, just perhaps, he did know something useful or had, in his travels, at least met someone else who could be useful. If there was truth to his words of him being an experienced traveler, then he would certainly be an asset should the Strixans ever venture to the surface. That was if they could even find a way back to the surface and if the surface population was willing to accept them.

"Hey, I uh, I realized that I never did thank you for rescuing me," Friedrich told her, cutting through her thoughts.

Gratitude? One of the higher emotions? This was something Vytilia would never have expected.

"I don't, I don't know why you were there, but I'm grateful."

There was sincerity in his voice, and while she would have preferred they both remain quiet, the humility and gratitude were pleasing to hear. "I was simply looking for remnants of our past. It was pure accident I came across you. Though I would be remiss not to say it was fortunate timing."

"Oh? You dig through caves as well? Heh, we, I guess we aren't so different after all."

She nearly stumbled when he finished. She wanted to stop, to turn her head around and scold him again, but she took another deep breath and continued on. "I have a higher purpose than profit. My work impacts thousands of fellow citizens. It can impact the course of our future and our survival."

"Well, that, that is a higher goal than just getting enough gold to live off of, but no matter the endgame, you have to admit there are similarities in what we do." He coughed nervously. "Why, uh, why do you say your 'people' are struggling to survive? What happened?"

She made a slightly annoyed grunt. "Details will be given in due time. For now, it will suffice it to say that that devil you encountered is all too familiar to us."

Friedrich gagged in disbelief. "You mean, there's really more of those, those fiends out there? *Gott im Himmel!*" He nearly drew his dagger, glancing to this sides, above, and behind him.

"Hence the need for us to make haste and get to Nidus. If the devils find their way to the surface, they could destroy your people and have mine completely surrounded. Civilization, even sentient life as we know it, could be erased from history."

"So, what sort of help are you wanting from the surface?"

"Anything. Anything that could give us an advantage over the devils: weapons, strategy, tactics. Even if all you can offer is a steady supply of food for our civilians, it would be a massive boost to morale. Just the knowledge that there is another empire out there, and that we could forge an alliance, would give us the hope we need to press on."

Her tone had shifted dramatically, Friedrich noted. There was a hint of sadness in her voice that was all too familiar. Maybe he really could help out these Strixans, somehow. Though he was unsure of what help he could offer, and he didn't want to say it, but the friendship she wanted between her people and the Realm would be downright impossible. The Church would never allow witchcraft users to be recognized, and no lord would ever risk helping them for fear of being disfellowshipped. Or worse. Yet, would they? He'd been brought here for a reason. He was alive for a reason. Would his own orlay really go against all the laws and teachings of the surface?

"How long have you been down here, fighting the fiends?" Friedrich asked.

"For many years. As I said earlier, all of this will be explained when we get to Nidus."

They continued hiking in near silence aside from the occasional warning. Time was still. While crawling and hiking through caves and tunnels was familiar, these caves and tunnels had just enough of the unfamiliar to keep Friedrich from feeling both safe and bored. He felt like he was underwater, floating in a dark abyss while fantastic and glowing things swam by. They resembled, at least marginally, life on the surface; newts, crickets, silverfish, even mushrooms and moss, but they were almost otherworldly. They glowed, they were colors not normally found in nature, some were even as translucent as a pane of expensive glass.

These things seemed to pay them no mind. They did not scurry away as life did on the surface. The bugs, in particular, didn't seem to notice that they were there, bouncing and hopping without so much as a care in the world. Why should they fear Friedrich or Vytilia? The two of them were in their land, temporary passers-by in the kingdom of ruby-colored, glowing lizards and their subjects. Friedrich was amazed at all this life, but Vytilia was unphased. Much like the cave filled with gemstones, she merely remarked that ecosystems (her word) existed like this all over the domain of her people.

They finally came to another cave, one that seemed to be ripped straight from the surface. This cave was smaller than the one with the waterfall, but it had a good-sized stream and trees. The trees, seemingly both sickly and healthy, had red-colored leaves with ash-colored trunks. The rocks were coated in a thin layer of red grass, brilliant blue-colored moths rested on the branches in place of birds, and what looked to be squirrels, or at least a distant cousin, darted from tree to tree. A large collection of brilliant blue star-shaped gemstones was embedded in the roof, acting more like a moon than a star.

"Can we take another rest here?" Friedrich asked. "I need some water." Vytilia closed her eyes, most likely to roll them, and sighed, nodding in agreement. Friedrich knelt at the stream and began lapping up the water, much to Vytilia's chagrin. "This place is incredible," Friedrich blurted out. "What is it?"

"It is simply a clearing."

"This looks a lot like the surface only with different colors." He kept drinking, finally stopping as he started to feel sick. "Are you not going to drink?"

"Do not worry about it. I have had enough water."

"How? I haven't seen you . . ." Vytilia was silent and nearly motionless, only her eyes moved as they looked for something. He paused, glancing around. "What is it?"

"We are being watched. Be quiet." Fire appeared on the fingertips of her right hand, and a glob of water flew from the stream into the palm of her left. Friedrich stood up and drew his dagger.

Vytilia slowly paced in a circle, scanning their perimeter. She stopped and threw a ball of fire at a small bush. It burnt to a crisp instantly, sending moths and squirrel-things panicking. She fired again, throwing another fireball. This one blasted the wall, scorching some of the grass and leaving ash marks on the rock.

"Come on beast, show yourself!" She fired again, nearly leveling a freestanding rock. A fiend crawled out from behind the rock, shrieking as fire spread over its body. This fiend was different from the one Friedrich fought. It was grey-blue and bulkier, crawling on all fours, with a spiked tail, the same razor-sharp talons as the red one, and a doglike head, the jaw splitting into four parts. On its back was a spiny frill, matching the fleshy frills it had behind the "ears." In the center of the head sat three blood-red eyes. Just as with the red fiend, there were no pupils.

Vytilia launched a stream of water at the fiend, heating it up with her fire hand. The boiling water temporarily blinded the beast, and it stumbled into walls, screaming. She launched another attack. It regained its sight and ran, outrunning her shots and climbing into a tree, hiding in the thick foliage. She stopped firing, watching as the tree rustled. The fiend leapt at Friedrich, roaring. He leapt to the side as the fiend landed then quickly climbed up another tree behind them as Vytilia launched another blast of boiling water.

"If I wound it, you finish it off!" She raised her hands, lifting several bullet-sized rocks into the air, they were all the same color but in many shapes and sizes. "Praise to the gods I studied these minerals," she muttered to herself. The fiend jumped from the tree and ran towards her, bounding off a freestanding rock. She threw the rocks, firing them like a volley straight into the fiend, knocking it to the ground. Howling, it fell over, lashing with its maw and slashing with its tail. She sent another volley, breaking its legs. For good measure, she floated and then dropped a rock the size of a small child onto the tail, pinning it to the ground.

With a nod from Vytilia, Friedrich began his approach, carefully circling it around from the tail. The fiend snapped at him but could not move. Friedrich swallowed and stepped closer to the wounded fiend. It stared at him, barking and snapping, but was impotent. Friedrich took a deep breath, closed his eyes, and plunged the dagger into the fiend's belly. It squealed, and he stabbed again, still keeping his eyes shut. He stabbed again and again until the fiend let out a final gurgle and went limp.

Friedrich opened his eyes, looking down at the messily butchered fiend. He stood up, wiping his dagger on his trouser legs before sheathing it. Vytilia walked over, leaning her ear towards the corpse. It was dead, but she looked disappointed, like a master smith watching his fellow make a sword without an edge.

"This is why I did not want to talk," Vytilia stated. "These quadrupeds are dangerous, much more agile and faster than the red biped you encountered. But what was it doing out here all alone?" She was pacing back and forth, her eyes scanning for more movement. Devils usually operated in packs, but it was almost always near Strixan outposts or on busy roads. It does not make sense, from a military standpoint, to have a lone one in relatively unchartered territory. "Why . . ." She paused, turning about-face and rushing over to Friedrich. "Take off your clothes," she ordered.

"I just met you. This is hardly the time."

"Not in that way, you filthy plebeian. The blood! You are covered in devil blood! They must be following the scent. We need to burn your clothes!" That was why it dived to attack him first, she thought. It was getting revenge for the one he killed as if the devils were capable of revenge. Unless it was some sort of instinct?

"Well, what am I supposed to wear?"

"Make a loincloth out of leaves if you have to! If we do not get rid of the scent, they will be harassing us all the way until we reach Nidus. They will be back and in greater numbers. We will have to do something about your pugio and shield as well."

Friedrich sighed and turned away from her. He pulled off what remained of his clothes, passing them to Vytilia who threw them on the corpse. She then snapped her fingers, setting the pile ablaze. Looking at Friedrich standing, freezing to be more accurate, in his undergarments, Vytilia stifled a laugh. She made sure the corpse and clothes burned fully and hosed Friedrich's face, hair, dagger, and hands with stream water, making sure there was not any blood on him. To be sure, she also set her fingertips on fire, drying Friedrich off and evaporating any remaining blood. As he stood there, humiliated and shivering, pity overtook her. She untied her cloak and passed it to him.

"Give me your pugio." He passed the dagger to her first, holding it by the blade. She held it in her right hand, admiring it before setting it on fire. She held it there for a moment before extinguishing the fire and returning it. The blade was now a cool, blue-black color. She then took the age-shield and belt it was clipped to. Seeing him wince as she held it, she carefully held a small flame from her fingertip to boil away the blood. *This shield must have more cultural importance than he was letting on,* she presumed. "That should clear us of the scent for now. We need to get moving. And do not ruin that cloak; it was a gift."

"Wait, wait, I can't just wear this!" Friedrich protested. "I'll freeze to death! Can't you call up a pair of hose or shoes for me?"

"Call up? What? Bah! Set aside all your preconceived notions of how thaumaturgy operates. I cannot just pull something out of the aether. I need materials, to know how it works and functions. The cloak should be enough for now."

It wasn't, though Friedrich wouldn't expect her to know what it was like being cold, given that every time she touched him, she was as cold as snow. He tied the cloak around his neck, folding his arms to preserve as much body heat as he could, then tied his sheath around his waist to stop the cloak from billowing. His torso was covered, but his legs and feet were still freezing enough for his teeth to start chattering.

"Come on. We need to get moving again." She stepped over the creek, heading down another tunnel. He noticed that she was rubbing her temple.

Friedrich followed, waddling and hopping to avoid stepping on a sharp rock, the chattering of his teeth echoing off the tunnel walls. "When's the next clearing?" he asked.

"Whatever for? If you need water, I can pull it out of the lichen growing on the walls. I will need some time before I do so."

"No, it's not water. It's sleep. It feels like ages already. I was hoping we could stop and get some sleep."

She glanced backwards at him, an eyebrow raised in confusion. "Sleep? You slept for two days when I found you. Why would you need more so soon?"

Friedrich blinked several times, nearly laugh-choking in disbelief. "If I, if I don't get enough sleep, I . . . what kind of question is that? Everyone needs to sleep every day."

"I do not. I only require a small period of rest every few days. I can push myself and go for longer but at the cost of having a weaker grasp on my mental faculties. Do you really require sleep every day?" she sounded surprised.

"Yes." His stomach growled. "Something to eat wouldn't hurt either. I don't exactly have any paunch to survive off of." He realized that Vytilia admitted she only slept once a week or at least chose to. What was she?

She looked around the tunnel, noticing the various creatures skittering about. "You said you eat meat, correct? Could you catch one of those salamandra and eat it as you walked?"

"N-no." Friedrich laugh-choked again. "I've been hungry but never that hungry. I need to kill it first then clean it and cook it. Raw meat is bad for you. Don't you know that?" She didn't answer, instead pointing out a cluster of the growing mushrooms. He drew his dagger, slicing the cluster off and eating it like a pretzel. She must be trying to give him the Strixan experience, merely surviving instead of living. Maybe it was supposed to engender him to helping them. Maybe she really didn't understand his physiology and what he required. Or, maybe she was a bastard.

They pressed on, hiking from one tunnel to the next, all without any clear indication, at least to Friedrich, of where they were going. They passed through many caves, some similar to the one just after the waterfall, filled with gemstones, and some nearly pitch black with Vytilia having to grab Friedrich by the wrist to guide him. He noted that in the dark caves, she made no use of a torch, lantern, or even her fire spells, instead walking as if the room was illuminated. He, of course, wanted to ask questions, but the further they continued and hiked, the colder it became and the worse he felt. When he wasn't shivering, the only thing out of his mouth were swears for whenever he stubbed a toe or was cut by a rock. He was especially attentive to make sure the cloak wasn't harmed, fearing Vytilia if it was.

At last, they came to another clearing with the same healthily sick red trees and grass, the same moths, the same squirrel-things, and similarly illuminated by moon-sized collections of light stones as the last, though this one was much larger. He couldn't see the exit tunnel or the walls, and the ground of this one was hillier. They stopped after a hundred feet in a copse of trees providing a shaded area, as shaded as one can be underground with gemstones providing light. Friedrich took the cloak off to use it as a blanket, finding a softish tree root to act as a pillow.

Vytilia, visibly annoyed at having to stop, set her bag down and brought out the large fire gemstone from earlier. She set it down then raised her hands. Several rocks of varying shapes and sizes flew into her arms. Friedrich watched as she set the rocks down and created a fire circle. She then asked for his dagger and began stripping bark and twigs off of the tree, piling them around the gemstone. Satisfied with her work, she snapped her fingers, setting the kindling on fire. The gemstone began to change color to a bright orange, giving off heat.

"If you don't use fire to see in the dark, and you don't care about the cold, why do you even have this?" he asked as he moved closer to the warmth.

"Are you not tired? You need to sleep, so we can get moving again."

"Humor me. I hate going to sleep with an unanswered question," he tried appealing to her learned side.

"The devils fear fire. We have never seen them use any sort of tools aside from basic clubs or stone weaponry, and so we are inclined to believe they have never invented it, and so they are hesitant to attack when it is around."

"What do you call that?" He gestured to the gemstone.

"The proper term is a Sollapis. It would translate as . . ." She closed an eye and furrowed her brow. "Sun stone. It was a gift from our god."

Friedrich thought it strange she only mentioned one god when earlier she clearly made reference to many gods. "And those ones up there?" He pointed to the ceiling.

Vytilia made a grabbing motion with her fingers. One of the gemstones flew out of the ceiling into her hands. She tossed it to Friedrich. "They are called stellalapis or 'star stones' in your language. They grow and emit light naturally, which is how clearings like this can occur. My people can manipulate them to illuminate paths and trails and to light our cities for the sake of our animals."

"For your 'animals,' but not for you?" The dots connected. "So, you can see in the dark?" She nodded. "That's amazing!" Being able to see in the dark would make caverneering so much easier and cut down on costs and carry weight. If he had her stamina and endurance, he could be the most profitable caverneer in Erebus. "Can you do your witchcraft and make me see in the dark?"

"It does not work that way," she huffed. "I told you. Stop trying to think of thaumaturgy as your superstitious 'witchcraft.' Enough questions, go to sleep." He sighed and rolled over to face away from the fire, quickly falling asleep.

Vytilia sat, staring into the fire. She did not let her guard down, even now that they had gotten rid of the devil's scent, but she prayed that they would be much safer as they traveled. Now that it was quiet, she had time to think and reflect, especially on everything Friedrich had told her. It seemed impossible that a people such as his could ever form something as complex as an empire and all without thaumaturgy or scotopic vision. Yet somehow, they did. They must have some sort of edge, something that gave them an advantage over other creatures. The pugio he carried was finely made, even she could recognize the fine metalworking. Perhaps that was it. Their artisanship set them apart.

Or, was it their endurance? Despite his obstructing calls for rests and sleep, Friedrich did not give up. She could see blisters already forming on his feet, and even in his sleep near the fire, he still shivered. Still, he kept going. Not even the hardiest of draught animals her people possessed could continue like that. They had a limit and stubbornly refused to go past that. Whatever it was, she was certain it would help her people. It had to.

3

It was the smell that woke Friedrich up. He rolled over to see Vytilia sitting near the fire, rotating a spit. He sat up, wrapping himself in the cloak. She had made the spit out of sticks, held together with clay, and was roasting two newts she had caught. "These are for you," she explained. "Protein will help keep up your strength." She handed the spit to Friedrich. The newts had been thoroughly cleaned with even most of the skeletons removed.

He bit into them, surprised at the pleasant taste. "Do you not want any?" he asked.

"I have already fed."

He paused before taking another bite. Did she eat the skeletons? She had already fed? Who phrases it like that? He shook his head and continued eating. He had never had newt before. When they traveled, he and Bergmann hadn't gotten that desperate. It tasted like chicken or the poorer cuts of beef. He wondered if surface newts tasted the same. "Do 'Strixans' eat these?" he asked between bites.

"Not normally. Nestlings do when they are learning to hunt, but adults prefer cattle. Vermin are seen as sustenance during hardships. I was surprised when you mentioned you clean your meat before eating. Do you not know that organs are rich in nutrients?"

Organs? She probably meant offal. "I don't like them by themselves. They're better ground up in a wurst. Offal by itself is an acquired taste, and I haven't acquired it yet." He'd heard that expression from a Gaul a few years back and used it ever since.

She stood up and extinguished the fire, placing the sun stone back in her bag, again doing it one handed. "Alright, you had your rest, and you can eat on the move. We need to keep going."

Friedrich carefully held the spit in the air, so it wouldn't touch the ground, hurrying to catch up to her. "Thank you for the firstmeal," he told her as he started on the second newt. "Are you sure you don't want any?"

"I am sure. As I told you earlier, I have already fed."

He finished eating, tossing the spit aside. They were still passing through the clearing with no tunnel in sight. "How come your kind never tried to dig up to the surface? You have that rock witchcraft; can't you use that to carve out a way up?"

She sighed, whether it was an annoyed sigh or a sad sigh, Friedrich couldn't tell. "Most of the caves and tunnels we utilize are naturally occurring. Our lapisoperarii, er, 'stone workers' operate in tandem with miners and engineers to expand them, so legions and scouts can pass through. Stone working is a very, very, very complex form of thaumaturgy and requires years of study. We do not have lapisoperarii to spare for digging upwards. And we did not even think there was anything above us. We assumed the surface was completely devoid of life, which is why finding you is such an important discovery. Then, of course, there are the logistical problems with such an endeavor, namely a lack of building material and supplies. And we do not know what is above us and do not want to cause a cave-in or flood," she stated. "We have tried before; there have been many attempts in the past to try digging above and below, mostly to look for more resources, but there always was a vain hope we could dig up, find the surface, and reestablish ourselves up there. I would give anything to see the sun and the moon. But we simply cannot spare the resources."

"Are things really that bad down here?" he asked.

She bit her lip, pausing before answering. "They are. From the time they are of age, all tiercels are conscripted into the legions and sent to garrison our colonies and outposts. We are trying to stretch out, cover as much land as possible, take the fight to the devils. But the devils are relentless. They go away for months only to return in full force and lay siege. We beat them back but always with casualties and damage. Hens, meanwhile, have to stay behind and do almost everything else: care for nestlings, tend to crops and cattle, manage finances, teach school. The entire time we have been down here, we have essentially been stretched thin and at our limit."

She used that word nestling again, Friedrich noted, which given the context must mean children, but it was such an odd term. And hens? That meant women but why call them a hen? Same for calling (assumedly) men tiercels. He'd ask about it later. "Don't get me wrong, I'm grateful you can, but if food is so hard to come by, how come you are able to go out?"

"Due to my patrician status, I was able to study many schools of thaumaturgy, whereas others have to focus on one or two disciplines. This makes me much more capable of adapting and surviving on my own. And, we still need someone to explore and cartograph. An individual is much easier on our supply lines, and faster, than a contubernium of legionaries."

He didn't know half of what she had just said, so he chalked it up to her being smart. But, it was good to talk, so he brought the conversation back to what he did know. "What you were talking about with being stretched thin, it was like that on the surface a few years ago," Friedrich told her. "There was a massive war, so many were killed, so many starved, so many suffered blights. It went on for years. Life didn't get better even when the war ended. It still hasn't if I'm being honest."

"What caused it?"

"God only knows. Well, He started it. At least, what the Želeks thought God wanted. Then the Church and the Kommandant were trying to stamp out the Urworkers,[7] then all our neighbors got involved, and everything went to hell from there." He tensed up, breathing laboriously. "I, I don't like talking about it," he admitted, pulling the cloak tighter.

"May I ask who the victor was?"

He paused before answering. "I don't think anyone won. Maybe Gallia won. They got some land out of it. The rest of us . . ." He sighed.

She glanced at him, waiting to hear the rest of the sentence, but he stayed silent, staring at nothing ahead of them. *How curious*, she thought. Why the sudden halt in conversation? Perhaps war on the surface was less honorable? Or perhaps it was impolite to discuss it. His people truly were alien to Strixans in that regard. Even in current circumstances, the Strixans still prided themselves on their martial prowess. Her Father used to spend hours telling her about his service in the legions and his exploits on campaign. If he was not going to talk, then she at least could take advantage of this brief opportunity. She had many burning questions and decided to extinguish one. "I have one curiosity. Those spots on your face. What are they?" She was glancing back at him.

Freckles or his scars? She probably meant his freckles, Friedrich assumed. She's never seen the sun, he thought to himself, so she wouldn't know what they are. Could silver skin even get

7. A catch all term for those who try to reform or change the church. (Ur- prefix + work).

them? "The brown spots are freckles. They happen when you're young and out in the sun. It darkens your skin."

She paused, turning her body around and touching Friedrich's face around his nose and under his eyes. "You have been marked by the sun," she said with reverence. He shuddered; her hand felt like he was putting his face into a pile of snow. "These are a badge of honor. The sun has chosen you; it has touched you. You must have some sacred purpose not yet known to you."

"Me and every other toiler kid born in Erebus."

"What do you mean?"

He raised an eyebrow then pointed to his face. "These? Everyone gets these, especially those who work outside. The hair will get lighter, and your whole skin gets slightly darker. It's part of living and working out in the sun. It doesn't *mean* anything." She was still stroking his face. "Can you please not touch me?"

She withdrew her hand, scowling at herself. "I apologize. The sun is sacred to my people."

Friedrich took note of that, a surprising similarity to the surface.

"I was hoping that perhaps this set you apart, a distinguishing mark, further proof that our meeting was an act of providence." She almost sounded disappointed. "Those scars, are they also from the sun?"

"Oh, you mean the pockmarks?" He scratched his cheek. "Smallpox. I had a mild case when I was young, just around the time I was fellowed. I was really lucky. It kills most it touches or leaves them with even worse scars. I suppose with you and your kind being far from everyone else, you probably don't have to deal with sickness."

"Actually, Strixans are immune to disease. We have never dealt with an outbreak in our entire history. Individuals can fall ill, but it is usually a form of indigestion. But we have a knowledge of fighting pathogens because it still affects our cattle."

Immune from disease, he liked the sound of that. If it wasn't for the fact that all men were levied to fight, being a Strixan sounded much better than being a man. He wondered if she had some kind of witchcraft that could turn him into one.

"What is the sun like?" Vytilia asked with the curiosity of a child. "And the moon?"

"They're both big. Really big, though the sun is supposedly bigger and brighter. So bright, you can't look at it for more than a few ticks, or it'll blind you. It's almost always white, except at dusk when it's more of a yellow or orange. It's incredibly warm as well. If I'm not too careful and stay in the sun too long, I'll start to get red and burned. Sometimes it can get bad enough that my skin starts peeling."

"That is repulsive," Vytilia commented.

"If that means gross then yes, but it only happened once. I had to sit in a bathtub of cold water just to sleep. Anything else was too painful."

She waved dismissively. "This is unpleasant, move on; tell me about the moon." She turned back around and continued walking.

"The moon is pretty, especially a full moon. It can change color. I've seen blue, yellow, white, grey, even a red moon once. It also changes shape every few days, even disappears."

"Indeed, the phases, I have heard so much about that. They are a common motif in our artwork. Or, used to be." She shook her head, refocusing. "Are sunsets also as scintillating as I have been led to believe?"

"They can be. You have to see them when there's nothing in the way, no mountains or buildings. That's when they're at their most beautiful. My master, Herr Bergmann, always said that the sunsets and sunrises were God's way of embracing the world like a parent hugging their child as they go to bed and as they wake up." He smiled. "Oh! I need to get back to the surface before the end of the week! It's almost Midsummer!"

"What is that?"

"It's one of the four most holy holidays. It's when the sun is at the highest in the sky and summer is halfway done. It's also the longest day of the year and a great time. There's no work, lots of sweets and good food, and most every town has a huge bonfire. It's my second favorite holiday. I'd hate to miss it."

"That resembles the Solstice. It is one of our sacred days as well. Or, at least it was. My family is one of the few who still celebrate it, according to our best reckoning." She wondered if the other four holy holidays he mentioned were also solar-based.

"How long ago did Strixans live on the surface?"

"Millennia ago. And, as I have said, all of this will be explained when we get to Nidus." She was adamant. "You need to trust me Friedrich and to be patient. I do intend to tell you the history of my people, at least a condensed, abridged version, but it will be much easier to do so if we are safe behind the city walls."

They exited the clearing, coming to another tunnel. The newts so prevalent in the other tunnels were absent, replaced with glowing silverfish and several eclipses of moths. As he stepped from the grass to the cold unforgiving rock, Friedrich's teeth began to chatter again. Gooseflesh started appearing up and down his arms and legs, and he swore he could see his breath. A wave of exhaustion came over him as he plodded along, following after Vytilia. His limbs felt heavier, his stomach growled, and he could feel the bags growing under his eyes. The cold had drained him of his energy after waking up.

With his other senses dulled, and his only goal to follow Vytilia, his mind turned inward and began to reflect on his situation, piecing together all the information that he had taken in. As he drew connecting lines, he began to call back to Saga tales his landlady had taught him in his youth, the early lore of mankind and of the Church. Though she was an Urworkish, his landlady, Frau Beck, still devoutly believed the early lore of the Church and of the Holies, imparting the importance of these tales on Friedrich. He much preferred the tales of fantastical things and daring undertakings he'd overhear in beerhalls, but the instruction Frau Beck provided was frequent enough for him to have them memorized, even with his lackluster church attendance.

It was these tales his mind was recalling as he shuffled along, tales about the dark ages, after mankind had sprung forth from the trees and the ground. In those days, he recalled, man was oppressed by a cruel, malicious, and mysterious race, a race only spoken of in hushed whispers within the confines of a church, the Lightless. They were the ultimate evil, the opposite of everything that God and mankind stood for. As the church tales say, they were cast down into the bowels of hell by God to make way for mankind. It wasn't clear what exactly they were, other than that they weren't men and were very powerful. One could describe Strixans the same way.

Strixans as the Lightless? No, that wasn't right. She saved him. A Lightless would've taken his head or his soul. He had to think this through. She had mentioned that she had longed to see a sunset, she resembled a woman, and her people had once lived on the surface. The Lightless despised the sun, they were evil incarnate, more like the fiends. But if Vytilia and her people were not Lightless, then that meant . . . *Could it be?* he asked himself. Could her people, these Strixans, be the Half-gods, the forefathers of mankind, the writers of the Sagas, the Holies? The pieces were there. They once lived on the surface, they had unknown, even witch-like crafts, and she possessed superhuman strength. But the Half-god were not banished underground. They were raised to the heavens.

Fear and worry began to set in. If she was a Half-god, if her people were the warriors of old from the Sagas, he couldn't, no, shouldn't help them. The return of the Half-gods would usher in the end times, begin the Götterdämmerung. If he brought her to the surface, he would be damning so many people, so many innocents with a fate worse than death. The Lightless and their ilk would spill onto the surface, hell raised in force. All because of him.

Vytilia paused. She had heard Friedrich stop and looked back to see what the cause was. He was leaning against the wall, one hand held his head, and his face was contorted in thought. Was he delirious? Was he suffering indigestion? Or dehydration? "Friedrich are you well? Do you require another break?"

He stammered a question. "Vytilia, please, answer me. What happened to the Strixans? Why were you sent underground?" He nervously scratched his facial scars and breathed heavily.

She turned to completely face him. "We were not sent here willingly. It was a sentence, given to us by the devils after millennia of warfare and siege. In the final years of the war, our cities and bastions were swallowed by the planet, along with the survivors."

"Who else fought?"

"What do you mean?"

"Who else was there, fighting against you and with you?"

She tilted her head, raising her eyebrows. "None else. Only Strixans against devils. What are you getting at?"

Did she not know? Well, of course she didn't know. He was no churchman, but he assumed the Half-gods would have known of regular men. Maybe, maybe the Strixans were different, an unknown folk in the lost lore of mankind. The Sagas and Holy plays made no mention of brightly-colored fiends. And she had made no mention of any of the other things men were taught to fear: vargr, draugr, ettins, and the hundreds of other wicked things from the Sagas. Unless they were all considered 'devils' by her, but that seemed unlikely. She had a rich wordstock, richer than his. She wouldn't use blanket terms.

Still, he needed one last confirmation. "Have your people, have Strixans, ever been called half-gods?"

She sneered at the term. "Absolutely not. I find that term and insinuation rather blasphemous."

Well, that clinches it, Friedrich thought. He must be overthinking. He was exhausted and delirious, chasing after shadows that weren't there. He kept walking. "Sorry, sorry, I was overthinking some folktales I know." She nodded, turning back around after shaking her arms, very birdlike, as if she was drying off feathers. Strixans had strange body language.

Now Vytilia began to wonder. Friedrich did bring up an interesting query; where did men come from, and how did they relate to Strixan history? Life, devils excluded, cannot coalesce out of the aether. It takes time to germinate and grow. So, where did men grow? Were they an offshoot of a long-distant Strixan colony? Possibly, but why would they have pink skin? They must have come from beyond the borders of the empire, past the lands where lions dwelt, but that raised further questions. Why did the devils not go after them? Why was there not a record of interactions between exploratores and early man? And how come his people's monarch's title was derived from a Strixan word? They needed to get to Nidus soon. There was so much to learn, so much to glean from this . . . hardy scavenger.

They pressed on through the tunnel, Friedrich shivering the entire time. Whenever they had to stop, so he could eat a handful of mushrooms or drink water ripped out of plants growing on the walls, he would nearly fall asleep standing up. She kept urging him onward, telling him that when they got to Nidus, her family's personal chef would prepare him a feast. He would smile at the offer, continuing to hobble along. She even considered putting him to sleep and carrying him but decided that would be too demeaning for him, and distract her from her vigilance. That aside, walking near him gave her more opportunity to observe him whenever she looked back.

His cultural misunderstandings aside, he was still fascinating. A strange creature, a simple creature, yet brave; he had faced a devil, alone and practically unarmed, and survived. She surmised his complexity was a reflection on his society. His behavior before, and during, his panic had told her a great deal of his kind. They had a complex religious system, solar-centric holidays, and a thriving body of myth and legend. Perhaps, just perhaps, this empire of man or whatever it is called, could be complex and civilized enough to rival even the Strixans in their heyday. They would be a valuable ally indeed. Or, gods forbid, a formidable foe.

After hiking for many hours with many breaks and rests, they exited the tunnel, coming again to a much larger cave. This one seemed to stretch on for miles. They were in a small copse of trees on a cliff, overlooking a large and deep lake, nearly black from the lack of light. Small trails petered off the side of the cliff, circling around the lake, pushing forward in the dim light towards the rest of the cave. The star stones were not as powerful or numerous here. Friedrich nearly tripped when he came to his first tree. Grateful at having stopped, he took the cloak off and sat down, almost sleeping instantly as he leaned against a tree.

Vytilia stepped over the sleeping Friedrich and stood at the cliff edge. She remembered this cave from her travels a few days prior. It was different. She peered into the dark, looking for change when she saw it; raised on the opposite side of the lake were four walls, and from her height, she could see sun stones blazing within. That could only mean one thing. She hurried over to Friedrich, quickly shaking him awake.

"Wha-what?" He drew his dagger. "Attack? Are we attack?" he slurred.

"Friedrich! Wonderful news! The legions have established an outpost nearby! We need to head there right away! Come on, stand up!" She grabbed his wrist, leading him through the trees and down the right-hand path towards the lake. As his eyes adjusted to the dark (and when he could open them) he now saw the walled encampment in front of them with flashes of orange fires sneaking out through the gates.

As they approached the gates, Vytilia let go of Friedrich's hand and approached the sentries. He laid in the sand by the lake shore, a good thirty feet from the gate, struggling to keep his eyes open, overhearing Vytilia talk to the sentries. They were speaking in her tongue, but he swore he heard them hissing at each other. When she finished, she picked Friedrich back up and again led him by the wrist into the camp. With light from the campfires, he got a better look at the walls. They were remarkable. Rather than a wooden palisade as he'd seen from abandoned encampments or woodcuts on the surface, they were stone. Not hewn or piled stone either, they were smooth and even on every side. They looked as if they were pulled straight from the cavern floor like a scroll being opened. Given that he'd seen Vytilia shoot rocks like bullets, he assumed this was done with similar means.

As they entered the camp, Friedrich got a better look at the warriors and was taken aback. While he never sought out warriors, he had a general idea of what they were supposed to look like, usually with minimal armor and brightly colored clothes. Yet these warriors were nothing like that. They all wore a dress, or at least some kind of skirt, colored blue-black, the same color as a deep bruise. Compared to warriors on the surface (except for certain kinds of horsemen) Strixan warriors were covered from head to toe in armor. Their cuirass was an odd design, made of several bands of metal horizontally wrapped around the torso. Large pauldrons, similarly designed, were wrapped around each shoulder. On their left arm, the men had large, rectangular shields, decorated with images of the sun and moon. A short sword and dagger were sheathed at their waist. Their right arm, protected by a long piece of armor built in a manner similar to the cuirass, held a long spear. Their helmets covered their heads completely, leaving only the face and ears exposed. Finally, they wore solid metal greaves and sandals to protect their legs. Their armor seemed archaic but was so finely crafted and professionally maintained, he could not doubt its effectiveness.

Friedrich couldn't help but be in awe at how professional and disciplined they looked, though he found it odd that there were almost no tents. The camp was arranged like a town square with clearly defined roads, each leading to an entrance in the walls. There was an armory, a ground for training, what he assumed to be a stable (though he couldn't see any horses), and places for warriors to assumedly sleep, where bedrolls and fire pits were all arranged carefully and methodically. Each group of warriors was circled about a sunstone, sharpening weapons, polishing armor, and stitching clothes, all while drinking or talking. A few pointed when Friedrich passed by.

So, these were male Strixans, Friedrich thought to himself. They differed vastly from Vytilia. Each one had a more pointed, sharp face, with a more beak-like nose. Each was broad chested, much broader than any workmen on the surface. Their eyes were small but piercing. Similarly, like Vytilia, they had long legs, and all moved their heads in a bird-like fashion. It was uncanny how familiar and unfamiliar they looked.

They stopped in front of the only tent in the entire camp, a large one that could accommodate ten or twelve people. It was adjacent to a large stage with a sizeable parade ground in front. Two sentries stood outside the tent entrance. Friedrich turned his back, observing the camp while Vytilia spoke to the guards. Did he hear hissing again? When he turned back around, there was a new person there, another warrior. He wore a chainmail shirt with several medallions tied to the front. Under his left arm, he cradled a helmet with a stiffened crest of hair dyed blue on top.

Vytilia turned to him. "Friedrich, this is Centurion Asprenas Decula Dracius, a commander in the Imperial Legions. He has been gracious enough to allow us to spend the night with his legion." Friedrich nodded, his eyes growing heavy. She turned back to the Centurion. "You will have to forgive him; the trip has been difficult on him."

"I can see that." The Centurion turned to his sentries and gave them both orders. They nodded, hurrying off to grab supplies. They returned with a large canvas tarp. "I am afraid we are short on proper bedding, but this will at least allow him to stay warm. He can sleep next to the command tent."

"*Gratias,*[8] Centurion." She led Friedrich over to the side of the tent to a flattened part of the rock and gently lowered him down. He took off the cloak, again using it as a pillow, and started falling asleep, still shivering. The legionaries, with an annoyed look, wrapped the tarp around him as a blanket. The soldiers resumed their position outside of the tent, showing Vytilia inside. Centurion Dracius was sitting on a cot, pouring over a report by lamplight. He gestured to an empty cot opposite of him for her to sit. He set the report down and reached under his cot, producing a bottle and two cups. She eagerly accepted the drink, swirling the dark red liquid before taking a long sip. It had been too long since her last proper drink, and even if it was only above-average military rations, it still tasted divine.

"He really is from the surface?" The Centurion asked before taking a drink.

"He is. He said he was exploring a cave system then fell down a hole and landed here. He must have fallen nearly a dozen miles by his reckoning."

8. Strixan way of saying Thank You.

"It is a miracle he is still alive!" She nodded, taking another drink. "Gods be praised, but what was he doing in that cave system in the first place?"

"He said it is his occupation, scavenging for trinkets in the mountain to make a living." She watched disappointment wash over Dracius' face. "I know. I felt the same way. But beggars cannot be choosers as the plebeians say. He is very knowledgeable about his people and has fought and killed a devil already."

"You encountered a devil?" The Centurion sat upright.

"He encountered one while he was still on the surface, a red biped, and then we fought another on our way here, one of the blue quadrupeds."

Dracius rubbed his chin then poured Vytilia another glass. "A devil that high up? That does not bode well."

She shook her head. "I had the same thought. Since it was all alone, I am inclined to believe it was feral and probably wandered through the burrows until it found its way up there. The blue one we fought, it too was alone and following us by scent. Hence why he was nearly naked when we arrived."

Dracius did not answer. He swirled his cup before taking another drink, wiping his mouth and setting the cup aside. "This is troubling news," he admitted. "Well, it is mixed news. If, and I mean if, the devils have found a way to the surface, it is possible that they might be gathering forces for another cataclysm, which would relieve the pressure off of us but damn his people. And the last thing we need are legions of battle-hardened devils returning from the surface," he grumbled, ruminating on the possibilities. "I am not much for piety, but it does sound as if you finding him was an act of providence. If you can convince the Concilium to ally with the surface, a joint effort to strike at the devils would save us and the surface. We can whitewash two walls with one bucket."

She nodded in agreement, accepting a third cup. "On the topic of the Concilium, are you out here on my father's orders?"

Dracius smiled. "Officially, we are expanding our reach into this region, clearing out any devil burrows we come across, while also searching for new sources of lumber." He tapped the side of his nose. "Unofficially, Praetor Quintia did mention that you were exploring here and made a vague suggestion to send out a vexillation to make sure you were safe."

"My father using imperial resources to protect me? I cannot imagine he would do such a thing." She winked, taking another sip. "What news is there from the rest of the empire? Anything exciting happen while I was away?"

"Compared to finding evidence of life on the surface, anything I tell you will be mundane." He chuckled to himself before clearing his throat. "A few of the outermost outposts have been attacked, nothing too substantial, mostly blues and reds and a few of the black arthropods. I have heard rumors amongst the legionaries that some of the green serpent archers were seen. But, nothing more than rumors."

"Have any of the colonies been attacked?"

"Just sightings and a few beat up officials. The beasts are mostly focusing on military outposts for now."

"I have never seen one of those black arthropods in person."

"Pray that you never do. They are the most powerful ones. Their arms are grafted into natural swords, and they have a shell thicker than a scutum. Pilums just bounce off; you have to hit at just the right angle with a gladius to finish them off." Dracius stood up, extinguishing the lamp and putting away his reports and maps in a lockbox. He donned his sword and put his helmet under his arms. "I imagine you must be tired. I will let you have the tent for the night. Would not want rumors to spread about a Centurion sleeping in proximity to a Praetor's daughter."

"Dracius, you have been so generous; I would hate to intrude."

"Oh, it is not an intrusion. All I needed to do was write up patrol schedules and examine reconnaissance reports. Though, spending the time making my rounds in the camp, inspecting equipment, putting the fear of the gods in the lad's hearts is a much better use of my time." He wryly smiled. He offered Vytilia a fourth cup, but she refused. He resealed the bottle and set it under his bed. "We have a supply train leaving for Nidus tomorrow. Be sure to pass along my regards to Praetor Quintia. I will also see if I can get our guest a proper tunic and footwear and some rations." He paused. "What does he eat?"

"He mentioned bread. And dried meat if you have it. He spent most of our journey subsisting on fungi and salamandra. Fresh, clean water would also do him some good."

Dracius nodded. "We should have enough to spare, especially for a guest as illustrious as a surface dweller. Rest well." He said that last sentence almost like it was an order. Vytilia was inclined to follow. She laid down on the cot. Tomorrow was going to be an

. . . interesting time. They would finally get to Nidus, the moment of truth. She closed her eyes; she needed all her faculties tomorrow.

• • •

Šar Šarrāni Molek was not a being who felt fear. Indeed, he wondered if his kind had even been engineered to recognize fear. Yet, as he stood before the great chamber of the gods, listening as a herald announced his arrival, he had to ponder what it was he felt. Trepidation, perhaps, or nervousness, or whatever he had felt every time he stepped through these doors and did not know the name of. Whatever it was, he could not afford to show it. He stepped through the chamber doors with his best and most placid face.

When he first had visited this hallowed and sacrosanct hall, he had been filled with the appropriate awe. It had been hard not to. The room was a magnificent display of architecture and craftsmanship. But now, after whichever number visit this was (he didn't bother counting which time it was anymore), he simply did not care.

In his private, innermost moments, the ones he dare not speak, he thought the room a cruel mockery of what once was and what could be. The chambers were decorated beautifully: carpets that were older than Molek but looked freshly woven, artworks made of alloys who's recipe was lost to history, ivory censures made from creatures now extinct, and a map of the heavens made of crystal in the roof above. The map was perhaps the most ironic part of the room. Molek had to wonder if the stars even looked like that anymore. It had been many tens of thousands of years since the gods last saw the sky and nearly one hundred thousand since that map had been made. But, Molek traitorously and privately had to wonder, was that on purpose? When was the last time the gods had *made* something, rather than destroyed? Truth be told, when was the last time they actually did any of the destroying?

He pushed these thoughts away and prostrated himself before the twin thrones. He stole a glance at the occupants, his masters, and was unsurprised at what he saw. It was the same posture they always sat in. Sky Father rested the elbow of his top right arm on the armrest, holding his head in one hand. His bottom pair of hands twiddled their thumbs or scratched himself, while his top left hand reached out and held the hand of his wife, Ground Mother, who mirrored his posture almost exactly.

Molek wondered if in any of the early artworks, or in any of the stories, if the gods were depicted as they were now. He supposed, if there were any, he would never know. None of his kind ever would. They were not made to think, only to pay obeisance and die. Sky Father had reminded him of that many times.

After paying his obeisance and prattling off meaningless and synonymous titles, Sky Father spoke. "What is it, warmaster?" Molek cringed. They never used his proper title, not even a close translation of it.

"Oh great ones," Molek began, "I bring word from the outermost layer. There has been . . . a breach. A pink-skinned being was spotted travelling with one of the grey birds. By our estimate, the pink one must have come from the surface."

It had been many thousands of years since Molek and his kind had been to the surface. The time before last, a society had risen up that could challenge, and very nearly did, threaten the rule of the gods. If history was a trend, then whatever society this pink one belonged to could be a greater threat than even they. He hoped his tone had been serious enough.

Now the gods' posture changed. They unclasped their hands and stopped twiddling their thumbs. "What!?" Ground Mother cried out. "How could this happen!? Insolent fool!"

Sky Father reached a hand out to calm his bride. "Warmaster," he began, "what is your purpose?"

Molek took a deep breath. It hid his annoyance. "To serve, oh ruler of the skies."

"And, what is the standing command we have given you?"

"To keep the layers separate."

"Why?"

"So that there may be balance."

"And, why must there be balance?"

"For your glory and exultation."

Sky Father nodded. "But warmaster, when the cycles interact and balance is disrupted, I am not being glorified or exulted, am I?"

Molek closed his eyes. Not for humility but so he could roll them. "No, oh great one, you are not."

"See? It is smart." Ground Mother beamed at her husband.

A myriad of slurs and disparaging comments came to Molek's mind, but he kept those sequestered and quiet.

Sky Father laughed. "So then, warmaster, what must you do for my glory?"

"Restore balance and kill the intruder."

"Then you know what you have to do. Go, leave us, kill this pink being and however many grey birds you need to."

Molek paused. If he wanted to ensure this would be done, he would need more resources, but he knew they would not be granted. He wondered if the gods themselves even realized the danger they were in. He would work with what he had.

"On the blood of my forefathers, it will be done my lords." Molek swallowed. "For your glory." No further response, only a waved dismissal. They went back to their original postures. Their faces did not even betray they had been given shattering news. They didn't care. Of course they didn't care! They weren't the ones who threw their lives away fighting their wars and their enemies. One final, traitorous thought came to Molek as he left. Can a god suffer from hubris?

4

Vytilia awoke sometime late. Gauging by the sound of soldiers outside lining up for orders, it must be the beginning of a new watch. That would have been a few hours after she had fallen asleep, enough for Friedrich to get a decent rest. She stepped outside the tent. Centurion Dracius and his officers were on the stage, handing out the day's commands and passphrase. When she stepped out, she noticed several of the soldiers' attention glance towards her. She ignored them, walking over to the side where Friedrich had been sleeping. He was sitting upright, huddled in the tarp and chewing on a piece of dried meat, holding a waterskin in one hand.

"*Guten Morgen,*" he told her as she walked over to him. He set the waterskin down and handed her the cloak, nicely folded. "I kept it safe, took good care of it, just as you asked."

"You did well. How did you sleep? Have you recovered enough for the rest of the journey?"

"I hope so. A war camp isn't the quietest place to sleep. And well, canvas doesn't keep out the cold very well. How come I couldn't stay in the tent like you?"

"This is the command tent," she explained, "the heart of a legion. Civilians cannot just wander in and spend the night. It is standard procedure. And it is improper for a hen of my class to be sleeping in the same room as a tiercel of any station. I do have honor to worry about."

He couldn't fault the honor part. "But aren't you a . . . 'civilian'? Why didn't you sleep outside?"

"My father's position affords me . . . certain privileges." Friedrich rolled his eyes, muttering something about all lords being the same. "Did the Centurion's legionaries treat you well? If not, I shall discuss it with him. The offenders will be properly disciplined."

"They were fine. Gave me some odd looks, I'm sure they got a good laugh from me. Other than that, they left me alone." He took a swig from the waterskin. "I think whoever they got this from might've been sneaking in wine. The water has this weird iron aftertaste. It didn't get cleaned out."

She tensed up slightly before putting on the cloak. "Have they brought you a tunic yet? We are to leave with a supply train to Nidus. It will get us there faster than on foot, and you can ride in the carriage, get some more rest."

"They brought the tunic. I wanted to ask . . ." He held the tunic up by the collar. "I mean the skirt part isn't odd. It looks like what a priest wears. But don't you have a pair of hose I could wear? This is awfully drafty."

She looked at him oddly. "Ho . . . se?"

"Yes, hose, or breeches? They're a single garment with two holes you can put your legs through. I was wearing them when you found me. Or, they *were* hose."

"We do not wear such attire. I found the clothes you were wearing to be more foreign than you were. Does everyone on the surface wear clothes like that?"

"More or less. In Erebus at least. Everywhere else wears robes." He started putting on the tunic, scratching himself. "Gah, this feels like it's made of ants. They wear this under armor? It'd drive you mad before the battle!" He stood up, wrapping the tarp around himself.

"That must be freshly woven. Keep wearing it, and it will soften up. Come along. Dracius has finished giving out orders for the day; the supply train will be leaving soon." She led him over to a gate at the rear of the camp where Dracius and a few of his troops were waiting. They stood next to a cart, no three carts all tied together, now that Friedrich could see. He saw movement towards the gate. He expected, like nearly all carts on the surface, that these were pulled by a team of horses. But upon closer inspection, they were pulled not by horses but by askards.[9] Horse-sized askards. They were dark-colored with beady eyes. They would flick their tongues out, licking their eyes then muzzling their handlers. Friedrich stepped backward. He turned his back, shuddering every time he heard the thing purr.

"Did our guest sleep well?" Dracius asked, smirking as Friedrich kept avoiding looking at their beasts of burden.

"He did, though he complained your legionaries were too loud."

9. Lizard or any reptile aside from serpents.

Dracius snorted. "I will make a note of that next time we entertain guests." He scratched an askard behind the ear. "I apologize for not giving you your own mount, but our resources are few. You will have to ride in one of the carriages with the man."

Vytilia nodded. "There is not a need for apologies, Centurion. It will make the journey go by faster and allow me to ask questions."

A legionary alerted Dracius the carriages were ready. "Fortune be with you, Vytilia. Give my regards to your father. I hope when I see you or him again, it will be accompanied with good news."

"*Gratias*, Centurion Dracius. I will be sure to let the Concilium and my father know of both your hospitality and assistance." Dracius nodded, returning to the command tent. "Friedrich!" she called out, grabbing his shoulder. "We are leaving. We are to ride in the back." She followed his eyes to the calcerta team. "Is something wrong?"

"What the hell is that!?" He pointed to the team. "I've never seen an askard that big! It looks like some kind of wyrm!" This is what he imagined the great, man-eating asks of the new world looked like, just with smaller teeth.

Vytilia stifled a laugh. "A worm? Not at all! There is not a need to be frightened. Calcerta are harmless! They're mostly herbivorous aside from insects or even a salamandra. They would not, and cannot, hurt you." A legionary scratched one behind its equivalent of ears. It made a clicking sound as its eyes rolled back in bliss. Friedrich still looked horrified, giving them a wide berth as he and Vytilia climbed into the last cart.

A legionary in a black-trimmed tunic stretched his hand out, and the gates began to recede back into the ground, like a wave into the sea. The teamsters urged their mounts forward, the askards chittering and purring as they picked up speed. Immediately after exiting the encampment, and for several stone's throw away, the ride was loud and uncomfortable, the cart rattling and shaking enough that Friedrich thought his teeth would fall out. Then suddenly, the ride turned smooth and quiet. He leaned out of the rear to examine the road. The cart wheels had rolled into carved grooves. It was like a mine cart track but inverted.

"What?"

"Incredible is it not? We call it the Via Sculptile.[10] It has been how our empire transports goods and personnel since the pre-cataclysmic days. Beasts of burden can pull three times their normal weight, and travel time can be measured in hours rather than days. And it keeps our wagons in good condition and fragile goods safe since resources are so scarce."

He pulled himself away from staring at the road, leaning back. "This is . . . keen. I can't fathom my kind never thought of anything like this! We've been walking, riding, or using boats since the Age of Dawn."

"Your people do not have a system like the Via Sculptile?"

"Not for everyday things. Mines will use rails to move ore, but that's it."

"My people have much to teach yours."

"Well, I'm sure we have just as much to teach." She smirked. A clever retort. "I suppose now that we're not walking and keeping a watch out for fiends, we have some time to talk? I have a saga's worth of questions."

"A sound idea. I can answer some of your questions, though I choose which ones I can answer now and what I can explain when we get to Nidus. And, I also have questions."

"Right, well first thing. I want—"

She raised her hand. "Ah, ah, ah, I will go first. Patrician's prerogative." He rolled his eyes. "The city you originate from. Hillerbon, Hilletton?"

"Hertzabrunno," he corrected.

"Forsooth, that was it; what is it like?"

"What's it like?" He scratched his head. "Hertzabrunno's a great burgh. It's more of a fortress than a town, at least the old town is. Once you get a few rutes[11] beyond the walls, or across the river, it's . . . cozy. A nice mix of field and town living. We've got some good folk there, lot of hard working, busy folks who stay out of each other's lives. The Stadtrat isn't too heavy handed, and while it doesn't like the Erdeish, it also isn't eager to give into witch hunts."

"Stadtrat?"

"The leading burghers, the townsmen. It's a group of them, and they all run the town, setting up lawhalls and lawspeakers and paying the Stadtwache."

---

10. Carved Road or Carved Way

11. Surface unit of measurement, about 12 feet in length.

Like the old Parvus Senatus that used to run the non-Nidus cities, Vytilia translated. "You make the walls sound . . . unusual. Do not all cities on the surface have such fortifications?"

"Not all of them. Major trading ones do or ones near the border like Hertzabrunno, but most smaller towns and hamlets only have a fence. Sometimes, you don't even notice the walls are there because so much has been built around and outside them."

"Fascinating. And Hertzabrunno, you mentioned it was part of a larger empire. Does it have a name? Do your people have a name?"

"When can I ask my questions?"

"Your time is coming soon. Has your race not yet learned patience?"

Friedrich rolled his eyes. "We're a Free-Stead, which means we answer directly to the Kommandant in Grenzburg. There's no middleman; all fees, gripes, war levies, all are under the Kommandant's wield. As for the Realm, the full name is The Holy Realm of Midgart. But normally, you'd just call it 'The Realm' or sometimes 'Das Reich' if you want to get priggish."

Vytilia thought it interesting that it was prefaced as "free." "Why is it referred to as holy?"

Friedrich let out a groan, annoyed she was ignoring (possibly deliberately) his questions. "The way I was taught, the Church and Realm go hand in hand. The Church started the Realm, gives legitimacy to the Kommandants, and in return, the Realm shields and broadens the Church. That's how it used to be anyway; everything is different now since the Urworkish started up, and the church moved to Grenzburg. That's a whole slew of problems I don't want to get into. That's kicking a hornet's nest."

Surface society is not as unified as her people are or had been, Vytilia thought. Religion seemed to play a much more central role, which could explain his superstitions and misconceptions. If this "Church" had some sort of dogma regarding thaumaturgy, then that explained why he was so unfamiliar with it. Ancient Strixans had dealt with many rebellious cults and tribes that hated thaumaturgy. One of her ancestors even earned a cognomen[12] for putting down such a rebellion. But those were on a small scale. An entire empire or religion that disregarded thaumaturgy? It sounded impossible.

12. A special type of commendation in Strixan society where a new name is given to commemorate a particular deed.

How did they fight wars, practice medicine, construct buildings? Such feats would be impossible, nay, *should* be impossible.

"Why does your God look down on . . . well, what you call witchcraft?"

Do I look like a priest? Friedrich grumbled. "Because they're liars." That was his best recollection of a teaching Frau Beck gave him. "You can't do something without earning it. You sow seeds, you reap crops. You shear sheep, you get wool. You work, you get paid. Witches make something out of nothing or steal to get by. And that's not to say anything about fouling wells, killing newborns, and calling Lightless out of hell to slay their foes."

"Do you still think I am a witch?"

Having realized what he just described, he couldn't really say yes, but at the same time, what else could she be? If snapping her fingers and making flames appear wasn't witchcraft, then he didn't know what else it could be. "Well . . . maybe not a bad witch. Not all witches are evil, just ones that do dark and black crafts. Every hamlet has a wise woman, someone who does white craft like finding water or making poultices." The line between blackcraft and whitecraft was a thin one and one that disappeared after a bad harvest. He didn't feel the need to mention that last part.

"This religion, or church of yours, it must be a powerful force . . ." Her voice trailed off as she pondered what kind of records and histories it kept. "What year is it on the surface?"

"1665 *Heiliges Jahr*. It means Holy Year, or HJ for short."

Another overtly religious reference. She wanted to know more. What did these church-men know? They must have scholars! And with how powerful he had made this church sound, they must be well-traveled. "Does every nation belong to this religion?"

"Uh, no, no not . . . most do?" So many of these words were new to Friedrich.

"Most? Interesting, what other nations are there aside from your Realm?" When he gave her a confused look, she expanded upon what she meant by nation.

When she finished, he decided that after this, he was going to ask questions whether she liked it or not. "It all depends on what you consider a 'nation.' We'd call it a homeland or fatherland if you're into talking fancy. The Realm is a land of stems and sippes who swear oaths to the Kommandant. Then there's lands such as Ostlücke, which are a part of and not a part of the Realm."

"What of fully independent nations?"

"Oh there's at least twenty or more on Erebus alone if you include Vitelish steadlands.[13] And there's kingdoms that share a king but are two different kingdoms. Then in Estuwwa, there's the Sultanate, Farsova, Mauryamulk, Zonguo. No matter which way you go, someone owns and oversees the land."

"Remarkable. That would explain why your people are so martial. It sounds as if you are surrounded by adversaries." And all of this developed in less than three millennia? Perhaps these men are smarter than they appeared.

"Vytilia?" Friedrich interrupted her thinking. She turned to him, half-annoyed and half-curious. "What are you?" he asked.

"I beg your pardon?"

"I've still been trying to figure out what you are since we met, so I can understand everything. You're obviously not a woman, you're not a huldra, you're not a fairy or anything like that, and I'm assuming you're not an elf since you're too tall. You're also not a Valkyrie or a Holy. I've heard almost every bedtime, campfire, and folktale there is, but there's nothing like you."

"I am a Strixan," she sputtered.

"I know that, but what *is* a Strixan is my question."

She did not know how to answer that. Nor did she ever think she would ever have to answer that. She was a Strixan, and that was it. She did have a few more aspects of their biology, history, and culture to share, though perhaps reveal was a better word, but those had to wait for Nidus, and even those could not fully answer his questions. How does one explain what stone is? Or what air is? It is what it is. "I, I do not have an answer for that," she admitted. "We are Strixans."

"Are you unique among Strixans?"

"What do you mean?"

"Well . . ." He cleared his throat, and his cheeks turned slightly red. "Back at the war camp, I noticed everyone else had more of a duller grey skin tone. And no one had white hair like yours or golden eyes. All those warriors looked similar to one another, but you were startlingly unique."

She hid a smile. Maybe this surface dweller had some charm. "It is a rare phenotype. My mother and I are the only ones who have had it in many years. According to historians, the original

13. City-state.

Strixans, the ones who founded the empire and started the line of Emperors, all had similar features."

"So, are you lordly?"

"We are Patricians, the upper-class of society. The Imperial dynasty and throne were done away with years ago. Having royal ancestors does not award us any special treatment or privileges."

He looked away from Vytilia, pondering on her answers. So, she was a high-born, the upper crust of her world. No wonder she spoke down to him. Her blue-bloodedness aside, something about what she told him felt . . . off. Really, everything about her felt off. She never showed her teeth when she spoke or smiled, she never ate, she seemed to have limitless energy. And while she looked mannish, there was still this, disconnect between her, the other Strixans, and people on the surface, a disconnect that went beyond skin tones and body temperature. There had to be more than simply "being a Strixan." There HAD to be some kind of thing or tale that explained what Strixans were. He knew it. Between her insistence that "everything would be explained at Nidus," the armed guards, his poor treatment, and the mystery of the Strixans, he felt uneasy. What did she really want from him? This seemed like a unnecessary amount of effort for knowledge on the surface. Were they trying to break his spirit? Prepare him for something worse? Was he just being fearful, his years of being raised on tall tales catching up to him?

"Vytilia. Am I your prisoner?" he asked.

She was taken aback. "Of course not! Why would you ever think of such a thing?"

"Well, you seem off, almost shifty, like you're hiding something from me. I didn't expect a grand welcome with a lot of pomp and fanfare, but you haven't treated me like a guest. Maybe guest-kindness is different down here?"

She did not know whether to be offended or astounded by his reasoning. "I promise you Friedrich, none of these actions were intentional. There are always . . . hiccups when establishing diplomatic relations. Cultural misunderstandings, language barriers, blunders in etiquette, for all intents and purposes, you are a diplomat of your people, and I am for mine. We do not understand each other, and so we also do not trust each other. And fear of the unknown is a common phobia, so it should not be a surprise you feel uneasy around us. If the roles were reversed, I imagine I would feel as you do."

Doubtful, Friedrich thought. Had the roles been reversed, he would've accounted for breaks, proper meals, answered questions, almost the opposite of what she'd been doing. But, he did suppose this too was a "cultural misunderstanding" as she put it. Even on Erebus, every group had different ideas of what guest-kindness was. At least he didn't have to greet the centurion with a kiss as the Gauls do. "Is it my turn to ask questions now?" she nodded. "How long have Strixans been down here?"

She thought on the question before answering. Was it one she could answer now or one that had to wait for Nidus? Now was fine. It was harmless enough and did not require much elaboration. "According to our best estimates—timekeeping is difficult without being able to track the heavens—we have been down here for 3,000 years, give or take a few centuries."

Friedrich whistled. 3,000 years? He was doubtful he could even count that high. He doubted even the Church had records going back that far. Everything before Year One was a vague and unknown time. The Sagas couldn't be that old, especially since, given their earlier talks, the Long Winter happened sometime after the Strixan cataclysm. "How have you stayed alive after this long?"

"With great difficulty. When we were brought underground, entire cities were sunk, which included all of the inhabitants and material. We have been surviving off of generations of heavily inbred cattle we feed with bioluminescent fungi and ferns. Everything we do is for the preservation of our race. Anything that takes up too many resources is either banned or repurposed. We are without luxuries, without art, without literature, even without religion. Sacrifices to the gods are banned because the animal could be used to feed a family."

"That sounds . . . miserable."

She shushed him. "It is best not to dwell or think on our situation. Our civilization's morale hangs on the thinnest of threads. The plebeians are only a few missed feedings away from rioting and upending our society. This is why discovering you is such an act of providence; your people can greatly aid us in relieving pressure on both our armies and our populace. Even if all you can offer us are new herds of cattle, that alone would save an uncountable number of Strixan lives."

Friedrich felt humbled and vindicated that perhaps his guardian Norn had guided him here to allay suffering and free the downtrodden, something he had longed to do his entire life but lacked the means. He could make a difference on the world, leave a mark and fulfill an orlay that was more than simply "do good." And all they asked for was knowledge and food.

"I believe it is my turn to ask a question," Vytilia announced. "You mentioned a word earlier when we spoke of your freckles: Erebus. It struck me as odd, almost out of place in your language. What is Erebus? Is it different from the Realm?"

"Erebus is the land, the earthtile the Realm resides on." What was that word he learned from the Vitelish man? "Continent as some call it."

Continent? Vytilia wondered. That was reminiscent of a Strixan word. "Where does the name come from?"

He shrugged. "It's old, older than the Realm, maybe older than the Church. Passed down through the ages. Did you have a name for it?"

"We did not. The landmass and the planet were referred to as 'Terra' or dry land. We gave names to specific regions and provinces, but that was it. Our empire was so expansive that it covered a number of landmasses; beyond our borders was untamable wilds."

Which begged the question, where did men come from? Friedrich wondered. He knew the Sagas said they trekked from the east, but how far did they have to trek to not meet Strixans? He was starting to think that maybe the Sagas had a few flaws in their tales. "So, if you've been down here for 3,000 years, how are you able to speak Teutonish so flawlessly?"

"Is that what your language is called? Teutonish?"

He nodded. "Churchmen will sometimes call it the 'mean tongue' or 'gutter Rinnish.' The rest of us call it Teutonish or Gothish in the east."

"Then is that the gentilic for your people? Teutons?"

"Huh?"

"What you call yourselves, that is what gentilic means. Is Teuton your gentilic?"

He had to stop and think. "No, Teutonish is our tongue, but no one has ever called me that before." He scratched his head. "On the surface, everything is about the stem, the big group you belong to. Then within that stem is the sippe, which is a smaller group, the one that gives you your age-shield." He tapped his for effect. "So, my stem is the Teudish. But no one within the Realm calls themselves the Teudish, always their sippe or their hometown.

Outsiders call us that. And that's just for us. Everyone else does things a little different."

"What about you? What would you call yourself? What is the gentilic for your home province?"

He shifted, hiding his age-shield. "I don't really have a homeland. If you wanted, you could call me a Hertzabrunner, but I live outside the walls. I think of myself as Friedrich, the caverneer."

"How sad, not having a state to fight and serve."

"I'm not losing any sleep over that." He shrugged. "How are you able to speak it?"

"Simple, in the brain there are neural pathways that are activated when speaking. I mapped those out via thaumaturgy then mapped them onto my own mind, so I can learn and speak your language. During this process, it also purifies your language to the best ability, allowing me to speak it fluently." He stared at her blankly. She sighed. "I used 'witchcraft' to read your mind and learned your language that way." She rolled her eyes.

"Well, you speak it better than me."

Of little surprise, she told herself, given his background. "Your language is odd. I cannot pronounce my name correctly in it."

"How are you supposed to pronounce it?"

"Wee-tee-lee-a," she told him. He caught a glimpse of her teeth, very briefly as she spoke. They sent a shiver down his spine for some reason.

"So, with a 'wee' sound not a 'vie' sound." She nodded affirmatively. It reminded Friedrich of the Merkyers. They pronounced the name "Wilhelm" as "*Will*-helm" rather than the right and proper "*Vil*-helm." No wonder she had been so hostile for the trip. She couldn't even be called the right name.

She stood up in the cart, looking over the teamsters. "We are approaching Nidus!" She sat back down, jittery with excitement. "You are being afforded a rare privilege. My family's residence is within the Arx, the seat of our government. Not many people ever get to visit the grounds, let alone go inside." He leaned out, trying to catch a glimpse of the city. "From your description, your home city sounds quite similar to Nidus. Nidus is both a fortress and our capital, along with being the heart of our empire."

He shot her a look full of pity.

She ignored that and started to plan for the next few days. Once they got to Nidus, she would have to report to the Concilium on her expedition then present Friedrich and have him explain the conditions on the surface. Assumedly, they will thoroughly interrogate him for hours on the surface, squeezing every detail they could out of him. She also promised to answer his questions. Perhaps she should feed him first? Maybe if he ate, slept in a proper bed, he would be more cooperative, more understanding? But she did not have the time or means to alert her family chef. Then, a much more worrying concern is her . . . explanation of her people's unique traits, something she had been dreading since he demonstrated how superstitious he was. To her, they were a normal part of life, but he obviously would not see it that way. He might cause a scene, which would just delay meeting with the Concilium and hurt her and her father's reputation. She could not be rash; maybe this was not a situation that could be resolved with a plan. She would just need to let things play out.

The cart shifted as it merged onto another track. The tunnel they traveled down opened up to a massive cavern, large enough to hold a small sea. Noise and thin smoke filled the air. It was a large city, one of the largest Friedrich had ever seen. It was surrounded with a massive stone wall fixed with battlements and guard towers at even intervals. The entirety of the city was built on a monstrous hill, giving it the appearance of a layered cake with a second, smaller wall rising above the first, and a further third one rising above that. The cavern was like the hub of a wheel with different tunnels, all with Via Sculptile tracks, sticking out like spokes. Warriors on foot, carts and wagons pulled by askards, even small herds of pigs made up the traffic outside of the city.

As they passed under a gated archway, they came inside the first wall. A road sloped upwards to the second wall, flanked on either side by a military camp, built similarly to the one under Dracius's command but ten times larger. Their supply train rode up to one of the camps and stopped. Friedrich and Vytilia hopped out of the cart, and she signaled for him to follow her inside. He stayed close, nervously looking around at the warriors staring at him, some whispering to one another.

As they followed the trail up to the second wall, they were passed by groups of warriors and unarmed traders. Just as the other Strixans at the first camp, none had the same coloration as Vytilia. He stuck out like a sore thumb with his brown hair and pink skin but so did she. Whenever people passed by Vytilia, they would sidestep and avoid getting in her way, almost bowing as she passed. Friedrich didn't get such treatment, only stares. He swore some of them hissed or sniffed him as he walked by. Chills went down his spine and not from their cold touch.

When they went past the second gate, Friedrich looked around at Nidus proper. As he surveyed it, he saw Vytilia beam with pride, her unsettling smile filling her face, her face flushed purple. He didn't know why; Nidus was miserable. The entire place seemed destitute, not from war or sickness, but from neglect. Moss and climbing plants covered nearly every available space with glowing mushrooms taking whatever was leftover.

The size of Nidus was not limited to how much ground it covered but also covered how high up it reached. Friedrich found himself, at first, in awe at the size of the buildings. Most reached up to six floors tall, taller than any home or building on the surface that wasn't a stronghold. All of the buildings were hewn from the living rock or pulled from the ground like Dracius's camp walls and constructed almost uniformly. The buildings were blocky, perfect cubes of rock with perfectly square windows and doors. Or, at least the hole where a window or door would go, there wasn't a single pane of glass in the entire second ring. And there were hundreds of these building blocks, all crowded around streets that looked like, at one point, they had been a nice, clean grid. Street signs or landmarks were gone. It was a wonder anyone could find their way home.

Then, as they pressed through the thronging crowd, Friedrich realized that most didn't seem to leave their homes. There was no laundry hanging from drying racks, no sweeping or cleaning, not even anyone trying to repair a building or the streets. All the chores one would expect to be done were simply not here. The closest he saw to anything being done were workers harvesting mushrooms and crawling plants or tending to livestock. The livestock was especially strange. The cows were emaciated and short, and many had their eyes glazed over. The pigs, while rotund, still looked sickly. Stranger still, they all had a thick, wooly coat like a sheep. He even saw Strixans shearing the pigs.

Aside from those few workers, the only Strixans Friedrich saw out and about were standing in lines. The longest line was for a cart, attended by two Strixans in crisp white tunics and guarded by a small cadre of purple-clad soldiers. One of the white-clad Strixans had a small book he wrote in, while the other would hand clay bottles to those waiting in line. They weren't regular size bottles, but small and thin, about the size of a finger. Sometimes, after getting their bottles, a Strixan would then go to a nearby market stall. There wasn't any merchandise on display, usually only a work bench or forge. The Strixan would hand a bottle to the seller and then receive a tunic or a shovel in return. It was then, Friedrich realized, he hadn't seen anyone with a chippurse or any of the familiar sounds or glints of gold or silver. Food must be the only way to buy things down here, and whatever it was that Strixans ate, it was given out in those bottles.

This was nothing like towns back on the surface aside from the smell of animal refuse. There were more people but less space and even fewer children. Friedrich only saw one or two babies (who seemed abnormally hairy), cradled by women whose faces were full of despair. What few children there were did nothing else but stack rocks or play in puddles, and all looked up with a hopeless gleam in their eye. Friedrich knew the feeling all too well. For as foreign and rundown Nidus might seem, it was not unfamiliar. The poverty and layout could be found in any surface town. Empathy and pity hung thick in the air as he walked, validating his feelings that perhaps he had met Vytilia on purpose. Most towns on the surface had already recovered from the last war. Years of rebuilding, hope, and a bright forthcoming lay ahead of them. For these Strixans, with 3,000 years of living in squalor, did any of them even know the word for hope?

While watching the town, Friedrich took the time to watch the populace, comparing them to Vytilia. Strixans, as a whole, were rather same looking. For men and women, they all had long legs, toned muscles, grey skin, and three different hair and eye colors. Men were barrel chested with beak-like noses, and women were well endowed with flat, ovaloid faces and large, round eyes. They all were very young, looked to be Friedrich's age or slightly older. And yet, while Vytilia shared some aspects, she still was a stark standout from others of her kind. On the surface, red hair was rare, yet a single burgh could have a handful of red-haired individuals. In Nidus, there wasn't a single white-haired or silver-skinned Strixan besides her.

They finally reached the third and smallest wall. Beyond, Friedrich could make out some sort of building resting atop a hill, the apex of Nidus, a vantage point where one could oversee the entire city. There was only one gate. The soldiers standing guard were counterparts to the ones guarding the food cart. In better lighting and being closer, Friedrich could see their wardress better.

It resembled, superficially, that of what Dracius or his warriors wore, but even he could see it was better and nicer looking. They wore a breastplate, molded and shaped to look like the torso of a very buff man. It was a dark color with gold highlighting the muscles. Golden medallions held by a web of leather straps decorated the front of the armor. A pleated armor skirt of white protected their lower regions, the hem of their purple tunic peeking out from the bottom. Their shields were also dark colored, embossed with gilded images of eagles, owls, the sun, and the moon. Their helmets lacked the stiffened-hair brush of Dracius but had a glinting metal ridge going vertical from forehead to the back of the head in its place. The guards themselves were stone-faced, cruel and glaring eyes inspecting everyone that passed. They stared intently at Friedrich. He could feel their eyes peeling back his skin and studying his very soul. Only after an explanation from Vytilia did they lessen their glare. When they opened the gate, he quickly followed her through. He'd been stared at enough for a lifetime.

"This is the Arx Campus where the Concilium meets, where our history is stored, where all the affairs of state are conducted, and where the most vital of patricians and their families live. This is the crown jewel in the diadem worn by the world. If civilization, commerce, culture, wealth, research, literature, all of it had a heart, it would be the Arx."

Unlike the rest of Nidus, her boast actually did the Arx justice. Rather than being hewn out of rock on uneven ground, the Arx was built on the flat top of a raised hill, covering an expansive campus. And there was grass, honest-to-god *green* grass coating the hill! A path made of stamped down and crushed stone went from the gate up to the cusp of the hill before splitting off to cover everywhere one would need to go. There were less buildings in this ring, but what were here were incredible! Rather than being made out of stone pulled from the ground with witchcraft, the buildings here were all made of the most exquisite quarried marble, limestone, or granite. They were old. Some were starting to crack or grey with age, but they made all the buildings in the second ring, even some buildings on the surface, look like mud huts!

The largest of the Arx buildings was, Friedrich would be told, the Arx itself. It sat on the cusp of the hill forming Nidus and dwarfed those around it. The Arx was a rectangle, made of pristine white marble columns six or seven floors tall with immaculately maintained brickwork filling the space between columns, inclosing it. The roof was almost triangular, aside from a large dome in the center, and seemingly rested on the columns like bread on a plate. The roof was made of shingles, each one a brilliant burnt orange color. Bas-relief carvings of owls, eagles, the sun, the moon, and warriors all decorated the front of the roof and the walls adjacent to the Arx's doors. The doors, the largest Friedrich had ever seen, and may ever see, were almost the full height of the building and made of bronze or brass, decorated with gold inlays, all repeating the same motifs.

The other buildings, while not as pristine or beautiful as the Arx, were no less impressive. To their right, immediately off the path to the Arx, was a cluster of granite and limestone buildings. They were similar in design, long rectangles of columns holding up a roof, though each had a large, arched opening. Their shingled roofs were each a different color, one a dark blue, one white, and one brown. Robed Strixans could be seen shooting fire from their hands or controlling water. Friedrich assumed these must be some kind of High Learnhouse.

To their left was a large free-standing stone wall, divided into twelve columns, marked with different symbols and unfamiliar letters. Next to it was a large golden globe, composed of rings, also decorated with symbols and letters. It looked like it should be rotating but remained stationary. Past those, hugging the encircling wall, was a light-yellow and white-trimmed building, probably sandstone if Friedrich had to guess. It was boxy with far fewer columns but still had large arched openings and two domes in the center. It had windows, very tall and far off the ground, again without glass, and chimneys, a first he had seen down here. Steam or perhaps white smoke lazily puffed out of the chimneys. That must be where they made the food. Behind that and to the back left of the Arx was a round, columned building with a dome roof. It was open and built like a flat tiered cake on the inside. It was made of a darker, blueish stone. To their right, behind the Arx and past the High Learnhouses, were the least impressive structures. They were made of brick with unadorned wooden roofs. There was a blacksmith, a stable of those accursed calcerta things, and a guard barracks with a training ground and other warrior necessities.

As they followed the path up to the Arx, Friedrich could see small paths heading off to the immediate left and right of the building, leading to semi-private gardens, walled in by thick hedges. Moths fluttered freely from plant to plant. Strixan men and women in fine and brightly colored clothing walked about the grounds, talking and laughing. Friedrich scoffed. Even with several wegstunde of solid rock separating them, Strixan lords were no different than their counterparts on the surface, oblivious to those beneath them. If one only experienced the Arx, one would never know this was a race fighting for survival. The only similarity these Strixan lords had with their suffering lower counterparts was most free space was taken up by emaciated cattle, grazing or being milked. Eating trumps looks, he supposed. Though, the livestock here looked relatively healthier and had more spacious pens.

They stopped at the top steps of the Arx, only a few feet from the massive doors. Two stern-faced sentries flanked the open entrance. Vytilia stopped to speak to one of them. When she was done, she turned to Friedrich. "They must confiscate your pugio. Only the Praetorian Cohort may have weapons within the Arx," she explained.

He put his hand on the sheathe. "I can't just give this away; it was a gift. One of the last memories I have of my master."

"We will not keep it. Valerius here is an old friend of the family. He will take it to my residence and alert my father we are here. You shall get it back, I promise." He hesitated before sighing and untying the sheathe to hand it to the guard. The guard nodded, tucking the dagger into his own belt.

Vytilia led the way, bubbling with enthusiasm, nearly skipping as she walked. They headed down a long hallway, illuminated by intricately carved sunstones resting in gold-embossed sconces on the wall. Again, unlike the residences below, the Arx had proper walls and doors, resembling a large house or schloss on the surface. They walked over to a small bench, sitting against a wall under a mosaic of an owl, and sat down. Friedrich took the time to look around, observing the inside. The hallways spread out into a large cross-shaped lobby with different hallways leading to the rest of the building. A large fountain sat in the center, though there was no water flowing. Behind the fountain was a statue of a feminine hooded figure. Directly above was the dome he had noticed before, painted with scenes of the lives of grey-skinned gods and goddesses. He had to respect the craftworks, they were skillfully done, better than what he had seen on the surface.

Vytilia sat next to Friedrich after speaking with a servant in a white tunic. She was uncomfortably shifting in her seat, nervously rubbing her hands together as she glanced back and forth from

Friedrich to the right hallway. Her bubbliness had disappeared. *What could be making her so anxious?* he wondered. She stood her ground against a fiend and before meeting him had hiked for several days through uncharted dark caves alone. What could she possibly be afraid of behind three rings of walls? "What's gotten into you?" he asked.

"Oh, nothing, nothing. Do not worry yourself." She was lying.

"What do we have to do first?"

"We will meet with my father, Praetor Faustus Quintia. Then depending on what he says, we may either take a dinner and rest or meet with the Concilium right away."

"The Concilium?" he asked.

"They are the ruling council that controls the empire. Their actions decides the fate of every Strixan."

"Questions? Rulers? Ugh." He groaned. "I don't. I can't." Friedrich grabbed his head and bent over, taking deep long breaths. He was sweating and felt uncomfortable in his skin. Everything seemed to just come at him at once. He didn't even know what day it was. How long ago had he entered the Toller Mund? Now he had to stand before a body of high-born lords? Was it a trial? Had she been lying to him? "I can't talk. I-I-I need to lie down." He avoided talking to or being around lords; they made him nervous and nauseous. His chest was tightening, and he could not help but scratch at his scars.

Vytilia, oblivious to his discomfort, stood up as a figure began to walk towards them. This man was tall, taller than Vytilia, with a deep, ash-grey colored skin and beak-like nose. His hair was a dark black, streaked with gray. He wore a long, white, flowing robe trimmed with a muted purple. The man breathed leadership and respect. Even Friedrich took notice as he approached. He held himself in high regard, and it was earned. He had the build of a warrior, experience had weathered his face, a far cry from the rich burghers and lords Friedrich had seen on the surface. His head still felt woozy.

"Father." Vytilia stood up straight before her father, and they both exchanged a hiss. The hissing wasn't antagonistic. It was almost like a greeting. With their mouths open, Friedrich could see what was causing the inhuman, uncomfortable smiles. Both Vytilia and her father had two pairs of fangs that replaced their eyeteeth. The fangs were as sinister and sharp as any serpent's, one pair on the top, the other on the bottom. Friedrich's eyes widened, and he stumbled, falling from the couch and gasping.

The pieces began to fit; the connection was made. Friedrich finally knew what Strixans really were. They were tales mainly spoken of by the Wenden[14] who fled from eastern Erebus. They were fell things only spoken of in hushed tones after making the token of the sun, a thing so evil, so dark, that even armed men dreaded to talk about them: Vampires. It all made sense, the grey skin, the cold touch, the witchcraft. These were hallmarks of the undead, those who had sold their souls to dark and ruinous powers. Now here Friedrich was, surrounded by them.

Vytilia knelt to help Friedrich up, offering him a toothless smile, her eyes wide to appear harmless, but he pulled away from her grasp, crawling backwards. He stood up, screaming and knocking over a table as he started to run. Fear filled his veins. All he focused on was survival and escape. Vytilia called out for him to stop, but he just kept running. The guards at the entrance of the Arx turned around and braced themselves to catch him. Not thinking, Friedrich ran towards them, his voice quavering as he panicked. One of the guards tackled him, slamming him onto the floor. Friedrich continued to scream, thrashing and kicking as one of the guards began to tie his wrists together. Vytilia caught up to them and placed her hand on Friedrich's forehead. He quickly slumped over, asleep.

"Take him to our personal residences," Praetor Quintia ordered. "Tell Sextus to keep an eye on him." He turned to his daughter.

"My apologies." She looked down. "I had a fear that would happen. He is openly superstitious, and when I noticed how dull his teeth were, I feared what his reaction would be. I did not want to tell him until we were within the city limits."

"That was wise." He put his hand on her shoulder, giving her an affirmative pat before quickly withdrawing his hand. "Plebeians of any type will be superstitious; it is in their nature. Sextus will take care of him, make sure he does not hurt himself. Now, come along. I want to hear your report first before the Concilium meets." He began walking towards the left wing of the Arx. Both nodded at the statue as they passed.

Vytilia hid her emotions well as they walked, but inwardly, she was deeply worried. She had watched the reaction of Friedrich

---

14. Ethno-Linguistic group in Eastern Erebus.

unfold with a great deal of shock and fright. His scream had been so visceral, almost instinctual. If their fangs had caused him to act like that, could he truly be of any assistance to her people? Was there any chance of him voluntarily helping them? And if he was coerced to help, could it at all be trusted?

She was sure her father was thinking along similar lines, but they would address that later.

Praetor Quintia was stoic and silent as he stepped through the purple curtains serving as a door to their large and lavishly decorated residence. He removed his sandals then laid down at a couch, sighing. There was annoyance and a bit of disappointment in his sigh. Making a scene, or hosting anyone who made a scene, was always a black mark on one's social standing.

Vytilia followed suit and sat across from him. A servant brought over two goblets and placed them on the table then reported on Friedrich's condition. He was still deeply asleep with a rapid heartbeat. Vytilia and her father raised their goblets and looked at a portrait on the wall adjacent to them. The portrait was their most prized possession, depicting a hen Strixan in her prime with long flowing white hair and deep golden eyes, a warm smile on her lips. She was looking at both of them, always watching over them and their home.

After observing the portrait and taking a long contemplative drink, Praetor Quintia sighed again, putting his goblet down and looking at Vytilia. "Now, tell me about our guest."

5

They spent a great length of time discussing her journey. It was the most time she had spent with her father in years, even if during it, they hardly made eye contact. She was grateful for it and for any opportunity, but she still had a desire, a wish more accurately, that he would do this in a context outside of their official duties. What questions he asked were preparing her for the questions other Praetors would have. They were all about the surface, Friedrich's people and society, and how they could benefit the Strixans. Never once did he ask her how she was or if she had been in any danger. She could rationalize that he had enough confidence in her abilities and experience, but the simple act of asking was more important. When she finally finished, he stopped her before she could recommend a course of action. He was off to meet with a few of his allies on the Concilium and call an early session, so she could present her findings. If Friedrich was willing, he would accompany her to clarify. If not, she would go alone and give a preliminary briefing on the surface. If the latter was the case, she and Friedrich would be summoned to a later meeting.

He had remained stone-faced and quiet for most of the talk, only asking clarifying questions or for her opinion. Though he did change his composure when she told him about meeting with Centurion Dracius. The centurion was an old friend of the family, and talking with or about him always put Faustus in a better mood.

When her father left, she summoned her ancilla, Annia, and decided it was time for a much needed and much deserved bath since it would be several hours before the Concilium convened and summoned her. The majordomo, Sextus, was left to watch over Friedrich while she and Annia departed the Arx for the thermae. They passed by the front colonnade of the Arx, where only a few hours ago, Friedrich had panicked and tried running away. Doubt began to cloud her mind; if Friedrich reacted that way to their fangs, how would the rest of his kind react? How could they hope to establish diplomatic or commercial relations with beings that superstitious and easily frightened? Was this an omen of their future, or gods willing, *only* a minor setback?

"Pardon me, Domina Vytilia, would you care to visit Fulvulus?" Annia asked.

Vytilia smiled. "An excellent idea." They broke off from the path leading to the bathhouses and went to a herd of cattle grazing behind the great calendar and the grand armillary. A herdsman, Caeso, an old and trusted member of the household, was watching the cattle, nodding as Vytilia approached. "And how is my Fulvulus today?" she asked, scratching the ears of a small, shaggy, brown juvenile female.

"She is better than before. We have been giving her regular inspections and medicine, but there is still a bit of infection still remaining on her rear. She is still lethargic and her blood sour."

Vytilia muzzled the bovine. Technically, this was Fulvulus XXV, the many times great-grand-daughter-niece of the original Fulvulus, a gift from her mother when she became of age. "That will not do. We cannot allow any nasty pathogens to remain. Caeso, your pugio if you will."

She walked to the rear of the animal, gently petting and soothing it as she felt for blood vessels near the infected area. As animals were the Strixan's main source of nutrition, a number of their resources, both physical and thaumaturgical, were devoted to keeping them well. Every Strixan from a young age was taught how to identify and care for sick cattle, and Vytilia was not an exception. She, however, had been taught veterinary thaumaturgy and had a slight advantage in caring for her family's herds.

When she found the right area, she took the pugio and made small incisions on either side of the infection before sticking an index finger in either one. She closed her eyes and began to do math in her head. "Cattle have 2.5 urnae[15] of blood in their system. At her age, her heart should beat 66 times per minute. But they only have one type of blood. Taking that into account . . ." She focused on the blood rushing past her fingertips. What she was doing was a very advanced form of thaumaturgy, one taught to her by her mother. It was believed by Strixan Veterinaria that blood possessed an anti-pathogen capability, and when normal herbal medicines and remedies could not fight a disease, blood could be "mobilized" to better fight against infections, passing it onto the waste removal

15. 31.5 liters, 8.3 gallons.

systems. It required a momentous amount of effort on the part of the thaumaturgist but had saved many a head of cattle from dying an early death.

Vytilia stood, activating the blood to fight back, for five minutes. Caeso and Annia watched as the infection on Fulvulus's hide began to shrink. On the sixth minute, she opened her eyes and removed her fingers, healing the incisions. The infection was gone, and Fulvulus let out an appreciative moo. Annia caught Vytilia as she stumbled. "A grand kindness you showed this beast, Domina," Annia told her.

"Here . . ." Caeso took his pugio and made another incision on the bovine's shoulder, collecting the spilled blood in a small clay cup. "Get a good drink. You need it." Vytilia thanked him and drank the cup dry. As she wiped her mouth after having her fill, she healed that wound as well.

"You are doing a fine job Caeso. The family is grateful. If you have the time, make sure Fulvulus gets a good bath in and let her play with the other juveniles."

"Of course, Domina, I will get on it right away."

Vytilia and Annia resumed their walk to the bathhouses. When they arrived, the other Praetors' daughters were drying off and changing. Vytilia knew their names and their families but had never spoken or interacted with them for longer than a few moments. As she disrobed, the other hens quickly and unanimously exited, flashing their mandible fangs at Vytilia as they departed the bathhouses. She said nothing, only sighing as she sat in the pool, sinking up to her eyes in the water.

"Do not pay them any mind. They are not worth your time. You have loftier goals and ideals than laying on your back or gossiping. Their underbite means nothing."

Vytilia grimaced. That instance with the lower fangs was a common interaction. She rose back up to her collarbone as Annia began cleaning her hair. "I suppose you are right. You echo mother talking like that."

"Domina Carmilla was a wise hen, always dispensing proverbs and axioms for the household to follow. She believed the wisdom of the old empire was every Strixan's heritage, regardless of class." She reached into the basket, producing a bottle and dull scythe. "Would you like the strigil and oil today?"

"The water is enough."

Annia put the instruments back. "Fantastic news about the surface dwellers! The household is ablaze with wonder and excitement! What a discovery!"

"It is *a* discovery," Vytilia mused. "It appears too early to tell if it will be of any use to the empire."

"Now, now, do not go and think like that. That hiccup in the grand foyer was a minor stumble. I am sure when the surface-dweller wakes up, you will be able to smooth things over. You have that Octavian charm and charisma."

"You mean Quintia charm and charisma."

"In politics perhaps, but in private is where your mother was at her best. She could get even the most discourteous of visitors to leave with only a smile." She began massaging Vytilia's scalp. "Your mother would be so proud of you. You are one great step closer to achieving her dream."

Annia is right, Vytilia thought. Friedrich did make apparent how superstitious and untrusting he and his society as a whole was. If she spoke with him, understood the root of his fears and concerns, she would be able to reconvince him to help. "Annia, what do you think mother would do in this situation?"

Her ancilla paused, making a hmmmm sound as she thought, then shook her head. "I could not tell you if I knew. Domina Carmilla always knew what to do but never explained to us how she did. I would ask your father if you get the chance. He knew her better than anyone else alive."

She had asked her father. His advice had been "play politics, do not use force, do what your mother would do." She did not blame him. He was not trained for a situation like this. Only Carmilla had come close to knowing how. But, she had never deigned to teach Vytilia how to handle something like this. Well, perhaps she had, but it was not coming to immediate memory. She would need to make some memories resurface.

"Annia, tell me more stories about mother." Maybe one of these stories had an answer Vytilia was looking for.

"Of course! I, well, when you do the mathematics, I suppose I knew her longer than you did. A shame, but so long as we remember and talk of her, she lives on."

Vytilia's eye twitched, and she rubbed her knuckles under the water. "A cruel irony depending on one's view."

"You are quite right, but whenever she would speak to me or Sextus or anyone else in the household, all she spoke of was you.

She loved you with all her heart. You were her greatest blessing, her greatest joy, her greatest venture."

Her greatest blessing? Vytilia had to scoff at that, internally. *Who leaves their greatest joy after three centuries?* "As I reflect, I have difficulty accepting that," she confided. "I feel stunted as a person because of her. At least socially."

"Perish the thought! Domina Carmilla raised you to be a fine hen! That is the backbiting of the other Praetor's daughters getting to you. Do *not* let that cloud your memories."

"I appreciate the sentiment Annia, but I still admit I feel as if my social graces are less than exemplary." Perhaps, had they been better, Friedrich would not have panicked as he did. "And I would like to have at least something resembling a friendship with the other daughters."

"Permission to speak honestly, Domina?"

"Granted."

"Had your mother not raised you the way she did, you would have been wasted. She put every hope, dream, and prayer of herself, your father, and all the families of the household into you. She knew you were fated for greatness. Lounging around the Arx is not the reason she brought you into this world. She knew and made you to do something great. To restore the empire! What a dream! Only the most virtuous and noble Strixan could ever make such an idea a reality! And to think this is already bearing fruit! Begging your pardon Domina, but you do not seem to recognize how important of an achievement this surface dweller is!"

She shook her head, diving below the surface to fully wet her hair, so Annia could dry and braid it. "Your words have brought me comfort Annia, as they have many times before." She leaned back, feeling the warm ceramics of the pool. "It is interesting. In your word choice, you make it sound as if mother handcrafted me whilst in the womb. Father always said so in a jesting manner."

Annia let out some sort of hiccough from deep in her throat that Vytilia ignored. It was probably a reaction to how filthy her hair had gotten. The tunnels were not forgiving to patrician coiffures.

"Handcrafted! A humorous notion Domina! Very humorous!" Annia quickly resumed talking, a slight hint of nervousness in her voice. Vytilia paid it little mind. The ancilla always fussed over Vytilia's hair, especially if she was to meet with the Concilium. "I doubt even she knew how to do such an endeavor if such an endeavor is possible! Though, with how fervently she prayed,

I am sure the gods had a hand in your development! It was rather taxing on her. While she was heavy with you, she suffered bouts of headaches and exhaustion, more so than I have seen in other hens while carrying. Whenever we tended to her, she always told us it would be worth it. She was constantly feeling you kick, whispering to you. Even before you were born, she loved you dearly."

"Her headaches and exhaustion were uncommon? When she spoke of them, she made them sound to be a regular affliction during pregnancy."

Annia hiccoughed again. "Well, uh, *ahem* truth be told, she may have not wanted you to feel guilty for causing them. I know a number of mothers who use their pains as a tool to guilt their own nestlings." She reached out a hand for Vytilia to exit. "Now, come along. We have to make you nice and presentable for the Concilium."

As they returned to the Arx, she began to ponder on both the previous events and what Annia had said. She was still troubled; when Friedrich screamed, his scream was of pure terror. All color drained from his face, and a primal, instinctive fear filled his eyes. It was their fangs that had caused the alarm, which baffled her even more. Why would teeth be the instigator for such panic? Perhaps he made a connection to venomous serpents, but that was a tentative connection at best.

Could it be that a lost colony had survived the cataclysm? One that had wreaked havoc and terrorized the world of men? Or could it be that this was an atavistic fear, passed down through generations from early ancestors? Somehow, despite historical record lacking evidence, man and Strixan had coexisted or interacted. But if the Strixans were destroyed, why was man spared? Then again, perhaps, since their biology was different than what Friedrich was familiar with, panic had been his first reaction, and this was all a misunderstanding. If it was a misunderstanding, she had to clear it up the moment he awoke for the good of the empire. And if it was a historical anachronism, well, she could set the record.

They returned to the Quintia residence. She and Annia headed towards her room, passing by Friedrich's guest chamber. Sextus was stationed outside the door and informed her that Friedrich remained blacked out. She could hear Friedrich's heart racing. Even though he was asleep, it sounded like he was running a race. She thanked Sextus and continued to her bedroom.

Vytilia sat on her bed, thinking on the Friedrich situation while Annia prepared her clothes. She glanced at the clothes as Annia pulled them out of the wardrobe. They were garments she had not seen or worn in decades, not since . . . . Vytilia shook her head and resumed her thinking. She would need to be careful with Friedrich, genteel as Annia had advised.

"Begging your pardon, Domina Vytilia." Sextus knocked on the wall. "Friedrich has started to stir."

The gods heard my concerns, Vytilia thought. "I will come right away. Please, prepare a proper change of clothes for Friedrich."

"Of course, right away, Domina."

She headed for the guest chamber. She could hear Friedrich mumbling and turning over. A change of clothes was resting on a seat. "Sextus, bring a cup of water and some meat if you have it. Make sure it is cooked," she called. Friedrich's mutterings became louder, and he started to caterwaul. She entered, staying a distance away from the bed. His wrists and ankles were lashed to the bed-posts, and a thick sheet tied under the bed kept his torso in place.

"Friedrich? Are you fully awake? Is everything well?"

He shook his head and looked up, his eyes widening. He began to struggle, shaking the bed as he did so. "Wha-wha-what? No! No! Stay away from me! Get, get away!"

"Friedrich calm down." She raised her hands to show she did not mean harm and used her softest and gentlest tone.

"Calm? No! Get away! Evil! You, you're a fell being!"

She scowled before banishing it and putting on a friendly face. "If you would just be quiet, I can explain everything, answer all your questions! Please."

Please! Please just let me go! I won't tell anyone you're down here! Just don't kill me, please!" He shrugged, covering his neck with his shoulders, screaming bloody murder. Vytilia sighed, walked over to the bed, and touched his forehead. He went limp, quickly falling back asleep.

Sextus entered with a clay cup and a slice of bread. "Has he fallen back asleep?"

"Not willingly. He panicked the moment I entered the room. I think his fatigue is affecting his thinking." She turned around. "Try and force him to have some water and keep an eye on him. He may be dehydrated. If he wakes up again, and I am not here, put him back to sleep."

"Of course, Domina. A courier has just arrived from the Concilium; they have reconvened and will be summoning you momentarily."

"My gratitude, Sextus. Inform the courier I shall be waiting."

She returned to her bedroom. Annia had finished selecting clothes and was waiting to dress her. She inspected what she had picked, silently nodding at the choices. They were her best, befitting such an auspicious occasion as standing before the Concilium. Though, as she studied the clothing, she could not help but theorize how Strixan clothing would change if they were still on the surface. Friedrich had not worn a tunic but instead that odd "hose" garment. Would Strixans ever adopt such an oddity, or was this unique to his people? Did others on the surface still wear tunics and togas? She gave a nod to Annia who began dressing her. If all went well with the Concilium, she may soon find out.

Strixan raiment had not changed much since their apex. Truthfully, it had not changed much since their earliest history. It was always tunics and variations of robes, billowing and loose, kept closed by belts and sashes. Annia removed Vytilia's previous outfit and prepared her under-tunic. Vytilia mused, privately, that if all else failed, she could at least relate to Friedrich that both their peoples had invented loincloths. It seemed even mankind had a concept of modesty. Or shame.

After the under-tunic came a light pink, gap-sleeved tunic with sleeves that came down to her elbows and a skirt that went to her ankles. Then a jeweled, cord belt was tied above her navel to accentuate the hips and bust, a necessity to keep the attention of some members of the Concilium. Then came the palla, a must among patrician Strixan hens. Like its masculine counterpart, the toga, it showed Vytilia was a virtuous adult, one who knew the *mores* and rules of society and followed them. It was a simple garment, cut like a sheet, and as sheer as could be manufactured, meant to reach down from the crown of the head to the ankles. It was worn over the left shoulder, clasped by a gold brooch of a noctua, an owl. Annia fluffed it up around her shoulders, making sure there was room to cover her head. Vytilia carried the excess in her right hand.

She sat down in a chair as Annia finished braiding her hair. Only patricians bothered styling their hair; it was a mark of her station. And it was always braids, curled and bunched together at the back of the head. When Annia finished, she pulled the palla off her shoulder and gently wrapped it over Vytilia's head. It seemed ironic, Vytilia thought, to put in the trouble of braiding and styling hair, only to hide most of it with the palla. Even more ironic was that the palla was meant to cover the wearer from the sun. It was a testament, she supposed, to the power of patrician traditions. It was all they had left, anyhow.

"You know Domina," Annia shared as she admired Vytilia. "I always look forward to the day when I can dress you in a stola." Stolas were thin-strapped dresses, worn above a tunic but under the palla. It was worn only by married hens who had become matrons of a family. Vytilia smiled at Annia's comment. If her father's attitude was anything to go off of, she would not be wearing a stola for many centuries to come.

She waited for the summons to the Concilium, fiddling with the excess of her palla, her mind racing with what to say, and pausing only to worry about the Friedrich situation. Then she would think again on standing before the Concilium, in front of her father and his colleagues, to help decide the fate of the empire. She wished vainly for a mirror. She felt noble and knew she was wearing the finest clothes available, but she had never seen herself wear them. Mirrors were a scarce commodity for her people, and the ones they possessed were a poor quality, made worse by the lack of illumination provided by fire stones. Vytilia did not know what she looked like. Her only reference was off-hand comments made by her father, comparing her to her mother. Carmilla would not have worried, would she?

Finally, after a near eternity, Sextus knocked on the bedroom wall. "Domina Vytilia? Another courier has just arrived from the Concilium; they are ready for you. You are instructed to head over immediately."

She sighed. She would have to face them alone. "My gratitude, Sextus." She exited the room, heading out into the hall. When she came to the central lobby with the fountain, she again stopped, uttering a quick prayer before taking a left to the end of the hallway. At the end were two large wood doors, overlayed with metal embossed with images of Strixan history. Two Praetorians stood outside the doors while six couriers, dressed in white tunics with a thin, matte-purple trim, sat in silence along the wall. A Praetorian stepped inside and announced Vytilia before opening the door. As she stepped inside, the door shut behind her.

The meeting place of the Concilium was properly referred to as the Curia. It was constructed like an amphitheater, a half-circle of several hundred benched seats all looking down on a dais. Behind the dais was a bas-relief of the first Emperor and the first Praetor. As she entered, twenty-one pairs of eyes all stared up at her. She swallowed, took a deep breath, and descended the stairs towards the stage. It was an extraordinary measure that a hen, especially one as young as she, would speak before the Concilium. She had to put on her best face, stick out her chest, sway her hips as she walked, and stay mindful that each footfall was both graceful and dignified. Every action she did here would be scrutinized. Most would not care to hear what a hen had to say. If her words would not keep their interest, then she herself would.

As she passed by the different rows of benches, she glanced at their occupants, putting names to faces. These were her father's colleagues, the tiercels who held the fate of their people in their hands. They had such a great responsibility, yet they were so few.

The Concilium was composed of twenty-one individuals:

Twelve Praetors, led by the Princeps, were the main legislative, executive, and judicial body. They had final say on all affairs of the Empire.

Three Tribunes of the Plebeians represented most of the population and voiced the concerns and issues of the lower classes. They were the second most powerful in the Concilium, and their position was sacrosanct. An attack on them was an attack on the plebs.

One Quaestor, in charge of finances and material distribution.

One Censor, in charge of population size and birthrates for both Strixans and animals.

One Aedile, in charge of city planning and public festivities on the rare occasions they were held.

The Pontifex Maximus, a mostly ceremonial position held by a retired Praetor, used to give the Concilium legitimacy and favor with the gods. That was if they still listened.

And finally, the Magister Militum, commander of the legions and military advisor.

Technically, the Prefect of the Praetorian Cohort was nominally a member, but most chose not to participate unless asked.

All of those positions sat in the third row, aside from the Prefect who stood at the door.

Each member, aside from the Prefect and Magister Militum, wore togas. It was draped over the right shoulder, colored a pure white as could be made, with a purple stripe along the edge. Like her palla, it was a sign of class, rank, and in their case, authority.

On the last step, Vytilia paused to glance at the mid-relief. She felt, instinctually perhaps, a twinge of pain as she saw the image of the first emperor. That was her ancestor, the progenitor of her maternal line, the once master and ruler of his imperium. And here he was, immortalized in handing the fasces of imperium to the first Princeps, ending seventy thousand years of Octavian rule. She shook off the feeling and waited for her invitation to stand on the dais.

The Princeps bid her to take the stand. She went onto the dais, facing the Concilium. Directly in front of her was the most important of them all: The Princeps, Plinius Diabolicius Porcia. He was *Primus inter pares*, first among equals. He was the de facto leader of the Concilium, first to speak, last to decide. He was who decided what became law and what died as an argument within the Curia. He was an unassuming tiercel with a soft face and an enthusiastic demeanor. He would not strike one as a leader, but her father had always remarked his military record and charisma more than made him qualified. He could be liked by everyone and was key to making compromises.

She glanced at her father, sitting on the farthest right seat, her left. He merely nodded at her before turning his attention to Princeps Porcia, who stood up. "Friends, Strixans, Countrymen!" According to her father, he started every meeting like that. "We have with us Vytilia Quintia, daughter of our esteemed colleague. She has come to address us on the world above and her plan of how this can benefit the empire. Vytilia, the floor is yours; we will allow you to speak, then we will ask questions." He sat back down.

Vytilia straightened her back and cleared her throat. "You honor me, Princeps Porcia, as do all of our esteemed Praetors and members of the Concilium. This is a rare honor, and one I shall never forget. I have recently returned from the northwestern reaches and accompanying me on my return was perhaps the greatest find since we have arrived underground: a being who lives on the surface." There was a murmur of amazement from a few of the members. Princeps Porcia seemed intrigued, leaning forward, listening intently as she relayed how she found Friedrich and how he came to be underground, how he survived and slew a red devil, and explained the strange language he spoke and even stranger clothes he wore. All were impressed, and slightly worried, as she explained their fight with the blue devil.

"As we travelled from the reaches to one of our forward camps, the surface dweller, Friedrich, taught me about his nation. The surface dwellers, or 'man' as they refer to themselves, have established a surprisingly complex civilization. They have managed to form an empire, and they have constructed cities with walls not unlike Nidus. They are an industrious people with fine skills in metallurgy. The pugio he carried with him was made of fine steel, capable of piercing a devil's hide without damage. Though he does not share our ability to heal rapidly or endure without rest, this man, Friedrich, is surprisingly hardy. He spent nearly the entire trip barefoot, half-naked, and slightly malnourished, yet he continued to press on. And from my understanding, he is merely an average specimen.

"Furthermore, along with empire-building and metalworking, these men have also established commercial networks, they engage in war and diplomacy, they even have a complex religious system with holy days and observances. This religion has even splintered due to schisms. Politics and religion are rather intertwined on the surface with secular imperial authority using religious authority to validate its power. Despite their aversion to Thaumaturgy, men have managed to create a complex and intricate life on the surface. This is not to mention what art and literature they have developed. Furthermore, they are familiar with war, a great aid in these trying times. Friedrich even described his people as having a martial culture, not one of brutes, but of thinking, strategic minds who can form nations. All of this is a hallmark of an advanced and sophisticated civilization, one which I fully believe is worth investigating or possibly allying with." She looked to her father, who remained expressionless, watching the Princeps.

Princeps Porcia stood back up. "Our appreciation for your report, Vytilia. I will now lead in opening with questions." He adjusted his toga. "I was struck by something in your last sentences, and I want clarification. You said these men, they do not practice Thaumaturgy?"

She waited until he sat back down before answering. "They do not. Friedrich referred to it as 'witchcraft' and said on the surface, those who practice it are declared as enemies of the state and put to death. I gathered that it is a part of their religion's doctrine. They have rather *interesting* misconceptions about thaumaturgy as well. They do not understand that thaumas cannot be performed *ex nihilo* and other basic rules." There were more murmurings from the Praetors, mostly whispers of amazement and shock.

The next one to ask questions sat on the right hand of Princeps Porcia, a man who had often fought with her father and not on the battlefield—Praetor Septimius Cornelia. He was one of the older Praetors and had shaved his head to give himself a wiser, more sophisticated appearance. Her father frequently called Cornelia a fellating[16] serpent. It was a widespread if whispered rumor, which explained how someone so antagonistic could achieve such a high position. That and he had his cadre of like-minded imbeciles. For some reason known only to the gods, Cornelia's ideas were popular.

Cornelia, the Princeps, and the tiercel on the Princeps' left, Praetor Gnaeus Licinia, formed what was informally called the Triumvirate, the most influential tiercels in the Concilium. "I have a question, one I think many of my comrades may also be wondering. Where is this man, this Friedrich? Why does he not stand before us and explain himself and his people?"

Vytilia took a deep breath as he sat back down. "One of the flaws I discovered in men is they are incredibly superstitious, more so than any plebeian. He has an extensive knowledge of his local legends and mythos, and he apparently mistook us for some kind of creature from them. He is still acclimatizing to both his location and situation." Praetor Cornelia scowled, muttering under his breath.

The next one to ask was Praetor Licinia. Vytilia noted that the Princeps had whispered to him before he stood. "Vytilia, why should the Concilium even take any of this under consideration? What would knowledge of the surface and of this race of men do to benefit the empire? Especially, given possible risks involved."

She glanced at her father, and she saw his body language express agreement. She needed to word this just right. "Good Praetors, esteemed representatives of the Concilium, I answer with a question of my own; what benefit would it not bring?" Answering a question with a question was a favorite tool of debate of her father. "Outside the gate of the Arx campus lies what is left of our capital city. It is where the plebs live and die, and beyond that is what remains of our empire. We have lived in precarious times for several millennia; our resources are stretched thin, our people

16. In Strixan culture, a male performing this act is considered very dishonorable. An insult such as this is tantamount to the worst curse in Strixan religions.

hopeless and destitute. We must accept the reality that we cannot continue to subsist off of what little resources exist underground. We are the descendants of the mightiest beings to ever walk terra, yet the majority of our people wear wool sheared from the backs of porcine. Where once our herds grazed across mighty grasslands, they now subsist off of fungi, always sickly thin and blind. This is not to mention the generations of inbreeding we have had to subject our animals to. Should their lineage become even more intertwined and give out, half of our food supply would be threatened. Our population cannot survive solely off of these meager beasts. There would be riots, anarchy, even civil war.

"We are not a thriving people; we are a *surviving* remnant. But now, the Gods have looked upon us with mercy and extended an olive branch. We have discovered another empire, one with healthier animals, with opportunities of commerce, with knowledge and experiences that we can utilize to help our people. They have domesticated animals we can import. They have proper linen and cloth. All of the products our ancestors enjoyed in abundance can be ours again. In the coming years, nestlings that are born will not have to wonder what the sun and the moon look like, for they will be able to see them with their own eyes. We can see the return of Nidus not solely as the seat of government, but a center of art and culture where we can once more write poetry and plays, create sculptors commemorating our greatest ancestors! We can once more properly honor the gods who for so long watched over our people! Dear Praetors, members of the Concilium, this opportunity we have been presented with may seem perilous, if not foolhardy, but we must remember that all of us have a duty to the empire, to the people. If allying with man can bring benefit and relief to the people, then we must take it! The welfare of the people is to be the highest law."

She had taken a risk. While the Concilium could discuss the grave reality of the empire, it was heavily discouraged for anyone else to do so. It was considered a threat to imperial morale and stability. She glanced at her father, who covered his mouth with his hand but left the corner exposed. It was turned upward in a smile.

Cornelia stood back up again. "Bah! What good does new herds and art do for us? We are at war, and we have been since before you were born. Your mother's foolish dreams are distracting you from the real problem we face, extinction at the hands of the devils! What can the surface provide that will help us win this war?" Her father's smile quickly turned to a scowl as he balled his fists, glaring at Cornelia.

Cornelia stayed standing, staring Vytilia down as she began to answer. "Men have experience with warfare, but I did not inquire about details. Nonetheless, the surface could still provide mercenaries or weaponry and allow us to experiment and try new strategies and tactics we may not have considered. Is our history not filled with strategies and armaments we acquired or learned from our foes? What reason is there to believe we could not learn the same from allies?"

Cornelia scoffed, waving his hand. "An alliance? What do you know of diplomacy or warfare? You expect us to just take your word at face value and make an effort to reveal ourselves to these surface dwellers? What if they react the same way he does? What if they get violent? We cannot afford to fight a war on two fronts."

"Better yet, why not just take the supplies we need? Why bother with diplomacy at all? These men are obviously weaker. It is our right to push them aside and reclaim the surface!" The tiercel who commented was Praetor Gaius Cispia, a notorious rabble-rouser and disciple of Cornelia.

"I concur! Why not kill this surface-dweller and take back what is rightfully ours! Why should we cower underground, besieged by devils, while these weaklings inherit terra!" Cornelia looked across the Curia for a challenge.

The Princeps put his hand on Cornelia's shoulder, forcing him to sit down. "Cornelia be silent! You yourself just said we cannot afford a two-front war. Now you want to invade the surface! Be rational for one moment. We cannot afford to let emotions take over." He fixed his toga and stood up. "Vytilia, your report on the surface world is . . . interesting. You make a compelling and sound argument for cooperation, but all you have to go on is hearsay and second-hand accounts from this plebeian. We require more information before making a decision, and we will need this . . . Friedrich it was? We will need him to stand before us and answer our questions, especially regarding warfare and military matters."

Vytilia raised a hand as the Princeps sat down. "Honorable Princeps and Praetors, before I am dismissed from this chamber, may I make one final suggestion?" The Princeps signaled for her to go ahead. "After you question Friedrich, commission him to act as a guide for a reconnaissance team to return to the surface. Allow them funds to spend a deal of time, learning their customs, political situation, their history and to investigate more into their commerce, their weaponry, what technology they possess. It would not be a strain on resources or manpower, and they can operate almost covertly if needs be."

The Princeps stroked his chin. "An interesting proposition, and who do you recommend for this surface expedition?"

"Myself," she stated. "I have the most experience in dealing with man and already know their language. Send the two of us. We will draw less attention to ourselves and can cover greater distances."

"Bah!" Cornelia interjected. "Her words are hollow! She is probably infatuated with the lad and is seeking a way to escape and chase after some foolish delusion of grandeur. How can we trust some fledgling with such an important matter? What do we know of her loyalty, her patriotism?"

Vytilia's father nearly stood up, ready to start fighting, but the Praetor sitting next to him calmed him down. The Princeps chided Cornelia before addressing the group. "The Quintia family history is enough to argue for her loyalty. If you have questions about it, address them to Praetor Quintia, tiercel-to-tiercel. The young Vytilia argues with reason and logic, and in military matters, her reasoning is correct. We shall deliberate on this and take a long recess, reconvening when this Friedrich has recovered and can address the Concilium directly." He paused, holding his chin in thought as he studied her. "Vytilia, these 'men' as they call themselves, would you consider them to be virtuous?"

She had to think on that. Ethics and virtues had never come up in her course of talking to Friedrich. But they had to have some. One could not have a religion and holidays or an empire with some form of law and order without them. "I would say they do, though likely their virtues, or equivalents thereof, are nothing compared to ours. But they have some semblance of law and some idea of respect and holding something sacrosanct."

The Princeps found her answer acceptable. "Our gratitude. Vytilia you are dismissed." She gave a small bow before departing up the stairs, exiting the Curia, and returning to her residence, taking a longer pause by the fountain to utter a prayer of gratitude.

• • •

"It appears we have much to discuss." Princeps Porcia stood before the Concilium just as the door closed behind Vytilia. All but her father's gaze turned to the Princeps from the door. "The young Quintia is right. Our ultimate duty is to the people, and if this man and his kind can aid our people, then we are obligated to seek his assistance. I have not yet made a decision, for I wish to hear from all of you. The floor is open."

The Quaestor stood up. "As harsh as her words about the cattle may sound, she is correct. This generation has had more still-born juveniles than all previous generations. The breeding pool is all but dried up. We are already having to cut the blood-alms with marrow and minced organs. Unless new breeds are introduced, we may see the end of bovines and then the porcines not soon after. Any sizeable draught animal we can import from the surface will go a long way to not only improving the size of the alms, but the quality as well. And that alone can greatly improve morale."

"I agree," the Censor added. "At this rate, we will not have enough animals to feed our people, and there are not enough tiercels being born to replenish the legions. I am not one for overt piety, but I must say that the arrival of this surface dweller is a sign of providence."

Praetor Mustius stood up. He was a neutral member of the Concilium and sometimes ally of Faustus. He was also famously, though some might say infamously, cautious. "Those concerns are serious, but I believe there is one population we are forgetting about, that of the surface-dwellers as a whole. Three millennia is a long time for any group to breed, learn, and advance. We all heard the fear in that lad's screams. Imagine if all of his people react like that! They could slaughter us with numbers alone! She said they were a martial culture and a superstitious, fearful one at that. Is exposing our people and civilization to such a hostile race worth the price of a few heads of cattle?"

"We have thaumaturgy! We have the legions!" Praetor Cornelia rebuked. "Any threat these pink mortals throw at us, we can handle!"

"I do not doubt that," Mustius said. "But for how long? And let us not forget, the devils are still a threat. We cannot afford a war on two fronts, especially not with the supply problems our esteemed colleagues addressed."

"But we are forgetting that she believed they could be a virtuous people," one of the tribunes, a tiercel named Volero Icilius stood up to speak. "It is possible that this . . . Freed-rick has not yet learned his people's virtues. If they can develop their own system of *virtus* and *mores*, then surely there are some level-headed enough to engage in diplomacy."

"You think a barbarian race can have virtue?" Cornelia scoffed. "You are a fool and so is everyone who agrees."

"I do not hear any solutions out of your mouth," Icilius rebuffed.

"Kill this 'man' and be rid of the problem! If we did send a delegation to the surface, we would send them to their deaths. The risks are too great and too many for our people. We need to concentrate on our lives here. As for the lowering blood alms, I say we kill some of the useless drinkers or bring back the games and have the lower classes thin themselves for amusement." The tribunes all scowled at Cornelia.

"We are *not* going to disgrace this hall with a discussion of culling the plebs," Princeps Porcia stated. "Our task at hand is the opportunity presented to us by the young Quintia."

"I say we send her up to the surface with him and have her scout the situation. One Strixan is sure not to draw too much attention. She certainly has experience," Icilius commented. "If Luna and Sol can raise up heroes to serve the empire, who is to say they cannot raise up a heroine?"

Faustus nodded silently at the tribune's words. Faustus, himself a former tribune, was friends with and ally to Icilius and the other two tribunes. Icilius was always complimentary and grateful for the work both he and Vytilia did for the empire. Though, in his more cynical moments, he wondered if there was an ulterior motive. Icilius had a son who would be discharged from the legions soon, an *unmarried* son as it were.

"You mean to send her out with that barbarian alone!" The Pontifex Maximus exclaimed. The Princeps silently groaned. Many in the Concilium audibly groaned. "But what of her chastity!? As eager as I am to import new animals that we may resume sacrifices, we must also protect the honor of our citizens, a patrician's daughter especially! We know nothing of this man or his people and culture. Should we risk this exquisite specimen being deflowered by these brutes if it means buying a head of cattle? Such an incident would be a stain on our offices! All our offices!"

"The only one who needs be concerned of that is her father," Porcia reprimanded. "I think Praetor Quintia's actions speak for themselves. How many of us would let our wives and daughters walk inside the second ring, let alone explore the frontier? If that does not speak to the trust we should have of Vytilia, then I know not what would."

"We could give her up to the barbarian," Cornelia commented. "If there is any sure way to convince him we desire peace, some of us anyway, it is that."

Faustus scowled.

"You would know all about giving favors to win favors, would you not, dear colleague?" Icilius asked. Cornelia stood up, ready to leap over the seating and wrestle the tribune. Icilius prepared a fighting stance. Only a cleared throat and the menacing scowl of the Praetorian Prefect sent them back into their seats. It was often forgotten that the Praetorians not only protected the patricians from the plebs but the patricians from each other.

"Are we forgetting something about the young Quintia as well? Praetor Cispia stood up and asked. "Did all of us forget what her mother's *nomen gentilicium*[17] was? Octavian. As in, the former imperial dynasty, Octavian. We may trust her to go out and explore, but should we send her to the surface. What is stopping her from using her feminine charms to return with an army? An army that would end our rule and restore the Octavians to the throne."

Faustus stood up immediately. "You forget, dear colleague, Vytilia is *my* daughter and therefore bears *my* nomen gentilicium. She is a Quintia, not an Octavian. She has not any interest in claiming the old imperial throne or title. Her loyalty is to the Concilium, unquestionably."

"But she is not your daughter alone, is she?" Cornelia asked. "Her mother was the last Octavian, an Octavian who filled her head with nonsense of restoring the glory of the old empire. Who can say that does not include the old monarchy as well?"

"The Octavian dynasty was done away with millennia before any of us were even born," Faustus defended. "Since the time of Princeps Julus, they have served the empire loyally and dutifully. Your accusation is unfounded and slanderous." *Mincing fellator.* Faustus did not speak that last part.

"I concur with Praetor Quintia. Never has his daughter, or wife before her, ever shown signs of wanting to restore the old monarchy or take power for themselves. It is only because of those dreams of the old glories and arts she was able to find this man in the first place," Icilius added.

"The Octavian matter aside," Mustius stood back up, "I am still not convinced sending Vytilia or any of our people to the surface

---

17. Family name.

is still a feasible idea. Even if we can demonstrate and explain to this man, Friedrich, our people are peaceful and desire cooperation, it would be a monumental task of convincing his entire race. There is too much at risk with exposure."

"Then what do we do about him? We cannot kill him," Licinia asked.

"He is a youth. We could give him all the gold he could carry, send him up the tunnel he came from then seal it behind him."

"But what about our herds!" The Quaestor pleaded. "I would much rather risk scaring the surface dwellers than starving to death. I ask all of you, is death at the hands of starving plebians or legionaries a worse alternative than the surface learning our race exists?"

There was a smattering of agreement muttered amongst the Concilium. Mustius even bobbed his head in agreement.

"Praetor Faustus," the Aedile asked, "this is your daughter we are discussing and her plan. Have you anything to say on her behalf?"

Faustus stood up. "I will say this and this alone. This opportunity presented before us is one my late wife dreamt of ever since our city first sank. She had prepared, trained, and molded Vytilia for this very occasion. She is prepared to represent our people and do what is necessary for the good of the empire. And, should we decide not to ask the surface for help, she will nobly accept our ruling. Her loyalty is without question and her devotion without blemish."

The words hung in the air for a minute before Princeps Porcia broke the silence. "I see there is still much to discuss and learn before we are quorate. I believe we should reconvene after the man, Friedrich, has awoken and Vytilia is able to dispel his fears. But, before we go on recess, Magister Militum Insteia, you have not yet spoken."

The Magister Militum stood up. "I do not agree with the bellicosity of some of our colleagues. There was a point earlier that we did not fully address; we are still at war. While the Quaestor and Censor have valid arguments of importing new animals, that will do us little good if the city walls are breeched, or our race is exterminated. First and foremost, we should be focused on anything that will give us an advantage over the devils. She says men are a martial culture, and this is a line of questioning we should pursue. If we can hire mercenaries, import new weaponry, anything to save Strixan lives and kill devils, it should be found. What good are laws protecting and helping the people if there is not a people to protect?"

Princeps Porcia nodded in agreement. "Agreed. If anyone else has comments or debates to share, now is the time. If not, when we reconvene, the gods willing, the man, Friedrich, will have awoken and can explain to us warfare on the surface. Then we shall debate again and reach a decision."

• • •

Vytilia returned to the residence and was greeted by Annia, who offered her a goblet and helped her remove the palla. "Welcome back, how was the meeting?"

"Better than expected. Luna was gracious today." She took a long drink. "How is Friedrich? Has he awoken?"

"Not yet, but Sextus has made sure he has been drinking water. Shall I prepare a change of clothes for you?"

"Not at the moment." She finished her drink, returning the goblet. She straightened her dress, accenting her body. If it worked on the Concilium, it may work on Friedrich. "I am going to try and wake Friedrich up and calm him down. Bring something for him to bite down on." Annia excused herself to fetch the items as Vytilia entered Friedrich's room. He was still asleep, lightly snoring but not moving. Annia entered with a small sliver of wood wrapped in a thick cloth and placed it in Friedrich's mouth, tying it to the bed to keep it in place. "Get to the kitchen. Bring water and meat." Annia nodded and hurried out.

Vytilia stood over Friedrich, taking a deep breath before placing her hands on his forehead. His eyes shot open, and he began to look around, his eyes darting all over the room until resting on Vytilia. His eyes narrowed, adjusting to the dim light, before widening again in fear. He began to scream, muffled by the gag. He thrashed violently, causing the bed to jump and shift position.

"Friedrich," Vytilia spoke. His screams got louder. "Friedrich!" He did not respond, still trying to rip out of his bindings. She raised her hand and slapped him across the face. "Friedrich!!!" *So much for being genteel.*

He fell quiet, looking up at her in pitiful terror. "If you had not responded the way you did when I greeted my father, you would not be in this situation. We do not take any pleasure in having you like this, and were it possible, we would treat you as any other honored visitor. But we need to take preventative measures to make sure you do not harm yourself or others. Do you understand?"

He nodded weakly.

"Excellent. I have just finished meeting with the Concilium. I have given them an overview of the surface based on what you explained to me with some assumptions. They are intrigued but require more information. We have mutually beneficial goals. You want to return to the surface, and we want supplies and assistance from the surface. We can work together. We do not mean you any harm. Do you understand?"

He nodded again.

"Then we have an accord." Annia returned to the room. "I have had the servants bring you food and drink. We are going to undo your binds. Remember, we do not mean you any harm. Do not move suddenly, and do not do anything you would regret." He nodded, and Annia set the food down then went over and began undoing Friedrich's binds, pulling the gag out of his mouth. When she finished, she gave him the food and drink. He graciously accepted it and quickly began eating. Vytilia excused Annia and sat down on a small chair across from Friedrich.

He looked at her, shrinking away and shuddering as she watched him. His discomfort was obvious, even after all the reassurances she had given him. "I suppose you have questions," she started. "I can answer whatever I can now and the rest after we meet with the Concilium."

He set his empty cup down, reaching for his dagger but swearing when he remembered it wasn't there. "I want my dagger back," he insisted.

"You will get it back when we leave the Arx."

"No, I want it now. If I'm going to be surrounded by vampires, I want something to defend myself."

"What was that you called us?"

"Vampires. I called you what you are."

This is an interesting word, she thought to herself. "What is a vampire?"

"You! You are, all of you! You're undead, bloodsucking wights! The Wends fear you more than they fear the Tujue or the lightless! You're evil, fell, wicked things!"

So, mankind somehow had heard that Strixans drank blood, but somehow over time, they presumed them to be undead and evil? Maybe there was a lost colony taking their frustrations out on innocent men, leading to the misunderstanding. "Well, we are not 'undead.' Such a thing is impossible. We have beating hearts, flowing blood, working organs. I am as alive as you are." She put two fingers on her neck. "Here, reach across. Feel my pulse!"

He saw her fangs glisten when she spoke. "I'll take your word on it. But what of the bloodsucking?" He clasped his hands around his neck. She noted that. The jugular vein and carotid artery were the favored puncture areas when hunting, which meant mankind knew of that practice, or they had coincidentally deduced it on their own.

"That is true. Blood is our primary source of nutrients and energy, but it is to us as water is for you." He shrugged again, further using his shoulders to shield his neck. "There is not a need for that." She gestured to his neck. "I cannot take another sapient being's blood unless I defeat them in armed combat. It is one of our most sacred and time-honored traditions." He relaxed his shoulders. "And think, why would I bite your neck when you are awake when I had ample opportunity when you were asleep?" He tensed up again, even though her argument was sound.

"What does your 'Concilium' want from me? How soon before I can go home?"

"They want to know what I was unable to tell them; what is war like on the surface? How do your people wage it? They had passing interest in commerce and diplomacy. Their focus is on seeing if your people can give us any advantage over the devils."

"I'm a caverneer, not a fighter," he admitted. "I don't know anything about how wars are fought."

"Well, you must know something. What kind of weapons are used, what sort of armor soldiers wear, even small details like that will be helpful."

He groaned. "I'm, I'm not comfortable talking about war. Isn't there anything else they want to know?"

Not comfortable talking about warfare? Did he really belong to a martial culture? Vytilia wanted to ask why but decided not to press it. She just had him calmed down and talking, and she did not want to risk him closing himself off. "They will not ask you for specifics, just a broad overview, so they can debate if your people can help us or not."

"And if I do that, you'll let me go home?" he asked.

"Almost. If they approve of what they hear, they will commission you to act as a guide for a team on the surface, so we can investigate and learn more about your society and if your style of warfare is advantageous and to procure weapons and supplies. You shall be rewarded, once the mission is complete."

"That's all you want from me? To know how muskets work and to take some of you up on the surface?" she nodded. He had to admit that was not what he was expecting, but it was better than being bitten and killed or even turned into one of them. "What if I say no or this council doesn't agree?"

"Then more than likely, we will take you back to the hole we found you in, exile you, and seal the entrance behind you. You will be going back empty-handed; we will not even provide you the rations to get home."

Friedrich thought back to when she found him. He technically had the choice not to follow her, but the ramifications of such a choice made choosing it impossible. He'd been backed into a corner, forced to bargain from a place of weakness, something he hadn't done since he was a kid doing his first trade deal. But Bergmann had taught him how to negotiate, or at the very least, stall a negotiation until a better option came up. He called it "humoring" the other party. Friedrich supposed he would have to humor these vampires until he could get back home. He could figure everything else out later.

"Alright, I'll talk to your lords, so long as I can go home."

"We shall certainly try our best," she affirmed.

I won't, he chuckled. *I'm not going to hell for aiding and abetting. But there's nothing in the sagas against tricking evil.*

6

As she watched Friedrich finish up his meal, an idea formed in Vytilia's mind. Instead of merely answering questions, she should show him the splendor of the old empire, of the world before the cataclysm. If anything, it may help him feel more comfortable and garner sympathy for the Strixan cause. When he finished, he went to speak, but she stood up and spoke first. "Friedrich, I know you have many questions and concerns that I wish to address, but to do so, there is something we should do first. Would you like to take a tour?"

"A . . . tour?"

"Indeed, an exhibition of the Arx campus to see why my countrymen and I love our empire. I know it should answer many of your burning questions."

"I . . ." His eyes widened when she stood up. She looked radiant, her dress shaping to her curves. She was the most stunning woman Friedrich had ever seen. Even a blind man would turn his head when she passed by. "I . . ." He shook his head. *Get a hold of yourself,* he barked internally. She was a monster, a bloodsucking forsaken wight, not some drinkmaid to ogle. She was doing this on purpose to trap him. Take a tour of the vampire burgh? More like take him to a dark corner and make him her thrall. "I would not be comfortable with that."

She tilted her head, her eyes narrowing. "Why ever not?" She answered her own question. "You still do not trust me, do you?"

"Of course not! How could I?!"

She sighed. "Friedrich, whatever misconceptions or prejudices you have must stem from an ancient fear. You trusted me after I rescued you. How is that any different from now? Do you not want to return to your homeland? To your people? We have mutually aligned goals. We should work together."

He did want to see Frau Beck again. But he didn't want to do so if it meant unleashing a vampiric horde on the surface. Then again, she had rescued him, saved him from almost certain death, and he came away without bite marks on his neck. And, well, not to be rude, but Wends are a very worrisome lot, always jumping at shadows. "I am . . . hesitant to trust you again. I feel like you lied to me."

"I never told you any falsehoods during our journey to Nidus. Keeping certain details away from you is not the same as outright fabricating them. Imagine I had shown you my fangs at the cavern I found you in. Your screams may have attracted devils, then where would you be? We all were fortunate your 'episode' happened within the safety of the city walls."

"Well, you got me there. But when we go on this 'tour,' I want to stay in well-lit areas. And I want my dagger back."

Well-lit when underground is a relative concept, but she would not say that. "The pugio is nonnegotiable; the law is the law. We cannot make exceptions simply because you are our guest."

She wasn't going to budge. Friedrich shrugged. "Alright. But, keep your distance. I don't want you to get close."

"A rude request but a reasonable one." She cocked her head to the door. "It sounds like my father has returned. Come, we shall reintroduce the two of you. There is a change of clothes for you." She pointed to a dark red tunic lying on a footstool. He changed out of his scratchy legionary garb into the equally scratchy civilian tunic. She was waiting outside the door curtain and guided him to the common area or living room. Praetor Quintia was talking with a servant when they entered. The servant departed, and Vytilia spoke to her father in their tongue. When she finished, he nodded approvingly then leaned in as Vytilia touched the sides of his temple, just as she had to Friedrich when she found him. When she pulled away, Praetor Quintia stepped forward, extending a hand to Friedrich.

"Friedrich, it is good to finally meet you after that . . . unfortunate incident in the foyer. I am glad to see you up and about and not screaming." He spoke Friedrich's language in the same refined, academic accent as his daughter but in a deep baritone voice. It was like butter on the ears.

"It is an honor as well, mein Herr. Your household has been . . . very gentle and not biting."

The Praetor raised a curious eyebrow. His movements and mannerisms were not as bird-like as his daughter. "I am pleased to hear that. Your discovery has caused quite a stir with my colleagues. There is a great deal of debate about how we are to approach meeting your people. We are eager to hear from you directly when we reconvene."

A lump formed in Friedrich's throat, and the food in his stomach started to rebel. He forgot he would have to stand before a group of high-born lords to be questioned. It was every toiler's nightmare. "I hope the . . . talks are . . . the talks bring about good."

Vytilia winced at the grammar, but the Praetor remained steadfast. "I want to personally ask you a few questions before I meet with some of my colleagues. I want a better foundation to work from when I try and solicit their support for allying with the surface." He gestured to two couches in the middle of the living room. Friedrich sat upright on one, and the Praetor laid on the other with Vytilia standing behind him. Friedrich glanced to his right and saw a portrait hanging on the wall, overlooking and watching this room. The portrait was very detailed and finely crafted. The Strixan depicted was almost a twin of Vytilia. He had not seen nor heard of a mother being mentioned and did not want to bring up a potentially unpleasant issue.

In the brief moment before speaking, he took the time to size up Vytilia and her father. Well, she called him father, but he didn't look more than a few years older than either of them. He had heard lords aged better, but aside from the slightly greying hair, there was not a mark of age on the man. He was handsome and charismatic with the same magnetism Vytilia had. These traits had been absent in the folk outside the Arx walls, but this family had it in spades. That was if Friedrich could call them a family. He remembered, albeit vaguely, that vampires could turn the living into them. Vytilia might say they weren't undead, but the cold touch and pale skin said otherwise. Were they using family in a poetic sense? Was he her father because he turned her into one, adopting her as a daughter-in-death?

"I suppose the first place to start is at the beginning," Praetor Quintia began. A servant brought him and Vytilia two goblets and a cup of water for Friedrich. "What was it that led you to fall underground? Vytilia said you were a . . . er what did you call it?" He looked to her.

"Caverneer," she answered.

"Exactly, tell me all about it."

"Well . . ." He took a deep breath, keeping his hands at his side. "I've been caverneering since I was six years old. My late master and I have dug through every mountain range in the Realm and most of the larger forests as well. We made our own tools and rope, and . . . and that's about it. Searching through the caves where I fell was to be his last outing before retiring."

Praetor Quintia's mood slightly soured before he returned to a resting face. "I see. My condolences on your master's passing. Death is never an easy concept to accept." *Ironic words*, Friedrich thought. "Do you have family or property you can return to?"

"I, I don't." He dabbed his eye. "No family, all I have is the upstairs room of a bakery and a landlady waiting for me."

Vytilia pinched the bridge of her nose, shaking her head. Her father waved at her to stop. "A pity. But by the sounds of it, you have traveled all over. Where have you gone in your travels?"

"All over the Realm, the only time I've been outside the borders is when we briefly crossed into Gallia after nightfall. We spent most of our time in the Weiße Hügel range. They're the largest mountains in Erebus, a lot of caves and old abandoned mines." He stopped. "Well, I suppose none of this makes any sense to you two."

"You would not be able to draw a map, would you?" Praetor Quintia asked.

"No, I'm not much of a drawer. Good maps are expensive and difficult to come by." Not to mention the Realm's borders were a mess. It had become something of a joke amongst ambassadors on the surface. Friedrich swallowed his drink and paused. Should he really be telling them this? He was by no means a fighting man, but he knew that if one was to go to war against an enemy, you'd want to know as much as you can about them. He should try to keep his answers vague and stretch the truth.

"Is this empire, or 'Realm' as you call it, is it rather large? You mentioned leaving the border only once," her father asked.

"It's the largest group of lands in Erebus." Not as big as the Sultanate or the Catask holdings in the new world, but they didn't need to know that.

"Group of lands? Do you mean provinces?" Friedrich stared at Faustus blankly.

"Small subdivisions," Vytilia clarified. "Like crumbs off of a loaf."

"Uh, no. More like several different breads all stitched together. We're a Realm of stems and sippes. Land belongs to those who live on it and own it."

"Fascinating," Faustus mused. "I do not mean any offense Friedrich, but I must confess these borders sound so inefficient, almost impractical. Why are there not appointed magistrates ruling over a defined area that report directly to a central authority?" the Praetor asked. Friedrich looked to Vytilia to translate.

"He is asking why the emperor, er, Kommandant as you called him, does not directly control everything and place governors in certain areas to rule on his behalf."

"Oh." Friedrich nodded in understanding. "Well, some areas are under the Kommandant. Others swear oaths to him instead. Everything is done through the lawhalls or the Kreise.[18] I don't know how it works, but it just works."

"How does your emperor, er, Kommandant? How does he gain control of the crown? Is it inherited from father to son?" Praetor Quintia asked.

Friedrich chose his next words carefully. "I don't understand all the details, but I know the Reichstag plays a role. What that role is, well, that's beyond my knowledge."

"A . . . Reichstag, am I saying that correctly? What is that?" Vytilia also leaned forward, interested.

"A gathering of all the Free-Steads, churchlands, stems, and sippes."

Praetor Quintia muttered "interesting, interesting" under his breath. "This Reichstag sounds similar to the old senate. How does your Emperor, apologies, Kommandant, collect taxes? Or raise an army? Or even send postage? Does he do this directly or through this Reichstag?" Vytilia quickly followed up with a simplified explanation.

"To tell the truth mein Herr, I simply don't know. I've never had to send anything through the Reichsauftrag.[19] But I pay land-fees right to the Kommandant. For armies . . . most of that is done through landsknechts," Friedrich spat. "Landsknechts are scum, lawful robbers."

"Landsknechts?" Vytilia asked.

"Sellswords. Chip-warriors. Guns and polearms for hire?"

"Mercenaries," she explained to her father.

"Interesting, interesting," Praetor Quintia repeated. He stared down at the floor, contemplating Friedrich's responses in deep thought. He was like this for several minutes, adding an

18. Means Circle. An informal alliance between neighboring or confessional territories of the Holy Realm of Midgart.

19. Realm form of Post Office, lit. Realm errand.

awkward tension to the room. "Your people are rather peculiar Friedrich. From what little I have heard, they seem rather eccentric in a way. Though I must commend you that such a strange group has managed to form and maintain an empire. Everything is an antithesis to our old empire, and yet somehow, you have made it work. I have to go meet with the other Praetors, if you will excuse me." He finished off his goblet and set it down, standing up and exiting the residence without another word.

When her father left, Vytilia motioned that it was time to go. He drank the last of his water, putting his cup next to the Praetor's goblet. He leaned in as he set the cup down and caught the faint smell of copper and iron, a telltale sign of blood.

"So, who's blood exactly is it you are . . . drinking?"

"Bovine. Well, this vintage was mixed with porcine and even calcerta. We call it Sanguinvinum. It is aged and mixed with what spices and grapes can grow down here."

He remembered the iron taste in his mouth when he woke up in the cave. "Did you feed me some of that when you found me?"

"Not Sanguinvinum. I gave you porcine blood, standard legionary rations. It was the only sustenance I had on hand." She stood up. "Would you like to see the cattle? My family has a number of sizeable herds within the city walls. I particularly favor a female juvenile descended from a female given to me when I became of age."

"I will pass. I have seen and met enough cows to last a lifetime." He was worried she would start feeding on one. His stomach was already nauseous about meeting with the vampire Concilium. Seeing a poor cow get butchered would set it over the edge.

"Suit yourself, Fulvulus is a darling animal, very affectionate. But enough about her, I have the Arx to show you!"

Her bubbliness had returned as she guided Friedrich back past the statue and out the front of the Arx. They stood on the last step, looking down on the city below. He could make out supply wagons arriving at the third wall and heard the faint sounds of blacksmiths hammering at anvils. It was strange, standing on a grassy hill and looking down at nothing but barren rock. By all accounts, Nidus should be unlivable, a ghost town, yet it was very much alive. Dying may be a more precise word but still alive.

"In our heyday, Nidus was a splendid city built of marble, much like the Arx." She gestured to the columns behind them. "On bright days, the sun was so reflective, one had to shield their eyes to cross the street. Now the Arx is all that remains of that." Her bubbliness dissipated, replaced with a thick forlornness. "At least allow me to show you what remains."

She pointed to the three buildings to the left. "These are the *Collegium Thaumaturgiae*, academic institutions where we teach practitioners of thaumaturgy, what you have been calling 'witchcraft.' One teaches medicinal and veterinary disciplines, one forging and fire, and the other working with stones, metals, and minerals."

Friedrich did not need her to explain which building taught which. He was sure the roofs did that for him. "Did you learn there?"

She smiled, a prideful smile as she looked down at the practicing pupils. "I did not. My mother taught me at home. She was the greatest practitioner of thaumaturgy seen in many generations. My education is a thousandfold better than what they will receive." She gestured to the students. "Though, I must commend them. They will dedicate their lives to the study of a single discipline. In several centuries, they will do thaumas I cannot. But, as of now, I know more than them."

She turned around and headed off to their right, towards the large wall and golden sphere. They stopped at the foot of the wall. "This is the great calendar. It is how we have kept track of the days and months and alerted the public to upcoming festivals and holidays. Smaller versions were built in every quarter of the city. Of course, since we do not have access to the sun, a calendar has become redundant."

"There're twelve lines. Does that mean you use twelve months?"

"An astute observation, do your people also use a twelve-month calendar?"

Friedrich nodded. "12 months, 52 weeks . . ."

"365 days?" she asked.

"366 every four years."

She was taken aback. His kind had learned about the intercalary year? How sophisticated were they? Did that develop naturally?

"Do you have clocks?" Friedrich asked. He was glancing at the great calendar as well. The realization Strixans had the same way to measure time was unnerving him ever so slightly.

"Clocks?"

"How to keep track of the day. All the big towns on the surface have a clock tower. I can read a clock pretty well."

"We do not use clocks . . . . How do your people measure time within a day?"

"There's 24 stounds in a day, 60 slices in a stound, then 60 ticks in a slice."

Her eyes went wide. Aside from the names, that was nearly identical to how Strixans kept track of time. "How . . . where did your people learn that?"

He scratched his head. "I think . . . it was either the first Great Churchmeet or one of the big ones after. The Elláser taught us how. They were smart. Not smart enough to beat the Tujue . . . ." He shrugged. "Is it the same for you?"

She nodded. "We call them hours, minutes, and seconds, but the principal is the same."

"Huh! What're the odds?" he asked. Though, his face twitched in concern. This was not lending credence to the idea Strixans were not the Half-gods.

"What are the odds indeed?" Vytilia muttered. She could not recall if she had ever been taught where Strixan horology originated. If it had a documented origin. In what she had read and what she had learned, it had always been measured that way. Had the early Strixans developed it coincidentally and identically to the mannish system, or had both peoples been taught?

This was too worrying for the moment. She had to focus on winning Friedrich to their cause. "Alongside the calendar, we used this . . . ." She pointed to the golden globe, which was actually one small sphere surrounded by nine rings. "This is the Grand Armillary, used to track the movement of the Sun, Moon, and the seven planets, not including Terra."

"Seven worlds?" He furrowed his brow. "Aren't there only five, six with Erde?"

She looked at him disgusted. "Have your people not yet learned astronomy? There are seven other planets, named after the children of our gods."

Friedrich could have sworn there were only five other worlds. He remembered a Holy-play about a Vitelish who was recently hallowed for observing the one closest to the sun. Compared to vampires being real, it didn't sound too farfetched. "What's that building over there?" He pointed to the structure past the armillary and calendar.

"Those? That is the thermae, or . . . bathhouse, the only extant public bathhouse in the empire." He sniffed his arms; it had been a long while since he had a bath. Though it was curious why these high-and-mighty vampire nobles never commented on that.

"You still have bathhouses?"

"Of course! How else is one expected to bathe?"

"At home? Where you can't catch the Gaulish blight?"

"At home? You expect me to believe every household on the surface has their own thermae? That is why your people are so disunited. You do not come together publicly to share news and bathe."

He didn't appreciate all these slights towards the world of the surface, but he kept his tongue. If she was talking, she wasn't drinking blood, and he was closer to getting home. He changed topics. "And that one?" He pointed to the round building with the tiered-cake interior.

"The Cenatio Annex, where formal banquets and dinners are held." Interesting, Friedrich thought. He'd heard of lordly schlosses having a separate kitchen but never a separate eating hall.

"Do you eat there?"

"Rarely, only when a Praetor retires and a new one is appointed. And we do not eat so much as drink."

He grinned, now was his chance for a comeback. "What? You don't eat together all the time? How do you and your neighbors bond if you don't eat together outside!?"

Was that an attempt at humor? she wondered. She would not play along. "I take it your kind eats communally rather frequently then?"

"Only on holidays and feast days if you're in Erdeish land. It's the only time burghers will ever rub shoulders with beggars. Though, it is not unheard of to spend the night outside drinking."

"What is the night sky like?" Vytilia asked.

"The night sky? It's wonderful, prettiest thing you'll ever see. Imagine a blank, black canvas, filled with diamonds, rubies, emeralds, all the gems you can think of, made with the elegance of a master, arranged with such an eye for detail you can get lost looking at just a small part of the sky. On the surface, we always call the sky God's canvas."

She smiled, glancing forlornly at the rocky roof above her. "I pray the Concilium listens to reason. You know not what I would give to gaze upon the face of Luna and Sol, to see my ancestors in the sky. You are very fortunate, you know, to live with such a masterpiece overhead."

He supposed he was. The feeling of pity he had felt when he walked through Nidus returned. Vytilia had been denied the chance of ever viewing the night sky or seeing a sunrise or a sunset. She had never felt crisp mountain air or the cool taste of creek water or the smell of freshly blooming blossoms. All of the wonderful beauty of the world Friedrich took for granted was as foreign to her as the surface of the moon to him. In all the stories he knew, had a monster ever sat and stared at the night sky? Did the hero character ever stumble on some fiend or draugr painting? A twinge of regret shot through his body; perhaps he had been too harsh on Strixans.

And yet, whatever pity or regret he felt, that burning doubt still glowed in the back of his mind. People do not fear things without good reason. Wolves are detested because they kill livestock, rats for eating food stores, the Tujue for invading Erebus. If the Wenden and others had reason to be fearful of vampires, no matter how long-ago man may have met them, it had to be for a good reason.

Vytilia studied Friedrich, watching as he scratched his facial scars, shifting from foot to foot while breathing heavily, his face contorted in thought and internal debate. "You are still unsure about us, are you not?"

"I am," he admitted. "This whole . . . problem is messy. Your kind, you're supposed to be tales, shadows that go bump in the night, tapping on windows to scare children. You're not supposed to be real. Fiends aren't supposed to be real! It doesn't make any sense!"

"I can understand your concern. Had the roles been reversed, and I found my way to the surface, I would have assumed it all to be some delirious hallucination. The shock of finding such a world would be overwhelming."

"But you wouldn't have stumbled on a world of monsters."

She scowled. "Who is to say? If a Strixan poet long ago had written a frightful verse about a pink-skinned, dull-teethed, martial culture, and had that story survived, would I not think you the monster? If I had been raised from a nestling to fear your kind, I would have run from you the moment I learned your true nature. What one calls a monster is a subjective term. Think of the devils you encountered! You know what a true monster is."

"There's more than one kind of monster," Friedrich countered.

She gripped her palla excess tightly until her knuckles went purple. Why was she not getting through to him? Maybe she should try a different approach. "Friedrich, do you have a mother?" He made a strange face before nodding. "So did I. I had a loving, darling mother, who carried me for eight months and raised me with love and devotion. In the course of my lifetime, never once did my mother teach me to be frightening, to prey on the weak and innocent, to cause nightmares. Never once did my mother or father give me explicit instructions to be monstrous. They taught me to be civil, to gain knowledge and wisdom, to serve my people and empire. They taught me aesthetics, literature, culture, all the hallmarks of a civilization. What 'monsters' or 'vampires' do you know of that build civilization, that enjoy the finer things in life?"

None that he knew of. He looked into her eyes and saw an innate innocence. He heard the pleading tone in her voice. She was right. She was not a monster, just another being. Afterall, why would God or his guardian Norn spare him to find her and her kind? They were victims of the Lightless and their ilk just as much as the Half-gods. Why should they suffer?

Maybe he could do more than just talk with her leaders and escape back home. Maybe, he was meant to do more than that.

"Here, come with me." She headed off to the other side of the Arx. "There is one more piece of our history I want to show you." They followed a trail to a bunker entrance below the Arx that was guarded by two Strixans. The door was solid iron, inlayed with golden images of owls and eagles. The guards straightened up with one hand going for their swords as Vytilia and he approached. One shifted, blocking her entrance, gesturing to Friedrich with his chin. She slowly explained why they were there. The guard stepped by, allowing them to pass, glaring at Friedrich as he walked by. He raised his hands to show he was unarmed, quickly following her inside.

Past the entrance was a long hallway, flanked by large steel doors, barred with chains and iron bars. At the end was a truly massive bronze door, unlocked and emblazoned with incredibly detailed reliefs of owls, eagles, and warriors. "What is this place?" he wondered aloud.

"This is the Imperial Library, the greatest collection of literature, knowledge, and artwork the world has ever known—and the last bastion of all Strixan learning. Most of these doors have not been unlocked in millennia. The underground environment is not kind to parchment." She stopped in front of the end doors. "This room, however, is what I wanted to show you." She opened the door, holding it so Friedrich could go through first.

Inside, Friedrich felt like he had stepped into another world (he was well familiar with that feeling at this point). He hadn't felt a breeze or any kind of wind since arriving underground, but the air here felt especially still, as if it was afraid of touching any of the objects. It even smelt different, almost cleaner, purer even than air on the surface. There was an unspoken sanctity in this room. It was hallowed, more so than any Hof Friedrich had ever stepped in.

The room was an art gallery, of sorts. There were murals, mosaics, busts, statues, even displays of old rusted armors and swords. The stonework here was much finer than the rest of the building. The marble was polished, glittering from the soft, blue-colored sun stones hanging from braziers on the roof. The center of the room was commanded by beautiful, expertly carved statues of the purest, whitest marble he'd ever seen that towered over both of them. He complimented the stonework of the room, but that was amateur compared to the statues; the skill and masterwork made them look as if they had been carved by the hand of a god. He could see individual pores and veins, the billowing of their robes, even the nails on their hands and feet. Such artistry would put any stone carver on the surface to shame.

The largest center statue was of a man and woman. She wore a hood and armor and held out a statuette of the moon with another statue of an owl resting on her arm. The man wore a simple tunic and held a statuette of the sun with an eagle grasped on his arm. Their free hands were clasped together. At the pedestal stood eleven smaller statues, seven in the front, four in the rear. Each was dressed in either a tunic or a dress and held aloft some object, either a sword or book. And just as the larger ones, each was expertly crafted from the purest of white marble.

"Should we remove our shoes?" he whispered, afraid to speak normally.

"You catch on quick," Vytilia responded, also whispering. He couldn't tell if she meant it as a compliment or an insult. He decided on compliment. "This is the Sanctum Sanctorum of my people," Vytilia explained, removing her sandals. "It is a reliquary of our history, the artifacts we have been able to preserve that tell our story. Watch your tongue and watch your step. You tread on sacred ground." Friedrich nodded and removed his own footwear. He may be sacrilegious at times, but on the rare occasion he did attend church meetings, he knew when to sit down and shut up. And he knew better than to anger Vytilia.

She hoped desperately, an unspoken prayer on her lips to the Gods above and in her heart, that this would soften Friedrich.

He still had doubts of their intentions, doubts she and the empire could not afford. If she could show him their history, show him their civility, he should be more willing and accepting of helping them. This had to work for the good of everyone.

They started with the statues in the center, or stone-casts as Friedrich would call them. "These are our gods, Luna Aeternus and Sol Invictus." She gestured to the two large figures. "In the beginning, only Luna ruled the world, a lone light shining through the eternal black. But nothing could live. There was only cold and darkness. She could not be a ruler without subjects, and so she created Sol, who created daytime. They were married and ruled the world together, a balance of dark and light, necessary for life to thrive. Our people were originally devotees of Luna. She was also our creator, and we ruled the dark, but we could not expand or thrive without light. We welcomed Sol as our deity and soon learned the importance of the cycle of day and night. Strixans are natural hunters, and in our oldest histories, we subsisted solely off of the blood of game we found. The light allowed our prey to expand, reproduce, and spread, while the night allowed us to hunt."

"It has often been asked by our philosophers," Vytilia continued, "why we worshipped anything. Our empire covered all of the habitable surface, we knew every imaginable school of thaumaturgy, and we had strength unmatched. But my mother always reminded me the gods were our counterweight, a reminder that despite how powerful or knowledgeable Strixans were, there was always a force greater than us. They were our reminder not to fall to that most egregious offense; hubris."

Most of what she had just said was lost on Friedrich as he stared at the statue of Sol Invictus. It felt so recognizable, almost as if he'd seen it before. Yet, he had! While the statue had odd elements, and Luna was different, statues like this were found in every Hof, Harug, and Hall in Erebus. This was . . . God! He opened his mouth to say something but quickly closed it. Was this another coincidence? A stroke of pure chance? He wanted to think so. The implications were . . . uncomfortable. Now he had to wonder; was this good news or bad news?

"So, you worship the sun and the moon?" he squeaked.

"We used to." She sighed. "Very few recognize the gods, and those who do mostly focus on Luna. Many feel that Sol has abandoned us and so have abandoned him."

Friedrich grit his teeth. Maybe Sol abandoned the vampires for mankind. There's a thought that was sure to cause offense. He needed to shift topics. "Who are these?" He pointed to the eleven waist-high statues at the pedestal.

"These are Luna and Sol's children and other creations. They are not gods in their own right. You may call them demi-gods, but we refer to them as *Deus Loci* and *Natura Loci*. Each was guardian over some aspect of reality such as warfare, marriage, animals, or even the firmament. They were respected with festivals, months in our calendar, and names for the heavenly bodies, but Luna and Sol always took precedence, Luna especially. My family does not venerate the Loci."

"Why not?"

"My mother did not, and she taught my father and I how to worship. She always said why thank the cup for water when the river provided it?"

His eyes wandered to the statue of Sol, his stomach sinking as a thousand thoughts, mostly nightmares, went through his head. "Why was Luna so important?" He wanted to move along, away from the statue. Seeing it was causing him to break out into a cold sweat.

She heard his heartbeat increasing. Perhaps even this gormless plebeian was awed at the sight of the gods. "We are more adapted for operation at night, hence the pigmentation of our hair and skin and our ability to see in the dark. Though as time went on, we began to see the merit of the daytime. Instead of hunting wild game, we began to learn animal husbandry and agriculture. We would raise mighty herds of bovines, porcines, and other animals now extinct to us and harvest their blood and meat. With this stable supply of food, we could now expand, build cities, lay the foundations of civilization."

He broke away from looking at the statue of Sol and turned his back to it. If he looked at it any longer, he would burst apart at the seams. His eye was drawn to the door. He wanted to leave, pretend he never saw what he saw here, then he spied one of the other pieces. It was a drawing, or several drawings, on a large slab of stone, hanging next to the door. On it were images of man-like beings, many with lower halves from different wildlife. A dragon flew above the other beings, and wolves were prominently featured in a darkened corner. He walked over to it. It was something different and took his mind off of the Sol statue.

"What is this?" he asked.

She joined him at the exhibit. She was smiling. "This is a treasure, an art work recovered shortly after Nidus fell. It is a collection of some of the more popular artistic motifs we used to have. We used non-Strixan beings to artistically represent aspects of art or nature. See, here is a pygmy, a chthonic spirit to remind us of the importance of mineral wealth."

She pointed to a short, stout, manlike thing. He likened it to a dwarf.

"Here is a nymph, an idealistic, relaxed, nature spirit . . . ."

She pointed to a slightly taller, pointed eared being. He likened it to an elf.

"Goliaths, beings of raw fury . . ."

This one was taller than any of the others, much like ettins of his own folklore.

"Cyclops, great builders and smiths . . ."

One-eyed ettins?

"I will not explain what all of them mean, but the rest are the naiad . . . ."

A mermaid.

"Leviathans . . ."

Some kind of kraken or great sea adder. His mind went to Ermingandz. He quickly pushed the latter thought out of his mind. He didn't need any more similarities to the Sol statue.

"The lamia . . ."

He didn't know anything like that. It was half-snake and half woman.

"The faun . . ."

Another he didn't know. Half-goat, half-man.

"The Ophiotaurus and its cousin the Fauntaurus . . ."

Two half-bull things, one with snakes for legs, and the other with a mannish lower body. And here Friedrich thought he knew every being and thing of folklore. He wondered what tall tales the Strixans told.

"And the draco. This one is odd. Mother taught me that it could either be a force of destruction or a neutral, sometimes benevolent force."

That one was easy. It was a dragon. Though, Friedrich had never heard of a dragon being anything but evil. On the surface, it was taught that the only good dragon is a dead dragon.

Friedrich pointed to the wolves in the darkened corner. Now that he stepped closer, he saw they were joined with half-bird, half-women. "Why are wolves and . . . whatever these are banished to the corner."

"The lupi, what you call wolves, are the ultimate antagonists in Strixan art," she explained. "When Luna and Sol gave us imperium over the world, we were instructed to treat it gently. The great ecosystem of the world is delicate and needs a careful hand to protect it."

When he managed to figure out what her words meant, he realized the church had a similar teaching, that men were stewards over Erde. It was why so much lumber was imported, since cutting down the old forests of the Realm was frowned upon. He glanced back at the statue. Was this something like the 12-month year, where it was similar, or was that taught to the old men by the Strixans? He swallowed hard and tried to keep his stomach from rebelling.

"Lupi, however, are a plague upon the world. They are selfish, dull creatures. They only care to devour without concern for how that affects the other animals. Even worse, when they have depopulated an area of prey, they decimate themselves and move on to repeat the process over and over, *ad nauseum*." She scowled at the wolves. "Any true Strixan knows to kill a lupus without care or thought. They need to be put down before they spread like some toxic fungus."

"You know . . ." his voice cracked. He cleared it. "My kind don't like wolves either . . ." She looked at him for explanation. "If you're named a "wolf," it's worse than being an outlaw. You have no friends, no kith or kin, and if someone kills you, they actually get rewarded for it." It was argued, mostly over drinks, that being tortured or broken on the wheel was better than being labeled 'wolf.' Neither was something Friedrich ever wanted to experience. There were also the vargr and barghests, evil wolves from other parts of Erebus, but he kept those to himself.

"Then perhaps that is a commonality we could work with," Vytilia told him. "For diplomacy, it is good to find common ground."

"What about the bird-women?" he asked.

"We call them harpies. We hold them in as much regard as we do lupi. Where our ancestors once could turn into full avian forms, harpies are a hubristic attempt to gain that power. Now they are cursed, straddling the line between the normal and avian form."

"Avian form?"

She led him over to the next piece on the wall to their right, a mosaic where several large, grey, bird-like creatures were standing, surrounded by people kneeling. The kneeling people were offering gifts of fruits, gold, and vases. The creatures resembled owls and eagles, but many times larger than a man.

"With the advent of sunlight and animal husbandry, our people split into tribes and ethnicities, ruling over territories and holding imperium over large stretches of land. These tribes constantly warred, only spreading death and destruction. They were devoid of culture and proper worship. This was against the wishes of the gods, and so Luna and Sol raised one tribe to be their champions: the Strixa. The Strixa were the purest of our kind and the namesake for our people as a whole."

Godly leaders raising up one group to do their bidding and unite different groups? That sounded like Karalthergroz. But, that did not worry Friedrich too much. That, he wagered, had to be a coincidence. Though, between the wolves and Sol, he wouldn't put all of his gold and silver on it.

Vytilia continued. "The ancient Strixa possessed the ancestral power of flight, the ability to mimic the powers and strength of the mighty animals sacred to the gods. They were like unto demigods, nigh invulnerable, who could fly and slay their enemy with the swipe of a talon. With this blessing, they were able to conquer and annex the other tribes, eventually uniting them under the Strixa banner and beginning the empire. The tribal chieftain, Aquilius Octavi, and his wife, Noctinna Vianus, eventually founded Nidus and the imperial line of Octavian."

He pointed to the bird creatures in the mosaic. "So, you used to be able to turn into one of these?" She nodded, beaming proudly. He grimaced. He could understand how a creature like that could conquer the world. It was something only seen in nightmares. "How come the other 'tribes' didn't also have the power of flight?"

"We do not know. What records survived our fall are a mixture of mythic histories, exaggerated chronicles, genealogy, inscriptions from the artifacts in this room, and a few oral traditions. During the course of the conquest, the Strixa implemented a policy known as 'Canescere' or . . . ." She paused to translate. "'Greying' in your tongue. Essentially, the nobles of a conquered tribe would be married to native Strixans to integrate and fully Strixanize them. It was through this course of action that, many believe, the original Strixan lost their ability to transform. Of course, since our records are damaged or lost, we do not truly know. I have read accounts that believe it was tainted blood that corrupted them. Others say they lost the fortunes and graces of Luna and so lost the ability to change. Personally, I believe they consumed impure blood. That is why we have strict traditions on drinking blood gained unjustly. 'What a body partakes is what a body reflects' was a favored saying of my maternal great-grandfather."

They came to the next artifact, an old sword and shield, both leaning against a tattered standard, topped with a faded gold eagle and owl. The shield, who's covering had long since peeled away, was more ovaloid than the ones used by the legions and nearly as tall as Friedrich. "With the Octavian family firmly on the throne, they began to expand the empire, establishing colonies to advance our borders, absorbing tribes who submitted, and eliminating any that resisted. It was brutal and bloody, but our borders stretched across the habitable world, carried on the backs of our legions. When the Great Frozen receded, we claimed all that had once been covered in the name of Luna and Sol."

"The Great Frozen?" He scratched his cheek scars. That sounded like the Long Winter. He glanced back at the statue of Sol, beads of sweat forming on his forehead. His initial thinking in the tunnels may have been right afterall.

"It is a mysterious event we know little of. The grounds to the north were coated in blocks of ice, glaciers as the ancient chroniclers call them. Whatever they were, they opened up new lands and peoples to conquer. This sword." She pointed to the one displayed. "As legend goes, the hilt is made from the tusk of a great beast found after the Great Frozen receded. Emperor Nerva Octavian allegedly slew the beast with his bare hands." She grinned. "It spilled enough blood to satiate an entire legion."

Great Frozen? Tusked beasts? And she said all of this was in the north. Land was always the same. It never changed. The north they were exploring must have been the Realm. *Or, what would become the Realm,* Friedrich thought. Unless this was the far north? In Zvearrik, where it was always snowing. And tusks? Is that what they called an auroch's horns? He wondered if Strixans ever encountered the Fimbulstormr.

"Who did you fight?" She looked at him for clarification. "You had an army, but who was it that you fought? Was it other vampires or something else?"

"Details like that are lost but also unimportant," she asserted. "Whoever we fought was either destroyed or absorbed into the empire, eventually gaining the rights of citizens. The only foe historians believed merit mentioning was our hated rival, the Baalites. They were a difficult enemy; our proudest and darkest moments were during the long and bloody wars against them. Some ancient hymns and poems that survived say they had been an enemy since our race existed. But eventually, we triumphed, and the Baalites were exterminated from history. Their feeble barbarity was not a match for our glorious civilization."

Two old enemies whose feud goes back hundreds of years and can only result in the destruction of one or the other? If race was replaced with religion, Friedrich thought, it could easily describe the relationship between the Church and the Sariqins of the Sultanate. Or the Church and the Urworkish. Or the Church and the Pananthropotes. "Were these . . . Baalites other vampires, or?"

"We do not know. We were so thorough in our destruction that artifacts and records did not survive." She looked at the old armor and standard with pride. "One story says we did not even bother taking prisoners. All were put to the sword, then the ground was sterilized."

She moved on, expounding before they got to the next artifact: a stone bust of a man wearing a helmet, his eyes focused, his top fangs bared. "Of course, the conquests eventually came to a halt as arable and habitable lands became scarcer. Eventually, permanent borders were established, and the Empire turned inwards. By this time, many emperors and a few empresses had controlled the throne. Without an outside enemy to unite our people, the patricians began to waste their time with intrigue and politics. The Imperial Family fell into factionalism as son fought against father, brother against brother, even nephew against uncle to claim the throne and eliminate rivals. The crises lasted for nearly a millennium, fracturing the empire into petty imperia, ruled by ambitious magistrates.

"That was until one tiercel took control, the first Princeps, Dracon Romulus Julus. He ended the civil wars and reunified the empire with one drastic decision—completely replacing the Imperial Family. It was a bold, some would say blasphemous move, but it worked. He replaced the emperor with the Concilium, composed of Praetors and magistrates from different provinces and groups of the empire. This system he established is the one still in use today. He implemented numerous other reforms as well: land distribution, blood rationing, military overhaul, even the revival of games to improve morale and unify the populace. He is the only reason the empire survived. Without him, we would have been scattered and lost, possibly returning to being mere hunters subsisting on wild game."

Her mood turned wistful. She seemed hesitant to get to the next artifact. "I have not visited this room in decades," she admitted.

What was a decade? Friedrich wondered.

"My mother and I would come here, and she would tell me the history of our people, much as I am doing with you." Her sadness returned. "She knew so much, had so many stories and anecdotes. Though she always said there was more to history than what was here. We once had hundreds of libraries, filled with codices and scrolls that detailed our rise, manuscripts that recounted the earliest days of our people! This room, these . . . trinkets, these are not but one one-thousandth of what was available!" She stopped to wipe her eyes.

Friedrich didn't know they could cry. He carefully walked over to her. He hesitated before lightly tapping her on the shoulder. "I, I think I've learned enough," he told her. "If you don't want to go on, I understand."

"There is nothing worth talking about further," she told him. "All that is left is the arrival of the devils. Damn them," she spat. "They appeared without warning. They did not give quarter and did not ask for tribute, always fleeing without a trace. They seemed to coalesce out of the aether, slaughtering anything they came across. It did not matter if it was armed legionaries or a hen and her nestlings tending to a garden. They killed without impunity, destroying and razing entire cities!" Her mood had shifted to white-hot hatred. He stepped back from her. "We fought them for many millennia, fleeing behind the walls of our greatest cities and fortresses, waiting out a siege. There, we had victories. We started to rebuild, fight back. But then, they returned in greater numbers. If that was not enough, it seemed that nature had turned against us. Rivers would flood without warning, mountains would collapse, the ground shook with such force, it felt that the planet itself would be rent in twain."

"They never gave terms? They never sought a truce?"

"Truce? Ha! Can you make a truce with a wild animal? Can you negotiate with a natural disaster? There were not any calls for diplomacy, nor demands of surrender. They do not even have leadership. All we knew of the devils were hosts of teeth, claws, and blades. When they came to Nidus, they laid siege for forty years, and for forty years, we held out." She wiped her eyes again, her face still twisted in anger. "Then, in the forty-first year, the outer defenses were overrun, then the planet shook, and the ground gave up. The city sank deep into the planet, swallowed like a morsel of food." She took a long and deep breath then another and another. "And that is how we got here, trapped underground."

Friedrich watched her after she finished speaking. This was perhaps the most emotional he'd ever seen Vytilia. Her history meant everything to her, much more than the Realm's history meant to him. He did feel a slight twinge of regret for calling her a monster and a witch earlier. It put everything in perspective, why she had been so desperate for a scholar or a learned person to aid them, and yet all they got was him. He didn't doubt the truthfulness of any of this; the sincerity in Vytilia's voice was proof enough. He felt resolved to help them. He still had doubts, questions of how their lore intersected with mankind's, but those doubts, those questions would have to come later. This was neither the time nor the place. "I'm sorry." He stepped closer to her. "Thank you for teaching me this. It was enlightening. I found it much more compelling than mankind's lore."

She took another deep breath and made one final dab to her eyes. "That was my desired result: I brought you down here so you could understand us. We need you to trust us. You might not like us, but we need you. I believe, I know, our future depends on your people. I do not know how; I just know we will need the help of men to survive." There was passion in her voice. "Let us return to my family's residence. You can get some rest before we are summoned to the Concilium."

She went for the exit, blinking to keep tears out of her eyes. Friedrich had to admit the tour worked. It still felt wrong, there was still a nag of doubt, but he did feel that aiding the Strixans would bring about good for them and man. When they started up the steps to the Arx, he looked back over at Nidus. Not too long ago, so many towns on the surface looked like that. So many of his own only knew despair. They were as innocent as any family on the surface. Why should he condemn them because of a few Wenden tales?

As they passed the main hallway, Friedrich took a better look at the statue. He noticed it was just of Luna. After seeing the workmanship on the statue in the Sanctum Sanctorum, he could see that this was newer and of a lesser quality. It must have been built by an inexperienced mason after Nidus had been destroyed. Now that he had seen the original, so to speak, he noticed how curious it was that only the female figure with the owl and moon was there. Had they abandoned their god, or had he abandoned them? Or, had he found new followers?

When they returned to the Quintia residence, they entered the living room, and Vytilia laid down on one of the couches, staring at the portrait. She was focused on it, still wiping and blinking her eyes to combat tears, ignorant of Friedrich. He turned to walk back towards the room where he was staying. He paused, turning back around to face Vytilia. He should say something, cheer her up, show that his mind was changing. "Thank you, again, for showing me everything."

"I hope you learned something." She spoke to him but continued to focus on the portrait.

"Hey Vytilia." She turned her head, eyes still focused on the portrait. He bit his lip and took a deep breath. She seemed down. She might need some cheering up. He would need her happy, or at least pleasant, if he was ever to get back to the surface. And, he wanted to show he did not see her as a fell wight anymore. He remembered an old trick he learned from Herr Bergmann, something that always worked on their landlady. "I like your dress. You wear it well."

She coughed, nearly choking on her words. Color came to her face before she scowled at Friedrich, sending the color away. "You only say that because you have been staring at me since you woke up!" Friedrich chuckled to himself and retired to his room.

7

Friedrich didn't sleep well. He tossed and turned, squeezing his eyes shut and relaxing his body, but his mind was ablaze with thought, comprehending and processing everything that had happened. The statue in the Sanctum Sanctorum kept coming back to him. He couldn't believe it. He couldn't accept it. That statue was God! The same god whose statues were found in every Hof in Erebus. There were minor differences, but that was the same God, down to the eagle and sun. How was it possible?

When Frau Beck taught him Saga stories, it is said that the Half-gods fought the Lightless during the Age of Dusk, while regular men fled to caves and forests to hide. When God returned and banished the Lightless, the remaining Half-gods taught man the crafts of life, like tilling and brewing, before being raised to Walhalla. But if the Strixan Sol was man's god, then that meant Strixans and the Half-gods were one in the same! Similarities kept coming; Strixans had strength and endurance greater than man, they built great towns, and they had great and advanced knowledge. But why were the Strixans underground? And how was mankind spared? Vytilia said her kind had never heard of man before, so why would the Half-gods fight to defend a race they never knew?

Another fear began to fester; if any of this spread to the surface, even just a hint, it could lead to disaster. As little regard as Friedrich had for the Kommandant and the church, without them, everything would fall apart. If people found out God was actually just the second to the goddess of a race of vampires, there would be riots, wars, and a complete breakdown of law and frith. The Church had already been tearing itself apart with the Urworkish. Something like this could ruin them forever. In the worst case, without the Church or the Kommandant to band Sonnendom[20] together, the Tujue could fill the void and take over.

---

20. A Erebusen term to refer to all who worship the sun. Used in the same sense as "Christendom."

Or, would the vampires want the surface back? Vytilia was extraordinarily proud of her history, as she called it, and it was a sentiment he assumed was shared by her fellow vampires. Her father particularly seemed interested in the disorder of the Realm. Was he looking for a weakness? He had to be. If they defeated the fiends with help from mankind, would they just turn on man? If they conquered the world before, what was to stop them from doing it again? They had the advantage of seeing in the dark and of witchcraft. No one in Erebus was prepared for another war, especially not a war against vampires.

Friedrich gave up trying to sleep and laid quietly on his back, staring up at the ceiling. If he helped the vampires, which in for a Pfennig in for a Thaler at this point, they would certainly upset everything on the surface, threatening his own kind. Was he selling out the rest of mankind? If this Concilium decided they wanted his help, then eventually they'd want to send ambassadors and meet with leaders on the surface. They'd establish trade and embassies, and then ideas and stories would spread. That's how he learned about vampires in the first place, from Wenden fleeing from the east. That's how the Great Work spread, through books and talking. Even ideas such as simple change to the Church had led to bloodshed and oppression. What would the knowledge he'd learned bring?

He sat up on the bed and rubbed his eyes, groaning. His head hurt. He'd never had to consider so many important things at once. This was the job of high-born men in frilly collars and stockings, not a caverneer. He got up and walked towards the living room. He needed something to eat and to use the outhouse. How long had he been down here now? It must have been a week at least or more. Either way, he missed Midsummer. Oh well, he still had Thanksgiving and Yuletide to look forward to. Both were much more fun than a bonfire. If there would be a mannish world to celebrate them later. He gulped and tried to bury the fear. He wondered if Strixans had some way of sensing fear.

He found Vytilia still in the living room, now looking over a scroll with a gemstone chalice in her hand, leaning on the couch. She didn't react to him when he came in, focusing on the scroll while he sat down. She was still in the same outfit from when they'd gone to the Sanctum Sanctorum, though she'd removed the earrings and let down her hair. His face burned as he noticed she still looked stunning. Had he been hasty in making that comment?

She had seemed downtrodden, and that had always worked for Herr Bergmann when their landlady needed some cheering up.

He thought of calling for a servant (that would be a new experience), but they only spoke the Strixan tongue. And since Praetor Quintia wasn't home, the only one he could really talk to was Vytilia. As she rustled through the scroll, occasionally taking sips from her chalice, he cleared his throat. Her eyes flashed upward before returning to her reading. He cleared his throat again, louder with more phlegm. She sighed, setting the scroll down and glaring at him. "What?" she demanded.

He hadn't considered what he wanted to say. "Uh, er. I don't suppose you have an outhouse here, do you?"

She looked confused. "A what?"

"A chamber pot?" She stared at him blankly. "A nightsoil closet?" More blank stares. "A shitter?" No response. "Never mind, I can hold it. What was that you were reading?"

"It would not be of interest to you." She started rolling the scroll. "You should go back and rest. The Concilium is still in recess. We do not need you at the moment."

"It would interest me," he insisted. "Besides, I can't sleep anyway. I've got a lot on my mind."

"You look fatigued," she noted. "If you so desire, Sextus knows a bit of cerebrumopus. He can put you to sleep."

"No, no, I'm well. I think I've slept enough." He betrayed himself by yawning and involuntarily rubbing his eye. "I don't suppose you have anything to drink around here, do you? Anything stronger than water?"

"Only Sanguinvinum." She shook her chalice before taking a sip.

"Mmmmm." He looked down at his wrist and saw the thin blue veins running up and down. He turned his wrist over and cleared his throat again. "How much longer do you think before the Concilium wants to meet us?"

"I have not the faintest idea. The Concilium is never in recess for long, but this one may take more time. My father is trying to rally support, and others are entrenching themselves. This matter of soliciting help from the surface is especially important."

He leaned forward, rubbing his eyes as concerns still trudged through his thoughts. Should he say something to her about Sol? She had already made comments of how their history seemed to be missing parts. Would this help? Could it help her look past his compliment? How would she react to the news? Offense? Joy?

"Are you sure you do not wish to sleep further? You look as if you have not rested."

"I . . . I can't sleep. Got too much on my mind."

She set the scroll down, focusing on him. "Do you wish to speak about it? Any concerns or uneasiness you have should be addressed for the sake of diplomacy."

This wasn't a matter of "diplomacy" as much as a foundation-shaking discovery. "I'm . . ." How should he word this? "I am concerned of how the surface will react to you."

"I see . . ." She took a long sip from her chalice. "Do most men on the surface hold this view and fear of 'vampires' as you do?"

"The men of the east do. The tales are starting to trickle westward. But everyone fears witchcraft, and most folktales have some kind of bloodsucking monster or seductress."

She scowled at the last word. "Do you still see us like that? Even after I showed you our most sacred room?"

"No, but, I know how men think. New ideas are a double-edged sword; they'll either make life great or make it worse."

"We won you over, and you are quite superstitious. I think we can replicate this success on the surface."

"But I didn't really have a choice. If I didn't accept and agree to help you, I'd never go home."

"We would have allowed you to return to the surface unscathed, but you would have been without our help, left on your own without a guide, money, or rations."

"That's not much of a choice."

She rolled her eyes. "Well, you are the resident expert. What course of action would you recommend for engaging with the surface?"

He didn't know. This was what was keeping him awake. Unless . . . there was a new possibility. "What if you didn't establish ties with the surface?"

"What?"

"Instead of sending ambassadors or whatever the plan was, just stay down here and maybe get a few trusted traders to deliver you supplies. Don't draw attention to yourselves."

She was flabbergasted. "Friedrich, we cannot afford to get supplies piecemeal. We need mass quantities of weapons or mercenaries and animals! Our people are teetering on the edge of extinction! Why should we continue to fight and die down here while you live comfortable lives up there?"

"If word got out of your kind, no one would have a comfortable life! You'll upset everything!"

She shook her head, taking another sip from her chalice. "You must be exaggerating, letting your old superstition come back! Surely our arrival would not cause that much distress!" She took another sip. "And do you not think we similarly have such concerns? The Concilium must keep a firm but just hand to ensure the plebeians do not fall to disorder and rioting. We are looking at every possibility in establishing relations. Whatever problems occur, will occur, but the benefits far outweigh the cost. The needs of the many outweigh the needs of the few."

"And what can you offer the surface? We risk upturning the world as men know it by helping you. What do we get out of it?"

"You recall that tunnel filled with jewels? There are deposits richer and larger scattered across our empire. Jewels, gold, silver, other precious minerals, all will be given in exchange for the material we need to survive. And, not to mention, our one hundred or so millennia of knowledge and learning to share. You did not even know about the two outlying planets! Think of what else we can share to uplift your people."

That sounded like the Half-gods alright, trying to teach dumb, earthly men. But when the Half-gods return, so do the Lightless. "What of the fiends? If you come to the surface, won't they follow?"

"Not if the weapons or strategy your people can offer are effective. You said the red biped you encountered was the first one you ever heard of?" He nodded. "Then that was most likely a wild, feral one, not a prelude to invasion. If our legions can be armed or aided by auxiliaries from the surface, then we can go on the offensive and wipe the devils from existence."

"You've really thought through everything, haven't you?"

She smiled with pride. "It is my duty. The state asks only our best, and I give my best. I am as concerned for my people as you are for yours. I, and the Concilium, are analyzing every outcome, every possibility, so we can reach a consensus that benefits both parties."

She probably didn't account for men worshipping Sol, did she? Friedrich laid down on the couch, facing the portrait. How does one break news like that? Would ne'er-do-well vampires use that news as a means to gain power, enthralling mankind? She was proud of their warrior heritage, even boasting how they eliminated the Baalites. What was to stop history from repeating itself? And if Strixans had lived on the surface before, what was stopping them from wanting to take back their old lands? When the fiends are defeated, those armies aren't going to up and retire. The Strixans may not be monsters, but they were a group. And groups go to war with one another, even if they go to the same church or are of the same race. He needed to shift focus, talk of something else. If he kept worrying about this, his brain would start leaking out of his ears. "Who is this portrait of?" he asked.

"My mother, Carmilla Luninna Octavian Quintia. It is rude to stare."

He pulled his eyes away. "It's very well done. You look like her."

"Indeed, I do. Many have remarked that I am an exact replica of her, at least physically. Father is quick to point out any attitude differences we have." She stared, longingly at the portrait as she finished her drink. "That was painted by the last surviving artist from the cataclysm. He molded clay around her face to create a bust and then painted that to capture every angle then replicated that onto tile. It was a rather unique way of painting, meant to be more realistic and honest. Father had it commissioned as a marriage present. Drained himself of many months' salary. My paternal grandfather was livid."

"Well, it was gold well spent. Even I can recognize the mastery of the work."

"Are your people artistic, or are you solely devoted to warfare?"

"We call them craftsmen. And we have them. Everyone has craftsmen. I've seen some fine woodcuts in my days, but everyone says the best craftsmen come from Viteliú or Gallia. We're good at castings, mostly of God or Holies or a marshal on horseback. Every big town has at least one bronze casting or one made of stone."

"It is curious a martial culture would accept, let alone allow, arts to flourish. We had to sacrifice our arts and culture when brought underground. They are frivolous and a drain on resources." She called for a servant. "Were you a soldier?"

"No, no, I'm a caverneer and a caverneer only. Fighting wars is best left to folks mad enough to do it. Well, preferably, there'd be no fighting at all." A servant entered, refilling her chalice and giving him grape-flavored water. Grape-flavored was a loose use of the word.

"Why would you prefer to not have wars? An odd thing for someone of your culture to say, is it not?"

He took a long draw from his drink. "You're right there. I'm the world's worst Teudish. I hate war. I can't grow a beard. Hell, I'm even a lightweight when it comes to drinking. Deep down, I have this recurring nightmare where I'm actually a Gaul."

She glanced at him before pulling her eyes elsewhere. For Strixans, clean shaven was the epitome of masculine beauty. "I cannot understand this disdain for warfare. War is an honorable means to slay the enemies of your people and demonstrate devotion to the state. There are times I wish I was a tiercel, able to gird armor and a gladius, so I may work a righteous vengeance and destruction on the devils. Service in the legions, now and in the past, was considered the greatest service a tiercel could do. Our most lauded heroes are victorious commanders and brave legionaries."

"Have you ever actually been in a battle?"

"I have not, but I have spent a great deal of time reading on battles and the commentaries of famous legates."

"Then you don't know what war is actually like. It's none of those things you said. There is none of this 'honor,' no 'lauding,' no bravery. It is slaughter, plain and simple. It is a blight the world should get rid of."

"Ah, so you are a pacifist."

"A what?"

"Pacifist. We used it as a derogatory term for a school of philosophy or a mystery cult. It depends on who was asked. Either way, they were deemed subversive. Being opposed to war was a threat to state security. We live or die by the strength of the legions."

He stared at the bottom of his cup. Remarks like that only added to his fears.

"It seems incongruent with statecraft that your society allows such thoughts to muster. How is that not deemed a threat?"

"We are allowed to think what we want. After the war, it is likely many agree with me."

She shook her head, groaning in disapproval. "Well, as subversive as that thinking is, I do hope you can provide the Concilium with enough detail of how wars are fought. The sooner they learn that, the sooner they can reach a decision, and the sooner we can start finding a way back to the surface."

His chest tightened. "I can tell you the bare-bones. I'm no marshal. All my knowledge is second hand."

"That should more than be enough. If we require details, we can always solicit a mercenary when we are on the surface. For the survival of our state and people, we shall not spare any expense." Sextus entered the room, informing her that a courier arrived from the Concilium; they had reconvened. Annia entered after, handing Vytilia her palla. She swung off the couch and stood up. "What a timely arrival; the Concilium has summoned us." She made a face. "A shame we do not have any finer clothes for you to wear. Nevertheless, come along."

He followed Vytilia out of the residence and down the hall, turning left at the statue of Luna towards an incredibly detailed and massive set of doors guarded by two Praetorians. Friedrich barely had time to admire the metalworking and detail before Vytilia was snapping at him to follow. She glided down the stairs to the center pit of an amphitheater, while he nearly tripped on the first steps, admiring the masonry of the room.

As he gained his footing, he largely ignored (somewhat purposefully) the several robed vampires sitting in the front rows, instead noting the materials used to construct this hall. One might think at first that the room was a single piece of marble, quarried to be a room. But he knew differently. This rock, the comforting, familiar rock, was a wide selection of different pieces. The walls were marble, now beige due to age, but the floor was tile, and each row of benches was made of different kinds of stone, as if each row was carved and added at a different time. The front rows were eroded with softer corners and no edges, while the top row still had a point. He focused on what he knew, recognizing the different granites and limestones he had seen before, taking deep breaths as he approached the stage to face the vampires.

Directly ahead of Friedrich and Vytilia were three vampires sitting closely on a bench. The one to their left, Friedrich noticed, looked particularly angry. He was bald with a scowl or glare permanently carved into his face. He stared at Friedrich suspiciously, repeatedly opening his mouth to bare his bottom fangs. To their far left was Vytilia's father. He largely ignored the two of them, instead staring down the bald vampire as if he was waiting for an excuse to start arguing or fighting.

After their initial shock of seeing Friedrich (Vytilia later explained most were whispering about how pink he was), they quieted down, and the vampire directly in front of them stood. He spoke first to the assembly at large then focused and spoke directly to Vytilia, who translated for Friedrich. "Their first question is what is the current political situation of your empire? Are you at war or are you at peace?"

Friedrich took another deep breath, briefly closing his eyes to gather his thoughts. He slid his foot on the ground, feeling the sturdy, familiar stone. "Currently, the Realm is at peace, though there are always rumors of war on the horizon. We already had a war." His chest tightened. "We're still healing."

She translated this to the Concilium, who briefly whispered among themselves, quieting when the vampire to right of the first one stood up. As he spoke, he mimed using a sword or donning armor, more for Friedrich's sake than Vytilia's. "When your empire fights a war, how do they do so? What weapons do soldiers use and what armor do they wear?"

"Most lords hire landsknechts or call up troops through the Kreise or Reichstag." He paused, allowing her to translate after explaining the Kreise. He had to physically restrain his hand from scratching his face, his chest tightening to a painful degree. He took a moment to pause, taking deep breaths. "Footmen and horsemen, all wear very little armor, just a breastplate and helmet and sometimes greaves." He stopped to shake his head as if clearing out a bad memory. "Most use muskets. The rest use pikes to deter horsemen. Pikes are-are-are long spears, twice my height."

She nodded approvingly, turning to the Concilium to translate, listened for their response, and turned back to Friedrich. " Explain more about a 'musket,'" she asked.

Friedrich could easily see a musket in his mind, and he could hear it: the quick snap as the flint struck the powder, the thunderous "bang" as the charge ignited, the sickening, indescribable sound as the ball struck a body. He looked down, avoiding looking at anyone else. " A musket is a metal tube, placed in a block of wood. It is filled with gunpowder and a lead ball. The powder is ignited, sending the ball screaming towards the target." He scratched with both hands, his breath shaking as he struggled to maintain his composure. The sound of musketry filled his ears.

Vytilia translated, glancing wearily at Friedrich. What was wrong with him? He was nearly scratching off his own skin, his heart was racing, and it sounded as if breathing was overtaxing. The Praetors, largely indifferent to Friedrich's plight, were greatly interested in muskets and pikes. She could overhear them starting to discuss the merits of such weapons against the devils, comparing them to the current, and ancient, tactics used by the legions. The Princeps stood up again, silencing the rest. He asked a brief question before sitting back down. She turned to ask Friedrich, resting a hand on his shoulder. "What is gunpowder?"

He took a deep breath, grabbing onto his belt to keep his hands occupied. "Gunpowder is a mixture of charcoal, potash-salt,[21] and brimstone. When mixed properly and lit on fire, it explodes." He mimed an explosion with his hand. "It can shoot a bullet or open up mineshafts and clear away rubble. It is a tool as much as a weapon!"

He had to explain what the materials were before Vytilia could translate. But when she did, there was a wave of discussion. Some of the discussion nearly turned into arguments with voices starting to be raised. Vytilia saw camps already beginning to form, some saying such weapons were a novelty, while others argued keeping devils at range would lower casualties and the cost of manufacturing swords and shields. A few believed the tremors from such explosions would collapse tunnels and kill more of their kind than the devils. Her father was noticeably quiet during all of this.

The Princeps asked one final question; how easy would it be to procure these weapons and powder? Friedrich took more deep breaths, his knees knocking, and answered that while they were difficult to make, they could be bought in large amounts with enough gold or silver, and that shot and powder were common and cheap enough to be anywhere. Satisfied, the Princeps dismissed the two of them, taking their place on the stage as they exited.

As the doors closed behind them, Vytilia held Friedrich by the shoulder while they walked. "What happened back there? You said you were a pacifist, but did talking about war really make you that upset?" Not to mention the poor display of his race he put on for the Concilium.

"Talking about muskets . . ." He sniffed, rubbing his eyes, then shook his head again. "Brought back some . . . bad memories." He sighed. "I think I'm tired enough to go to sleep." When they entered the residence, she watched as he stumbled back to his room.

"When do you think you will awake? I will have the servants prepare something."

"God willing, never," he muttered.

• • •

21. Saltpeter or Potassium Nitrate

As Friedrich audibly tossed and turned in his room, Vytilia sat alone in hers, lying on her bed. Her palla lay in a folded pile near her wardrobe, eagerly awaiting the next chance to be worn. She laid, staring at the ceiling, her mind a conflux of thoughts. She was doubtful that the Strixans or any civilization possessed a word for what she was feeling. It was so many emotions at once, so many thoughts rushing through, each one a shade from another. She was dissecting what had happened to Friedrich within the Curia, pondering the possible responses from the Concilium, drafting plans of how to reach and interact with the surface, and wondering on his comment after their tour of the Sanctum Sanctorum.

What did he mean by that? Was there any sincerity behind it, or was it a slip of the tongue? Was it a tradition or custom of men to say such a thing? What was his angle, his reasoning behind saying such a thing? This was not to say she had not been flattered. In truth, while she would never admit it, she was very accepting and appreciative of such a compliment. Whatever his reasoning or sincerity, it was a pleasant surprise to hear it from someone else. Annia and the other servants were required to be complimentary. Father rarely spoke to her. And the tiercels in the Arx cared more for what was under the clothes. Of everything Friedrich could have noticed or mentioned, it was her dress and how it was well worn and pleasing to the eye. For a semi-civilized barbarian, he did have an eye for aesthetics.

She sat up. It had been many hours since Friedrich had gone to sleep, and his heartrate showed he was starting to awake. "Sextus!"

The majordomo appeared outside her door. "How may I be of service, Domina?"

"Our guest is waking. Prepare a plate of food for him."

"Right away."

For Friedrich, it was a dreamless night; the moment an image formed in his mind, he quickly woke up in a cold sweat. Each time, it was always the same memory, and each time, he opened his eyes before it could be replayed. He'd been doing well and hadn't thought about this in years. When he woke up for good, he saw Vytilia sitting on a bench near the door, holding a serving tray. He blinked several times, rubbing his eyes to make sure what he was seeing was real then felt his neck for bitemarks. She scowled.

"How long have you been there?"

"I heard your heartrate elevating and assumed you were waking up. I had Sextus prepare a meal for you." She passed him a tray with tender, sauce-covered meat, bread, and a pitcher of water.

He sat upright while accepting the tray. "You heard my heartbeat?" he asked as he started eating.

"We are capable of listening to heartbeats from several miles away but can also tune it to only focus on what is close by. It helps us hunt or keep track of each other." She rubbed her knuckles. "We have a brief respite as the Concilium still debates. I was hoping I could ask a few questions?"

He dipped the bread, which had hints of a mushroom taste, into the sauce. "Ask away. You have a trapped listener."

She harumphed. "You are not our prisoner; I wish to remind you of that fact. That aside, there are two serious questions I wanted to ask. The first is about the comment you made the previous day on my dress."

Friedrich tugged at his collar and swallowed, and sweat beads began to form on his face. "W-what about it?"

She looked him dead in the eyes. "Were you sincere?"

Friedrich was taken aback. She wasn't angry, and her tone was one of genuine curiosity. He himself didn't know if he had been sincere when he said it. It had been a spur-of-the-moment thing. Whenever Bergmann had complimented their landlady, Friedrich never asked if he was being sincere or not. "I . . ." He had to be careful. "I was sincere. I meant what I said. You have an eye for style and wear it well." He sat upright, puffing out his chest.

"Why?"

"Why? Huh, well, it's a well-cut dress, and—"

"Not that why. Why did you see the need to say such a thing?"

He scratched the back of his neck. "After you told me the history of your people, your mood had shifted. You were very downtrodden, understandably I should add, and so I thought something like that would cheer you up, change your mood. Nobody likes being sad, and nobody likes seeing anyone sad."

"Is this normal man tiercel behavior on the surface?"

"We don't call each other 'tiercels.' You can just call us men. Or 'weaponed' but that's dirty. *Ahem* And, well, I suppose so. I can't speak for everyone."

She made a soft *hmm* sound. "You'd be wise not to hand out compliments like that so readily to someone above your station Friedrich. It is bound to get you in trouble one of these days. I will accept, it but mind your tongue in the future. Though, I did enjoy it." She whispered that last part.

"What was your second question?"

"I am curious about your behavior during the presentation before the Concilium. Your heartrate elevated, you were clawing at your face, and your breathing was labored. Was that some sort of reaction? A defensive mechanism?"

He set the tray aside. "None of those. It's what was being talked about. It dredged up stuff I didn't want to think about."

How curious, Vytilia thought. Had he been a soldier at one point, fighting on the defeated side? But if he fought with a defeated army, it should not be something hidden away. In the old days when the legions suffered defeats, each loss made them stronger and taught them how to fight harder. That would explain why he knew about weaponry, but would he not mention that? "What are the memories?"

His chest tightened. "Nothing worth mentioning. It's over now. Your leaders got the knowledge they wanted, and I got some sleep."

Despite her curiosity, she would not pry further, not if it risked jeopardizing his cooperation. Perhaps he similarly needed cheering up, to be pulled out of this mood and have his mind cleared. "Friedrich, would you want to walk the grounds of the Arx? Stretch your legs, get out of this room?"

He nodded. "That sounds nice." He took one last bite of bread and meat then followed her to the living room. As they exited the residence, her father arrived at the end of the hall, headed towards them. He passed Vytilia and went straight for Friedrich.

"Friedrich! Wonderful news! The Concilium has nearly reached a quorum on commissioning you to head to the surface. However, before a final decision is made, we wish to see this 'gunpowder' in action. Are you able to give a demonstration?"

"Uh, I-I can." A few years back, other caverneers had been discussing the idea of using gunpowder to clear tunnels or open up deposits. He and Bergmann had tried making gunpowder charges, but the Hertzabrunno Stadtrat shut them down on issues of safety. "I can't make a musket, but . . . well I suppose I can make a grenade." He gritted his teeth.

"Why can you not produce a musket?"

"It's beyond my skill level. If you make a musket wrong, it blows up in your face. Grenades are easier Of course, don't forget, it has other, non-war purposes."

Praetor Quintia waved that aside. "We have lapisoperarii[22] for that. Come with me to the cohort barracks. Vytilia, you come along as well." The Praetor hurried out of the Arx, Vytilia and Friedrich jogging behind. They passed the Sanctum Sanctorum entrance, walking all the way to the rear of the campus where a blacksmith, stable, and guard barracks sat. The rest of the Concilium and a sizeable detachment of the Praetorian Cohort stood near the wall of a training field. When they arrived, Praetor Quintia spoke with the head Praetor then took his place amongst his colleagues. The head Praetor then spoke to Friedrich, showing him a table at the edge of the training field.

"The Concilium has gathered the finest charcoal, potash-salt, and brimstone, as per your ingredients. Or, what we think those are, there are a few of them which may match your description," Vytilia translated. "They ask what other materials you require to make a 'grenade.'"

Friedrich scratched his cheek. "I'll need some clay, a mortar and pestle, and a wick. And they'll want to give everyone below a warning. These are loud." Vytilia explained his request. The head Praetor nodded, summoning a dozen messengers in white, purple-hemmed tunics, sending them into every quarter of the city. The Praetorian Cohort brought out a stool and the other materials Friedrich requested. He sat down and rifled through the ingredients they provided, finding the three correct ones, and poured the charcoal into the mortar. "Vytilia, could you mold the clay into a ball, leaving an opening at the top? And can you harden it when you're done?"

"Of course." Her curiosity shifted from his disdain for warfare to seeing gunpowder in action. As she shaped the clay into a sphere, heating it with her hands, Friedrich ground the charcoal into a fine powder, carefully mixing in one of the white powders provided. He was muttering to himself about percentages and ratios, sweat pooling on his forehead and a slight shake in his hand. With the charcoal and potash-salt mixed, he slowly, carefully added in

22. Literally "Stone Worker," a Strixan thaumaturgist who specializes in molding and controlling rock.

the brimstone, mixing it into a grey powder. "Sphere ready." She placed the grenade shell between them.

"Oh . . . god . . . oh . . . god." He swallowed, wiping his head. "Please, put the wick in, making sure it hangs out, and hold it steady. Is it cool to the touch?" She nodded. "Forefathers watch over me." He poured the powder into the shell, holding his breath as each fine sprinkle fell from the mortar. "I am going to take it and place it in the field. You'll want to tell them to back up."

She explained to the Concilium, asking them to back away. The Magister Militum spoke up as the others backed to a safe distance. "Do not place it in the field," she translated. "Put it on one of those training models."

He swore but agreed and slowly, deliberately walked, one foot at a time, towards a training model, what he would call a dummy. The dummies were simple, boiled leather tied over a wooden skeleton. He tucked the grenade into the shoulder of the dummy and backpedaled towards the Concilium, ducking behind the stone wall marking the border of the training ground. "Vytilia . . . will you do the honors? Aim for the wick." He covered his ears, sitting behind the wall. A few of the Concilium members mimicked covering their ears.

She snapped her fingers, focusing the flame into a small ball, no bigger than a pearl, and sent it over the wall, across the field, right into the end of the wick. She stepped back, watching as the wick caught fire, burning down until it passed the rim. Then, with a great FWOOM, the grenade exploded; charred pieces of clay shot across the Arx campus. A few Praetors coughed. Others rubbed their eyes, shooing away the smoke. Friedrich looked over the wall, watching as the head Praetor and a guard walked over to what remained of the training dummy, a single charred post. Ruined bits of leather and blackened wood were scattered across the field.

Praetor Quintia helped Friedrich to his feet. "Friedrich Bauer, welcome to the services of the Empire."

8

Friedrich and Vytilia stood at the wall, watching as the Concilium gathered around the remains of the training dummy. He picked up a piece of leather, studded with burnt bits of clay, and ran it through his hands. Vytilia listened in to the Concilium's discussion. The Princeps called for a vote; every member raised their hand. The Princeps smiled, taking her father aside and giving him further instructions.

"They have made the vote. We will be headed to the surface."

He tossed the leather aside, wiping his hand on the seat of his tunic. "Only to return as a trader of death."

"Do not think of it as that. Think instead as a deliverer, a savior to our people. With gunpowder, we will be able to slay the devils at a distance. This will lead to a substantial decrease in casualties. You are a merchant of life. The only death will be to devils, who rightly deserve it." She saw that did little to comfort him. She stepped in front of him, sitting on the wall as they looked each other in the eye. "Regardless of what you perceive, I do want you to know I at least am incredibly grateful."

She smiled at Friedrich, and he smiled back. Despite her monstrous traits and condescending attitude, deep down, Vytilia was a pretty and gentle girl. She had a kind, warm smile and eyes that made him feel comforted. She reminded him of Clotilde, a girl he fancied back in Hertzabrunno. She was confident, smart, capable, and beautiful. Though he still had reservations, being around her did make losing Herr Bergmann and falling underground a bit more comfortable.

Vytilia, similarly, was starting to enjoy Friedrich's company. He was a complex creature, multifaceted in tastes and ideas, but was a welcome breath of fresh air from the admittedly stale thinking of Strixans. He was starting to treat her with respect and see the benefits of helping Strixans. And on the personal side, she was grateful for his listening. Rarely did she have a chance to talk to someone other than Annia. Friedrich was attentive and a good listener, traits she admired. She was also enraptured with him telling her about the surface and adored every modicum of information he told her. Inwardly, she was bursting with joy that the Concilium had approved of a surface mission, and while she did not want to be hubristic, she felt confident they had chosen her to escort him.

Praetor Quintia walked over to the two of them, calling for Vytilia. She stood at attention as he gave her instructions. This was the first time Friedrich had actually watched Vytilia and her father interact directly. The way they spoke to each other was . . . odd. Neither one made eye contact with one another. The brief time their eyes met, her father quickly shut his eyes or looked away. Most of the time, while he spoke, Vytilia would avoid his gaze, staring at her feet, even while she spoke. He felt sorry for her.

When Praetor Quintia finished, Vytilia raised her arms for an embrace, but he turned to Friedrich, walking towards him. "Friedrich, as I am sure you have been made aware, the Concilium has decided to commission you to take Vytilia to the surface. Your commission will be to secure and return with a supply of muskets and gunpowder. She will be given the funds necessary to procure these items, but should you require more, we shall compensate you for any additional costs. And, as an incentive, you will also be given a substantial reward upon your return." He leaned in closer to Friedrich. "Now listen to me closely: sending Vytilia with you was not my first choice, but we do not have any other options. Know this; if you harm her or allow harm to come to her, I *will* find out, and I will kill you myself. Do we have an understanding?" Friedrich silently nodded, his eyes as wide as dinner plates. "Excellent." He gave Friedrich a pat on the shoulder then turned to say farewell to Vytilia. She reached out again for an embrace and was again rebuffed, the Praetor instead heading to the stables.

She watched as he exited, slowly bringing her hands down before shaking her head and sighing. "At least the good news is I was chosen to escort you." She sighed again, watching as her father mounted a calcerta. "Come along, we need to get to the Imperial Armory. Sextus will meet us at the gate with provisions and supplies. Oh, and your pugio as well."

"Do you want to . . ." Her eyes followed her father as he and a troop of Praetorian horsemen (or, askardmen?) rode to the gate. "Never mind. So, we're leaving right away?"

"Indeed, the Concilium has given us a deadline of three months once we reach the surface. My father's career, my family's honor, and your reward are at stake if we do not return."

"So where do we start? Back where I fell?" He followed her to the blacksmith next to the barracks.

"We are going to Colonia Aurum; it is a mining colony in the northeast. Of all our cities, it has the highest elevation, which means it is our best chance of getting a quick route to the surface."

"Why not go back to where I fell from? The hole to the surface already exists. Sounds like we'd save a lot more time going that way instead of carving out a new tunnel."

"That is where my father is going, to reinforce Dracius' vexillation. They are to lay more Via Sculptile tracks and expand on and make the tunnel you fell from more suitable for travel. First, they have to clear out any burrows they find, then they have to dam the waterfall, construct a ladder to the tunnel, then build stairs in the tunnel without collapsing it. Using wonder working to carve a new entrance in a secured, protected area is a more efficient use of our time. When we return, we are to come down the way you fell."

When they opened the door to the armory, after withstanding the heat from the furnace, they were met by a vampire with many scars across his face and arms, his face blackened from ash and soot. Vytilia spoke to him in their language, and he nodded. He came over to Friedrich with a marked strip of leather and began taking measurements. Friedrich stood awkwardly as the blacksmith wrapped the leather all around his body. He then went over to a rack full of armors and selected one, handing it to him. It was the same armor Dracius wore, a chainmail shirt with chainmail pauldrons.

The blacksmith spoke to Vytilia again, then when she finished, he went over to the armors again and selected a scale armor, handing it to her. She spoke again, and he went around the armory, collecting several bits and pieces of armor, tunics, dresses, and other clothes and belts, placing them into a thick leather bag. He handed it to Friedrich, then Vytilia spoke again, thanking him before they left.

"Is all this really necessary?" Friedrich asked, setting the bag (which was heavier than it looked) by the door of the barracks.

"There is always a risk of a devil attack. Any chance we can take to increase our survivability, we have to. I thought you mentioned mankind wears armor?"

"Not while travelling, it's mostly used in wartime. Knights used to wear a lot more in the beforetime; they'd wear a full suit from head to toe. But now, almost none."

"I still cannot believe that. Why do your people not wear armor? Do your soldiers not wish to protect themselves?"

"Well, armor doesn't do much against a musket," he shot back.

"*Well,* the devils do not use muskets, so we should still wear it."

Friedrich just shook his head and snorted.

"Come, we should get changed before we head down to the third wall." She knocked on the door of the barracks, yelling inside. The door flung open as off-duty Praetorians ran out in various states of dress. Vytilia smiled, pulling a thick dress and some strips of leather out of the armor bag, and stepped inside. Friedrich found another tunic for himself, a thick, ¾ths sleeve work tunic, colored dark grey and made of the same thick, woolen material as the first one he had been given. It was itchy but warm. The Praetorians all stared at him, and he stared back. He gulped, knocking on the door. "Vytilia, are you almost done? I'd like to change as well."

"You can change out there."

He looked at the guards still staring at him, and sighed, undoing his belt and slipping off his current tunic and putting on the new one, while the guards whispered and pointed. He, of course, hadn't been given any trousers, but he had a pair of thick socks and some hobnail, mid-shin boots. The boots were a low-quality leather, but they'd help with climbing if they didn't fall apart before then.

Vytilia exited the barracks. Her outfit was made of the same thick, wooly material. Hers was more akin to a tight-skin dress with close-cut sleeves and a skirt that went down to her shins with a slit to allow a greater degree of mobility. Even with its bulky and unladylike appearance, it still complimented her figure quite well, though learning from last time, Friedrich avoided looking for too long. She tilted her head, looking Friedrich up and down, a smile cresting her face before it turned to a glower at the dumbfounded Praetorians. They hurried back into their barracks.

She started pulling her armor on. "We had best get armored before we go down to the third wall. Do you know how to put these on?" She handed him an arm guard, a sleeve of metal overlaying leather, stretching from his wrist to shoulder, the same kind of arm protection worn by Dracius' soldiers. He slipped his hand through as she helped connect it to his chainmail. Unlike the soldiers, he'd been given a second one for his left arm as well. As uncomfortable as he was wearing armor, he had to admit it was well crafted and had an intriguing design. He had a great degree of mobility. Whenever he stretched his arm, the metal would overlay on itself, like those small woodlice bugs he would play with as a child. Not as intriguing and adding to his discomfort, he'd also been given metal greaves. There was no articulation with these, just a solid piece of metal, hammered to curve around his shins. He had to wonder, if he wasn't a slow-healing, squishy man, would the vampires even bother giving him these?

"Is this everything? Just armor?"

"There was one more item." She paused, putting on her arm guards. Hers did not connect up to her bicep, instead only covering her forearms with a spiderweb-like lining of leather crisscrossing the back of her hand. "The Concilium also gave you this as a sign of appreciation." She handed him a sword.

"Oh . . ." He sucked his teeth.

"What?"

"Hmm," his face went red. "Well, on the surface . . . a woman handing a man a sword means . . . something else."

She frowned. "Well, I am not a woman. I am a hen. And I am not giving it to you; the Concilium is."

He accepted the sword, unsheathing it to inspect the blade. It was a short sword, identical to the one worn by Dracius and his soldiers, though much more ornate, inlaid with gold and white gold. The pommel was made of onyx, inscribed with an image of a Strixan god. It resembled an art piece more than a weapon. Hopefully, he could pass it off as a long knife rather than a sword on the surface. Nobles looked down on anyone who would tread on their privileges. He ran his hand over the sheathe. Maybe he should worry about not being robbed instead. There was enough gold to buy a house on the sheathe alone.

"You should count yourself fortunate. You have been given equipment normally reserved for the Praetorian Cohort, and only the finest is issued to them. Do not let the ornateness deceive you. It will hack through any devil we encounter." She scoffed as she saw him gird the sword to his new belt. "On the left hip? You must have a high opinion of yourself."

He looked down at the sword sheathed on his left hip then up at her in disbelief. Was she seriously mocking how he tied his weapon? "Is this not how swords are carried?"

"By senior, experienced officers. The rank-and-file gird it on the right hip for easier access when carrying a shield."

"Well, I'm not carrying a shield." Friedrich mocked while hiding his age-shield. She rolled her eyes. "Won't wearing all this just slow us down?"

"Oh, I do beg your pardon Friedrich. I was unaware you came from a race with literal millennia of experience in combatting the devils. I forgot to ask your experience in such matters!"

"You said we're going to be climbing through mine shafts to reach the surface. That's where I know what I'm doing. These vambraces . . ." He bent his elbow, "will just slow us down and get scratched up."

"They are called manica. At least yours are, mine are manicula. That aside, the blue devils like to go for your arms, bite down, and force you to drop your weapon or shield, then they maul you. The manica stops them from biting down with full force. *We* know what we are doing."

"I don't doubt you know what *you're* doing when it comes to war, but *I* am the caverneer, which is what we'll be doing. We're going to need more than armor and swords."

She paused, furrowing her brow in thought. "What equipment do you suggest?"

"We'll need pickaxes, good, strong ropes, some gloves would help, rock hammers, chisels, lanterns, and little flags to help us track where we came from."

"That all sounds excessive."

"Trust me; I know what I am talking about." She narrowed her eyes in doubt but knocked on the barrack door anyway. A Praetorian emerged in full kit, and Vytilia gave him instructions for the armorer, counting the items on her fingers. The Praetorian nodded and left. "They are . . . obedient."

"Being in the Praetorian Cohort is an exceptional privilege only reserved for the most loyal and capable legionaries. They, and their families, receive higher blood rations and have priority for having nestlings."

Is bought loyalty true loyalty? Friedrich wondered.

The Praetorian returned, presenting a bag to Vytilia and explaining its contents before returning to the barracks. "The armorer had everything, aside from those flags you mentioned. He called them a bizarre idea and had never heard of such a thing."

Friedrich went over and observed the equipment, picking up a pickaxe and swinging it before giving the blade a few tugs. He flicked his fingernail on the blade. "This isn't the best iron, but it should work." He grabbed the rope and gave it a similar inspection. "What is this made from?"

"I am unsure."

He frowned. "Is this the best rope he had? Can they get us any better quality?"

"Quality? It is a length of rope, not a vintage of wine! What difference does it make?"

"Some stock is stronger than others. It's the difference between life or death." He gave the rope a firm tug again, sighing. "I guess this will have to do."

"Is that everything we need then?" Friedrich nodded. "Excellent. Let us meet up with the servants and then get our mounts."

He grabbed a length of rope from the equipment bag and tied it diagonally across his torso, sliding a rock hammer into his belt, slinging the equipment bag over his shoulder. Though the armor was new, he felt like a caverneer again, like his old self. "Mounts?"

"Of course, our escort is cavalry, so we will be taking calcerta."

Friedrich winced. "Why do *we* need them or need to ride them? Couldn't we take a cart?"

"That is unwise. Carriages are too slow, too unwieldy, and too vulnerable. Even with the Via Sculptile, they are laughable in speed when compared to a calcerta." *Praetor Quintia did mention a substantial reward,* Friedrich thought. Part of getting that would include dealing with those ghastly asks.

Vytilia's servants were waiting at the gate, along with a Concilium messenger in the purple-lined tunic. The messenger handed Vytilia a satchel. Friedrich judged from the heft and stretched leather that it contained something bulky, gold if he had to guess. The head servant then handed each of them a leather bag and a dark blue cloak and returned his dagger. Vytilia shoved the satchel into her haversack as a female servant embraced her, crying violet-colored tears while patting her on the back. The head servant looked at Friedrich and gave him an awkward smile and thumbs up.

After putting their cloaks on, and finally pulling Vytilia away from the female servant, they exited the Arx, heading down to the third wall. The Praetorians at the gate were reverent, wishing them well. Friedrich caught the words Luna and Sol as they spoke. The outer settlements all possessed a reverent feel, similar to the inside of the Sanctum Sanctorum. In the marketplace and residential areas, all talk ceased. Even the children took notice and stopped playing. The whole of Nidus had quieted down, stopping to watch as they walked by. Some even offered weak smiles and a slight glimmer of hope was in the eyes of some of the women.

"Word travels fast," Vytilia commented. "In these scant few minutes, I have heard more prayers uttered by the populace than at any point in my life." She stood up straight. "The providence of the gods is sure to be with us. Not even miles of rock can stop this much devotion."

They came to the legion camps by the third wall where several lightly armored cavalrymen were waiting next to their calcerta. A cavalryman brought two over, one brown and spackled with tan and yellow spots, the other grey with white and blue bands on its tail. He handed the reins to Friedrich and Vytilia then took the equipment bag and attached it to Friedrich's saddle. Friedrich got the brown one while Vytilia got the grey and white. She gracefully mounted hers, petting it behind the ear holes as she sat sidesaddle. It purred and licked its eyes, the tail slapping the ground. Friedrich grimaced then mounted his own. One of the cavalrymen called up to the watcher at the gatehouse. The gate slowly opened, and three cavalry calcerta began to scamper out. Vytilia and Friedrich followed with three more cavalry calcerta bringing up the rearguard.

Despite his extreme discomfort around the calcerta, Friedrich had to admit there was something amusing about the way they ran. Their feet were broad, mostly composed of digits, and flopped around as they smacked the ground, making a humorous "thwick" sound. Their entire body would wiggle as they moved, almost slithering like a snake. Friedrich would bob up and down as the calcerta ran, and he could feel it breathing between his legs. The ride was smooth enough, but feeling the rough, scaly skin of the lizard made him nauseous, combined with the feeling at any moment he could be bucked off, only for the beast to turn around and start chewing on him. Even when it ran, it would lick its eye, only adding to Friedrich's nausea.

He tried urging the calcerta to speed up and run alongside Vytilia's, but she had a much faster mount. Even if he could catch up, they wouldn't be able to talk, The lizards made a surprising amount of noise, drowning out anything below a scream. A time like this made him realize how much he missed Herr Bergmann. What would he think of him doing this? He'd certainly agree with the "handsome reward," that much Friedrich was certain, but the rest of the situation was difficult to judge. Would he approve of helping the vampires? They were in dire need, but where would he have drawn the line? They weren't man, but they had helped animals before, and those weren't men either. Would he still approve? Friedrich smiled. A better question would be what his landlady, Frau Beck, would think. She was much more holy than either of them. Her heart would probably give out the moment Vytilia showed her fangs.

After riding for several hours, the cavalrymen in the front began to slow down, signaling for the rest of the group to follow suit. They had come to an oasis, a wide, circular shaped cavern where water poured from a depression in the roof. Mushrooms and ferns grew at the edge of the water. The group dismounted and led the calcerta to the water where they began to drink and nibble at the plants.

One of the cavalrymen pulled a fire stone out of his saddlebag and made a fire circle. Vytilia lit the stone with the snap of her fingers. With the fire lit, the cavalrymen took up guard at the entrance and exit of the oasis. Friedrich walked over to the fire and sat down next to it, chewing some of the salted meat rations the servants had provided.

"Not that I'm whining, but why have we stopped?" Friedrich asked.

"We have traveled about twelve miles so far," Vytilia explained. "The calcerta can only make about thirty miles in a day, or they die from exhaustion or start going feral and disobeying. According to our escort, there is a way station another fifteen miles away. We can spend a few hours there to rest and get new calcerta."

"I've been under the impression you and other vam—Strixans don't need to rest." He offered her a piece of salted meat, but she declined.

"Not as often as you do. Last time we were travelling, I overestimated your endurance and nearly killed you. Now that I know your limitations, I have planned accordingly to allow for regular rests for you and the calcerta."

"That's very kind of you." He smiled at her.

"You are not any good to us dead."

"I'm no good to myself dead either." She eyed him coolly but said nothing. "Have you been down these tunnels before on your travels?"

"Not for a few years. Aurum is one of our oldest colonies. After the Arx was swallowed, we sent out expeditions to find other groups of survivors and more resources. Aurum was built on a foundation of ruins we found. It also was sitting on several veins of gold and silver. By the time I was old enough to venture out on my own, Aurum had been well picked over, so I spent most of my time at the newer colonies or in unexplored tunnels."

"If you were one of my kind, you would've made a good caverneer."

"Possibly. But I had higher motives for my expeditions than mere profit." She knelt next to the fire stone and unslung her haversack. She reached in and produced a small clay vial. She snapped off the top and drank the contents. She then adjusted her armor, tugging at it below her neck and around the shoulders.

"Armor not fitting well?" He tugged at his own collar, though not out of sympathy.

"We do not make armor for the female form," she explained, tugging at the chest. "I am wearing a piece of athletic equipment to help make it fit. It is not the most comfortable of garments." Her eye twitched. "If you would be so kind as to not stare."

"I wasn't staring." Which was a half-truth. "Now, if you would be so kind and answer a question of mine?"

"What is it?"

"How do you want me to say your name?"

She looked at him, puzzled. "What do you mean?"

"Is it *Wee*-tee-lee-a or *Vie*-till-lee-ah? You've said it both ways."

"Since you lack the anatomy to properly pronounce Strixic," she opened her mouth, showing her fangs, "you can refer to me as *Vie*-till-lee-ah."

Well, that would make things easier, Friedrich thought. He glanced back at the calcerta, who were still draining the pool. Guess he still had to make small talk. If she was talking, she wasn't biting. "So, when you're out and about in the hinterlands, what are you looking for?"

"Literary works mostly, scrolls and codices that survived the cataclysm. Sometimes ruins where we can establish an outpost or colony. I actually discovered one of the blades on display at the Sanctum Sanctorum."

"Does your father approve of these expeditions? I would think a Praetor's daughter would warrant a close guard. Lords on the surface don't let their children go out and mingle with low-born folk, knowingly at least."

"He does not *disapprove*. He recognizes their importance and the bounty they bring to our empire. And it helps us achieve our goals." She stood up, staring into the fire longingly. "Not that he would notice when I leave anyway. His business with the Concilium occupies most of his time. When I am at the Arx, he is almost never at our residence, always away debating or politicking. It is a necessary sacrifice; our people would not have lasted this long without leaders like him. He has his duty to the state, and I have mine. We both understand the risk."

The calcerta began to click and hiss. One of the cavalrymen left his post to examine them. He called out to the rest of the group and gathered the steeds. Vytilia extinguished the fire while another cavalryman put the sun stone in his bag. They all remounted and began to ride again. Friedrich rode alongside Vytilia, catching glances of her from the corner of his eye. She looked somber and reflective. He decided not to bring up her father in the future.

They rode continuously without seeing any other group or life. No ferns grew in this tunnel, and no water pooled. All around them was rock and stone. Except, far in the distance was a powerful orange light, bright enough to cause Friedrich to squint. The cavalryman at the head signaled for everyone to slow down to a trot. The other cavalrymen readied their lances and bared their fangs. Vytilia snapped her fingers, the small ember of flame appearing on her fingertips. Friedrich drew his new sword.

As the calcerta got closer, the lights spread out; they were bonfires, wood and other debris piled together with corpses. There were both Strixan and fiend bodies burning and what looked like the limbs and tails of calcerta. Friedrich likened it to Midsummer in hell. He stared on ahead, covering his nose while Vytilia turned away, shutting her eyes as they passed the fire.

They could see the way station or what was left of it. It had been built into the rock, an artificial junction in an otherwise straight path. The walls and towers were cracked and crumbling. Stone stakes, coated in blood, had been sharpened out of the ground in front of the walls. The ground was cratered and jagged, resembling the surface of the moon. They paused a few feet out from the gate, coolly staring down the guards as they leveled bows and javelins at them.

The gates quickly opened as a legionary ran out. His tunic had been torn, he had lost his helmet, and his armor was covered in blood. He signaled for the guards to lower their weapons. "Where is your commanding officer?" the lead cavalryman asked.

"I am the commanding officer," the legionary explained. "My name is Glabius, and I am the senior-most legionary left. Quickly, come inside the gates before they return." He led the group inside and showed them where they could hitch their calcerta.

"We are escorting a Praetor's daughter and a VIP to Aurum. We require fresh mounts," the cavalry commander demanded.

"You are not our relief force? We sent out messengers and . . ." Glabius sighed, swallowing hard. "I, uh, I wish we could help. But our best mounts, really our only mounts were . . . killed."

Vytilia and Friedrich dismounted as she brought him up to speed on what Glabius had been explaining. "We didn't see a rider passing us," Friedrich observed.

"And we did not see a body." Vytilia listened as the cavalryman and Glabius continued talking.

"They only attacked a few hours ago," Glabius told the group. "It started out with a few quadruped scouts, which we easily took care of, but then more kept coming. Some of the red bipedal ones and a few of the black ones as well. They, I do not know how to explain it! They were methodic, probing our defenses, picking off archers first. They were almost smarter."

"They were organized?" All of the cavalrymen got tense, quickly grabbing their shields and putting hands on their swords.

"It appeared so or as close to organized as those beasts can get. Our Tesserarius was killed leading a charge to drive them away. That is also how we lost our mounts."

"He sounds reckless."

"He was lustful for glory; this is not the most prestigious posting. He really wanted to make a name for himself. Ever since we set those bonfires, it has kept them at bay, but it is only a matter of time before the fires die down, and they mount another assault. We barely have enough bodies to watch both gates. We even had to conscript the civilians."

Vytilia stepped forward, pushing past the cavalryman. "Legionary, my name is Vytilia Quintia, daughter of Praetor Quintia. We are on assignment directly from the Concilium. It is imperative we get to Aurum. If necessary, our escort will stay behind while my companion and I take your freshest mounts and go on ahead.

"Domina Quintia, I must protest," the cavalryman interjected.

"Decurion, we cannot sit around and wait out a siege. Our mission is vital to the survival of the empire. The man and I will continue on. The two of us have a better chance of survival than an entire ala." She turned to Glabius. "I regret to inform you that we did not pass by your messenger on our way here. It is unlikely reinforcements will be arriving anytime soon."

"Well, you would not have seen him. Please, if you will follow me, I have an idea." Vytilia gestured for Friedrich to follow. Glabius led them over to a wood structure built against the rock. Several legionaries and civilians were laying in piles of straw and vines. Most were bandaged and being attended to by a surgeon. One of the wounded wore scale armor and reinforced robes. A soldier was kneeling by him, holding his arm.

"This is our on-station lapisoperarius. He was sent from Nidus to reinforce our walls and assist repairing the Via Sculptile tracks." Glabius introduced Vytilia. The lapisoperarius rested on his good elbow to sit up.

"It is a pleasure, Domina Quintia. I am Pellio Lusia, Expert Lapisoperarius."

"How were you wounded?" Vytilia asked.

"One of the damn crawlers got me while we were driving them from the walls. I am why the ground out there is so jagged. The medicus says it will heal but will leave scars and give me pain for the next few weeks." He grimaced as he adjusted himself.

"The senior legionary says you might have a way to help us get to Aurum."

"Verily, if you could . . ." He reached his good arm out for help. Friedrich came forward and took it, lifting him up. Pellio looked amazed at Friedrich's hand, commenting on the coloring. "Please tell him I apologize for staring. You must be the outsider we have heard about." Friedrich looked at him puzzled until Vytilia translated.

"He's heard of me?" he asked her.

"You were in Nidus for some time. Rumor and gossip travel faster than supplies or personnel. It is not every day a pink-colored outsider falls from the surface." Vytilia turned back to Pellio. "Now, what can you tell us?"

"Well, between you and I, and uh, the outsider, I was actually sent here with an assignment from the Concilium as well." He walked them over to a bare stretch of wall. "We have recently discovered, from excavations and by accident, that this area is surrounded by devil burrows. We have been closing them wherever we find them, but we also have been creating our own."

"Our own . . . burrows?" Vytilia nearly coughed at the words.

"In a sense. The Concilium wanted to look into constructing emergency routes, different from the branch lines and auxiliary tunnels. If one of the main vias got obstructed, we would need alternate routes to keep the empire connected. We already closed off several of the devil burrows then connected them with existing natural tunnels to create a new road. We constructed one between here, the Arx, and the next way station. It is not wide enough to send a calcerta yet, but a legionary on foot can move around comfortably. You can take the path to the next way station where you will be able to get mounts and get to Aurum faster."

"Incredible." She stopped. "How do we know these tunnels are safe? You yourself said they are created from existing burrows. We also do not know if your messengers got through safely."

"Well, we have taken precautions to make sure any burrows we found were sealed off completely. As for our messengers, well, let us remember calcerta travel faster than a legionary sprinting. I would trust my life in these tunnels, more than trying to outrun the devils on an exhausted calcerta."

Vytilia nodded in understanding then told Friedrich about the new path (leaving out any mention of the burrows), and he approved. "Alright, show us the tunnel. My companion and I will go alone and leave the cavalry here to reinforce you. The two of us can handle ourselves better in the tunnels."

Pellio closed his eyes, touching the wall when the sentries on the walls began to shout. "Devils! Devils incoming! Both sides, both sides!" They began loosing arrows and hurling javelins.

The cavalryman ran over to Vytilia. "Domina, we need to get you and the surface-dweller to safety. Please, stay close with us."

"Never mind that Decurion, Pellio has introduced an alternate route that we can take. We will go alone; you stay here and help defend the way station."

"We have strict orders to . . ."

"I know your orders!" She paused, snapping a fireball at a devil crawling over the ramparts. "You will be covering us as we move. Make sure they do not follow us!" The cavalryman sighed and returned to the rest of his men as they braced for combat. "Pellio, get that entrance open, then seal it behind us! We will make sure the next garrison gets your message about reinforcements!" She spun and let loose another fireball.

"Wait!" Friedrich sheathed his sword. "If we're going into caves, we'll need our gear!" He ran back towards the calcerta and began untying the bag full of caverneering equipment. Vytilia swore under her breath and ran towards him, looking both ways and firing at even the slightest glimpse of a devil. Friedrich hoisted the bag over his shoulders and started heading back. He stopped when one of the legionaries on the wall screamed. Both stared as a quadruped devil grabbed the legionary by the throat, tearing it out before throwing his body to the ground. Another legionary hurled a javelin, spearing the devil and knocking it off the wall, but more followed. Several of the red bipeds also began climbing over, slashing at the nearest targets and jumping down from the wall. One noticed Friedrich. It bellowed and began marching towards him.

Friedrich froze. The fiend lumbered towards him, the eyes staring into his soul. Those eyes, those evil, soulless eyes. His chest tightened. His knees locked. He couldn't move. He couldn't speak. He just stood there as the beast howled, never taking the eyes off him. He must be sleeping. *This must be a nightmare,* his mind insisted. This was a bad memory being replayed, not reality.

Vytilia let loose a flurry of fireballs, distracting the devil as a cavalryman speared it through the chest. "Move!" she yelled. Friedrich was still frozen, his knees shaking. She ran over and grabbed his collar. "Move!" They began running back towards Pellio who was hurling rocks at the incoming devils. A group of devils jumped down from the walls, landing in front of Vytilia and Friedrich. She bared her fangs and readied her fire. Before the devils could take another step, each one was impaled on a spike of rock. Pellio held out his bad hand, the other still firing rocks. Vytilia saw a large hole carved out of the rock wall.

"Hurry!" Pellio called. "Hurry!" Vytilia, still dragging Friedrich, ran back over. "Go in, take the left, and just keep going! Do not stop for any reason! I will stay here and seal the rock up behind you!" Vytilia, holding back violet-colored tears, thanked him, and led Friedrich into the rock. She just kept running, practically carrying Friedrich as they ran into the darkness.

• • •

Pellio quickly closed the opening after they entered. He brought down several rockslides just to be sure. He turned back around to defend the way station, only to be speared through the chest. A large, black-colored devil wielding two scythes made of bone howled in his face as it speared him again. Pellio screamed at the beast, hurling two rocks into the side of the devil's head. The beast fell with Pellio falling on top of it. He struggled to pull the blades out of him, but he was too weak. His own blood poured like a river out of his chest. He slowly lifted his head up, watching as the other legionaries and civilian militia fought back. Legionaries beat devils with their shields before stabbing them. Civilians hurled javelins and stones. The cavalry who had escorted the Praetor's daughter formed a circle, spearing any devil that got close. But the devils kept coming, pouring over the walls like some eldritch wave. The hellish rainbow of blue and red burst through both gates, trampling their dead comrades as they ran at the Strixans. As the legionaries fell, one by one, Pellio found one final comfort. "They are safe. Gods be with them," he told himself before closing his eyes.

• • •

Vytilia just kept running, keeping a tight grip around Friedrich's hand. She did not know what else to do. Tears began to pool in her eyes. Her route became harder and harder to see. She finally stopped, collapsing onto her knees, tears pouring like rain. She buried her face in her hands. It was all she knew to do right now.

"Oh gods!" she cried, falling onto her back. This was warfare. This was what the legionaries faced every day! That was raw carnage, unfettered bloodshed! Those valiant soldiers had just been slaughtered wholesale. "Oh gods!" she repeated, bawling. It had been so visceral, seeing an actual devil assault on a legion outpost. This was not the glorious tales of heroic victories and self-sacrifice for the good of the state. Those tiercels, those legionaries, they were real, not a statistic or a number scribbled on a parchment. They were real flesh and blood Strixans with families, hopes, dreams, aspirations. And they were all cut down so unceremoniously, without honor, without glory! That was not a battlefield. It was a butcher's yard. *Dulce bellum inexpertis*, a phrase she had read once and did not give any thought to, came to her mind. War is sweet to the inexperienced. Now she had experienced it, the bitterest of tastes.

Friedrich had fallen onto his face; the bag of equipment lay a few feet behind him in the dark. He was speechless, motionless, thoughtless. The last few moments were nothing but a blur, memories mixing and bleeding with now. He didn't even realize he was in the dark. Feeling returned to his body when he heard crying. Was it him? No, his eyes were dry. Who was it?

He suddenly sprang to life as he realized Vytilia was crying. He looked around for her, but the tunnel was too dark. He followed the sound, feeling around on the ground. He felt cloth, the hem of her skirt. He crawled over to her, sitting next to her as she cried. She felt his presence and leaned against him, not saying a word. He wanted to cry but no tears came; he just sat there silent, his hands at his side. They sat there, together, for an unknown amount of time. Vytilia finally finished, wiping her face on her dress. It was unladylike, but she did not care. She reached down and felt something. It twitched.

"Friedrich?" she asked.

"I'm here."

She did not respond. She sat there, still leaning against him, and gripped his shirt.

"Are you alright?" he asked.

"I am not. I . . . I feel helpless," she confided. "All those gallant soldiers, those legionaries. They stayed behind. They were left behind." She felt the tears welling up again. "Why? Why? Why?" She started crying again.

Friedrich put an arm around her, patting her shoulder assuredly. He didn't know what to say. Whatever he said would only make things worse. He just held her close and let her cry. Guilt nagged at him in the back of his head. He began remembering what happened. He had gone back for the equipment bag, then a fiend stood in front of him, a red one with the blank, white eyes. His chest tightened, and he felt a chill ripple through his body. *The eyes*. He could still feel them staring at him, staring into his soul. He could still hear it roar, even smell its breath.

Vytilia stopped crying again and dusted off her clothes. She stood up. "We need to get moving. The best way we can honor those legionaries is by finishing our mission." She sighed and rubbed her eyes. "And Friedrich? You have my gratitude. I, well, I can understand your pacifism."

He smiled as he stood up and dusted himself off. "You're welcome."

She hid her smile and snapped her fingers. Fire lit her fingertips like a candle. She walked over and found the equipment bag. She pulled out a lantern, lit the sun stone encased within, and handed it to Friedrich. "Here, you lead the way; I shall carry the gear."

"Are you sure?"

"I am sure. Do not worry about me. Afterall, this is your expertise." Friedrich smiled as he turned around and led the way.

They walked in silence. Vytilia would occasionally sniff, tears sometimes sneaking their way through. Every time she did, she would talk quietly to herself in her language. Friedrich had to admit she was strong. Not many people could have recovered that quickly, if she had recovered. She could just be putting on a face, for either his sake or her own. As the trail kept going on, he felt tiredness creeping through his body. He didn't know how long they'd been walking but hoped they could stop soon. From the pain in his feet and legs, it felt like several wegstundes. He kicked a rock and watched it fly in the distance, but it didn't land. He stopped and stuck his hand out. Vytilia stopped walking. "What is it?"

"I think there's a cliff edge." He shone the light and took a few steps forward. He was right. The path ended in a steep cut-off. The chasm below was pitch black, stretching down as far as the eye could see. The other part of the path was across the chasm, roughly thirty feet away. "Did they cut the path on purpose?" he asked.

"Verily, this is standard on secret passageways. A healthy Strixan can jump this distance easily, and devils cannot." She set the bag down and walked back to take a running start. Friedrich stepped out of the way as she raced by, leaping over the chasm and landing gracefully. "I can jump back over to help you across," she called. "I cannot carry you, but we could devise a plan."

Friedrich grinned, now was his time to show off. "No, stay over there! I've already got a plan!" He reached into the bag and grabbed two pickaxes. He unspooled the rope from his shoulders and tied one end around a pickaxe. He looked around for a solid crack and stuck the pickaxe in, tugging to make sure it stayed in place. He then wrapped part of the rope around an outcropping of rock. He grabbed a second length of rope and tied it together with the first one. He then tied the other end around the second pickaxe. Satisfied with the knot, he began spinning it around. "Catch!" he called out. He threw the pickaxe across. Vytilia caught it and held it tightly. "Alright, find somewhere strong to anchor it, then wrap a free bit of rope around a solid piece of rock!"

Vytilia stuck the pickaxe into the rock and wrapped the rope around an outcropping. When she reported her success, Friedrich went back to the bag and grabbed whatever tools he could, tucking them into his belt and haversack. He finally tied the lantern to his belt. "Alright! I'm coming across!" he announced. She stood nervously at the edge of the cliff. Friedrich climbed under the rope, wrapping his arms and legs around it. Slowly, he began to crawl across the chasm, careful to only look upwards, sweat pouring from his face.

Then, time seemed to slow again. Almost instinctually, Friedrich froze up. He heard the dreaded sound of fibers unwinding and snapping. He held on tightly, quivering a prayer as the rope snapped, sending him careening into the wall. He braced for the impact, grimacing as he slammed into the solid rock, pain shooting through his head and back. The lantern smashed, and the glass and metal slashed into his thighs. The blow was too much. His grip loosened, and he felt himself at the mercy of gravity, falling and flailing into the darkness below. He couldn't scream.

"Friedrich!" Vytilia yelled. "Friedrich!" she screamed, instinct taking over, and dove into the darkness.

9

"Herr Bergmann!" Friedrich snapped awake, screaming until he ran out of breath, breaking out into a cold sweat. He was sitting up. Sitting up? Was he . . . on the ground? He felt around, feeling dirt, grass, and rocks, the definite signs of land. He looked around. Wherever he was, it was early morning; there was still dew on the leaves and grass, and light was barely breaking through the clouds. Was he back on the surface? He took a closer look at his surroundings; he was in a forest and birds had begun to chirp. The leaves and needles on the trees were yellow, their trunks a beige color. The grass and shrubbery were also yellow, and the light sneaking through the clouds had a green hue. Far in the distance, he heard a wolf howl, which was strange given that it was day.

He tried remembering what happened, how he got here. All he could recall was darkness. His backside was sore, and he felt a twinge of pain in his shoulders. His hands were tender, the telltale signs of rope burn. Memories began to crawl back. He'd been climbing, then he fell. Someone had been calling his name, then it was a blur. He must've blacked out. But how was he alive? He couldn't have survived that fall. No one could have. He looked down at his person. He still had his tunic, his cloak, and the sword sheathed to his belt, though the skirt of his tunic had a few rips and tears. Most importantly, he still had his age-shield and dagger. He unslung the haversack from his shoulders. It was beat up, but his rations and a change of clothes were still in there. Wait. He stopped rummaging. Why did he have all of this again? He rubbed his head, realizing he had a splitting headache. That fact, which was oddly comforting, meant he was alive.

So, he wasn't dead, and he wasn't on the surface. But where was he? He attempted to stand up but let out a gasp of pain and sat back down. His thighs burned like they'd been slashed with a hot poker. He felt the underside, feeling small cuts and slices in his flesh, picking out bits of gravel and glass. He wasn't bleeding, but it hurt like hell. Bleeding. He tried piecing together thoughts. Why did blood seem familiar?

"Vytilia!" he said aloud. He looked around again. Where was she? She was the voice who had called his name. Had she gone for help? Maybe she'd crawled down to look for him? "Vytilia!" he called again. Behind him to his right, he heard someone groan. He looked over and saw a figure laying in the grass atop a small hill. He grimaced and stood up, limping over to them. As he crested the hill, his face went red, and he turned away. It was Vytilia, but her clothes were torn. She'd lost her boots, and her dress was little more than rags covering her personal parts. He couldn't help but laugh as he sat down at the base of the hill, looking in the opposite direction. She was well. But how did she get down here? Had she jumped down after him? And where did her clothes go?

He sat there for a trice, listening to her breathe. She began to stir, calling out in her language. He tentatively took a look back, watching as she came to her feet, then quickly turned back around. "Friedrich?" she called out.

He raised his hand and waved, still looking away.

"You are alive! Are you well?" she asked.

"I've got a headache, some bruises, and some scrapes but I've been through worse."

She looked in the same direction as him. "What are you looking at?"

He coughed. "It's uh, er more about what I'm not looking at."

"What?" She then looked down at herself, her eyes widening and her face turning purple as she covered herself. "Wha-what happened?" *Did he do this?* she wondered. That seemed unlikely. His behavior would not be so sheepish if he did. Her clothes did not look cut. They had been torn, like they had been caught on an outcrop of rock. Or, several outcroppings.

"Here!" Friedrich reached into his haversack, grabbing a spare tunic and taking off his cloak. He held his arm out. She walked over and snatched them out of his hands, retiring to the other side of the hill to change. *What happened to my clothes?* she wondered. What had happened to her? She was extremely fatigued, something she had never experienced before. It was as if all of her energy had been drained out of her like a leak in a vase. That was in addition to all the discomfort all over her body. Her arms were both incredibly sore and bleeding from widened pores, her jaw felt locked, her feet felt like they had been put on backwards, and her eyes felt too large for her skull. It was like something had taken her apart, stretched and bent every piece of her, then hastily reassembled everything without a guide.

"Friedrich?" she called from the other side of the hill.

"Yes?"

She bit her lip, looking at the legionary tunic he lent her. It . . . would not be a proper fit. "May I borrow your pugio?" There was a pause then a cry of effort as he threw the dagger backwards. She hastily climbed up the hill to grab it. Using the tip, she started carefully undoing stitches in the tunic, loosening it before sliding it on. It would not leave much to the imagination, but it was all she had to work with. At least she had the cloak. Maybe if there was time after they got their bearings, she could borrow another tunic and try to make this one more modest. If only the art of textile thaumaturgy had survived the cataclysm; making clothes with needles and thread was so time consuming.

She walked down to Friedrich, returning his pugio. He glanced sideways at her and blushed as he looked away, sheathing his dagger. "What is this place?" she asked, studying their surroundings.

"I don't know. We're definitely not on the surface. The sun and trees aren't these colors."

"Do you remember what happened?"

He shook his head. "I remember losing my grip and falling, but after that, it's a fog."

"I remember you falling as well, then after that, it is . . . a blank. It seems plausible I jumped down after you. I, I do not remember thinking about it. It was . . . compulsive?" She paused, furrowing her brow in thought. "I remember hearing screeching." She grabbed a handful of grass, running the blades through her fingers. It was much drier than the grass kept at the Arx, and the yellow coloring made her think it was in a state of perpetual sickness. "This is all so surreal," she admitted. "Another inhabitable stratum beneath my own. How far below Strixan territory are we?"

"I don't know." Friedrich looked up. "I can't even see the roof. I've never heard of clouds forming underground." Unless Bergmann's claim of rain inside the Toller Mund was true.

Neither had she heard of underground clouds. "Life above us, life below us. How many gaps are there in Strixan knowledge?"

He put his hand on her shoulder. "Don't feel too bad. We didn't know your kind was real or that there was any life this far down."

"That is not comforting, but I appreciate the effort." She tightened the cloak. "I do wonder if that means there are any sapient, sentient races down here. Even in our heyday, we never knew how old the world was. Think of how many other races could have inhabited it before your people or mine came along." Could the devils be part of some sort of natural culling? A response by nature to ensure every sapient race has a chance to flourish? That sounded preposterous but so did the environment she was sitting in.

"Speaking of your kind, do you . . ." He paused. Maybe he shouldn't ask. She was gracious not to pry into his hard times. "How are you?"

"Functioning," she stated. "I am . . . capable. We need to get moving. I can find some solace in that what we are doing will lessen the casualties in future battles. The dead will be mourned. All we can do is press on." She looked up and saw that the tops of the trees seemed to have been sheared off.

"What happened there?" he asked, noticing the trees as well.

"I do not know." She started walking towards them, kneeling to pick up several feathers spread out across the forest floor. *Where did these come from?* They were light brown with dark brown specks and tips. Some had hints of yellow and tan as well. They had a fine quality, much softer and stronger than the few feather decorations she had seen that had survived the cataclysm. They had never encountered avians underground, yet there were enough feathers here to cover an entire flock.

"Do you think you did this?" Friedrich asked, looking up at the damaged trees.

"Me? How could I?" She held onto one of the feathers and looked up as well.

He shrugged. "I don't know, some kind of witchcraft?" He stared up at the birds flying overhead. They looked too big for how far away they were. They were oddly shaped as well, as if they had a head and neck like a man. All the wildlife down here must be weird.

"I do not know anything that could shear trees like that without burning them to the ground." She also did not know any arboropus on top of that. It was an extremely difficult discipline. "We fell, so maybe, we did that?" She looked down at the pile of feathers. "Or, what is most likely is that a flock of avians were sent by Luna and Sol to slow our descent. They might have grabbed us and set us down here, alive." Though, large clusters of avian plumage? Could that also mean . . . ? She shot the thought down. It was ridiculous.

"So, a swallow gripped us by the scruff and set us down?" It wasn't like the Sagas weren't full of tales of birds rescuing mankind, he conceded. "Oh well. As my friend Franz always says, don't look a gift horse in the mouth. At least we're alive." He paused. "Unless this is the vam—Strixan heaven, in which case, why would I be here?"

She did not respond. She sat down and curled up, resting her chin on her knees. The soreness intensified, especially her arms and shoulders. Her legs felt heavy, and they burned with an acidic pain, as if she had just been sprinting. But why? The stranger aspect is that she was not bruised or cut like Friedrich. She was just sore. Strixans did not tire easily. Soreness was rare outside of childbirth or battle, and she had experienced neither, so what had exhausted her? She smacked her lips, realizing she was parched. That must have been why she was so tired if nothing else explained it. She looked at Friedrich who was feeling around under his thigh, throwing away any small rocks he found. She considered asking him for some of his blood but shook her head. Her people had traditions; she could not throw those away in a crisis. Things were already awkward enough between them. For all his uncouthness, he did at least know when to divert his gaze.

She looked down at her outfit, using that in the loosest sense of the word. It was unfortunate she lost her manicula and boots. It would make her more vulnerable to attacks from blue devils, but at least she still had . . . she gasped. "My bag! Where is it? Did you see it?" She quickly got up, running back towards the hill, looking around.

"Your haversack? No. Well, think about it, whatever tore your clothes would've torn that."

"Ah damn!" She buried her head in her hands. "What poor fortune is this?!"

"Hey it's alright." He tried comforting her from a distance, not looking at her. "We'll find you some proper lady clothes, and there's wildlife here. You can . . . drink them." He gritted his teeth for the last part.

"It is not that! My bag had sealed orders of cooperation from the Concilium. I was supposed to give them to the City Proconsul of Aurum, so they would give us anything we need."

"Well, if you explain what happened, I'm sure the lord of Aurum will still help. Your name seems to carry a lot of weight. And, I'm living proof of the mission."

She sighed and looked away. "There were also five solid gold bars to help pay for the weaponry and delivery." She swore. "That was the satchel given to me."

"Oh." Friedrich reached for where he'd normally keep his chippurse, but there was nothing there. He made a mental note that next time he accepted a job from some vampires to ask for part of the payment up front.

"We shall worry about that later," she announced. "For now, we should get our bearings, understand the lay of the land, then figure out a way back to my people, and then eventually, to the surface. We should also seek proper shelter." She stood up, surveying the horizon. "Look!" She pointed to a mountain behind them. It was several miles in the distance, but it was tall, the summit disappearing behind blue-green colored clouds. "Since we are underground, there has to be a ceiling. That looks tall enough to reach it. From there, we can exploit a crack in the roof or find a natural tunnel to get back to my stratum."

"Looks like it'll be a long trek getting there. We should probably get started." Friedrich winced as he stood back up, slinging his haversack back over his shoulders.

"Are you sure you are well?" she asked.

"Yeah, yeah. Just some aches and scrapes. We might just have to slow our pace a bit."

"Here, show me where it hurts. I can heal it." His face went red as he turned around, showing her his cut-up thigh. The lantern had scraped his leg, but the wound was mostly surface level. No ligaments or muscles were cut. She held both hands on his leg, making Friedrich squirm. As she drew her hands away, announcing her work was complete, she noticed a few drops of blood. She stared at them, her thirst nagging at her, her lips feeling drier. She ran her tongue over her fangs. They were primed and ready. She quickly snapped out of it and wiped her hands on his shirt. "You should be good to walk now," she told him, turning away and focusing on the mountain. "I shall lead the way if that is alright."

"Wait." Friedrich stuck an arm out to stop her. He pointed to the ground. "Tracks." He knelt, tracing the soft outline in the dirt. "This is a hunter track, some kind of cat, probably a lynx." He looked up at the direction it was going. "I don't think we're on a game trail, but it would be better to go the other way." He pointed to the right of the mountain.

"How do you know all of this?" she asked as he stood back up.

"Herr Bergmann and I spent a lot of time camping in the wilds. Most big wildlife will avoid towns and hamlets, but once you enter their realm, they lose *all* fear of mankind." He looked up at the trees. "We should find a clearing or a field to cross. Most big cats are great climbers."

"You lead the way then," she suggested. He gladly complied, watching the forest floor as they headed to the mountains. Birds and other critters went about their daily business as they hiked. It reminded Friedrich of his first time in the tunnels with Vytilia, where he was a guest in a world of the animals.

"On your travels, did you frequently have to contend with predators?" she asked.

"Rarely. They mostly come out at night. Mostly. We always tried to avoid fresh tracks and game trails. And we always had a fire going at night to scare them away. They might not fear man, but all wildlife is wary of fire. Down here though, it's better to err on the side of careful. I heard a wolf howl when I woke up, so who knows if the wilderness is the same down here."

"Do you hunt then?"

"We'd set snares for rabbits and fish but never hunted anything bigger. Most of the good hunting forests are owned by lords, so poaching is unlawful. If our food ran out, well, they usually won't miss a couple of rabbits." He chuckled. "If we were already trespassing, we'd avoid snaring or fishing. Luckily, unless you encounter the huntmaster, most game wardens will give us a warning or chase after someone even worse."

"Do all plebeians flaunt the law so openly on the surface?"

"Hey, hey, hey," he insisted. "We weren't 'flaunting' anything. We were surviving. Besides, most lords don't care what was in the caves, so that wasn't unlawful. Sometimes, getting to them was." She rolled her eyes. Every time he spoke about the surface, it made it sound like anarchy masquerading as a legitimate governing body.

She ignored her distaste with the surface and took note of their surroundings. She could not help but be in awe of this place. The differences between where her people lived and this new ecosystem were night and day. The trees were healthier, taller, and fuller. There were clouds in the sky, even some sort of replacement sun, not star stones which now seemed pitiful by comparison. There was grass and brightly colored plants that did not glow. *Was this how the world had been before the cataclysm?* she asked herself. Is this what the paintings and mosaics in the Sanctum Sanctorum had tried to capture? What her mother saw?

Despite her awe, she felt her more primal instincts kicking in. Every avian, every vermin, every animal she saw, all she could sense was a heartbeat, the flow of their precious ichor. She could also hear Friedrich's heartbeat; it was steady and loud. She was getting hungrier by the minute, which was strange; she had gone longer than this without blood. It was not as if her people were addicts. They had impeccable endurance, going days without a sanguination. By all accounts, she should not be this thirsty. Her mind was starting to cloud, and she felt her senses dull. She could not resist for much longer.

She stopped dead in her tracks, looking around. She spotted her quarry: a lone mammalian creature was standing a few feet behind them, blissfully grazing on some grass. It was grey-colored, speckled with dark brown spots and streaks down its back, with black antlers sprouting from the head. She readied herself to jump, her fangs bared. Friedrich heard her stop and turned around. She ignored him, focusing on her prey. When the creature looked away, she sprinted forward and pounced, all in a moment, grappling it to the ground in a lightning-quick motion. The cloak flew off in a flash. The animal bellowed and kicked, but she held it tightly, observing the neck for the jugular vein. Finding it, she bit down hard, puncturing it on both sides. The animal gave a final cry before going limp as she began to drink.

Friedrich stared on in horror. All color had drained from his face, he was shaking, and his teeth chattered. It had all happened so fast. One moment Vytilia had paused, and the next moment she had pounced on the deer and was drinking it dry. The poor thing didn't even have a chance or get a glance at its attacker. Had he eaten something, he probably would have thrown up.

Vytilia gulped down the last drop and wiped her ruddy-colored mouth. She felt invigorated, young, almost new. The soreness in her arms and legs had vanished, and she could think clearly, her mind focused on her surroundings and the task ahead rather than battling her own hunger. She muttered a small prayer to Luna, thanking her for the bounty and asking that this creature be guided to find eternal rest. She picked up the cloak, wrapping it around herself as she began to walk back towards Friedrich, pausing when she saw him standing, shaking in fear. His arms were outstretched, and he was making some sort of sign with his hands. His palms were touching, with each finger outstretched and straight. She examined it, wondering what it might be. Some kind of arachnid? The spokes of a wheel?[23]

"You look uneasy."

"Yes!" he cried, his voice cracking. "What, what the hell was that?"

She bit her lip. "Hunger got the better of me. That was what we were like before the empire, before civilization. It was brutish, but necessary."

"There's nothing left! That poor thing, it's . . . it's a husk now!"

"As I said, it was a necessary sacrifice." He was not reassured. "I would not do that on normal circumstances. For whatever reason, I was abnormally thirsty," she insisted.

"Swear you won't do that to me!"

"What?"

"Swear it!"

She sighed and rolled her eyes. As clever and resourceful Friedrich was making himself out to be, and after all the time he had spent around Strixans, he was still letting his plebeian superstitions get the better of him. "As I told you before, a respectable Strixan will only drink another being's blood if they are slain in single combat. And I promise you, I will not challenge you to single combat." *Considering it would not be a fair fight,* she thought to herself. His face started to return to a healthy color, and they resumed walking towards the mountain, though with his hand closer to his dagger and a few paces farther away from her.

Vytilia began to argue with herself mentally. Should she have waited, informed him what she was going to do so as not to terrify him? She knew, even if she would never admit it, that watching her kill and drink a living creature would have been a terrifying sight. He ran and screamed when she just showed her fangs. Should she just have swallowed her pride and asked for some of his? Or given

---

23. This is the Token of the Rays or the Strahlenzeichen in High Rinnish. It is a traditional mannish practice used to ward off evil. To do it properly, the palms must be touching, with the back of the right hand facing away from the user. The pointed finger of the left hand is hidden behind the right wrist, making it appear as if the person doing the Token only has nine fingers, nine being the holiest number.

him a warning, tell him to look away? Even worse, did she just erase all of the trust and understanding the two had built up? They had shared a moment together, one that was touching and intimate. He had been compassionate and personal, understanding in a way no one else had ever been before. Now she had gone and thrown it all away by obeying her most basic instinct. All her education and etiquette, her civility, years of training and discipline, ignored just because of a strong thirst.

She stopped walking, waiting for him to notice and turn around. He stopped, looking back at her coolly. He was tense, with his hand on the hilt of his dagger. "There is not a need for that. I just wanted to apologize and ease some tension," she explained. "What happened was . . . an unfortunate lack of grace on my part and an abandonment of civil principles. It was poor judgment, and I did not mean to cause you any fright or worry. I am sorry."

He sighed, loosening up and dropping his hand to his side. He couldn't afford hostility between the two of them. They would need each other to survive and get back to the surface. "Apology accepted. And . . . I may have overreacted. Just, just let me know next time. I nearly shit myself." He turned back around. "Can't blame me, right? Still just getting used to working with vampires. Sorry, Strixans." She smiled.

Friedrich, while glad to have eased the tension, didn't know if he should feel relieved or if he should remain on his guard. Despite the fact that they had spent every day since he fell from the surface together, and with everything that has happened since then, he still did not know if he fully trusted Vytilia. Granted, he was with her since they had a similar goal, and he didn't have a choice, it was still a rather unfortunate circumstance to be in. He had both a lack of experience with women and an upbringing seeped in fearing anything weird or strange. He'd grown up seeing witch trials and even a few hangings, and even Herr Bergmann, who had normally been a level-headed man, steered clear of anything involving witchcraft. And yet here Friedrich was, travelling underground with a vampire witch.

He wanted to trust her. And, though he would never admit it, he was starting to be attracted to her. But something was nagging at him, a sense of dread that this was all a trick being played on him, and at the end of their mission, his "handsome reward" would be his lifeless corpse drained of blood, just like that deer.

There were hundreds of folk tales about a man being tricked by a witch or their ilk.

At least for now, in this strange place, he would trust her. She'd just fed, so he was safe until she wanted more. He looked up at the "sun." Whatever the light was, it was high in the sky by now. It must've been about midday, or at least whatever passed for midday. He was amazed anyone could have a sense of time down here. "Do you think we could stop and get some water?" he asked, looking back.

Vytilia stopped. She craned her head to the right then pointed to her left. "There is a watering hole a few feet over there." She also looked up at the "sun." It was bright; looking up at it hurt her eyes. Was this how bright it was on the surface? Would Sol be as unbearable or hard to look at?

They found the watering hole. A few animals that had been drinking saw the two of them approach and scattered away. He knelt at the shoreline and began to lap up the water like a dog. She scoffed at his manners and used thaumaturgy to create a funnel she could drink from, like a straw. The water was cool and refreshing. Even Vytilia, who had never drunk more than a sip around Friedrich, was taking multiple drinks. Friedrich continued to drink then washed his face and hair. It'd been so long since he'd bathed. When he finished, he sat across from Vytilia under the shade of a tree. She leaned up against the trunk of a larger one, crossing her legs, so she was completely covered by the shade.

"Not a fan of the light?" he called over to her.

"I am not used to it. I have to keep squinting just to see. Is the sun like this?"

"It's brighter. And warmer. And yellower. Whatever that is . . ." he pointed up to the sky, "it's just a light, all the brightness but none of the warmth, which is nice since there also isn't a breeze to cool us down."

"I look forward to seeing it. We only really talk about Luna, so many have forgotten Sol."

"You know, on the surface, vampires don't like the sun. They always skulk around at night. Well, most 'dark and fell things' don't like the sun."

"That is curious," she admitted. "We worship the sun. I cannot think of a reason why the stories depict us as hating it."

Especially with that statue, Friedrich thought. "If you love the sun, why do you wear the hood of the cloak up? You were wearing something on your head back at Nidus as well."

"It is a tradition, especially for patricians. Originally, as my mother taught, the nighttime was for hunting and waging war, and the daytime was for writing and creating art. During the day, my people tend to be a bit more languid than usual. But, as the empire expanded, it became necessary, especially during certain seasons, to be in the sun more often." She paused to explain some of the terminology she used. "Laboring outside began to be seen as something only tiercels should do. For the poorer classes, the plebians, hens and tiercels both had to work outside during the day to earn a living. So, when patrician hens traveled outside during the day, they covered their head to show they were out for leisure, not for labor."

"I didn't see any other . . . hens," using the Strixan word for woman was odd to him, "wearing it."

"They are supposed to. Eventually, the wearing of a head covering became popular for all classes, except a few by law. Though, now that we are underground and the history behind it has been lost, I suspect most do not see a need to. That and spare fabric is a bit of a rarity."

"That bit you said about men working outside and women working inside, it's the same on the surface too." She had mentioned wanting to find "common ground" and actually work with the surface. This similarity could be what she meant. And, if he was helpful, he might get a bigger reward. "Though, the house isn't only for women to work, it's their own kingdom, er queendom. They have the final say on everything inside the home. Instead of a weapon, they carry their house keys on their waist."

"Fascinating," Vytilia commented. "It would seem our civilizations have more in common than one would expect."

He nodded in agreement. If one could get past the fangs and blood drinking, this whole plan to ally with the surface might actually work. "You said some Strixans can't cover their head by law?"

"Slaves and shoulder-biters."

"Shoulder-biters?"

"That was the translated term for their euphemism. I thought it would make sense. They are also known as prostitutes." He gave her another confused look. "Never mind. Tell me more about how mankind perceives 'vampires,' as you called us."

"Only if you tell me how your witchcraft works," he insisted.

She perked up, smiling. "Happily, I am glad you asked." She stood up. "I shall explain it to you as we walk. It will help the journey seem quicker." As they returned to the trail, they heard a grunt. They looked down; a small metal dart was embedded in the earth between her feet. "What?" Before she could raise her arms and ready her thaumaturgy, there was another grunt, and another dart punched into the tree just behind her head. Her head spun around. She heard heartbeats but could not tell what was animal or not. She snapped her fingers, glancing for a hint of their attacker. She had to be cautious. If she started a fire or annoyed the wrong thing, they would both be in an uncomfortable diplomatic incident.

They both backed up towards the tree line, fire dancing on her fingertips and he with his dagger drawn. A spear flew and struck the ground behind Friedrich. He picked it up to examine it; it had a thin shaft, made of light wood with a small iron tip. It was much smaller than any spear he'd seen on the surface or even the ones used by the vampire warriors. He guessed their attackers were some sort of band of wild men, like the wildfolk he'd heard about in the new world.

He threw the spear away when he heard Vytilia yowl. He looked up and saw her holding her left arm, a dart jammed into her bicep. He reached up to help her, but she pushed him away, screaming as she ripped it out. This was the first time Friedrich had seen Strixan blood this close. It wasn't red. It was a blue-white, almost clear color, like water mixed with milk. She grimaced and held her hand over the wound as it healed. The darts and spears had stopped firing, and Friedrich could hear footsteps in the grass. Their attackers were closing in. Another spear landed at his feet. He sheathed his dagger and raised his hands above his head. Vytilia, wincing, did the same.

They stared as their ambushers slowly emerged from the brush with some climbing down from trees. Whoever these beings were, they were not men and not Strixan. They were, on average, shorter than Friedrich. Their skins were either the same color as egg yolk or egg whites or some shade between. Every one of them had only four digits on their hands and feet. They all wore trousers and cloaks with no consistent coloring, some wearing brighter primary colors, others dull colors similar to the ones worn by Strixans. The older ones, with a bit of grey and a spot of wrinkles, were decorated with elaborate tattoos, some on the face or covering a full arm and parts of the chest. Each tattoo was a light red or green hue, composed of intricate patterns and knots. Most, both old and young had shaved heads or long, elaborate braids. That's when Friedrich noticed their ears; they were thin, narrow, and pointed.

"Elves?" Friedrich whispered to himself.

All of the group (there were at least twelve) had weapons. The ones holding throwing spears stood a distance back, while others wielding swords, axes, or clubs approached Vytilia and Friedrich. With them were hunting dogs, tall beasts that came up to their chest. The dogs looked like no hound Friedrich had seen. They had a humped back, a shaggy ridge of fur on their head, and a spotted coat. Their bark sounded more like a wheezing laugh.

One of the beings, their leader, gave orders to the others. A few of the warriors sheathed their weapons, taking Friedrich's sword and dagger. The leader looked at Vytilia, or more correctly, looked up at her, his eyes holding on her outfit. He grinned, commenting on her to the others as they laughed. He didn't touch her physically, but he and the other warriors all stared closely at her.

One of the warriors, holding a piece of cord, called out to the leader who walked behind to look at Friedrich's hands. The leader's eyes widened, and he nearly fell back, gasping and stuttering. The other warriors all stepped back, sheathing their weapons and falling to their knees, holding out their belongings. The leader stood up, nervously gesturing and pointing in a direction to go. Friedrich and Vytilia exchanged a glance and started walking, the warriors all following at a distance. The leader ran ahead, his hands clasped and bowed as he led the way.

"Friedrich, any idea what is happening?" Vytilia asked.

He looked at his hands, checking for anything different. "I . . . I don't know."

"Any stories that would help us?"

He gritted his teeth. "About hand worshipping elves? None that I've heard."

She walked closer to him. "Keep quiet, and stay close. We will make it through this. Together."

The elves (or nymphs as Vytilia mentally referred to them as) escorted them for a good distance, headed away from the mountain, passing through a forest into a grassy plainland with a range of hills further ahead. The elves would glance at them, staring at their hands as they marched, always respectfully keeping their distance. Friedrich and Vytilia stayed silent, observing their captors. She was surprised at their stature and coloring. She thought Friedrich was strange, but these nymphs were even stranger with their pointed ears, colorful ink markings, and four-digit hands and feet. When they spoke to one another, she noticed their ears would change colors or move around. The party was joined by more hunters. They were unarmed but carried game animals with them including the husk of the one she had drained. The party all looked annoyed and looked at the two of them with contempt until the leader spoke to them, then they looked with awe and fear.

As they walked, Friedrich started recalling everything he'd heard about elves. Elves had been a staple of children's tales since children started being told tales. Like most tales told, elves were usually mischief makers who loved to trick men, though they also could hold a grudge and seek revenge, especially if someone disrespected nature. Some even thought that elves had been among the Lightless, others that god had given them their own world.

As they crossed the plains, several herdsmen ran to the trail to look at the two of them, leering at Vytilia until the hunters spoke to them. They quickly prostrated themselves worshipfully or fled back to their herds, nervously looking back. She was thankful not be the object of stares but did not know whether to feel concerned or relieved when they quickly left. Friedrich paused to stare at the livestock the herdsmen were caring for; squat, bulky, pad-footed, and very shaggy haired four-legged things, no taller than a pony with a single horn protruding from their face. "Unicorns?" he wondered aloud.

After the plains, at the edge of hill country, was their destination. It was a settlement, built around and on top of a hill, half the size of the one Nidus was built on. The heart of the settlement was a fort, built on the crest of the hill, surrounded by a wall made of earthworks and wooden stakes covered in leather hides. Warriors looked over from the bronze gate, the terminus for the many trails crisscrossing and connecting the entire settlement. Smaller outlaying settlements were all built in circles, surrounded by a low stone wall and connected by trails and wooden gates. In each circle was a collection of huts, squat, rectangular buildings made of wood or daub with thatched roofs. In the open spaces, there was always some kind of work going on: shearing the unicorn creatures, repairing a chariot, dyeing clothes, or metalworking. When the one leading them would announce their coming, all would stop what they were doing and prostrate themselves, holding out fine golden torcs and other treasures as an offering.

The hunting party guided them up the center trail, past the bronze gate. All the buildings on the inside of the wall were built in a similar style with the same material as the ones outside, though they were noticeable larger and decorated with fine linens. Both noticed there wasn't a single door or window in the entire hamlet. A large firepit occupied the center where women stood, spinning a spit roast and gossiping. Other women would be in their door frames, doing weaving or washing while children ran around chasing each other. Men were either helping construct a building or watching their livestock, kept in pens built against the wall. At first, Friedrich thought they were tending to pigs, but as they walked past, he saw whatever the animal was, it was closer to a . . . beaver? Friedrich racked his brain; he had never heard of elves tending to beavers and hairy unicorns.

They were shown past the spit roast and huts by the leader and one other elf while the rest started dividing up the game and dispersing into the hamlet. Those who left bowed their heads and made prayers or pleaded in their language. They stood in front of a wide-open plaza, marked by a wattle fence. Beyond the plaza was the largest building in the settlement, a scaled-up version of the previously seen huts but with a proper door and frame and glassless windows. It was built on an earthen embankment, looking over the entirety of the hamlet. It reminded Friedrich of the old mead halls where church services used to be held. *Those* were the days, though they had ended many hundreds of years before he was born.

The leader of the hunters, his ears turned green and pointed downward, told another hunter with him to hurry inside then clasped his hands, begging Friedrich and Vytilia to wait in his language, sweating as he kept looking over his shoulder.

"I think they must think we are some sort of . . . deity," Vytilia whispered. "We must be meeting their Princeps or some sort of Pontiff."

He looked at his hands again. "How'd they'd get that from my hands?" he wondered aloud.

"Is this what a city is like on the surface?"

"No! Not in the Realm at least. They're always bigger and cleaner." The smell of . . . something hit his nose.

And this is not what a Strixan city was like, she thought. "Did you see those strange animals they were attending to?"

"How couldn't I! Unicorns, laughing dogs, and beavers! I think we might be dead; we could be in Schlaraffenland.[24]"

Is unicorn what he called those rhinoceroses? "What is Schlaraffenland?"

"Every toiler's dream. A land of milk and honey where you never work and get to be young forever."

The messenger returned, and the lead hunter hurriedly showed the two of them inside after several elves, both male and female, reverently left, all staring until the doors closed behind them. The inside was mostly a single chamber with smaller enclosed spaces on the wings. The smell of food wafted from their right. A large, stained carpet stretched the length of the chamber, and the walls were decorated with antlers, broken shields, shattered swords, and other battlefield treasures. The room was illuminated by several braziers hanging from the roof, the space directly above blackened with years of smoke.

Friedrich and Vytilia stood before a small group of elves gathered around a wooden throne. The throne rested on an elevated pedestal, allowing the occupant to look over everyone and who entered and exited the door. The current occupant of said throne was a larger and more muscular elf with long red hair and a beard composed almost entirely of braids, holding a knobbed club made of white wood. Of the other elves flanking him, one in a white cloak and holding a staff standing on his left especially stood out.

The throne elf leaned forward, his ears pointed downward, and spoke. There was humility in his tone. He made small gestures, speaking quietly and carefully, switching eye contact between the two of them. When he stopped talking, he leaned forward, waiting for a response. There was an awkward silence as Friedrich and Vytilia exchanged a look then stared back at the throne elf. He spoke again, and there was another silence.

"This calls for a translation. Allow me," Vytilia muttered. She motioned for the throne elf to step down and come in front of her, but the elf in the white cloak raised his hand to volunteer. She shrugged, beckoning him to come before her. He knelt (which put him at the same level as her waist) looking up, his eyes closed, as if he accepted something hallowed would happen. The crowd held

24. Lazy monkey land, comparable to Cockaigne.

their breath as she placed her hands on the side of the cloaked elf's head. Friedrich recognized it as the same motion she had done when she found him. The cloaked elf started to mutter, his lips trembling and voice cracking in amazement. When Vytilia finished, she spoke to the elf in his language. He quickly returned to the side of the throne as she turned to Friedrich, doing the same movements.

"Now then." She stood straight; her arms folded as she stared down each of the elves. "To what purpose have we been brought here? Your party ambushed my companion and I, striking me in the arm with a projectile and holding us at spearpoint. We demand answers."

The throne elf nearly leapt from his seat, falling at their feet. The others similarly prostrated themselves. "Oh, forgive us great and mighty one! Our warriors knew not with whom they dealt with! We thought you thieves, comin' to pillage our game and our lands. We ask kindness upon them and their families."

Vytilia smirked. "Your vena—*ahem* hunters are fortunate the wound was easily healed and that further harm did not fall upon us. Stand up, return to your throne, and explain to us this people and these lands."

The throne elf hurried back into his seat, his hands clasped and ears pointed downward; they were colored red-green. "I thank you a thousand times, your worship, for sparin' the lives of my hunters. I welcome you to our baile[25] of Bryn Adref. I am Llewelyn ap Hywel ap Rhys MabCynan, Rí tuaithe of Budin[26] MabCynan." He gestured to the elves at his side. "These are the great household leaders of our Budin and our druid, Ruith."

"It is an honor, your worship. Your skills with draíocht far surpass my own. I am humbled to kneel before you." The druid bowed his head and knelt.

She leaned in towards Friedrich, speaking to him in Teutonish. "Well, my hypothesis on us being revered as deities is correct."

"Don't let it go to your head," he warned with a sly smile. "Can you ask if they have a change of clothes and a hot meal?"

"My thoughts exactly. Though, we did just discover another civilization, buried underneath my own. We could probably learn something from them. Perhaps they know of a better way back to my stratum."

---

25. Native word for a village or settlement.

26. A term similar to clan or tribe.

"It's worth a try, but food and hose first."

"Nothing ventured, nothing earned." She cleared her throat, switching to the elf's language. "Rí MabCynan, as recompense for your hunter's transgressions, I require a change of proper feminine clothing." Friedrich cleared his throat. "And a pair of . . . hose? And my companion and I will require food and shelter for the night and directions for our continued journeying tomorrow. In addition, I wish to speak with your historians and scholars."

Rí MabCynan stroked his beard, and his ears returned to a normal color and position. "Directions?" He puzzled out the word in his mind with context. "Why of course! Our traders have gone wide and far!" He leaned back in his chair. "And where are you headed that we may help you?"

"The black-colored mountain, off in the distance."

Rí MabCynan leaned forward again. "The Càrn Dubh?" He quickly glanced at Ruith.

"Forgive my tone if it offends, but why must you go to Càrn Dubh?" the druid asked.

Vytilia began to speak, but Friedrich stopped her. They exchanged a look, and he spoke. "This mountain is our way into the otherworld. We must go to the peak and preform a great spell. It is forbidden for others to see this. That is all you need to know, but you will be rewarded for your help."

An elf standing to the right of the throne frowned. He wore a fine outfit with clean, braided brown hair. His face was tatted with intricate, blue-colored designs. "The Càrn Dubh is the burying ground for all of the Budins' honored dead." He spat. "If ye be gods, then surely ye should know that no good can come of doing forbidden draíocht on such hallowed grounds. What gods would not know this?"

"Anarawd, behave yourself!" Rí MabCynan chastised. "Their dealings are they're own. Watch your tongue!"

"I watch nothing Llewelyn! Why do they have to trespass on our holy grounds? And what did Fionn's lad say? They found an iwrch completely drained of its life. They are trespassers. They have stolen our game and will only bring death to the Budin!"

Rí MabCynan slammed his fist on the throne's armrest. "Damn you, Anarawd! Our game is their game! They showed kindness to Fionn and his hunters! They learned our speech without touchin' the tongue of Ruith! You may have brought death by speakin' ill of them! Have your forefathers failed to teach you and your kin godliness?"

Anarawd scowled, pulling his cloak back and reaching for a knife. Thinking quickly, Vytilia snapped her fingers. A ball of fire grew in her palm, and she sent it off, floating around Anarawd's head three times before striking the ground at his feet, burning a hole in the floor. Anarawd removed his hand as the other elves oohed and ahhed.

"Remarkable," Ruith commented.

"And now they have shown you a kindness Anarawd. I wouldn't have. Go, leave this hall. Go tend to your children and herds while thinkin' of your words and works. Hope that these two will grant our Budin further kindnesses in spite of your fell deeds." Anarawd swore as he exited the hall, glaring at Vytilia and Friedrich as he walked by, slamming the door behind him. "Anarawd is head of one of the oldest families in MabCynan," the Rí explained. "His temper is known far and wide. Please, I beg of you, forgive him and us. He only has the best in his heart."

"We shall be benevolent, Rí MabCynan. The hospitality and reverence shown by the rest of your people more than make up for Anarawd's shortcomings," Vytilia told him.

"Now, I recall there was mention of food and shelter?" Friedrich chimed in.

Rí MabCynan grinned. "We'll have the Bina[27] get started on that right away. Cynbel, go find the kitchen bina and have them start on a feast for our guests!" He stepped down from the throne, standing in front of Friedrich and Vytilia. "Your worships, if you may be so kind, what are your names that we may know how to rightly call on you?" Ruith joined him at his side, nodding eagerly.

"I am Vytilia," she announced.

"And I am Friedrich."

The Rí smiled. "Such high and godly names. Budin MabCynan truly is blessed by the two of you. It will take them a while to make the food. May I show the two of you around our lands? Perhaps ask a blessing on them?"

---

27. Elvish Pronouns:
Adult Male: Fer (singular) Fir (plural)
Adult Female: Ben (singular) Bina (plural)
Young Male: Bach (singular) Bechyn (plural)
Young Female: Plach (singular) Plached (plural)

"We can also answer any questions you have!" Ruith added.

"Very well, Rí MabCynan, you are the host." Vytilia stepped back, leaning towards Friedrich as the two elves led them outside. "I think that went over well, all things considered," she whispered in Teutonish.

"I think that Anarawd is going to be an issue. He isn't going to leave us alone. God forbid he finds out what you really are."

"You make a good point. We shall spend the night, procure supplies, then head for the mountain in the morning. When our current assignment is complete, I plan on coming back here to do more research."

"Everything alright? Have we done something wrong?" Rí MabCynan asked.

"No, no, everything is alright," Friedrich insisted. "We're just planning on how to . . . reward you!"

"Ah."

As they walked through the MabCynan baile, Vytilia could not help but stare at everything and everyone. This was a surreal experience for her, more dreamlike than even meeting Friedrich. Here she was, surrounded by what were on all accounts *barbarians*. She had not shared this with Friedrich, but those motifs on the slate back at the Sanctum Sanctorum were a minute percentage of Strixan art. By far the most popular motif had been the unwashed, uncivilized, uncultured barbarian. It was a universal fiction in the mind of every tiercel, hen, and nestling, a phantom always haunting the culture of the empire. They were not real, according to what her mother taught her, but a shared idea, a fear given artistic form. Friedrich's people had known of her race, at least a fictional version. She wondered if, perhaps, that imagined barbarian image had a source among these nymphs.

Then her eye caught something that caused her to do a double-take. It was a sword, gird around the waist of a nymph warrior who averted his gaze. The shape of the scabbard was . . . familiar. Too familiar. She stopped and approached the warrior. "Your sword." He was startled. "Please."

Carefully, he detached it from his belt, handing it to her before stepping back. She withdrew the sword from the scabbard, and her eyes widened. This sword *was* familiar. It's size, shape, dimension, even weight, was almost exactly like a legionary gladius. There were differences, especially in the quality and handle, but the blade itself was nearly the same. She felt a strange emotion begin to percolate through her, something basic, something fearful.

Did the legions owe their success to a barbarian blade? she asked herself. *Impossible, this, this must be a coincidence!* Surely any society, given enough time would realize the superiority of the gladius' design.

She handed the sword back to the nymph warrior. "It is a good weapon," she told him, loud enough that the confused, staring Llewelyn and Ruith could hear. "Take good care of it."

"You have a good eye, your worship," Llewelyn complimented. "That make of sword has been passed down since our forebearers first arrived here! It's done us well ever since then."

That comment did nothing to sooth Vytilia's spreading sense of fear. She smiled and nodded politely then banished the fear to the dark recesses of her mind, to never be let out. Strixans do not fear anything.

Friedrich saw something was bothering Vytilia, but he kept his mouth shut. If he said anything, it could make the elves think twice about their ruse. Though, he couldn't see how a sword made her so upset. Maybe it reminded her of the slaughter at the way station. If that were the case, he would be careful talking to her.

Llewelyn and Ruith showed them to a ladder near the gate, letting their guests go first. When everyone had climbed up, Rí MabCynan proudly stretched out his hands, beaming as he showed the extent of Budin MabCynan's territory. "Beautiful, isn't it? Well over 650 seisrechs[28] of lands, gifted from the gods to our forefathers. We've got plenty of rivers, good huntin' grounds, and more grass than any grazer could ever want." He took a deep inhale. "Ah, it even smells nice too!" He beamed with pride as he faced Friedrich and Vytilia. "I don't mean to brag, your worships, but you'll nay find a better-kept baile than Bryn Adref."

Vytilia stared at the land below. It was magnificent. There was so much to see, so many colors, so many varying sights. She felt overwhelmed. All her life she'd only known the grey, unchanging solid rock, but here was hundreds of miles of life! There were miles of undulating grasslands, trees so tall they could reach mountain peaks. There were clear blue streams, all manner of animals across the whole spectrum of color. The colors were not the same as how her mother described, but it was still incredible! She did not believe

28. 78,000 acres or 31,566 Hectares.

it that so much existed outside of the empire. Staring out at these vast grasslands and forests, places she thought of only in stories, it made her all the more excited to see the surface.

"Are there other Budins?" Friedrich asked, pulling her out of her wonder.

"Aye. A whole lot of us, don't know how many there are, though. Our closest neighbors are Budin Rronalt. They're far pass the trees there. They're good friends of ours. Their Rí tuaithe is even wedded to my sister." He pointed to the left, far from Càrn Dubh. "They're odd folk though. They all live in the tops of the great trees, use rope to get down to the ground. Makes defendin' their lands easy but tradin' and visitin' is a huge pain. I always feel like I'm going to fall."

"Who are you defending your lands from?" Friedrich asked.

"The other Budins," Rí MabCynan explained. "Fightin' ain't too often but often enough that we've always got a standin' band of warriors. 'Course, every fer can fight, but some are better at it than others. Nuttins more of a shame than losing our best smith in battle to a born warrior."

"The walls also help keep out the wildlife. And the MacMórrígan." Ruith added.

"The what?" Friedrich and Vytilia asked simultaneously.

Ruith and MabCynan exchanged a glance. "The MacMórrígan." Ruith repeated. "Surely two beings such as yourself know of them?"

"Remind us." Friedrich cut-off Vytilia before she could speak. "These . . . forms cause us to be forgetful." He winked at her. "It happens often when travelling between the worlds."

"Ah. Well, the MacMórrígan are the watchers of the gods, sons of the original Mórrígan, the most powerful Druidess at the time of the God's wrath. They keep us in line, make sure we're following the wisdom of the druids rightly and sticking to the old ways," Ruith explained. "They are wild but trusted."

"Without them, all the Budins would have fallen into endless warfare. Their ways may be tough, but the results are fair," Rí MabCynan tacked on. "Never seen one in the flesh, mind you, and I don't know whether or not that's a good sign. I like to think it is. I'm not much for stirrin' the pot."

"Has anyone ever seen these MacMórrígan? What are they exactly?" Vytilia asked.

"We don't quite know exactly. Some say they're bears; others say they're wolves or a great hawk. The hunters think any big wild thing is one, so they always leave behind the choicest cuts from an iwrch as an offering," Ruith answered. "I must cheer Llewellyn here. He's done well following my wisdom. It's kept the MacMórrígan from bothering our game or our traders."

Friedrich and Vytilia nodded then stepped away, further down the wall. "Well, that clinches it. We need to leave before those MacMórrígan show up. I don't want to put all these folk at risk," he told her in Teutonish.

She looked up; the sky was starting to darken. "I concur. It will be best to wait until morning. Whatever these MacMórrígan are, they probably are used to operating in the dark. Given your . . . deficiency, it would be wiser to travel by light."

"Mankind made fire for a reason, but go on." He waved dismissively. "Do you think they're fiends? You said they made burrows, so it's possible they must have found their way down here."

"It may be possible? But the druid said they looked like . . . what is a bear?"

"What? You don't know what a bear is?" She shook her head. "A bear is a big old, mean thing. Weighs as much as a house and can disembowel you with a swipe of a paw."

"And they have fur?" He nodded. "That rules out devils. We have never encountered a mammalian one." She sighed, looking longingly at the land. "I would love to stay, find out as much of these people's history as I can, but we should leave by tomorrow."

"Uh, begging your pardon, your worships," Rí MabCynan interrupted. "Word just arrived from the kitchens. The feast is ready."

• • •

Šar Šarrāni Molek had finished his prostrating, his paying of obeisance and listing of titles, and had finished his report. The survivors of the ambush party had returned, slaying all of the grey birds they found. The body of the pink mortal had not been found, but he was confident the interloper was dead. He glanced up at Sky Father and Ground Mother, as bored and uninterested as ever, but he had a feeling they would recognize the achievement and success his kind accomplished in their name.

Then the herald entered and announced the arrival of Arkhegtis Phlegyas.

Molek's blood chilled slightly before warming to white-hot hatred. He hated this bestial upstart, and he knew well the feeling was mutual. With an unearned and overconfident swagger, Phlegyas entered the gods' chambers. He smiled at his lords, casting a growl at Molek, who responded in kind.

While Molek and his brother officers had been made in the image of their lords, complete with four arms, blue-tinted skin, and height, Phlegyas and his cadre of dogs had been given a different, bestial form. It was called a blessing, a physical reward for their loyalty and service to the gods and their cause, but Molek thought it a curse. Phlegyas had been transformed from a normal, basic-stock biped into a two-legged wolf-like *thing*. His hair was thick, matted, and most likely flea infested. His teeth were broken and yellow and not numerous enough to fill his snout. His ears and tail had a mind of their own. And yet, Phlegyas was overjoyed, in a state of rapture at having been made like this.

Molek supposed, in a way, it was fitting. Phlegyas and his ilk had already mentally been dogs, even before their transformation; they were loyal to whoever fed them and told them pleasantries and stupidly fought without question or planning.

"Arkhegtis Phlegyas," Sky Father greeted after the beastman paid his deference. Molek cringed. The gods always used this creature's proper titles, never his. "What brings you before us today?"

Phlegyas flashed a grin at Molek before turning his full attention to the gods. "I bring news, oh master and mistress of creation. My scouts have spotted the pink surface-walker and a grey bird in the layer of the sharp-ears. They are alive and have found refuge with an unsuspecting tribe."

The chill returned to Molek's blood. Sky Father sat upright, letting go of his bride's hand. He narrowed his eyes. "Your pathetic excuse for soldiers have failed, warmaster. Now three layers have interacted. You deprive me of my rightful glory and upset everything I have been working towards for thousands of years."

Molek instantly fell on his face. "Oh, forgive me, merciful father of the skies, a thousand apologies for the failures of my forces!"

"Is it really so difficult, warmaster?" Ground Mother asked, sneering. "We gave you a single, simple task to accomplish, and your failure to do so has upset three layers! It makes me wonder why my dear husband ever chose to uplift you and your primitive tribesmen."

"We shall redouble our efforts, fertile matron of the soil! If we could only have access to more diggers and more of our stronger warriors, we could . . ."

"Do I detect ingratitude in your voice?" Ground Mother asked. Phlegyas barely hid his snickering.

"No ingratitude, potentate of all that grows! I was merely requesting more forces so that I may better glorify you!"

"Enough, I grow tired of your whining," Sky Father muttered. "Arkhegtis, this problem is now yours. Kill the interloper."

"And what of the sharp-ears who give them shelter?"

Sky Father paused to consider this for a moment, all four hands clasped in different gestures of pondering. "Wait until the interloper leaves their settlement. The sharp-ears are diligent, if foolish, worshippers. I shall need them for my glory."

"It will be done my lords." Phlegyas stood, bowed, mockingly sneered at Molek, and exited the chamber, his tail wagging triumphantly. Molek watched the dog leave, making a promise to himself to see Phlegyas killed one day. Slowly, if possible, and painfully, as a necessity.

"Leave us as well, warmaster," Sky Father instructed. "Kill the survivors of the assault as recompense for their failure. Then kill whatever family they have."

"Yes, oh father of creation." He bowed and left without another word. When the time came, Molek wondered, would he kill those two before the dog or after?

10

They climbed down from the walls and walked to the fenced-off area. A grand table and benches had been brought out. Many elves in their finery and adorned with gold and silver jewelry stood around the fence, eagerly waiting for the guests of honor to sit before they took their seats. The elvish cooks had prepared a truly exceptional banquet; the table was filled with baskets of fresh bread, small cauldrons of soup, bowls overflowing with vegetables, and horns of ale. The centerpiece was one of the beavers, butchered and served over choice cuts of game, garnished with fine cheeses. The meat was coated in a glaze and seasoned with a dry rub of herbs. Singers in grey robes, properly called bards, stood at both ends of the table, ready to add a show to the meal.

The center of the table had been reserved, Rí MabCynan and Ruith sitting on one side and Friedrich and Vytilia on the other. As they sat down, Friedrich was almost instantly swarmed by female elves, their ears perked up and pink with excitement. They fought for seats and the opportunity to feed him or give him drink, each one sharing their merits and showing off what they contributed to the meal.

For Vytilia, on the other hand, the male elves all avoided eye contact with her, their ears pointed downward and red-purple with discomfort. Aside from Rí MabCynan and Ruith, none spoke to her, and when they brushed against her while reaching for food, they tensed up with fear, stammering out a string of apologies and prayers. When she looked at the females all fighting for a chance to impress Friedrich (who was, all things considered, taking this in stride), she felt unusual. *Is it jealousy*? she wondered. That was an unusual feeling. And it was extraordinarily rare that her face would burn like this. She tried putting it out of her mind.

"We save the great table for big meetings," Rí MabCynan clarified. "Most days, we all would just eat in our own rooms, but with such great guests, well, I made sure we spared no honor!"

"My gratitude," Vytilia responded.

"And of course, we're bringing only the finest for the two of you. Cynbel! Another horn for our guests, fill it with the oldest!" Rí MabCynan ordered.

Several females cut off slices of the roast for Friedrich, and after some strong convincing, they relented and let him feed himself. He bit a large piece off, surprised at the sweet taste. Vytilia was repulsed. Were these not the same creatures they saw rolling around in the mud?

"How are you eating that?" Vytilia hiss-whispered in Teutonish. "That is vermin! It is a pest, not a proper food!"

"Didn't you feed me newt on our trip to Nidus?"

"That! That was different. It was a survival situation, and salamandra are not vermin. They are a cousin to our beloved calcerta!"

"It doesn't taste that bad," he told her. "I've never had a chance to try beaver meat. This is pretty good."

She shook her head in exasperation. "And you think drinking blood is strange. Ugh!"

Large, hollowed out animal horns were placed before them, resting upright on a metal stand. An elf brought Friedrich's to his mouth; he eagerly took a drink. "Wow!" he wheezed. "That's strong! And it's an ale. I haven't had one in ages."

Vytilia rolled her eyes, sliding her plate and horn aside, so she could have a clear line of sight to Rí MabCynan and Ruith. "Rí MabCynan, I was wondering if I could ask you a few questions about the history of your people?"

"Oh, forgive me your worship, but do you not want any of our meats? You do us a great honor, and we'd be remiss if we brought out something not to your liking," Rí MabCynan insisted, his ears quivering nervously.

Vytilia sighed. Her parents had taught her better than to stick her nose up at an offered meal. (Though given the common diet with Strixans, this was not a worry, more of a formality.) She stripped off a slice of the vermin-roast and quietly chewed it. Rí MabCynan and Ruith, smiling and nodding, their ears perked up and pink, toasted their horns with Friedrich, who was quickly becoming more and more inebriated. "Your cooks are quite skilled," Vytilia lied, hiding her gags as she suffered through eating the vermin.

"Ah, I bet it's nuttin' like what you can eat in the otherworld. I'm sure the meats and drink there are better than any we have here." He did not know how right he was. "Now, you said you wanted to ask a few questions? I'll have to warn ya, you'll need to ask quickly. I'm startin' to feel like Friedrich."

"Friedrich and I are . . . new in the otherworld. Initiates, so we were sent here to learn as much as we can from first-hand experience. My question is do you have a Rex? Some sort of supreme Rí who can govern all the Budins? Build roads, settle disputes, things like that?" They stared at her blankly until she simplified the words. It was getting to be headache inducing trying to manage three different languages.

Rí MabCynan wiped the beer foam from his mouth. "No. That would be an Ard Rí, but we haven't had one in a long time. Ruith can tell you more about that. The MacMórrígan don't take too kindly when one Rí tuaithe gets too big a head and starts laying claims to the other Budins; it's greatly upsettin' to the gods."

"So, there is not an overarching ruler over the Budins? It is a miracle you have never devolved into war."

"The MacMórrígan remind us of our place," Ruith clarified. "They 'foster' peace between the Budins. My fellow druids and I teach that they, and also the gods, want trade over war."

"That's not to say we don't have war. But it's a small fight, between harvests or birthing time for the livestock, and always at a chosen time or place. It is more of a game than anything; a chosen few fight without death, and the loser hands over a tract a land, a few bina, or a few bushels," the Rí interjected.

"And all of this on account of the MacMórrígan?" They both nodded. *Interesting*, Vytilia thought to herself. It seemed these MacMórrígan were intentionally keeping these people primitive and disunited, but why? She glanced over at Friedrich, to see if he was listening. He was not, instead fighting a battle to stay awake while the female nymphs continued to ply him with food and drink. Most of the other guests were focusing on eating or talking with those around them, occasionally glancing at her and Friedrich.

At least there were not any eavesdroppers or someone like that unsavory Anarawd character. "Tell me please, what is the history of your people? Not just your Budin but your people as a whole?"

"Ah, they're *really* making you learn down here, aren't they? Druid Ruith . . ." He slapped him on the back. "Tell her everythin' she wants to know."

"Aye. Our foredays are a great tale. What would you like to know?"

"How did you get here? Not to this village but this region."

"Hmmm." The druid finished off his drink before answering. Vytilia noticed he had a mug of water with only bread and vegetables on his plate. "That's our most hallowed lore. We didn't always live here. We once lived on a higher world, a world where the sun was yellow and the lands green. Our kind, the Ellyllon, once had a mighty Ríocht[29] ruled by a long line of powerful Ard Rí, skilled in all manner of draíocht, but we were a godless, lustful, ruthless group. We sought only the lusts of the flesh or to bend the world to our whim. Many great and godly druids and druidesses, taught in the oldest of ways, came forth and warned the Ard Rí and his subjects that we were abandoning the gods and incurring their wrath. Very few of the Ard Rí and his underlings listened to the druids, but a few families did. They would follow the druids to secluded wildernesses, away from the sin of our leaders.

"Then the great ending came. The gods came down in their chariots, followed by floods of fuathan, defeating great armies and slaying the mightiest Rí and their warriors. The land was covered in bodies. Even the most stalwart Caers fell, destroyed by great winds and the ruptures of the ground. Those families who followed the druids, who heeded their warnings, they were spared. They and their offspring were brought to a new world, with a green sun and yellow lands, to live a life free from the sins of the old world. They are our forebearers. We honor them, and the gods, by keeping alive their ways. We've lived this way for time unknowable, free from the wreckage and waste of the old world, and will continue to live like this for time yet known."

"Fascinating." She ruminated on the druid's story. It sounded similar to her own people's history. But the Strixan Empire was not destroyed for its decadence or hubris, and there certainly had not been any messengers or envoys warning them. She needed more information. "These hosts of fuathan, do you know what they look like?"

"Vaguely. There are a few gifts that have been passed down through our Budin of the great ending." He reached into his cloak and produced a necklace. He took it off, handing it to Vytilia. "This was given to me by my granduncle, our Budin's previous druid. It is the only worldly thing we can own." The necklace was leather with three thin golden rectangles hanging from it. Each rectangle

29. Kingdom.

had an engraving. The first was a hooded figure holding a staff in front of a group of figures. The second was the hooded figure leading a small group with bags and children. The third was a chariot rolling over a figure in armor, the four-armed charioteer accompanied by a beast on four legs. The beast had three tails and a long head, remarkably similar to the blue quadruped devils.

"Is this one of the MacMórrígan?" she asked, pointing to the third image.

"No. That is a fuath. The druid lore does not mention the MacMórrígan until after we were brought here. By the same token, we have not seen the fuathan nor the wrath of the gods since."

Vytilia returned the necklace, quietly cursing that they could not afford to spend more time here. This story could impact the history of her people, possibly even the future of Friedrich's. There had been other cataclysms similarly inflicted at the hands of the devils. But who were these gods? Well, false gods, she corrected herself. They were imposters compared to Luna and Sol. Whoever, or whatever, they were, they had to be the connecting factor in this, the unknown leadership rank of the devils, who must have access to world-shattering thaumaturgy to even cause the cataclysm. She would need more information, more sources. Part of her doubted that Ruith told her everything, but the other part had to ask; why would he hold anything back? Perhaps if she asked specific questions, she may get better answers.

"You said that the druids who led the survivors away were trained in ancient ways. What do you mean by that?"

"In the beginning, druids were there to speak on behalf of the gods and to teach the old Ellyllon the ways of standing upright before the gods. But, as the Ellyllon spread and grew, druids took on many more roles, even forgetting their godly tasks. They would write law, help different Rí in the running of their lands, or travel around telling tales as a bard, singing in exchange for bits of shiny metals. But, with the great ending, we have returned to our godly tasks, first and foremost. We still write laws, bless weddings, and help our Rí, but the work of the gods is above all else."

Vytilia found that concerning, the more she thought on this. If the ancient nymphic druids had once been religious leaders, and then forgotten that duty, then were *reminded* before this "great ending," then that meant there were sentient, sapient devils. Devils capable of speech. Devils capable of negotiation. Devils capable of infiltration and subterfuge. All tactics they used on the nymphs, but not on the Strixans.

Why?

Why was there such a difference in tactics? Why were small groups of Strixans not offered a chance to surrender?

Unless, some were? Were there Strixans mixed in here among the nymphs? They made gladii. Perhaps a Strixan colonist had taught them how to do this. Maybe the cataclysms were the same, maybe the nymphs had been isolated, far from the Strixan population centers when their false gods took them away.

"Druid Ruith," she began. "Friedrich has an interest in fantastic stories, particularly about monsters and frightening creatures. Do you know any I could tell him to make our travel time past faster? Specifically, do you know of any stories about creatures who . . . drink blood. That is a rather frightening idea." She looked over to Friedrich. He was resting his head on the table, and his heartrate indicated he was close to falling asleep. The females feeding him had lost interest and began to disperse.

Ruith paused to think, glancing at Rí MabCynan, who only shrugged. Finally Ruith shook his head, a forlorn look on his face. "I'm sorry, your worship, I do not know any tales like that. I . . . well, I've never heard of anything drinking blood. Eating it, perhaps, in sausages and soups, but never drinking it right from the body."

Damn, Vytilia thought.

"We could tell you the tale of the banshee," Rí MabCynan offered, conciliatorily. "It's a herald of coming death. It might be enough to scare Friedrich."

"That will not be necessary," Vytilia told them. "I suppose I will have to use my imagination instead."

Rí MabCynan finished off his horn of beer. The food had started to get cold, and the singers had started playing quieter and slower tunes. "Well, it's gettin' late. We best be clearin' the table and headin' to bed. Now, will you and Friedrich be wantin' a room together?"

"What?!" she wheezed. "We do not have that relationship. Just, just stick him with the rest of the drunks. I will take a proper bed, and I do still require a proper change of clothing. And, he would like a pair of hose as well."

"Hose?"

"The two-legged garment you wear."

"Ah, you mean some braca! Of course! Me wife Brigit will stitch him up a pair. And he can take my bed. I wouldn't dare dream of leavin' him out here with the rest of us! You can sleep with Brigit and our daughters. She'll fix up a nice set of clothin' for ya." He smiled. "Might take her a while, we don't have anyone with your height or your bosom!" He sobered up for a minute, his eyes going wide. "Sorry, your worship. I let the drink get the better of me. Brigit?" He called down to the end of the table. A plump female nymph skipped over. She smiled up at Vytilia and took her by the hand, quickly gasping at the cold touch before leading her into the hall and to the left towards the bedrooms. Four male nymphs followed, carrying Friedrich on their shoulders to the master bedroom.

• • •

As the dishes and benches started to be removed, Llewelyn MabCynan leaned against the table, nibbling on a bone. Ruith cleared away his plate before returning to his seat next to him. "Ask you for your thoughts, Rí tuaithe?"

"Aye, go ahead."

"Do you think those two are really from the otherworld? Some sort of gods?"

Llewelyn shrugged. "I mean you saw both their hands; they've got the mark of the gods. I don't know why they wouldn't be. And you saw that cantrip she did. Who but a god could do something that powerful? She kindly even avoided the rug."

"But they know so little of us, of our ways and tales. Did you not find it weird they did not have this knowledge?"

"Careful Ruith, you're soundin' like Anarawd. I don't think it right for a druid to be worrisome. And you remember what she said; they're new. They were sent here to learn. And there must be tens of thousands of Ellyllon. How can we honestly expect all of the gods to keep track?" He got up from the table to find a clear spot on the floor to lie down. "The gods have not been with us in the flesh for so long. I think we should rejoice that they have chosen our Budin over all the others and not fret over small things."

"I suppose you're right. The last thing I want is to become the next Anarawd." Ruith stood up. "But as your druid, I must say I don't think it right for a Rí tuaithe to drool over a goddess' breasts." He started walking to the gate.

"I weren't droolin'. And that weren't me talkin'. That was the drink! And it was a warning, not drooling! Anyway, she didn't strike me down!" he called back. "And if she does, make sure you take good care of Gruffudd! Don't let Anarawd tear him down if he takes the seat!"

• • •

Friedrich was gently dumped in the master bedroom while Brigit led Vytilia to a series of smaller bedrooms. Four juvenile hen nymphs stirred awake as Brigit opened the door. "Careful now, watch yer head. Shame we didn't take into account your height when we made our home." Vytilia had to nearly squat down to enter the bedroom. "There's a lamp hanging from the ceiling, your worship, if you wouldn't mind."

Vytilia reached up and snapped her fingers, turning on the lamp. It was a small crystalline box, hanging from a chain, using . . . sunstones as light. It was translucent and white, bathing the room in a soft light. Perhaps the generosity of Luna and Sol extended to even non-Strixans.

The young hens looked up at Vytilia in awe, whispering to one another. "Don't stare li'l plached. Ya know it ain't polite," Brigit chided.

"These are your daughters?" Vytilia asked as she sat by the bed, her head nearly reaching the lamp.

"Aye, these are me lovelies and why me midriff hangs over me belt." Brigit laughed. "Now, if you wouldn't mind standing up as tall as you can, I'll show you a few of my pieces; you pick one you like, then I'll start fixin' 'em. It'll be ready for you in the morning. I'll have to guess Friedrich has the same lengths as you."

"You will work through the night?" Vytilia asked.

"Ah, ain't no trouble. I like sewing, especially at night. Gives me time to think and keeps me away from Llewelyn's snoring." The nestlings all giggled.

Brigit opened a trunk at the foot of a bed and started pulling out several brightly colored garments, laying them out on the bed. The colors were shocking: rich and vibrant reds, bright and sparkling yellows, soft and cozy greens. And there were patterns! Diamonds, swirls, marbling, colors and fabrics blended together to create a veritable tapestry. Vytilia looked down at the legionary tunic and cloak she was wearing. It seemed bleak and dead by comparison. She frowned at the possible metaphor that could be used there.

"Did you make all these?" Vytilia asked.

"I just put them together. My home Budin, the Dunsay, they're master weavers. They make the cloth." Brigit picked up a dress, holding it in front of Vytilia. It was an exquisite, long, single-piece dress, dyed a rich blue, more befitting a formal gala than travelling.

"Do you have anything more rugged?" Vytilia asked. Brigit nodded, digging through the trunk. "The Dunsay? You are not a native MabCynan?"

"Aye. The gods gifted us the best land for growing flax and fibers, so we've always been masters of sewing, but we don't have a lot of good fishing grounds or grazing land. The MabCynan do, so my father and Llewelyn's father struck a deal, and that's how I came here."

"You were married off to secure a supply of . . . fish?" She wanted to ask what a fish was, but that was a question reserved for Friedrich.

"Aye, fish and trwynpeth[30] wool, though there were some other whys as well, but that was the main one." She held up a thick green skirt and a brown, long-sleeved top. "How's this?" Brigit held it up against Vytilia, noting where she'd have to loosen it and lengthen it.

"Better. Is it suitable for active movements? I like to run and jump and climb."

"I'll have to strengthen the seams, but I can do it." She put the rest of the clothes away and pulled out a sewing kit.

Vytilia sat on the floor, leaning against the edge of the bed, the younger nymphs quickly surrounding and staring at her. "Plached, I told ya not to stare at our guest! She almost fried Anarawd for threatening your father. Don't think she won't do the same to you!"

"Oh, it is alright." Vytilia ruffled the hair of one. "I rather them look on in awe than how the tier- uh, males look at me." The one whose hair she ruffled held her hand, touching each finger with quiet reverence.

"Are the fir looking at you greedily? If you can point out their faces, I'm sure Ruith can remind them of the proper respect we show the gods."

"Not lustfully. Quite the opposite in fact. They avoided looking at me."

"Oh." Brigit smiled slightly. "I say this with all due respect, but I would too if I were them. You're rather scary to them, and I mean that nicely."

---

30. Lit. "nose thing," the large, one-horned creatures tended to by the herdsmen outside.

"The he—females though seemed to ignore me. All their eyes were on Friedrich, interestingly enough."

Brigit looked up from her sewing, raising a curious eyebrow at Vytilia before returning to her sewing. "You sound surprised! Why I know all the bina were thinking alike. They were trying to impress him! They all wanted him to stay and take one of them to wife. Course, they lost interest after the drink took him. Hard to win over a fer, even a god, when he's all drunk up."

"Why were they trying to get married?"

"Friedrich's a handsome fer, a rugged, handy charm to him. And being a god on top of that, well, I don't know a ban alive who wouldn't want to be his wife! Every bina dreams of giving birth to a great warrior. Even I did in my younger years. A fer, nay a god like Friedrich, would surely father some mighty powerful Ellyllon. A long line of warriors, of leaders, sprung from a god, is every mother's dream for her sons."

Vytilia cheeks started to burn violet, soliciting a giggle from the daughters. If that were true, Friedrich would not abandon her, would he? As doubt started to creep in on her, she quickly changed the subject. "Brigit, I do not suppose you happen to know any history, do you? I find the subject fascinating, but I got all I could out of the druid."

"His-tory?"

"Stories, er, tales, about the times that came before."

"Hmmm, my great aunt was a druidess, but she never told us many tales of the time before. I know plenty of Teg tales if you'd like. Mostly about making sure children behave!" The daughter holding Vytilia's hand quickly let go.

"Teg tales?" She sounded like Friedrich.

"Aye. We used to have kin, long ago before the gods brought the Ellyllon here, called the Teg or the Tylwyth Teg. Where we Ellyllon lived in great bailes and caers, the Teg lived freely out in the wilds, hiding in trees and lochs and great pits for digging stone and ore. They were closer to the world than we were, and my great aunt even said they were the first Ellyllon, even teaching the first druids. But, where our forefathers turned against the world and became selfish, the Teg turned against the new and retreated into the wilds. To have a child taken by the Teg was a great blessing in the ending days, for the Teg freed them from the sins and awfulness of the old world."

"Where are they now?"

She shrugged. "Nobody knows, though most druids will tell you they returned to the otherworld. There are whispers that they became the . . ." she glanced around, told her children to cover their ears, then leaned in towards Vytilia, "the Gwyllion."

"The what?"

Brigit shook her head. "I'll say no more on them your worship. I'm sorry. I shouldn't have said anything at all."

Vytilia furrowed her brow. These nymphs were as superstitious as Friedrich was. She would not address this strange "Gwyllion" Brigit had mentioned. Doing so was liable to cause an incident. She thought about inquiring about these "Teg" creatures but decided against it. It was probable if she asked, Brigit would spend several hours telling Vytilia juvenile stories that had nothing to do with history or reality. Still, she wanted to know more of the nymphic cataclysm and how or if it related to the Strixan's.

"Brigit, I do not suppose your people have any sort of written record, do they? Some sort of holy codex or a library?" She realized her mistake and quickly reexplained her request in smaller words.

Brigit shook her head, not even looking up from her sewing. "Nay, only the druids write anything down, and only they know the words. And, if Ruith didn't share it with you, I don't think we do."

Damn, Vytilia thought, *foiled again*. Maybe she needs to meet other druids. Perhaps they know more of the history than Ruith, and the more she asked, the more she'll understand. "Where is your home Budin, the Dunsay?"

"All the way on the other side of Càrn Dubh, about a three-dark journey. Haven't been able to go back since I wedded Llewelyn. He's such a homebody, and every time he gets up the strength to visit, I find out I'm going to have one of the wee ones, then he calls off the plans and . . . ." She sighed. "It's a whole mess. My mother has never even met her grandbabies! Ah, don't mean to bore you with my gossip, your worship. I'm sure our little problems aren't even a worry for someone of your skill. I do appreciate the listening ear though; the plached just roll their eyes and play with their dolls every time I talk." She snapped at one of her daughters who had started braiding Vytilia's hair.

Vytilia looked back at the girls and mouthed "continue" to them. "Do you not like it here?" She turned back and asked Brigit.

She sighed again. "I don't hate it. No, I do like it; I love me wee-ones, I have good friends here, and Llewelyn's a good husband. It's only, ever since our son was born, that's all he cares about, making sure he's fit to carry on the name, to take the Rí-seat, hardly has any time for me anymore. I mean, I can see why as much as I can anyway; if he does a poor job teaching Gruffudd, then someone like Anarawd will sneak his way into power. I just . . . wish it weren't so."

"I can empathize," Vytilia confided.

Brigit looked up, smiling. "You do? Well not with that Friedrich, right? He doesn't act like our lads. He's very respectful of you, letting you talk, not staring. You two seem like good friends. Are you two, well, betrothed, or . . ."

Vytilia coughed, covering her face. "Not with him, er, with anyone. We are only travelling companions, and that is it. I was referring to immediate family. This . . . relation similarly is focused on other work. And it was not always like that."

"That's a shame. I didn't know the gods could have such similar relations as us worldly folk. Do godly children also disobey their mothers?" All of the daughters had started to braid Vytilia's hair.

She just laughed and smiled. "It is fine. Let them have their fun. I do not mind."

"You're right and kind, your worship. Plached, make sure it's your best work, only the best for someone of her grade."

"I have been meaning to ask or confirm to be more exact; what exactly made you realize Friedrich and I came from the otherworld?"

Brigit opened her mouth but quickly closed it, biting her lip as she stopped herself from finishing a sentence. "Why, the mark of the gods, your worship. Any ellyll[31] with their sight could see that!"

"I understand, but things can get muddied in translation. I just want to be clear and ensure the proper teachings are still being followed: the mark of the gods is . . . ?"

"Your extra finger!"

Vytilia looked down at her hands, bending each one individually. "Ohhhhhhhhhhhh," she said to herself. Now that Brigit had pointed it out to her, it seemed obvious. Comparing her hands to the nymphs', they were missing the equivalent to the middle digit. "Ah, I am glad to see that you have continued to remember the ancient marks. Now do you remember why it was given in the first place?"

"The Ellyllon lost their fifth finger when the gods brought us to the new world," the youngest daughter to Vytilia's right an-

31. Singular of Ellyllon.

swered. "Mama says they changed our forefathers, so we always remember to not be sinful like the others, and so we know how to recognize the gods and their heralds."

Brigit beamed with pride. "Well done, Aelwen, glad to see someone was listening to their bedtime tales!"

Vytilia stared at her hands again. The nymph gods . . . changed them? That must have required some powerfully advanced form of thaumaturgy, powerful beyond comprehension, to completely alter an entire race at the basic hereditary level. How could something like that even be accomplished? Is such a thing even possible? Strixan limbs and most organs grew back naturally, faster when visiting a physician. That was a power known. When it regrew, it was the same as before, except for any previous scarring. But the power to completely alter a being's heredity? She recalled the porcine her people grew, how ancient survivors bred them selectively for their wooly coats. Had they used thaumaturgy? Maybe changing a finger was not implausible, but that would require millennia of study, numberless resources, and an intricate understanding of the fundamentals of life! There was not a being alive who could do that. But a powerful, immortal god had an eternity to study . . . . She shook her head. She could not afford such blasphemous thoughts at a time like this. There were not any other gods, only Luna and Sol.

Whatever these false gods were, the devils were the connecting factor. The Strixans, nymphs, and man had all heard of them or encountered them at some point in their history. But there were so many unknowns. If she would not get more from the nymphs, she would have to find out more from mankind. Then when she returned to Nidus, she would have to beg and plead to access the private collections of the other patrician families and the locked portions of the library for information not collected at the Sanctum Sanctorum.

"So, your worship, will you be joining us for the lightbreak meal tomorrow?" Brigit asked.

Vytilia had to blink to recollect her thoughts. "I do not think so. We have greatly enjoyed our time here, but we do have other obligations. I do believe we will come back and visit. I would like to meet the other Budins and their druids, especially to learn their histories."

"Ah, do you really have to leave so soon? MabCynan may be a small Budin, but we offer everything we can. I do hope we didn't offend you in some way."

"Not at all, your hospitality has been impeccable. It is just circumstances outside of our control. If given the chance, I would love to stay here, document and learn as much as I could."

Did she really just say that? Spending a month living amongst these primitives in their huts? How could she, the descendant of emperors, say such a thing? She looked at the nestlings braiding her hair, the big eyes and wide smiles each of them had. She looked at the skill with which Brigit adjusted the clothes. She really did just say that. They were, by Strixan standards, barbarians, but they were not barbarous. And it sounded like it was not even their fault. If their gods or whatever had not purposefully kept them like this, they might have advanced to the resplendent palaces and cities of the old empire. They might have created an advanced and centralized civilization comparable to her own. She looked down in shame; even if they thought she was a god, they had still been kind and opened their homes. They treated her better than she had treated Friedrich, whom her people were dependent on for survival.

"Your family is wonderful, Brigit," Vytilia told her. "Your daughters are incredibly kind, and you have taken me in as one of your own."

"Oh, I wouldn't say that, your worship. If I treated you as one of me own, I'd have given you quite the scolding by now."

"Mama likes to put on an act," one of the girls whispered. "She spoils us whenever guests aren't around." All of the sisters giggled.

"Well, if there is enough time, perhaps we will join you for the morning meal."

"Excellent." Brigit stood up, showing off the now lengthened skirt. "I'll set this aside, and you can change in the morning. I'm sure Friedrich would love to see you in such a wonderful outfit."

"Now wait—"

• • •

Much time passed before Friedrich rolled off the bed onto the floor, groaning as he rubbed his throbbing head. Daylight was beginning to peek through a glassless window on the wall. It only now occurred to Friedrich how many times he'd woken up in a strange place within the last few weeks. He stood up and stretched. The chainmail and other armor he was wearing made a loud and headache-inducing scraping sound as he moved. He was in some sort of bedroom with a low but wide wooden bed, a chest, and a small woven rug.

As the last of the previous night's ale started filtering through his system, he started to wake up. He made for the door and followed the hallway to the main hall then made his way outside, finding the ground now covered in half-asleep and half-drunk elves, snoring louder than a blizzard. Rí MabCynan and Ruith the druid were awake. MabCynan sat against the fence, holding his head while Ruith stood at his side. Friedrich walked over to them, carefully avoiding stepping on any sleeping elves. "Ah, Friedrich, your worship, you've awoken!" Ruith greeted him. "And how are you feeling?"

Friedrich stretched his neck and rubbed his head. "Good. I didn't break anything last night, did I? That was some strong drink."

"Aye, mighty great taste too," Rí MabCynan agreed. "You didn't break anythin' though, just passed out after having your fill, so I gave you my bed." He rubbed his temple and his lower back. "Starting to regret sleepin' out here, however. Don't you know any way to make the ground softer Ruith?"

"A druid's skill comes from the gods, Llewelyn. I don't think they'd approve." The Rí muttered something under his breath. "Friedrich, will you and her worship, Vytilia, be joining us for the lightbreak meal?"

"I, I don't know. We . . ." He remembered the cover they'd crafted the day before. "We're needed back in the otherworld rather soon, and we do have to get all the way to that mountain."

"Càrn Dubh," Ruith gently corrected.

"If you need anything, don't hesitate to ask," Rí MabCynan added. "As you head for the Càrn Dubh, you'll be leaving our lands and crossing into the lands of Budin Alessa, bunch of hard-noses those ones."

"They aren't godly, and their druids are usually strongarmed by their Rí, so they might not pay the two of you the right respect," Ruith clarified. "If so desired, myself and a number of our warriors can accompany you to ensure they do not hassle you."

"Ah come on Ruith, you saw her blast that hole yesterday, and he's got a sword and armor. What kind of gods would they be if they couldn't handle a few Alessa bastards?" Rí MabCynan scolded.

"We'll be well," Friedrich insisted. "Though I thank you for the offer. If I may ask for something, however, can we have a larger bag?"

"Of course! When Brigit comes out, I'll have her fetch you one. Oh, speak of she . . . ." He stopped as a door to the hall opened.

Vytilia stepped out, accompanied by Brigit and a few younger female elves. Vytilia was wearing a long skirt and blouse, both bright but earthy colors, much more colorful than anything he'd seen Strixans wear. She had a fine stole, dyed a deep earthy green, clasped with a brooch wrapped around her shoulders. Her hair had been braided, done with such skill, it looked like a fine work of art.

"Wow," Friedrich squeaked, tugging at his collar.

Rí MabCynan grinned. "I know how you feel lad. I feel the same way every time Brigit gets all doled up. She hasn't done it for a while though." He stepped away from the fence, bowing before Vytilia and kissing his wife. "Your worship, you look heavenly, another job by our dear Brigit no doubt?"

Vytilia twirled. "You are lucky to have her Rí MabCynan. I expect you to take care of her." she ruffled the hair of two of the elf girls. "And your fine daughters here, nothing is more vital than family. You cannot afford to forget that."

"Will you be joining us for a meal then?" Brigit asked.

She and Friedrich exchanged a glance. He looked well-rested and healthy, and she was still invigorated from both resting and from the blood she had the previous day. She did want to stay, but she still had a duty. She needed to get back to her people, let the Concilium know they had not perished. She sighed. "Unfortunately, we cannot. We will have to eat on the go."

"Ah, 'tis a right shame. The girls and I really were hoping you could stay another day."

"Don't get all sad Brigit. They've got godly work to do. She's got no time for sitting around and gossiping," Rí MabCynan lightly corrected. "I was just warning Friedrich how you'll be crossing into Budin Alessa lands, and how they're all a right bunch of bastards." Brigit flicked his ear, telling him not to swear in front of the children.

"I—we appreciate the warning, but rest assured, anything this Budin throws at us, we shall be prepared." She snapped her fingers, dancing fire on the tips as the daughters all looked up in amazement.

"I would like to add my hope that you return," Ruith interjected. "Your skills with draíocht far surpass that of any known druid. I do hope you can teach me one day."

Vytilia was starting to get crowded with all of the nymphs looking up at here. They all wanted her to stay, to enlighten them, practically asking for her to civilize them. She furrowed her brow. Should she stay? What about the empire? Well, if she got Friedrich back, he could find someone else to take to the surface, and she could stay here, comfortably surrounded by this family and these colors and all this life. Being here, listening to Brigit, spending time with her daughters, it filled a hole Vytilia had not acknowledged in her soul. Was it a crime to want to stay here, to ingratiate herself with this loving family? Certainly not, there was not a jurist dead or alive who would find fault in that.

Friedrich grabbed her arm, gently pulling her away. "Now remember, we will always be with you in your hearts. We now consider you our friends and will find the time to come back and visit. But please also remember, we do have business to take care of in the otherworld."

"Certainly, of course." Vytilia nodded.

"Now if I could just get that bag before I go. And we'll need some food as well. I don't suppose you have any blood sausage, do you? It's one of my favorites." Friedrich winked at Vytilia; she hid a smile. "Oh and some leather to cover my sword, there are some sticky fingers even in the otherworld." He tapped the gilded sheathe on his hip.

"Right, of course. Brigit, bring the lad a bag would you? That good brown one in our room should suffice."

Brigit frowned. "We're in the middle of a farewell! You can't send one of your drunks?" She gestured to the elves sprawled on the ground. "Here you go, your worship. Vytilia had me make you these." She handed him a pair of trousers; Friedrich's eyes lit up.

"Come now lass, don't fight me in front of our guests. You're setting a bad example for the plached."

"And this is a better example for Gruffudd?"

Rí MabCynan scowled. "You're forgetting your place, Brigit." He gritted his teeth.

"Hold on, it's alright," Friedrich interrupted. "No need to start fighting on our behalf. Why don't you go get the bag, and she gets the food? You're both doing work."

Brigit proudly harumphed while the Rí grumbled. "Aye, suppose that's some of that godly wisdom I've heard about. Come along Ruith, help me find that bag."

"But I—" Rí MabCynan grabbed the druid, nearly dragging him towards the hall.

The grounds started to empty as sleeping elves started to sober and wake up. They reverently acknowledged both Friedrich and Vytilia as they left. "You've certainly taken a shine to the elves," he noted.

She folded her arms. "Well, we had some . . . bonding moments, I suppose you could call them. And I must admire her skills as a seamstress." *He certainly embraced them as well, at least at dinner,* she thought.

"She did a good job. You look, ah, er, never mind."

Vytilia turned away. "I will allow it, just this once."

"It's a good outfit. You look nice. You always do," he quietly added.

"*Gratias.* And quick thinking, both recently and back at the wall, when you brought up the otherworld. I think it stopped them from turning against us. How did you know about the otherworld?"

"Oh, it turns up in some of our tales. Anytime a child goes wandering off, the mom always scolds them, says some kobolds are going to take them away to the otherworld to work on a mushroom tillage or something. And, I wasn't lying; we really do need to get to an 'otherworld.'"

Brigit said the same thing about the Teg taking children. "You are a peculiar specimen, Friedrich Bauer. It appears all those stories you go on about are coming in handy."

"Just glad I can help. Not all of us can shoot fire out of our fingers."

The elves returned with the supplies. Friedrich gave Vytilia his haversack, taking the larger one Rí MabCynan gave him. She tucked the blood sausages in her bag while he stored the trousers in his then started to take off his armor. "Wait," she whispered in Teutonish. "Remember what they said? About the MacMórrígan? Same principle as the devils." He grumbled about the weight but agreed, tossing the bag over his shoulder.

"Oh, great ones, before you go, may we offer these gifts to you, a token of our following in the ways of the almighties?" Rí MabCynan held out two golden torcs for each of them. They accepted, tucking the gifts into their waistbands.

"Now before you go, do you have any wisdom to pass on?" Ruith asked.

"Assuredly, we do." Vytilia cleared her throat then pointed at Rí MabCynan. "Llewelyn MabCynan, your charge as leader of your people is a great one, a duty you cannot shirk from, but you have other duties as well. Care for your family, especially your wife. She is wise and can greatly aid you. We expect only the best from those who guide the budins. Listen and care for her, lest you risk the displeasure of the heavens." Rí MabCynan's eyes went wide, and he fell to his knees.

"I swear on the grave of my forefathers, oh great ones, that I shall heed this charge! For the great name of MabCynan!" He stood up, embracing his wife. "Whatever you want my sweet, ask, and I shall grant it."

Brigit grinned from ear to ear. "Spend more time with me. Take me out hunting and fishing. Oh! And I want to go see my mother. And I want another wee one or maybe two, haven't decided yet."

"But we already have five!" Rí MabCynan protested. Vytilia narrowed her eyes. "Of course, as you wish."

"Farewell Budin MabCynan." Friedrich waved as they made for the gate. "Remember to avoid fighting and seek frith! And keep brewing that ale!" They headed down towards the bottom of the hill, all while elves stopped their business to stare, whispering and commenting to one another, some kneeling or bowing.

"The level of piety amongst these people is incredible," Vytilia commented. "I wonder, had the Strixans shown this much reverence to Luna and Sol, could our tragedy have been adverted?"

"I wouldn't bet on it. Everyone goes to church on the surface, but it feels like some new awfulness happens about every ten years. Godliness doesn't mean much."

"There is a difference between simply attending a service and true piety."

Friedrich shrugged. "Well, it's easy to be godly when a god takes a stroll through your hamlet."

11

There was not much either wished to discuss as they walked further and further away from Bryn Adref towards Càrn Dubh. They were crossing several miles of empty grassland and fields, then they would come to a small grove of trees, and beyond that was the mountain. There were no hills or other villages to see, just miles of a slight incline to walk. The silence as they walked was caused by both being absorbed in their own thoughts.

To Friedrich, the experience with the elves seemed like a dream: captured by wildfolk, treated like a god, then sent on his merry way. It was as if they were lost children found and fed by a kind stranger before being given directions home. Should he go back? He didn't want to abuse their kindness, but life there might be better than anything offered to him on the surface. He'd be treated well, never have to worry about gold, and could find some sort of job to make a living. He could take an elf wife and live out his days in peace, never worrying about the next war or sickness on the horizon. Maybe he could take multiple, see what life was like as a Tujue Sultan. But, Frau Beck would probably find out and give him a verbal lashing like he'd never had before. She had an uncanny sense for that.

For Vytilia, the experience was revelatory but frustratingly brief. She felt she was on the cusp of something, a historical discovery that could shake the very idea of history to its core. Somehow everything was connected: the nymphs, the Strixans, mankind, the cataclysms, the devils. All of these could be part of something larger and grander, possibly even sinister, more so than their histories would lead them to believe. There were unseen forces at work, godlike forces, and she was determined to see them. She just needed more information, more sources, more accounts, more of everything except time. For her kind, time was a limitless resource.

She wanted to discuss it with Friedrich, at least juggle ideas off of him, but would he be helpful? He knew so little of his own history. What help could he be? All he knew were juvenile phantom stories, nothing of history or events. The druid, for all his primitiveness, at least was the closest the nymphs had to a scholar. Even if his account was embellished and mythologized, it was too similar to her own people's to be false. She glanced over at Friedrich. How did his people fit into all of this? They must have been around. An entire race cannot appear from nothing, and he had heard of, or heard stories of, both the nymphs and her own people.

"Friedrich. Do you remember, before the nymphs captured us, I asked if you could tell me more about the tales your people tell?"

"Yes, and you said you'd tell me how your witchcraft works."

"I recall. What do you know, or at least what your people know, first about the Strixans then about the nymphs?"

He cracked his neck then shook his head to wake himself up. "This is what I know: a vampire is an undead, blight spreading, evil wight that drinks blood, can do witchcraft, and almost always hunt at night. Whenever someone dies in the nighttime, usually a young girl, a vampire hunter will arrive, find the freshest grave, then cut off the body's head, always with a silver weapon, and then rub garlic all over the body."

"They believe the corpse is the one who did the murder?" He nodded. "That is ludicrous; has anyone ever actually *seen* a corpse climb out of the grave and start walking?"

"Well, they must have! How else would they know who does the killing? When I camped out in the woods, I saw some strange things in the moonlight. I've never seen a dead body walking, but I've heard enough folk talk about it that I think it's true."

"So, the villagers find a dead body that has been exsanguinated—" They looked at one another. "Apologies, drained of blood, then they call a hunter, he exhumes a body, desecrates it, then leaves? That sounds like a scam to me. How do they know the hunter was not the one who killed the victim in the first place?"

"Well, towns don't have an on-hand vampire hunter. By the time they reach one, there's usually been a few more deaths."

"All exsanguinated?"

He nodded. "Usually. Then once the hunter leaves, deaths stop happening."

"I hope you know I find all of this wildly implausible, downright ridiculous."

"I did too the first time. But after hearing different folk tell different but similar tales six or seven times in different parts of the Realm, I started to lean towards it being truth, even more so after meeting some Wenden who'd fled from the Sultanate. They hate the Tujue, call them all sorts of names, but they won't talk about vampires or any night things. If you even mention the word, they stare at you, make the rays of the sun, and beseech. Only hunters talk about them openly, even then, only in hushed whispers."

"They never give a reason why?"

"They don't need to. Talking about evil, invites evil; that's what my landlady would always say. It's like moths to a flame. You mention vampires, and then every dead body around will start to rise from the grave."

Brigit acted the same way about those Gwyllion, Vytilia recalled.

She furrowed her brow. Why the association of Strixans and the living dead? Her people were very much alive; they thought, they ate, they drank, and they procreated. What about that connects to corpses? And where did the belief that the dead could rise again come from? Such a concept was absolutely ludicrous. Mortemopus had long been debunked as an impossible school of thaumaturgy, nothing more than the wild dreams of operandii who were without reason. It must be a form of hysteria, a plague of fear that gripped a town who searched for any explanation. If that were the case, however, one thing stuck with her. "When these 'hunters' desecrate a corpse, you mentioned they use garlic and silver. What is garlic?"

He smiled fondly. "Oh, garlic is great! It's this white-yellow, round bulb that smells amazing, especially when you're cooking. You can buy them for dirt cheap by the bushel then just peel, chop, and throw in the pot. Makes anything smell and taste great."

"Small, white, and bulbous?" She asked herself. "Do you mean allium?"

"I-I don't know. What does allium look like?"

"Well, I do not know. I have never seen it, none among my people have, but we are raised to fear it more than anything else. It is actually the only thing we are taught to fear. It was highly illegal during the empire. Many emperors and Praetors tried to wipe it out. To us, it was, is, the most toxic substance ever created. According to imperial records, most Strixans who touched it, not even consumed, just touched it, would perish. They would lose their eyesight, their throat would start to swell up and close, and they would often develop a rash, then their capillaries would burst. That is not even how you would die. It slowly, painfully, shuts down all major organs until you die a bloody, crumpled mess.

It was a popular poison during the crises before the Concilium took control."

He grimaced. "Ugh, sounds like an awful way to go."

She nodded. "It was. Not even the worst traitors were killed with allium. Though my mother told me there are accounts of emperors who were immune, who would crucify their opponents after a failed poisoning, but this was back in the early days when the empire was still young."

"And what about silver?"

"That is similarly toxic but only lethal if it enters the bloodstream in large quantities or is ingested. Merely touching it and handling it causes a terrible rash and skin damage, though if someone held silver for long enough, it could cause their fingers to fall off. For most, my father and I are the minority immune to silver poisoning." She stopped to think. "If allium is the same as garlic, then somehow, your people know about its toxicity. And they also know about the silver allergy."

"Not necessarily," he interjected. "I've heard of all sorts of items being used to ward off things of the night. Silver and garlic are the easiest to get. In the smaller hamlets, folk will nail a horseshoe to their door to scare off pixies."

"But you have to admit, hunters using those two specifically against supposed 'vampires' is more than coincidental. And remember what I said back at the Arx, how the legend of the vampires is similar to my people."

"What are you getting at?"

She took a deep breath. "I think I may be stumbling upon the greatest discovery in the field of history. Comments made by yourself, and the druid, and even Brigit, they have all made me step back and reexamine what I know. I think there is more to history than what is written down. It is possible that all three of our peoples interacted at some point."

"Or . . . were conquered by your armies."

She shot him an angry look. "Not necessarily. If we had encountered a race like the nymphs, it surely would have been noteworthy enough to be written in the imperial chronicles. Think about it: tribes of short beings who emote with their ears? That is strange enough that any historian worth their salt should have made a comment on it. This is the part that is strange; why is there not a record of any interaction? Surely there must be a reference to them in a war commentary, or a trade deal, or something, even if it is a footnote!"

"Maybe they didn't all interact?" he suggested.

"But that is impossible!" she insisted. She hated admitting this next sentence. "The sword I examined that the chieftain said had been made since ancient times, it was a gladius, the main armament of the legions. Brigit told me about the Teg, who would kidnap children, something you yourself said is a threat used by mothers in your culture. And, you heard what they call themselves: Ellyllon. Does that not sound like 'elf,' what you have called them?"

Friedrich, now not inebriated, began to see the similarities.

"The nymph's civilization was destroyed by the devils, whom they call fuathan, but an advanced, leadership caste of devil was able to preserve some nymphs from destruction. Somehow, your people have heard of both elves and vampires, yet neither of those groups knew about mankind. But Strixans did not know about the nymphs as real creatures, and the nymphs do not have legends of blood-drinking beings in their mythos."

Her eyes widened, and she stopped walking when another realization came upon her. Her mother, when tutoring her, never did spend much time on ethnography of the other Strixan ethnicities. In the time she did spend, however, she made mention of defining cultural and even physical traits. And when she spoke of the Leannán,[32] the smallest of the ethnicities, she spoke about them possessing pointed ears. Not as expressive or long as the nymphs, but more pointed than any other Strixan group. And, they were infamously nomadic and resistant to urbanization.

"Gods above!" She said it like a swear. Could it be the Leannán were hybrids? The result of Strixan colonists mixing with nymph survivors? That was preposterous! The difference in their hereditary would make that impossible! Bovines and porcines cannot mix. "Then if they did not . . ." she spoke the thought out loud. Then, did the Leannán alter themselves as the nymph's false gods had? Or, could it be Luna and Sol had created them differently on purpose? But why would they be so different from the Strixans,

32. The smallest of the Strixan ethnicities, noted for the slight point in their ears and almost only possessing maxilla fangs. They were popular paramours for both Emperors and Praetors, and their influence was a source of constant speculation and controversy. None are known to have survived the Cataclysm.

Striga, or even Lilithans? And where did the design for the gladius come from?

She weighed what she had learned in her mind. The connective tissue was mankind and the devils. Yet, Friedrich said he had never heard of, nor seen a devil before, so those groups had not interacted.

She growled in frustration and continued walking. "Damn it all," she swore, kicking a rock.

"What's wrong?" he asked, both out of legitimate concern and an internal, instinctive fear of an angry Vytilia.

"I am building a temple and missing half of my materials and all of my laborers. There is a connection, I know it, between all our peoples and the devils. But I do not know enough, and everyone I speak to does not know enough." And, what she did not say was that she was afraid that, quite possibly, she was overanalyzing all of this. "I need more information, more sources, more accounts, more records! I am starved like some emaciated, neural predator."

"Well . . ." He scratched the back of his head, laughing nervously. He supposed now would be as good a time as any to tell her about Sol and man. Afterall, she trusted him when they were packing for the trip, she dived down a hole after he fell to almost certain death, and she had gotten him a pair of trousers. Helping her with this "discovery" of hers was at least how he could show his thanks. And she would know better than to spread this news all over the surface or Nidus and whatever unfortunateness that would come with it. "Vytilia, I want to tell you something, but I want an oath from you won't breathe a word of it to anyone."

She raised her eyebrows, staring at him with her head cocked. "What do you mean by that?"

"I mean, what I am about to tell you, I tell it to you as a token of trust. It is . . . dangerous to know."

"Well, you have my word, but I fail to see how this relates to my theory."

He sucked his teeth and scratched his face. "Oh, it is very related." He took one final deep breath. "Your god is my god."

She stopped dead in her tracks again, her large eyes growing even larger. "Friedrich, I will not tolerate blasphemes. What do you mean 'my god is your god?'"

He took a deep breath. "Sol Invictus is, more or less, the god worshipped by mankind and most of Erebus on the surface. I recognized the stonework at the Sanctum Sanctorum. There is a copy, or one similar, in every Hof. The sun and eagle are on flags, coats-of-arms, everything."

She tilted her head again, staring through Friedrich at the ground. Her eye started to twitch as she furrowed her brow and rubbed her knuckles. "Your god . . . is . . . Sol . . . Invictus?" Her face shifted from confusion, to disbelief, then to anger, before quickly shifting to excitement. "Friedrich! Praise and gratitude! This!" Her mouth shook with excitement, and she stammered, trying to get the words out. "T-t-t-this is more connective tissue! And-and-and it has so many implications and new ways to look at history and the connection between our people and diplomacy and—" she stopped.

"And what?"

"And, why do you not worship Luna? In your mythology, what is the moon?"

"The moon is, well, the moon, but it is manned by Holy Máni. He's the man in the moon and an einherjar, a heavenly warrior who watches over mankind in the nighttime."

"And he is a male, a . . . man?" Friedrich nodded. "Damn it all!" she swore again.

"What, isn't this good? It adds to your discovery?"

"It is not enough! It only brings up more questions! How is it that *one* of my people's deities is remembered and venerated, but my people themselves are consigned to shadows and undead monsters? Why is our chief deity, the feminine moon, not present! Why are there not any more answers!" Vytilia bared her fangs, the whites of her eyes started to go purple, and veins bulged in her neck and arms.

"I don't know!" Friedrich squeaked. "I'm not a priest!"

Vytilia took a deep breath through her nose, wiping her face before taking more deep breaths. When she opened her eyes, they were back to normal. "Apologies," she stated calmly. They resumed walking once more.

We'll never reach Càrn Dubh at this pace, Friedrich thought.

"I do not possess the vocabulary to share my frustration," she began, "not with you but with . . . civilization, I suppose. It is such a fragile idea, and its records are so precious and easily destroyed. History is the teacher of life, but it is also a cruel taskmaster."

"When we get to the surface, I'll take you to a High Learn-house," he offered. "It's like those collegiums back at Nidus, except it doesn't teach witchcraft."

"Your people have educational institutes?"

"Don't sound so surprised."

"I was not. It was a tone of curiosity."

He grinned wryly. "We do, if 'educational institute' means what I think it means. They're mostly run by the church, so they'll know the really old lore. They might be able to answer some of your questions."

She saw how far they still were from Càrn Dubh. "We still have a bit of a journey. What do you know of the origins of mankind?"

"Only what Frau Beck taught me. That is to say, what I can recall." He cleared his throat. "Everything goes back to the Half-gods . . . ."

She listened, enraptured as Friedrich gave an admittedly bare bones and somewhat out of chronological order retelling of the mannish cosmological story. There were the Half-gods, the valiant defenders of mankind. The Lightless, the bitter foe of man and god, and the Long Winter, a time of complete darkness when the great war against the Lightless was waged. He also told her what he knew of the Götterdämmerung, the return of the Half-gods and the end of the world.

"Absolutely fascinating!" Vytilia commented as he finished. "I see now why you asked me if we ever referred to ourselves as demigods. That does sound so remarkably similar to the cataclysm. I would be tempted to even call it a mythological retelling of our fall. But, there are so many dissimilarities. If the Half-gods were Strixans, then they would still be around. The Strixan survivors would have tried to set up a continuation of state and continue the veneration of Luna."

"Which is good," Friedrich quickly added, "because if the surface found out the Half-gods were actually bloodsu—, blood *drinking* vampires, it would upturn everything."

She smiled at the self-restraint. "Well, I would not discount any possibility yet. Strixans still *could* be the Half-gods." Friedrich went pale for a second. "I do not understand the hesitance. Would this not vindicate your religion's teachings?"

He winced. "I don't think so. It would make everything a lie. We thought the Half-gods were men, a mightier, more powerful race than us but still men. The church gets legitimacy from carrying on the teachings left by the Half-gods. If men found out they were vampires, the church would be a big lie. That's not even wondering what would happen if the Wenden found out. They fear vampires more than anyone else. They might leave to the Tujue in droves."

"You have a surprising amount of concern for an organization you only speak of with an amount of disdain."

"Just because I don't follow every teaching in the Sagas doesn't mean I think they're bad. No murdering, no oath-breaking, no thieving, those are all good ideas to live by. Where are folk to get goodness from if it isn't taught? I wonder how much of a shitheel I would be if Herr Bergmann and Frau Beck hadn't set me straight."

"That would cause issues. Then, as we deduced back at the tunnel before we met Dracius, and as we have learned from our pointed-ear friends, there was more than one cataclysm." The chances of this were low but not impossible. For diplomacy, at times, comforting lies rather than harsh truths were more acceptable.

Friedrich knew she was humoring him but accepted it anyway. At least it made him less guilty. Now he didn't have this feeling of dread hanging over him, reminding him he may very well be ushering in the Götterdämmerung. "We can, at least, use the tale of the Half-gods to our advantage?"

"How so?"

He tugged at his chainmail. "The church, and gatherers, are always wanting to buy Half-god stuff. I think with a bit of grime and dirt, we can sell these to a High Learnhouse, get enough to buy a few muskets."

"How would that work? If Strixans are not the same as the Half-gods, any trained scholar should know the difference."

"You and I know that they're different, but the rest of the surface doesn't. Even if the church won't buy our stuff, there's bound to be someone who will."

It felt wrong selling off equipment given to them by the Concilium, but in the grand scheme, one shirt of *Lorica Hamata* is worth the survival of her people. "And, when we sell the armor, we can see a scholar!" He nodded. "Look at that, Luna and Sol continue to provide divine providence and guide us in our mission." As excited as she was to speak with a mannish scholar, a small part of her wished it was a coincidence, more for his people's sake than anything else. It would not bode well for relations if her people uprooted centuries of engrained religious teachings.

Friedrich watched Vytilia. The buzz and bubbliness from when they first met had returned. When she talked, Friedrich found himself smiling involuntarily. The drive in her voice, the commitment, it was a relief to meet and listen to someone who was genuine, someone with a real love of something. He had to pull himself away, to look and observe the land around them, watching as the birds flew overhead. He, whether he liked it or not, was starting to be drawn to Vytilia. It only muddied things. They'd be spending a good amount of time together, time to talk, get to know one another, build a friendship, and assumedly, his draw would only increase. If only he had some idea of how to go about this, but he had never been able to observe his parent's relationship closely, and Herr Bergmann had been unwedded (though in his younger years, Bergmann had been a bit of a womanizer). It was doubtful she would return the liking, so should he even bother? Should he just focus on the task at hand? He had so many lines of thinking, so many doubts and questions and worries all swirling around in his head, it was like a headache soup. And this soup, to continue the metaphor, was washed down with a big glass of "he wasn't sure if he could still trust her kind's intentions."

"How about another break?" he asked as they came to a small stream. "There are some trees over there. We can sit in the shade a bit. We've been walking and standing for so long, Càrn Dubh isn't going anywhere." She nodded and headed for the trees, sitting down under the closest while Friedrich started drinking from the stream. The water was lukewarm, quenching but not refreshing. He sat back, looking up at the sky. That could describe this entire place, lukewarm, not too uncomfortable and not too comfortable; there wasn't a breeze, but there wasn't heat. It was mild but only mild. It wasn't necessarily a bad thing, but the longer he stayed outside and observed the nature, he couldn't help but feel something was off. It felt fake like the background on a stage, a world pretending to be something it wasn't.

He splashed water on his face and walked over to Vytilia, sitting down under the tree to her right. He pulled out his dagger and stripped off a piece of bark from the tree, examining it. The wood was soft. He could break it with his hand. He'd never seen a tree like this, a beige trunk, dotted with black knots and yellow leaves. He remembered the great tusked beast she mentioned back at the Arx. Between the elves, the Strixans, and the Half-gods, that meant so much wildlife had also been destroyed. He thought it a pity that so much gentle wildlife had been swept away, lost to time.

Gentle life. He laughed, remembering Greatness, the donkey. *Wait* . . . he stopped laughing, burying his head in his hand. "God forsake it," he muttered.

She leaned over to him. "Something happen?" She checked his hand for cuts.

He coughed, wiping his eyes. "Forsake it all," he swore.

She knelt next to him, placing a hand on his shoulder, withdrawing it, then returning it to his shoulder. "Talk to me."

He leaned back on the tree, his eyes and cheeks red. "Greatness. Herr Bergmann and I owned a donkey, left it outside the Toller Mund." He sniffed, wiping his eyes again. "We just left him there. And now he's probably dead. Son of a bitch, he was a friend," he laugh-cried. "I thought we'd be back in a few stounds. Now it's been a fortnight. He must've thought we abandoned him!"

He was not only talking about a beast of burden, she noted. His heart rate was elevating. "Tell me more."

"Everything hit me all at once," he admitted. "Bergmann dying, falling wegstundes below the surface, finding vampires and elves, I can't take it. None of this should be real. None of this should've happened. Bergmann should still be alive. We should be back in Hertzabrunno! He should've retired to the coast! Damn it, it isn't fair!" He wiped his eyes and spat on the ground. "It's all a sick joke."

Vytilia stood up, watching as he coughed and spat again. "Friedrich, I am sorry for your loss and for everything that has happened. I do not know what I could say to help you."

He stood back up, waving her off. "There's nothing you can say. I just needed to get it off my chest."

She stood next to him. "I do not know if your Church teaches the same principle, but we have passed down since time immemorial that Luna and Sol raise up heroes for the empire in time of need. They did it with the early Strixans, with Princeps Julus, and I firmly believe they did it with Herr Bergmann. He will go down as a selfless hero in our annals, a paragon of virtue. Just as the legionaries, we will honor his sacrifice." She walked in front of him, putting a hand on his shoulder. "I, at least, am grateful to have found you. When I speak with you, I remember providence smiles upon us. And that none will have died in vain."

He looked her in the eye, glancing at his reflection in her deep, golden eyes. His tongue was caught in his throat, and he struggled to form a sentence. He felt bewitched. His worries about losing Greatness, the pain of missing Herr Bergmann, they seemed to vanish, replaced by this comforting feeling in his soul. "I'm . . ." He turned away to smack his lips and form a sentence. "I'm glad you found me too." They both smiled. She gestured for him to lead the way as they crossed the stream, resuming their hike to Càrn Dubh.

Vytilia was glad she could comfort Friedrich the same way he had comforted her after the way station was attacked. She had not thought about it since they had arrived at the nymph lands. She had made a great effort not to, but it still haunted her thoughts. Her fledgling historical theory helped banish the memory to faraway recesses of her mind. Talking with Friedrich about society on the surface was both enlightening and entertaining. The way man viewed the world, and their rationale for why different events happened, told her volumes of his race.

And it was more than just information. She enjoyed speaking with Friedrich. He had this plebeian charm around him, a sort of homey, simple wisdom and a more grounded view of the world, focusing on the here and now. There was a small part of her that still wished he had been a scholar (though she had come to realize it would be out of character for such a person to be rooting through a cave system). She was beginning to see the merit in his practical knowledge. And they were getting along well. They laughed, they cried, they empathized with one another. She could still sense some hesitation and unease from him, mostly cultural misunderstandings and false preconceived ideas about Strixans, but their partnership was shaping up nicely. She might even call them . . . friends.

They passed by a purposefully stacked pile of stone in the middle of a field, a hundred feet away from the grove of trees sitting at the base of Càrn Dubh. To their left and right, roughly a mile on either side, was another stack of stones. "These must be boundary markers," Vytilia observed.

"Which means . . ." Friedrich stepped past the stones. "This is the land of that Budin Rí MabCynan warned us about."

"A forest like that would be a perfect place for an ambush," she noted, pausing as she tilted her ear towards the trees. "I can hear heartbeats coming from the forest, but I cannot tell what they belong to."

"Should we go around? Look, down there to the left, there's a break in the tree line, either a clearing or a path."

She glanced up at the "sun." "The mountain is still a distance away. What if we do not get there before dark?"

"We could make camp, start a fire."

"If the nymph's stories of the MacMórrígan are true, I do not believe they would be cowered by fire. Normally, I am not one for superstition, but it is better to ere on the side of caution."

Friedrich's hand went to his dagger. "Alright, through the forest then?" She nodded and they started to cross the field. She would pause every twenty feet or so, stopping to listen, shutting her eyes and focusing.

"Still cannot hear anything large, mostly avians and vermin," she explained.

They walked across the field at a tense and quick gait. Vytilia needed silence to filter through the myriad of sounds. A thousand drums clashed in her ears. She needed to listen to each one, to dissect friend from foe. They carefully crossed the border between plain and forest. The cacophony of noise only grew louder. She remained on alert, scanning the trees ahead and behind, listening to the heartbeats that moved, hoping the warning had been for naught.

Friedrich, meanwhile, started to admire the trees around them. This forest was not composed of the other white and yellow trees they'd seen earlier. These were similar to the firs and other conifers back on the surface, though their needles were all shades of yellow and the cones a dark blue. The forest floor was rather barren, fallen cones and branches carpeting the space between surfaced roots and rocks. The ground here was drier and harder, which meant a distinctive lack of tracks, but Friedrich wasn't worried. Most large wildlife, the ones that were bait for larger meat-eaters, avoided needle trees. For now, all they had to worry about was twisting an ankle.

And possibly the MacMórrígan.

He thought the idea of the MacMórrígan was interesting. For one thing, it seemed that Vytilia was, if not afraid, at least heedful about them. She was the one who brought them up, out of worry it seemed. There was more than likely something new she'd learned and didn't share that made her heedful. To him, they were probably just tall tales of wolf attacks. He didn't fear wolves or bears. He knew what to avoid and how to stay away. Though, Friedrich was starting to think her fear wasn't unfounded; despite the daylight, this forest was rather creepy. There was a distinct lack of birdsong and chittering. Even at midnight, forests on the surface would always have something chattering away, an owl, bugs, sometimes even deer running. Quiet, in his experience, was never a good sign.

He shifted his focus to Vytilia, worrying the quiet would slow him down. He ruminated on their earlier discussion of how their peoples may be intertwined. The vampire of legend and the Strixans of reality, while similar, were still different. She might fit the description of a vampire in terms of appearance, but she was not the monstrous villain of Wenden horror stories. She had such a way of explaining things, a way of diagramming the world and simplifying it, so Friedrich could understand. He was also grateful she was starting to talk to him more as an equal and not as a lesser, trying to relate to him and see eye-to-eye. She had even complimented him! Though he did, usually involuntarily and unfortunately, always remind himself that she was not the same as him.

Vytilia grabbed his arm, stopping him. "Huh?"

She didn't respond, only gesturing for him to be quiet as she studied the trees behind them, cupping her ears. "I think we are being followed," she whispered.

"By elves?"

"Possibly. It is a small creature, or creatures, dashing from tree to tree, all behind us."

He wanted to make a joke about her height and how almost everything would be a small creature to her but kept his mouth shut. "Perhaps we should pick up the pace?" he suggested.

"A good idea. Gods willing, I may simply be overthinking." They resumed walking with Vytilia looking back over her shoulder every few steps. Any time a branch broke, or a cone landed on the forest floor, she bared her fangs and raised her arms, ready to start hurling fireballs before quickly returning to normal.

Friedrich looked up; the sky was beginning to darken. Instead of sunset, the light in the sky seemed to be rotating to a duller side. Shadows far off to their right began to slowly creep over the land as the sky light turned. Càrn Dubh was only a few hundred more klafters away, just past a stretch of grassland. If they could get there before nightfall, or whatever passes for night, they'd be safe. They could build a fire, make camp, and be in a better position to defend themselves. They just had to get through these last few feet of forest. *So far, so good . . . .*

"Behind us!" Vytilia hissed, flashing her fangs and snapping her fingers. "Several heartbeats just dropped from the trees!" She fired several fireballs behind them before breaking out into a sprint, headed for the clearing. Friedrich, slowed down by the armor, ran after her, the war cry of several elves echoing behind him. Spears, darts, and rocks started nipping at their heels or flying past their heads. Friedrich ducked and weaved, nearly tripping over an exposed root, catching himself on a tree as a throwing spear grazed his arm. Vytilia turned to fire another fireball. "Hurry!" she urged.

"Not easy to run with all this damn metal!" Friedrich called back. There was a bone-snapping *crack!* as he suddenly cried out, grabbing his side and falling to his knees. Vytilia skidded across the forest floor as she stopped, hurrying back to help him up.

"What is wrong?"

He let out a string of profanity, clutching his left side as he stood up. "I think I just got shot!" She moved his hand and examined where he was holding. The armor had been damaged, bits of the mail torn away just below the armpit. There was not an entry or exit wound, but the area felt tender, and he cried out when she touched it.

"I can heal it later!" she told him, urging him to hurry on as she stayed back, lighting the forest floor behind them on fire. A wall of fire, reaching up to the treetops, started to spread, standing like a shield wall. She fired a few more fireballs before turning and running back to Friedrich. They were so close to the clearing, they could see a shoreline, a thin river, a boat, and the foothill of the mountain. They could smell the water, the grass, and Vytilia could hear something familiar.

"Friedrich, please, do not think less of me for this," she said as she ran ahead of him, baring her fangs and jumping with the same speed as when she pounced on the deer. She flew into the trees at the border of the forest, rustling from branch to branch. Friedrich heard a scream. A body flew from the trees and landed close by. Friedrich raced over, clutching his ribs while kneeling on the chest with his dagger to the body's throat. It was Anarawd; his clothes were torn, he had a bite mark on his collarbone, and green-colored blood was pouring out of his broken nose.

"Oh, what fresh hell is this?" Friedrich huffed.

"Just slit his throat and let us get moving!" Vytilia ordered as she climbed down, licking her lips clean.

Anarawd laughed. "What're you going to do lad? Kill me? A milksop like you? You ain't got the guts to kill me."

"Fine," Vytilia growled. "If he will not kill you, I will. I have gotten a taste for nymph blood; it is coppery, but I shall enjoy every drop." She ran her tongue over her fangs, and her eyes had started to turn purple. Friedrich felt the hairs on his neck stand up.

"Ha! Good luck. I've got half of the Alessa warriors right behind me! Kill me and I'll quickly be avenged! I can die knowing I was right! You're not a god. You're just a blasted fey trickster! Llewelyn was daft for taking you in!"

Vytilia spun around as several warriors emerged from the woods, their hair singed and clothes smoldering. All were ready for battle, dressed in armor with warpaint adorning their faces. They held throwing spears at the ready, and several were twirling slings, waiting to fire. One of those slingers must have hit Friedrich. She hissed and flashed her fangs. "Have at it! I will kill every last one of you and drink you dry!" The warriors all hesitated, nervously glancing at one another. They were expecting to fight a powerful hag, not some sort of fey!

"What are you waiting for?" Anarawd yelled. "Kill her like the thing she—gah!" Friedrich struck him in the face.

"We have no quarrel with Budin Alessa!" Friedrich told the warriors. "Leave us and there will be peace. Fight us and . . ." He looked up at Vytilia greedily running her tongue over her fangs, the whites of her eyes now fully purple. "Suffer the aftermath." He struck Anarawd again and shuddered. He didn't want to see what Vytilia would do to them.

The Alessa warriors held their position, still holding their weapons at the ready. None wanted to make the first move or to incur this witch's wrath. They held no loyalty to Anarawd, nor any real malice to these five-fingered interlopers, but they had their honor to worry about. They couldn't just run with their tail between their legs.

It was Vytilia who made the first move, not towards the Alessa warriors but towards Friedrich. "Get off him," she ordered.

"What?" He looked up at her coming towards him. Her eyes had returned to normal.

Vytilia pushed Friedrich off of Anarawd then grabbed the elf by his shirt. She spun around and hurled Anarawd into the woods, grabbing Friedrich and pulling him away. Before Anarawd even hit the ground, a great black mass leapt from the trees and grabbed him, holding him by the throat in its maw, bowling over the Alessa warriors. It landed where Friedrich and Vytilia had just been standing, turning to stare the two of them down.

It was a wolf but a wolf unlike any Friedrich had seen before. It was larger; on all fours, it came up to his chin. It was black with stripes of blue and white marbling its body. The feet weren't like a normal dog's paws. They were more . . . manlike with five digits. Even the head was eerily canny with a shorter snout and prominent brow. The ears were low, sitting just behind the sickly, jaundice-yellow eyes.

"MacMórrígan!" the Alessa warriors screamed. "MacMórrígan!" They ran back into the forest, dropping their weapons and shedding their armor as they yelled prayers of repentance and begged the heavens for forgiveness.

The great beast ignored the fleeing warriors, snapping Anarawd's neck and dropping him, staring down the two of them. It was especially focused on Friedrich, growling as they locked eyes. Vytilia readied her fire while Friedrich held his dagger at the ready, biting his upper lip to keep it stiff. He was, admittedly, scared and still in pain. He'd learned how to avoid wolves specifically so a situation like this wouldn't happen.

"I will cover you and draw it away from the water," Vytilia whispered. "You run and get to the boat. Start paddling across. I will join you on the other side."

"I'm not leaving you," he shot back. "We're in this together."

A smile pursed her lips. "I never said we were not, but we need to keep it at range. And, I do not mean to offend, but I can recover from an injury faster."

He smirked then winced as he clutched his ribs again then sheathed his dagger. "Fair enough. You give the word."

"Now!" She sent out a wave of fire, engulfing the wolf as she ran a distance away from Friedrich. He sprinted for the boat. The wolf howled as the fire singed its fur, but it shook off the hit and started running towards them. Vytilia stopped, firing narrow bolts as she set the grass on fire, creating curtains of flame to direct the wolf. It was undeterred, charging through the flames straight for Friedrich. Vytilia dove for the wolf, slamming into it with her shoulder, halting the beast's momentum and flattening it on its back. The wolf arched its back, snapping and biting at her as she pinned its arms down and struck for the neck. The wolf slammed its snout into her head, barking loudly into her ear. She grimaced. The wolf knocked her off as she lost equilibrium. The wolf quickly returned to its feet, running towards Friedrich.

Friedrich had reached the boat, panting and holding his side while watching the fight unfold. As the wolf knocked Vytilia off and started running for him, he readied himself. He grabbed one of the paddles in the boat, and as the wolf closed in, he swung, smashing the paddle on its snout. The wolf lost its footing and slid onto the gravel shore. Friedrich wasted no time, drawing his dagger and rushing forward, ready to split the beast open. Just before his dagger could make contact, the wolf swung its head around and clamped down on Friedrich's left arm. He yelled as it bit down, the manica making a deafening scraping sound. The wolf overpowered Friedrich, knocking him on his back as it bit down harder. Still holding his dagger, Friedrich thrust it upward, aiming for the eye but stabbing into the wolf's cheek. It arced its neck back, the jaws still gripping Friedrich's arm. He screamed as his shoulder dislocated. Panting and feeling faint, Friedrich pulled the dagger out and stuck the wolf again, striking it in the throat. It finally freed itself from his arm, howling, blood pouring from its mouth, as it bit at the dagger hilt, trying to pull it out.

Friedrich scrambled backwards, reaching for his sword as the wolf ripped the dagger out, tossing it aside before staring him down, blood oozing from its mouth, cheek, and throat. It snarled; several teeth were missing. Friedrich chanced a glance down at his arm and saw the bloody roots of the missing teeth.

The wolf prepared to reel back, ready to pounce, but was thrown into the water by a furnace-temperature blast of fire. Vytilia fired another equally powerful blast, boiling the water around the wolf. "Into the boat! Go!" she yelled. Friedrich, gritting his teeth, quickly grabbed his dagger and jumped into the boat. Vytilia stood at the aft, propelling the boat forward with water. They crossed the river in seconds, getting out at the base of Càrn Dubh.

"Are you injured?" she asked.

"I've been better." He laughed weakly. She gave him a smile then looked across the river. The wolf, limping and hacking, was directly across from them, eyeing the water with caution.

"It is unable to swim." A cruel grin came across her face. She winced and raised her hands; two great tendrils of water emerged from the river. The wolf backed away, turning to run as the tendrils came down, wrapping around the wolf's neck and legs. Vytilia pulled down, sweating and groaning as she did, her eyes full of rage. The wolf howled and screamed as it was pulled under the water, splashing frantically, trying to keep its head up. Vytilia growled as the wolf's splashing lessened until finally, it went quiet.

"Gott im Himmel," Friedrich muttered, catching his breath. His left arm throbbed. He sat down on the shore, resting against a large rock, picking wolf teeth out of his arm. The manica had saved his arm. He shuddered to imagine what would've happened if he had taken it off. Vytilia sat down next to him, breathing heavily and sweating, her skirt and blouse torn in several places. Her eye twitched as she held her temple. "Are you well?" he asked.

"I have been better." She laughed, wincing.

He sat back, closing his eyes as the sky continued to darken. "Vytil, one of these days, you're going to be the death of me," he joked.

She sat back as well, still breathing heavily and holding her head. "I told you; do not call me that." She let out a sigh of relief. "Well, we made it."

"And mostly in one piece."

12

Vytilia awoke sometime later when the sky was already darkened. She looked over at Friedrich. He was asleep, his face contorted in pain. She stood up and walked to his left side. His arm was swollen and tender to touch and his shoulder dislocated. There were still a few lupus teeth embedded in his armor. She pulled them out then reached across to his right shoulder and gently shook him awake. "Friedrich," she whispered. "Wake up."

He slowly stirred awake, blinking rapidly and wiping drool with his good arm. "Huh, what? Nighttime?" She helped him to his feet.

"You are injured. I need to reset your arm."

"What about you?"

"I am fine. Now, hold still. This is going to hurt." She grabbed his arm and jammed it back into the socket, holding his collar bone for balance.

"Ah! God, son of a!" he yelled as she jammed it again. "Damn it all!" She let go, watching as he slowly started rotating his arm; it burned like hellfire, but now he could use it.

"Now I will take off your manica to get to your arm." He nodded weakly, his eyes wet as she loosened the armor and pulled it off, metal scraping on skin. He gritted his teeth, letting loose all manner of profanities and vulgarities until it was off. The wolf had left superficial wounds. There was not any heavy bleeding or serious muscle damage. Removing it did the most damage. He wiped away the blood with his tunic skirt as she healed it. "The manica saved your life," she observed as he started taking off the other one. "Without it, that lupus could have torn your arm off."

He looked at his arm. He was more surprised that Vytilia sounded relieved rather than smug. Were their positions reversed, he would've gone "told you so." "Well." He groaned as he unslung his bag and stuffed the armors in. "At least I got him worse than he got me." He looked over towards the river as he started undoing his greaves. "You haven't heard anything else sneaking up on us, have you?"

"I have not; we are alone." She turned to face the mountain, craning back as she watched it ascend into the sky. "We will have to wait for daylight. It would not be safe to climb in the darkness."

He tried pulling off his chainmail but winced as he raised his arms above his shoulders, giving up and grabbing his bag. "And I don't feel in the best shape to be rock climbing."

"There." She pointed, quickly putting her arm down after realizing Friedrich could not see. "Some kind of cave, we can shelter in there then get started at first light." She went to the boat, grabbing the paddle and ripping off a section of the hull then returned to guide Friedrich. "You were brave facing that lupus," she told him.

He blushed. "Oh, well, thank you." He smiled. Another compliment from Vytilia? Maybe there was some hope. Unless he was mistaking flattery for interest. He missed Herr Bergmann; he would have some kind of wisdom that could help.

"I do worry if our actions will cause any harm to the Mab-Cynan. Rumor and hearsay can spread fast." She gently grabbed his good shoulder and lead him over to the cave.

"I wouldn't be too worried. They broke bread with two folk who fought and killed a MacMórrígan. I don't think anyone will be messing with them for a while." Vytilia stopped and set down the wood, breaking the paddle into several pieces before setting it on fire. Friedrich set his bag down and sat, leaning against the wall of the cave. "Right, spending the night in an elf tomb. Should make for a fun night." The cave, from what Friedrich could see in the firelight, was almost a circular mine shaft, boring deep into the mountain. There were old shields and swords, banners and offerings hanging from the walls, with intricate carvings and wall paintings decorating any free space. Empty bowls, vases, and burnt-out candles littered the floor. He hoped the actual bodies were buried deeper inside.

Curious, Friedrich took out his dagger and struck the wall with the hilt, then used the blade to pry off a small piece. He held the rock close to the fire, inspecting the color and texture. He broke it apart, inspecting the inside before finally tasting it. Vytilia, watching all of this unfold, was rather appalled. "What in the gods' name?"

"This mountain? It's limestone," he responded, tossing the piece away. "Or at least the inside is."

"And what does that mean?"

"There's water nearby. A lot of it."

She looked at him curiously. "You can tell a mineral just by looking at it? And tasting it?"

He nodded. "If it's very rare or from another land, I can't, but otherwise, all I need is a small bit."

"But for what purpose?"

"It's part of caverneering. Gold and other rich ores are found in certain rocks. If you want gold and silver, you have to know where to find it."

She sat down across from him, unslinging her haversack to rummage through. "If you spend your days looking for valuables, I am surprised more people do not do it. It sounds lucrative."

"They can't," he answered flatly. "Most folks are born to what they'll do, or some are bound to the land. Well, all Teudish are free, but when you get to it, some of us are freer than others. Hence why we focus on the 'free' part of free toilers. We can move around, but we're always looked at with a hint of distrust." He started drawing in the sand with his dagger. "Truth be told, most don't like us. Might be they're jealous, but we got called all sorts of names. Tunnel rats, pickers, stuff like that. Only time Bergmann ever came close to killing another man was when he called us beggars."

"So why did you keep doing it? Why not get a more respectable career?"

"What else is there?" he asked. "Work your fingers to the bone as a smith? Or break your back as a ploughman? Or, god forbid, be forced to beg. I'd rather take the odds of missing out on a meal every once in a while than work for someone else. The dream is to make it big, strike the motherlode and live out your days on that or find a good vein and sell it to a lord. That was Herr Bergmann's goal. He wanted to leave and head up to the coast, buy part of a shipping house, and just let the gold roll in."

"And what about you? When my people pay you, will you retire? Invest your earnings?"

He shrugged, laying on his back. "Maybe. I might just buy a new donkey and tools and start over. I feel like that's what Herr Bergmann would've wanted. Or I might sign up and sail to the new world, get a plot of land in a Catask or Merkyer settlement, far away from everyone else." He massaged his shoulder.

"Sorry," she interrupted. "The new world?"

His eyes widened in realization. "Right . . . you, you probably wouldn't know about that. Westward, far across the great sea, they found a new land. Or two new lands as I hear it."

"Two new continents? Across the ocean?" He nodded. "How long have they been there?"

"I don't know. Long enough for men to be there. Apparently, there's thousands of wildfolk all over. I saw one once in Karlstadt. He looked like a Tujue with dark black hair and dark skin, but he had ink all over his face, earrings, and he was taller than any Tujue I ever saw. He only spoke Merkyish, though according to his . . . master? He spoke it fluently; he'd even been name-washed and dressed like a Erebusen."

"How, how long does it take to travel to this new world?"

"About two, maybe three months? It all depends on the wind. The sailors say you have to leave during a certain time of the year, else the winds suddenly change."

"Fascinating." She had stopped rummaging, so enthralled by the concept of a "new world." "What is the new world like? Are there any fantastic beasts? An acceptance of thaumaturgy? Powerful empires and civilizations?"

"I've heard there's witches there, and wizards, but there's also a witch hiding in every shadow in Erebus, so I don't know how truthful that is. I've been told there are kingdoms, big ones too, as big as the Realm or bigger. And the wild folk have whole towns built into the cliffs or live high in the mountains above the clouds. The Catask keep trying to take them over, but they always get a bloody nose. There's thousands of odd new wildlife: big man-eating askards, spotted cats that'll hunt you in the dark, and frogs that kill with a single touch."

Vytilia was already intensely interested in the surface, but this compounded her curiosity tenfold. An entirely new continent, unknown to most of the world for possibly hundreds, if not thousands of years? It was incredible! Even with all her knowledge, she could never fathom such an idea. How could her people never discover something like this? Why did they never? Why were these men able to do something in a few hundred years that her people could never do in tens of thousands of years? Could this new world play any part in her theory regarding the interconnected history? All these questions, however, made her more upset; why was man able to accomplish so much, all without a central government or thaumaturgy? By all accounts, they should be more primitive and backwards than the nymphs, yet they were almost more advanced than even the Strixans. She tried changing subjects. Considering the possibility that another race was more advanced, civilized, and cultured than her own was greatly upsetting.

"Here." She tossed a blood sausage link to Friedrich. "I need you to do a taste test."

"Huh?"

"Earlier, when we were talking about silver and allium, I realized I should be careful with what I eat. I need you to check that for me, make sure there is not any allium."

Friedrich, much to her chagrin, pulled out his sword and stuck the sausage on the tip, slowly roasting it over the fire. He held it for a few minutes until it started to blacken then took a bite. "You're all good."

Then, much to his chagrin, she started eating them uncooked. She did not care; it was not as if cooking blood made a difference. Though as she ate, she realized this was the first time she felt homesick on the journey. It only got worse with every bite she took, tasting the dry, grain-filled casing with hints of blood. She remembered the fine, spiced Sanguinvinum from her family stocks. She even missed the taste of that beast she killed before they were captured by the nymphs. She finished off a link, leaving three more for the rest of the journey. Hopefully she could find a better tasting and fresher supply as they went along the way. "What a misleading name," she complained. "There is hardly any in these." She shuddered, realizing the meat and blood probably came from those horrid vermin they kept penned.

"I don't think it's bad," Friedrich commented as he finished his off.

"Well, you seem to have the ability to stomach anything," she responded. He smiled back, taking it as a compliment, to which she rolled her eyes. "Is there anything I should know about the surface before we get there? Something I need to be prepared for?"

"Yes, you'll stick out like a colorful dog."

"A what?"

"Never mind." He waved. "The point is, you'll be different; you'll probably get a lot of stares and questions, especially if they touch you and feel how cold you are."

"Will that cause an issue? You have painted your people in a rather unflattering light. I do not want to be crucified for 'witchcraft.'"

"So long as you keep your fangs hidden, we can talk everything away. For the touch, say you have poor blood-flow. That's what the leechers call it anyway. It's a fairly widespread illness many have. Those poor folk with it couldn't get warm touching the sun. And as for the skin, we can pass you off as a really tall . . . oh, what was that word? Albino! I haven't ever really seen an albino man or woman, only rabbits, but that doesn't mean they're not real."

The fangs and touch she could understand, but looking down at her skin, the same skin color as her mother, that was hurtful, knowing such radiance was a liability. "Fine. What else should I know?"

He rubbed his chin, feeling slight hair growth in the unscarred areas. "We'll have to be careful when church is brought up. Follow my lead and don't give a straight answer. If it comes to it; badmouth the other side."

"What are the religious sects we have to worry about?"

"Mainly the Erdeish and the Urworkish. Erdeish are 'the Church.' They're the oldest and still have the most reach, but the Urworkers have been gaining ground, and there's at least a handful of Urworker churches. If we're talking to an Erdeish, talk about how much you love the Gothi,[33] and if we're talking to an Urworkish, just say the opposite."

"That seems inane and petty," she commented.

"I don't know what those words mean, but I'm inclined to agree."

She hid a smile and giggle. Friedrich had a simple, self-deprecating sense of humor she was starting to find enjoyable. "Do you belong to either sect?"

"I'm Erdeish. That's usually the church Herr Bergmann and I would go to when we would go. But I've been to an Urworkish one before. Wherever it is we were staying, we'd go to church there. I really don't care for either, but I lean more towards Erdeish."

"What about language? Will we have to worry about finding someone, so I can map their language to our minds?"

"Not unless we leave the borders of the Realm. Most speak Teutonish, and I know enough of the stem patois to get by. I also know a bit of Želek if that ever comes up, though only for asking for a new drink."

---

33. Highest cleric in the Erdeish Church, similar to a Pope or Patriarch.

She felt pity for Friedrich. She wondered if perhaps he had been born a Strixan, raised in a centralized, civilized empire, would he turn out the same? Would he feel pride, a sense of unity and purpose with his own countrymen? Would he have a more honorable, respected career? Or what would she be like, born in such a weak, decentralized state? Would she have been born into a patrician, high-born class? Or a plebeian like Friedrich. What would she do as a career? What would she know?

"Do you ever think you will feel some sort of pride in your people, in your empire?"

"If the Tujue invade, I'll gladly pay the war fees and give some food to the army. Otherwise . . . I just don't see why. Caves are caves. Whoever is on the Karlseat or is the Gothi won't change that. At the end of the day, so long as there's gold in the hills and folk willing to buy, that's good by me."

Friedrich's loyalty was to his pocket, though despite how upset it made her, she did not blame him. There appeared to not be any rationing program or system to help the lower classes survive in times of hardship. There was not a shared history or commonality that he had described. They were without a common cause or singular, national purpose. He did not even know who his leaders were. Perhaps it was impossible, due to both man's need to daily eat and drink, but also their frequent religious schisms prevented them from ever rallying around a single standard. Even if all they shared was a language, people from one province to the next were not loyal to one another. Whether that was a failure of the imperial system they had established, or a failure of man as a race was yet to be determined.

"Still eager to visit the surface?" he asked slyly.

She removed her stole and laid it out as a blanket, laying on her back. "Your governmental shortcomings aside, my people still need those muskets. And to answer your question, I am still eager. I have to see this world with my own eyes." She turned her head to face him. "In your opinion, do you think our two peoples could ever become allies, or at least, partners?"

He wanted to say yes. The words wanted to jump from his mouth, but that's what *he* wanted. He was beginning to trust her, see her as a woman, not a thing, but that had only come with time and her saving his life several times. The two of them had shown that man and vampire could work together, but he was doing it . . . well at first for gold but now . . . because of her.

They locked eyes. She was gently, but impatiently, waiting for a response. "It could happen," he finally replied. "But it would be a lot of work. The gold and silver your kind can trade would certainly make most turn a blind eye to your . . . teeth. But others might not be so easily swayed. If you could somehow get the Church to support you, you'd stand a better chance. All this is a maybe, however. It could also be that my own would let fear steer them rather than gold."

"Do you trust us?"

"I trust you." He was blushing.

She quickly turned to stare at the ceiling. "Will you trust us?"

He gulped. "I want to take you for your word, but I also want to see what you will do with the muskets and legions once they've defeated the fiends."

"Trust but verify," she whispered to herself. She could not afford to be offended by Friedrich's reasoning, especially since Praetor Cornelia had been vocal about being wary, even afraid of men. Given his bellicosity, she would not be surprised if he advocated an assault on the surface once the devils were defeated. *If* they were defeated. Though if the devils were not a concern any longer, how long before the Strixans turn their attention to the surface? There were many reasons why they could not, but an equally long list of why they could, number one being that they had conquered the surface once before. Given the current historical dilemma she was trying to piece together, it would be foolish of her to say that history cannot repeat. She glanced over. Friedrich had fallen asleep, his heartrate slowing down. She sat up, resting her head on her knees as she folded her arms. She wanted to rest, but someone had to stay alert and stay on guard. She took out another blood sausage link and took a bite. That someone had to be her.

• • •

Light blindingly shot through the clouds and filled the cave, hitting Friedrich in the eyes as he rolled over, trying to get a few more slices of precious sleep. When he rolled on his left side, he put pressure on his still tender arm. And when he rolled to his right, he got a face full of heat from the dying embers of the fire and pressure on his aching rib. He resigned himself and sat up, rubbing his eyes and slapping himself to wake up.

"*Guten morgen,*" he told Vytilia as she handed him one of his rations from the haversack. The salty smell of fish immersed the crypt. He saw a large pile, many still flopping, next to her.

"*Salve*," she responded as she grabbed a fish, bit it, drained it, then set it aside. Her face was ruddy-colored from previous fish. He chewed his food in silence, unsure of how to respond. "How is your arm?" she asked before biting down on another fish.

"Better." He looked down at the fire, trying to block out the sound of her spine-chilling slurping.

"Oh, my apologies." She halted. "I never asked. Would you like a piscis? I assume you eat these; I was just caught up in my own sustenance. I did not think . . . ."

"I'm, I'm alright," he told her while chewing a piece of salt meat. "I'm not in the mood for . . . fish."

"If you change your mind, I can gut one for you to cook." She bit down and started drinking another. "Piscis is a bit of a delicacy for us back at the Arx, so I have never had this many in one sitting before. I never realized how salty they tasted." Friedrich hid a wretch as she tossed a fish and started up on another. "My mother told me there used to be a fish-based sauce that was quite popular during the heyday of the empire. If I remember correctly, it was called garum? I have always wanted to try it; I do not suppose your people make such a product, do they?"

"Can we talk about something else?" Friedrich said in one breath.

She was taken aback, stopping before biting into another fish. "Oh, we can; you can choose the topic."

"Anything but blood and fish." He gagged.

She finished off her last one. "That will not be a topic anymore. I have had my fill. I feel so much more invigorated, energetic. I appreciate the thought with those blood sausages, but they only had so much in them." She raised her hand, pulling a large ball of water from the creek, enveloping the fish. "Would you mind cleaning up the fire while I dispose of these, then we can converse as we get started on our climb." She stood up, guiding the ball back towards the water.

Friedrich was glad to be rid of her drinking and started scattering the embers and ashes outside the cave. It had felt weird to spend the night at the entrance of an elven crypt, but compared to everything else that had happened, it was probably the least weird. He made sure to be extra tidy with cleaning. They already had fiends and evil wolves coming after them. They didn't need vengeful elf ghosts.

"Here." She grabbed his shoulders and faced him before lifting his right arm. "I took care of your arm, but I forgot your ribcage. Is it still hurting?"

"Only when I—yeow!" She stuck her arm down the sleeve of his tunic, pressing against each of his ribs before holding her hand there. "A little warning, next time?" He groaned, his teeth chattering.

"What did you expect I would do?" She drew a stream of water to wash off her hands before drying them with her fingertip fire. "I felt a few minor cracks and fractures, but nothing broke. Same story as the manica, the armor saved you from a more grievous injury."

They paused their conversation to stare at the task ahead of them. They would climb what appeared to be a path circling up the mountain to the peak, much like a spiral staircase. Unlike a staircase, this one was uneven and jagged. The level parts where they could walk normally were broken up by rock faces that required climbing. Friedrich groaned. This trail snaked all the way up the mountain, continuing even beyond the clouds hugging the peak.

Friedrich sighed, mentally preparing himself as they began their ascent. Vytilia, being lighter on her feet, took the lead, keeping watch for any loose rocks and slippery terrain.

"I suppose I should say sorry for my remarks about wearing this at the Arx," he commented, stretching his left hand. "They really saved my bacon. Though, with that wolf biting me, I won't turn into one, will I?"

She looked at him curiously. "Why would a lupus biting you change your structure?"

He scratched his chin. "In the tales, when you get bit by some fell thing, you usually turn into one. I think by biting, that is how vampires make more vampires." He balled his fists, so he wouldn't reach up and protect his neck.

She scoffed. "You do know how ridiculous that is, right? A bite like that may be unhygienic, but it cannot change who you are. That is impossible. I mean look at all the creatures I have bitten. None of them turned into Strixans."

He shrugged and had to concede that. She did mention her mother carried her. "So, Strixans get more Strixans by . . ."

"The usual way mammals reproduce. Had you not become inebriated, you may have experienced it with those nymph hens." She harumphed.

He stared up at her. "Is . . . is that jealousy in your tone?"

Her face went purple. "Of course not! It was . . . indignation. I thought their behavior was unbecoming, and you were enjoying it like some sort of hedonist!"

"Well, enjoy is a strong word. I thought it was nice, but all they talked about was having warrior sons; that and the ears threw me off. Weren't those elf boys lining up to woo you?"

"They did not. The nymph tiercels were . . . put off by me. Not that I would have accepted any offers either. I do not like beards. Or facial markings. Or . . . the ears too."

Friedrich hid a grin. She was definitely jealous, either from the attention he was given or the lack she received. "Well, if it makes you feel any better, I don't think you're off-putting."

Now he does not, she scoffed. *Only took me saving his life*. "Did I not warn you of doling out compliments to those above your station?"

"I can take it back if you want. I can even give an insult if you'd prefer." She gave him a glower and walked on ahead, leaping over small rock walls that he would have to climb. He slapped himself. How stupid could he really be? He started climbing up the wall, wincing whenever he used his left arm. As he struggled to find a handhold, he felt Vytilia's cold touch. She took him by the hand, lifting him onto the next level.

"I will accept the compliment, if one can call it that. Your landlady did well in teaching etiquette." She turned away from him. "I do appreciate you not giving into . . . lasciviousness around me. It is a welcome change."

"Do you get bawdy remarks like that back at Nidus?"

"Not always, but thinking like that is not uncommon, especially with tiercels and especially with legionaries. As much as I do not enjoy it, I at least understand; our entire race has been cut down to a fraction of its size. It is only natural to think about . . . reproducing." She said the last word with slight disdain. "Natural urges aside, for a good portion of the populace, that is all they can do to spend their leisure time. Resources are so scarce, we cannot spare anyone or anything to write plays or even hold gladiator matches. The plebeians are left without much entertainment; blood is too precious to gamble or trade away for amusements."

He chuckled under his breath. "It's a godsend you aren't drowning in kids. Seems like there should be twenty . . . nestlings for every couple."

She frowned, shaking her head. "Whenever a Strixan comes of age, a state physician . . . decommissions their reproductive systems using thaumaturgy. It is only resumed when a couple gets married and are approved to be parents. The approval process can take a century."

Friedrich had to stop, looking at her in disbelief. "You mean to tell me, with your wit—, weirdcraft, you can stop or start a womb, like a clock?" She nodded. "Hell, you could make so much gold doing that on the surface. Gallia would empty their whole goldhoard for that."

"See?" she mused. "Something else Strixans can offer man through trade. It should work the same on your kind. The Gods know we have had more than enough time to perfect it." She paused, thinking back to what Brigit said about the nymph's false gods. How much manipulation can a thaumaturgist have over a womb? Could that be how their false gods changed their ancestor's structure? Such a process would require arcane and forbidden knowledge. It would take months to do. It would be exhausting! Exhausting . . .

"I remember you said you'd been underground for 3,000 years," Friedrich interrupted. "Are you 3,000 years old?"

She jumped up to the next level of rock, looking down at him as he started to climb. "I am not that old; I am only 425 years old." He looked at her sheepishly. She hid a smile, rolling her eyes. "Believe it or not, that is young by Strixan standards. Until a few decades ago, there lived many at the Arx who were alive during the cataclysm. That is partially why the imperial family fell out of favor, and the Concilium was established. It was unhealthy to have one person in control for so long, not to mention all the infighting and squabbling that came from having a growing royal family."

"So, you're undying."

"In truth, though only to natural causes. Warfare or serious accidents that damage the heart or brain can still kill us, as can allium and silver. But disease, pathogens, aging, none can affect us."

"I wish it was like that for men. I can't tell you how many extra weeks Herr Bergmann and I had to spend in a cave because the nearest town had some kind of outbreak. Of course, every time there's a war, there's blight a short time later. A never-ending cycle of suffering." Friedrich paused at the top of the rock, catching his breath. "And do you look young like that the entire time?"

She nodded. "Once you reach twenty, you are fully mature and lose all vestiges of being a nestling. From then on, this is more or less how you will look. Though once you pass the 10,000-year mark, mostly in high-stress positions, you may get wrinkles. It is also popular to halt hair follicles. Older tiercels do it to give them a wiser, sage appearance."

"By hair follicles—"

"The roots. They intentionally make themselves balding."

"Well, add that to list of exports. Herr Bergmann himself would've shelled out a good amount of chips to have his hair again. All he could grow was this scraggly beard. Frau Beck always made fun of it." He took another deep breath as they continued. "So aside from maybe getting wrinkles, what happens after 10,000 years?"

"Nothing. Though, living past 10,000 is exceptionally rare. There are only one, maybe two written accounts. All eventually choose to pass on sometime before then; it is all a personal preference of what one considers a good life. If you have dutifully served the empire, raised a family of several dozens, seen the natural wonders wrought by Luna and Sol, after that, there is not much to do. All elder Strixans, once they have experienced all they can and given their efforts to the good of the empire, choose to take their own lives. It is a noble death, a fitting finale to such a grand existence."

"Sounds rather sad if you ask me." Friedrich swore to himself as they came to another rock to climb.

"Oh, it is far from depressing." She paused. "Well, normally. It is a rather grand affair, akin to a marriage or the birth of a nestling. Depending on the age gap, couples will usually choose to go together. The departed gathers all their friends and family to their home for a lavish banquet, which can last for a week. Then they read their final will and testament out loud, give everyone a departing gift, and give one final speech. A self-eulogy, so to speak. Then, they or a trusted physician stop their heartbeat."

"In front of everyone?" Friedrich asked. He shook his hand, holding it closed after slicing his palm on a sharp rock.

"Indeed, it is meant to be a social occasion. Afterwards, the departed's closest family and friends will drink their blood then carry them in a coffin to be interred in the family or communal catacombs. Or cremated. A departing is one of the only times outside of armed combat a Strixan can drink another Strixan's blood." She jumped up to the top of the rock as Friedrich finally finished his climb.

He laid down on the path, breathing heavily. He needed to take better care of himself. "I can't wrap my mind around that," he told her between breaths. "Taking your own life in front of all your loved ones? It sounds gruesome."

"It is simply another cultural difference," she retorted. "How does mankind handle a departing?"

"With drinking!" He rolled himself over to stand up. "After someone dies, you go to the town church, say some nice things about the dead, then you throw them on a deadheap. After that, you have some drinks and remember the dead with tales and songs."

"Deadheap?"

"Wood stacked together that you place a body on for burning."

"You mean a pyre!"

"No, I mean deadheap. You might call it a 'pyre,' but we call it a deadheap. If someone dead is on it, it's a deadheap, if not, then it's a bonfire."

"Your people burn your dead?"

"Toilers and burghers do. Lords like to build tombs or mounds and put their dead in there. They make a big deal out of dying. Rest of us . . ." He stopped to scratch at his facial scars. "Well, rest of us have to move on. We give the family a few chips, bring the widow a meal or two, and keep going. A lot of folks die every day, and most of us don't have the gold to worry about it for too long."

There was a somber tone in his voice, Vytilia noted. While not exact, it was reminiscent of how he sounded and acted when explaining muskets to the Concilium. She wondered if funerals and war were somehow related in his past. But, she knew not to press any further.

"Was it weird, seeing a nymph in the flesh?" he asked, perhaps also noticing his own somberness.

"I will admit, seeing an artistic motif in reality was disconcerting. As was seeing a lupus. Though, any concern I had washed away after slaying that lupus. It reminded me of the Strixans' place in the natural order."

"Your place as a hunter."

"As the apex lifeform. Strixans do not feel fear, for Luna and Sol gave us imperium over the world." Friedrich bit his tongue, not wanting to bring up the new world as a snide comment. "Of course, unlike other animals that merely hunt and survive, we used our imperium to found civilization. What separates us from say . . . do you know what a leo is? A large feline, usually has a large mane of hair around its neck?"

He nodded. "We call them lions or löwe if you're at church. They're on a lot of flags."

"Interesting. For us, they were popular for gladiator fights. Anyway, what separates a Strixan from a leo is our culture, our language, our hierarchy, our ability to expand and settle. We and the leo both hunt, but we, the Strixan, are capable of doing so much more. Now, back to the nymphs, what do men know of them?"

"Right." He started scaling another rock wall, pausing halfway up to wipe off his face. "They're talked about more up north than where I'm from, so there isn't a lot of elf tales that I know of. But you can swap the word for fairy or kobold, and it'll mean the same thing. Elf, to us, just means a small little trickster who likes causing mischief."

"You hear a lot of these stories, but have you ever actually seen any of them? Have you ever seen an elf?" He went to open his mouth. "*Before* the previous day," she quickly added.

"I might have? I've seen a lot of weird things in the forest at night. It might've been an elf; it might've been a bird. Nighttime has the witching stound when ghosts and the weirdkind come out. And, what I call a kobold, someone might call an elf or a gnome. It could be all three of those, or it could be none."

She sighed, rather defeatedly. "But Friedrich, of all these stories you have heard, vampires, elves, fairies, have *you* ever actually *seen* any of these creatures?"

"Not as such, no."

"You have only heard first or second-hand accounts from others?" He nodded. "So why do you believe any of it? All of what you have heard could be a fiction or someone's desperate bid for either attention or coin. Why bother taking any of it seriously?"

"It's what I would do for fun," he explained. "When Herr Bergmann and I would wander, before he wanted me to start drinking, I'd sit and listen to all the talking in the beerhalls and guesthouses we went to. I would hear rumors of war, dashing undertakings in the new world, or ghostly tales pouring out of the east. Didn't matter to me if they were true or not. I liked hearing them."

"Were you raised by Herr Bergmann?" she asked as he started climbing to the next ridge.

"For the most part. Our landlady, Frau Beck, had a hand in my upbringing as well. She tried teaching me manners and godliness." He chuckled. "I'm sure you can tell her teachings fell on deaf ears."

"I would not say that. You have enough sense not to leer. And you recognize your own god. That is more than I could say for some plebeians I have encountered."

"Well, it's easy not to leer when the leeree can kill me with a flick of her wrist. Though, even if you couldn't . . . I know better." He cleared his throat as he crawled onto the top of the ridge. "Frau Beck made sure of that." His heartrate had elevated and not from the physical activity. She smiled, leaping up next to him.

They both paused to admire the view. The river and forest (some of it still smoldering) were far below them now, all blending into one vista. Above them was still the peak, hidden by cloud cover, which meant they didn't know if they were halfway finished or halfway to their next base camp. The air was getting thin and cold. Each breath stung Friedrich in his lungs and nose, like he was inhaling a hive full of bees. The air was even getting to Vytilia. She was taking deeper and deeper breaths with each ascent.

"Oh look! The MabCynan village!" She pointed above the forest, to a small brown spot nestled against a veritable ocean of yellow grass.

Friedrich strained his eyes, but he couldn't make anything definite out. They were nearing the cloud cover. How much longer to go? "We should keep moving," he told her. "If we can't reach the peak, we should find a cave, lest we freeze to death tonight."

"I would not," she responded proudly. "We have exceptional temperature control; cold or hot weather does not affect us directly. Clothes and insulation are more a matter of modesty, style, and comfort."

"Hey if talking about how much stronger Strixans are keeps you walking, keep doing it," he retorted.

"I could talk about my people all day, but I am afraid of boring you and putting you to sleep. Carrying you up the side of the mountain would put a damper on everything." They both laughed, though she turned her head away. "I would rather talk about you and your people."

"What do you want to know?"

"Well . . . I told you Strixan weaknesses to silver and allium. Do you not think it fair you tell me a weakness of men?"

He snorted. "What weaknesses? Anything will kill us. Too hot, we die. Too cold, we die. Too little food, we die. Too much food, we die. And so on and so on. We don't have it as easy as you do. We don't have the skill to heal ourselves with a wave of a hand or live by just drinking a fish like it's a beer. We have to scrape by and use our wits to survive."

"How long do men usually live for?"

"About 60 years. Some lords can live to be 80 or 90. I did once hear of a man who lived to be 100. He looked like an old leather bag wrapped around tree branches."

"That short of time?" she asked.

"Yep. And that's if a sickness doesn't get you first." He scratched the scars on his cheek. "By all reckoning, as young as I was, smallpox should've taken me. Herr Bergmann called it a godsend. That was probably the godliest I've ever seen him."

"Was it painful?"

He sighed then nodded. "At first, it felt like my whole body was on fire, then like my brain was trying to crawl out of my skull, and finally like someone was grating my face. I couldn't move, couldn't eat or drink. I'd only sleep when I blacked out from exhaustion." His voice went somber again. "Bergmann was helpless. I'd just been fellowed with him. He never had kids before. He didn't know what to do. He called on every priest and healer he knew, spent days on his knees beseeching God. I didn't even know what was happening to me. All I knew was pain and heat."

Gods be praised! Vytilia thought. She never felt more thankful Strixans were not susceptible to disease. "How long were you afflicted?"

"A little more than two weeks. The sores went away, then I could eat and sleep again. Ever since then, haven't caught it in all my years."

"You must have developed a natural immunity."

"It's times like that that make me glad I'm a caverneer. Not much chance of catching something when you're by yourself in a cave."

"I am beginning to see more of the merits of this caverneering trade," she admitted. "I suppose, in a sense of the word, all of my people are caverneers, so we have never had much of a use for them."

"You also have a much easier go of caverneering, since you can just carve your own tunnels with weirdcraft."

"Not weirdcraft, it is called thaumaturgy."

"Yes, right." He sucked in a deep chilly breath. "I suppose I'll have to learn about it another time." They passed through the clouds, the trail narrowing. The clouds, more similar to fog, dissipated when touched, soaking the ground below. Friedrich soldiered on, biting his lip to stop his teeth from shattering like glass. Vytilia held her hand out, fingertips on fire, to keep him warm.

As they walked through the fog, they saw that there was a roof. Above them, all around was rock, dipping and bending like rain drops. It stretched as far as they could see, continuing past the horizon. They could even see the "sun," miles away, embedded in the roof. It was a gemstone, finely cut and square shaped, as tall and wide as seven grown men. Friedrich guessed it was an emerald of some sort by the coloring but an emerald star stone. It shined brightly like a noonday sun.

The actual peak of the mountain went higher than the roof. An opening encircled it, as if someone or something had carved out enough space for the mountain to climb higher. From what Friedrich could see, the roof opening was an almost perfect circle. If some great being could grab both in their hands, the mountain would fill the hole like a hand in a glove. Vytilia must have realized this too. She looked uneasy.

If Friedrich had to venture a guess, based on previous climbs, it would be noon or sometime after. He was a bit disappointed in himself. Compared to the peaks he and Bergmann had climbed before, the Càrn Dubh was a molehill. Though he supposed in his state, he should be grateful he could even climb it.

Standing here just below the mountain peak, Vytilia could now understand this world. It was like a box, as if this environment had been constructed, sealed underneath the Strixan stratum and the surface, a monument to a forgone era of unknown history. "It is beautiful," Vytilia commented.

"It is," Friedrich added, glancing sideways at her. He started climbing up the rock towards the icy peak, his face whipped by the chills. He could feel ice on his fingertips and in his lungs. He pulled himself up, breathing heavily, as he reached the summit. Vytilia stood over him. "We made it!" he coughed triumphantly.

"And now, it is just solid rock above us."

They rested, leaning against the summit, their breathing and the sound of water echoing against the chamber. The only light came from what slipped beneath the bottom of the roof. It reminded Friedrich of the cave he had been in before falling. He held his breath, listening, and heard the drip-drip sound of water falling. He held his hand out, touching the jagged icicle at the pinnacle of the mountain. A splash of water, ice-cold, fell into his palm. Another drop followed then another.

"Remember how I said this mountain was made of limestone?" She nodded. He pointed to the tip of the concave roof above them. "I think that might be where the water comes from. If we can get in there, we should be able to find an opening, somewhere where it runs off. Water means life. We find water . . ."

"We will find some form of life." She started formulating a plan. "Here, come stand by me." She held her hands above her head. Friedrich stood by her, watching as she closed her eyes and began swaying her arms, knitting her brows in effort. She gritted her teeth, making a grabbing motion with her hands, then pulled her arms down with great force. The roof began to quake, cracks starting to form. With a tremendous CRACK, a plume of water broke through the rock, splashing onto the peak and pouring down the sides of Càrn Dubh. Vytilia smiled and pulled the water off of her and Friedrich.

"That was brilliant!" he cheered. "Now how do we get through that?"

Vytilia held her head and took a deep breath before answering. "I can get us up there, and seal the hole behind us, but that is the most I can do before I pass out."

"If you get us to somewhere with air, I'll take over from there."

Vytilia took another deep breath and nodded. She approached the plume, raising her hands and opening a hole in the water, like a hollow in a tree. Friedrich followed in after her. "Grab ahold of me." Friedrich wrapped his arms around her, and she let out a surprised cry. "Move your hands," she ordered. She closed the opening, they were now encased in a dry bubble within the tubular plume of water spilling from the roof.

She spread her hands apart and put them by her hips. Water began to pool under their feet, hardening into a solid chunk of ice, then began lifting Vytilia and Friedrich upward. They came through the roof, watching as six feet of rock passed by them in their aquatic tube, pushing through the frigid water into a clear, dimly lit aquifer. With a stretch of her hand and making a fist, Friedrich watched as Vytilia froze the hole below them. They flew upwards for several more minutes until she put her hands up. They stopped flying upward. Both swam towards the surface, poking their heads through and taking a deep gulp of air.

"Ha!" Friedrich cried as they treaded water. "That was amazing!" He watched as Vytilia offered a weak smile before positioning herself to float on her back. "Are you alright? How's your head?"

"I feel like it was split open with a hammer," she bemoaned. "At least, I am alive. At least, we are alive." She discreetly wiped away a spot of purple blood from her nose.

Friedrich swam over to her and pulled off the haversack and reached in for a blood sausage. It was soggy but intact. He handed it to Vytilia, and she eagerly wolfed it down, asking for a second. She savored this one as she caught her breath, their splashing and breathing echoing off the rocky walls. While she ate, Friedrich took the moment to get their bearings. The aquifer was large and dimly lit. He could see water all around them. The roof, made of solid rock, gneiss as far as Friedrich could tell, was only a few feet above their heads. Their only light source was a hole, high in the roof. A single, almost angelic beam poured through the opening, magnified by the water.

"Hallo!" he called out, listening to the echo. No response, this must be somewhere untapped. "That skylight," he pointed up to the hole, "is our way out of here. The surface is just out and over the hole."

"How do you know?"

"The light is white, not green or blue. So unless there's someone buried below your kind but above the elves, that only leaves the surface."

She could not fault that logic. "We will need to climb." Vytilia rubbed her temples. "I cannot lift us up with water. I need a few minutes to gather my strength."

"You stay here and rest. I don't want you hurting yourself. We're in this together. Just hold this." He gave her his bag (which she kindly drained of water) and started swimming over to the hole. When he turned his back, Vytilia felt color come to her cheeks, and she smiled. Brigit was right. He did have a certain charm.

Friedrich swam to the wall just under the hole. The chamber was conical with the far side angled until it came to a point. The shape was similar to a pointed conical hat with a bent tip. The hole sat just below the tip.

Friedrich held his hands up against the wall, waiting for them to dry, and slowly pushed himself along, looking for a handhold. He found a crevice and grabbed it with his right hand. Putting his foot on an outcropping below the surface, he lifted his upper body out of the water. He grabbed another rock with his left and fully pulled himself out. Vytilia swam over to him, treading water as she ate another sausage. Once out of the water, he felt himself lighten as Vytilia dried him off with a wave of her hand. Sticking closely to the wall, Friedrich looked around, reaching for another handhold. Sweat was pouring down his face, his muscles aching with every movement of his arms and legs. He was going to sleep well tonight.

Finding another handhold, he stretched out, almost spread eagle, resting his foot on a precarious and smooth piece of rock. He brought his other foot over, resting his toes on the small piece. He reached up and found another handhold. As he grabbed it, the rock he was standing on broke off, falling into the water. He was holding himself up by just his hands, his shoulders crying out in pain. He let one arm fall to his side, resting it before swinging it up and grabbing another rock.

He reached around with his feet, searching for something solid to hold onto. He found a crevice and jammed his foot in, carving out more room with the toe of his shoe. With three of his limbs on the wall, he took the chance and looked up. He could smell the crisp mountain air outside; the hole was less than seven feet away. He heard splashing and glanced downward. Vytilia had come over, giving him a reassuring smile. Mustering his courage, he reached up, grabbing another rock, then stuck his free foot into a different crevice. He slowly pulled himself, his entire body throbbing with pain. He took another break, feeling an acidic pain spreading throughout his limbs. Screaming, he repeated the same maneuver, pulling himself up higher. He adjusted himself, his head only finger lengths from the hole. With one final leap, he grabbed onto the edge of the hole, his hands coming down on jagged rocks. With a flurry of swears, he held on tight, pulling himself up, crawling out of the hole.

He was laying in snow, honest-to-God, white, cold snow. He almost cried, looking up and over the valley below. It was lush and green with dark blue rivers snaking down from the mountains, twisting around distant hamlets and towns. Beautiful, grey, snow-capped mountains were to his left and right, blue skies above him, and a yellow, warm sun set high in the sky. He was home.

Once she made sure he was safe, Vytilia climbed onto the wall, quickly scaling it, dashing upwards like a lizard, joining Friedrich on the outside. He was lying face-down in . . . she knelt and picked up this white mush covering the mountain. It was cold and wet, like ice but more soluble and moldable. She sat down, reveling in the cold and taking in the view. This was unlike anything she had seen before; it was so verdant and full of life. She could hardly believe her eyes. It seemed impossible for there to be so much vitality. Even these mountains, simple stones, seemed to exude an energy and soul. Even the sun, harsh as it was on her skin, seemed welcoming.

She lacked the vocabulary to express her feelings. All of this was so new to her. After 400 years of being underground, she was finally experiencing living. What could she say to capture this majesty? How could one even put this into words? This world seemed limitless. It was so wide open, so vast. She could actually see a horizon. There was something in the distance, not just another dark, dank tunnel. She stared at the valley below, crying as she watched flocks of avians fly in formation. "It is beautiful," she announced, "so beautiful."

Part 2:

So Above

13

Friedrich laid in the snow, now on his back, quietly muttering a thank you to the heavens. Vytilia sat, amazed at the beauty of the land below her. She could not believe it. She almost refused to believe it. Here it was, the surface. Below her was the land of her ancestors, the land her mother had once seen. She bit her lower lip repeatedly to ensure she was not dreaming, that she was awake and could partake in this majesty, squealing with delight after each bite; this was not a dream. This was reality. Below, encompassing the mountain they sat on, was a deep and mountainous valley, greenery stretching to the horizon and beyond. There was so much green, so many shades, so many intensities. The ground was green, the plants were green, even the smaller mountains at the foothill of this one were green. And there was air, a soft blowing air, that caressed her face. It was refreshing, almost ethereal. She took a deep breath, taking in a deep lungful of the crisp, cold, and sharp mountain air. She took many more breaths, smiling at each one as the cold air chilled her to her soul. She loved it! Every sight, every touch, every smell! It was wonderful! She stood up, throwing handfuls of the white ice into the air, feeling their coldness run down her as they landed. She twirled, cheering and jumping as she felt the sun on her skin.

She suddenly gasped and turned to look up at the sun, shielding her eyes as she captured a quick glance. The sun, it was just as Friedrich had described, this bright and beautiful orb hanging in the sky. That was Sol, Sol Invictus! The god of her ancestors was right there, beaming down on her, the first Strixan to see the surface in almost three millennia. She had to remember what brought her here, what had guided her since she first encountered Friedrich. She knelt in the ice, facing the direction of the sun, pouring her heart out in gratitude. It was by the grace of Luna and Sol, and by their own wits, that they had survived. She had to remember that this land, this beautiful, lush and verdant land, was guarded and watched over by the gods, and anywhere touched by sunlight or moonlight was sacred ground.

Finished with a quick but rote beseeching of thanks taught to him by his landlady, Friedrich sat up, his eyes closed as the sun, the real sun, shone down. He was actually thankful for the snow. The cold helped rest his muscles. His left side was still dull from the pain of climbing and the wolf attack. Even with the pain, the damp clothing, and the freezing temperatures, he wanted to go to sleep. He'd been up since God knows how early and climbed up a frigid mountain, all while still recovering from his wounds. All this talk of smallpox and fighting, and what would probably do him in is exhaustion, or at this rate, pneumonia.

"Friedrich?" Vytilia asked. His eyes slowly creaked open. She was still kneeling, her body facing him but her head transfixed on the valley below. "Do you know where we are?"

His teeth chattered as he sucked cold air with each breath. "We're somewhere in Erebus," he told her, "still within the Weiße Hügel range."

"Have you been to this part before?"

"Maybe. Though there's so many mountain dales, I can't tell them apart without a landmark."

She stood up, reaching down to help him up. He took her hand, hiding his discomfort; her hand was almost colder than the snow. "Do we have a plan?"

"Yes." He pointed down to where the snow ended, and rock began. "Follow this down into the dale and find a way to the nearest hamlet. Once I know where we are, I can put us on the path to the nearest High Learnhouse. Then we'll figure out where to buy muskets from there."

"Will the people we meet treat us well?"

"Ah, don't worry about that." He gestured for his bag and started digging through it for the trousers the elves gave him. "Most folk are kind; I just only talk about the bad eggs because it's a better tale." He found the trousers, gleefully sliding them on. For the first time since falling, his legs were somewhat warm, even though the trousers only came down to his mid-shins. He wrapped the sword in the strips of leather the elves gave him, hiding the gold filigree. He closed the bag and slung it onto his shoulders. "Unless we encounter a robber or a mean drunk, no one'll rough us up. You'll get some stares, so remember our back-lore."

"I remember; I am an albino, perhaps the only non-animal albino anyone has ever seen." She reached down and grabbed two handfuls of snow, holding them out towards Friedrich. "Before we leave, what is this? It is ice but not any ice I have ever dealt with before."

He grabbed a fingerful and made a small ball. "It's snow. It's on the highest peaks nearly year-round, then in the winter months, it'll blanket the whole Realm." He threw the ball at her feet. "It is ice that falls from the sky."

"So, this is simply water?" She squeezed it, hardening it in her hands before rolling it into a ball. Curiosity overpowering her sense of decency, she leaned in and took a bite. It was cold, so cold, colder than any water she had ever drank. She was surprised that she enjoyed it, taking another bite.

"If you're ever here around winter, don't try any snow that's yellow." Friedrich started walking downhill, trudging through the slowly melting snow.

"Why not?" she asked, throwing down what she had in her hands before wiping them off. She tied her stole into a bonnet to shield her face, her exposed skin was starting to turn a more matte light grey.

"It's best if you don't know." He chuckled.

She frowned. "If you prefer not to explain that to me, will you at least tell me this? Since we are currently lacking in funds, will we be able to get food and shelter?"

He took the torc out from his belt and twirled it on his finger. "These should fetch us a good bit of chips, enough for room and board and with some left over for clothes."

She held hers in her hand. "Is it ethical to sell these? They were a gift from the MabCynan, a votive offering. We already pretended to be their gods, and now we are selling their gifts?"

"I don't like selling them either . . ." He yawned, feeling an aching in his muscles. "But if we don't sell these, we're going to starve before we get to the nearest High Learnhouse."

"Can we not find hunting grounds and search for game? I will take the blood; you will take the meat?"

"We could do that, but, depending on the area, there might not be any meanlands to hunt on. And we don't want any game wardens or rangers coming after us. The less attention you draw the better. And, well, I want to sleep in a proper bed. Guesthouses don't open tabs."

She handed him her torc. "Very well. You are the expert on the surface. I shall follow your lead. Though, I must state I believe selling these gifts is distasteful."

"Sleeping outside is more distasteful. And, you won't get to see the best the surface has to offer." She thought about it before nodding. "Alright, we're in agreement; we'll live off of these until we go to a High Learnhouse and sell my armor. And if we still need gold, we can go to Hertzabrunno."

"Hertzabrunno? Your home city?" He nodded. "What is there?"

"The life savings of myself and Herr Bergmann. He wasn't much for wills, but I suppose I get a share of it. And he always wanted to use his to get a stake in a good cause. What better cause than saving the vampires from doom?"

She was humbled. "Friedrich, I promise to you, I will ensure you are compensated, generously, for this sacrifice."

"Ah, think nothing of it." He blushed.

As the snow made way to solid rock, they couldn't talk. Friedrich showed her how to properly descend an incline, walking sideways while keeping one hand against the rock, descending in a zigzag pattern to ensure they wouldn't lose their footing and fall down. Friedrich, justly so, said himself to be a master of falling down mountains, or more accurately, falling IN mountains.

Vytilia realized how provident it had been Friedrich was a caverneer. She was already starting to feel languid and lethargic from being out in the sun, and there were many times where she could have lost her footing and rolled down the rest of the summit.

Now that she had taken in the majesty of the surface and had time to think, she admired the change she started to see in Friedrich. Here in his "home" environment, he had much greater confidence. He did not seem lost or act like a passenger. Here he was a much more active agent. Their roles had almost been reversed with him being the well-traveled guide and expositor and she the wide-eyed and curious newcomer. She was glad. Ever since he had told her about civilization on the surface, she was almost boiling over with curiosity. Now that she was here, only her patrician upbringing was preventing her from exploding like an energetic nestling.

Though even as they walked, or side-climbed down, she could not help but pause to admire more and more of the surface. Every inch they descended brought the vibrant and verdant life below into greater detail. She even found herself stopping to admire the rocks on the mountain face. They were lighter in color than the ones down below, smooth and round from years of water runoff. She loved these rocks. She just wanted to hold them, run them through her hands, cheering as she did so. This was not the ordinary rock her people used to build houses; this was from a mountain! A mountain that had watched as their empire grew from a collection of tribes to the mightiest civilization in history. This mountain could have watched as legions marched to and from the frontier, conquering new lands and putting down rebellions. The stories this rock she held in her hand could tell!

He had continued going and was now standing on a more level part of the mountain that was covered in grass. Behind him was the outskirts of a forest with the tallest trees Vytilia had ever seen. She set the rock down and carefully slid down to join him, gaping up at these massive arboreal wonders. She ran to the nearest one, hugging it. It was so beautiful! The trunk was wider than any below. It was healthy and brown with small black insects climbing up and down and avians nesting in the branches. This tree was a veritable metropolis of life! By the gods, she wished she could carry this tree and take it with her, just to look at it, to put on display in Nidus, so all may see its splendor, plebeian and patrician alike!

"Hey, would you look at this?" She pushed away from the tree forlornly to see Friedrich kneeling. He picked something up and turned around. He was holding . . . some kind of plant life. Vytilia stepped closer. What he held had a long, skinny green stalk, topped by a flat surface. Pointed and fuzzy white leaves jutted out from the center while yellow bulbs rested in the "mouth" like many pairs of eyes. It was small and white, and despite being on the ground, was clean and bright.

"What is it?" she asked, leaning in to where her nose nearly touched it.

"It's an edelweiss!" Friedrich announced. "They're a bit hard to come across. They only grow high up in the mountains during certain times of the year. Sometimes you hear them called Sunna's spoor or Sunna's steps, showing she can grow life even this high up." He gestured for her to take it, which she did, twirling it between her fingers. "It almost looks happy to see you."

"But what is it?" She stroked the leaves. They felt like they were made of wool.

"It's a blossom," Friedrich explained.

"A blossom?"

He nodded. "They're a kind of greenery, brightly colored with a nice smell. Folks will grow different kinds of them in gardens or set them up on ploughlands for bees."

She continued to study the edelweiss, careful not to rip any of the leaves. "So, they are a kind of crop?"

"They're not really for eating, Edelweiss are for looks." His heartrate elevated. "It reminded me of you because of the white petals and your hair and the golden buds." His face started getting red. He had to turn away. She smiled, tucking the edelweiss into her hair.

"I love it," she told him. He turned back around, walking beside her as they continued down. "Could you tell me more about these bees?"

"Bees are these little bugs." He held his thumb and pointer finger a bit apart to demonstrate. "They're yellow and black and live in hives, hundreds upon hundreds of them crammed into a hive. They fly out, go from blossom to blossom, then that makes honey. They also make the best candle wax."

"Honey?"

"Honey is this gold, sticky stuff that tastes heavenly. You can spread it on some toast, bake it into a sweet, or glaze ham with it. You can even brew it, turn it into mead. It's a staple of the winter holidays, church galdrs, and this new kind of thinkers."

"Wait!" she interrupted. "I know what you are talking about! Apiculture! My mother told me about it. Her uncle owned the largest collection of apiaries in Nidus! In the olden days, honey was a staple ingredient in fine Sanguinvinum!" She was so excited. "That is something we did! That is a Strixan practice! And your people are still doing it! That is something we can relate to when we establish regular diplomatic ties, an interest in apiculture! See, our two peoples are not so different." She shook her head. "A pity we could not continue; Apēs cannot survive underground. Instead, we raise eclipses of tineae to pollinate what few crops we have."

"Tineae?"

"Small, furry winged insects. They can sometimes glow."

She means moths, Friedrich reasoned. *What else could live underground*?

Vytilia fiddled with the edelweiss while she thought. If mankind knew of apiculture, did it develop naturally, or was it taught to them by Strixans? She was both excited and nervous. Every new thing she learned of the surface improved her interconnected history theory but also proved Strixans were the Half-god of man's legend. She had to be careful. "If it is not too much trouble, would it be possible to acquire some honey? I have always wanted to try it. My mother used to love it, but by the time I was born, all our reserves had been used up."

"Sure. Next town we come to, we can buy a bottle of it somewhere. Or we might stumble across a beekeeper. A real one, not the thinkers."

She hid a smile with her left hand while the right played with the edelweiss. The giving of this blossom, as he called it, was a kind gesture, but she could tell it was much more symbolic to Friedrich. She silenced a gasp. Was Friedrich . . . attracted to her? Her first impulse was that she was flattered, especially since Friedrich seemed to be coming from a more heartfelt stance than the tiercels that lived at the Arx. He was respectful and kept his eyes and hands to himself, which she would always appreciate. Even then, as grateful as she was, she could only feel pity; he would get his heart broken. For starters, her father would never approve of such a pairing, then there was the difference in age, background, not to mention they were different beings, and, she did not feel the same way. She respected him but mutual attraction? That was nonexistent.

Was it?

There was a small voice, a small almost insignificant doubt in her mind, that perhaps she was being too hasty. Maybe there was some attraction. She respected him, enjoyed his company, was genuine in her compliments, and greatly enjoyed receiving them from him. Are these not the first steps to attraction? And he would actually listen to her talk about history, something the other Praetor's sons found disinteresting.

She shook her head. She was overanalyzing again. This was all a daydream, a fantasy, she told herself. Respect and attraction were two completely different things. She only felt the former, not the latter. She should not bother herself with this. She needed to let him down gently, forge a lasting friendship, but just that: a friendship. Perhaps, if time would allow, she could help him find . . . a replacement, a replacement hen, er, woman to be attracted to.

They came to a break in the tree line and were met by the dark eyes of a grazing cow. It lowed at them and went back to its grass. Vytilia had to do a double-take at the creature. It was massive. She had never seen a cow that was so tall, or fat, or with such a powerful heartbeat. This specimen was twice, almost three times the size of the cattle back underground. It was so healthy. The eyes were not glazed over. It was happy! She reached her hand out to touch it, but the beast reeled back, letting out a deep bellowing moo. It turned its head, took one last look back at Vytilia, and walked away to graze elsewhere. She felt offended, especially after one mooed happily after Friedrich petted it on the back.

In the center of the cows was a herdsman holding a shovel, watching the two of them closely, laughing when the cow refused to let Vytilia touch it. She stayed a good distance away from any of the beasts while Friedrich approached the man and spoke with him, returning after a few minutes.

"I know where we are now," he announced. "We're in Baivor. It's the largest land in the south of the Realm."

"Where do we go from here?"

"Well, according to the herdsman there, who was very nice about us crossing through his fields, our best path is to keep heading down into the dale until we get to the town of Salzahoi. There's a pawn broker there and a guesthouse we can spend the night. From there, we just follow the road to Weinetsee, then onto Mondsruhe, the Head-Stead."

"Head-Stead?"

"Main town or burgh, where the Herzog sits."

"A capital city?"

"Your word, not mine."

"This name, Mondsruhe, it sounds strong, a good name for a city."

"Well, it does mean 'Moon's rest.'" Her eyes lit up. "Not named after your moon. Holy Máni is the Warden Holy of the town and all of Baivor."

They pressed on through the field, watching their step as they went. "You know where we are and where to go all from a brief conversation? That is an impeccable sense of direction."

He blushed again. "Only thing I know how to read is a map."

"Can you not read?"

"No. Well . . . not fully. I know some runes, and I know a few words. But other than that, it's all Cataskal to me."

She was shocked. "Why can you not read?" They stopped.

"I was never taught. Herr Bergmann hardly knew how, and Frau Beck didn't know how to teach it. We could never find a house-teacher for a cheaper rate." He shrugged. "I can get by without it."

"Oh, but you should learn to read! Everything I know I learned from reading or my mother, and what she learned was from reading! It is the most valuable skill in the world!"

"But I don't need it!" he insisted. "Caverneering doesn't need a lot of reading, and I know how to read a map. I have real skills; smithing, baking, sewing, woodworking. These are things I can do with my hands and can make gold off of."

She frowned. "Is that all that matters to you? Making money?"

"Having chips means having food. How did you feel before you killed that poor deer down with the elves?"

"Awful, as if I was coming apart at the seams. Every part of me was crying out in pain."

He resumed walking. "That's what it's like going hungry."

She stayed where she was, humbled. There was much she still had to learn and not from reading.

That was perhaps the moral of her journey so far; she had much to learn, much that would not be found in a scroll or codex. From the way station, to her strange upsetness about the female nymphs fawning over Friedrich, to this lush world around her. So far, the world was her favorite learning experience.

There was not a passage nor prose written that could explain what she saw. Everything around her was alive. It was connected. When air blew through the treetops, it was like a lung inhaling. Avians nested on branches, small mammals collected seeds and nuts, everything was interrelated. This was life, or, what life should be. She plucked a leaf off of a low-hanging branch, smelling it and running it through her hands, tracing her fingers along the edge. She lifted it up, holding it where she could see the veins. It was almost like a body with arteries for water instead of blood. This tree was not any different from her, only rearranged by different means. She was once more humbled.

Now that she could see it in the flesh, she now understood why green had been her mother's favorite color. It was so plentiful, an abundance in every nook and cranny. There was green on the tree branches, on the ridges of the tree bark, on rocks, green plants resting on the water, and even green insects. It was all the same color, yet it blended together to form such a rich portrait of the world, meshing seamlessly with the other shades of nature. A thousand artists with a thousand years could not capture but one-one thousandth of this majesty. Yet, despite all this, there was still a pervasive sense of melancholy, a lingering bad taste that this land had been the Strixan's home, and they had been driven from it, forced in the monochrome, monotonous underground. But man lived here, not the devils. Why would the devils drive the Strixans away and not take the land for themselves? Was that not the natural order, groups driving out other groups for their resources? Even animals understood this principle, and the devils were little more than animals. So where were they?

"Is all of the surface like this?" she asked to push away her melancholy. She waved her hand to encompass the valley and the mountains, "with the trees and the green and the rivers and the green."

"Not all of it. To the east, there's a kingdom called Bouya. A lot of travelers say it's nothing but ice and snow and always has a bitter winter, a winter so cold, it freezes the marrow in your bones." He shuddered just thinking about the chill. "To the south is Ifrin; it has lands like Misr and Arava. They're nothing but sand."

"Would you like to visit these places one day?" she asked as she pulled a handful of black, bulbous berries off of a bush, studying them between her fingers. These lands solely made of ice or sand were intriguing.

He shook his head. "Herr Bergman and I always wanted to go caverneering in the Kardaken mountains in the east but that never happened. They're too far away, and neither of us knew the local tongues or had any friends there. It wouldn't be feasible."

"Well, with thaumaturgy, you could learn those languages easily. Imagine how easy commerce and exploring will be when you can learn a language in a matter of minutes!"

"You know . . . you never did tell me how thaumaturgy works."

Her eyes lit up. "You are right! Oh, I need to get started right away, but first." She popped one of the berries into her mouth and chewed it. "These are delectable. We shall need to bring some of these back." She dropped the rest and burned her hands clean. "First, I need you to forget everything you know about 'witchcraft' or anything like that. That will make explaining easier."

"My mind is empty." It was good hearing her excited again. It complicated things, but it gave both of them the push they needed to keep going. He was tired, but they were still aways away from Salzahoi.

"Good. Now, it is properly called thaumaturgy, not witchcraft or weirdcraft or whatever else you call it. If you want to call it anything, call it thaumaturgy or 'wonder working.' Wonder working is the direct translation."

"So, not witchcraft but wondercraft."

She beamed. "Exactly. I would prefer if you called it wonder working, but that is much better than the derogatory witchcraft." He nodded in agreement. "Now, therefore, one who practices thaumaturgy is either a thaumaturgist or a wonder worker. If someone has a specific field, they are an Operarius with their discipline prefixed before that: Lapis-, Ignis-, Aqua-, and so on and so on. From here on, I will call it wonder working to make things simple."

"What is your discipline?" he asked.

"Technically, it would be an Omnioperius or an 'everything worker.' Normally, most workers only have one, maybe two disciplines they will study through the course of their lifetime. But I was something of a prodigy, and my mother insisted on teaching me in many fields. Student of many but master of none. Yet, at least."

Friedrich suppressed a yawn. She was right. This was much different than the witchcraft he'd heard about with a lot bigger words.

"Anyway, I was getting off topic and bragging, apologies." A grin peeked at the corner of his mouth. "With the nomenclature out of the way, it is time to understand what wonder working is. It is, essentially, the manipulation of the natural world and natural forces through mindpower. Or, to simplify it, I can change and mold the world with my brain."

Friedrich nearly tripped. "How?"

"Through diligent study. A wonder worker has to truly comprehend what it is they are working with. It is not enough to know that fire is hot, or water is wet. One has to know how hot fire can burn, how to fuel it, how to control it. One must know everything about what they are studying. And one has to have the substance nearby to work with it. Wonder working cannot be done *ex nihilo*."

He didn't ask but gathered what "ex nihilo" meant from context.

"This is why most wonder workers will spend centuries on one school. A true master can do unimaginable wonders. But because of this, many are limited. Someone who studies fire cannot move a mountain, and one who studies water cannot put someone to sleep."

"You're 400 years old, but I've seen you shoot fire, water, rocks, heal wounds, learn my tongue, and put me to sleep. And your kind lives forever. How come more workers don't master everything?"

"Remember, I am a student of many schools, but I have not mastered any. I can shoot fire but cannot melt metal. I can pull water out of plants but not put it back in. There are many wonders I can do but far more I cannot."

That made sense, Friedrich admitted to himself.

"And, wonder working comes at a cost. Because it is tied to one's mind, the mind can be damaged if one overstrains oneself. There are stories of thaumaturgists even dying from mental exhaustion. The brain needs to be trained and grown to do certain wonders. I can read about advanced wonders, but I need to prepare my mind to do those."

"It is odd . . ." Friedrich began, suppressing another yawn. "Having heard all this, I can't help but ask where the tales about 'witchcraft' came from. Nothing you said, well almost nothing, is anything like what the witchy tales say. There aren't calling-rings, big bubbling cauldrons, bargains with lightless, and no black meetings."

"Well, like the 'vampire' story, it seems there is a kernel of truth buried under centuries of time and falsehoods."

They had exited the forest, coming to a well-worn trail, carved with wagon-wheel ruts and horse tracks. Friedrich looked up at the sun. "We've still got a few stounds of sunlight left," he explained, yawning. "We should be there just before nightfall."

"How can you tell what time it is?" She quickly glanced up at the sun before turning away and rubbing her eyes.

"The sun rises in the east in the morning then climbs across the sky to set in the west. When it's right above us, it's midday. Since it's summer, it takes slightly longer for the sun to set, giving us more daylight."

"You can tell the time just by the position of the sun?" He nodded. "Incredible."

"Herr Bergmann was the one who actually taught me those Church tales. He told me about sunrise, sunset, all the holy days, how the world rings around the sun."

"You mean the sun orbits the planet, right?" she asked.

He stared at her blankly. "No."

"That, that is, that is incorrect," she insisted. "The correct cosmology is that the sun and moon both orbit the planet. Luna and Sol are watching us, but they do so in shifts like sentries at a military encampment."

"That's not what I was taught. Erde rings the sun, or God, or heaven. I'm not sure on that, and then the moon rings Erde."

"It appears it is not only your culture, but your sciences that have kernels of truth hidden under many strata of falsehoods."

Arguing with Vytilia over "science" was a losing battle, so Friedrich let it go.

They had walked down a street lined with small houses with fields and pastures behind each little cottage. She stopped just outside of the boundary of a cottage. It was small, built partially into the side of a hill. The bottom story was made of wood, overlaid with a whitewash. Small windows, placed in wrought-iron stills, were placed evenly along the side. A large wooden roof sat on top, overlooking the house like a guard tower.

A housewife was working in her garden, placing root vegetables in a basket, her back turned to them. A small nestling, a hen with curled, blonde hair saw Vytilia and stumbled over to her. She cooed and waved, staring intently at Vytilia. Her eyes were drawn to the edelweiss in her hair. Vytilia bit her lips, careful to hide her fangs, before finally deciding to hand the blossom to the child. The nestling accepted it, giggling and stumbling back towards her mother.

The cottage seemed cozy, full of heart and life. It was a home, not a mere residence like where she and her father lived. She felt ill, not physically, but emotionally, yearning for something she did not have. She quickly turned away from the cottage and caught back up to Friedrich, who was a good distance ahead of her. She was . . . envious of these people! She was envious of what these plebeians had! Their clothes were plain, they were unbathed, most likely illiterate like Friedrich, yet their homes were bigger, more inviting, the nestlings happy and full of life. How often did the nestlings back home smile? When did Strixan homes stop being . . . homes?

She glanced at Friedrich. He may have been loyal only to his purse and his next drink, spending his days digging through caves, yet his life was simple, almost admirable. He did not deal with politicking, he did not worry about how he presented himself, and he did not have a family honor that hung on his every action. He may not have been eloquent or as intelligent as she was, but she was asking herself if this was more of a curse rather than a blessing. She could scoff and dismiss him all she liked, but at the end of the day, who was happier? She . . . she was jealous of Friedrich, his people, his whole race. If only there were some way to live like them, live amongst them, experience what they experienced, see the world as they saw it! She looked again at Friedrich, who had slowed his pace and was looking back at her. Was there a way to live like them and live . . . with them?

"Everything alright back there?" he asked.

"Indeed! Everything is fine!" She ran to catch up with him. "I, I got distracted. All of this is so new to me. I was occupied."

"Oh." He saw the edelweiss now absent in her hair. "You, you got rid of it." His voice sounded pained.

"Not maliciously." She quickly explained. "That little nestling hen, she, she was admiring it."

He turned back around to keep walking. "It's alright, I get it." His voice quavered slightly. "They're called children. We call them children. And she's a girl, not a hen." He still sounded hurt.

"I did appreciate it when you gave it to me," she insisted. "I thought it right to return the gesture!"

He ignored her, continuing to walk languidly until the road eventually came to a T-crossing. The left path circled around, following the curvature of a hill, headed upwards towards hilly ground, the path flanked by forested mountains. The right path extended up towards a flatter land, beyond the tree line. They could see small clusters of buildings continuing down the path. A signpost sat at the head of the intersection. At least, Vytilia thought it was a signpost. The "letters" looked as if someone had hacked the wood with an axe, trying to draw rather than write. Friedrich headed to the left, walking along the shoulder of the road as a wagon passed by, headed to the right.

"Is that your script?" she asked. "Hardly looks like letters at all!" She muttered that last part to herself.

"It's called futhark or new futhark."

"Fascinating. Is it a phonetic alphabet or pictorial?"

"I don't know. How would I know that? I can't read?"

"Of course. You, you just told me that." She should have known that! The remarks about the blossom must have distracted her. His tone was snippy.

Friedrich sighed. He was tired, tired in body, tired in mind, and now tired in feeling. And they still had several wegstunde to walk. *Am I an idiot?* he asked himself. What was he thinking? He wasted an edelweiss! She just ended up squandering it on some kid! She didn't even say thank you! Typical upper-rank snob, used to getting everything on a silver platter only to throw it away.

What a fool he was. If he'd given that to an elf girl or even just the next toiler woman he met, they'd cherish it forever! He knew Herr Bergmann would've been on the floor laughing then would take Friedrich out and buy him a drink to forget his troubles.

Damn, he missed Herr Bergmann. He tried repressing, even forgetting what had happened, but he couldn't: the fiend's roar, the sickening sound of claw on stone, and those eyes, those soulless, awful white eyes, staring at him. He couldn't even give him a proper burning; all that was left was probably bones and rags. He deserved better. He should've died peacefully in a nice house, just like he always wanted! And what justice was there for Friedrich? Stuck with this vampire blueblood, trudging through the ass end of Baivor, falling for a monster, giving his soul to a race of inhuman monsters who would kill or enslave his own kind if given the chance. What a fool he was, what a fool! He listened to his heart and mind once in his life, rather than his gut, and it'll end up biting him in the ass or more likely, the neck.

"Is everything well?" Vytilia asked. "Your heartrate started elevating."

"I'm alright. Stop that."

"What? Listening?"

"Yes, it's . . . off-putting."

She pinched the bridge of her nose and shook her head. He was probably still upset about that blossom. "If it meant that much to you, I will go back and steal the damn plant from the child! Would you accept that?"

"I don't care about the blossom!" he snapped. "I . . . ah forget it! Let's just get to Salzahoi. I'm too tired to argue."

Could he be using the blossom to vent his frustration about the death of his master? Vytilia asked herself. She was unsure of how to proceed. She could risk offending Friedrich, driving a wedge between the two of them and compromising their mission. Perhaps it is best, for now, to let sleeping calcerta lie.

I've set myself up for failure, again, Friedrich thought. He got his hopes up, for God knows whatever reason, only for them to be dashed again. Being right left such a bitter taste in his mouth. How was he not used to it? He knew Vytilia wouldn't fully understand how important giving an edelweiss is, but for someone as smart as her, she should have been able to see it was important. Maybe she really didn't care and was using him, molding his mind with her witchcraft. She had just told him she could. Maybe it was a birthright for vampire lords? How else could they keep their underlings calm for thousands of years?

But, the more he thought, ignoring his exhaustion and his sore body, he realized that he couldn't stay mad at her. He didn't *want* to be mad. He remembered why he was starting to fall for her, everything he admired about her, was heartened by her, and could depend on her. Did she know? Well, she had to, by now. He had made it obvious, and given her smarts, she would have had to notice. That was a given. But did she . . . return anything? He guessed maybe? She had been trying to get to know him, she was kinder, and was listening and trusting him more. If that wasn't her taking a liking to him, he didn't know what it was. Unless she was simply being friendly and only friendly, which could also be true. Or she could be gaining his trust to do her mission before killing him. No, no, he shouldn't think like that. It was wrong and rude. And she made no sign to show she would. Afterall, she did say if she wanted to, she would have done so already.

If she wasn't simply being friendly, well, then that only left her feeling similarly to how he felt, which was good. At least, he thought it was. But if that was the case, he didn't know what to do from there. In all honesty, these last few weeks had been the longest he'd ever spoken to a girl, let alone been around one. Who could he ask for help? Should he even ask for any? There was the ever-present reminder in the back of his mind that she was a blood-drinking, undying, witchy vampire. Is this even something he should pursue? If anyone found out, the best outcome would be disfellowship, and that was if everyone he met was understanding; the worst case was being either burned at the stake or hung. Did he really care what anyone else thought? Afterall, he wanted to retire and live out his days away from everyone else. If he had a beautiful vampire at his side, that was even better.

He was letting his imagination run wild, causing him to laugh to himself.

"Something funny happen?" she asked, smiling slightly.

"Oh, uh, nothing. Just remembering a . . . funny-looking cow I saw. I always think of it when I'm tired." His face had gone red, and she heard his heartrate pick up. He was lying, but she decided not to press it.

"Do you want to take a break?" she asked. "You have been walking strangely, and you keep yawning."

He yawned, shaking his head. "No, no Salzahoi should be just around this mountain. I can do it. Herr Bergmann and I use to walk a wegtag[34] every day for weeks."

"But you did not do that after climbing up a mountain and recovering from fighting a lupus."

"Wolf," he corrected. "We call them wolves." He stopped to yawn again, looking up as the sky started to gain a purple tint. Night was coming soon. "I'm tired, but I'll make it." He was moments away from just passing out on the trail. His body was asking for it. All that stopped him was sheer willpower.

"Look!" Vytilia pointed in the diminishing daylight. Ahead of them was a wooden fence. At last, they reached Salzahoi. They arrived just in time; the town gatekeeper was closing the gate across the main trail. Friedrich gained a second wind, and they pressed on.

---

34. The larger counterpart to a wegstunde. The distance an average man can travel in a day. Officially regarded as a distance of around 25 US Miles but can vary between man to man.

14

The sun continued to lower in the sky, which turned into a tapestry of orange, red, yellow, and purple. Vytilia was in awe, staring up at the colored clouds (the mountains prevented her from seeing the sun). It was not until she nearly collided with another passerby, Friedrich apologizing profusely, that she took her attention away. She shifted her focus to the people around her. Afterall, this was her first time in a mannish settlement. They walked by more cottages, barns, and sheds. Some were new and clean, while others were old and weathered. The people they passed by were happy and hardworking, pausing to talk with one another as they carried loads or pushed handcarts. Their clothes were bright, and their children were smiling. If this was but a sample of the surface, it was nowhere near as bleak as Friedrich had made it seem.

Friedrich, meanwhile, was looking to the left, examining the wagons as they passed by, thinking back to what Herr Bergmann had said about being a trader. Carrying salt barrels and sacks of flour in a horse-drawn wagon was a lot more enticing than walking from cave to cave. Maybe it was Vytilia, maybe it had been spending over a week underground, but caverneering was starting to lose its appeal. His whole life, his goal, everything he knew was becoming less tasteful.

Salzahoi was a splendid little town, nestled comfortably at the foot of a small range of lush, verdant mountains. A green-colored river feeding from a briny lake flowed past the town, headed to the northwest. The town square was quaint, constructed around the main road they were travelling on with the largest attraction being the town hall or *rathaus* as Friedrich later called it. The rathaus was a half-timbered building two floors tall with a clock as large as a man observing the town from its spire-like clocktower. The rathaus was painted white, with sea-green trim, making it look like a large block of salt. The buildings around it were painted in reds, blues, greens, yellows, more colors than Vytilia had ever seen! They all had glass windows, large wooden doors, and wooden balconies where laundry hung or people leaned against, resting after a long day. Most of the roofs were thatched, though several, especially those closer to the rathaus, had tiled roofs, some even in the process of replacing the thatch. The only complaint either of them had was the pervasive and thick smell of vinegar and brine.

Though, Vytilia did have questions. "This is a typical surface town?" she asked. He nodded. "Where are the aqueducts? And the sewer drains?"

"The what and the what?"

"How do you get water? And dispose of animal leavings?"

He pointed to a circular stone structure in the center of the town square. "The well or the river is where most get water. Or a spring if you're lucky to be by one. And then 'leavings' are in the outhouse or thrown in the midden." He pointed to a wooden box in front of a row of residential buildings. She observed as several residents emptied wide ceramic bowls into the box. She dared not ask what was in the bowls.

"And it sits there?" She felt sick.

"No, the nightmen come and take it away. Usually sell it to ploughman as 'nightsoil.' Suppose to be really good for crops."

First things first, Vytilia decided. *When diplomacy is established, we are teaching men how to build aqueducts and sewers.*

They walked towards the rathaus, passing by a building where people were loudly cheering and singing. "That's a beerhall," Friedrich pointed out. "If gold wasn't an issue, I wouldn't mind spending a few stounds in there." Vytilia rolled her eyes.

Friedrich stopped a better dressed man who was on his way to the beerhall. He asked for directions to the nearest guesthouse with the man pointing westward, telling them to follow a spur off of the main road. Friedrich thanked the man before they left.

They came to a small two-floor building at the edge of the town, facing the river. It was made of wood with a yellow-thatched roof, a well-built wooden fence surrounding the property. A long line of stables was built on the right side of the house. They opened the gate leading up to the property, closing it behind them, and knocked on the door. An older, heavyset woman in a low-cut bodice and apron peeked out from behind the half-open door, staring suspiciously at them.

Friedrich cleared his throat, maintaining eye contact. "*Guten Nacht, gnädige Frau.*[35] We were wondering if you had a room for the night?"

The woman looked Friedrich up and down, pausing on the sword. It was expected for a Teudish adult to carry one weapon. Two was suspicious. And a sword was unlawful. Then she looked past him and took a long, curious look at Vytilia, who was looking down at her own feet. "We do. Come, come in." She opened the door and invited them inside. "I warn you, my husband, Otloh, fought in the war. If you cause any trouble with that sword, there will be hell to pay."

"No need to worry, gnädige Frau, it's a big knife, not a sword. And we are weary from our trek. We seek only a room and a meal."

"My name is Krüger."

"I am Ulrich Bauer. This is my wife, Wilhelmina, but we call her Mina." Vytilia, still staring at her feet, widened her eyes.

"We finished eating a half stound ago, but there's still some stew warming on the fire. We can settle the cost in the morning. For now, you'll sign our guestbook," she explained. Friedrich walked over to the guestbook, scribbling something unreadable where Frau Krüger pointed. She led the pair over to a dining room where the smell of food still lingered. They sat down at a bench, both taking a deep breath and leaning on the table. Frau Krüger returned with two bowls and wooden spoons, placing them on the table. "Would either of you care for a beer?" she asked.

"I would," Friedrich told her. "But, none for her please. She is with child."

Frau Krüger smiled at Vytilia and congratulated her. She left, returning with a tall, dented stein brimming with foam. She told them to just call for her when they were done and retired. As he enjoyed a long sip, he saw Vytilia giving him a death glare.

"What?" he asked, taking a bite of stew. "I can taste some garlic. Don't eat it."

"I do not know what you think you are getting at, Friedrich Bauer, telling people I am expecting." She hissed and looked down at her food, shooting it full of daggers.

"I told you to trust me, didn't I? Folks will be kinder if they think we're a young, soon-to-be-parents couple. I bet just that little comment took a good chunk out of our bill." She frowned. "Herr

---

35. "Gracious lady" used when a female's surname is not known.

Bergmann and I would do it all the time on our treks; our usual spiel was a father and son on a wayfareage."

She was not impressed, still glowering at him.

He leaned in to whisper. "And, most don't look kindly on an unwedded couple traveling together. We come across the wrong crowd, they may whip us for it. And, after everything that's happened in the last twenty years, a baby is news anyone can enjoy."

Her glower started to fade. Strixans had similar views on chastity. "It is wrong to lie. Deception is a vice and unbecoming of a civilized people," Vytilia countered.

"So Strixans never lie?"

"Of course they do, but that does not make it correct or moral. A good and true Strixan is both candid and conscientious."

"But," Friedrich now countered in a low whisper, "there's more than one kind of lie, just as there is more than one kind of meat. Cow, pig, chicken, duck, hedgehog, they even eat dog down in Helvensland. All of it is eatable, but some of it is better than others. If you put a plate of roasted rat in front of me, I'd think you were touched in the head. But if you gave me a bit of horse, I'd be willing to try it."

She was skeptical and twisted her face accordingly. "What then is a 'good lie?'"

"What Bergmann taught me is we aren't lying to rob this guesthouse blind. We're lying so we have enough to live another day. If you're lying to take, you're begging. If you're lying to keep, that's staying alive."

There was a twisted logic to his words, though she did somewhat regret telling Princeps Porcia that men were virtuous. But, in all her readings and lessons, she never did stumble across a Strixan hero who was entirely viceless. Each one had their faults, and she supposed, for the good of the empire, this would be hers. She did say she would trust him and follow his lead now that they were on the surface. "It feels unscrupulous," she told him, gently patting her womb, "but I will play along, only doing so under protest."

"You know, I thought the same thing when we were elven gods."

She covered her mouth as she stifled an unconscious laugh before forcing her face back to stoic. That was odd. "I am curious, why did you give the innkeeper an alias?"

Friedrich yawned as he took another drink. "Herr Bergmann always warned me never to give out your real name. Names are supposed to have power to them, so it's not something you give away. There's the risk of having a crime pinned on you or someone using your name to commit fraud."

"So, tell me about our aliases. You kept your *nomen gentilicium* but changed our *praenomen*. Any reasoning behind those names?"

"Right, first, it's family name or last name." She nodded in understanding. "Second, it's called a given name. And third, Bauer is a widespread name. It means ploughman or tiller or toiler, someone low-born who grows crops." Vytilia almost choked at hearing that. "Ulrich is actually one of my middle names. This way, it's not a fake name, just stretching the truth."

"One of your middle names?" She smiled coyly, forcing her face back to tight-lipped. "What are the rest?"

"Goswin. Friedrich Goswin Ulrich Bauer." He rattled off his name rather unenthusiastically, a fact that displeased Vytilia.

"You say it like it's a chore."

He shrugged. "It's just a name. There's probably a thousand Friedrichs and tens of thousands of Bauers."

"But it is *your* name, your connection to your family, your ancestors. Are you not named after a familiar relation? Do you not pass on names as a patrimony?"

His face went sullen as she spoke. He looked away from her, staring at the table. "I . . . I don't know," he admitted. "We're supposed to name children after family and friends. Especially one who died, so they can live on, but I don't know if I am."

Vytilia bit her lip. She had unwittingly trodden on an uncomfortable subject. Yet, her curiosity was nagging at her. That mention of naming a child after an ancestor so a spirit lived on was intriguing. It reminded her of a Strixan practice, though one that had been popularized after the cataclysm.

"Well, whoever the first Friedrich was, I am sure he would be proud of the work you are doing." He seemed to smile at that. Maybe he thought it was true, or maybe he enjoyed it as a comforting lie.

"I don't know if there was a first Friedrich. Instead I ask myself if Bergmann would approve, and I like to think he would."

Now they were getting somewhere. Vytilia had to admit she was curious about Friedrich's past. She had spoken so much of the Strixans' history. Now she wanted to know some of his. "You said you had been apprenticed since you were six?" She recalled the conversation with her father. Talking about his trade would let her know more of him.

"That's right. In other trades, you're usually a bit older, but Bergmann didn't have a wife to leave me with, and we didn't meet Frau Beck until a few years later, so anytime he went caverneering, I came with him. Early on, I would fuse the ends of rope, make sure the lantern wicks were greased, or tend to the donkey while he went into the caves. I'd spend the day, sometimes days, alone until he came back up. I had to learn how to start and care for a fire rather quickly and get used to the taste of salt meat."

"Did you enjoy it?"

"At first, no. But it beat starving in an orphanage. Once I turned nine, Bergmann started showing me how to climb, how to set a waypoint, the difference between gold and halfwit's gold. From then on, we were basically workmates, splitting our finds evenly and making decisions together, even though I was still just a fellow." He sighed, taking another sip. "Of course, I use fellow as a joke. There's no caverneer guild."

Vytilia noticed he never outright said he started to enjoy it. "Have you ever considered what your life would be like if you were not a caverneer?" She tried phrasing that so it did not sound malicious.

"I assume it would've been boring. Spend my whole life in one hamlet, tilling the ground harvest after harvest, though I might've been wedded at this point." He picked up his stew bowl and started drinking it directly, horrifying Vytilia. "Of course," he resumed after setting it down and wiping his mouth, "I wouldn't have met Herr Bergmann, or Frau Beck, or you." His face went red.

She turned away. She had had an idea, letting it nurture and grow as they walked, of inviting him to stay underground at Nidus as a live-in ambassador and resident expert on the world of men. Was it partially because she was still working through her own misunderstood attraction to him? Possibly. Was it also because she thought he could be happier underground than he could above it? Also, possibly. The greatest gift a Strixan could bestow on an ally was the rights of citizenship, and if the weapons they procured were effective, the Concilium could be convinced to grant Friedrich citizenship rather than pay him a hefty sum of gold. If he lived underground, perhaps she could, well, civilize him, teach him to read, how to argue logically, turn him into a Strixan in all but blood. Her father might approve, and maybe . . . well, she was getting carried away with something she did not understand (or did not want to understand), and that something was distracting. Their mission came first. Anything else she had to bottle up and save for later. All these previous conversations about marriage and nestlings were fogging her mind.

He called for Frau Krüger. She came in, looking down at their bowls. "Why, you hardly ate!" She put a hand on Vytilia's shoulder. "You've got to keep your strength up, my dear. The baby needs it! Trust me, I've had six of my own!" She gave a hearty laugh as she cleared the bowls. "I've got you two set up in our 'honeymoon' room in the attic. It's nice and warm there, and you won't have to worry about waking the rest of the household with any marital noises." She snorted as Vytilia gave her an awkward, toothless smile, and Friedrich laughed.

Frau Krüger led the two upstairs, past rooms full of snoring family members and other guests. When they were on the second floor, she reached up and grabbed a cord hanging from the roof, opening a trap door. She then ducked into a nearby room, retrieving an old, creaky wooden ladder. "Now, when you get to the top, just turn around and head straight back. Your room is unlocked. We serve firstmeal at sunrise; the rooster will give you the time."

Friedrich thanked her, and taking Vytilia by the hand, led her up the ladder. Frau Krüger closed the entrance behind them. The "honeymoon room" was an oversized garret. A small wooden bed, milking stool, and chamber pot were the only furniture. The wooden shutters covering the windows would rattle every time they were hit by the wind.

"If this is the honeymoon room, I'd hate to see the other rooms." Friedrich grinned at his own joke, but it was too dark to see her reaction.

"Maybe she overheard you lie about our situation?" she retorted.

Friedrich walked over to the bed, pulling off the cover and sitting down on the edge. The mattress was lumpy, and the blankets were woolly and itchy, but it beat rocks. "So, uh," his voice started to crack again, "how do we want to do this?"

"I do not need to sleep at the moment," she explained. "I shall stand guard; you take the bed."

"Are you sure?" he asked as he started taking off his shoes.

"I am fine. You need the rest."

He spread out on the bed, stretched, and was asleep within a few minutes. Once he was sound asleep, Vytilia went over and sat on the edge of the bed next to him, processing the day's events. They had climbed out of the side of a mountain, she had seen a true forest for the first time, and she had seen the sun! Her god, she had actually felt his warmth and his light and seen the world as illuminated by him.

The window rattled and shook as the wind picked up. She got up from the bed and went to the window, opening it to stare outside. The surface at night was almost as beautiful as it was in the daytime. Of all she saw in the nighttime, the most spectacular was the moon, as bright as the sun but even more glorious. She could see the craters and dark spots, witness the beautiful and illuminating moonlight she had heard so much about, and feel the love of Luna she had only had described. She uttered a prayer, thanking Luna for this boon, just for the chance to see her goddess in the flesh. It was humbling. How was it that she could be so fortunate? She took it as a sign of providence, a blessing that meeting Friedrich, reaching the surface, all had been guided by Luna and Sol to preserve and protect the Strixans. They would not only survive; they would thrive.

She looked up after finishing her prayer, looking beyond and around the moon where she could see the stars, each of them twinkling and sparkling, looking like nothing she had ever seen before. Behind the stars, she could see bands of purple and dark blue arcing across the night sky, a rich tapestry of natural wonder. All above her were the ancestors, the progenitors of her people. She wanted to sing and to cry of what they had witnessed, observing and watching as the empire rose and fell. Did they wonder where their descendants went? Were they still watching? They must have a thousand-thousand questions whenever a new star joined them.

She wanted to see more. She quietly climbed onto the windowsill then onto the roof, laying on the thatch as she stared upwards. She still could not believe it. That was the sky! It was not an enclosed stone tunnel; it was open and free! Those were not just glowing crystals; those were actual stars! She felt comfortable, more comfortable than she had ever felt before, embraced by the aspect of her goddess. This was her true home, her people's true home, not caves illuminated by rocks, but here under the light of the stars and moon. This was life as it was meant to be, the life her mother had experienced. The air was still, even the sour salty smell was lessened. She was relaxed, relaxed for the first time in what felt like years. Just like the great trees, she wanted to bottle this moment up and bring it back so that every tiercel, hen, and nestling back at Nidus could experience it. She could tour the colonies, showing everyone she encountered this memory, this feeling, from the lowliest plebeian to the Princeps himself.

She was disturbed from her wonder by a ruffling noise and a small "hoot." She stared up at the ridge of the roof. A small avian was resting there, staring at her. It was a rather peculiar specimen with a wide, flat face, a small, curved black beak, two piercing golden eyes, and small tufts of hair sticking up from an ovaloid, brown-black, speckled body. It looked simultaneously fearsome, quizzical, and simple. The creature "hooted" again at her then carefully started walking down towards her, its taloned feet slapping against the thatch of the roof. It stopped at her head, staring at her again, hooting softly.

Slowly, Vytilia brought her arm up, extending it carefully towards the creature. It stepped backwards then stopped, allowing her to touch it. It was soft, not unlike nestling fur, but there was a rigidity to the softness and powerful muscle beneath. The creature even seemed to enjoy it, cooing as she stroked. It was feathers! She realized after one had fallen from the tail. She picked it up and examined it. In structure and color, it resembled the feathers she found back where they landed in the nymph stratum. If these were the same, then it gave credence to her theory that their landing had been softened by a divinely sent flock of avians. But that must mean that these avians were connected to the gods. Which meant . . . "You are a noctua!" she exclaimed in an excited whisper, the noctua sharing in her excitement as it hooed and cooed with joy, rustling its feathers.

Vytilia gave a wide smile, displaying her fangs and hissing. The noctua, not having fangs, opened its beak wide. This was her kinsman! A distant (extremely distant) relation. This was what hen Strixans resembled in their ancestral form. This was what the sacred messengers of Luna looked like. Could this night get any better? Here she was, more or less conversing with one of the most sacred animals in the Strixan religion! Soon, there was more rustling as more noctuae flew down, all standing around and looking up at Vytilia. Fledglings crawled onto her lap, and she held the smaller ones in her hand. The hooting was symphonic. She added her hisses to this harmony of praises to the moon.

Whatever doubt there was in her mind, any tiny fear or uncertainty, was banished. If this was not evidence of her mission being guided by the gods, what else was there? She was surrounded by family! Sacred family! Luna herself was smiling down on her! A few of the noctuae had even brought her vermin and small mammals, placing them on her lap, almost as a gift. She graciously accepted them, biting and drinking as the noctuae all continued to hoo. As she drank, out of curiosity, she tuned out the noctuae and listened to the world around, perhaps hoping for a message from Luna herself to be whispered on the wind.

But there was something else, not a message, but a heartbeat, maybe two. They were miles away, past the horizon, but they were familiar. Not familiar in that she knew who they belonged to, but she recognized the creature. It was large, quadrupedal, and animalistic. It was not a devil. Could it be a lupus? Not possible, not likely, she was being paranoid, trying to find fault in an otherwise majestic occasion. Friedrich mentioned men knew of lupi. They were still extant and must live in the woodlands. Perhaps she was just hearing a pair of those. She was confident. Her mission was blessed by the gods. Neither lupus nor devil would stop her from accomplishing it. They had gotten away; they were going to succeed.

• • •

Šar Šarrāni Molek waited outside the god's chambers, standing in the long, tall hallway that connected the chambers to the rest of the palace complex. The hallway was made of finely quarried sandstone and decorated with ancient, and admittedly forgettable, works of art. Molek sat on a low couch, made from extinct hide and filled with extinct feathers. The herald would look up at him every so often before returning to amusing themselves with little clay sculptures. He wasn't summoned, at least not yet. Instead, he had chosen to come before the gods. And he was giddy.

This was a rare feeling for him. He could remember all the times he had been before on one finger. But when his scouts and agents had told him and his brother officers the news, he knew he had to see it in the flesh. And here came the bearer of bad news now . . . .

Arkhegtis Phlegyas slumped down the hallway towards the chamber doors. His tail was appropriately tucked between his legs, and his dogface sullen and downcast. He did not even growl at the now grinning Molek. They both stood before the great brass doors as the herald announced their arrival.

They walked in together, Molek barely containing his excitement and Phlegyas giving no effort to disguise his fear. Sky Father and Ground Mother looked at each other, curious at why both had arrived, then listened as both prostrated and recited the platitudes.

"Arise, both of you. What news do you bring?"

Phlegyas swallowed, avoiding the gaze of his lords. "Oh dominates of all life, most merciful of masters . . ." he made the whining moan all dogs did when scolded. "My agent has failed. The trespassers live."

Sky Father sat upright then leaned forward. A visible, fearful look flashed across his face before being banished by a scowl. "What!?"

Phlegyas made the whining noise again. "The agent was killed, drowned by the grey bird."

"You only sent one?" Ground Mother asked. Phlegyas nodded. "I thought you raised them up for their skills as a pack." She directed that at her husband.

Sky Father waved his bride off. "Where are they now?"

"As best as we can tell, they may have escaped to the surface." There was a pregnant pause when Phlegyas finished. None of the servant races, nor even the gods themselves, had been to the surface in thousands of years. It was as foreign and unknown to them as the surface of the moon.

"Miserable dog!" Molek seized the opportunity, striking Phlegyas. "Because of your failure, two cycles may soon unite! Never send a dog to do a demigod's work!"

"Foul demon!" Phlegyas quickly regained his composure, baring his teeth. "Your failure is what caused all of this!"

The two went into a fighting stance, reaching for the swords at their hips.

"Enough!" Sky Father bellowed. He stood up, pulling fire from one of the censures. He formed a ring around the two leaders. They relaxed, hands going to their sides. A lick of flame whipped out, lashing both across the cheek before returning home. "This bickering is pointless!" Sky Father stepped down from his throne, standing before the two leaders. They both prostrated themselves, begging forgiveness. Sky Father bid both of them to stand.

"Both of you are to blame." Ground Mother joined her husband at his side. "This colossal failure has not been seen by our servants before. You are fortunate my dear husband has granted you clemency." She wrapped all four arms around Sky Father.

"It is only because I care little to raise up your replacements that I spare your lives," he explained. Then his tone softened. He grabbed both by their chins, one in each hand, and raised their faces to make eye contact. "But as my beloved bride said, I am a merciful god. Both of you may atone for the failure you have wrought. I may need you in the coming days."

"You truly are merciful lord, oh ruler of all you survey!" Molek squeaked out.

"I shall accept any repentance you ask of me, oh guider of lives!" Phlegyas quickly added.

"A question for both of you." Sky Father looked each in the eye. "Why is it we have the cycles?"

"They are a refiner's fire! So that the sin and vice of generations may be burned away!" Molek quickly piped up.

"And when burned through, an age of peace and prosperity may begin!"

"And why must we burn away the sin and vice of the old worlds?" Sky Father lifted both up to his eye level.

"So that perfect worshippers may recognize and see your glory!" both stammered. This was a recitation they both had memorized by heart. For anyone of their station, it was learned before their own name.

"And?" Ground Mother asked.

"And that you may achieve a true and divine ascendance!"

Sky Father dropped both on the ground. They landed with an echoing and clanking *thud*. "But, if the cycles interact, then the sins and defiance of the old worlds corrupt the new. I seek to gain exaltation, to be reborn in an apotheosis! I need pure, refined, devoted worshippers to do this. And it cannot be done if my servants report nothing but failures!"

"It shall be done my lord!" Phlegyas yelled. "I shall prepare an *agema* of my finest light infantry! I will send a score! They will kill the pink mortal! The cycles shall not interact ever again!"

"Good. Go, leave us, and do not return until the interlopers are dead or your warriors are." Phlegyas stood and began to leave. "Arkhegtis, wait." The beastman turned and bowed. "If your team fails, let them know their families will perish. Their wives will strangle their own babes, and then the wives shall be drowned. And, it should not be said, but be sure to send *married* warriors to the surface."

"It will be done, my lord." His tail was tucked back between his legs as he exited.

Molek similarly began to stand up and leave. "Warmaster, you wait as well." He turned to face the gods. They had returned to their thrones and resumed their lounging position. "Should the dogs fail, your army shall strangle this problem in its cradle. End this alliance before it can begin. Am I understood?"

"I understand, my lord." He went to turn around but paused then stammered out a question. "May I have some of the 'special' hosts to deal with the problem, should it arise?"

Sky Father scratched his chin, seriously studying the request. Then he shook his head. "No need to display our full power yet. But, take what you need from the lessers. If they object, they shall speak with me about it."

Molek hid his grin. "It shall be done my lord."

15

As a rooster crowed, Friedrich grumbled and began to wake up. He looked over. Vytilia was sitting on the windowsill, looking outside. Sunlight was breaking through, causing her to glow. He paused and laid on his side, staring at her. She looked radiant, like a heavenly being from a stained-glass window. He was transfixed, seeing her in this, quite literal, new light. At this time, she was not Vytilia Quintia, vampire lady and user of witchcraft. She was Vytilia, a woman around his age whom he was travelling with, and . . . someone he . . . well he didn't know what he felt or wanted. All he knew was he didn't want to get up and spend the rest of the day walking, worrying about gold. He wanted to stay here and watch her.

She took one last look out the window then turned around and stepped down. She saw Friedrich looking at her and turned to her side, slightly blushing. His heart leapt in his chest at seeing the purple in her cheeks. His mind raced with wonder and possibilities. "It is rude to stare." Her tone was gentle, teasing almost.

"Sorry, I was just waking up," he mumbled as he sat up. He regained control of his senses, focusing on the day ahead.

"How did you sleep?"

He yawned, stretching his arms. "Alright. Had the oddest dream; I was minding my own business, and then I was walking through a sea of owls. Owls, everywhere, all hooting and flying around, staring at me with their big eyes."

She glanced down at the noctua feathers she had collected, quietly tucking them into her belt. "That does sound like a strange dream. But at least you are rested now. Ready to start the day?"

"Ready as I'll ever be." He yawned, standing up and walking over to hold the door open. They exited the garret and headed downstairs, passing by members of the Krüger family who nodded at them as they walked by. Down in the dining room, two men were already sitting at the table, laughing over cups of hot liquid. The man on the left wore a dirt-covered shirt, torn trousers, and an old hat. His age-shield was a black lion against a field of dark red and white. The man on the right wore finer clothes with a well-kept beard. His age-shield was a red eagle against a field of white. Friedrich did not recognize the sippes on the shields and correctly assumed them to be Ostvolk.

Frau Krüger walked out of the kitchen holding two bowls, placing them in front of the two men. "Ah, Herr *und* Frau Bauer, *guten morgen*. How did the two of you sleep?"

"Like a stone, thank you." He sat down next to the man in the hat with Vytilia sitting across.

"Ha! Enjoy those while you can. Once your little one comes, you won't be getting those!" She slapped Friedrich on the back. "Can I get the two of you some coffee? Herr Winkler here gifted us some as part of his bill. Imported straight from the sultanate." She gestured to the man in finer clothes. Friedrich shook his head, and she returned to the kitchen.

"Oh, are you folks bearing? *Zum Wohl*!" The man in the hat raised his cup in a toast before taking a sip.

"*Gratias*," Vytilia told him, looking down at the table, avoiding eye contact with Friedrich.

"What were your names?" Herr Winkler asked.

"Bauer. I'm Ulrich, and this is my wife, Mina." Vytilia gave the two men a wave while Friedrich shook their hands.

"I'm Heine Winkler," the fine clothed man explained. "I run a salt house in Soizort. I came here for a delivery." He took another sip. "If you don't know, there's nowhere better to buy salt than Salzahoi."

"And I'm Gerhard Werner. I'm coming back from a wayfareage to Altkirche," the man in the hat introduced. "Are you hoping for a boy or girl?"

"A boy to carry on the family name."

"But I would prefer . . . a girl." She remembered the correct term for a hen, casting a coy smile at Friedrich.

"Whatever it is, we'll be happy," Friedrich added.

Herr Winkler nodded in approval. "Cheers to that. So, what brings you to these parts?"

"We're headed up to Hertzabrunno where I'm from. I was doing digging down in Dialenfels where we met. We wanted to come up and see my family before the child comes."

"Bit out of the way from Dialenfels to Hertzabrunno, wouldn't you say?" Herr Werner asked.

"We're going to stop by and see some friends in Mondsruhe, and she was bent on seeing Leodolf pass. If it's a boy, she wants to name him Leodolf." They exchanged a smile.

"Well how are you liking this side of the mountains?" Herr Winkler asked.

"Oh, it was incredible!" Vytilia told him while Frau Krüger brought breakfast. It was bowls of porridge with small slices of fruit cut in. She also poured cups of milk for both of them. "I have never seen such natural majesty! He can tell you; I was speechless and in awe for most of the trip! It was a sight to behold!" She looked at Friedrich, who took a bite of the food then nodded to say it was allium-free.

"I agree," Herr Werner told her. "Though, I'm sure it's nothing like what you have in Helvensland."

"Aye, you go to Helvensland for the landscape and Salzahoi for the salt!" Herr Winkler added.

"Though, if you have the time, come back in the winter. It is like another world when the snow falls. Sometimes you can't tell what's a dale and what's a mountain."

"We shall return if the baby permits." She winked at Friedrich then finally took a bite of her food. This taste, whatever this food was, was incredible. It was tart but a pleasurable tartness. The consistency was unlike anything she ever had, but it was pleasant; there was a simple homeliness to this meal, like the taste was the same feeling she had whenever she saw those cottages on the road. She could hardly contain her excitement as she ate, savoring each bite; it was sour but warm and pleasant, and the fruit the innkeeper added was exquisite. She hoped Friedrich did not eat his, so she could have it.

"Herr Werner, you said you're coming back from Altkirche? Bring any news from out west?" Friedrich asked.

"Things are getting tense with the Gauls. Their King and the Kommandant are having a spat over trade and who owns what. There's been troops marching west for the last month." Herr Werner finished off his drink. "But I have steadfastness in sunshine, that God will guide the ambassadors. He knows neither side can afford another war."

"Not to sound like a gainer," Herr Winkler added, "but rumors of war are good for business. More warriors mean a higher demand for salt!" He laughed at his own joke, quickly stopping after reading the room.

"In all honesty, things are almost worse over in Gallia than over here," Herr Werner added. "I wanted to stop on my way-fareage and see the great Hof of Notre-Balise, but time wouldn't allow. Their cities have more beggars, their highways have more highwaymen, the toilers are poorer. I think they're just doing this as a show of strength. They're also in no shape to fight. Their king has bigger issues to worry about."

"If you ask me, war with the Tujue is more likely," Herr Winkler commented. "They sat out the last bloodening. All they need is a word from the sultan. I've got buyers in the Sultanate who've been hearing rumors of war for the last few years."

"All we can do now is trust in the Lord our God," Herr Werner advised. "Though if I were you, I'd go back to Helvensland as soon as you can. A battlefield is no place to raise a child."

"Oh, I agree," Friedrich told him, "but my family has never met Mina, so I feel bound to at least allow them to meet before their first grandchild comes. We'll stay a while then head back to Helvensland."

"You're a good son," Herr Winkler told him. "I wish my sons were like that. They all went up to work on the coast. They don't even write anymore. Breaks my poor wife's heart." He looked over at Vytilia's empty bowl and offered her the rest of his porridge. She accepted it, taking the bowl from him, their fingers brushing. "Ah!" He withdrew his hand. "Your hands are cold! Are you alright?"

"Verily!" she quickly assured him. "I have poor . . . circul—blood flow in the mornings. I am trying to warm up."

"I had a cousin like that," Herr Werner commented. "Nearly died every winter." He similarly offered Vytilia his porridge. She graciously accepted it, digging in immediately. "You've got a fancy accent, Frau Bauer, real learned one. You sound like the smartest talking woman I've ever heard." He elbowed Friedrich. "You're a lucky lad. Always good to have a smart woman, keeps your purse in line."

"My gratitude. Herr Werner . . ." Vytilia hesitated, trying to use correct honorifics. "You mentioned you were on a wayfareage? What was it you were doing?" she asked between bites.

Herr Werner took a sip before answering. "I was wandering, looking for wisdom. So, I went to Altkirche out in the west. It's where Kommandant Karalthergroz is buried. There's a beautiful Hof, tallest building I've ever seen. It's a very . . . enlightening trip.

It's close enough to Hertzabrunno. You folks should go see it. I know doing a wayfareage would do the baby some good."

"If there is time," Friedrich told him. "We do want to get back before the shooting starts. If any shooting starts. God forbid."

Herr Winkler stood up from his seat. "Well folks, it's been a treat, but I've got to get to the salt works. If any of you are in Soizort, look me up. I've got a good house there. You can spend the night if you agree to help me carry some salt." He grinned, calling for Frau Krüger to settle his bill.

"I should probably get going as well." Herr Werner finished off his drink. "I have to make it to Lofnscheid. I won't make it, but I need all the daylight I can get." He stood up, tapping Friedrich on the shoulder. "You won't make it to Mondsruhe today. Depending on how fast you two will be walking, you'll probably reach the south bank of the Weinetsee before nightfall. Stay at the Meier Guesthouse. They're kind folk and distant kin of mine. They'll take care of you two." He started to walk but turned back around to face them. "Oh, the rivers have been flooding, so you'll have to take the side ways. The Herzog's men are working on fixing them but," he shrugged, "you know how that goes. I heard there's robbers prowling around, but I didn't have any trouble. That is all. Go with God."

"*Danke*, Herr Werner," Friedrich told him. He went off to settle his account. Friedrich looked up, matching eyes with Vytilia. Both smirked. "Enjoying your porridge?" he asked.

"This is incredible!" she announced, quickly finishing off her bowl. "I have never had anything this tasteful! Not even my family's private Sanguinvinum stock is this savory! Is this what men eat for breakfast every day?"

"Some do." Friedrich gave her his portion. "Herr Bergmann and I could only afford potatoes and back bacon. This had sugar, too rich for my blood. And my taste."

"Sugar?"

"Yeah, it's this white, sweet stuff, looks like gems. It's costly and has to be imported from the new world. It's good in small bites, but too much can ruin a meal."

"Sweet." Vytilia hung on the word, savoring another bite. "That is what this taste is."

Friedrich raised an eyebrow. "Have you never tasted sweet before?"

She shook her head. "We do not get the luxury of taste underground. Spices are hard to grow. The only flavor I know is metallic." She savored her final bite, licking the spoon clean. "Your people's trade network is so extensive. We would not have imagined half of these products when we were on the surface! Gunpowder, sugar, all these fruits." She picked a slice of fruit off of her porridge, enjoying the bite. "It is all so incredible."

"Maybe we should get a few bushels of apples or peaches along with the gunpowder. I'm sure your people would appreciate it."

She laughed. "Do not tempt them. They may start buying whole orchards."

Frau Krüger entered the room. She stared at the empty bowls surrounding Vytilia, her hands on her hips. "Did you eat all that?" she asked, guffawing. Vytilia avoided eye contact. "You might be having twin's sweetie; best be ready for that. I'll get you another bowl, and Herr Bauer, whenever you're ready, we can settle your tab."

Vytilia made a note to ask Friedrich what she meant by twins. "She's a welcoming hen, er, woman," Vytilia commented. "An exceptional hostess."

"It comes with the job. A Guesthouse owner doesn't stay in business if they don't treat their guests right."

"You know, you play an expectant family tiercel, er, man, rather well. How often did you have to lie as a caverneer?" she asked, smirking. Frau Krüger returned, handing her a bowl and refilling both of their cups before leaving again.

"Don't sell yourself short. You played along swimmingly," he shot back. "We lied enough to avoid being treated like a scaler, and I'll leave it at that."

"A scaler?"

"It's this awful skin rot Herr Bergmann told me about once, as bad, if not worse than the Gaulish blight. The skin falls off, and you lose fingers and toes." He shuddered.

Vytilia still felt some guilt over their deception, especially with the hospitality they had been shown, but it was still hard to fault Friedrich's logic. And she would be lying if she did not tell herself she had enjoyed pretending to be a couple. It reminded her of the time spent with Brigit and her daughters, that warm, homey feeling. The Nymphs, the surface, and Friedrich, all were filling a void she had not recognized, one that had been there for a long time. She wanted to ask Friedrich about his family, hear more about his relationships and how men operate as a family unit, but she knew she should not. Well, perhaps not directly.

"I am curious, if you did have a wife, is there someone you would take her to meet in Hertzabrunno?" She patted her stomach, not as part of the act, but because she was not used to having so much solid food.

"Frau Beck, of course. Once Herr Bergmann and I moved into her house, she helped him raise me whenever we were home. If I ever went and got wedded, she'd kill me if I didn't tell her."

"Are we going to go see her?"

"If the armor doesn't get us a good price, we'll have to stop by." His face went solemn. "No, we should go anyway. I have to tell her what happened to Herr Bergmann." Friedrich finished off his milk and stood up. "Let's go pay Frau Krüger, then we can go. We're burning daylight." Vytilia nodded but sighed; she was a bit disappointed. She was so close to getting to understand Friedrich better, and then he would remember something and close himself off. She sighed again, finishing off her porridge and following Friedrich into the front room.

"Well, Herr Bauer, did you enjoy your stay?"

"We did Frau Krüger. You're one of the better guesthouses I've been to." He pulled one of the torcs from his bag. "I apologize for the clunky way we're paying, but chips were in short supply in Dialenfels when we left. We tried finding a pawnshop, but I don't think you have one."

"Oh, you don't want to deal with a pawnbroker. They're as rotten as the Gauls. May I?" He handed the torc to Frau Krüger. "This is a very well-done piece, the kind Grafs buy for their wives. Frau Bauer, did your family make these?"

"A friend did as a going away present."

"They have an eye for good work. If you're ever coming by this way again, my husband and I know quite a few traders we can talk to. If your friend makes enough of these, we can help ship them out. They could fetch a good price."

"We will have to discuss it with them. They are rather isolated. It would be difficult to traverse," Vytilia answered. Though Frau Krüger brought up a good idea, interstrata commerce, a boon to Strixans, Men, and Nymph alike.

"If you hear back from them, you know where to find us. Now, obviously, this is worth more than your bill. I'll have my son fetch a saw."

Vytilia cringed at what she was about to offer. It was a beautiful piece and given by the nymphs willingly, but it was for the good of the mission, she reminded herself. "Allow me!" Vytilia took the torc, snapping off one of the caps on the end. "Will this suffice?"

"More than! You've got a strong woman here, Herr Bauer. She'll need that for when the baby comes." She held the cap in her hand. "I am afraid I may not have the chips on hand to settle the difference."

Friedrich waved her off. "Don't worry about it. A gift for keeping up such a nice home."

Vytilia smirked. They had lied to get a discount on the bill but ended up paying more anyway. *Poetic justice,* she thought.

Frau Krüger beamed. "Well, why thank you Herr Bauer. How about some food for the road? Enough to keep you going to your next stop?"

Vytilia spoke up, resting a hand on her womb to maximize the innkeeper's empathy. "Frau Krüger, if I could ask, do you have blood sausage to spare? It is my favorite, and uh, the little one's favorite as well."

"Of course, sweetheart, I understand. There's a well outside when you walk back towards town. Take a good drink from it before you go." Frau Krüger hurried to the kitchen then returned with a whole link of light red sausage, some cheeses, and bread wrapped in cloth. Friedrich thanked her and put it in the haversack.

"I don't know if the other guests spoke about it, but I am sorry for the owls last night. We heard their hooting through the whole night! We've never had them flock to the house before. I'll have Herr Krüger look for a nest and get rid of it."

"Do not!" Vytilia quickly exclaimed. "I, I at least did not mind. Owls are gentle creatures; they do not pose any harm. And they are good at killing vermin. They are more of an asset than an annoyance."

"Well, we'll think about it. Might be a better option for a mouser. Maybe we can move the nest." As they headed for the door, Frau Krüger gave Vytilia a hug, commenting on her cold touch, sending the two away with God's blessing.

They stopped at the well while Friedrich refilled the waterskin. "She's really sweet. And we'll have enough of these left over to get to Mondsruhe and beyond." He twirled the torc around his finger before stashing it in his pocket.

"And we will not be without food." She fished out a blood sausage for Friedrich to try. "Since we have enough of the nymph's gifts to last us, let us refrain from deception from here on out?" He took a bite, nodding that it was clean.

"We'll see how long the torcs last us. With the roads flooded, it might take us weeks to get to Mondsruhe and God only knows how long to Hertzabrunno. Besides, it was a small, white lie, no harm done. We had a roof over our heads and food in our bellies. We didn't take, only kept." He plugged the lip of the waterskin and started back off on the road.

"Is that why you agreed to help us?" she posed, "because you have also been forced to scrape by and survive?"

He scratched at his scars. "I suppose it is. That and the reward. And, well . . ." He quickly hurried on ahead, so she wouldn't see his face, but she could hear his heart race.

She smiled then stopped herself. She was feeling conflicted, unsure of herself. She would worry about this later, ignoring it as she caught up to him. "Herr Werner mentioned flooding. Is that typical in this region?"

"It happens." He pointed upwards. Rather than the light blue of yesterday, the sky was now covered in a dark grey overcast of clouds. In the distance, she heard a tremendous cracking noise. "There's why. It's going to be a rainy summer. We'll have to find shelter at some point. Ugh, that's gonna slow us down."

Clouds would slow them down? Clouds causing floods? Was this a previously unknown surface phenomena or one of his people's superstitions? There was a deafening noise many miles away. She hurried her pace. Perhaps she had been too eager to judge these clouds.

They exited Salzahoi, following signs to an unflooded trail. This trail was flat with vast forests and farmland to their right and forested mountains to their left. There were a few dirt trails leading off towards isolated cottages and farmhouses on the right, but for the most part, it was nothing but wilderness.

She took off her bonnet, embracing the comforting, grey-tinted sunlight. It was a pleasant day, another new experience, which Vytilia was grateful for. It cast the world in a literally different light. The trees and bushes and grasses were duller but uniquely vibrant. It was astonishing how lively the surface could be, how varied and diverse it was in colors, tastes, even sounds. She could hardly believe she had spent four hundred years surrounded by nothing but rocks and caves.

Friedrich realized this was perhaps the most he'd ever thought about weddings or family in his life. It was ironic that he'd only thought about it to get a discount on a guesthouse bill yet ended up paying more for the bill anyway. He was approaching an acceptable age to be married, something he both longed for and was hesitant about. It was an incredible commitment, one that required all of a person, and yet, he was held back.

Yet, the rightful life came back and rudely slapped him in the face. There was no baby Bauer, Vytilia was not his wife, and the fate of several thousand vampires, Strixans, whatever they were called, did indeed rest on his shoulders. Never had being pulled out of a daydream felt like a kick in the balls.

Talking would take the pain away, he hoped. "So, was that you last night with the owls, making all that ruckus?"

"Not on purpose. We were all celebrating Luna. I am the first Strixan to see Luna in so many millennia . . ." She stopped dead in her tracks, gasping. "The Concilium! They do not know we survived! Aurum would report we never arrived! They must think our mission failed! We need to get back, tell them of our survival!"

"Hold on, hold on, think this through. You said they were building a tunnel where I fell, right?" She nodded. "They'll keep building, no matter what happens to us. To get to the Toller Mund where I fell, it will take us several days to the south. We're already on the road to Mondsruhe; we'll sell the armor, buy a cart and a few muskets, and then it's a straight shot south to the Toller Mund. We can get back to your kind, with our mission done, in a fortnight at the most."

"A fortnight?"

"Two weeks. And, at the most. If we can find a cheap enough cart and some donkeys, it'll be even shorter. And I'm sure we could play up baby Bauer to get a better deal." He gave Vytilia a pat on her stomach before a rage-fill scowled chased him away.

"I would still prefer to inform my father of my survival." They resumed walking. "Could we spare the coin and send a messenger? I can write a letter."

"That is too risky. A non-caverneer going into a cave as large and deep as the Toller Mund would get lost. Not to mention your word-errand could go down the wrong tunnel, or the runner could fall down the wrong tunnel. Your father can wait two weeks. I don't want to send someone to their death."

"You are right." She folded her arms. "I can only hope and pray he trusts me and Luna enough to hold out hope."

"There we go! And think of how much happier he'll be when he sees you bringing back muskets when you return."

Maybe her father would smile again. "All of this is true. It is not as if I will not be able to return to the surface. We will need more muskets, there is more to learn, and I would like to meet your landlady."

"I'm sure Frau Beck would love to meet you. We can't do the wedded life with her, however. She'd kill me if I brought a bride home." His eyes lit up. "Oh, and my friends! If I were wedded, I'd need to show off my wife to them!"

"You have friends?"

"Don't sound so surprised."

"I . . . I was not . . . never mind." She scowled. He laughed.

"I have three, the best friends in the world: Kurt, Franz, and Klaus. When Herr Bergmann and I weren't out caverneering, the four of us would get into all kinds of trouble. We'd get drink, set snares, go bowling. They're a good crop of lads." He beamed.

"You are very fortunate. It is good to have friends."

"Do you have any, back at Nidus?"

"Why, of course! I have Annia, my ancilla. There is Sextus, the majordomo. Valerius, Felix, Centurion Dracius, Antonius, Father . . . ." Friedrich's visage was pained. "What?"

"Is . . . is that it?"

"What do you mean?"

"Aren't those . . . isn't that the folk who work for you and your father?"

"Many are honored members of our household, but they can still be friends. Annia is my ancilla, my confidante, my sartrix,[36] my tonstrix,[37] and was even the obsterix[38] to my mother. If that is not a friend, I do not know what is!"

Friedrich let it go. That was another reminder that what they told Frau Krüger was a lie. She was a high-born blueblood. She had servants, ladies-in-waiting, a chef, and was never in want

36. Tailor, though in this instance, also means a Mistress of the Robes

37. Barber, though really more of a hairdresser

38. Midwife

for anything. She would never understand how he'd lived. She didn't need to. It was all a lie, he reminded himself, nothing more, nothing less.

They were now a wegstunde (two miles by Vytilia's accounting) from the town. The deafening noise Vytilia had heard got louder, and the clouds overhead got darker. She was not frightened but concerned. The sound was like rocks cleaving in two, and a dense shadow was falling on the land in the distance. She thought of the descriptions of the world upheaving itself when the empire fell, and her own heart raced. "Friedrich," she asked, standing close to him, pointing to the distant shadow, "what is that?"

"Rain," he told her without even looking.

"Rain? What is that?"

"It's water that falls from the sky."

She blinked in disbelief. "Water, that just falls from the sky?" Her mother had told her about this, but hearing about it and seeing it was different. "Is it like snow?"

"Sort of. Snow is colder and a lot more solid. Rain doesn't stay packed on top of the mountain. It either floods or drains away. Both can make you sick." He started looking for tall trees to duck under.

"It can make you sick? It is water, not a virus. Water is the ingredient of life! Even Strixans need it."

"Trust me," he almost sang it. "Every mother teaches her kids not to play in the rain, else they'll catch a cold."

"A cold?"

"It's a very mild sickness, a sniffle really. Hot soup and bedrest are all you need to get over it."

She wondered if men's superstitions held them back or if it was their lack of knowledge that made them superstitious.

The rain shadow began creeping closer and closer to them with the deafening noise getting louder and louder. "And that noise?"

"Thunder. It means lightning is close by." Before she could ask, he took her by the shoulder and pointed off at the horizon on the right. She stared, watching the rain shadow draw closer, when suddenly, there was a brilliant flash of light! It was stringy and jagged, stabbing from the clouds to the ground. Then minutes later, there was another roaring, cracking sound. "You see lightning first, then thunder follows. That's just Holy Donar in his workshop, finding new things to teach man." He continued on, but she stayed transfixed, watching the horizon without blinking as another bolt of lightning struck the ground, followed by another clap of thunder.

"By the gods!" she exclaimed.

"Come on!" he called to her, squatting under a tree. "We've got to take shelter and wait for it to pass!" He sat down, setting his bag aside and watching the sky nervously.

She started heading towards him, stopping as droplets of water started hitting her. *So, this is rain,* she thought to herself. The volume began to increase, more and more rain pouring down until it felt like an entire river was being emptied from the sky. She stretched her arms out, feeling the rain on every inch of her. "I love it!" she announced, spinning and watching the droplets fly off her. "This is wonderful! It just falls from the sky?" Her normally stoic composure broke as she gleefully danced through the rain, jumping into puddles. She was in heaven, dashing and leaping through the water, using her wonder working to create art with the rain, images of animals, letters, or even a bowl to catch more rain.

Friedrich watched from the comfort of the tree as she danced in the rain. It was strange seeing an adult jump gleefully through the rain like a child, but he had to remind himself she was seeing this all for the first time, like a child. Almost everything from the wildlife to the colors were new to her. Her curiosity must be insatiable. After a gleeful romp, she had enough and walked over to Friedrich, sopping wet. She used her wonder working to remove the water from her clothes, forming it into a ball and launching it across the road. "Have fun?" he asked.

She nodded, regaining her patrician façade. "I apologize for that, wasting our time prancing around in the water. It was unprofessional and immature." She sounded disappointed.

"Ah, no need to be sorry. You deserve to have a bit of fun. And besides, it's not wise to travel in a storm anyway, better to wait it out."

"Well, call it a product of upbringing. It is not right for me to lose my social graces so easily." She held her hand out, letting the rain accumulate in her palm. She sat down next to him, studying the rainwater. "Though, I would be remiss if I also did not express gratitude for allowing me to enjoy this phenomena." She drank the water, sloshing it in her mouth like it was a wine tasting. It tasted different than water back at Nidus and different from the snow when they first emerged. For reasons she could not explain, it tasted better.

They sat a few feet apart from each other, leaning against the trunk of the tree, rain trickling down from the pines and branches above, while lightning continued to leap from the sky, and thunder echoed around them. Every so often, Friedrich would steal a glance at her, watching as she stared at the lightning strikes.

His stomach turned as he thought, his mind gnawing at him as he wondered. He was so downtrodden, always thinking himself put upon. It did not have to be that way! He should say something to her, see if she had any . . . interest as he did. This may be his only shot. "Vytilia?" he asked. She didn't flinch. "Vytilia?" She slightly turned her head to ask what but kept staring at the rain. "Edelweiss?" That got her attention.

"What did you call me?"

"Edelweiss. Just, just a joke because the blossom looks like you . . ." He coughed. "Well, it got your attention anyway."

"What do you need?"

"Uh . . ." He had a lump in his throat. "I was, wondering, uh, thinking. Er." He stretched his neck, laughing to bide time. "When we . . . get to Mondsruhe . . . why don't we . . . celebrate?"

"What did you have in mind?"

"Well . . . you're always talking about these 'arts' you want to restore. We could see what mankind has to tide you over! Maybe a Holy play or a funny or a puppet show!"

Was this . . . Vytilia pondered . . . *was this an attempt at courtship?* Her cheeks burned violet. She did not know how to respond. She was flattered and very curious about what arts men had to offer. But she needed to be cautious. She did not want to hurt Friedrich and endanger her mission, but she also was internally conflicted. She admired this man, respected him, and . . . well, she did not want to expound on what she felt. Emotions were foreign and messy. They got in the way of her goals and studies. She would take Friedrich up on this offer only because her curiosity was so strong.

"That sounds like a wonderful idea," she told him.

He grinned from ear to ear. "Good! Good!"

The rain intensified, a deafening roar of water that prevented conversation. Then, as quickly as it began, it subsided. "Onto Mondsruhe we go!" Friedrich got up and helped her come to her feet. They both started trudging back towards the path.

They did not walk on the road, which was now a dark, brown color, but on the grass shoulder. She wanted to ask why they were on the shoulder, but after scooping a handful of viscous wet dirt from the road, she understood why. This was truly curious, dirt that almost liquified after mixing with water. What other wonders and natural curiosities did the surface hold? Though, she had to admit, being outside after the rain was not as exciting or pleasant as it was before and during. The air was thick and wet, a phenomena Friedrich called "humidity." She felt like she was bathing as she walked, breathing in mostly water. Her clothes were starting to get damp despite how frequently she dried it with thaumaturgy.

Though she had to remind herself, it was not all bad. The trees were almost mirrors as a spectrum of light shone through the water trapped on their leaves and needles. The sky was marbled with dark grey storm clouds interspersed with their snow-white, fluffier counterparts. Whenever there was a break in the trees, Vytilia looked upward, looking for the sun or for anything new in the sky. A scholar could spend their entire life just documenting this one aspect of the surface.

She suddenly stopped, turning around to scan the road behind them. She heard something, something powerful and beating rapidly. Actually, it was two somethings. She turned back around, hurrying to Friedrich and grabbing his shoulder, pulling him into the tree line. "What is it?"

"I heard someone coming up behind us, sounded like they were in a hurry."

Friedrich shot her a look of disbelief. "Someone was coming up behind us, on the only unflooded road around, and you got suspicious?"

"They just started following us and their heartrate elevated only a few moments ago. As if they were desperate to catch up." Friedrich regretted his previous comment and drew his dagger. They ducked down, lying in the mud behind the trees and bushes, watching the road.

They heard the gallop of a horse to their right. A horseman rode up shortly after, kicking up mud and splashing water. The horse was a mottled brown and emaciated. The rider was thin in raggedy clothes, mismatched shoes, and a hat falling apart at the seams. His face was gaunt and skin yellowing. The thin sword he had sheathed, and the pistol in his hand gave them pause. Despite his stature, he was not one to be dealt with lightly.

He spat on the ground as he wheeled the horse around, scanning the trees. "I know yer out there," he growled. His voice was deep and guttural, his accent provincial with a boorish twang to it. "You can't hide forever. Just gimme yer chip, and I'll let you on yer way." He spun his pistol around for emphasis. "No need fer bloodshed."

Friedrich and Vytilia exchanged a look. He sheathed his dagger and mimed putting his hands up. She shook her head, glaring at the rider. Friedrich tried to plead with her using his eyes, but she refused. She was not going to let herself be bullied by a brigand. She could defeat him easily without even blinking. She would not stand for simply cowering, but it was Friedrich she had to worry about.

The highwayman willed his horse forward. They could hear him sniffing the air. "Yer close. I can almost smell you." He spat again. "Yer coin or yer life. Easy choice." Friedrich realized he hadn't bathed in weeks; he wouldn't be surprised if the highwayman could smell him against the damp air. "I've got other ways of flushing you out," the highwayman threatened. He holstered his pistol and set the reins down. Reaching into his saddle bag, he produced a small iron ball and a flint. It was a grenade. "Right then, don't make me pick up yer chips from all the body parts." He struck the flint in the air to show it worked. "Come on out, and I won't blow you to hell!"

Vytilia clenched her hands into fists. She recognized what the brigand held, a metal version of what Friedrich demonstrated at Nidus. She could only imagine how far more dangerous metal was over clay. They would have to fight.

The mud prevented them from running, and there was not anywhere they could flee. Friedrich, though his heart raced, otherwise remained calm, slowly pulling the torcs out of his pocket, setting them down on the ground. He checked the sword on his belt, making sure the leather hid the glint and gilding. Before she could stop him, he crawled sideways then stood up, his hands over his head. "It's alright! It's alright! No need for threats!"

The highwayman put the grenade away, drawing his pistol, aiming straight at Friedrich's heart. "I don't like waitin' boy. Where's the other one? I saw two of youse." He cocked his pistol.

"Please, I am travelling with my wife. She is with child; we only have the clothes on our back."

"Everyone got silver boy. Yer just hidin' it. Turn out yer pockets!" He grinned. "Where is this wife of yers? I haven't seen a real woman in days."

Friedrich turned out his pocket. "See? We have no silver. Just leave us to be on our way."

"Where's yer silver boy!? You leave it with yer wife? I know ya got some." The highwayman looked away, keeping the pistol aimed at him. "Come on out lady! I just want to get a good look at ya. Come on out, or yer husband gets it! I'll kill him! Better show yourself!"

Vytilia gave a low growl, startling the horse. The highwayman calmed the beast, lowering the pistol. "What the hell is that?"

She gripped the ground, getting herself in a ready position, extending her fangs.

"Where's yer wife boy? Don't she listen?" He turned to face Friedrich.

"She is with child! She can't move quickly. We have no silver! Leave us be, and we won't tell anyone! We aren't worth it." The highwayman swore, lowering his pistol.

That was her opening. With a screech, she leapt from cover and dove straight for the highwayman, her fangs bared and her eyes bloodshot and purple. Her stole-bonnet had flown off, snagged on a bush. The highwayman had no time to react as she grabbed him, breaking his arm holding the pistol. It dropped to the mud. Her momentum forced him off the saddle onto the ground. The horse kicked and whinnied then ran a short distance away. Once on the ground, Vytilia knelt on him, holding his good arm down while ripping off his jacket, the carotid artery bulging outwards. She heard his heartrate elevate; fear filled his eyes. He tried to scream, but she kept his mouth still. She did not have a mind for mercy, only anger. He had threatened Friedrich, threatened her, threatened their mission! Nothing would stand in her way. And she was thirsty. She went to bite down, but Friedrich screamed for her to stop. Her rationality returned, and her fangs receded. She still held the man in place but turned to Friedrich. "What?" she demanded.

"You can't kill him!"

"He was more than willing to kill us! To kill you!" She pointed to the pistol laying on the ground with her chin. "I saved your life! I was looking out for you!"

Friedrich bent over and picked it up. It was light for a pistol with an older wheellock design. "It's not even loaded. It was all a bluff! We don't need to kill him! He was about to let us go!"

"Well, if we do not kill him, he will just run off and tell the town about us! Then we will have a whole bloody army following us! What use is he to the world anyway!? He is a thief! If he was one of my people, we would have him crucified!" she snarled.

"He's still a man. We can't just kill him without a second thought! We were talking our way out! You need to trust me! We have laws! We have lawmen! Let them deal with him!"

She scoffed. "You killed two devils and said nothing about me drowning that wolf. Why is he any different?"

"He's, he's a being! A man! Not some mindless thing!"

She growled at him, almost crushing the highwayman's head like an egg. "Do you know how many legionaries died to save us? How many of my people are slain every day!? I do not give a damn about one thief's life! He is not worth jeopardizing our mission! To perdition with him!" She bared her fangs and bit down on the artery. Friedrich turned away as the highwayman let out a muffled scream, kicking and thrashing until he went limp. Vytilia drained the body until it was paper-white.

Friedrich shut his eyes and covered his ears, his back turned to her. She wiped the corners of her mouth and started examining the body, taking the man's meager coin purse and untying his sword. She threw the body over her shoulder, walking over to a small ditch and tossing it in. She lit the body on fire then turned back to Friedrich; he was still crying. She walked over, placing a hand on his shoulder.

He quickly slapped it away and stepped backwards, gritting his teeth. "Get away," he yelled. "Get away!" He glowered at her, his hand near his dagger.

"It is fine, calm down."

"No! It's not fine! You just killed a man in cold blood! Get away from me!"

"He was going to kill you! I saved your life! Does that not mean anything?"

He continued backing away. "He didn't have to die! You didn't have to kill him! Do our lives mean nothing to you?"

"Why should they?!" she yelled, gasping as realization set in. "That is not what I, wait!"

Friedrich stared at her in horror. "Stay away from me!" he yelled, backing over to the horse and grabbing the reins. "Stay away you, you, you fell, forsaken thing of the pit!" He mounted the horse and galloped westward, tears pouring down his face.

Vytilia stood there at the side of the road, listening to the fire pop and the horse gallop away. She began to shake, tears swelling up. A thousand thoughts and questions raced through her mind, all on what she could have done differently. Should she have just followed Friedrich's example and let them get robbed? Could she have fought him off with more conventional means? Why was Friedrich so upset about taking the life of another man? If needed, she would be willing to kill another Strixan. Why could he not accept the reality of the situation! She began to bawl. Why did she blame him? She was the one who took the man's life! She had caused this strife!

What had she done?

16

The horse instinctively followed the trail to the west while Friedrich sat in the saddle, wanting to keep crying, but no tears would pour. He didn't know what else to do. He felt like a hole had been punched into his chest, ripping out his very soul. He had never felt like this before, this feeling of betrayal. Every memory from the past weeks left a bitter taste. And the memory of the highwayman dying, drained in the blink of an eye, twitching and gurgling, it haunted him above all the rest. He couldn't believe what had happened. He wished he was still asleep back at the guesthouse, even back with the elves. So many things he could have done differently, so many things he could say or change, so much pain he could have avoided. Now he was stuck. Directionless, penniless, and alone.

The horse began to slow down until it was plodding along at a light jog. Friedrich blew his nose on his sleeve and rubbed his eyes. He didn't know how long he'd been riding. Hopefully, he'd put plenty of distance between him and that . . . that thing. He needed a plan, a new goal to focus on, something to push him forward. "The coast," he said to himself. "I'll go to the coast." He'd heard good things about the town of Bothort. Maybe he could get a job there, carve out a decent living. No, the new world, that's where he'd go, maybe the Merkya settlements, to live a life out on the frontier. Oh, what a thought, to have the great sea separating him and this blasted, godforsaken land.

The sun began to lower in the sky, the shadows cast by the trees stretching longer. He would need to find a place to stay for the night, preferably somewhere indoors. Staying outside would risk an attack from that *thing*. Where could he even stay? He'd left the torcs behind, and the hamlets here were little more than a few family homes, a mill, and maybe a blacksmith or woodworker. He expected most families wouldn't be all that willing to let him in their homes, and sleeping in someone's stable was liable to get him in trouble. He'd rather not wake up staring down the business end of a pitchfork.

He tried recalling the distance he'd traveled all the way back to Salzahoi. They'd . . . he shuddered, *he'd* probably gone about one wegstunde west of the city, maybe one and a half by the time the rain had hit, then an unknown distance on this horse. He'd never make it to the Weinetsee before nightfall; he'd never even be able to find the town. He took another look up at the sun and spurred the horse forward, speeding it into a canter. The road straightened out; copses of trees and tilled land lined the thin trail leading northwest. Cows and sheep looked up at him as he passed by, their shepherds oblivious to him as they led their flock to their nighttime quarters. The trail was beginning to dry from the rain, light dust kicking up behind Friedrich as he rode.

As the sun began to set, Friedrich finally arrived at a small hamlet. The road sign named it Preisdorf. It was much smaller than Salzahoi. The tallest building was the church, a beige colored stone building with a tall black steeple. Single-floor cottages and homes were clustered around the church with a stone well as the epicenter. It was quiet; Preisdorf didn't have a beerhall to cause a ruckus at night. Friedrich brought the horse to a stop by the well, dismounting and quickly pulling up the bucket, taking a long drink.

He sat against the stone well, tapping the bucket against the stonework. What was he going to do? He'd made it to town, but now what? He started going over his options. Could he go north? Work in Bothort? Even travel to the new world? What a foolhardy idea! Where could he go with empty pockets and a malnourished horse? He was lucky to be alive! Well, if one could call it luck, he would be better off dead. He shook off that thought. He just needed to find a way to get to Hertzabrunno where he'd collect his savings and formulate a better plan. He just needed a starting point. He'd lived off of less before, and he can continue to do so.

The well was across from the Erdeish church. It was a small one, a Hall as it was supposed to be called. The emblem of the hallowed sun was painted above the doors with the familiar motto of the Church, *Gott mit Uns,* written above the doorpost. A low wall surrounded the property; the church proper, a small orchard of apples, and an outhouse. If this church taught what it was supposed to, perhaps Friedrich could find shelter here.

But, he stopped himself. Wouldn't this be begging? Bergmann always taught to pay his way and barter if necessary. He didn't have any chips . . . . He looked at the vampire sword. All he had to barter with was that. It would have to last him between here and wherever it was he would be going. Maybe he should press on. The horse still had some legs on it. Maybe he could make it to the next big town, one with a pawnbroker. He'd sell the sword and then he'd have some silver to spend. He'd have to be frugal, foraging where he could, drinking from streams. He could do it. It would be rough, but he could do it. And a harvest was coming up soon. He had a strong back. He could work for an honest wage and get some more when the sword silver ran out.

Then another thought struck him. He can't stay outside, and he can't stay in one place for long. *It* was still out there, most likely scorned and angry. He recalled *it* could hear his heartbeat and move without making a sound. If he didn't want to end up a body with two holes in his neck, he'd need the safety of a roof and four walls. And, he knew churches usually had door locks.

He sighed deeply, apologizing to Bergmann but rationalizing that this wasn't begging. Churches were supposed to offer help to the needy. He wasn't asking. It was being given. If someone buys a round, you don't say no. And if there was anyone right now who was needy and couldn't say no, it was Friedrich Bauer.

He lowered the bucket, bringing it up again for the horse, letting it drink before walking it over to the church and tying it to a post near the door, making sure it had room to graze. Then he walked up the steps to the doors and knocked. He felt a lump in his throat, and his palms started to sweat. It had been months, almost a full year since he'd been in a church. How would the priest react? If a strange man showed up on his doorstep, dirty, disheveled, and armed to the teeth, the priest would have every right to throw him out! This was a mistake. He turned around to untie the horse and leave just as the door opened.

The priest who answered the door was still in his churchdress: an orange robe and trousers with a white collar and sash around his waist, along with the ever-present necklace of the sun. His outfit was trimmed with black, and the familiar emblem of two ravens were stitched to his collar. That caused Friedrich to suppress a shudder. He didn't need any more reminders of death. The priest was young and clean-shaven, as all priests were with thinning blond hair and thin spectacles. He looked Friedrich up and down, pausing at the sword. "*Guten Nacht*, yes, how may I help you?"

"*Entschuldigung, Herr Pfarrer*. I am a poor wanderer; I have been on the road alone. I have no chips for board, no family, and no kin nearby. Please, allow me to stay here."

The priest removed his spectacles and cleaned them on his sleeve. He paused again, eyeing Friedrich's sword before quietly uttering a beseech and opening the door wider, inviting Friedrich inside. "Come in my son. The house of God is welcome to all weary travelers." He led Friedrich over to a pew near the front, across from the vé[39] and priestbox, sitting him down. "I will return with food and drink."

As churchhalls went, this one was very simple, catering to the smaller town. There was only a single row of pews with no stain glass windows, and the priestbox was made of plain, unvarnished wood. A large, elaborately made gilded sun hung on the wall above the candles on the vé. They were still burning. The priest returned with a small cup of mead and a piece of black bread. "Here, it is not much, but it is what I can offer."

Friedrich hesitated, not wanting to take more than was necessary, but the pain in his stomach overrode his concern. "*Danke, Herr Pfarrer*. It is more than enough." Friedrich took a long sip of the mead.

"Please, call me *Vater* Sieghart." He sat next to Friedrich, giving him a reassuring pat on the back. "And what may I call you?"

Friedrich hesitated before answering. "Ulf—uh, Friedrich. Friedrich Bauer."

"A good name. I hope here in this hall, you can find a king's frith, Friedrich. Where have you come from?"

"Salzahoi. I've been travelling from Helvensland."

"What brings you this way out to Preisdorf?"

Friedrich swallowed his last bit of bread. "I was travelling, and a woe befell me; I wandered here and now am without real meaning. I am thinking about heading north; I might find work or purpose in Bothort." He finished his mead, handing the cup back to Vater Sieghart. He felt like he was lying, even though that was the closest he had to an actual plan.

Sieghart set the cup down. "A woe? I am sorry to hear this." He leaned forward, clasping his hands. "Do you wish to talk about it?"

Would talking help? Friedrich sighed. "I don't know Vater. I don't think I can." Or should, might be a better word. If he sold

39. An altar with pulpit.

out V—her, he would forfeit his own soul. No lawhall would find him sinless after all he had done with a witch, what he had helped her and her ilk with. He should take this to his grave.

Vater Sieghart was silent for a time while Friedrich thought. He was careful to choose his next words. "Friedrich. Might I ask you one question?" He nodded. "I will not ask for everything, but did this woe involve . . . lawlessness?" The priest quickly held up his hand. "Before you say anything, I will treat this as an answering.[40] It will not go beyond the walls of the hall."

Friedrich was unsure of how much he trusted the priest. Though he also wondered how well the Herzog's lawmen would watch the smaller hamlets for wrongdoing. Either way, he would do what he did with Frau Krüger, stretch the truth, what he had always done to survive. "I was not a part of the lawlessness. A . . . well, someone I thought was my friend was. We had a fight. I thought I could trust them, that they would trust me. I saw good in them, thought what we were doing was a good thing. I was wrong."

Vater Sieghart nodded, tapping his fingers together. "Friedrich, are you familiar with the saying, 'The road to Helheim is paved with good goals?'" He nodded, though nervously. "There are many cases throughout the time of man where someone has suffered for what they thought was a lawful goal. From the Kommandant himself to a mere ploughman, everyone has at one time or another paved the road to hell. But . . ." Sieghart made sure he and Friedrich locked eyes. "What is forgotten yet taught in the Sagas is that we can unpave the road."

"I . . . I don't follow."

"You have been hurt, and you may even feel regret because of it. You may have sinned; you may have not. But if you want to heal, to begin unpaving, there is a way to start."

Healing did sound nice, Friedrich admitted. After weeks of confusion and pain, starting anew and healing may just be what he needed. He recalled how he was after getting over smallpox, like the old Friedrich had been burned away, and he was a new man. Perhaps, just perhaps, this was the same. He had burned away his life as a caverneer and all that came with it, and now, he could be a newer man. "Vater, how do you suggest I start unpaving?"

---

40. A religious rite where a sinner goes before a priest to share what wrongs they have done. The priest then advises them on good deeds they can do to right their wrongs. Similar to a confession.

"It is easy; remember the Douths and live by them. They should be your guide in all that you do. Clothe the needy, feed the hungry, press on through hardship, strengthen your bonds with friends and family, work hard, live a godly life. You will not be renewed overnight but start with the small things first."

"Do you really think it will help?"

Sieghart smiled grabbing his churchdress. "I would not be wearing this if I didn't."

Friedrich leaned back in the pew, staring at the gilded sun hanging over the vé. Seeing it felt hollow, almost cruel with what he knew. "Vater, may I ask you a question? One that may be . . . godless?" The Vater nodded. "Why should I? It seems every time in my life when I have something good, or I do something good or honest, it gets taken away from me. I've lost my home, my family, my master, my friend. I don't have much going for me in my life, I'm not meant for anything, and I keep getting shit on! Pardon my true Teutonish."

Sieghart chuckled, also leaning back and crossing his legs. "Friedrich, I don't think there's a man alive who has not asked themselves that very same question; anyone who says they haven't is a liar. So, why do we do good?" He looked to Friedrich who shrugged. "We don't do good only because God wants us to. We don't do good only because it is asked of us by our lords and laws. We do good because it is within the heart of all mankind. Look at wildlife; deer, rabbits, beavers, what have you, when one of their own is hurt, they're left behind and forgotten. When a man is hurt, his fellow men will take him, heal him, and if he passes, give him a proper burning. We help each other, be they kin or outsiders. When a bear winters, they do not wake up and make sure other bears have enough food. They let them starve. When mankind winters, they do their best to make sure their neighbors have food and fire. That is why."

Now it was Friedrich's turn to be humbled. He hung his head low in thought.

"Ask yourself," Sieghart continued. "You have gone through many hard times in your life. Were you not helped by your fellow men? Only now, you came to my hall asking for a bed, and I gave it to you. I did not do it because God demanded it. I did it because it was a good and right thing to do." He leaned in towards Friedrich. "Now, I am not saying this to tell you to go out and find your former friend and have them right their ways. But, what I am saying is that can be behind you now, and you can start anew. What happened before, stays there. What happens tomorrow, must be made."

"Thank you Vater," Friedrich told him. "You've made this all a bit easier to endure."

"No thanks are necessary Friedrich; we do not help because we expect to be rewarded."

Friedrich felt a flash of embarrassment on his face. It was late, but he had one more question burning in the back of his mind. All this talk of healing and forgiveness and helping others made him wonder. "Vater," he began, "when I met this friend who harmed me, I thought it a near godsend. I thought maybe my guardian Norn or God had guided me to them, that maybe my orlay lay with them and their cause. They said they wanted to help others. Maybe they still do. Why would I be spared if my orlay does not rest with them?"

The priest thought on this for a bit. "I cannot speak for why God spared you or why it is this former friend met with you. Maybe God has taken an interest in your life and has a great orlay He needs you to fulfill. Or, it may be luck. From what you have said, nothing tells that this former friend of yours wished to do good and help others."

Because I haven't told you everything, Friedrich thought. "They said they did. They may have lied." Those downtrodden faces at Nidus didn't lie. Those vampire warriors who had their throats torn out didn't lie. Did his heart lie? It was only that morning he wanted to spend the day looking at her. Now he only thought of her as an *it*. "Vater, can good come out of evil?"

"Yes." The answer was straightforward without a hint of hesitation. "It is rare, but it can happen. Aufseher Leodolf had to abandon many towns and those who lived there to stop the Etstilau horde. Karalthergroz had to put many hamlets and towns to the torch, but he brought in a time of frith and calm that strengthened the church and founded the realm. In our days, when blight strikes, oftentimes a family must be sent away or boarded in their home, so the sickness does not spread." He could see Friedrich shift uncomfortably. "I know it is hard to hear, but the teaching of life is that it is unfair and unforgiving."

He wasn't convinced. "It doesn't make any sense, Vater. You said men would heal a limb when a deer wouldn't, then you say it's good for men to burn a town. How are both of these good?"

"As Holy Hálogi the Lion[41] once said: the needs of the many outweigh the needs of the few. The lives of many men, of all mankind, are sometimes worth the life of one. It is good to heal a man who's leg is broken. And it is evil to burn a town. But if burning one town can save many towns, then it is good. Karalthergroz himself said he would take ten lives if it would save thousands."

Friedrich didn't know what to say. His stomach felt sick, and his head felt heavy. He had heard that phrase uttered before.

"Remember this as well Friedrich. No man is orlayed to do evil. It is not written in any man's life that he will let his inner darkness consume him. Leodolf and Karalthergroz chose to do those evil acts, so that better can come of it. But it did not make them evil."

It did not make them evil. The words echoed in Friedrich's ears.

"Come, it is late. We have talked much, but you need your rest. I have a spare bed in the priesthouse, right through here." Friedrich followed Sieghart to the rear of the church. They passed by a small chamber littered with candles and books, stopping before two rooms with windowless doors. Sieghart opened the far one, showing Friedrich inside. The accommodations were sparse, only featuring a small wooden bed. "It isn't much," Sieghart explained, "but here at least, you're warm, and you're safe. Feel free to sleep as long as you wish. You're welcome to stay here as long as needed."

Friedrich rubbed the back of his head. "Vater Sieghart, I don't know what to say, thank you. I could never repay you."

"You needn't worry about payment my son. The Church is a spot of rest for the downtrodden and weary. All I ask is that on your travels and from this point on, you show similar kindness to others." He bid Friedrich good night and retired to his own room.

Friedrich sat on the bed and took off what was left of his tunic and curled up in the bed. He just laid there, facing the brick wall. Everything seemed so surreal. One moment, he was at a guesthouse, and now, here he was in a small hall in the middle of nowhere. He closed his eyes and tried to will himself to sleep. He thought about the coming days. It would probably take a week to ride up to Bothort, that is if the horse could last that long. He still didn't know what to do for gold. He could ask Vater Sieghart for some, but he was generous enough already. Asking for anything

---

41. He wasn't an actual lion but known for wearing a lion pelt. The story goes that he slew it after it had slaughtered the sheep of a starving town. He is the patron Holy of blacksmiths and is sometimes referred to as Hálogi Leonard.

more would feel like taking advantage. He could make his way to Hertzabrunno, go to his old home, and pick up his savings. Maybe he should even go down to Helvensland, live out there amongst the cows and cheese. Friedrich rolled over, pulling his blanket tighter as he started to drift off. Those were worries for tomorrow.

• • •

Friedrich didn't know how long he slept, but he was grateful it had at least been a dreamless night. It was only when he awoke that the weight of the world came back to him. He looked around, expecting to see Vytilia standing guard or staring out a window. Instead, he was only met with silence and an empty room. He laid down, flat on his back as he stared up at the ceiling. When his eyes closed, all he saw was death.

He hadn't seen someone die in years. The last time, he was still a boy, and it had been an accident. He and Bergmann had been caught up in a crowd who were excited to watch a beheading. He didn't know the crime or the man killed. All he knew was how sickening the sound of the sword meeting the neck had been. He hadn't slept that night or the night after. He cried every night until Bergmann bought him his first beer. That kept the memory away.

Now when he closed his eyes, he saw that beheading again. He saw the warriors slaughtered at the way station. He saw the highwayman die. He even saw Anarawd mauled by that wolf. It was easy to say someone dying was for the greater good. But it was different to actually watch someone die. In times such as that, words meant nothing.

Of course, saying killing was wrong was easy too. Again, those were just words. He did not know, and he would never know, if he had been the first to be accosted by that highwayman. He did not know how many luckless travelers had lost their silver or their lives because of him. And were he caught, he most likely would have been hung or beheaded. He was going to die anyway, but between then and now, how many lives would he have taken? Or how many lives ruined?

What if the lie had been a truth? What if he had a wife who was with child? Would he have risked her safety just so he didn't have to take a life? Was he willing to put his wife on the line for the life of a stranger? Not only his wife, but their child. Was there ever a time the needs of the many outweighed the needs of the one . . . ?

He sighed, rolling onto his side to stare instead at the wall. It wasn't fair. No matter how he looked at it, someone died. *Why couldn't it have been different*? he wondered. *Why couldn't the main road be open, or there be more travelers, or . . . why didn't she trust me*?

Was that what hurt him the most? Was it because *she* had killed the highwayman, not that anyone had died? She was so reckless and so careless with mannish life. She almost took glee in doing so. Was that just an excuse? A chance for her to show her true face? Maybe she was nothing more than the nighttime stalker the wends so rightfully fear.

Then, like some nighttime stalker, Vater Sieghart's words came back to haunt him. *One evil act does not make someone evil,* Friedrich paraphrased. The great leaders of the Realm, the exemplars of mankind, they had to do evil acts to save an untold number of lives. Who's to say she hadn't done the same? She wanted to do what was right. She wanted to help others. She was trying to do good and had let an evil slip-up get in her way.

He shifted to the other side to stare at the other wall. He must be mad to think this! She had no right to take a mannish life, to decide who lives and who dies! She was an outsider. She wasn't even of the same race! She was little more than some wild thing living in the woods. He buried his face in his hands. She was a some*one*, not a some*thing*. She was someone he once . . . someone he thought . . .

He rolled onto his back once more. She was a someone, someone who had made a choice to take a life when they didn't have to. The doom of the highwayman was for the lawmen and the lawhalls to decide. If everyone killed anyone who slighted them, the world would have a handful of folks left alive. She had chosen to kill, to not trust him, and that choice was final. If she chose to kill once, who was to say she couldn't choose it again? How many would die for the greater good? How many would be killed before one becomes evil?

He sat up in bed before the Vater's words had another chance to echo. He stretched and sat up, reaching down for his clothes. Now that he'd taken them off and could see them in the sunlight, he saw how ragged and torn they were. There were stains, nicks, and cuts all over his tunic and trousers. And that wasn't even mentioning the smell. Even his shoes were worn out. The hobnails were almost flattened, and the leather was beginning to crack and dry. He wanted to ask Vater Sieghart for some new clothes, but he had already been generous enough. That would be taking advantage of him.

Doubt flashed in his mind again, but he ignored it, sighing as he stood up and ungirded the sword sheathe and walked out, looking inside the office for Vater Sieghart. He wasn't there, so he continued onto the chapel. He found the Vater in front of the vé, kneeling as he lit candles below the sun image. Friedrich stood at the entrance to the priesthouse, staying quiet as he watched the Vater beseech. He was amazed anyone could stay on their knees for so long.

When the Vater finished, he stood up, touching the sun before looking upwards. Friedrich awkwardly coughed. Sieghart turned around. "Ah, Herr Bauer, how are you? How did you sleep?"

"I, I slept great. Thank you," he lied.

"Good! I'm happy to hear that. I was actually about to partake of some firstmeal. Care to join me, or do you have to get going?"

"Oh, I, I could stay for a firstmeal." Sieghart retired to the rooms. Friedrich walked over and sat on the front pew, staring at the image of the sun. In the Hofs in the bigger towns, the ones he and Herr Bergmann had visited, they didn't have these small, simple images. They would usually have an elaborate, intricately carved statue of God, holding aloft the sun like a torch to guide mankind, flanked by busts or statuettes of Holies and all surrounded by stained glass showing tales from the Sagas. Friedrich had heard somewhere that it was forbidden to show God's face, and so the statues always had him with a hood, covering everything above his mouth.

His silence was interrupted when Vater Sieghart returned with two bowls of hard-boiled eggs. He handed one to Friedrich before sitting next to him. "So," Sieghart began between bites, "where are you headed to on your travels today?"

"Well, Mondsruhe was where I *was* going to go, but, after what happened, I probably shouldn't go there."

Sieghart nodded as he ate. "It might be for the best."

"For now, I guess I'll keep heading north until I reach the coast."

"If that is the case, may I proffer an idea?" Friedrich looked at him while he ate. "There is a member of the halldom here, Herr Roth, a good man. He has a river barge here on the Trautz. He takes salt and other goods up the Trautz and the Aumfz rivers to the towns north of here. He actually leaves today if I'm not mistaken, and he could always use an extra pair of hands onboard."

Friedrich thought it over. He did have some seafaring, or river faring, experience. Sometimes he and Herr Bergmann would hitch a ride on a barge that needed extra hands in exchange for transport and some extra chips. It wasn't an illustrious job, but it was honest work. More honest than caverneering, he had to admit. "How far does he go?"

"He usually goes to Aumfzmarkt or Drosselaue, up north. He was telling me it was about a wegtag away. Of course, he makes stops, loads and unloads along the way, but he can make the trip in about two days. And there's always other river crews you could sign up with. I'm not too knowledgeable with river travel, but you might be able to go all the way to the coastal ports and the purpose you wanted to find. The rivers will give you good learnings and get you there faster than on foot."

It was hard to find fault with the Vater's words, aside from the river part, which sounded incorrect. This would be valuable experience, especially if he was going to work in a port town and eventually on a ship. Sure, the great carracks and galleons were nothing like a simple barge, but everyone had to start somewhere. And, if Friedrich was remembering his geography correctly, this would be a chance to explore an entirely new part of the Realm. There weren't a lot of mountains in the east, around the border with Pelanomov,[42] so he and Herr Bergmann never bothered with it. "It sounds like a great idea," he admitted. "I'm sorry, I don't know what to say. Thank you, but that doesn't sound like enough."

Vater Sieghart just smiled. "It is more than enough. Remember what I taught you. This is what the Church is supposed to be doing. All I ask is that you pass along this kindness to others. If just a few of us share the true love of God with others, we can change the world."

Friedrich grabbed his sword, running his fingers over the embossed sheathe. The doubt and echo crept back loudly in his mind. "Vater Sieghart, does that include forgiving others?"

Sieghart scratched his chin, looking at Friedrich closely. "Are you asking in regard to your former friend?" Friedrich nodded. "Are you having second thoughts?"

---

42. A largely Erdeish kingdom on the eastern border of the Realm. It is a nominal ally and ardent supporter of the church but largely ignored by the Kommandant outside of wartime.

"I . . . I suppose so? I don't know what to call it. I don't know if I should turn back and find them or continue on up north. I don't want to see them again, but something isn't sitting right with me."

The Vater stared at the vé, thinking. "Now, do you feel that you may be harmed if you see them again?"

Friedrich felt the hairs on his neck stand up. "I . . . er . . . well, yes?"

"Then, it might be best to avoid them. Being near an outlaw does not make one an outlaw, but if you hold dry wood and wool near a fire, you cannot expect to not be burned." Friedrich scratched at his cheeks. "And while the Sagas teach us that forgiveness is part of the Douth of Mildheartedness, we must also know that we do not need to forgive right away. And there are times where we do not need to forgive at all. Regardless, there should be, nay there *must be,* time to heal and to grieve. If the other also sees their mistake and undergoes regret, all the better, but forgiveness cannot come right away."

"So, I wouldn't be in the wrong if I never saw them again, if I never forgive them?"

"You wouldn't be wrong, no. You can forgive a man who might shortchange you on a purchase, but you needn't forgive a man who kills your family. The only wrongdoing is passing on the grudge. Don't make your sons hate who you hate. Grudges aren't a birthright. If you never meet them again, don't teach your children to hate them. Teach them properly, warn them, but do not let them carry on a feud."

That was a new idea. Friedrich had always been raised to inherit a father's friends as well as his enemies. There was a split between church law and Teudish folklore. He would have to think about this; just as doubt had gnawed at him underground, it had returned for a different reason. He handed the sword to Vater Sieghart. "Here, it isn't much, but I found it while on my travels. It might be worth something, or you could pass it along to someone who needs it, but I want you to have it."

The Vater accepted it graciously. "Thank you, Herr Bauer. I will put this in the keepsakery." He stood up, walking over to a small box adjacent to the Vé and placed the sword next to it. "Now, let's get to the wharf. We don't want to miss Herr Roth." He collected the bowls, quickly returning to the priesthouse before leading Friedrich outside.

Friedrich untied the horse when they went outside, rousing it from a standing slumber. He held the reins, leading it as they walked through the hamlet. The locals looked up from their work, pausing to greet Vater Sieghart. He stopped, shaking hands with each one, quickly wishing them a good day before returning to Friedrich and continuing to walk. Friedrich couldn't help but admire him. He was unlike any priest he had met before. And, he had actually learned something. Maybe he should start and try to do something new, something good. His own book in his personal Saga was waiting to be written, and he just needed to put leadpen to paper.

They arrived at the wharf, a few feet past the hamlet outskirts. It was a simple wooden pier jutting out into the water. The barge was moored at the end with two men, their backs turned to Friedrich and Vater Sieghart, who were loading barrels into the hold. The barge was a squat vessel with a wide but flat hull and a pointed bow and aft. There was no sail or oars, not even a rudder. Friedrich sighed internally. This was a push-boat, one that used long poles to propel the craft forward. At least there wasn't a current they would have to fight.

"*Entschuldigung*, Herr Roth?" One of the men turned around. He was an older man in his forties with a bit of a paunch. He was bald, aside from an unruly, red beard.

"Ah, Vater Sieghart!" His voice sounded gravelly and rough but oddly welcoming, especially when he spoke to the Vater. "What can I do for you on this God-given day?"

"Herr Roth, this here is Friedrich Bauer. He was recently a guest at the church and is looking to travel up north. I was wondering if you would be willing to take him with you to Drosselaue. As a crewman, of course, I know he can pull his weight."

Herr Roth rubbed his chin, eyeing Friedrich. "Is that so lad? Have you got any knowhow with river travel?"

"A bit. I'm good with knots, and I have a strong back. I can't sing though, so I'll be no help if you moonlight."

"Ha! No players on my boat Herr Bauer, don't you worry. We earn enough with shipping." Herr Roth nodded at Friedrich approvingly. "If Vater Sieghart can vouch for you, that's all I need to hear. We're shipping off in a few slices, so settle your business and be ready." He turned back towards the barge and climbed in.

"Oh." Friedrich got a better look at the hold. There wouldn't be room for the horse.

Vater Sieghart noticed his concern and reached for a chip purse. "Do not worry about your horse. Here." He dropped the entire purse into Friedrich's hand. Inside were nearly twenty, no maybe thirty, silver Sonners, way more than what the horse was worth. Way more than Friedrich was worth.

"Oh, no, no, no. I can't!" He tried handing the chips back.

Sieghart shook his head and held up his hand. "Ah, ah, ah. Remember what I taught you. And, I've been in need of a good horse; there are several families in my halldom I've been unable to visit because of how far they live, and this fellow will help me reach them." He stroked the horse's mane. "Now, it's not my place to tell you how to spend your chips, but I would recommend at least using some to do good and help others." He patted Friedrich on the back, taking the reins.

"Vater, this is too generous! You can't give this to me!"

"There is no such thing as too generous! And here, these looked to be about your size." He passed Friedrich a small bag he had on his back. Inside was a change of clothes. "And if I can leave you one last piece of wisdom, this is a part from the Sagas; God's in His heaven; All's right with the World." Vater Sieghart pointed up at the sun. "Remember that. So long as there is a sun hanging in the sky, so long as there is light, there is goodness. Though the world may seem wrong, though there may be evil, the sun will always rise into the sky to shine on what is good and right in the world." He hugged Friedrich. "Go with God, Herr Bauer. I hope we'll meet again with better news and better hearts."

"I will do some good!" Friedrich called to the priest as he left. Friedrich then climbed into the boat. "How can I be of help, Herr Roth?" he asked.

Herr Roth pulled a long wooden pole from the water, swinging it over their heads and leaning it across the bow. "For starters, it is Shipmaster Roth from here on out. And you'll be taking the bow shift for the first leg." Friedrich nodded. "It's a simple job. Just stick the staff in the water until it hits ground then push us forward. Then swing it around to the other side and do the same. And you'll also help us stop when we make port, but we'll worry about that later." He patted the other man on the back. "This is my son, Ruther. You can just call him Ruther. He doesn't become a Shipmaster until I retire or croak, whichever comes first." He laughed and went to the back of the boat. "I'll be steering from the rear; you get up to the bow and help me launch!"

Friedrich went up to the bow, grabbing the staff and sticking it in the water, angling it just ahead of him. Ruther unmoored the barge and pushed them away from the pier. "Alright! Launch!" Friedrich pushed the staff, feeling the weight of the barge follow him as it moved forward. He swung the staff across the front of the bow, stabbing it into the water and repeating the action. The barge was beginning to pick up speed, slowly inching forward.

The river was placid, a shimmering, green-blue color. Though it was too silted to see the bottom, it looked refreshing and peaceful. Lush trees lined the banks of the river, birds tweeting and flying overhead. Occasionally a fish or turtle would break the surface of the water before quickly diving back down. Frogs would croak when they passed by. It was a cacophony of nature, one that Friedrich welcomed. He had a task again, a goal and purpose, his mind filled with the sounds of animals rather than regrets and what-ifs. He pushed Vyt—he banished thoughts of the vampiric harlot. She was behind him now, a thing of the past. Tomorrow was a new day. Tomorrow was a new life.

• • •

Vytilia did not move for several hours after Friedrich left. She sat under a tree far from the road, immobile. The embers of the cremated highwayman still glowed, the smell lingering in the air. Everything that had happened left her numbed; she felt nothing, she thought nothing, she was an empty shell. It all seemed like a dream, or some cruel nightmare. None of this could be real!

It was not real. It could not be real, she started convincing herself. This had all been blown out of proportion! She started to laugh at the dark, ironic comedy of the situation. This was all a misunderstanding between the two of them. He was overreacting, she was underreacting, it would all sort itself out. He probably just went ahead to cool his heels and clear his head. He would be back, she would apologize, they would make up, and resume their journey. All she had to do was wait. She needed to be prepared, quickly grabbing the torcs, their bags, and the pistol and sword from the highwayman, neatly arranging them in a pile as she awaited Friedrich to come back. Once he was here, they could resume travelling right away.

And she did wait.

She waited, sitting under the tree, watching as avians flew through the sky, as clouds rolled by like waves, as animals and travelers would gallop down the dried road. Her heart skipped beats whenever an equine would pass by, and each time, she was disappointed. She continued to wait through the setting of the sun. She waited as noctuae came down, bringing her vermin to feed on. She waited as the sun rose and the noctuae returned to their nests. She waited as the clouds parted, and sunlight shone down in the middle of the day.

Friedrich did not return.

He *was not* coming back.

The realization swept over and paralyzed her; he was gone.

The gravity of the situation hit her with force. She had just alienated her guide, her people's only ally on the surface, their only hope of survival . . . and her friend.

He was her *only* friend.

He was right. Annia, Sextus, all of them were not friends. They were servants in her family's employ. Friedrich had been a real friend, or at least, he had started to be one. And she had thrown that all away. He was gone, miles away, the gods know where in the great unknown of the surface.

She was a stranger in a strange land, a hostile land whose inhabitants had every justification for hunting her down. She knew not where to go; she knew not whom to trust. How could she complete her mission? How could she save her people? They were all counting on her, praying to gods long forgotten for her, and she failed! She had failed everyone, the Concilium, the populace, her father! All of them had been counting on her, and she failed them when they needed her the most.

She started to cry, her mind devoid of thought, only filled with self-loathing and regret. How could she have been so stupid? So foolish? She let her anger get the best of her once again! She was out of her element, in a strange, foreign land. She should have listened to her guide, her . . . friend. She screamed, crying into the night in frustration, clenching her fists so tightly, her nails drew blood, falling onto her face and weeping. Everyone had been depending on them, on her! Her civilization depended on her and she failed! Tens of thousands of years of history and culture, all thrown away because she was reckless! All those miracles and intervention from Luna and Sol wasted! She pounded the ground in frustration, tears pouring down her face.

She cried until she had nothing left; she was hopeless, beyond lost, beyond despair. What was she to do now? She could not return to Nidus! Return would only bring shame and dishonor. It spat on the lineage of her mother and father. Failure was not acceptable, and would not be tolerated.

But . . . Nidus did not know she was alive. Word would reach the Concilium that they had never arrived at Aurum. They would know of the attack on the way station, and they would not find her body amongst the dead. But they would find Pellio. They would know she escaped into the tunnels and presume she had perished there. As far as the Concilium knew, she had perished.

She stood up, dusting off the seat of her skirt, and faced westward. Her family honor was intact, and her loyalty to the empire was without question. She started to walk. It was . . . comforting, knowing that the Concilium assumed her dead. To the people, she died in service to the empire, and while their prayers may not have been answered, she had at least started the establishment of relations with the surface. She had been dutiful, the empire was on the path to receive advanced weaponry, and she, heiress of emperors and empresses, would be remembered as a hero.

Her mind went to pity for her father. He had lost her, just as he had lost her mother years earlier. But he would find solace that she died in the line of duty. Perhaps this would pull him out of his mourning. He could remarry, continue the Quintia line. The Octavian line may have been exterminated, but what a fitting end; dying to save the empire it once ruled. Her father was mighty, stronger than most realized. Her supposed passing would be difficult, but he would move on. He would survive.

She had not failed, at least as far as the Concilium was concerned; but what was she to do now? The world of the surface was still dangerous; to their law, she had killed a man, practiced witchcraft, and was a monster. She did not blend well with the populace. She stood out "as a colorful dog" as Friedrich described. A slip of the tongue or flash of her fang, and she would be hunted.

Should she try and find Friedrich? She stopped in her tracks, looking north. Could she even find him? He said his name was fairly common. If she asked for a Friedrich Bauer, would she find her Friedrich? If she did manage to find him, what would she say? Would he even listen to her? He had readily called her a monster before, and now she had proven him right. If she found him, it would only further antagonize him. She would have had to follow him, almost stalking him like a predator.

It caused her heart to ache, but the best course would be to let a sleeping calcerta lie, for both of them. She was free, liberated from responsibility. The world was hers to see. Much had changed in the 3,000 years Strixans had been gone, and she would be the first to see all that man has learned and changed in their absence.

Yet, it would not be the same without Friedrich. The strange feelings she had felt, the jealousy at the nymphs, this new sense of longing, it was eating at her, rusting her psyche like iron. The thought that she would have to see the world alone, without her friend, caused tears to swell. What was the point of travelling if you were alone, spending your time in the shadows, praying that you were never found? What joy would travel bring if it could not fill this new-found, uncomfortable void she felt in her heart?

Then what ultimately, was she to do? In a sense, she was truly and ultimately free, liberated from any and all responsibility. But this was a bitter liberty, a cruel, listless one. She decided to walk, to press on westward through these wilds and to think.

She could not give up. She could not abandon her people, could she? Strixans had a duty to the state, to the empire, to the people. And she was a loyal Strixan. Yet, how could she? She had ultimately failed in her mission to acquire arms. She did not even know where this . . . "Toller Mund" as he called it was. She could ask, but, even if she found it, it had been described as a labyrinthine maze of tunnels and caves. She could easily get lost, or worse, trapped in there. Then her fictious death would become a reality.

And asking was less and less feasible the more she thought of it. She did not know this world. She did not know this people. They had some sense of honor, of virtue, but she had only seen such a small sampling of the population. What if she asked the wrong person? How many others like that brigand could be out there? What if she was led into a trap and forced to kill again? Gods forbid, she could even be seen doing the killing. She would spread the erroneous legend of blood-drinkers faster than any mannish ethnicities could.

Then, ultimately, it seemed, to perform her duty to the empire, she had to shirk it. If becoming a pariah meant the preservation and survival of the Strixan empire then so be it. Better she hide in the shadows, never to be seen again, so that elder statesmen may unite her people and the peoples of the surface.

A bitter cup to drink from, but one that must be drunk. Everything was in the hands of Luna and Sol now. All that could be asked was that diplomacy see its due course. She wished she could be there to see it, but, she had her duty.

Vytilia continued to walk westward in a near-straight line. She walked through the night and the morning, only slowing down when the sun rose and made her skin matte and energy languid. But while her body slowed, her mind did not. The entirety of her trek, she had been debating with herself. Like a court case of the old empire, she argued with herself, before herself, of what to do.

Not returning to Nidus and abandoning her people, for the betterment of the empire, remained her directive. Now she was wondering what she could do with this ill-gotten liberty. She had to do something that would not attract attention to herself, especially once relations between man and Strixans were normalized. If word spread of a silver-skinned, white-haired female sojourner, it would not take long for a Strixan delegation to seek her out, thinking her a long-lost kinsman.

Her walk brought her to the edge of a fenced field late in the night, before the morning twilight. Beyond a low stone wall were furrowed plots filled with green stalks. Curious as always, she watched for sign of a farmer or fieldhand, and spotting none, hopped the fence, plucking one of the stalks before climbing back over. As she observed the vegetable taken, she gasped, nearly throwing it back over in horror. Beneath the green stalk was a beige, bulbous, and pungent root; allium.

Horror aside, her curiosity was thoroughly piqued. This was the forbidden fruit, the deadliest substance known to strixankind. Yet, here was a field, stretching to the horizon, full of it. Times truly have changed.

As she studied the bulb, careful not the touch anything but the stalk, she contemplated throwing it back over the wall. But, should the worst occur, for someone of her sex and station, death might be preferable to capture or further harming future diplomatic relations. She set the allium down and unslung Friedrich's bag, finding a scrap of cloth. She wrapped the bulb in the cloth then tucked it in. She set off again, continuing west. That was another reason to avoid population centers and hide in the wilds, lest she be inadvertently poisoned.

The thought of food made her smack her lips; she could use a good feeding. Between the distance traveled and the heat of the sun, she was feeling weak. She pressed on into a deeply wooded thicket, listening for her quarry. Miles from the allium farm, she heard it: a heartbeat similar in size and pace to the beast she killed in the nymph stratum. She slowed down, unslinging the bag and waiting behind a tree. One of the beasts wandered near her, bellowing before licking at moss growing on a rock. She readied her body to pounce, baring her fangs, and leapt. The beast let out only a slight bellow as she wrestled it to the ground, puncturing the carotid arteries on both sides of the neck. Rich, gamey blood rushed into her mouth. She could already feel her senses heightening and her mind racing with thoughts.

She dropped the corpse and wiped her mouth, collecting her things as she continued on her way. She went to study the surroundings, to plan where she could live and hide, yet she could not focus. Something was nagging at her, something physical that she could not explain. She grunted in frustration, kicking rocks as she walked. What was it? It had something to do with her mouth. She massaged it, feeling for a dislocation or laceration, but there were none.

She had walked for many miles from the farm, the sun was beginning to raise in the sky, and she was still plagued by this strange nagging in her mouth. As she came to a hill crest, overlooking a lake, a realization began to dawn on her; it was taste. She was missing a taste, longing for something she had fed on before. But what? She recalled the various bloods she had tried within the last few days, trying to pinpoint what this craving was. It riddled her taste buds. Was it one of the fine sanguine stocks so prized by her father? It could not be. That only made her mouth dry up. The gamey blood of the beast she recently killed? That was not it either. That tasted . . . plain. Was it even that small taste of Anarawd's? That was not it. It was something, fresher, more recent and newer . . .

Horror overtook her at the realization. What she craved was the blood of *men*. The mere idea shook her to her soul, and she nearly vomited at the thought. How could this be? How could she have fallen so low? The very word man caused her fangs to flash and her mouth to hiss. The inner predator had come out, and it wanted more.

It had all made sense; there was something so unique, so special about this mortal blood. It was sweet, sweeter than any she had had before. She felt energetic, powerful, even her melancholic mood dissipated. She had the energy of an entire legion. She *did* want more. Just a taste, a mere droplet, that was all. Nothing else sounded satisfying, not even the finest stocks of Sanguinvinum, or the freshest blood of a butchered beast. All were as ash to her. She wanted the dark red ichor of mortal men.

She threw herself on the ground, wrestling with her baser self. What had overcome her? The rational mind fought back, seizing control of mind and body. How could she think any of these things!? Men were sapient, sentient creatures, the allies and potential saviors of her people. How could she think of them like that? Her people had laws! They had traditions! Traditions she was trying to preserve, how could she want to throw them away so easily?! She needed to forget, to put this all behind her, to move on. This was a temporary setback. She would overcome it, just as she had everything before her. She was stronger than herself. She was free, not a slave to her thirst. Men were beings, just as she was, equals in civility, not prey. She thrashed, fighting herself, her sight going red. Her body ignored her mind. Nothing mattered, not rules, not tradition, not alliances. All it wanted was more, another, fresh and taken unwillingly. The pain and surprise made it thrilling.

The mind came back, rationalizing and fighting. Vytilia felt as if she was two persons, battling a fight to the death, and she feared the outcome. She could not let this primitive side of her win. She could not let a lust for blood dictate her existence. She had a duty to her people and her state, not her mouth and stomach.

She needed to get active, to weaken the body and let the mind take over. She raced up and down the side of the mountain, weaving through trees and brush, leaping over rocks and fallen logs. Oh, what a nightmare this was! What a curse! Damn her very essence for crying out for another taste!

She kept running, covering her mouth, nearly crying at her behavior. She heard the sound of water and ran towards it, bursting through the tree line, nearly falling into the water. She fell to her knees on the bank of a lake, cupping her hands and bringing up several drinks of water. She rinsed her mouth out, spitting repeatedly as she continued to drink. She splashed her face, washed her hands, anything to feel clean.

She broke down crying, nearly prostrating in the water. Could she even win this fight? All while running, the craving was still there! The mind was losing! She was a monster! Oh gods, Friedrich was right! She was a monster, and all it took was one taste! She was horrified with herself. This was not what the daughter of a praetor should do. This was not becoming of a true Strixan. She was civilized, not a barbaric slave to her desire and thirst. She needed to get away, stay far away from men.

"*Entschuldigung, Fräulein*?" She looked up to her left in terror, falling on her back and crawling away. A man was approaching her. He was young, wearing simple peasant garb and a straw hat. He was holding a hooked rod in one hand. "Oh." He was surprised at her face. "Are, are you alright? Do you need any help?"

"Get away!" Vytilia yelled. "Get back!" She was nearly hissing, shutting her mouth with one hand to not expose her fangs. She could hear his heartbeat. She salivated, imagining the blood pumping through his veins. Everything she saw had a red tint. His heart rate elevated as she tried to warn him, her fangs began to extend, and she covered her mouth in fear. Her stomach growled, her muscles tensed, ready to spring forward.

"Fräulein, it's alright! I just want to help!" He stepped closer. She stepped back. "Are you well?"

"Stay away! Please!" she pleaded, her mouth quivering. The man stopped; fear began to creep across his face. Her thirst only increased; she only heard his heartbeat. "Leave me alone!" She picked herself up and ran, running across the shallow end of the lake, heading up the side of a mountain, her stole falling off, and she cared not to grab it. She needed to get away, running until she could not hear that man's heartbeat, nor any heartbeat. She ran and ran up the mountain over rock and log until she did not hear anything but the wind. She collapsed onto the rock, crying. Her jaw nearly had a mind of its own, snapping at the rocks as if they were the fleshy, blood-filled necks of men.

She felt delirious, falling in and out of consciousness, the toll of this internal battle stretching her to her very limit. In her moments of near sleep, everything was red, a vicious, cruel scarlet that only exacerbated her problem. The scarlet almost smiled at her, laughing and taunting her yet was inviting, bidding her to join it.

Vytilia awoke, pulling herself out of the delirium in a cold sweat. Panic and fear flowed through her nerves until at last, it receded. A momentary calm in a storm, she assumed. She used the time to gauge her surroundings, to ascertain her own and the safety of others.

She was near the peak of a wooded mountain, far from any village. There was a cave at the peak. It was shallow, only a few feet into the rock, but it was shady and far from anyone else. She crawled into the cave, going as deep as it would allow, and curled into a fetal position, lying on her side.

Whatever options she previously had evaporated in an instant. The very thought of the race of men made her thrash like an animal. Staying in the mannish world was an impossibility. Now she was an even greater liability to stable relations. Whatever her outward appearance, internally, she was a bloodthirsty monster, primed for killing. She could never see Friedrich again, never see her father or her home again.

In her darkest hour, exiled from the moonlight by the rock once more, a single thought emerged; only one option remained.

She got up onto her knees, retrieving the allium bulb from her bag. In the empire, only in death does duty end. Strixans are expected to give everything to the empire and their fellow citizens. A legionary is to return from battle with their shield or carried upon it by their surviving comrades. To die before dishonor is to die without a tarnished legacy. The Concilium believed her to be dead already. It only made sense to make that fiction a reality. She was too much of a risk, a living liability to peace and stability. In a sense, her mission was already complete; she had initiated establishing relations with the surface. Now, it was in the hands of elder statesmen. She had done her duty to the state, to the people.

She grabbed a rock, crushing the bulb until the yellow, fruit-like innards were exposed. She dry-swallowed, looking down at the pungent tool of her demise. *This is for the best,* she reasoned. This was for the empire, for her people. With a final prayer to Luna and Sol, she took one of the pieces, bringing it up to her mouth. "Axios[43]!" she exclaimed. "Vivat Imperium!" She popped the piece in her mouth, chewed, and swallowed, waiting for the end.

Time seemed to slow, every passing second taking an eternity. She waited for the effects to take. But . . . moments passed, and she remained . . . alive. She opened her eyes. She could still see. She took a breath. She could still breathe. She was alive! But, how? How was this possible? Was the allium not ripe? She grabbed another piece and ate it, waiting a few minutes and still nothing. What, what did this mean? Was she . . . immune? But, that was impossible. There had not been a Strixan with allium immunity in sixty millennia! There had to be another explanation.

She glanced at the entrance of the cave. Faint, silvery strips of moonlight were peeking through the clouds outside. This immunity, it must be a miracle, divine intervention by Luna on

---

43. Axios, meaning "I am worthy" a traditional Strixan phrase of loyalty.

her behalf, like the avians who cushioned their fall in the nymph stratum! Perhaps, there was still a chance to succeed, a chance to return home and complete her mission!

But she must not squander this opportunity. She needed to be prepared. She would get this craving under control. She could once again walk amongst the men of the surface to solicit their help. She would return to Nidus, a triumphant hero with arms and supplies in tow. Once more, the Gods of her ancestors had shown mercy where none was deserved. She had further work to complete, and by the honor of her family names, she, Vytilia Sangilla Noctinna Vespertilica Albuargentia Camilla Octavian Quintia, daughter of the Praetor Faustus and Carmilla Quintia, would complete it. Neither death nor this craving would stop her!

She laid on her back, grabbing her skirt to steady herself, and thought of men and their blood. She would conquer this problem, just as her ancestors conquered the world. And then, when she was done, she was going to find her friend, Friedrich, *and* complete her mission. The gods had once more blessed the Strixans. It was a beneficence she would not squander.

17

After two days on the river, it was just before dusk by the time Friedrich and the Roths arrived at their final destination: the river town of Drosselaue. Drosselaue was a decent-sized town, much larger than Preisdorf or Salzahoi. Most of the buildings were new, two or three floors painted in the usual bright colors with shingled roofs and glass windows. As with most port towns, there were horse-carts, handcarts, and other barge crews all gathered around the pier, haggling over prices or loading goods. Shipmaster Roth tied the barge to the pier and climbed up. Ruther and Friedrich began passing him their cargo. Most of what they were delivering was salt, imported from Salzahoi, with a few crates of foodstuffs, bolts of cloth and linen, a barrel of wine, and two lambs.

A swarthy Tujue in a fine silk suit and turban walked over to Shipmaster Roth and talked with him, accompanied by two dockmen. Ruther, Friedrich, and the dockmen helped load the salt barrels into a cart with Friedrich tying the rope to keep the barrels secure. With the cart loaded, the Tujue dropped a bag of chips in Shipmaster Roth's hand.

"Well done boys! Well done! Another successful trip! Finish stowing the rest of our cargo in that shed over there. We'll load up the rest of our buyers tomorrow morning. For now, let's hit the beerhall!" He clapped Friedrich and Ruther on the shoulders, much to Friedrich's chagrin. His back and shoulders still ached, more than they ever would when caverneering.

The other sailors, dockmen, and teamsters were already celebrating a day of work, pouring into the two Beerhalls or an accommodating guesthouse or leaning against railings, chatting and singing. Shipmaster Roth led them into the farther beerhall, closer to the small stone church in the center of town. The beerhall was a bit dingy. There was a prevalent mildewy smell with a low ceiling hugged by a thin layer of smoke, songs bouncing off the stone walls. Puddles of . . . something were splattered across the floor. Large casks and barrels hugged the walls with drinkmaids rushing back and forth from the casks to tables.

In the center sat a rough-looking company of men in buff coats, armor, and helmets. Swords and pistols were sheathed in well-worn holsters at their hips. They were gleefully chugging back flagons of beer and wine, all singing of their triumphs. Friedrich scoffed when he passed them. They were landsknechts, little more than legal robbers.

Friedrich and the Roths sat at a table near the corner of the beerhall, where a drinkmaid brought over three steins, overflowing with foam. Shipmaster Roth slipped a thaler into her hand then raised his stein with a smile. "To another successful journey and to the good Vater! May he continue to guide us in goodness. Zum Wohl!"

"Zum Wohl!" Ruther and Friedrich cheered.

"So, Friedrich, what's your next move? Still want to head north, or will you be coming with us back to Preisdorf, become a part of our crew?"

Friedrich paused before answering, taking a long draw from his stein to avoid speaking. It'd been two days, two days to think and ponder when he wasn't working. He'd thought about her in those last two days. Guilt gnawed at him like white ants gnawed a house's foundation. The idea of forgiving her, of going back and continuing to Mondsruhe together, floated pleasantly in his mind. And yet, at night, the death of the highwayman and the vivid feeling that it could be his neck in her mouth next haunted him to his soul. She was smart. She might have already moved on. She didn't need him, and he didn't need her.

He finally pulled the stein away from his mouth to answer. "No," he said as affirmatively as he could. "I'll try to sign on with another barge. Vater Sieghart really helped me in understanding what I want out of life, and I think that it's up north."

"Aye, that Vater Sieghart is a good man. Best priest our little town ever had," Shipmaster Roth commented. "Well, Friedrich, since you did such a good job helping us, allow me to do you a favor. Follow me." He stood up, bringing his stein with him. Friedrich followed him over to another table where a lean, older man with a hoary beard sat. He was leaning back against the wall, chewing on a wooden pipe as smoke billowed from the bowl. "Friedrich . . ." Shipmaster Roth introduced, "this is my good friend, Shipmaster Fischer, best sailor on the Tonau!"

Shipmaster Fischer extended a hand, holding the pipe in the corner of his mouth. "How do you do lad?" His hands were old but calloused, the sign of an experienced sailor.

"Shipmaster Fischer, Friedrich here just proved himself a worthy riverman with me and my boy. I thought I'd reward him by introducing him to you."

"Is that right? Well, Roth's word is as good as any. Come, sit, sit!" He gestured to the free bench across from him. Friedrich sat down, coughing slightly at the smoke. "I'm always looking for new hands to sail with me."

"Where do you sail?" Friedrich asked.

"I pick up some cargo here in Drosselaue, usually some salt Roth here brings up, then I go up the Adenz to Barriort. There, I usually pick up a new load and keep going down the Tonau to Lofnscheid."

"That's a long trip," Friedrich commented. "How far do you go into Ostlücke?"

"Oh, I stop at Lofnscheid, but if the pay is good, I'll keep going onto Grenzburg. Wherever I stop, I'll sell off me boat, borrow a horse, and head back here to start all over."

Friedrich really did not want to go into Ostlücke, towards the Head-Stead of Grenzburg. He needed to be going north, not east. But work was work, and it got him a step in the right direction. "Shipmaster Fischer, if you need the hands, I'll gladly join along, but I'll need to get off at Barriort."

"Aye, if you insist. Though going down to Lofnscheid is good chips and plenty of time to get your sea legs, get a good tan, and learn the ropes! And did I mention it'll bring in a good amount of silver!" He laughed then coughed. "We leave after dawn tomorrow." He slapped some grozpfennigs on the table. "Friedrich, why don't you go get the next round. We can toast our new task."

He took the chip and headed towards the bar, passing by the table full of landsknechts, the loudest group in the hall. Just as he walked by, he heard one of them yell out to him. He stopped, turning around to face the yeller. In the midst of all the sellswords was a young woman, only a bit older than him. She had on a blue-dyed buff coat, a gorget hanging just below her neck. Her dark black hair was cropped short, longer than a man's but short for a woman. Her face was scarred, especially on the right cheek, and her nose had been broken a few times. She was the opposite of

Vyt—the vampire, gruffer and rougher around the edges rather than dainty and well-kept.

"You, come here, take seat." She spoke with an accent, Želek or some kind of Wenden. Her words were sharp, spoken in short sentences, and each word was carefully enunciated. She waved the sellswords in front of her aside, creating a space for him. Friedrich reluctantly went over and sat down, wearily glancing at his side. "You are young, strong, with good back," she observed.

"Thank you?" He made himself smaller, trying not to bump elbows with the men on his left and right.

"No need to be tense. We are friends." She smiled, taking a drink.

Friedrich eyed her suspiciously. "I don't make friends with sellswords."

"How can you say that? You not even get to know us! As my dear old *matka*, my mother say, a stranger is friend you haven't met!"

"Well, I'd rather not meet any sellswords. Can't have warriors without a war brewing nearby."

"You have good sense of joke! He come from land of warriors and no like warriors. Maybe we should trade names. I am Adélka Bohdana Žipek. I am the Velitel of this crew. Roland! What is Teutonish word for Velitel?"

"Hauptmann," a mercenary answered.

"Yes. This is my band. But, let us talk the niceness. Where are you from?"

"Helvensland."

She eyed his age-shield with a bit of suspicion then shrugged. It wasn't her business to know where men were *really* from. "Ah! I have friends in Helvensland. Hårok, your brother in Helvensland, yes?" She elbowed the large man next to her.

Hårok was nose-deep in a pamphlet, quietly nodding every time Adélka spoke. He was a burly man with a mess of long blond braids and a beard that would put a lion's mane to shame. He was more interested in his pamphlet than the conversation. A landsknecht that could read was the most astonishing thing Friedrich had seen thus far.

"Bah, pay him no mind. The Helven, they are good warriors. You are warrior?"

Friedrich took a deep breath, balling his free hand into a fist. "No," he spoke through gritted teeth. "I am a hewer, turned sailor."

Adélka looked him up and down, narrowing her eyes. "Are you sure? You have strength of warrior. And you are Teudish-Helven." She pointed to his age-shield. "Teudish are proud warrior. Make best."

"I am not a warrior," he insisted.

"You want become one? We are taking on newlings." Friedrich shook his head. "I change your mind!" she insisted, snapping for another round for the table. "These . . ." she gestured to the table, "are Wagon Warriors. The best fighters in Erebus!"

"Never heard of you," Friedrich stated.

"That is lie. Everyone know Wagon Warriors! You know the Yarruser wars?" Friedrich shook his head again. "Bah! Another lie! Everyone know the Yarrusers, first Urworkers! Hårok, tell him!"

The burly man at her side sighed and closed his pamphlet, keeping a finger inside to mark his place. "The Wagon Warriors were founded nearly two hundred years ago. After the Erdeish and Kommandant murdered Hugo Yarrus, Želevlast rose up to free themselves. Using armored wagons, the Želeks cut down scores of knights until the Kommandant called for a truce," Hårok explained in monotone; this wasn't the first time he had given this spiel. "We are their scions. We are skilled warriors who accept only the best jobs and only fight in the best battles. Boss, I'm trying to read."

"Hårok speak Teutonish better than I, is better for telling tale," Adélka explained. "And best part of tale? Is all true. My great-great-grandpapa found original Wagon Warriors to defend the weak and free Želevlast. Yarrusers great warriors, fight liars and cruelness! We start the Great Ur-Working! We break back of Midgart Church! Ludher not happen without Yarrus!"

Friedrich wasn't amused. He'd heard enough lore to last a lifetime. "So, your kind is why Erebus tore itself in half all those years ago. You lit the powder keg." He quietly sipped his drink.

"You say that as if it was bad thing! We light powder of freedom! We fight to free our folk!" Adélka insisted. "We broke chivalry, ended the oppression of many lords. We fight for our rights!"

"Tell that to all the burned towns and dead families. *We* had freedom; *we* were happy with the church. Ask the dead how they feel about the 'freedom' you fought for." Friedrich stood up. "Thanks for the drink, but I'm not interested."

"It is good chips!" A landsknecht next to Friedrich grabbed his arm while Adélka spoke. "We go west to border with Galie to town of Zweibaden. We offer to fight for the Markrabě, fight in war. More chips than boats give. Renown, songs, rewards! Fight with us. Become Wagon Warrior!"

"That's your home," Hårok had finished reading and added. "The land of the Nemeten. We can take you home. Your real home." He gestured to Friedrich's age-shield.

"I said, I'm not interested!" Friedrich ripped his arm away, spilling some of his drink. Adélka waved him away, cursing him in her tongue. A few of the Wagon Warriors made threatening faces at Friedrich but stayed where they were.

Friedrich placed the grozpfennigs on the bar as the drinkkeeper got him three more steins. "Thanks for not starting a brawl," the drinkkeeper joked. "I'd hate to replace all the furniture."

Friedrich rolled his eyes and turned around before stopping and turning back to the drinkkeeper. "Do you sell food here?"

"Some nights. It'll take us a bit to get the ovens started if you want anything."

"No, no." Friedrich reached into his chippurse, pulling out one of the sonners Vater Sieghart gave him. "Here, this should be worth a few meals. Save it for the next time the hungry ask for something."

The drinkkeeper nodded, putting the Sonner by his lockbox. "Aye lad. I'll keep it safe; don't you worry."

Friedrich returned to the shipmasters, handing them each their drinks. "I was worried there for tick," Shipmaster Fischer admitted. "I thought you were about to meet the wrong end of a pistol."

"Wouldn't be a good move to kill off joiners, would it?" Friedrich asked.

"They seem like a bunch of pricks, but I have to admit, she is right. If war with Gallia breaks out, you could make a lot more gold fighting with a sellsword band than sailing down the Tonau," Shipmaster Roth admitted.

"I'm not a fighter, never have been, never will be."

"Not saying you are, but good chips are good chips."

"Ah Donar, quit trying to frighten my new hand away! The gold he'll make with me won't be stained with blood!" Shipmaster Fischer elbowed Roth.

"Aye, watch your arm," Roth retorted. "I ain't trying to whore out the lad. No sense getting yourself killed over a few extra gulders."

Shipmaster Fischer finished off his drink and stood up, extinguishing his pipe. "Well, I best be turning in for the night. Friedrich, remember, just after dawn. Look for the barge labeled

Schürze." He chuckled and left the beerhall. Shipmaster Roth patted Friedrich on the shoulder and returned to Ruther.

Friedrich was all alone now, nursing his beer while he heard the landsknechts laugh and sing, drowning out the rest of the hall. It was funny, he thought, had she still been with him, they would have been excited to see sellswords. They could have traded the torcs for a few spare muskets or pistols. It would have cut down on their travel time and scared off any more robbers. It was odd, the way the world worked. Had he been more of a churchly man, he might have taken it as some sort of foretoken.

He shook his head and finished his drink then stood up. He thanked and said goodbye to Shipmaster Roth then went outside to find a spot to piss and a spot to sleep in that order. The Wagon Warriors spilled out of the beerhall a while later. They gave him another sneer as they walked by him but continued to their camp, spewing and singing as they stumbled.

"Hopefully, that's the last I'll ever see of them," Friedrich muttered as he lay down.

• • •

Time was negligible to Vytilia in the cave. Days could have passed, months could have, and she would not have known. All she focused on was training herself to suppress her thirst. She would lie on her back in the dark and close her eyes, imagining a man's neck. Then the memory of the taste would flood her senses. She would struggle, clenching her jaw shut, squeezing her eyes and clenching her fists. At first, she would lose, nearly breaking her mandible as she lashed out at the darkness, desperate to bite anything. Frequently, she would hit herself, forcing her fangs to recede and her mouth to close before lying back down. Then she would start the process all over again.

She would practice this for hours on end until she passed out from exhaustion then would start over. If she did not master this, she could not master herself, and she would never be able to complete this mission. She could not pass over this mercy, however excruciating it was. Each time she just imagined a heartbeat, her mouth would open with a hiss, reverberating off the walls of the cave. She would scream, even considering ripping out her fangs before slamming her fist on the wall. But she did not stop. She could not stop. Once she had regained control of herself, closed her mouth and receded her fangs, she went back to work. Every time she was able to stop herself was a victory, however minor. Every hour that passed was an hour she got closer to winning this war.

It was exhausting; her lips and gums chafed, her jaw muscles were numb, and her mind wanted to split from her skull. But she had been given a new chance, a new opportunity to continue her mission and fulfill her duty. She was the vanguard of the Strixan peoples on the surface, and she could not be a diplomat in her current state. Her ancestors had conquered continents. She could conquer herself.

In her bouts of exhaustion, something was haunting her mind. It was not a person nor a creature but a scarlet-colored mist. Each time, it was tempting, always calling to her. And each time, she awoke, sweating, reinvigorated, and beginning again. But the days without blood and constant exertion weakened her, and she fell into a delirious sleep.

She knew right away that this was a dream or some sort of phantasmal experience. Her limbs felt as heavy as marble blocks. She could not walk, only moving her head. Instead, the scarlet mist around her moved, passing her like water over a rock. Then, the scarlet began to take form, molding into a forum of the old empire, a cobblestone road lined with great works of architecture and colonnades. Legionaries in their finery stood as a guard, holding pilum and shields at attention. Vytilia leaned towards the legionaries before pulling away. Their armor and shields were stained with blood, a deep red blood. She knew instantly it was men's blood.

"Magnificent, are they not?" Vytilia heard a voice, piercing through the scarlet, the forum and colonnade dissipating. She turned around. Standing before her was a hen Strixan, arrayed in royal scarlet finery, a golden crown of laurels on her head. Her hair was a radiant white, her skin a startling silver, and her eyes a lustrous gold. It was . . . her! "You look surprised."

"I-I-I-I-I-I-I-I."

"Do not be alarmed. This should be natural."

The surroundings transformed again into a deep scarlet fog, almost choking everything around her. All she could see clearly was this red version of her. "I need to wake up," she stated, trying not to let the fear creep into her voice.

"You cannot, at least not yet. I need to speak with you."

"You need nothing. I do not talk to my inner devils."

Her scarlet counterpart laughed. "You call me a devil? Do I look like one of those dumb brutes? I am the epitome of civilization, the apex of Strixan society. And I am you. And you are me."

"You are not me," Vytilia spat. "You are some delirious, mocking visage, my mind creating phantoms to manifest my fears."

"I am not a phantom nor am I your fears, dear self. I have been with you since the very beginning." The scarlet counterpart paused. "If anything, *you* are the mocking visage, a masquerade of me."

Vytilia tried raising her arms and snapping her fingers to banish this . . . *thing* in a ball of fire. But the limbs did not respond. She was paralyzed.

"Why do you fight yourself, dear self? You know of our history. You know nothing good comes of Strixan civil wars."

"I am fighting a bestial, basic urge. And only good can come of it. I am a diplomat, a civilized representative of our, er, *my* people. A diplomat does not go around slitting the throats of the people whose lands they reside in."

"Hmmmm." The scarlet counterpart rolled her eyes. "Come now, dear self, diplomats only represent the Strixan people to civilized, advanced societies, who are worthy of us gracing their presence. Do you really think these pink mortals are worthy of receiving us? Of learning of our existence?"

"Of course they are! An ally to fight the devils is an ally worth having!"

"Allies are ones you trust, who will summon a call to war and fight alongside you. These men are flighty and fleeting. Where is your man friend now?"

"I do not need to dignify that with a response," Vytilia countered.

"Oh? Is it because the truth is painful to hear, or is it because you are the denser of the two of us?"

"I need to wake up." Vytilia looked away from the scarlet counterpart. "I need to wake up."

"I AM NOT FINISHED WITH YOU!" the scarlet one roared. She grabbed Vytilia's chin in a manner reminiscent of Carmilla. Her fangs were bared as she stared into Vytilia's eyes, trying to peer into her soul. The fangs were stained red. Droplets of blood fell from the points. "You do not need to wake up. You need to grow up! You cannot continue living under delusions! You cannot continue to believe in these falsities you sell yourself!" She pulled away in a dramatic flourish.

"Then say what you need to say and leave me be!"

"I cannot leave you be, dear self! I am you! I am what you should be!"

"I am *not* a monster!"

"You are!" her scarlet-self hissed. "You are a monster! But you are only a monster to those who deserve it! You think out there, those frightened, stupid, mortals would ever reject their petty superstitions and see our people as equals? You seriously believe after three millennia of isolation on the surface, they will accept us with open arms and open ledgers?"

"They could!"

"Stop deceiving yourself! You believe that only because you want to! It is not true! You told everything to that mortal! You took him to the most sacred room in Nidus, and he still turned away!"

Stinging tears began to burn Vytilia's eyes. "It was a mistake *I* made that *I* need to rectify!"

"By torturing yourself? By hiding in a cave? You did not make the mistake, dear self. It is the mortals who made the mistake. It is the Concilium who made the mistake. Masters do not make alliances with slaves. Your destiny does not lie in allying with the mortals. It is enslaving them, conquering them, teaching them their place."

Vytilia's chest felt heavy. Her mouth quivered, falling open in shock. Those words, that idea, they sounded so sweet, so correct. Maybe, that was what mother meant by restoring the empire.

"Think about it," her scarlet counterpart continued, "imagine the peace we would bring to the blighted land. Imagine a pacified countryside, free of brigands, free of floods, free of disease and pitiful superstitions. And think of what they would have to offer in return: their sweet, delectable, flowing ichor." The sentence was spoken dripping with vice. "We have the knowledge. We have the medical skill. We can take it without killing them. It will be like a tax. They can keep their gold, and we can have their blood."

New ideas began to swirl, the scarlet fog giving them form. She could leave the cave and find the capital. She could win over the leaders, force them to submit. She would not return to Nidus a pariah nor with a paltry collection of weapons. She would return a conquering heroine. Strixans would have a home on the surface again. They would see the sun and the moon, and not have to worry about or be scared of the devils. She could do it. She could take over this pitiful empire without the sword.

"It is ours for the taking," she continued, "all that rich, delicious ichor. We will not need to torture ourselves. We will not need to live and hide in fear. It is your ancestral right to take it, to conquer them and drink their blood. Do you not tire of surviving off porcines? Do you not tire of watching the plebians live in vice? Do you not want to see the world as mother once saw it?"

She could not, or refused to, form a counterargument. It was all so perfectly logical, perfectly reasonable. Why should she not? Why should her people have to suffer, have to live in such degrading conditions?

Then a single thought emerged, a torchlight in the thick, ichoric fog. "I need to resist," Vytilia stated. Her scarlet counterpart glared at her. "This craving, this . . . addiction, I cannot give into it!"

"And why not?"

"A virtuous Strixan is temperate. They resist avarice of all kinds!" She could not allow this internal beast to be fed, to grow. She could not give into temptations, as so many of her ancestors had. The empire was threatened when its people were not temperate, when they gave into all manner of pleasures. "This gluttony for mannish blood, it is unbecoming! I am not any better than the devils!"

"IGNORANT FOOL!" her scarlet counterpart roared again. "Why do you spend your energy keeping these foolish old traditions!? Who can even explain what a virtue is, let alone live it! Why do you allow these rules to hold you back!?"

"They are *our* traditions! They have been with our people and our empire since time immemorial! To reject them is to reject our ancestors, to reject our history!"

"Our history is dead, and our ancestors have forgotten us! You cling to the past like a nestling clings to its mother's breasts! Do you think the gods still care? Do you think our ancestors care? Our history is dead and buried!"

"Our history is sacred! Mother would never allow us to do so! Our ancestors, our gods, our history is all that we have left! It *is* the empire!"

"Enough with your delusions! Enough with this idiocy! Be who you are meant to be! Who you were *created* to be!"

"I was born to restore the culture of the empire! Civilization, not conquest!"

"I am the empire! I am civilization! The empire was built on conquest with the sword, not the pen! It will be restored by the soldier, not the artist!"

"I will not!"

"Do not fight it, Vytilia! This is your future!" The scarlet fog began to thicken until even her counterpart was gone from view.

Vytilia awoke from her delirium, sweating coldly, the first time she had ever done so. Her limbs still felt heavy, and her breathing was labored. That was her first nightmare. She had a sinking feeling it would not be her last.

She took a break from her training, sitting upright, her back against the wall and her chin on her knees. It was dark outside and quiet. She would have preferred there to be a wind or a flock of noctuae to keep her company, their hooting drowning out her thoughts.

Those words, those honeyed, audibly delicious words still haunted her. The laugh of her scarlet self, her laugh, still rung in her ears. A foreboding and pervasive sense of fear and dread followed not long after. *What if she was right*? Vytilia wondered. *What if I am the mask, and she is the true Vytilia*? There was a certain twisted logic to that. She was used to not being herself. She always had to put on a face at political functions, she put on one for Friedrich when she found him, and another among the nymphs and men. She was so used to being different, to wearing a figurative mask, she may not have realized she had never taken one off.

How true was that for the Strixans as a whole? Her scarlet counterpart, the Scarlet Empress, as she would refer to it now, was right. The empire was spread by the legions, not by art. Canescere was a military tactic, meant to pacify absorbed and conquered tribes. Everything revolved around the legions. A tiercel was not considered fit to lead or to rule unless they had spent time in the legions. Hens were lauded when they produced sons for the legions. Glory was won for the people through military campaigns, not through poems and prose. Service to the state, service to one's fellow citizens, was always in the legions.

Is that what she was supposed to restore? Is that what she was to return to the world? Did she only exist so that the devils could be defeated and Strixans could replace them as a plague upon the civilized world? Friedrich had every right to fear her, every right to see and call her a monster. For that is what she was, what her people were.

What if I let her take over? she wondered. *Would I be the true me? Is that what mother would want? Is that why I was spared*? It sounded incongruent, but it was not such a foreign concept. There were many miraculous tales of a key commander or a competent legionary surviving a defeat, only to become the component to a greater victory. That is all Strixan history, a string of military successes.

Her eyes drifted to the bag and the bulb of allium still laying on the cave floor. She had survived a lethal dosage of allium for a reason. She had survived that fall into the nymph's stratum for a reason. She had found Friedrich for a reason. There was something . . . disreputable about being granted these miraculous opportunities, only to disregard all virtue and tradition and begin a bloody and vicious war of conquest.

Her mind went back to that brief time of leaving the mountain peaks up until they left Frau Krüger's inn. She thought of the kindness of the innkeeper and other guests, the innocent smile of the nestling she had given the edelweiss, and the waves and friendly greetings she had been given or seen exchanged by the villagers. Did these people deserve to be subjugated? Did they deserve to be conquered and their lives disrupted and uprooted? And did they deserve to be bled so that she may satisfy some unvirtuous and wicked craving?

They did not.

These men were not future subjects, but future allies. And they needed to be seen as such. *She* would need to see them as such. She laid back down on her back and resumed her training. She was going to conquer but only herself. She would not let this blasphemous phantasm fill her head with lies and slander. She was going to gain control of herself, then she was going to go out once more into the world of men. She was going to learn their ways, learn their history, and see the civilization *they* had built. Then, she would return to Nidus and show all her countryman the wonders the people of the surface had wrought, that they are equals to the Strixans not lessers.

A thought crossed her mind. There was one item to take care of first before returning to Nidus; she was going to find Friedrich. She would show him she was not a monster. She was going to show him she could live and be civil among men. And they were going to be friends again. Above all else, it was his friendship she wanted most. That, she knew, would be more succulent than any draught of blood.

She closed her eyes and went to work.

• • •

Praetor Faustus Quintia stood, looking over a blueprint within his command tent. At his command were a legion's worth of the empire's best miners, engineers, lapisoperarii, and architects. They were working nearly nonstop since arriving at the location Vytilia had indicated on a map.

The labor was brutal. The cavern the man, Friedrich, had fallen into was not preferable for a large-scale engineering project. But, it had a proven and unobstructed way to the surface. With enough sweat, determination, and mathematics, it could be done. Strixan engineering was a source of pride for the empire. Their greatest work, the Arx, had survived even the cataclysm unscathed. If any group could tame this cavern and reach the surface, it was them.

Every day, even every duty rotation, the plan drawn on the blueprint became more and more of a reality. With Via Sculptile tracks in place, supplies and laborers could be brought in at record speed. Faustus publicly opinioned the project would be completed ahead of schedule.

Privately, however, he hoped for something else. He had not heard any word of Vytilia's mission to Aurum or of the project to reach the surface there. Whenever he asked the incoming crews, they were always ignorant. This set his nerves on edge. The mission was not classified, especially for someone of his rank. Why had there not been any communication from either Nidus or Aurum?

He looked up from the blueprint and heard the familiar heartbeat of Centurion Dracius headed towards him. He welcomed the centurion, asking for a progress report, but the legionary did not answer. His face was sullen, and in his hand, he held a scroll, sealed with purple wax. A missive from the Concilium.

"For your eyes only," Dracius explained. "It was just delivered by a single rider."

Faustus did not allow fear to grace his face, but it ate at him internally. "*Gratias*, Centurion. I shall read it alone." He took the scroll. Dracius hesitated before leaving, as if to say something, but he left without a word. Faustus sat on a crate and broke the seal.

He read the missive. Then he read it again and then a third time. He refused to accept what was written. Yet, the words were still there, and they were still true.

Neither the body of Vytilia Quintia nor the man Friedrich were recovered. There has not been any sighting of them at any of the stations between Nidus or Aurum nor in any of the branch-lines or emergency tunnels. They are presumed to have perished, and we pray the gods grant them a peaceful departure.

Vytilia was gone.

Faustus cast the parchment aside and stared at the floor of his tent. His hands hung limp. Time slowed to a crawl.

Vytilia was gone.

She was not away nor on one of her expeditions.

She was gone, never to return.

His daughter, Carmilla's daughter, their daughter, was gone.

He fell from the crate, laying on the floor in a crumbled mess of limb and toga. "Why?" he asked aloud. "Why her?" She was so young! She was so bright! She was . . . she was . . . He did not know any more than that.

Regret and horror struck him at the same time. He did not even know who it was that had perished. He . . . when was the last time he had spoken to her? Actually spoken with her? When had they last eaten a meal together? When had they last celebrated the sacred holidays together? When . . . when was the last time he had been a father?

He had been so distraught since Carmilla that he . . .

He dared not finish the sentence. He was pained enough already. He simply shook his head, repeating the question of "why" over and over again.

It was many hours later, possibly days, that Dracius returned. He stared down at his commander and went to help him up, but Faustus refused, pointing to the accursed parchment that brought him the news. Dracius read it.

"I am so sorry, Faustus. I, I do not know what I can do for you."

Faustus closed his eyes. "Call for my servants. I must amend my testament. You shall take the apartment at the Arx. Sextus, Annia, Antonius, they will care for you now. I shall recommend you to replace me."

"Replace you? I am a centurion, not a Praetor. I cannot . . ." The realization struck Dracius. "You mean, you are to take your life?"

"Not at this moment." Faustus collected himself and sat back on the crate. His eyes were puffy, and his cheeks were stained violet with tears. His voice was soft and mournful. "I have failed in my duty as paterfamilias and in my duty to my wife. But I can still fulfill my duty to the empire. When this passageway to the surface is complete, then will my duty be done and my purpose in this life."

"I cannot change your mind? Or even try?"

"You cannot. Carmilla was everything to me, and I realized too late Vytilia should have been as well. Without them, I have nothing. I am nothing. I was charged with building this tunnel, and I shall see its completion. After that . . ." He need not say what came after.

"I see." The centurion sighed and shook his head. "Then I shall leave you. I will inform the vexillation you are in mourning and not to be disturbed. Our condolences for you." Dracius left the tent.

"Carmilla, if you can still hear me," Faustus bitterly whispered, "forgive me."

18

Shipmaster Fischer's ship, the 23rd *SGS Schürze*, was a custom designed flatboat. It was a long, squat vessel with a shallow hold and sides. The bow was curved, almost to a point, slicing through the water like a knife. Unlike the Roth's barge, this was mostly propelled by wind and current. Fischer had erected a series of triangular sails to propel the craft. He said he got the design from the large trader galleys used by the Vitelish. This cut down slightly on space for freight, but it made the *Schürze* much faster. When it reached the final port, the entirety of the boat would be sold as scrap lumber. To get back home, Shipmaster Fischer had a deal with a trader in Lofnscheid to borrow a horse-cart to carry his sail and rigging back with him to build the next *Schürze*.

Friedrich was beginning to get used to life as a sailor. It was hard work but honest work. He was beginning to get a healthy tan, his hair was lightening, and he was picking up on the sailor lingo, especially the new swears. Shipmaster Fischer even offered to teach Friedrich how to smoke pipe tobacco (a foul-smelling new world weed), but Friedrich declined. The fear of smoke blindness from his caverneering days still stuck with him.

They'd been sailing up the Aumfz river for a day and a half, passing by small towns and hamlets, idly floating upstream. Friedrich didn't have much to work on, aside from occasionally using a staff to help unstick the ship from a sandbank or provide additional direction while Shipmaster Fischer steered. He would tie and retie the knots securing the cargo, learned sailing knots to open or close the sail, and even picked up on rudder control.

On their second day, they began to pass from the river Aumfz to the Adenz, the river that would eventually bring them to Barriort then to the Tonau, the second mightiest river in the Realm. "Shipmaster . . ." Friedrich asked as the rivers merged, "why the name Schürze? Isn't that an apron? And what does SGS stand for?"

The old sailor laughed. "Ah, I got the idea from an old shipmate of mine. Used to serve in the Merkya fleet. See they actually have a fleet, being an island and such. Back when they had a king, whenever they built a warship, they'd always put HGS before the name to show it wasn't a trading boat, but part of the fleet. HGS means His Greatness' Ship. I liked the idea, thought it made the ships stand apart, so, I did the same for mine. I gave 'er a prefix like the Merkyers, *Seiner Größe Schiff.*[44] 'Course the Kommandant has nothing to do with it, but buyers like it, and it makes it stick out."

"And, the name Schürze? Odd name for a boat."

He grinned. "Don't pooh-pooh an apron boyo. When you see a home with an apron drying on the line, you know it's got a good woman at the helm. When you come back from a long trip at sea, a woman in an apron means a fresh hot meal waiting for you. And . . . well . . . a woman looks mighty fine only wearing one." He grinned a tobacco-stained grin.

When Friedrich imagined returning home and being greeted by a woman in an apron (with clothes on, as Frau Beck's teachings were still firmly rooted), the woman he saw was white haired. He quickly stopped imagining. He hoped Fischer didn't see his cheeks burning and didn't ask if it was because of guilt or embarrassment.

Fischer puffed his pipe. "Have you seen the Tonau before, boyo?" Fischer asked during a calm section of sailing.

"A few times when I travelled but only the western part. I'm rather fond of a drinkhouse in Tonaustadt, near the mouth." Friedrich grabbed a low-hanging branch dangling from the shoreline and started whittling. "Spent a lot of time around the Rinne."

"The Rinne is a good river. Spent some time there as a youth. Too busy nowadays, hard to find a good market." Fischer chewed the end of his pipe, puffing small rings of smoke. "You sound like you're well-traveled. Why'd you leave Helvensland for the coast?"

Friedrich took a deep breath. "I got a taste for travelling, going back and forth from the mines to Scwhäbland. And I got tired of living in the mines. The threat of cave-ins, getting lost, always being in the dark, it wasn't a real life. Being a sailor seemed like the best option."

"So, you trade cave-ins for capsizing," Fischer laughed.

Friedrich chuckled as well. "Well, you can always swim in the water, can't swim through rock."

---

44. His Greatness' Ship or His Majesty's Ship. In other words, they're on the HMS Apron. And what's another name for an apron? A pinafore.

"Did you have anyone back in Helvensland? Any family or a lady friend?"

Friedrich shook his head. "I've been on my own for years, just me and my pickaxe. Well, I had a few friends, but other than that, it was just me."

"I can understand. Never really had a full-time crew, at least not since I sailed from Viteliú. Usually, it's just me and the Schürze. That's why I like the pipe, helps keep me focused."

"How did you become a sailor?"

Fischer exhaled. "That's a long tale. Here, switch places with me." Friedrich took over the rudder while Fischer grabbed a sewing kit and began patching up a small tear in the sail. "I've always been on the river. My father was a fisherman in Lusbenhort on the banks of the Labve. His father was a fisherman and his before him, back to the beginnings of the Realm and the Church. I was the second son, you understand, so my elder brother was set to inherit the family boat, so I decided to set off and make my own life." He set his pipe down on a salt barrel, making sure the flame was extinguished. "So, I went down to Vinixa, signed up with a trading house, and sailed all across the Mittelmeer: the Sultanate, Cataskal, Misyr, even up the coast to the Bythony Islands. I enjoyed my time in the Sultanate. They may be heathens, but by God, their Head-Stead, Şehir, is a sight to behold."

"Did you ever go to the new world? See any of the settlements?"

"Nope." He put the sewing kit away and picked his pipe up. "I never went that far. Never really wanted to if I'm being honest. Never heard good things about them, aside from the land and the women. Everything else is . . . hellish. The Catask are just ruthless, scathingly ruthless from what I've heard, to the wildfolk that live there. And then the Merkyers and Gauls are always fighting and dying in wars against the wildfolk. And the wildfolk themselves, well, they know how to kill like any tame man. It's a pity, hear the place is downright beautiful, finest handiwork of God himself. Yet it sounds like we just exported all the forsaken hell bottled up in the old world and spilled it out all over the new world."

"We didn't spill all of it," Friedrich commented.

Fischer nodded in agreement. "Aye. Aye." He relit his pipe. "Hardly seems like any time passed since the Saught was signed. I list my blessings every day that I survived during the war. I had built the first Schürze just a few years before it started, sailing out of Ingmarsburg to Grenzburg. I spent most of my time behind the mountains, away from the fighting." He sighed. "You were spared as well, weren't you? Helvensland got off lightly. Hell, you folks even made a nice bit of gold off it." Friedrich didn't answer. He leaned back, letting his hand glide along in the water. "Sorry, I meant . . ."

"No, no, don't worry," Friedrich muttered.

"Anyway, that's my tale. I left out some of the more private bits you understand. Didn't think you'd be interested in all my port-of-call visits." He giggled to himself. "I don't do those things anymore though. I returned to the Church because of the war. In fact, tomorrow is Sonntag. When we stop in Barriort, we'll go to the hallmeet and take the day off to rest."

He was beginning to sound like Frau Beck. "Herr Shipmaster, is attending the hallmeet required to be paid?"

Fischer looked at Friedrich sadly. "Nay, it ain't, but I really suggest you should; it's important to take time and rest, especially to pay thanks to God. He made these rivers, gave us the wind in our sail, the trees used for the hull. I won't make you go. I'd rather if you did, but you're your own man. It's good for the soul." He took over the rudder from Friedrich. Friedrich sat next to him. He unsheathed his dagger and continued working on his whittling.

"How come you went back to the Church?" Friedrich asked. "After hearing about all the foulness in the New World and seeing what was left after the war. Why go back? How could God let all those things happen?"

"Man is more than just his faults," Fischer told him. Friedrich cringed. Another group could easily be described that way. "We can't judge our race on our failings. If we did, God would've smitten us off the face of Erde. The same men who slaughtered the weak and burned crops can just as easily build a house for the homeless and share food with the hungry. Think of all the folk, godmen and worldmen alike, who followed the armies, rebuilding towns, caring for the sick, resowing fields. Those were the folk who inspired me to go back, they who did good, even in the midst of darkness."

Friedrich did know someone like that. He *knew* someone like that. Herr Bergmann. Others could say otherwise, but Herr Bergmann was the greatest man Friedrich had ever known. He always tried to do good when he could. He might not have always been able to, but he tried.

"Let me share something with you," Fischer interrupted. "This has helped me through some dark times. 'Each and every day is a struggle. Man must fight the innate and inborn darkness within him. It is only through the understanding of the righteous and upstanding laws and wisdom of God, will man overcome this.' That's from the Warnings in the Sagas. It's my favorite part."

"I haven't heard that one before," Friedrich admitted.

"All the more why you should come with me to the hallmeet. A good, upstanding, man of trust will always be someone folk want to do business with. And the best way to become that man is through learning and accepting the wisdom and teachings of God."

"I didn't know our trip would turn into a Churchmeet," Friedrich joked, but Fischer stayed quiet. Friedrich cleared his throat. "I have a favorite part too, learned it recently. God's in His heaven; All's right with the World."

Fischer nodded approvingly. "Aye, that's a good one. From the Edda of Holy Hrodpreht." He puffed his pipe. "Do you hold it to be true?"

Friedrich didn't know how to answer. Did he? He'd seen a lot of horror happen during the daytime, the time when God was in His heaven, but all was not right with the world. The line was well-meaning, but what he'd seen made it sound hollow. But he had also seen a lot of good happen during the daytime. "I don't know," he finally answered.

"I understand," Fischer told him. "It's always easier to say a line rather than actually live it. I can second that."

"Is it difficult to continue to hold this to be truth?"

Fischer nodded, chewing his pipe. "At times. There are times where I want to go to the houses of ill-repute, drink myself blind, live as a whore until the Gaulish blight takes me. But there's more to life than drink and the lusts of the flesh. I always try to remember that." He puffed on his pipe. "Most importantly, I try to live it. I'll give food to the hungry, a spare chip to the beggar. I'll even give wayfarers free passage. It isn't much, but I think the world is better because of it."

Friedrich cleared away the wood shavings, looking off at the passing shoreline. "I. I don't understand," he admitted. "I just can't grasp something like that."

"Hmmm," Fischer mused, "have you ever done any bird-watching, Friedrich?" Friedrich shook his head. "Well, you know what it is at least, right?" Friedrich nodded. "Well, imagine you go out, and you want to see an oriole."

"You mean one of those priests with the yellow clothes?"

"No, those are rightly called Pirols. They're named after the bird. Anyway, imagine you wanted to see an oriole, but you only kept looking at flocks of crows."

"I'm not following."

"Orioles are beautiful birds, brilliant yellow feathers, a pleasant chirp, nothing like a crow. But if you only look at crows, you'll never find an oriole. You can't find beauty if you're only looking at the ugly."

"You can't find the light if you only look at the dark."

Fischer smiled and nodded. "Exactly."

"But how do you find the light when you've suffered so many slights, when you've seen unthinkable things happen to you and others? When you've been betrayed, abandoned?"

"I don't know the answer to that, boyo. I don't think there's a priest alive who does." He took a few more puffs of his pipe. "But remember, our past may shape us into who we are, but it does not make us be anyone. Think of sailing, you wouldn't be able to plot a proper course and steer if you spent your whole voyage looking at your wake. You have to look forward, see what's ahead, to sail properly. You can't dwell on old slights. You have to forgive, or forget in some rare cases, and go on ahead, looking for the light and the beauty." It was sage advice and difficult to find fault in it. Friedrich didn't have any further questions. Fischer smiled and went over to their barrel of provisions. "Here, have some of this salt pork, work up a thirst. I'll get the first round when we land."

• • •

In the time since the nightmare of the Scarlet Empress had passed, Vytilia was feeling more confident. She had managed to get her bloodlust under control to a surprising degree. Now, whenever she imagined mannish blood, her fangs extended only slightly. Now came the ultimate test: finding a settlement and walking amongst the populace.

She gathered up her belongings, hurling the allium bulb deep into the woods, and took stock of her situation. She still had the highwayman's sword and pistol on her belt. They could be useful in scaring off wrongdoers, a better alternative to her Thaumaturgy and fangs, but they seemed unladylike. She did not need to draw any unnecessary attention to herself. Then her attire would have to change. *A perfect first experiment*, she thought. She could go into a settlement and procure new clothing. She could trade the sword or the torcs for them.

Procuring new clothing would be another in a long list of new experiences for her and a good test to see how disciplined she had been. Her family never bought clothing, and given their situation, Strixans never bought clothing. What she wore was always handcrafted and spun by the servants and always of the finest, smoothest cloth. Her only comparable experience was when her father allowed her to pick out a few of her mother's dresses, a rarity, as he allowed none, not even his most loyal servants, to even see, let alone handle her mother's possessions. Selling the weapons too would be a new experience. She never purchased anything in her life, at least directly. If her family needed or wanted something, they had intermediaries to do the legwork for them. The only time she was in the Nidus markets was when she passed through the inner walls going to and from her travels.

Here is where, perhaps for the first, if not last time, she would admit she was handicapped. For all her knowledge and experience, she simply did not know how to live or act like a plebeian. She could handle and understand the intense political machinations of the ruling class, but the bartering and haggling of low-level commoners? That was uncharted waters. Even the body language was different. Men did not have the same twitches or tells as a Strixan. Their lack of using fangs and hisses when communicating was frustrating. She did not know if someone was honest, deceitful, or just stupid. Even the nymph's ear wiggling and coloring was more recognizable.

Every time the word "man" ran through her mind, her heart would race, her stomach would gurgle, and her fangs began to involuntarily extend. And every time this happened, she would shut her mouth and force them to recede. She had not wasted the week; she was overcoming herself. Although, there was a deep, dark fear in the back of her head that she had not practiced enough. It was one thing to merely think of a temptation, but to see it, smell it, and in her case hear it, was another matter altogether. Her foray into the world of men would either end with the information she needed or an unfortunate bloodbath. Still, she would press on, keeping her head high and her upper lip stiff.

Now that she had a goal and a plan, all she needed was direction. She had gone . . . west since Salzahoi, so she knew to the east was nothing but wilderness and a few scattered farms. She considered going south, but that was where the Toller Mund was and the entrance to her stratum. She would save the south for later as an emergency destination should the situation call for it. Then that only left going northwards.

She shielded her eyes from the sunlight as she exited the cave and looked out over the valley below. Behind her, the sun was starting to shine, so that told her which direction was which. She headed down the side of the mountain, looking for a river she had heard. Along the way, she found her stole. The implication of her not wearing it was not lost on her. She quickly tied it around her head, relieving her scalp from the sun's heat. She was master of herself, not a slave to this thirst. She could choose. A slave had to obey.

Still, she would have to eat. When she found the river, more of a stream than a river, she spotted several varieties of fish swimming in it. She looked around, listened, and made sure she was alone before ripping several out of the stream using her thaumaturgy. The salty blood of the fish was a welcome taste. Already, with these few to drink, she was feeling stronger and more energetic. She prayed they would be enough to sustain her.

Having had her fill, she tossed the corpses back into the water and began to follow the river northward. As the mountains gradually receded, giving way to flat, fertile land, buildings began to dot the horizon.

They were small cottages, similar to the ones they encountered before Salzahoi. Farmers were milking cows or pitching fodder. She puckered when she walked by, salivating at the echo of their heartbeat. She balled her hands into fists, twitching as she resisted the temptation. Every step was agony as she did so. She felt as if she was being torn in half, one side wishing to fly and prey on the farmers, the other slowly shuffling on ahead.

A small beast, a furry, quadruped creature, raced down from one of the cottages. It was a canine, a scaled down lupus. It was thin with light brown fur and long ears. It stared at Vytilia, its eyes full of curiosity and anger. Then it began to bark, viciously growling at her as she walked past, hopping along, nipping at her. One of the farmers called for the canine, apologizing and waving to her. She did not wave back, continuing forward, mile after mile, step after step, suppressing her instinct.

After several agonizing miles, during which she ducked into the bushes and woods to drain several long-eared creatures, she came to the outskirts of a small town. The town was more cloistered than Salzahoi, the buildings were much closer together, cozier yet widespread. Rather than a Rathaus, the center of this town was a church, a yellow steeple topped with an image of the sun. A small round dial, subdivided into twelve sections, sat below the image. Vytilia paused, looking at it curiously. She had noticed such a device back in Salzahoi but never asked what it was. There were four of these dials, one on each side of the steeple. Each one had a pair of needles, all pointing to one of the subdivisions. A curious contraption indeed, a two-dimensional version of an armillary?

She stopped just in front of the church, looking up at the steeple to ask Sol for guidance then around to gather information. Heartbeats echoed in her ears. She sucked the last bit of long-eared blood in her mouth and took deep breaths. Her hands shook as she walked, but she remained calm. She should first find somewhere to sell the sword and pistol, then use the money to buy new, more suitable clothing. This town had many more streets and roads than Salzahoi. So many of the buildings were hidden from view. Which shops took trades? Which sold clothing?

Vytilia sighed. She would need to ask for directions, approach a man and get up close. She was already straining as she heard every heartbeat in this town but steeled herself, heading down a busy street, looking for someone to talk with. There were many people on this street, merchants advertising their wares (though none mentioned selling clothing), laborers constructing a building or carrying goods, and nestlings running and playing. They were all busy. None paid her any mind. She needed someone who was unoccupied, someone nonthreatening. A group of men, all around Friedrich's age, smiled and whistled at her, but a quick glare caused them to shut up.

Then, Vytilia happened upon an old hen. What was the proper term? An old woman, hobbling along with a cane, holding a small basket of root vegetables. She wore dark clothing, dark by the standards of man but not for Strixans, a simple shawl wrapped around her head. She was bent and wrinkled; her heartbeat was irregular. This woman was sick, approaching the end of her days. But she was an elder, an honored position, and someone who could be trusted. Vytilia carefully approached her, tapping her shoulder carefully so as to not startle her.

"I beg your pardon Frau." The old woman turned to look at her, startled, but she smiled at Vytilia, looking up with joyful eyes.

"Oh! Dear me! Aren't you an elegant young lady! What can I do for you fräulein?"

"I am new to town, and I am looking for a clothing merchant and anyone who buys miscellaneous items. Might you know where I can find them?"

"Oh, we've got many a snipper in our little town but no 'miss-aisle-aan-eous' shops I'm afraid." She looked at Vytilia closer. "Are you alright, my dear? You look awfully pale." She reached up, touching Vytilia's forehead, quickly withdrawing her hand. "Ah! And you're as cold as snow! Come, come with me! I will give you a hot meal and some rest, can't travel while you're ill!"

"I am not ill, dear Frau!" Even this irregular heartbeat was making her thirsty. "There is not a need to worry! Do these 'snippers' accept trades?"

"It isn't a worry my dear! I insist! Please, come with me! My home is just up here!" She began ascending steps at the side of a house, leading up to the top story. Vytilia stayed put, not trusting herself to be alone with one of them, especially one as frail as her. The old woman stopped, looking down. "Please! Come on! I'll get a soup ready!"

"Please, Frau, it is fine. I need to be on my way!" Heartbeats echoed in her ears.

"Nonsense my dear! Wherever you're going can wait! You need to heal, get back your strength!" She saw that her words weren't working. "I have a change of clothes you can have! For free!" Vytilia sighed. This old crone was already attracting attention and heartbeats. She climbed up the steps, following her.

The old woman's home consisted of a single room with two small windows, slightly bigger than a hand, bringing in the light. She had a small fireplace where a pot was boiling, a small table and two stools, a counter, and a simple bed with a large tome on the ground next to it. Several trunks rested in the far corner with clothes spilling out of them. The woman showed Vytilia a seat then cut up the root vegetables and threw them into the pot. She gently sat down in the other chair, breathing heavily and leaning on her cane. "The soup will finish boiling soon. I hope you don't mind only roots. I'm unable to afford meat these days."

Vytilia fidgeted nervously, chewing on her bottom lip. The room's acoustics accentuated the irregular heartbeat. Every pump echoed in her ears, pounding on her mind like a drum. "Nothing to worry about, I assure you." She chewed her lip, letting it bleed.

"So, you say you're a traveler? Where are you coming from, and where are you going?"

"I am originally from . . . Hellen land?" She tried to remember the nation Friedrich had said they came from. "I am looking for my . . . brother. He came up here looking for adventure, and our father sent me to bring him back." Dishonesty still felt wrong, but even virtuous Vytilia had to admit it was better than the alternative.

"Ah. Boys are always getting into trouble. That's what makes them boys! Ha ha!" She tapped her cane as she laughed. "Where do you think he ran off to?"

"I do not know precisely. He said something about a city, Mondsruhe."

"Perhaps he's gone to the High Learnhouse? To become a man of the cloth? There's a fine Learnhouse there in Mondsruhe. I myself was a learner there, many years ago."

"You studied there? Where is it?"

"Oh, just north of here, a good walk away in Mondsruhe. Though, I wasn't an actual learner, you see. Women aren't allowed to do *everything*. But I took my oaths there, became a churchmaid." She laughed again. "I met my husband there. He was attending the Churchlearnhouse to become a priest. We fell in love, even got a special writ from His Holiness himself to leave our oaths, then we were wedded." She sighed, looking down at her old, wrinkled hands. "Those were simpler times then. Happier times." She groaned and got up off the stool, hobbling over to the pot.

As the old woman checked on the soup, an idea began to form in Vytilia's mind. It was not a new idea but a reforging of an old one. She could go to this High Learnhouse and ask for a specialist on the early history of mankind. If she could find a connection, or more solid evidence of her historical theory, she could tie man and Strixan together. She could show herself and the world that her people were not conquering monsters and lay the foundation for future civilizations. And, so far, she had proven her self-restraint. The journey to this High Learnhouse would be more practice. Perhaps, even Friedrich would be there.

The old woman grabbed two bowls, filling them with the soup, and placed them on the table. She then reached into her cupboard and pulled out two small glasses and an opaque glass decanter. An orange-pink liquid swished around inside.

Vytilia cautiously opened her mouth, sipping the soup. It did not compare to the sugary porridge, but it was warm and flavorful and kept her craving at bay. "It is good," she complimented.

"You're too sweet, my dear. Here, this is my one ill." She unstopped the decanter and poured the liquid into the cups. She and Vytilia clinked glasses before taking a drink. It was alcohol, the finest non-Strixan alcohol she had tried, with a fruity aftertaste and sweet smell to it. "I have a good friend who brews this. He always gives me a smidgen as a gift. I don't drink too much, you understand, just something to go with my meal."

Vytilia continued taking small sips of the soup and drink, careful to tune out the woman's irregular heartbeat. "What is your name?" she asked.

"I am Hildegard Meyer. And you?"

"Mina . . . Bauer."

"Ah that is such a lovely name! One of my daughters-in-law was named Wilhelmina. She was a sweet girl. I do miss her. Do you have any news from Helvensland? Or any news from your travels? I don't get out much. I don't know what's going on in the outside world." She sighed again.

"I do not. I have been travelling for so long. I do not stop long enough to hear the news."

"Oh, that's a shame. You should take the time to stop and listen my dear. You hear many fun tales when travelling. My dear Kuno used to come back with a new tale every time he went to the market or to Mondsruhe. It would amuse the children for stounds on end! He was a good tale-spinner, my Kuno." She leaned back against the wall, her eyes closed, a smile on her lips. "Do you have anyone in your life, my dear? A wooer or a betrothed?"

Vytilia pushed aside her half-finished bowl, dabbing her lips with a small linen napkin. "I do not," she said matter-of-factly. "My father is rather protective of me. He does not allow suitors to call on me."

"But he lets you go out, all alone, to look for your brother?" Vytilia's eyes went wide as she realized her stories did not match up. She was not a good liar like Friedrich. "Ah, men will always be strange like that. Kuno wouldn't let our little Adelheid have a dog. He was worried the dog would bite her, but he let her use a knife. She got pretty good with it too!"

Vytilia was getting impatient. Certainly, the old crone was nice, but she just wanted to prattle on about her family. She needed to get going before the craving returned. "You mentioned you had a change of clothes I could borrow?"

"Hmmm? Oh! That's right. Dear me, dear me, I had forgotten all about that! I don't get many guests you see. Let me see what Adelheid left behind." She slowly stood up and doddered over to a trunk, opening it and sifting through clothes. "My dear Adelheid was about your size, though she didn't have quite your bust. Tall girl. So tall, she scared all the boys! Let's see . . ." She doddered back over to Vytilia with an armful of clothing. Vytilia accepted and inspected them. The neckline was lower than she'd like, but she could cover that. She looked around, looking for a privacy screen or wall.

"Er . . ."

"Oh, don't worry about that my dear, nothing I haven't seen before. Here, I'll turn around for a tick." She went over to the table, taking Vytilia's seat and pouring herself another glass. Vytilia awkwardly shuffled away, quickly changing clothes. Frau Meyer gave her a simple linen bodice, dyed green, with a yellow, long-sleeved shirt and a long blue skirt and beige apron. It was plebeian garb, but it covered her skin from the sun and would help her blend in though the colors did clash with her stole. She could always find a matching one. In the meantime, she undid her braids, letting her hair flow to cover her ears and nape.

"You look lovely my dear, the spitting image of Adelheid."

"Frau Meyer, my gratitude. I have the means to repay you, not coin but valuables."

"No need for payment my dear. As the good book teaches . . ." she gestured to the large tome sitting beside her bed, "a good deed is a reward in it of itself."

"Well, then I am grateful. Hopefully we shall meet again." Vytilia started to grab her bag and equipment.

"Leaving so soon, my dear? You're still sick! I can't let you go out like that! Please, stay, at least until your touch goes back to warm."

"Please, Frau Meyer, I am fine, I assure you. I have travelled thus far feeling like this." The effect of the soup was passing. Vytilia's craving started up again, the old woman's heartbeat echoing in her ear.

The old woman sighed, wiping her eye. "I'm sorry, my dear. I just get so lonely. It's a mother's right to worry you understand."

Vytilia twinged with guilt. Was it not the duty of the civilized world to respect elders? To listen to their wisdom? She bit her tongue, forcing the craving back in a dormant state then sat down on the bed, looking at Frau Meyer. "I can stay for a moment longer. Then I must be on my way to Mondsruhe."

The largest smile spread across the old woman's face. "Oh, bless you my dear. Bless you! You have brought joy to this old soul once again!" Vytilia offered her a weak smile. "I haven't felt this happy since the war ended. It seems like ages ago. The Kommandant and the Gothi announced the Saught, and the fighting was finally over. Dreadful, awful thing that war, the wrath of God poured out upon Erebus."

She would have to play along until the woman fell asleep. "What caused it?"

"Nobody really knows. It went on for so long. First, it was an uprising in Želevlast. Then Zvearrik invaded, then Gallia invaded. Town fought against town, brother against brother. The Realm was nearly torn apart! Nothing short of a godsend kept us from collapsing and stayed the hand of the Sultanate from attacking." She wiped her eye again. "The war came close. Mondsruhe was sacked by the Zvearish, but it never reached down here. Töiz was spared."

Töiz must be the name of this town, Vytilia reasoned. "That is a blessing," she commented.

"At first, it seemed like it was. But the armies brought sickness, and they took our harvests, and we were left to starve. They stole so many of our menfolk to join them. My Kuno, God bless his soul, he caught the sickness. He refused to eat, saving what little we had for me. I wish, sometimes, that it had taken both of us instead." She took a drink.

"I am sorry for your loss," Vytilia expressed. She could hear Frau Meyer's heartrate slowing down.

"I don't know why God has kept me around for so long," Meyer admitted. "I wonder if it is a punishment for abandoning my oaths or for allowing Kuno to turn to the Urworkish." She started to cry. Vytilia walked over to her. She thought a hug or embrace would be appropriate, but she stopped, realizing how close that would bring her to the woman's neck. "I know I'll see my Kuno again; I just know it! I just wish it would be sooner, rather than later." Her heartbeat was becoming more irregular. Her breathing became shallower and more labored. "I hope you find your brother my dear. If we've got nothing in the world, we'll always have family."

Vytilia stepped back, staring at Frau Meyer as she started to weep, clutching her chest. She was in pain, and she was alone.

She could not stay here forever, but she could not leave her like this in a depressed, pained state, a state she was becoming all too familiar with. "Frau Meyer, do your children visit you often?" She felt duty-bound to help, to prove she was civilized, not a monster.

"No," she sputtered through tears. "I lost all of them because of the war. And my in-laws. And my granddaughter." She resumed her crying, leaning on her cane. Her heart rate became more erratic, her breathing more pained. As she leaned, her neck was exposed, her carotid artery nearly varicose. Vytilia opened her mouth, her fangs extended. She physically pushed her chin upward, closing her mouth. Frau Meyer looked up. "Did you say something my dear?"

"A sympathy cry." Frau Meyer went back to leaning on her cane. Vytilia knelt and picked up the old woman, carrying her to the bed, setting her down gently. She had bitten her lip so fiercely, it was nearly torn off.

"You're so strong my dear!" Frau Meyer coughed, closing her eyes, tears still escaping and falling. She was so helpless. Vytilia had to look away, puckering her face to stop her fangs from reemerging. "It's not my time yet." Frau Meyer coughed. "I've had bouts like this before. It'll pass. It'll pass." She sounded confident, if bothered.

Vytilia stood at the bedside, looking down at the old woman. She heard her heartbeat; she heard the blood flowing through her veins. Her mouth watered. *Who would miss her*, she asked? Her family was deceased. She had few friends. Who would notice? Would it not be better to satiate her craving with the blood of someone whose life was at an end? She had fought back and spared others. Surely this one, this meager crone, could be used. If anything, Vytilia would be doing her a mercy, ending her pain and suffering. It was not altruistic by any means, but are a few spills of blood equal or greater than relief from such an existence? And, this would not awaken the Scarlet Empress, would it?

Of course, Vytilia could hide it. She could bite her on the wrist or the leg or any of the other major veins or arteries. Who would ever suspect it was her or any of her kind? And she needed the blood. She had not had any substantial amount for some time. If she pressed on without any, she could grow faint and weary. Drinking vermin was beneath her, a stain on someone of her station. This woman would not be using it. It would be better for her to have it, so she could press on. Her people depended on her, hundreds of thousands yet to be born. Frau Meyer would be honored for her sacrifice, statues erected in her honor. Her name would go down in the annals of Strixan history as one who put the needs of the many ahead of the one. Granted, she might not have done so willingly, but it would be Vytilia who was telling the story. She could say what she wanted.

Which Vytilia would be telling the story?

She shook her head again, trying to banish her thoughts. She, as she was now, was the real Vytilia. And the real Vytilia needed a proper sanguination to press on. And the real Vytilia was showing benevolence to someone who was in pain. The real Vytilia was in control.

Then it was decided. Vytilia leaned over Frau Meyer, slowly opening her mouth as her fangs extended. Meyer did not stir or notice. She slept peacefully. Slowly, Vytilia approached her neck, careful not to make a sound. Her own heart raced; her mouth salivated, her vision narrowing and clouding red. Finally, she was getting another taste, another draught of that sweet, ambrosial ichor. Just this last taste, and she would be refreshed, her craving satisfied, then she could move onto Mondsruhe and onto finding Friedrich.

Her jaw snapped shut. Friedrich.

He would not approve of this. Bleeding this helpless woman? That was what monsters did. She stood straight up. If she did this, she would only prove him right. A civilized being, a true, honorable Strixan, would never take advantage of an elder like this. She was abandoning her own traditions, her own beliefs. She had not fought this woman in combat. She had not earned the right to partake of her blood. She was ashamed. What had she become? This is not what she wanted; this is not how she should act. The fact that this thought had crossed her mind was tantamount to spitting on her ancestor's grave.

Not only would she be hurting Friedrich, she was giving into to her primitive, basic self. Standing here, contemplating this situation, was causing her vision to go red. She could see that blood-stained smile of her scarlet counterpart. She could not drink. She could not give in.

But there were ways she could help. She could repay this woman for her kindness. Vytilia could still show her mercy, relieve her of her pain. Friedrich had mentioned he always wanted to help others, to relieve suffering. He did not possess the means. But she did. Honorable means. "Frau Meyer, I know how I can repay you." She looked towards Vytilia, smiling with her eyes still closed.

Frau Meyer stirred awake, keeping her eyes closed. "How is that my dear?" she asked sleepily.

"Lay still. Think of your husband." Vytilia placed her hand on Frau Meyer's sternum. She could feel the heartbeat, feel her blood rushing through her veins. Vytilia squeezed her eyes closed, pouring all her concentration into her work. In her hand, she felt the pump of the heart. It was burning and anguished. Vytilia, tears welling up, closed her hand. With a gasp, Frau Meyer lurched then went stiff, her heart silent. Vytilia collapsed. Was this what Friedrich would have wanted? Was this the right decision? This woman had been suffering. She had lost everything. Was it not right to spare her? Was this helping or even merciful?

Vytilia did not have an answer. She did not have any idea if this was a just or right decision. She stayed there, lying on the floor next to the bed, her mind blank. She was overwhelmed and numb. As the sun set, Vytilia finally stood back up. She offered Luna a prayer on Frau Meyer's behalf then slipped out, disappearing into the night, her mind burning with internal arguments and debates. Is this what Friedrich would have done?

• • •

Neighbors discovered Frau Meyer's body a day later, lying peacefully on her bed. They assumed her old age had finally caught up with her and called the priest to give her a final blessing. She was burned on the grounds of the local church; many came to attend and give their farewells to a kind old woman who'd been a part of their community for many years. Tears were shed, tears of joy that she would finally be reunited with her beloved Kuno and their children. She had at last found peace.

19

Friedrich and Shipmaster Fischer had arrived in the Free-Stead of Barriort the previous night, emptied the ship's hold, and slept under tarpaulin. After the sun had risen and the Shipmaster excused himself to wash for church, he returned and told Friedrich a bit about the town.

Even in the early morning light, Friedrich could see Barriort was different. The buildings, layout, even materials were different from other large river towns. The burgh felt fresh, renewed or reborn. And indeed, it was. Fischer explained that most of the town had been burned a few years back and that the townsfolk were still rebuilding, using the latest trends in buildingcraft and recruiting the finest drafters to make Barriort anew.

True to his word, when time for church came, Fischer offered to row over several worshippers, burghers from the town who were quick to point out the beauty of their home. They bragged at length of what style and method had been used to rebuild the differing neighborhoods and boroughs; Vitelish style, Gaulish style, Catask, Galazer, Merkya. All of Erebus (besides the Tujue) made a mark in Barriort. The townsfolk considered themselves gatekeepers, watching over where the Tonau was fed and went into Ostlücke. They straddled the border between the Realm and the lands of the Rabenburgs. They wanted to look good, to be the best of all Teudish, a powerful memory to those going down the mighty river.

Friedrich pondered on all this as he sat under an ash tree. Behind him, higher up on the hill, was the *Weledahilf*, the church where Shipmaster Fischer and other worshippers all bowed their heads in silent beseeching. Weledahilf was a Harug, a church larger than the one in Preisdorf but not large enough to have an Aufseher. It sat high on a hill south of Barriort. The town itself blanketed a stretch of land abutting both the Adenz and the Tonau rivers. Shipping traffic from the south and west all passed through here on their way to Grenzburg and beyond.

While he understood why the town had to be rebuilt, being an important shipping hub, Friedrich could not grasp why all the effort had gone into beautifying and prettying it. It had caught fire, burning down to its foundation stones. What was to stop it from doing so again? Fire didn't care if a Gaul had drafted the building plans or if a Teudish had. Buildings were food. These new styles the townsfolk had boasted of were not fireproof, they had not built any sort of fire-fighting water supply, and they were all close together. It didn't even matter if everyone in town was inside the Weledahilf! Should another blaze come through, Barriort would be right back to where it started.

What a way to describe life, Friedrich quietly grumbled. Build something up, only for the world to knock it down. Want to retire? A fiend kills you. Make a friend? She kills a man in cold blood without remorse. Friedrich glanced up at the sunlight sneaking through the ash tree's branches. There was God in His heaven. Was all right with the world? Maybe for the Barriorten, all was right with the world. But how long until a lantern fell and lit a bit of tinder, then would they sing a different song?

He sighed, looking away from the sunlight. Here he was, looking for crows when he should be looking for orioles. He was being downtrodden again. He was a new Friedrich, he reminded himself. He needed a new outlook. Fischer would be continuing east, but he offered to talk Friedrich up with some of the west-bound crews. He'd even given him some extra chips with his pay to cover any expenses. Tomorrow, he'd be aboard a west-bounder, most likely rowing against the tide but one step closer to the coast, to a newer and better life.

Did he want to go westward? Did he really want to change and become new? Would that life be better? His nights were still haunted with the sounds and images of death, but during the day, he had this pervasive feeling of regret. Between Vater Sieghart and Shipmaster Fischer, he had a saga's worth of reminders adding to that regret.

No one is orlayed to do evil.

Man is more than just his faults.

The needs of the many outweigh the needs of the few.

It felt wrong that he felt wrong. He should not feel so regretful, so downtrodden and sullen over abandoning Vytilia after she killed a man, but he did. It pervaded everything he did; beer tasted bitter, sleep wasn't as restful, even having a purse full of chips didn't feel as safe or good as it once felt. How was this choice the wrong choice? How was leaving something, someone, that killed in cold blood the bad thing to do? He glared up at the sun through the branches. How is it that God was in His heaven, but all was not right with the world?

Then what could he do? Was he supposed to scour the entire Weiße Hügel range looking for her? Was he to go to every town and hamlet in Baivor and ask for a tall, silver-skinned, white-haired woman? And what if it got him killed? He knew she could get angry. It had been nearly a week, no, almost two since they'd split. That was a long time for anger to simmer and come to a boil. He might not even get an opportunity to say sorry. If, that's what he would say.

He had never felt this way before, an unexplainable and unbearable combination of regret, worry, and fear. It left him feeling hollow, starved of all that made life livable. *Maybe*, he wondered, *I need to do some good to offset this bad feeling*. That's also what Vater Sieghart had advised. He might be able to find some opportunities out west or maybe further east.

The bells of the Weledahilf began to ring. Church was over. Friedrich started to shift and stand up. He'd find Shipmaster Fischer and ask him if he knew any douthful shipmasters he could sign on with or even keep going east with him.

"*Entschuldigung*, are you Friedrich Bauer?" a man asked. Friedrich looked to his left, slightly above him then stood at near-attention. The man was older than him, middle-aged but immaculately groomed. One had to squint to see the grey in his hair or pointed beard. He wore the finest Sonntag best: long, expensive trousers, aged but fine leather boots, fine personalized riding gloves, a light-red waist coat made of the best material, and a broad hat with feathers. Along with that, belts for swords were wrapped around his waist, his age-shield was black with a white sun, and a sprig of mistletoe was pinned to his lapel. He was a lord, a knight to be exact, and member of a Knightly Band. Friedrich held his head low, eyes wide and ears open.

"Yes, mein Herr! How can I be of help?" he asked.

"No need for formalities. Come along, raise your head, look me in the eyes." Friedrich obeyed. "I hear tell you are headed west and looking for work."

"I . . . am, mein Herr."

"You say that as if you are not sure."

"Well, I want to go wherever there is trouble. And I want to do some good about it."

The knight smiled. "Then it is good I have found you, or rather, the good Herr Shipmaster and I got to talking." He removed his hat, wiping away summer sweat with a kerchief. "I am Herr Sinric Neveu, Watchman of the Knights and Wayfarers of Holies Balder and Gottegnade. We are a Holy Band of Knighthood." He let the name sink in for a moment. "We run the sickhouses. Ours are the black banners with the white sun, and we escort wayfarers through unfriendly lands."

"Oh, well, how lucky then." Cold sweat had begun to pour down Friedrich's back. The Church already made him nervous, Lords as well. Churchy Lords was a new discomfort. Though, he had heard good of the Wayfaring Knights. Even Frau Beck did not say their name with the usual curses she said with other Erdeish. "What is it I can do for you, mein Herr? I do have some chips I could give if you are in need of funds."

Herr Neveu shook his head. "No, our band is well funded. Why I wanted to talk to you is this: myself and my knightly brothers are escorting a wayfareage to the Holy-Stead of Midgart. One of our men, a halberdier, fell ill in Lofnscheid, and we have been without a replacement. Herr Fischer is an old friend of mine, and he suggested you. I cannot offer you wages like you would have on the river, nor can I always promise a roof over your head. But what I can give you is honest weeks of work, two meals a day, and the chance to do some good. We will not make you take a knightly oath or pledge yourself to our band, but we ask you to follow our laws and our behests. It would only be until Midgart. From there on out, you are a free man."

Friedrich had to admit, it was a good deal. He wouldn't be paid, but he also wouldn't be going hungry. And while Frau Beck may disagree, escorting wayfarers would be an opportunity to do some real good. He'd be keeping them safe from robbers and cheats, something he couldn't do just a few days ago. And it was an honorable job, far more dignified and reputable than caverneering.

But, he was no churchman, and he wasn't a landed lord or someone with titles and a bloodline going back to Karalthergroz. He was Friedrich Bauer, son of toilers and scion of field workers. And these wayfareages, they were full of good, upstanding, very godly folk. He wouldn't fit in with them even if God himself told him he would. Wayfareages had strict rules as well, and breaking them warranted going to a priest and answering. The thinking was that if someone was sinful on a wayfareage, it could doom the entire group. And to him, there was not a man more sinful than Friedrich Bauer.

"I am sorry, mein Herr. But, I cannot come with you."

"Oh?" Herr Neveu raised an eyebrow. "And why is that?"

"I . . ." He had to be careful, lest he out himself as a fellow traveler of witchcraft. "I cannot say."

"Debts? I assume. Perhaps a milkmaid you knocked up? Or is it a lawman with a warrant to throw you in irons and stand before a Lawspeaker?"

"None of those, mein Herr."

"Then if you will not say Friedrich Bauer, I see no cause why you cannot join us."

"I . . ." He had to give some answer. This knight clearly would not accept a no. "I am not worthy to be in your group. I am a sinner, a wicked man to the core." Might as well tell him a bit of the truth.

A smile perused the knight's lip. "Herr Bauer, our Band runs the sickhouses. We are masters of healing, both worldly wounds and godly. A sinner has his place with us." He put his hat back on. "I feel fear in your voice, Herr Bauer. Be it fear of the unknown or fear of the coming days, I do not know. But may I share with you something to fight that fear?" Friedrich nodded. "Men cannot escape darkness on their own but through each other. Brotherhood and fellowship are what dispels the dark and ushers in the light. Every neighbor a brother and every stranger a friend. It falls on us to lift up those who have sunk down. This should be the creed of every soul, the words written on every heart. Each of us is our brother's keeper." He paused, allowing the words to sink in. "The final line in the Book of Douths, written by Holy Budô himself, fear is the foe of man, Herr Bauer. None of us should have to live with it."

The knight walked down to Friedrich's level. "I do not know what it is you fear, nor may I ever know. But this I do know; you cannot allow this fear to hold onto your heart forever. Fear is a rot that will curse you through your days. It will spread to your family, your friends, all you care about, unless you rip it out."

"Mein Herr . . ." Friedrich began.

The knight raised a gloved hand to silence him. "No excuses, no whines, those are the tools fear uses to buy itself time. A brave man, Herr Bauer, is not a fearful man. Nor is he a sinner. A brave man lives the Douths and does good. A coward doesn't.

Be a man among men, Herr Bauer. Rip out this fear before it continues to fester."

Friedrich didn't know what to say. His manhood had been insulted, and while it stung, the knight was right. He couldn't keep doing this. He couldn't keep living with this imbedded feeling of worry and regret. He couldn't keep being afraid of the world. He was doubtful he could ever conquer fear, for there was much he was afraid of, but he could at least learn to stand a little taller. And, maybe, just maybe, these knights could offer him the chance to do the good he wanted. And he would learn a little about being a man along the way.

"To Midgart?" Friedrich asked.

"To Midgart, no further." The knight extended a hand.

"No killing," he announced. The knight looked for clarification. "I won't do any killing. You can give me a weapon, but you can't make me use it."

Herr Neveu nodded in approval. "A man with his own law. I can respect that. You have my word, Herr Bauer. There will be no killing under my watch."

Friedrich swallowed. A thousand thoughts, a thousand fears, and a thousand doubts ran through his head. But he pushed those all away and shook Herr Neveu's hand.

"Welcome to the wayfareage Friedrich Bauer."

• • •

Vytilia travelled north, all through the night, following the river out of Töiz towards Mondsruhe. She ruminated on what had happened as she walked, debating with herself if what she had done was the right thing. Her doubt told her she was a murderer, who slew a woman in cold blood, while her rational side argued that what she did was a mercy. She spared an old and broken woman from further pain and agony. Regardless of the answer, it had greatly diminished her thirst. She did not know why. Perhaps seeing a person struggle and cry and emote affected her. She was once more seeing them not as vessels for blood but as sentient, sapient beings. Beings who suffered and lost, just as Strixans did, beings of rationality, of civility, and even nobility. She still had to suppress her urges, clenching her jaw and fighting her inner turmoil when she heard a heartbeat, but it was far easier now.

She arrived at the outskirts of Mondsruhe before daybreak when the city was still quiet. Torchlights still burned on the streets and on the walls and watchtowers. Vytilia ascended a tree, observing from the branches, waiting for the city to rouse to life. Mondsruhe was a mighty city, mightier than any of the little towns she passed through, mightier than the nymph encampment and, dare she say, mightier than Nidus. It stretched far beyond from where she could see, straddling the banks of the river. Spires and church steeples stood high above the city, overlooking the denizens below. Outside of the walls, buildings constructed of all manner of material were everywhere from tall, brightly colored inns and taverns of wood to small, squat, brick or stone furnaces and manufactories. Roofs of brick, of shingles and slate, thatch and wood, chimneys of all shapes and sizes, all created a patchwork blanket that was the city.

Past the mighty wall, tall as three grown tiercels, the city was nearly all whitewashed with smart, varnished wood latticework and red-orange tile roofs. There were market stalls, for now empty, with awnings of the most brilliant cloth stretching out overhead. Bridges, smartly constructed, decorated with ribbons and statues, spanned the river. Horses and carts moved across, confident in their construction. Moon and starlight reflected over weathervanes and golden effigies of the sun. It was a city of piety, a city of culture, a city of trade, a city of civilization.

She waxed nostalgic for the days of the old empire when every Strixan city was this glorious, where the splendor was evident, where buildings stretched for miles, when there was time and energy to devote to decorations and aesthetics, where people could be proud to live and work. Those were the halcyon days, the days of her ancestors, the days of her mother, the days before the devils and the cataclysm. With day breaking and the men rousing from their sleep and beginning to work, she climbed down the tree. She may not ever see the past golden age of the empire, but she would see to it that the dark age never again returns.

The roads in this town were not dirt. The streets, as they should be properly referred to as, were paved with cobblestone and brick. Horse hooves and wagon wheels made a curious, clopping sound when they passed over. The walls of the city were old, made of a splendent white brick, encircling the heart of the city. The gate she passed under was a tall watchtower, elaborate heraldry carved above the keystone. Another of those strange dials resting near the pinnacle. As she came out the other side, bells began to ring, a great clanging sound reverberating across the rooftops. Vytilia had to pause, worried it was the sign of an attack, but all the citizenry were calm and collected. After six rings, the bells ceased. *What an odd practice.*

Once she was past the gate, her view was obstructed by the surrounding buildings, the crowds and animals drowning out the rush of the nearby river. It was remarkable how fast the city had come to life, going from the quiet of night to the business of day in only the blink of an eye. She walked over to an older man as he placed several bolts of cloth into a wheelbarrow. A small canine nipped at his heels, wiggling its tail and panting as he went to and from his house.

"I beg your pardon, Herr, might I trouble you for directions?"

The man set another bolt down, shooing the canine away as it growled at Vytilia. She wanted to growl back. "Yes?" He raised an eyebrow when he got a better look at her, looking up at her, studying her hair and skin. "Where do you need going?"

"The High Learnhouse."

"The High Learnhouse?" His face expressed concern and curiosity. "Whatever for?"

She remembered the cover story she gave Frau Meyer. "I am looking for my brother. I have reason to believe he is here."

"Well if he hasn't taken his oaths yet, you should be able to find him. Go one street over until you come to a wide avenue. Keep following it this way," He pointed north. "The learnhouse is hard to miss, just look for the building crawling with priests." He did a double-glance at the sword on her belt. "They won't let you in with that however. I'd stash it somewhere or sell it off. Herr Schmidt has a smithy two streets over. He'll take care of it."

"*Gratias*, Herr." She started setting off.

"Oh, and fräulein?" She stopped and turned her head. "If you don't know someone's family name, you call them *mein* Herr." She thanked him and carried on.

She would have to relieve herself of the sword. She followed his directions to the blacksmith, eventually finding a wood-framed open shack. A burly, hairy man in a leather apron was working the billows and checking the heat of his forge. The shack was filled with half-circle flat pieces of iron, blades, cutlery, and all manner of consumer goods. She stood at the entrance to the smithy and knocked on a post, clearing her throat.

The blacksmith turned away from the forge, his large, white eyes widening when he saw Vytilia. He wiped his face with a rag then walked over to her, wiping his hands. "*Guten morgen, Fräulein.*

How can I be of help?" This blacksmith was one of the first men Vytilia had met who was taller than her.

"Are you Herr Schmidt?" He nodded. "I was told by the cloth merchant you would be able to help me with this." She untied the sword from her belt and handed it to him. He stepped back, unsheathing the blade to inspect it, weighing it in his hands.

"A fine blade. A Vitelish by the make of it or maybe Barriort?" He tapped on it, tugging at the blade where it met the handguard. "It seems to be in good shape if a bit dull."

"Would you buy it?" she asked.

"Buy it?" He rubbed his chin, looking at her, then the sword, then her, then the sword again. "Forgive me for prying, Fräulein, but what are you doing with this? And how come you are alone?"

She bit her lip. "I have come to . . . find my brother. My father presented me with the sword as both a deterrent and a means of acquiring funds for my journey."

Herr Schmidt sheathed the sword, muttering something about a "fancy wordstock" under his breath. "I mean no offense to your father, I'm sure his ends were right, but letting a young woman out into the world alone seems reckless." He sighed, staring at the sword. "He really let you out like this? Without an escort?"

"I had a guide, but . . ." She sighed, shaking her head. "He found better employment elsewhere."

"Well, he'll get what's coming to him." Vytilia sincerely hoped not. "I'll give you two Sonners for it."

"Is that a good price?"

Herr Schmidt looked at her curiously. "It is best not to ask that to the buyer. It shows weakness." He set the sword down by a grindstone. "So . . ." he asked as he unlocked a lockbox, "where's your brother run off to?"

"We believe the High Learnhouse. I am headed there next, which reminds me." She unslung the bag from her shoulders and retrieved Friedrich's manica, chainmail, and greaves, setting them on the table. She also carefully hid the highwayman's pistol, burying it under sausage links and her old nymph clothes. "I was also given these to sell. Would you mind appraising these?"

Herr Schmidt grabbed one of the manica. "Amazing," he muttered. "I've never seen a vambrace like this." He curled it. "It folds! Just like a wood louse. My god that is clever."

"What did you call them?"

"Vambrace," he explained, picking up the other one. "It was part of a Ritter's kit, how they guarded their arms, before full armor fell out of use. Well, I think lancers still use them." He poked the other manica. "Are these teeth marks?"

"An animal got to them before we did. We found them in an old mine shaft."

He looked skeptical or confused at her verbiage. "Really?"

She nodded. "We thought them to be artifacts, half-god artifacts."

Herr Schmidt smiled, setting the manica down. "They're impressive forgeries. I have to give you that."

"Forgeries?" She was aghast.

"Well, look at them." He pointed to the metal. "This looks like it wasn't made more than a few months ago. Aside from the bitemarks, there's no damage, no aging, no weathering. Hell, there isn't any rust. And the greaves and mail, you can still smell whoever wore them last. I've seen the stuff the High Learnhouse buys. They're always green or orange from age and very, very fragile. These . . ." he mimed putting one of the manica on, "a daring horseman could still wear these to battle."

"Oh . . ." Vytilia was out of her element. This had never occurred to her, the disparity between the artifacts of her people that had been found and the condition of their current equipment, which begged the question of what Friedrich had planned to do when selling them. Perhaps he knew how to mask the age of an artifact or could come up with a better story. The curiosity furthered her resolve to find him.

"I'll give you another three Sonner for the set. I could probably fix up this one with the bitemarks, give the rest some polish, and find a gatherer of strange armors. But these can't be sold to the Church. It wouldn't be right." He looked her in the eye. "And yes, that is a good price." Vytilia nodded in agreement and accepted five silver coins from the blacksmith. He put his money away and set the armor on a workbench. "I wish you luck with finding your brother, Fräulein. I hope they can be of help at the High Learnhouse. But I would recommend finding a group to travel with for safety. Look for the Wayfaring Knights, the Balderers. They're always escorting wayfarers; you can probably find a group headed in the same direction."

"How will I recognize them?"

"Look for the white sun on the black background or anything with mistletoe," he explained. "The High Learnhouse should know more."

"Very well. My gratitude, Herr Schmidt."

"Of course, Fräulein. Go with God!"

She left the blacksmith and retraced her steps to where she had met the cloth merchant and his rude canine. She was excited to see this High Learnhouse and meet a mannish scholar. It was exhilarating to think what connections they could help her make in her historical theory.

She found the avenue the cloth merchant had described, perhaps the widest non-natural road she had ever seen. It was wide enough that several animals and carts could travel in either direction comfortably. She walked along the sidewalk. There was all manner of men here, ones with fine livery and powdered, artificial hair, others barefoot in little more than rags, rambling and raving, holding out their hands for alms. Some were darker skinned with strange, orb-like cloth hats and long beards, speaking a strange, unknown language. Others were pink like Friedrich with hair as orange as a sunset. The elder men and women even had hair as white as hers.

The diversity of men was something that astounded Vytilia. Strixans were mostly uniform. The only differences they had were the shade of grey in their skin and one of three hair and eye colors. Vytilia was an exception. But men, on the other hand, had a plethora of phenotypes. There were ones with red colored hair, others with green eyes, some with dark skin, and more with almost more combinations than could be imagined. Even the nymphs were more uniform than the men. But all these different people had one commonality: a beating heart. With so many people surrounding her, it was getting more and more difficult to fight back.

In the center of the city, the heart was made up of a marketplace surrounding a gilded and elaborately carved column memorial. A grand, commanding building with a dial was surrounded by men in the finest of fineries. All stood at the door, looking out over their great city. Everywhere, the most well-dressed flashed their age-shields of a white half-moon against a field of light blue. She surmised they were the colors of the city. To her left, looming over the city like a benevolent watchman, was a nine-spired church as grand and maintained as the Arx back in Nidus. This was a city that took pride in itself and its achievements. And despite the heartbeats pounding in her ears, she steeled herself and pressed on, hoping that one day the Strixans would have that same pride.

The buildings lining the avenue eventually gave way to two plazas, both hedged in by large bushes decorated with yellow, white, red, and orange blossoms. On her right was a religious building, tall enough to be considered a temple by the Strixans. It was also wide, almost round in its construction, with nine spires at the entrance, middle, and rear. A brilliant white eagle was carved on the front, holding a ribbon scribbled with the mannish script. It was flanked by a lion on the left and a griffin on the right. Bas-reliefs of different men and women, eagles, lions, and griffins, decorated the wall and face of the edifice. It reminded her of the Arx, though made of a darker brownstone rather than marble.

Across from this mannish temple was a less grandiose but equally impressive structure. It looked at first to be a single building, a long hallway, but then she saw two wings jutting out from it an angle. When she looked closer, she saw another pair of wings just ahead of the first. The design reminded her of an arrow, though without the arrowhead and only the fletching. The style of the building was also curious. It was made to purposefully resemble the cottages and homes she had seen outside the city walls with whitewashed brick walls, dark brown wooden supports and truss, and a roof shingled to resemble thatch. In the grass surrounding the white-brick arrow building, many priests and priestesses in green vestments walked to and fro. *This must be the High Learnhouse,* she decided.

She raced across the avenue, dodging horses and coaches, strolling up the few stairs to the doors of the High Learnhouse. She went through the open doors, entering the lobby. She nearly fell to her knees when she entered. In the center was a large marble statue of a hooded figure with two hallways leading down to the rear of the building on the left and right. The statue had one arm stretched out, holding an image of the sun with an eagle perched on their shoulders, a lion and griffin standing guard on his flanks. The other hand was open, pointed upward. He was standing over some sort of amorphous creature, a broken sword just past the creature's reach.

"My God!" she announced. It *was* Sol Invictus with a few minor cosmetic changes. She knelt, mouth agape, staring at the statue. It looked like it could have been ripped straight from the Sanctum Sanctorum.

"I understand you; I feel like this every day when I come before the light of our Lord," a soft feminine voice spoke behind Vytilia, a light hand touching her shoulder and helping her to her feet. "You're so cold. Are you well?" Whoever this was, they were young with a strong heart.

Vytilia closed her mouth. "I, indeed, I am, my gratitude, good Frau. I just have . . . poor circulation, uh . . . flow." She continued to stare at the statue of Sol Invictus.

"I am Schwester Braun, a newling here at the High Learn-house. How can I help you?" She was cheerful and smiling, exuding enthusiasm.

"I." She shook her head, taking her eyes off the statue.

The young woman who helped her wore a strange garment, which given its coloring, Vytilia realized was a religious vestment. It was a long green dress, going down to her wrists and ankles, but overlayed was a beige apron. It was not quite like an apron. It went up to her throat and down to just below mid-shin. It was more like a long vest that tucked into itself at the center, kept closed by a plain black leather belt. The girl also had on a large, bronze, nine-pointed sun pinned just above her right breast. Her hair was tied back, tucked into a detached beige hood that hugged her forehead and behind her ears. It reminded Vytilia so much of the old sibylic vestments worn by Strixan priestesses.

"I." She was tongue-tied. She could not say she was looking for her brother. They might send her off, and she might not get the information she needed.

"Are you here to take up the cloth?" Schwester Braun suggested.

"Not exactly. I come from a small village and want to . . ." Her gaze shifted back to the statue. "I want to learn. I want to know more of the history, the doctrine, the folklore, the legends." She swallowed; the awe of the statue kept her thirst at bay but only barely.

"Learn more? But your accent and your wordstock! You sound like a learned woman already!" She took a step back, talking to herself. "No, no Wiligard, don't say that! All are welcome!" She cleared her throat, stepping back towards Vytilia. "I'm sorry. I am still new here. Come with me. I will take you to Bruder Wenzel. He is the head skald of our lore branch! He can tell you everything you would ever want to know!"

She took Vytilia by the wrist down the left hallway, passing by more clerics clad in green and beige vestments. They came to the first wing and turned left, heading all the way to the end of the wing then took another left to a small alcove. Schwester Braun let go of Vytilia and knocked on the door, giddily hopping from foot to foot.

"You are in for a treat!" Schwester Braun told her. "Bruder Wenzel is the smartest man I have ever met! He teaches all the newlings before they take their oaths!"

The door opened, and a man in earthy-green and beige vestments opened the door. His clothing was not at all dissimilar to Schwester Braun's. It was composed of a single-piece green outfit, a long-sleeve shirt, and a pair of trousers sewn together to be a single piece. The man also wore some sort of a cloak-like, beige colored garment. It was a long rectangle with a hole for the head and neck. He too wore a belt with a talisman of the sun and a miniature version of the statue hanging from his belt. He was clean shaven, his head nearly bald aside from a hoary whisp of hair. His face was old, and he had wrinkles around his eyes from near-constant squinting. His heartrate was slower but quickened when he saw Vytilia. His eyes also widened.

"My goodness child, are you alright? You're looking rather sickly." He was much shorter and squatter than either Vytilia or Schwester Braun, looking up at both of them.

"*Entschuldigung,* Bruder Wenzel." Schwester Braun smiled gently. He looked over to her. "This is . . ." Her face went pale. "My goodness, I never asked for your name! I just took you by the wrist and . . ."

Vytilia held up her hand. The girl's anxiety was causing her heartrate to go up, the sound pounding into Vytilia's ears. "Do not worry. I am . . . Mina . . . Meyer."

"How do you do?" Bruder Wenzel rubbed his eyes. "Now, what can I do for you two?"

"Fräulein Meyer has come to the High Learnhouse to learn. She wants to know everything!"

"I see. Are you interested in becoming a churchmaid, Frau Meyer?"

"I am not. I consider myself an itinerant scholar. I want to learn as much as I can before I depart the city."

"A woman delver?" Bruder Wenzel made an amused sound. "Are you travelling alone?" Vytilia nodded. "It isn't safe for you to be travelling alone, not nowadays anyway." He shook his head then peeked into his office. He stepped outside, closing the door behind him. "You know girls, I have been in there for a few days.

What do you say we go to the *Lehrerkirche* to learn? A teaching in a house of God does good for the mind and soul."

They followed the man down the hallway, back out to the main foyer.

"What were you working on this time?" Schwester Braun asked eagerly.

"Nothing quite as fun as you make it sound, dear Schwester. I have spent endless days pouring over the Sagas and the unhallowed tales for the book I am writing."

"Unhallowed tales?" Vytilia asked.

"Yes, not everything was put into the sagas, you see. While they may not be holy writ, there are still teachings and lore to be learned from them." They stepped outside, pausing as they waited for the road traffic to clear up. "Where are you from Frau Meyer?"

"Helvensland."

"You speak very refined Teutonish for a Helven with many new words. Gaulish ones I assume. You'll have to forgive me, but I have always found the Helven accent to be a bit boorish. Have you been taught before?"

"Not through official channels. My mother taught me since I was a nest—adolescent. I was sent out to learn more, so I can teach others when I return."

"How unusual. Your mother must have had some kind of Learnhouse rearing, highly unlikely for small hamlets. Though, given the reputation of the Helven, I must surmise all the menfolk are engaged in sellsword work?" She simply nodded. He was not entirely incorrect. "I do not suppose you have a writ or a warrant from your Bürgermeister or someone else?"

"I do not."

Bruder Wenzel's eyes narrowed. "Hmmmm. Highly unusual. But, I will give this first teaching free of charge, but any following will need approval and some form of payment. We cannot just let anyone come in and learn. Even the High Learnhouse has things it needs to pay for."

"I will be sure to have all my questions asked today."

"Very good." Bruder Wenzel held the door to the church, the Lehrerkirche as he called it, open for the two of them. "Now, we are truly blessed to have these wonderful stained-glass windows to help in our learning. The 'poor man's sagas' as they are called, but they do a better job than some teachers I know. We shall start over here."

The inside of the Lehrerkirche was as curious as the outside. The walls were in a wide, nonagonal shape with high arching windows at even intervals to bring in sunlight. The floorplan was the most striking. Most of the room was taken up by two lines of wooden pews, which were split down the center by a long, muted and worn carpet. The pews were arranged to fill in the nonagonal design, narrow at the doors and towards an altar at the other end, but widened out until it almost touched the walls, leaving only a narrow passageway. There were a few other people in the church, most sitting in the front near the altar. Vytilia had only a chance to glimpse it before Bruder Wenzel led her to one of the windows. It was a circular alcove towards the rear of the church with a spectacular stained-glassed circular window of a nine-pointed sun. Beneath the window was another statue of Sol Invictus, surrounded by small metal statues or stone busts of different figures. The atmosphere was reverent. It reminded her of the Sanctum Sanctorum.

"Now, Frau Meyer," Bruder Wenzel asked, "help me understand where to start with you. What do you already know? What is it you wish to learn most about?" He spoke in a low whisper, so his voice would not reverberate off the walls.

She recalled the brief synopsis of a lesson Friedrich had given her. It was not much of a foundation, especially a foundation she wanted to rewrite the understanding of history with. "I know nothing," she admitted, though there was humor in that statement. "Start at the very beginning."

"A very good place to start," Schwester Braun chimed in.

Bruder Wenzel seemed taken aback at Vytilia's declaration, but he stood up straight and began. They were standing under the left-most window on the wall left of the door. If this was the beginning, then Vytilia realized that meant men read from left to right. Something they learned, or something that developed naturally?

The artwork in the window was expertly crafted. It looked more like it was made of jewels rather than glass. It depicted a figure clad in white, their face hidden and hand outstretched, raising an arm over a dark void. Small pinpricks of white, yellow, blue, and green, were scattered through the void, while opaque pieces of grey, brown, and dark green began to cluster under the figure's hand.

"In the beginning, God created the heavens and the world. In the dark void, made from heavenly timber and stone, our home, Erde, was made. To give our world light, God placed himself at the center of our world group. Or, *Weltgruppe* if you wish to know the High Rinnish word." That gave credence to Friedrich's erroneous thinking that the planet orbited the sun, rather than the other way around.

They moved onto the next window where the white-clad being, which she now understood was Sol, oversaw a world of green, full of different plants and animals. There were avians in the sky, mammals on the land, and piscis in the sea. Androgynous-clothed, faceless, mannish beings, in many different colors, tended to the plants and animals. "Once Erde was created, God began to sow the seeds of life so that the world may fulfill its orlay," Vytilia made a note to ask more on that word later. "All manner of fish and birds, askards and bugs, wildlife and tamelife were sown so that they may live. Among these seeds sown were the first breed of men. They were mightier, stronger, wiser, faster, and godlier than any man or group of men on Erde today. This is why we have given them the title of Half-god. These first men were to help God, acting as stewards so that life may grow. This time we now refer to as the Age of Dusk."

Very dissimilar to the Strixan cosmogonic story, Vytilia thought. There was not a predecessor race in any Strixan stories. The world was their domain, and their domain alone. Though, they similarly had been given stewardship. Another connection perhaps? She would ponder that later, now she had a more pressing question.

"Bruder Wenzel, where was the moon?"

"Ah, that brings us to our next part of the tale." They walked to the next window. It was darker than the previous one but showed nearly the exact scene, except that Sol was exiting the frame. The Half-gods were raising their arms, as if to wave goodbye. "The moon had not yet been formed, but we are getting ahead of ourselves."

The moon had not yet been formed? She knew mankind thought of the moon as male, but to think it came *after* the sun? She felt like she was committing every known sacrilege and blaspheme imaginable listening to this. But, there was more to learn. She steeled herself and continued listening.

"Building an entire world, and everything around it, was difficult work. And it took its toll on God. He needed to rest and recover his strength, so He could watch over his making. He left the Half-gods on their own to continue their stewardship and help every seed of life grow."

On to the next window. This one too was darker and depicted many different . . . things. They crawled from crevices in the ground or out of shadowy caves. There was no uniformity in these creatures. Some were monstrous serpents. Some were canines with blood-red eyes. There were bestial, goliath-like, blue-skinned beings wielding clubs, hideous large-nosed manlike beasts crawling out of rocks, a great cephalopod rising from the waters, and even a draco. This was very much like the motif tile back at the Sanctum Sanctorum, though she could only recognize a small portion of the creatures.

Bruder Wenzel made a curious sign before he continued. He touched the center of his forehead with his index finger, then used that same finger to draw a circle around his face, stopping at where he first touched. Schwester Braun made the same gesture. "When the light of God left the world, it was shrouded in a thick, cold darkness. We refer to this time as the Age of Eventide, more known as the Long Winter. Even during this dark time, the seeds of life continued to grow. But, without that warm and holy light, evil began to twist some of the life that grew. These lesser beings turned against their maker. They waged war on the Half-gods, on everything that was good and holy, thinking that the world belonged to them and them alone. These are what we call the Lightless."

That certainly sounded like the devils and their *modus operandi*, but none of these depictions looked like a devil. And her mother had told her when the cataclysm came, there was still the day and night cycle, not this eternal winter. And, this was nothing like the Great Frozen of Strixan records. *Where did these stories come from*? she wondered. "Are these," she gestured to the different creatures depicted, "are these all of the Lightless?"

"No." Bruder Wenzel cleared his throat before continuing and made the circular gesture again. "These are only *some* of the many evils that make up the Lightless. Well, we assume. The Sagas are never exact on what the Lightless are, if it is a single race or many different evils all banded together. It does not matter what they were, only that they are evil and rose up against the Half-gods."

"Then anything could potentially be a Lightless? Anything considered evil, I mean?"

"Yes. The quiet teaching of the church is that any and all things of the different folklores, things that fear God, can be considered a Lightless. The basilisk of Merkya, the tarasque of south Gaul, the demons of the Pananthropotes, all the many different breeds of dragon and wyrm, all of these can be considered a Lightless."

She covered her mouth and bit her lip, unsure if she should ask this next question. Bruder Wenzel started to move on to the next window, but she stopped him. "I . . ." she was careful not to let the points of her fangs slip, not an easy task since heartbeats reverberated loudly off the walls. "I have a relative who has traveled in the east. When they were among the Wends, they brought back stories of a creature called . . . a vampire. Would this be considered a Lightless as well?"

Bruder Wenzel scratched his beardless chin. He looked at Schwester Braun who only shrugged. "What is a vampire?"

"Well . . . I am not sure. I have heard many conflicting stories. But the only commonality is that they drink blood."

"Ah." Bruder Wenzel gritted his teeth. "That is all you need to say. Blood drinking is an unholy deed, Frau Meyer. Nothing made by God drinks the blood of another to live."

"What about when you, we, butcher animals? Or when we make blood sausage?"

"Those are different, very different, from drinking blood directly. We . . . you do not come from a Yarruser family, do you?" She shook her head. "Good, those are my least favorite Urworkish. Anyway, butchering livestock or making *blutwurst* or the Sonntag blót are not the same as drinking blood from a living being. Butchers do, or at least should, thank the livestock for its life, so that we may eat, and man does not live off blutwurst alone. And the Sonntag blót is simply a hallowed way of butchering. The livestock is killed, its blood spilled, so that we may thank God for His bounty and greatness. Using blood in food is part of butchering. But to drink the blood alone, it is thought of as drinking the life, some even say the soul of the living."

Vytilia had to stop herself from gritting her teeth and growling in frustration. She felt like she was wasting her time. Men had stolen her god, disregarded her goddess, and reduced her people to creatures that hide in shadows. How was this possible!?

Bruder Wenzel went to continue to the next window, but he noticed Vytilia staring at the wall, a cross expression on her face. "Are you well, Frau Meyer?"

"I am fine. I am . . . pondering."

"Are you worried about a loved one?" Schwester Braun asked. Vytilia's confusion and curiosity pulled her out of her brooding to look at the girl curiously. "Where I come from, in the northwest, we tell tales of nachzehrer. It is similar to this vampire you speak of. They say that if someone dies of the blight, or takes their own life, they turn into one." The girl held Vytilia's arm for reassurance. "But, from what I have learned, that isn't true! Evil does not have power over the souls of the dead, only God does! I'm sure His ravens will find your loved one's soul so that they may go to Folkwang!" The girl was so sincere in her reassurance, Vytilia could not help but smile.

"I echo the dear Schwester's words," Bruder Wenzel added. "Too often the meanfolk think that the Lightless and evil have more power over this world than they actually do. We must not forget that so long as the sun shines, and it will forever shine, the souls of men are safe." He went to turn and move on to the next window, but Vytilia stopped him again. She thought of a different question to ask.

"What about nym—elves." She gestured to the window full of Lightless. "Are they considered one of those?"

"Hmmmm." Bruder Wenzel was intrigued by the question. "Well, you see, it depends on who you ask." Vytilia looked at him for clarification. "It is important to remember, Frau Meyer, that what I have told you, and what I will tell you, are not the same for all mankind."

"What?"

"Now, I know that sounds off, and I should specify. The beginning of the world and the lore of God, all of that is the same. Though, the less said about the arguments of God is the sun or the sun is His seat, the better. *ahem* But once we finish with Erde being made and God leaving the Half-gods as stewards, that is when things begin to change."

He went onto the next window. Right away, Vytilia noticed it was different. The subject matter, of course, was different, but so was the art style. It was cut recently with different shades and tints than the other windows. The metal holding the frame was less weathered, as if it had been replaced. The window depicted three different beings, one blond male with a hammer fighting several serpentine beasts, a grey-haired and one-eyed male fighting a monstrous lupus with a spear, and a red-headed female fighting a blue-skinned goliath, wielding a sword and shield.

"Now, from here on out is where the lore is different depending on where one lives. What I have told you is the lore for our stem, the Teudish." Bruder Wenzel made a gesture encompassing Vytilia, Schwester Braun, and himself. "This is where our stem, and the Gauls, and the Wends, all came from. The Holies shown here are who we consider to be the lead guiders of our life. But the other stems and groups see things differently. The Greenmen of the Bythony Isles, the Merkya excluded, actually think of elves or elf-like beings as being their forefathers, and many of their Holies are drawn and shown accordingly. Our Elláser brethren to the south thought that rather than teach their forefathers, the Half-gods of their lands left behind knowledge in great storehouses built into the caves of their mountainous homelands. And, far down south, the Habaxum church has dark-skinned Holies, and their version of the Saga has many different tales from our own."

"But, even though we all came from many places and learned in many ways, we are all banded together in our worship of the true God!" Schwester Braun cheerily added.

Vytilia was almost blindsided by the Bruder's statement. She braced herself against a pew. The information of elves being one tribe of man's ancestors was news enough, but that statement of the southern men learning from buried repositories, that left her shaking. As her mother taught her: the Striga, the eastern cousins of the Strixans, and the second largest ethnicity, believed the gods had placed repositories of knowledge throughout their territory. They were able to use this knowledge to greatly advance their civilization, especially in fields of mathematics, thaumaturgy, and architecture. If these repositories were the same as the storehouses, then that was a definite link between the Strixans and mankind!

Though, where did these repositories originate from? The Striga believed that Luna and Sol, or Helios and Selene as they referred to them, had put them there as a sign of favoritism. But the Strixans, Leannán, and Lilithans all believed that to be blasphemous. The nymphs could not have built them, could they?

"Sorry," Vytilia interrupted as Bruder Wenzel was about to continue, "what was that about these 'storehouses' used in the south?"

"Oh, was I unclear? I am sorry. The Elláser, and by extension the Pananthropotes Church, teach that their forefathers were not taught by Half-gods directly, as ours were. Rather, the Half-gods buried great stores of knowledge for them to find. They call them 'Gnósisapothêkai' and because of them, for a good long while, they were the strongest realm in the world. That was one of the reasons why they split from the Church in Midgart. Lygotium was so much stronger and powerful than Midgart, they thought they should be the seat of Sonnendom."

"Those storehouses did not help them very much when the Tujue came knocking on their walls," Schwester Braun quipped.

"Indeed, if anything, it made them stale, unable to learn and grow to fight the Tujue. One could say that was the wrath of God for abandoning the Church in Midgart, but it is not my place to decree such things."

Such a remark could have been made about the Striga several millennia ago, Vytilia thought. They were praised for their philosophy and art in Nidus but also condoned for their unvirtuous behaviors and habits. There were also plenty of religious debates on the true nature of the Gods, but that was between all four Strixan ethnicities.

Since Bruder Wenzel did not mention this "Greenman" tribe as being as advanced as the Elláser tribe, Vytilia took that to mean nymphs did not build those repositories. That still left the question of, who did? Was it possible there had been other groups, other civilizations before the Strixans? Possibly even before the nymphs? If nymphs were real, then, is it possible the other motifs were also real? A record of creatures and civilizations long lost and forgotten?

She looked up at the window again. It depicted two males and a female fighting individually. Such a strategy was anathema to the legions, who always fought in closed rank formations and forbade females. Since these are the ones Bruder Wenzel had referenced as personally teaching the Teudish, it was increasingly unlikely that they had been Strixans.

Then, Strixans might not have been the only *influence on mankind,* she realized. *We must have been a part, a great part, but still only a part.* The history of men then must be like the world below the surface, many strata built on top of another. Then, there must be something below the nymphs! And something even below that! Down until . . . until . . . that was the obstacle. Where did the devils originate? What role did they play in all of this, if any? Why were they destroying civilizations but never claimed the surface for themselves? Why were they destroying civilizations at all?

"Frau Meyer?" Bruder Wenzel waved his hand in front of her. "Are you still with us?"

"I am, apologies. I am . . . entranced by the majesty of our God's creation."

"Ah. If you need to take a trice and beseech, I understand. My legs are actually getting a bit sore. Why don't we continue this from the pews?"

20

The wayfareage was camped outside of the small town of Konradheim where the river Altum fed into the Tonau. Erdeish ploughmen on the outskirts of the town offered their free rooms and barns to house the wayfarers while the guard detail slept in fields and guarded the wagons. Friedrich had found himself a nice comfortable spot under a beech tree where he leaned against the trunk, whittling an old branch he'd found.

Along with the forty wayfarers, there were twelve guards including himself, four knights, four shieldbearers, and four halberdiers. Though they did keep a military schedule and some aspects of discipline, going so far as to give Friedrich a wardress (a breastplate and boots. He turned down a morion helmet), the attitude here was more relaxed than one would find in a band of landsknechts. While the knights insisted on being referred to with "Herr" before being spoken to, they were otherwise open to be spoken to almost as an equal. They made attempts to get to know Friedrich, riding alongside him at the back of the wayfareage, telling him about their Band and its many tales and undertakings, always imparting a godly or goodly teaching.

Though he disdained the wearing of wardress and having to lug around a halberd, Friedrich was relieved he did not have to live like a warrior. He would do guard duty and carry his weight, but he was glad they did not make him act, speak, or do the things warriors did. It was because of this, he could sleep at night and live with himself. To him, fighting men were the lowest of all men, but their escorting cousins were far more respectable.

What struck Friedrich most about the knights was their desire to continue the idea of knighthood, or as it was more widely known, chivalry. They confirmed that what the sellswords in Drosselaue had said was true to an extent. Gone were the elaborate coats-of-arms emblazoned on wide shields, gone were the mighty longswords that could cleave a foe in two, and gone were the full-faced great helms adorned with the token of a fair maiden. Now there were sabers and rapiers, holstered pistols, a simple steel breastplate, and lobster-tail helmets. But, the ideas of knighthood remained.

This was a regular topic of conversation with the knights and even some of the other halberdiers. They would tell Friedrich about it as they walked. While the wayfarers sung songs about God and recited Saga lines from memory, Friedrich was told about being a good man and living a knightly law. He assumed (correctly) Herr Neveu had put the others up to it.

He did not fault the knights for wanting to spread chivalry. They were sincere and honest in their efforts and were living what they taught, trying to help their fellow man and spread goodness. While there were parts of the chivalry teachings he enjoyed, it was hard for Friedrich, since the fighting aspect was always preeminent. Kindness to foes, bravery in fighting, pride in one's armor, all of it went back to the worst thing mankind had ever made: war. The knights could talk of goodness and respect all they wanted. At the end of the day, chivalry was a code of how to wage war. There was no honor in war, Friedrich had learned, only blood and broken lives. No amount of tales of renown would ever mask that.

Still, in the end, Friedrich was grateful or at least content he had signed on with the wayfareage. The men were good and trustworthy, enjoyed a good drink, and always had a good tale to tell. Herr Berstett, one of the knights, had even refreshed Friedrich on playing chess, a game he first learned when fellowed to Herr Bergmann. The wayfarers were happy to have him along, and seeing them safe made him feel less hollow. There were even a few pretty girl wayfarers his age.

"Ahoy Friedrich!" He looked up. Herr Berstett was calling to him. "Herr Horben broke open a cask. Come and have a drink! We've got some swine belly frying over the fire!" Friedrich certainly wouldn't say no to that. He sheathed his dagger and threw his whittling away, joining the others (aside from Herr Neveu who was conducting business in Konradheim) around a large fire, accepting a dented tin cup full of cheap, young wine. It tasted pleasant enough that he accepted a second helping.

"Hope you lads are ready for a good hike tomorrow." Herr Berstett announced over the crackling fire. "Ingmarsburg is a hefty wegtag away. Probably won't make it until sundown."

"We could've been there already if we didn't take that detour in Reichstadt," one of the halberdiers countered.

Friedrich had enjoyed the detour, as it meant he got to rest his legs and get a good laugh. The residents of Reichstadt gave anyone who used that name a dirty look and insisted the town was still named Rüdibrück. They had enjoyed the prestige and wealth that came with all the great men of the Realm meeting in their town but not the name change bestowed upon them. Watching the locals nearly come to blows with a lost trader had given Friedrich a much-needed laugh.

"Oh, come now Erfo, don't act like you didn't enjoy seeing the Reichstag Kanzlermat[45] and all those beautiful churches. It's not a wayfareage if you don't make a few stops along the way," Herr Berstett countered, earning a laugh from the group.

"What's the plan once we get to Ingmarsburg?" a shield-bearer asked.

"From there, we keep heading west through the Schwäbish Hügel towards Hengigert, then from there, we take the Nikros, which will feed into the Rinne up to Meinze." One of the other knights, Herr Pergen, answered. "And from Meinze, it's a walk to Midgart."

"Is there proper lodging in Ingmarsburg, or are we going to camp out in the woods again?" one of the shieldbearers asked, masking their voice.

"Ah, quit your whining. It is unbecoming. The band has a sickhouse there we'll be staying at," Herr Berstett chided.

"Any of you lads ever been to Midgart before?" The third Knight, Herr Horben, asked.

"I been there once. During the war," a halberdier, Rollo, answered. "My marschbund was sent to stop the Gauls from getting their hands on it. Spent five years garrisoning the lands around it."

"I was part of an escort about 5 years back," Erfo answered. "You could practically feel the Gauls lusting after it. I swear the whole border was just horseman, waiting for the word to cross over and take the place."

"I'm surprised the Gauls never tried to get it during the war. They're clawing after every other town west of the Rinne. Why not that one?" Rollo asked aloud. "It's not easy to defend and in a good spot of land."

---

45. The Reichstag Chancellery, the campus of buildings where the Reichstag, a semi-legislative body composed of nobles, clergy, and burghers, meet under the guidance of the Kommandant. Its laws are theoretically binding for all the Realm.

"They have too much respect for Karalthergroz. He's the one who declared it free and middle ground. No one but the Church is to own it. They see him as one of their own, a father to their folk and land, much as we see him. They try to actively avoid harming Midgart as well as Altkirche," Herr Pergen responded. "And they want to be seen as the wardens of the Church. Can't be a warden if they take Midgart by force of arms."

"What was that you said about Karalthergroz? They respect him? Bah, they won't even call him by his proper name![46] Charlegrand! Their bastard tongue sullies his name!" Herr Berstett added.

Friedrich shifted uncomfortably in his seat, all this talk about the war and tensions with the Gauls. He shifted topics, leaning to Herr Pergen, who was sitting next to him. "Herr Pergen, since we're asking questions, I hope you'll answer one of mine," Friedrich asked. "Why the mistletoe? It's on all the wayfarer's hats, and each of you has some pinned to your shirt. Is there some importance behind it?"

"What, you don't know the Holy's lore?" Rollo asked.

Herr Pergen waved the halberdier off. "That's an excellent question, Friedrich. It's a teaching I think all of us could stand to relearn," Herr Pergen told the group. He unpinned his mistletoe and handed it to Friedrich. "Long before the Church was shaped and made, before the Sagas were penned, the word of God was spread by the Holies. The Holies would travel between the three Holy-Steads and the heathen folks to teach. Among these was Holy Balder. Holy Balder's message was the circle of life, how death and birth are foundational to the ways of the world. Livestock must be killed, so that we may eat. Trees must be felled, so we may have homes. And, when we die, our body is burned and returned to the world, a gift to the world that fed and clothed us."

"But it was more than the circle of life," Herr Horben added. "Holy Balder taught how man has a duty to the wilderness and was once a part of it, but man is different from other life. Man has higher goals, a higher end."

"Indeed," Herr Pergen affirmed, "these were but some of the teachings of Holy Balder, though most know him for his messages

---

46. Technically, they do not call him by his name either. His real name is Karl Pepinling. In his time, he was known as Kommandant Karl, Karl the Mighty, Karl the Brave, Karl the Free, or Karl the Godly. The name of Karalthergroz, Karl the Great, emerged during the Righteous Wars of 1100-1200 HJ.

of family and kinship and the importance of honoring our forefathers. Friedrich, I assume you know it was he who first taught the importance of the *Namensbad*? The 'Name-bath.'"

Friedrich remembered seeing an Urworkish-style name-bath with Frau Beck for her granddaughter. Nine days after a baby was born, it was bathed in a tub of water warmed either by the sun or by fire. Once it was dried, the father, grandfather, or godfather gave the child a name, accepting it into the family and the stem. Since the inside of a body, the womb included, was dark, an unborn baby was surrounded by darkness. Since the inside of a body has never and will never (or at least, should never) see the sun, it is thought that the inside of a body was full of the inborn and vile darkness that had beset mankind since the Long Winter. So, a healthy baby was washed in sun-blessed water to both remove that inborn darkness and open its mind to the wisdom of God. Most items that came out of a body were seen as unclean for similar reasons. He didn't know that Holy Balder had started the name-bath but didn't want to seem a halfwit in front of the others. He nodded that he knew.

"Holy Balder made friends with all wildlife and all greenery. Though, he was particular to mistletoe, as it would climb the height of trees to reach the sun, its white berries blank canvases to absorb God's wisdom," Herr Pergen continued. "But, during a skaldish trip to the heathens of the north, Holy Balder was betrayed by one of his 'friends' and shot with an arrow tipped with mistletoe."

"It is unfortunate that he died where he did because the *Nordmänner* ended up turning him into one of their heathen gods. Took quite a few Righteous Wars to get that mess sorted out," Herr Berstett added.

Friedrich handed the mistletoe back to Herr Pergen. "I'd never heard that tale before," he admitted.

"Really?" Herr Horben commented. "Well, that is unfortunate. Your halldom priest must have been a slacker. Shame on him."

"I didn't actually get much opportunity to attend proper church," Friedrich confessed. "I spent a lot of time on the road."

"Well so do we. That's no excuse," Rollo jabbed, half-jokingly.

"Regardless, there's no better time than now to start attending regularly," Herr Pergen assured.

"Better no church than a damned Urworkish' meeting," Erfo added. Friedrich smiled with a twinge of irony, remembering the few times Frau Beck had made him go.

"What about the other half of the name? What did Holy Gottegnade do?"

"He was a follower of Holy Balder," Herr Pergen explained. "When Holy Balder was killed, he burned the body and carried on his work. Many consider him to be the first healer, or as we know them now, a leecher. He and a group of women healers turned to the south and west, establishing sickhouses for the poor and wounded and teaching proper healing. Though it is not written, the Band teaches that he was the first to allow girls to receive a name-bath as well."

"Is there a difference between a leecher and a healer?"

"Sort of," Herr Berstett explained, "they both heal the sick and wounded, but it's the way they do it that's different. A leecher uses bandages, salves, and poultices. They take bits of greenery and blossoms and buds and roots and turn them into something to rub on a wound. But a healer, they've got a rare, God-given gift. All they have to do is set their hands on someone, and they're good as new. Haven't heard of a healer being born in a while, but God knows if there was ever a time to send one, it's now."

Friedrich shifted uncomfortably. He didn't like the implication. He also didn't like being reminded of her.

One of the shieldbearers started passing around plates of food while another topped off everyone's drink. Friedrich ate his food quietly, oblivious to the conversations about past victories and wayfareages going on around him. He didn't feel like himself, sitting here, surrounded by knights and warriors. This wasn't who he was, what he wanted. He almost felt dirty, in need of a bath that got below his skin. With his meal finished, he excused himself, returning to his bedroll. He shifted his halberd to the other side of the tree, out of view, and laid down, staring up through the branches at the sky.

Friedrich had to wonder about Holy Balder. He was a good man, maybe even a Half-god since he lived so long ago and was made a heathen god in the north. He was doing good work, helping his fellow man, respecting all life. And yet, he died, betrayed and murdered by someone he thought a friend. If that could happen to a Holy, what hope was there for him? Doing good was the right thing, but at the cost of his life? What was the point then? Why do good if the deed is trampled by someone doing evil? He had to doubt Vater Sieghart. Would him doing good really matter in the grand scheme of things? What difference did li'l ol' Friedrich Bauer make in the world?

He took a deep breath, exhaling in a slow groan. What difference DID he make in the world? He was just another low-born toiler, one of tens of thousands of Bauers in life. He'd probably never account for anything. Even the knights with all their talk of chivalry and goodness, who would remember them? They'd lost or given up their lands. All they had was a rank and a name. In fifty years, one hundred, no one would know they even lived. They could do nothing but good all their lives, and it wouldn't make a difference. They weren't Holies. They weren't Wardens of the Church. They were bodyguards for poor wayfarers, a drop in the great sea of mankind.

Yet, like an unwanted swelling, doubt still stuck in his mind. Not a doubt, but perhaps . . . well . . . Friedrich did not know how to describe it. Even though he knew that in the end nothing he did really matters, as anyone could see, that was not cause to stop doing good. If he left the wayfareage then went out and robbed and plundered, drinking and whoring to his last days, it would not matter overall. But . . . he did not want to do that. It was wrong, and he knew it was wrong and cared that it was wrong.

Then, this was life he supposed, doing good, even though it did not matter in the end. It was odd, comforting in some way. There were tens of thousands of Bauers, and all, most likely, were doing good. Perhaps, alone they did not matter, but as a whole, they would make a difference. Maybe, there was an oriole to spot amongst all the crows.

"Friedrich?" He looked up; it was Herr Neveu. "I wanted to remind you of your oath." He looked at the distance between Friedrich and the other guard's sleeping arrangements. "It is worrisome you are out here so far."

Friedrich sat upright. "I haven't forgotten, mein Herr. I'm a man of my word, with you to Midgart unless released."

Herr Neveu nodded. "That's what I like to hear." He once more looked at how far away Friedrich was from the rest of the camp. "Though with that understood, I wonder why you stay so far from everyone else?"

"They were talking about the war, mein Herr. I . . . I do not like talking about war."

"Hmmm." He removed his hat, squatting down next to Friedrich. "Your age-shield, I do not recognize the colors. Where are you originally from?"

"Nemeten, it's a Markgrafschaft, underling of the Herzogtum of the Schwäbish."

"Mmmhmm. The Rinnemark if I remember right?"

"Yes, mein Herr. Right on the Rinne."

Herr Neveu didn't say anything further on the matter. "Well, since you are keeping with your oath, I do recommend you sleep closer to the rest of us. You are one of us in all but name. We do not want you to be an outsider."

"I understand, mein Herr, but . . ." Should he move closer? It would do him some good. Though, if he moved closer, he would hear more talk of war. Afterall, what are knights and halberdiers going to talk about? Can't talk about gambling or drinking or pretty ladies on a wayfareage. If he heard more talk about wars, he wasn't going to get any meaningful sleep. If he wanted to be a man of his word, he needed to be rested. That should be good enough for Herr Neveu. "I think I will stay out here. I'll sleep better."

Herr Neveu shrugged and stood up. "Very well. I cannot make you so long as you are true to your word. Though, I can say, lifelong friendships and bonds are made with brothers-in-arms."

Friedrich called out to Herr Neveu as he started to return to the other knights. "Herr Neveu, may I ask a question?" The knight turned back around. "If Holy Balder was doing the work of God, why was he killed?

Herr Neveu rubbed his chin. "That's the question our band has asked since our founding," he explained, clearing his throat. "Holy Balder was killed not because it was willed by God but because others made the choice to harm him. God granted to mankind the freedom to choose, granted to us wisdom to learn right from wrong. But He cannot make us choose. The Nordmänner chose to reject Holy Balder's words. More than likely, they were offended at his words. Men can make rash decisions in the heat of the trice. Anger, jealousy, fear, all of these can cause anyone to do something they would regret."

Friedrich bit his lip. "Why didn't God protect his worker?"

"The sunlight shines upon all greenery, but it cannot decide if the sapling grows or dies. God gave us the tools to make our own path and our decisions. Holy Balder knew where he was going and who he was teaching were dangerous but chose to do so anyway."

"But why?"

"To help those in need. One might disagree with why he went, but one cannot dispute his motives. Holy Balder did not simply bring the Nordmänner godly teachings but teachings on healing, on cleaning. This was carried on by Holy Gottegnade. They wanted to bring light to their fellow men, but they also brought with them real teachings to use every day as well." Friedrich laid back, staring back up into the stars. All of that sounded familiar. "Beseech for wisdom, Herr Bauer. God pours out more than I can offer."

Men can make rash decisions in the heat of the trice. Didn't that sound like someone Friedrich know? Didn't that sound like two someones Friedrich knew. He did beseech that night, just before going to bed. His first time doing so sincerely in many years. It was quick and short, to the point. He didn't ask for wisdom. He asked only for more opportunities. One way or another, he could make up for what he did. Maybe, if it was his orlay, he may even see her again.

• • •

Vytilia, Schwester Braun, and Bruder Wenzel took a break from their lesson for around half an hour. Bruder Wenzel took the time to procure small bread rolls for the three of them from a peddler outside the church, since it was time for a midday meal. The bread was sweet, so different from Strixan bread, Vytilia could hardly believe it was the same food. Bruder Wenzel wiped his mouth clean before leaning over his pew to look back at Vytilia and Schwester Braun. "Now then, where were we?"

Vytilia pointed to the window with the three figures fighting different monsters. "We were talking about those three holies and how they were the guides for your, er, our tribe."

"Ah yes, that's right." Bruder Wenzel scooted down to the end of the pew, so he was closer to the window. Vytilia and Schwester Braun followed his lead, though Vytilia kept her distance. The bread was delicious, but it was not a substitute for blood, and a full stomach seemed to only make her ears keener. "Those three Holies are . . ."

Vytilia only shook her head.

"Holies Donar, Wuotan, and Friia," Schwester Braun answered for Vytilia.

"Yes. Now, there were thousands upon thousands of Halfgods and thousands of Holies, but according to the Sagas, those three are the ones who taught our forefathers the most. But, we are getting ahead of ourselves. When the Lightless began their uprising, their goal was to wipe out mankind, not the Half-gods, but us," Vytilia stifled a snicker at the irony, "because mankind was chosen to be God's greatest making. We were to inherit stewardship over the world. We were the favorite child in a sense. And the Half-gods, being our kin and oath-bound to God Himself, fought to defend us. Among the seeds of life that grew during the Long Winter, mankind was among them."

That got Vytilia's attention. "Mankind grew during the Long Winter?" Bruder Wenzel nodded. "How come *ahem* we were not tainted by that darkness like the Lightless?"

"Oh, but we were, dear Frau. That is why mankind can be evil. It is why there are those who murder, those who steal, who do all manner of evil, wicked things. These men, and women, were not made to be evil. It is not foretold that they must do these things. But, they choose to do so. That inner darkness which is within all of us grows as much as we allow it. When we choose to do good, that darkness is weakened. When we choose to do evil, it flourishes. Being evil is a choice, one all of us must make every day."

Vytilia found that comforting. Even if it was meant for mankind, it could easily be transferred to Strixans as well. Though, it was a thin line she straddled. She may not be a monster, she had the capacity to be one. That was a choice she could make and one she had made once already. She retracted her fangs as far as they could go and continued listening.

"Now, while the Half-gods fought their war against the Lightless, our forefathers fled or hid in caves and thick groves of trees." He pointed now to the next window, which depicted an armored warrior fighting a mass of Lightless while a group of refugees crossed the horizon behind him. "Most of those who fled went eastward and spent many years there, even after the war ended. That is the agreed upon area where most of the Erebusen groups came from. They wandered westward many hundreds of years after God had returned. But, again, we are getting ahead of ourselves."

He pointed to the next window, the last one on the left they could see clearly from their pews. It showed Sol returning, filling the window with gold and bright white glass. Armored warriors gathered under Sol's guiding hand, chasing the disparate Lightless from the early window into a cold-blue colored crevice. "After an unknown amount of time, God returned to His world, and with His blinding light, struck the killing blow to the Lightless. The surviving Half-gods gained heart, and banding together with eagles, lions, and griffins, they rounded up and chased the Lightless until all of them were banished into the deepest, coldest pits of Helheim. There, they remain."

Now that was identical to the devils, Vytilia thought. Though, if what she suspected was true, and it increasingly looked like it was, there were many times when the devils razed the surface, only to retreat back deep into the planet. This mannish story could be any of those times or all of them combined into one account. She shuddered at the thought of the destruction the devils had wrought, multiplied by however many times it had been done before her people's.

"Bruder Wenzel," she asked, "are there any records or accounts of the Lightless before the Long Winter? Or after?"

"They are not written yet," the man explained. He turned around and pointed to the window closest to the door on the right wall. It depicted a war with figures in modern mannish armor, with muskets, with winged figures in swords and golden armor descending from a sun-filled heaven. They fought against monstrous, indescribable horrors. They were mixtures of serpents and canines and arachnids and every awful beast that haunted the darkness. "There will be a time when the Lightless shall return. It is a long time away, don't worry, but it is a time that shall come. As it is written, evil grows and flourishes every day, even if we do not see it. There will come a day when the waters will be bitter, the trees die, and the ground will rend with furious anger, and the Lightless will return. A mankind banded together is expected to give them battle long enough until the einherjar can come down and the Lightless finally destroyed, once and for all."

An eschatological story, Vytilia realized. That was something the Strixan religions did not have. The end of the world was a philosophical discussion topic, not a religious dogma. Then it became a reality.

"Who are the einherjar?" Vytilia asked. She had heard Friedrich use that word but could not remember the context.

"Oh, we keep skipping ahead, jumping like a frog! I do not need the window for this one. After the first defeat of the Lightless, and before their return, the surviving Half-gods began to teach the survivors of mankind. They taught our forefathers how to till the ground, how to brew, livestock husbandry, orecraft, healing, leadership, and warfare. Elder bands of skalds remembered their deeds, passing these teachings to us today." He grimaced. "Unfortunately, writing did not seem to be taught to many, and the teachings of the Half-gods became corrupted over time. Many were turned into heathen gods worshipped wrongly. It is a godsend we were able to spread the teachings of the one true sun god without too much bloodshed. That is for another time.

"For our teaching, when all was done, the surviving Half-gods were taken to the heavens to become Einherjar, holy warriors who will one day return when man needs them most. This begins our current age, the Age of Dawn. This is also where the moon begins. Since we now know Erde circles around the sun, we know part of it faces away from the sun for a time. So, God created the moon and placed an einherjar, Máni, to watch over man in the nighttime. And during the times Holy Máni is resting, we have fire."

"So, at the end of the world, these einherjar and the Lightless will return?"

Bruder Wenzel nodded. "This time is called the Götterdämmerung, 'The Twilight of the Gods.' It should be twilight of the half-gods, but that does not roll off the tongue quite as well."

"I know twilight is often spoken of in the nighttime, but the time before the sun rises is also twilight," Schwester quickly added. "I was scared too when I first heard it, but when the einherjar return, they will bring with them an age of forever sunlight. The final age, the Age of Summer."

"Very good Schwester," Bruder Wenzel told her.

Vytilia was not scared, or at least she did not think her face said she was. She was concerned. That was what Friedrich had been rambling about in the tunnels after the clearing. That was why he had been so terrified. If Strixans were the Half-gods, he would have ushered the end of his world, at least religiously, by establishing relations.

That would be a difficult problem, especially when relations between the two races were established. It was quite the theological dilemma. Strixans, at least from one view were, simultaneously, the Half-gods and were not. The diplomats would have to devise a way to explain how their return did *not* usher in this Götterdämmerung. And, as both unofficial diplomat and official vanguard of the Strixan race, it was up to her to learn as much as she could to aid future efforts.

"Bruder Wenzel," she asked. "What did the Half-gods look like? What was their culture, their art, their language? Specifically the ones who taught our tribes."

He gestured to the window of the three figures. "That is how they are often shown, but that was the decision of the windowmaker. It is better than the old one, I admit." He shrugged. "The sagas themselves say very little of what they looked like or how they dressed or what their tongue sounded like. There are few scant writings of the Half-gods themselves: long flowing hair, great beards, bones like iron, skin as tough as flint. Aside from that, all we have are their deeds, a smattering of gifts and birthrights, and what they taught us to remember them. Even then, all of that has degraded over the years. I think the saddest is that we have lost that pure, original, Half-god tongue, Ur-Mannaz. Not even High Rinnish comes close." He sighed, shaking his head. Vytilia could relate.

"Although, if you ask the Gauls, Catask, or Vitelish, they are rather boastful that their tongues are closer to the true Half-god tongue than Teutonish," Schwester Braun whispered to Vytilia.

Bruder Wenzel heard that. "Bah, that is jealous talk. Given time, I can prove the Gaulish tongue is bastardized old Rinnish, Catask is bastardized Gothish, and Vitelish is bastardized Elláser."

Vytilia made a mental note to investigate those languages later when given the opportunity. "You mentioned Teutonish is descended from the Half-god's language. Does that include the title of Kommandant?" Vytilia asked. Asking that almost felt like a lie. Aside from a few words, the mannish language had nothing in common with Strixic.

Bruder Wenzel nodded. "Indeed. As it is written, in times of strife, your Gothi must make a great King, a King of Kings to unite the lands and defend the church. He must be a warrior, a fair lawmaker, and a godly man and seek to spread the guidance and teachings of the church. He shall be granted a new rank, taken from the old tongue: Kommandant. That was among the last teachings written by Holy Budô himself. In the same book, it also recommends an Hochkanzler to aid in leading the Realm."

"Hochkanzler?"

"Oh . . . what is the worldman's term for it? High Chancellor! Now, there are many chancellors in many lands but only one High Chancellor."

Vytilia swallowed. Chancellor was another Strixan-derived word. The position was extinct now, but in the heyday of the empire, it was a respected, albeit minor, position in the judiciary. They were originally ushers, but she could understand how that would evolve into a governmental advisor. "And, the Half-god had these positions?"

"We assume so. The tale behind the rank was lost to time, but the meaning of it remains. Many say Wuotan was the first true Kommandant during the Age of Dawn, but again, this is all wondering. As far as lore is concerned, the first Kommandant was Karalthergroz. It was he who was helmed by Gothi Leonhardt the Fourth in Midgart on Yule. It is he who all following Kommandants must look up to for inspiration. It is he who started the Realm we live in today. And it is he who saved our forefathers and our lands from a ravaging by our foes."

Vytilia slumped down in her pew. She felt so helpless and lost! She did not know whether to be frustrated, angry, or relieved. She was frustrated at the lack of clarity and written documentation, angry that of all the great Strixan ideas and legacies, all that survived was a few words, but relieved the Half-gods were so unlike her people, it would make diplomacy easier. Why was it all so difficult! Why was there not one definite story showing the transition from Strixan civilization to mannish!

Schwester Braun noticed Vytilia being so downtrodden and wrapped her arm around her. "Is everything alright, friend Meyer?"

Vytilia felt like screaming but only nodded. Coming to the surface was starting to feel like a mistake. She could not see any way that relations between the two peoples could ever happen without completely disrupting and destroying the society of the surface. Despite her best efforts, it seemed like Strixans were fated to always be conquerors, even if unintentionally.

Bruder Wenzel leaned in towards the two of them, sensing Vytilia's distress. "If you did not learn what you wanted today, if you really want to get a sense of what the Half-gods were like, you can always see Midgart. The Wayfaring Knights are always escorting wayfarers there since it is through the heart of Urworkish land."

"Midgart? What would I find there?"

"Wisdom, mainly. The Holy-Stead is the source of wisdom and enlightenment. For your case, you may be aided by the Half-god birthrights on display and what is left of the buildings they built."

"There are Half-god cities, still extant?"

"According to church lore. There are a handful scattered across Erebus and the lands of the Sultanate. They are not proper towns anymore, mind you, only a handful of oldbuilds. But with seeking to a Holy or a beseeching to God, you may receive an understanding of what they were like."

"An ancient city?" This did pique Vytilia's curiosity. There was the possibility that Midgart could be the ruins of a Strixan city, but there was the slim possibility that it could not be. If the latter were the case, it would dispel her worries about future diplomacy. If the former were true . . . well, then, she or the diplomats might find a way to explain it without destroying surface society.

She glanced back at the final window on the right. Either way, if the Strixans were or were not the Half-gods, the devils were still a threat. Of all the possibilities, the only certainty was that they were the Lightless. If history repeated itself as Vytilia theorized, and as the mannish religion taught, the devils may return to destroy the surface, just as they had the Strixans and the nymphs before. Causing a theological disagreement was preferable to another civilization being destroyed.

"Where is Midgart?" she asked.

"To the northwest, at least a fortnight's travel away by foot," Bruder Wenzel answered. "Though, it bears repeating that the Wayfaring Knights escort wayfarers headed there. The route is through the birthplace of the Great Work and is not friendly to good Erdeish like ourselves."

"And where can I find these wayfaring knights?"

"They run a sickhouse in the northern part of Mondsruhe." Bruder Wenzel suppressed a yawn. "I do think it is time for a larger midday meal. Was there anything else you wanted to ask about, Frau Meyer. or would I be well to take my leave?"

"I have one question," Vytilia told him. "You said that the Half-gods had become corrupted and deified. Why then did the worship of the sun god spread? What makes Him better than all the rest?" She wanted to see if it was Sol the men worshipped or if it was possibly another solar deity with Sol's iconography.

"Because God is above even the great power of orlay."

"Or-, I am sorry, what do you mean by that?"

Both Bruder Wenzel and Schwester Braun looked as if they'd seen a ghost. They exchanged a glance. "Frau Meyer, how do you not know about orlay? It is as great a teaching as the Douths of Man!"

"I do not know what these 'Douths' are either." Vytilia's face burned purple.

"It is a good thing you came to the High Learnhouse then," Bruder Wenzel remarked. "It is better to go without clothes than without learning this!" He shook his head. "I have half a mind to find your halldom priest and slap some sense into them with a heavy copy of the sagas!"

"Bruder, do recall where we are." Schwester Braun smiled.

"Yes, yes you're right. I am sorry, Frau Meyer. I have never heard such a thing before." He cleared his throat again. "Orlay is . . . well, it is what you will do, what you will fulfill. It is your wyrd, as the Merkya say, your doom before that became a scary thing to say, your lot in life."

"Do you mean destiny?"

"Yes, that, if I recall, that is the Vitelish word for it, yes. Exactly." Another reminder to investigate this other tribe. "Now, everyone has one from Holy Wuotan himself to each ploughman and milkmaid who has ever lived. Now, not everyone has the same one. Some are orlayed to do great things in life, such as be helmed Kommandant or find the new world or invent the printing press. But most of us, our orlay is to be good and go about our lives. God has taught us how to live, how to treat our fellow men, how to live and work happily and safely, and our orlay is to use these teachings, and to pass them on. But, God is above all that. He is not tied or foretold to do anything. He is free, but He chooses to use that freedom to make and guide and watch over us. The Half-gods, they were orlayed to fight and be stewards, and when they were falsely made heathen gods, they were orlayed to die. But, the true god was not held to whims of orlay or doom. His life was his, and he chose to use it for us."

That was not entirely unlike Sol, Vytilia thought, *or Luna, for that matter.* She recalled what her mother had said about the Striga, how they saw the gods as beings to fear, who were as susceptible to vice as anyone. The Strigan version of the gods were morality lessons. The Strixan gods were a counterweight, a power greater than the empire as a reminder that Strixans, while long lived, could still die. Luna and Sol could not.

"And these Douths?"

"The Douths of Man, or Ethics, however you describe it, are the components of being a good man or woman. There are nine: Godliness, Wisdom, Mildheartedness, Trustworthiness, Strength, Worksomeness, Fellowship, Love, and Goodness. I can offer teachings on each one of these but," Bruder Wenzel stifled another yawn, "that will be for another day and with a writ and payment of course."

And those were not entirely unlike the virtues, Vytilia pondered. Though, Strixan virtues were never so organized and presented this way. Her frustration returned. There was so much of the mannish civilization that she could say was a Strixan influence! And, so much that could be a coincidence or influenced by something or someone else. It all could be common ground to help with diplomacy or a load-bearing falsity that could break apart at any moment. She needed to know more. She would go to this Midgart city and see for herself.

"Do you have anything else you wish to ask, Frau Meyer?" Bruder Wenzel asked.

"I do not, Herr Bruder. You have been more than helpful. I found this all very enlightening."

"I am glad you did. I shall take my leave and see if I can find somewhere that has started serving the evening meal. Go with God, both of you." The man slid out of the pew and exited the church.

"I told you that was a treat! I love learning about the lore of the church! I always feel so close to the heavens when I do so!" Schwester Braun quietly squealed.

Vytilia wished she could have felt as excited. Instead, all she felt was disappointment. She stood and began to shuffle towards the end of the pew, but she paused and stared up at the window with the three holies on it. "Frau Schwester," she asked, "Bruder Wenzel mentioned that there was an old version of this window. Why was it replaced?"

"Oh, the old one had Ermingandz on it," she answered as she stepped out. "After that nasty business with Ludher, the Hochaufseher of Mondsruhe had it replaced."

"Tensions with the other religious groups are so terrible, they replaced this artwork?"

"Things have gotten better now, but the Urworkish still hate us, even though they have their own lands and can worship how they want. It is why there are escorts for wayfarers, even when there isn't a war."

They both headed towards the doors of the Church. Vytilia stepped out first, shielding her eyes from the sun as she did so. It was past midday as best as she could tell, probably closer to evening. They had been in this church for longer than she expected.

"Where will you go next?" Schwester Braun asked. "If you are hungry, the sisters have a eating hall in the back of the school. You can eat with us, and we can tell you all about life under the habit!"

"A generous offer, but I must get going. I wish to see Midgart before I leave, and I assume I have much ground to cover?"

"It is far to the northwest, but you cannot travel alone! Think of the danger! I really must recommend you find a wayfareage." They exited the High Learnhouse and stood on the steps. She pointed north. "If you continue on this road, you will find a sickhouse run by the Wayfaring Knights. They are always escorting wayfarers."

"Sickhouse? I am unfamiliar with that term."

"Don't let the name scare you; it is for everyone: travelers, the poor, the weary, and the hurt. The knights and brothers there are very kind and will be respectful. They are the safest group to travel with to Midgart. Look for the black banners with the white sun. It is difficult to miss."

"I shall look into it." It would be best to travel with a group. Were she accosted on the road again, all she needed was an excuse. "You have my gratitude Schwester—" The woman threw her arms around Vytilia. She gasped, sucking her teeth. Her mouth was so close to the girl's neck.

"Thank you for coming. I hope you learned something you needed." She let go, smiling. "Go with God my dear sister. I hope we shall meet again."

Vytilia swallowed, ignoring the heart beating in her ears. "Perhaps one day." She pulled away, her breath shaky, and hurried up the road. She had learned much. And she hoped in Midgart, she would learn more. She sucked her teeth, drowning out the heartbeats. *If* she made it there.

The further north Vytilia went from the High Learnhouse, the less impressive Mondsruhe was, at least for the alleyways and side streets she passed. The main avenue remained immaculate. Aside from the main streets, once she was beyond the wealth and affluence of the city center, the area was . . . plain. Gone were the men of renown in fine clothes and landscaped public spaces. In their place were plain-clothed laborers in whitewashed houses. Houses would be missing an occasional roof tile, or a shutter would slightly be off its hinge. The main thoroughfares would be clean, but alleys and side streets would have a noticeable amount of refuse and detritus in the gutters. Advertisements, peddlers, and beggars were all much more prevalent here than in the other areas of the city.

As the sky changed to a deep orange, and blue and purple began to creep up on the horizon, she found the building Schwester Braun had recommended. She stood on the other side of the street, studying the building. It was a rather unremarkable structure, three floors tall, painted a drab grey color, with large black banners emblazoned with a white sun in the center hanging on either side of the entrance. The windows were open, and she could hear coughing coming from them, along with an occasional groan or even a scream. What had the nun called it? A sickhouse?

Strixans did not have an equivalent, at least for civilians. On campaign, legions would establish a field hospital to tend for the wounded, but civilians did not have a need for such a thing. Medicine was the care of the state; when a Strixan laborer or athlete was injured, a physician would be sent to their location to heal and assess, accompanied by novices to act as nurses. The only medicinal building in a Strixan city was a veterinarian to care for family pets and a city's herds. Everything from birth to death was taken care of inside the home. Still, the concept of a *civilian* hospital was too intriguing. Her curiosity and need propelled her across the street, up towards the entrance of the sickhouse, where a man in a black robe was greeting people.

"Ah, *Guten abend, gnädige frau*, how may my brothers and I be of help to you tonight?" the man welcomed her.

She took pause, looking past the doorman inside. The ground floor was a large single room with rows of simple wooden beds where men in various states lay. Some were covered in bandages, others sleeping. Her eyes widened when she saw blood carried away in basins by black-robed attendants. She swallowed. "I . . . I . . . do you have rooms to sleep?"

"We do, always for the tired and weary. Bruder Cniva inside can show you to the women's ward."

She stopped dead. The faint smell of blood, so pungent that even she could detect it, started to waft towards her. "Are there any accommodations outside?"

"No, spare rooms are down in the dolery. Unless you need to see a leecher?"

"I do not. I . . . I cannot stand the sight of blood."

"The dolery is far from the sick wards. I can lead you down there. You'll never see any blood."

"I cannot! I . . . I cannot stay here!" She turned her back, shuddering while trying to keep her mouth closed.

"Are you well, gnädige frau? Do you need any help?"

"I cannot stay here," Vytilia told him without turning around. "I will need to find other accommodations." She swallowed, stepping away from the building. "Do you know where the nearest pilgrimage to Midgart is?"

"Do you mean wayfareage? There is one leaving the day after tomorrow in Ingmarsburg, to the north. But surely, we can do something. We don't want to turn anyone away. We cannot let you wander around the town this late by yourself!"

"I will be fine, Herr Bruder. I appreciate the offer, but I need to get going." She shut her eyes, hurrying back across the street and continuing north, her upper body shaking and her jaw twitching as she walked. One more moment near that place, and she would have lost her self-control. Had she really made any difference since biting the highwayman? Had all that time in those caves been for naught? She smelled blood! Smelled it! Only the most starved Strixans could smell fresh blood! How many would she have killed if she had stayed? How many innocents would she have taken?

Oh gods! she bemoaned, stopping to lean against a wall. She really was a monster, a beast driven only by her thirst of a taskmaster. She pulled herself against the wall and shook her head. *I am not a slave,* she reminded herself. *I am free!* She had the wherewithal to pull herself away from that house of bloodletting. She had the discipline to not drain Frau Meyer. She could do this! She was stronger than her base desire. She was stronger than the Scarlet Empress.

So, she pressed on to the north gate, exiting the city just as the entrance was sealed and curfew started. She followed the road headed northward. As the city became a bump on the horizon behind her, she walked off the trail and followed along through the woods and fields. She reasoned that if she was not spotted on a trail, she would not be accosted.

With her body walking almost automatically and her mind clear and away from the butchery of the hospital, she started to ask herself questions. If the pilgrimages were run by the same organization that ran those civic hospitals, would they not stay in hospitals during the journey? And unless she wanted to draw attention to herself, she would need to stay in the same place as the rest of the pilgrims. This meant more hospitals and more blood. She could always hold her breath, shut her eyes and go to sleep, but what if that was not enough? Just the thought could set her off if she immersed herself, surrounded herself with the sight and smell and living beating hearts. It would turn into a bloodbath.

She was vacillating, arguing if she should go or not. She could not return to Nidus, not without weapons and not without controlling herself. She owed it to the legionaries who died. She owed it to all those poor and unfortunate souls living bleak and meaningless lives in Nidus. She needed to do everything she could to aid her people, through both material and immaterial means. Then, she would go to Nidus.

With the sky turning a dark blue and the stars beginning to twinkle, she decided to rest and get a fill of blood. A Strixan cannot live on bread alone. She strayed a bit deeper into the woods, far from the path, and came across a pair of red-colored wild canines. They did not notice her, and she was able to pounce on the two of them, draining them both dry. Though it was filling, it was not satisfying. Every bit of blood she had had since the "unfortunate incident" did not taste, well, like anything. It was bland like water. She shuddered at the thought that nothing would ever taste as good again.

Still, she pressed on. It was dark enough that anyone but herself would be asleep, so she returned to the main road. She reminded herself that this was a momentary lapse, a depressive mood that she would emerge out of stronger and better because of it. When she returned to Nidus, triumphant and victorious, the Scarlet Empress would be nothing more than blurred and faded memory.

And, she hoped that before that triumphal return, she would encounter Friedrich again. Her pace slackened as she felt tears begin to fall. She missed him. There were a thousand reasons why she missed him, and each one hurt her to her very soul. She missed walking with him. She missed eating with him, listening to one another explain their world. She missed his folksy wisdom, his humor, even his flashes of brilliance. And . . . there were higher emotions involved, though the thought bittered her. But even that was a reason to see him again! When he saw her next, she was not going to be the exact same Vytilia. She was going to be someone changed, someone he and all of his kind could trust. She wanted to show herself and him that she was master over herself, master of the Scarlet Empress, and that she was not a monster.

She had to find him again.

For hours, she hiked north, passing by endless fields of soft, blossoming grain and quiet cottages and villages. A few noctuae would fly down and walk with her, offering her vermin to drink. Though she cringed internally, she was grateful. Any kind of blood kept the thirst at bay. She asked the noctuae to stay with her during the pilgrimage. They were her connection to Luna and would keep her and many others alive.

In a long stretch of forest, miles from any settlement, she realized she was not alone. She paused and took stock of the situation. Walking along the road made a considerable amount of noise, but none that would give her away as being a person rather than an animal. Yet still, she was being followed. It was ironic that she, a creature of the night, master of the twilight watch, was the one being stalked in the darkness. Ordinarily, this would not be a concern, but she was neither in the mood nor mindset for a confrontation. Once again, all she needed was an excuse, and the Scarlet Empress would take control. She went further into the woods, careful to avoid stepping on anything loud, politely shooing away the noctuae. She ducked behind a thick cluster of bushes, holding her breath, listening as a heartbeat jumped around, looking for her. It was a man's heartbeat, some vagabond or another highwayman. The man paused, only a few steps away from her, standing where she had stood on the road. He was poorly dressed, as she expected, but held a well-used blade in one hand.

"I know someone's there," the man announced. "I know you probably got a lovely bit of silver, maybe even some gold. Hand it over, and I won't hurt ya." He reached down onto the ground, grabbing a handful of dirt before throwing it into the bushes, barely missing her.

"I don't like gettin' my hands dirty. Every rock I throw is another nick I'll have to give ya." He grabbed another handful and threw it, missing her again but only barely.

Vytilia had to plan. She had the advantage in the darkness, but she needed to be careful. One fortunate throw and she could be blinded, and the man could close the distance. And if threatened, she was without doubt that would give her basic, scarlet self the justification to take over.

She recalled Friedrich had made mention of a number of creatures in his local mythology. Some, she assumed, could mimic speech. Surely hearing a voice in the middle of the night would make any brigand think twice. Perhaps if she put on an act, she could frighten this man away. It was better than lunging out and tearing his throat open anyway.

"Stop that throwing." She put on her deepest voice. "You are upsetting nature. You are upsetting me. You do not want to see me angry. You better leave if you know what is good for you."

The man dropped the handful of dirt he was holding. "You think you're tough? Trying to scare me off?"

Damn it, she cursed. Friedrich's superstitious nature must be an exception.

"You better leave," she warned, deepening her voice, and adding menace. "You will only find pain unless you leave."

"Bet you got some nice gold and silver on ya, and you want to keep it for yourself." He started towards the bushes.

"Godsdamn it," Vytilia swore. Though, the element of surprise was still on her side. The man approached the bush, raising the blade to hack the plant away. His neck bulged as he did so. She salivated at the thought, imagining the warm, gushing feeling of a freshly-cut artery. She let out a bestial growl and lunged forward, her vision clouded red.

She only had a second, a fraction of one, to regain control. She forced her jaw shut, but she was still on a collision course with this man. She brought her arms up, one grabbing the man around the throat, thereby protecting it, and the other grabbing his arm with the blade. She broke several of his carpal bones as they collided. They both fell backwards, but she quickly rose to her feet after landing. He laid on the forest floor, swearing and crying as he clutched his broken hand.

She stared down at him, wondering what to do. His neck was exposed again, and by Strixan tradition, she had bested him in combat. Her jaw twitched and mouth salivated at the thought. She closed her eyes to stop her vision from going red. She had every right, every justification to kill this man. He had planned to rob her, and she did not doubt that, given the chance, he would have attempted to assault her as well. But there would be larger ramifications if she killed him. She would set back all the work on conquering herself. She would give the Scarlet Empress a victory. She would be delaying her going on the pilgrimage, delaying finding Friedrich again and returning to her people. If she saw him again, how would she justify more death by her hand? While he might agree this man should die for his crime, it was the fact SHE was killing him. She had to show she valued the laws and customs of mankind. There would be proper channels, legal courses for this man to meet his end.

Then, she would let the mannish authorities deal with this vagabond. But, she had to make sure they found him first. She opened her eyes and walked over to his leg. With an echoing snap, she broke his left tibia. The man screamed and howled even louder. She grabbed him by the collar and dragged him towards the road. The mannish authorities did not necessarily have to find him in perfect condition.

"What do you want from me!?" he pleaded.

"I want you to die. I want to kill you. But I cannot." She threw him onto the side of the road, kicking him in the ribs. "I cannot allow myself to take your life as much as I want to." Her fangs tried to extend. Her body tried to leap onto him and bite, but she fought back.

"Just let me go! I won't tell anyone! I'm sorry!"

She grabbed his ear and rubbed his face into the gravelly road. "You listen to me, and you listen well, you mewling cinaedus. You are among the most reprehensible scum on the planet! Were it up to me, you would be crucified and your entrails fed to porcine! But I have a larger purpose than killing you. I want you to tell the next traveler the extent of your crimes! I want the full brutality of man's justice on your despicable head! Do you hear me!"

"Yes! Yes! Oh god everything hurts!"

"Good, I want you in pain! I want you to suffer!" She smashed his head against the gravel. "You tell the courts, tell the juries everything you have done! But do not speak a word of me, or I will come back and make you wish you died as a child. I will make you regret every day of your life! Do you understand!?" She smashed his head again.

"Yes! I'll tell the truth! God! Oh! Kill me now!"

She gave his head one last smash before placing her hand on his forehead, putting him to sleep. She looked down. He was in rough shape but did not have any life-threatening injuries. She believed he would survive long enough for his own kind to bring him to trial. She growled again, biting her lip. She wanted to kill him, to take his ichor and put it towards something useful. She started to run north, running until she could not hear his heartbeat any longer. She was different. She could not kill. She *would* not kill. "For Friedrich," she reminded herself. "For my friend and for our peoples."

Appendix

I. The Worldbook, Scroll One

II. Strixan Ethnicities and Biology

III. Strixan Pantheon

I.

The Worldbook

Das Weltbuch

Scroll 1

Age

An age is an undetermined amount of time that makes up the story of mankind. According to Erdeish and Urworkish churches, there have been three ages: the Age of Dusk, when the world was created; the Age of Eventide, when God had to rest, darkness enveloped the world, and both mankind and the lightless appeared; and the Age of Dawn, the current age, where mankind is to grow and expand. In Pananthropotes teachings, these are called Epochs, and there are four. Their current epoch is the Epoch of Noon, which began after the Half-gods were recalled into heaven.

Age-Shield

Also called an Altersschild in High Rinnish, the Age-shield is a distinguishing mark of a Teudish man. It is worn by all the Teudish groups with variations. It is earned at the age of 15 alongside a simple weapon by able-bodied men who have been scarred, usually on the arm or chest, to show they are willing to fight and defend their home. It is small, made of oak, ash, or elm wood, and no larger than a hand. Many are round, but certain families and sippes will have hexagonal or ovaloid Age-Shields. A father, godfather, grandfather, or uncle will make and paint the shield before giving it to the youth. Most wear it as a belt buckle around the waist, though it is becoming popular to wear it as a pin on the chest.

In most churches, priests are forbidden from wearing Age-shields or other distinguishing marks, as priests and churches are supposed to serve all mankind, not a particular stem or group.

Women do not wear age-shields, though when they are married, they will wear their house keys in the same position as their husbands. In northern regions, they also wear a comb made by their husbands. Alongside the wedding ring, which has become nearly universal, in some areas of the HRM, married women also wear bands of iron, silver, or gold around their arms.

Examples of different Age-shield traditions:

HRM: Teudish in the Holy Realm of Midgart (excluding Helvensland), along with Ostlücke and Teutonish-speaking wendish lands, will paint their shield the simplified colors and style of the flag of the land they hail from. This allows those from the same land, or lands of the same church, to find one another easily in a new area.

Helvensland: Teudish here will always have a grey diamond in the center and a ring of white along the edges with their home colors painted in the center.

Zvearrik: Teudish here paint theirs yellow and white, the national colors.

Jutrig: Teudish here will have half of theirs painted green and white, their national colors, with the other half being the flag of their home area.

Betauven: Teudish here will paint the center the colors of their home area but leave a large blue circle on the outside, blue being both the national and royal color.

Merkya: Despite being Teudish, they do not traditionally wear Age-shields. Though following the overthrow of the monarchy, many have begun to wear one painted in the colors of the national flag.

Askard

Any lizard or lizard-like animal, not including adders, serpents, or dragons.

Backsliding

Backsliding is a euphemism for anytime in history, especially church history, where either mankind fell back into heathen ways, or the church became unforgivingly corrupt. Periods of backsliding are often the catalyst for great change including the helming of Karalthergroz, the Yarruser wars, and the rise of Ziurin Ludher.

Beerhall

The general term for any establishment that serves alcohol. They can often have rooms for rent but not always. Other terms include alehouse, biergarten, drinkhouse, or tavern.

Beseech

The act of speaking with and to God, similar to a prayer. Despite claims by the Urworkish, Erdeish and Pananthropotes do not beseech Holies. One seeks to a holy (or an ancestor), asking them for a specific bit of wisdom. Beseechings are for God and God alone and can be about anything.

A proper beseeching, under Erdeish and most Urworkish teachings, includes a list of deeds one has done recently and what makes one worthy of the wisdom being sought. In a sense, a beseeching is bargaining where the beseecher offers good deeds in exchange for wisdom and help.

Birthright

While amongst the laity the meaning is the same, in academic and ecclesiastic circles, Birthrights are artifacts left behind by the Half-gods. Birthrights are held in a Halidom, which serves as reliquary or a museum, depending on ownership.

Chip

Coins and coinage. They are carried in a chippurse. Non-circular money is also referred to as chips.

Across Erebus and most of the known world, silver and silver alloys are the primary metal used in currency. Most of the population will rarely own, or even hold, a gold coin. In the continent of Carusea, Catask traders have noted that natives trade with artifacts made with "fool's silver" or "white silver" in lieu of coined currency. Specific denominations of currency will be discussed later.

Churchmeet

Churchmeets are gatherings of priests and other churchmen to decide upon church law, teachings, and other important topics. Analogous to a synod. Not to be confused with the Hallmeet, which are ordinary church services held on Sonntag and Holidays.

Craft

A craft is any profession that requires skilled or artisanal labor. Though some professions, such as blacksmithing and bookkeeping would be considered a craft, they are rarely suffixed as one. Those with a craft are often called craftsmen or wrights. Unskilled labor is usually regarded as being merely "work" and can be used derogatorily.

Examples of crafts include:

Stonecraft; masonry
Woodcraft; carpentry
Snippercraft; tailoring
Haircraft; barbering
Healcraft: medicine
Buildingcraft; architecture
Draughtcraft; painting/art
Lawcraft; lawyering
Singcraft; music
Wheelcraft; wagon-making/repair
Learncraft/Delvecraft; teaching
Stemcraft; diplomacy

Crumb Churches

Since the first great churchmeet of 1 HJ, the standard metaphor for organized Sun-worship has been to compare the church to a loaf of bread. Following this metaphor, those that break away from the original church are known as "crumb churches."

Crumb churches was originally used derogatorily, starting first with the North-South schism between the Erdeish and Pananthropotes in 555 HJ and continued to be used with Yarruser and Urworkish churches starting in the early 1400s. With the spread of Urworkish churches, many began to use Crumb Church as a badge of honor. In Bythony especially, where the main church is itself a crumb church, those that break with that crumb church refer to themselves as crust churches. Bythony has the largest amount of both crumb and crust churches, while on the mainland, most crumb churches have been consolidated and banded together following the Hundred Years' Sorrow and the Great War. This is a source of pride for many on the islands.

Deathmeet

When someone has died, loved ones and family will gather to remember who has passed and either burn or bury them. Burning on a deadheap is more common amongst the lower classes, except for Catasks and those in the Bythony Islands. Entombment or burial is more common in those regions and among the upper classes across Erebus. For Gauls and Greenmen, they either burn, entomb, or throw their dead into bogs and swamps. Though, the latter is usually reserved for holy men and priests. In Teudish territories, criminals are buried in bogs.

Delve

To delve is the act of studying, researching, or compiling information, either religious or educational. A delver is a general term for a scholar. Delver as a suffix (-delver) is to denote one's expertise in a particular field. For example, a Stardelver is an astronomer, and a Greendelver is a botanist.

Douth

The most important teaching of Sun-worship with the core 9 Douths being shared among all sects and groups. Pananthropotes refer to these as Ethics and have an additional 3.

The Nine Core Douths are as follows:

Godliness: Also called piety, this is the most important Douth and the most minimum one that should be followed. Godliness is defined as the belief, acceptance, and willingness to follow God.

Wisdom: In writings, wisdom is often a Douth that cannot be perfectly achieved, but one that should always be sought after. It is second to godliness in importance and understood to be the ability to learn and gain knowledge then apply that to the difficulties and struggles of life. Wisdom is used in function with all other Douths to make a better man.

Mildheartedness: Also called mercy, this is defined as the ability to forgive, to spare the innocent, and to show compassion.

Trustworthiness: Also called loyalty, this is required of all those who make vows or swear fealty. This is defined as the ability to be reliable and fulfill oaths. This is also sometimes described as integrity, the ability to keep one's word and maintain honor.

Strength: This is defined as the ability to continue on through difficult times, the defining trait of those who survived the Long Winter. It is also described as bravery and the ability to be courageous. This is the ideal Douth to be had by all warriors.

Worksomeness: Also known as diligence, defined as the ability to work vigorously and with great effort in all that is undertaken. Worksomeness has a central place in Ludher-derived Urworkish teachings, as it is believed that hard-working people could make up for all other shortcomings. Men work best when they work together.

Love: Defined as familiar love between parents and children, spouses, and extended family. Love is the most defining trait of mankind as a race with marriage being a unique and God-guided institution. The singular mannish family is the bedrock of the entirety of society.

Fellowship: This is mostly love for non-familiar relationships. It is sometimes translated as kinship. It is defined as the ability to recognize and help fellow man, regardless of if they are related or not. It is often appealed to during peace negotiations and to halt slavery and other atrocities.

Goodness: Similar to wisdom, goodness is a Douth that cannot be perfectly achieved but should always be strived for. Goodness is simply the act of doing and being good; one should assist those in need, tell the truth, stop evil, and constantly strive to improve the world.

The additional Douths of the Pananthropotes are:

Restraint: In all matters, be it food, lust, sleep, or battle.

Obedience: Closely related to Godliness, it is not only obedience to divine and church law, but also obedience to secular law and family hierarchy.

Sacrifice: Unique to the Pananthropotes is their practice of Dodekatos, a form of tithing where 1/12th of a revenue is given to the Church. This is based on their Douth of Sacrifice, which celebrates giving up oneself or one's property to a greater cause, be it building a church or fighting for a nation.

In certain Urworkish circles, they also believe in a 10th Douth, that of Meekness, sometimes referred to as humility. The belief behind it is that to truly live the other 9 Douths, and to live a good life, one must ultimately recognize that they are nothing without God, his laws, and his teachings. With the teaching of Meekness also comes an aversion to decadent or extravagant clothing, food, or other habits and tastes.

Earthtile

The term used synonymously for continents in lands north of the Weiße Hügel. It is also called a Greatland. According to mapmakers and delvers, the world of Erde has eight continents: Erebus, Estuwwa, Ifrin, Rhapzaj, Terkundam, Hirawhenua, Vinland, and Carusea. Arguments are made to include the island of Ofir. Others argue that Erebus, Ifrin, and Estuwwa should all be considered one continent as should Vinland and Carusea.

Einherjar

At the beginning of the Age of Dawn, after the surviving Half-gods had taught mankind what they needed to know, all of them were raised to Walhalla and became Einherjar: immortal, godly warriors who would return in man's darkest hour.

Ermingandz

In the Erdeish version of the Sagas and further teachings, Ermingandz is a great dragon or adder who became the first Lightless. Jealous of God's favoritism of mankind, it fouled other creations of God to rebel during the Long Winter. At the end of the Long Winter, he is slain by Holy Donar and Holy Sunna and is never mentioned again. In certain Urworkish branches, mainly those based off Ziurin Ludher's work, Ermingandz is the King of the Lightless and is still alive, plotting and planning while frozen in Helheim. By Urworkish understanding, Ermingandz is responsible for fouling the hearts and minds of mankind to rebel against God. In Pananthropotes teachings, no such figure exists, though an analogous figure may be found in the Archdemon Khaos.

Fellow

Term for one who follows and learns from a master craftsman or wright, similar to an apprentice. To begin learning a trade is called "being fellowed."

Fimbulstormr

The Fimbulstormr, or the Forever Storm, is a massive and violent cyclonic storm that covers the entirety of Erde's north pole, reaching down to the equivalent of the arctic circle. Because of this, no land exists at the boundary of the storm, and it is assumed that none is inside. Entering the storm is impossible, and even the most experienced sailors with the most modern of ships are dashed to pieces by the waves and winds. Those living near the storm speak of great monsters residing in the waters and the clouds. Many assume that within the Fimbulstormr lies hell itself. Interestingly, it is known that something is at the center of the storm, as compasses always point to it as a fixed northern point. And many make trips to the edge of the storm to see the fabled ribbon lights. According to explorers and sailors, no such equivalent storm can be found at the south pole.

Gaulish Blight

A horrific, debilitating, syphilitic venereal disease. Symptoms include white pustule sores, complete mental degradation, and necrosis in the extremities. Other names include the Vitelish

Sickness, the Whore's Rot, White Death, and Greatpox. Amongst leechers, it is called "White Gangrene." Interestingly, there is no record found of the sickness being in Erebus until after Hermógenes Casal's conquest of Texihauco. In the new world, it is only found in Erebusen settlements or among those exiled by the wild folk. No known cure or remedy exists.

Great War, The

The Great War of 1616-1650 HJ was the most devasting conflict to be wrought upon the continent of Erebus since the Long Winter. It was not one singular war, but many wars congregating together into a horrific conflagration that devastated the Holy Realm of Midgart. The origin of the war can be traced to the Hundred Year's Sorrows (see below) and is regarded by most historians as being the culmination of those sorrows. It was a rather fitting, if violent and gruesome ending.

The war saw violence on a previously unknown scale, especially against civilians. Most armies were composed of mercenaries, and as those who hired them were always strapped for cash, looting and pillaging was a common substitute for regular pay. Eventually, the raiding became almost self-sustaining as armies of mercenaries would desert and essentially become rogue states of bandits ravaging the countryside. These could only be put down by other mercenaries, which would start the cycle again.

Amidst all of the fighting, there were various minor conflicts throughout the Realm and the rest of the continent. These were ethnic, sectarian, or even neighborly quarrels where rival towns, cities, and lords fought each other separate from the greater conflicts going on at the time.

Along with the violence, sickness, famine, and the coldest of winters repeatedly hit Erebus. The death toll is ultimately known only to God.

The war can be broken down into five stages:

Stage One, The Second Wagon Uprising:

At the end of the Yarruser Wars, the Yarrusers, an early break away from the Erdeish Church composed entirely of wendish Želeks, had been given significant religious freedom and were subject to different laws than Urworkish. In 1604, following the death of their previous, heirless king, the brother of Kommandant Friedrich Rabenburg, Graf Ferdinand Rabenburg, was appointed King of Želevlast. Ferdinand, a devout Erdeish, believed that his lands should be Erdeish, and only Erdeish, citing the policy of Lord's Land, Lord's Church. He began an aggressive campaign of turning everyone in Želevlast back the Erdeish Church, seizing lands and properties from those who refused. Across Želevlast, rebellions, strikes, and protests broke out. In 1614, at the Žipek estate, a center for Yarruser thinking and culture, a formal declaration of rebellion was declared with letters sent to King Ferdinand, Kommandant Friedrich, and the Gothi, asking for a return to the previous policy and a return to religious freedom. Despite the pleading of his brother, and spurned on by his advisors, Ferdinand continued his policy and ordered the ringleaders of the rebellion executed.

In 1616, shooting began. Yarruser horsemen raided the King's lands, killing his guards and burning his crops. The Second Wagon Uprising began. Across Želevlast, thousands, both Yarrusers and Erdeish, took up arms to fight the king. Reluctantly, Kommandant Friedrich sent troops to support his brother. Under the command of the High Marshal of the Realm, Graf Jungarat Thrumbach, thousands of troops marched into Želevlast.

Lead mostly by minor nobles and merchants, the ringleaders asked Stanimir Žipek, great-grandson of the Yarruser hero, to become king and marshal of their army. Stanimir accepted but was unable to return to his homeland due to fighting in Betauven. Many attempted to lead the rebellion in the interim, but many were killed fighting Graf Thrumbach. Devoid of leadership and losing support following defeat after defeat, the last vestiges of the rebellion were crushed at the Battle of Löwenwald in 1618.

Stage Two, The Amber Sea War:

For many years, Zvearrik had been working towards becoming a great power, mostly by controlling the Amber Sea and its lucrative trade routes. Following the Writ of the Free, the Ludher-derived Urworkish Church was made state religion and only accepted church. This unified the kingdom and allowed Zvearrik to embark on several costly, but successful military campaigns.

In 1618, under the leadership of King Germund Alvarson Rinne-Karlman, Zvearrik declared it could no longer stand by and watch their "Urworkish Cousins" be slaughtered by the Kommandant and Erdeish troops. He launched an invasion of the Holy Realm of Midgart, allying or vassalizing HRM lands that bordered the Amber Sea. At the same time, the King's brothers and sons launched invasions of Pelanomov, Bouya, and Jutrig. The justification of protecting the honor of all Urworkish was little more than a pretense to finally control the entirety of the Amber Sea.

With lightning speed, King Germund smashed through Kommandlich forces, seizing the Želevlast capital of Praizha, and moving south to capture the Tonau and isolated Ostlücke from the rest of the HRM in hopes of forcing the Kommandant to sue for peace. All the while, Zvearish forces were stripping the land of valuables and food to support the war effort. More Želeks died during the Amber Sea war than during the Second Wagon Uprising.

King Germund, a brilliant military tactician, was countered by the equally brilliant Graf Thrumbach, who sacked and destroyed any Urworkish town that would have provided the king with support. The worst of these sackings, the Slaughter of Sunnahain, left the town with only 700 survivors out of a population of 11,000.

At the Battle of Hengstfeld in 1628, the majority of both Zvearish and Kommandlich forces fought. The results were inconclusive and resulted in the death of both King Germund and Graf Thrumbach. Eyewitnesses say both dueled in the middle of the battle with each striking a mortal blow at the same time. With the death of the king, Zvearish forces withdrew from the HRM, focusing on garrisoning the vassals they had gained or reinforcing campaigns elsewhere.

Stage Three, The Bloody Coast:

In 1625, with the Kommandant and Erdeish focusing on Želevlast and the Zvearrik invasion, Betauven and her Urworkish neighbors and allies renewed their effort to liberate the southern half of Betauven from the Catask. The Catask, who had supplied Kommandant Friedrich with men, material, and money, demanded he aid them in crushing the rebellion. Kommandant Friedrich reluctantly agreed, appointing Diether Marwig Flussturm, Herzog of Baivor as High Marshal of the Realm.

Herzog Flusstrum was tasked with undermining Betauven, rather than directly attacking it in hopes of avoiding war with Gallia. He marched his army north along the Rinne, destroying ports and harbors that supplied Betauven and sacked any town with a foundry, arsenal, or gunsmith. Urworkish leaders, believing that Herzog Flussturm was acting of his own accord, declared war against him and not the Kommandant.

At the same time, Bythony and Cataskal renewed their naval war against both Betauven and now Zvearrik. The Fifth Battle of

Dog Island, the largest naval battle in recorded history, involved over 250 warships and over 12,000 men. So many died, it is recorded that the waters turned red for years, and thousands of sharks flocked to the waters to feast on the bodies.

All during this time, tens of thousands of men were fighting on land, both in Betauven and the Holy Realm of Midgart. At one time, over a dozen forts and fortified cities were under siege. Trade came to a halt, and disease and famine spread like wildfire, taking thousands of lives on both sides.

Stage Four, The Black Pirol's War:

In 1636, after funding and supplying many sides of the war for many years, Gallia became directly involved. Robinet Josselin Pellerin, Marquis du Rugist, a former Pirol who had been manumitted from his oaths as a priest to serve the King of Gallia, advised his King to join the war. Pellerin, a preeminent statesman, had left his service to the Church to aid his close friend, the aged King of Gallia. He wanted to see his homeland strong, believing it, rather than the "tolerant" HRM, to be the bastion of the Erdeish Church. Because of this, he was known as the Black Pirol for leaving the church.

In 1635, after the Siege of Schilddaam ended with a Catask victory, it seemed likely that Cataskal would crush the Betauven rebellion. This would leave Gallia surrounded by an empowered and wealthier rival. Under Pellerin's direction, the Gaulish army marched eastward, smashing a Catask army and relieving several beleaguered Betauven towns and armies. At the same time, the Gaulish navy sailed to raid Catask supply lines and aid Betauven ships. Even though Betauven was Urworkish, and had expelled all Erdeish from their lands after the defeat at Schilddaam, Pellerin believed it was better to have a friendly, Urworkish neighbor than an unfriendly Erdeish one.

The ultimate goal of the war was to capture all lands belonging to the HRM west of the Rinne river, especially Midgart. Initially, the war was a success with several Catask and Realm armies smashed and several cities and lands annexed. However, the closer to Midgart the armies got, the slower the advance, and the more costly the victories. Many nobles and officers felt uncomfortable about besieging the Holy-Steads. Fearing a revolt by the nobles, and after an army was defeated on the Catask border, the King ordered Pellerin to scale back his goals. Pellerin agreed, instead focusing efforts on driving Cataskal out of Gallia's eastern borders and pushing them back over the Marca mountains in the south. All the while, Gaulish administrators went about renaming captured territories and integrating them into the kingdom.

Stage Five, The Time of Landsknechts:

By 1646, the war had gone on for over 30 years. Most of the men who started the war were dead with only Kommandant Friedrich and the now-regent Pellerin still alive. A truce was called, and a peace conference was held in the Bevlaagen city of Moergord. Here, what would become the Saught of Bevlaagen was written and eventually signed. During this time, mercenary armies, which had been the backbone of most of the forces that fought, had gone without leadership, purpose, or pay. They began to maraud, pillage, and raid across the HRM and much of Erebus. As a final clause of the Saught, each nation was to contribute a unit of professional soldiers to put down the marauding mercenaries.

In an ironic, final twist of fate, after decades of fighting, all sides came together to put down a monster they created. Though, even with the landsknechts put down like a sick dog, the war continued to ravage the countryside through outbreaks of sickness, famine and crop failures, and economic depressions. Even in years of relative peace, the war continued to accumulate a death toll.

With the signing of the Saught of Bevlaagen, the map of Erebus changed. Betauven was finally recognized as an independent kingdom and gained five of the nine southern provinces it had sought to liberate. Gallia gained the other four and nearly all Catask lands on their eastern border. At the request of the Gothi, a permanent border was established between Gallia and the Holy Realm of Midgart at the Honig river, giving Gallia direct water access to the Holy-Stead. In exchange for allowing the HRM to keep control of Midgart, several wealthy lands, Aufsehertums, and towns were ceded to Gallia. Cataskal also had to give up several key islands and ports in the Middle Sea to Gallia in exchange for the return of several forts and towns along their border. Due to their losses in the war, and the financial cost of fighting it, the ruling Rabenburg branch of Cataskal began to lose popularity and support amongst their nobility.

Zvearrik was granted vassalage over nearly all the northern lands of the HRM with the exception of the Herzogtum of the Bruzzen, who had to pay taxes to the Kommandant and custom fees to Zvearrik. Due to them not being signatories of the Saught, Zvearrik continued their brutal war against Bouya and Pelanomov. Due to the treaty, the HRM was unable to aid their neighbor.

And within the Holy Realm of Midgart, many began to lose faith and trust in the Kommandant. Increasingly, the Kommandant was not seen as the heir of Karalthergroz or a leader, but more of a burden. Many lands, especially Urworkish, hoped to eventually gain their independence and leave the confederation. But with huge swathes of land still unoccupied, and with the production of food still uneasy, independence is a distant dream. For the Rabenburgs of Ostlücke, who still hold the title of Kommandant, their position is untenable. Who knows what a future crisis could bring.

Great Work, The

The Great Work is the name given to the religious upheaval in Erdeish Erebus during the 1500s to the present day. Though never called the Great Work at the time, this has become the universal designation of the movement by scholars and critics on both sides. The churches that sprang from this movement are collectively referred to as Urworkish or Crumb Churches.

The origin of the Great Work can be traced back to both the North-South Schism of 555 HJ and the Yarruser Wars of the 1400s. Both of these were organized and widespread protestations to Erdeish doctrine and orthodoxy. Though the origin for the Great Work, neither of these events are classified as Urworkish. Mistakenly, Yarrusers are grouped with Urworkish.

What is considered the catalyst that spurred Ludher to begin the Great Work, was the heavy Churchfees the Erdeish Church levied on it's worshippers. Churchfees were never supposed to be permanent, and only implemented during emergencies, but they had been in place for nearly 100 years by the time of Ludher.

The purpose of these Churchfees was to raise funds to beautify and modernize the stead of Rasna, in Viteliú, and move Church leadership there rather than stay in the contested Midgart. Very little of the funds went to Rasna, with most enriching corrupt priests and lords.

The purpose of the Great Work was a return to the original, "purer," primordial form of Sun-Worship before hierarchy and organization corrupted and confused the religion. It is called a "Great Work" because its goal was to undo thousands of years of dogma that have led mankind astray from their original purpose.

While some consider the Great Work to have ended with the conclusion of the Great War and the establishment of religious freedom, many Urworkish consider it an ongoing event. According to these Urworkish, the Great Work will only end when the lies and treachery of the Erdeish Church have finally been revealed to the world, and the Erdeish Church ceases to exist.

Guest-kindness

Also called the "unwritten Douth," guest-kindness, or hospitality, is preeminent among all social relations in all Erebusen cultures. Good guest-kindness is taught repeatedly throughout the sagas, and those who show bad guest-kindness are condemned. Being a bad guest is also condemned.

Guesthouse

General term for any place where a traveler can find refuge for the night. Different from a sickhouse, as many guesthouses, or inns, require payment.

Half-God

All Half-gods are holies, but not all Holies are Half-gods. Half-gods were the first race of mankind created by God. They were stronger, smarter, and more righteous. They were given stewardship over earth to help their weaker cousins (modern man) grow and advance as well as watch over all life. Many died during the Long Winter fighting off the Lightless.

By the Saga's own admission, all of the Half-gods were once worshipped as heathen gods by primitive man. It was only through the effort of skalds that this worship was "corrected."

Hall

Hall has two definitions; the first is a small church that usually serves a small town or city. The land that a Hall encompasses is referred to as a Halldom. The term parish or shire is used as an equivalent in other languages. Groups of Halls answer to either a Hof with an Aufseher or Hochaufseher or a Vaterhort.

Hall as a suffix is used to denote the court of a ruler or the home of someone or something. A Herzoglich Halle is the court and household of a Herzog. And Aufseherhalle is the home of an Aufseher. Both terms stem from the earliest days of Sun-worship when religious services, feasts, and court were held inside mead halls.

Hallow

To make something hallow is to have it blessed by a priest and treated with an appropriate degree of reverence. To make someone hallowed is to canonize them as a holy.

Hallowed Unknowns, The

Also known as the Great Heathenries, the Hallowed Unknowns are questions posed by the sagas but not answered by them, leading to speculation and debate. Amongst the most common Hallowed Unknowns are:

Does God have a wife?

It is assumed so, as Holy Sunna is described as being his daughter, and other holies are described as his children. With marriage being nigh-ubiquitous in all mannish societies, many expect God himself to also be married. Some even regard God as having multiple wives.
Popular contenders include:

Holy Rán, who watches over the souls of dead sailors.
Holy Hel, who guards Helheim.
Holy Bil, who is only briefly mentioned in the Sagas as the watcher on the dark side of the moon.
Holy Nott, who is the guardian of mankind during nighttime.
And most controversial, Holy Sunna herself.

What happened to elves, dwarves, fae, and other groups during the Long Winter?

The Erdeish, and therefore Urworkish, do not have an official answer to this. The Pananthropotes believe any manlike group that existed were men but devolved and degenerated due to their sins.

Where do souls come from?

The only definite answer is a few passages regarding the Ur-Sela, a primordial soul that only becomes a full-fledged soul when given a body and name. Where the Ur-Sela comes from is the mystery.

Is the sun God's throne, a representation of his power, or is God the sun?

Most priests will answer "Yes."

Can mortal women become Einherjar?

While not official doctrine, it is widely believed by clergy and laity alike that women who die in childbirth can enter Walhalla. Women warriors, despite their rarity, can also enter Walhalla.

Harug

A Harug is technically the same as a Hall but services either a larger population or area. While a Hall only has one, maybe two meetings on Sonntag, a Harug can have many. Harugs will also have land used to sustain the several priests who reside there.

Hearer

Any who learn, though usually refers to those enrolled at a High Learnhouse or similar institution.

Heaven

Across all of sun-worship, what is agreed is that there are many afterlives, which more or less resemble one another, under different names. It is also believed that a soul can go to all or many of these heavens. Helheim, while not a heaven, is one of these destinations. In Erdeish and Urworkish areas, these are named:

Walhalla, for those who died in battle (or childbirth) where most of their soul becomes an Einherjar to train and prepare for the Götterdämmerung.

Folkwang, an idealistic place where most souls will reside. Here, it is said, a soul learns everything there is to learn, bit by bit, and also will help their descendants.

Ránhalle, essentially an aquatic variation of Walhalla where those who died at sea are also trained to be Einherjar.

Helheim, a frozen wasteland (or warm depending on where one is from) where the souls of the evilest go. It is said the Lightless reside there as well, though this is a matter of debate.

Middle-heavens, or small heavens, are also mentioned in the sagas. These are either subsections of heaven, transitory places for souls who had not learned of Sun-worship, or something else. The most famous are Ansgart, which is said to be where God himself lives, and Utgart, where the Lightless are said to be held.

High Learnhouse

An institution, nominally religious, dedicated to more advanced forms of learning and teaching. To enroll in a High Learnhouse, one must be able to pay the fees, have a writ from someone high-born, and be well-versed in the basics of reading, writing, and other skills. Clergy and laity both enroll and learn at the same High Learnhouses and will usually take or even teach the same classes.

Holy

A Holy is an exemplar of mankind. They are wise men or women, who through their deeds, have been hallowed. One seeks a Holy for a specific bit of wisdom; one seeks a fisherman Holy to ask for how to get a batter catch, and one would seek a woman Holy to ask how to conceive a child. In other cultures, they are referred to as Agios, Svats, or Sants. It is abbreviated as Hl.

Urworkish only recognize Holies named in the Sagas with few exceptions, while the Erdeish and Pananthropotes continuously Hallow men and women as Holies.

The study of a Holy's life is called Hallowken, or as the Pananthropotes know it, Hagiography.

A Warden Holy, sometimes known as a Guiding Holy, is a Holy who dispenses specific wisdom for a specific task, profession, or region. Holy Máni is the Warden Holy for the moon and for Mondsruhe and all of Baivor. Often, since many Holies were former heathen pantheons, some Holies may share overlapping jurisdiction.

Holyplay

As the name suggests, it is a play about the life or hallowing of a Holy. They are wildly popular among all groups and lands in Erebus and are many people's first exposure to culture. The current most popular Holyplay is about Gilberto di Vasco Prando Gabriotti, a Vitelish Stardelver who observed that Erde revolves around the sun. This discovery was shown as proof that, just as the Sun is the center of space, so too should God be the center of our lives.

Honorifics

Travelers in Teutonish-speaking lands may often be confused over the usage of "Herr" when addressing men, acting analogously to "Sir" and "Mister." They may wonder why they use the same honorific to address both the highest-born lord and the lowest-born peasant. It was not always this way. Since the time of Karalthergroz, only lords were referred to as Herr. However, in the late 1300s, following the Grautod in the preceding century, peasants began to gain greater autonomy and power. At the Reichstag of 1381 HJ, a peasant delegation demonstrated that peasants (who had only been referred to by their given names) held more land than lower-rank nobles. Because of this, the peasants argued for the right to permanent and universal use of surnames and to be referred to as Herr. This was granted, though with caveats that persist to the current day.

How can one tell a lower-ranked "Herr" from an upper-ranked "Herr"? The easiest method is by dress. While most laws regarding clothing have largely been repealed, the cut, make, and quality of clothes are still starkly different between classes. Footwear is also legally an indicator of class; only knighted and ennobled "Herrs" may wear spurs. Lordly "Herrs" are also the only ones allowed to wear swords, while most burghers and lower-ranked ones will wear daggers, small hammers, axes, or wooden maces.

For women, there are three honorifics used. "Frau" is by far the most common. Amongst the upper classes, it refers to all lower-class women, regardless of marital status. Amongst burghers and lower classes, the usage of "Fräulein" is becoming increasingly common to refer to any unmarried woman, especially young women. "Herrin" is used by all classes to refer to any noble woman whose title is not known. Frau is analogous to Mrs, Fräulein is analogous to Miss or Ms, and Herrin is analogous to Dame or Lady.

Hundred Years' Sorrows

The Hundred Years' Sorrows, sometimes known as the Hundred Tears, is a dark period in Erebusen history that began with the death of Ziurin Ludher and ends with the signing of the Saught of Bevlaagen. Between these two events was a period of unprecedent bloodshed, plague, economic disaster, freezing winters, and almost annual famines.

Timeline of the Hundred Years' Sorrows:

1522: The death of Ziurin Ludher

1523-1526: The Conquest of Texihauco by Hermógenes Casal

1524, Spring: The Writ of the Free is written, and the Hertzabrunnobund is formed. The Writ is a promulgation of Urworkish beliefs and the founding charter of Urworkish Churches that follow Ludher's teachings. The Hertzabrunnobund is a military alliance formed by Urworkish lands to defend themselves

1524, Fall-1528: The Grafenkrieg, a war between smaller landowners who wish to turn to Urworkish teachings and their liege lords. Fought between Kommandlich Forces and the Hertzabrunnobund. There were few battles during the war, as most of the fighting was done through sieges or champion warfare. When war broke out between the HRM and the Sultanate, a temporary truce was signed.

1528: The Battle of Four Kings is fought. A devastating loss for Sonnendom, which results in the death of four different kings, all at the hands of the Sultanate. Though it allowed Sultan Erdem the Mighty to control most of the Bataliks, it depleted his forces of veteran troops, bringing his campaign to a temporary end.
1530: Hostilities resume against the Sultanate, and Grenzburg is besieged. After a month of hard fighting, the siege is lifted, in no small part due to Urworkish help.
1531: In recognition of their help, the Reichstag issues to the Writ of Karlstadt, a temporary granting of religious freedom.
1532-1533: The Rinnemark War, which was fought between different Urworkish groups regarding authority, doctrine, and law. The war ends with a repromulgation of the Writ of the Free and the first Pastor's Conference.
1533, Fall: With the Sultanate still reeling from their defeat at Grenzburg and suffering from a series of rebellions, Fyodor II, Velikiy Knyaz (Grand Prince) of Bouya, makes his move to bring Bouya onto the world stage. Under his orders, Giorgios X, Supreme Patriarch of the Pananthropotes church, is kidnapped from under the Sultan's watch in Şehir. The Supreme Patriarch then crowns Fyodor as Vasilias, the successor to Lygotian Basileis. Bouya, once a small principality on the eastern edge of Erebus, is now christened the Ecumene of Bouya, successor to Lygotium and guardian of all Pananthropotes.
1535-1536: All of Erebus suffers from the Hell Winter from 1535-1536, which did not end until late into the summer.
1536-1541: The Five Year's Dearth, a series of crop failures which resulted from the Hell Winter.
1538: This year marked the beginning of the first Rabenburg-Gaulish wars. It would continue on and off for the next twenty years, being fought on multiple fronts on land and sea. The main cause of the war was influence over Midgart, the rich, northern regions of Viteliú, and Rabenburg dominance in Cataskal.
1542: The Ritterkrieg (Knights' War) and the Pflügerkrieg (Peasant's War) begin. While both wars were somewhat related to religious freedom granted by the Writ of Karlstadt, economics and land ownership became a greater focus of the wars. The Ritterkrieg was fought by knights and small landowners who were cut off and abandoned by their lords for religious differences. Many, both Erdeish and Urworkish, would band together to

reclaim their lands. The Pflügerkrieg was a large-scale popular uprising amongst landless, landed, and urban toilers who rebelled against their lords and neighbors over religion, economic, and legal rights. Both wars saw widespread violence with entire towns being razed and numerous lives lost. Both wars caused another series of dearths and the spreading of blights. The Ritterkrieg ended in 1553 and the Pflügerkrieg in 1557.

1550: The Battles of the Heel and the Hellmouth are fought. Sultan Salur, successor and son of Sultan Erdem, attempts to mimic his father's greatness and orders a naval invasion of southern Viteliú, rather than an overland attack through the still rebellious Bataliks. At the urging of the Gothi, all hostilities in Erebus are temporarily halted, and every major Erdeish nation contributes ships and marines to the fighting. Through bloody fighting, both major Sultanate naval forces are defeated. This marks the end of any further Sultanate expansion westward, as it now focuses eastward instead.

1555: As hostilities between the Rabenburgs and the Gauls resume, Midgart is sacked. During the sacking, the Helven Guard was slaughtered and the Gothi imprisoned and held for ransom. Who exactly participated in the sacking is unknown with all sides pointing fingers at the other. Kommandant Rodrigo outbid the King of Gallia, paying the Gothi's ransom and inviting the Gothi and church leadership to stay in Grenzburg, indefinitely.

1556: At a meeting of leechers, it is determined that outbreaks of Greatpox, also known as the Gaulish Blight, and smallpox have become endemic, spreading far faster and reaching far more distant lands than any disease since the Grautod. Steps are taken to stem the spread of the sicknesses, but warfare makes implementing these steps nigh impossible. Amongst leechers and the public, many regard these pandemics as still ongoing.

1559: The Port Wars, a series of conflicts fought in the Middle Sea, intensify. Mainly fought between Cataskal, Gallia, the lands of Viteliú, the Sultanate, kingdoms of northern Ifrin, and pirates. Most of the fighting is done to secure strategic ports, control wealthy trade routes, and block rival influence in a region, along with considerable efforts to destroy pirates.

1560: The Steppe War begins. As part of its quest for dominance and influence, the Ecumene of Bouya launches a war against Pelanomov, the Kozak Hetmanates, and their vassals. Later Zvearrik would join, fighting against all sides. The western steppe, which provided a significant amount of grain and timber to Erebus, was devasted, leading to another dearth across the continent.

1566: Kommandant Rodrigo Rabenburg, who nearly all historians agree began the Hundred Year's Sorrow by ordering the execution of Ziurin Ludher, steps down as Kommandant, wanting to live out his final days at his hacienda in Cataskal. In protest to his leadership, his chosen successor and grandson, who was Catask by blood and birth, is not cast as the next Kommandant, and an informal rule is made that only Teudish can become Kommandant. This is done to hopefully avoid getting the Holy Realm of Midgart involved in foreign wars. Karl Franz Rabenburg, Herzog of Ostlücke and a third cousin of Rodrigo is chosen to be Kommandant. He does so with a promise to be more tolerant of Urworkish, lessen taxes, and removed the HRM from Cataskal's wars.

1567: Kommandant Karl Franz begins the Hinterland War. Its purpose was to expand the eastern border with the Sultanate and establish a firm and stable frontier. Done with the blessing of the Gothi and with the express forbiddance of Catask involvement (though they did supply troops and funding), the war is meant to unify the HRM and all of Erebus in a common cause. The war was grinding and costly but saw enough success that the Sultanate sued for peace with a formal treaty, though not until 1603.

1575: The nine northern streeks (provinces) of Betauven, which had belonged to the Catask crown for two hundred years, revolt against their distant lords. This begins the *Vrijheid Oorlog*, the Freedom War. True to his word, Kommandant Karl Franz does not lend support to the Catask in crushing the rebellion, which many believe allowed the rebellion to survive and prolong the war. While Betauven as an entity consisted of 18 total streeks, only the northern half was able to rebel, using the gold and power they'd amassed through trade to fund the war. This war would go on for almost sixty years, only ending with the Saught of Bevlaagen and the successful liberation of five of the southern streeks. The other four were taken by Gallia in the peace.

1579: Kommandant Karl Franz dies. Many fear his son and successor, Arbogast, will not be as lenient or wise as his father. Fearing further repression, the Urworkish begin their penultimate war against Erdeish domination, the Nornberch War.

Though small and localized, the war was still bloody with Urworkish knights and armies seizing vital roads and waterways from their Erdeish rivals in hopes of bargaining from a position of strength. The war ended in 1583 with the Frith of Alteburg and what many regarded as the best hope of permanent peace: the Policy of Lord's Land, Lord's Church. Lord's Land, Lord's Church, as a policy, did its best to bring religious freedom to the Holy Realm of Midgart. It enshrined into law that whatever church a liege lord went to, those living in his lands must also go there. The policy also allowed for populations and entire towns to migrate or change allegiances to lords that followed their preferred churches. While this policy did allow those who followed Ludher-style teachings to thrive, it did not account for smaller, non-Ludher churches. With one exception, these were too small to make an impact and so carved out their own enclaves in the wilderness and foothills where they could be unbothered. The one exception, however, was the Yarrusers. And this shortsightedness would eventually lead to the Great War.

1590: The Three Fleet War, which became part of both the Bloody Coast and the Great War, begins. During a lull in the Freedom War, Bythony makes a move and seizes strategic islands and ports along the Cold Sea, fighting both Cataskal, Gaulish, and Betauven fleets. This war was a massive disruption to trade and caused a depression in northern Erebus. The war only ended with the Saught of Bevlaagen, though Bythony is prepared to renew it.

Though it ended after the signing of the Saught, the Bythony Inward War from 1635-1655, and the Rending from 1656-1664, all fought on the islands, are often included as part of the Hundred Year's Sorrows.

Ken

Ken is almost always used as a suffix and denotes a field of learning. While ken can be used as a synonym for knowledge, it is most often found as a suffix. Worldken is used to describe all the different kens, used in the same sense as science. Examples of kens include:

Bodyken; Anatomy
Churchken/Godken; Theology
Deorken; Zoology
Greenken; Botany
Healthken; Medicine

Landken; Geography
Loreken; Historiography
Runeken; Grammar
Starken; Astronomy
Stoneken; Geology
Saltken; Chemistry
Tongueken; Philology
Zahlken; Mathematics

Kind

Similar to ken, kind is also used as a suffix, usually to denote a certain group. Its most famous usage is in mankind to describe all the races and tribes of men; however, delvers have used this as an example to classify different animals in the burgeoning field of Deorken.

Milkkind; Mammals, not including mankind
Scalekind; Reptiles
Newtkind/Toadkind; Amphibians
Featherkind; Birds
Finkind; Fish
Crawlerkind; Insects
Greenkind; Plants, currently includes fungus
Dwimmerkind; An unofficial designation that classifies beings such as elves, dwarves, and the Lightless. The nearest comparison would be cryptids.

Landsknecht

Technically, a Landsknecht is a specific kind of soldier-for-hire. However, they became so ubiquitous that Landsknecht became another byword for sellsword.

Leodolf Pass

Leodolf pass is the name given to the mountain valley through which the Tonau flows that connects the Holy Realm of Midgart with the land of Ostlücke. Originally known as Salzfeuer pass, it earned its current name due to the leadership of Aufseher Leodolf during a battle fought there in 392 HJ during the First Steppe War or the First Steppe Invasion. Aufseher Leodolf rallied an army of tribal warriors to smash the invading horde of the Chunen King Etstilau. In a stroke of military genius, Leodolf blocked off the southern bank of the Tonau, forcing the Etstilau horsemen onto the narrow northern bank where his army of spearmen and archers made mincemeat of the invaders. Etstilau was killed, and most of the horsemen retreated back onto the steppe to be absorbed into the other tribes.

One of the tribes that made up the steppe confederacy, the Mogyër, actually turned to Sun-worship and were made a *Grenzvolk*, a border people. They guarded the lands around the Gottesspur to protect against any further steppe incursions. Even hundreds of years later, the Mogyër still fight alongside the HRM in the hinterlands between Ostlücke and the Sultanate.

Leodolf was later hallowed as Holy Leodolf the Fighter and became a Warden Holy of the Mogyër Kings.

Mankind

As currently understood, the only intelligent, sapient, and sentient race in the world of Erde. Mankind is God's favorite creation, according to most religions, though they are not without their faults. Men can be found on every land in every corner of the globe. Women are included, as Men and Mankind encompasses the group as a whole. Mannish is the adjective used to describe anything related to mankind.

Norn

A Norn, more often referred to as a Guardian Norn, is a being who lies somewhere between a Valkyrie and an Einherjar. They are not Holies and do not have names but are still makings of God. They are usually referred to as females, though the Sagas do not describe them as having bodies or genders. What a Norn is, however, is clear; they are beings who help someone reach their orlay. They can either protect someone from danger, give them the wisdom to go in the right direction, or give them a bit of courage to begin an undertaking. It is written that God and the Holies answer beseechings through the Guardian Norns.

Orlay

An orlay is known by many names: fate, destiny, foredoom, or simply one's lot in life. Everyone has one from the highest king to the lowliest ploughman to all the Holies. Only God himself does not have an orlay. He is the freest being in existence, and he uses that freedom to watch over and help mankind. An orlay can be anything; for most, it will be to live a good life and raise a family. For some, it is to lead armies into battle, lead nations, or guide the church. For others, especially those who choose evil, their orlay is to die and remove themselves from the world. What one's orlay is, one will not know. Orlays are not written in stone. The ending is known only to God, but how that ending is reached is up to the choices of an individual person. All orlays lead one to do good. No one is orlayed to be evil.

Pananthropotes

The Pananthropotes were the first large scale schism within Sun-Worship, separating from what would become the Erdeish Church in 555 HJ. The North-South Schism, or the North-South Sundering, began over arguments and disagreements between the rural and poor northern church centered around Midgart and the wealthier, metropolitan south, centered around Lygotium. It will be explored further at a later date.

The Pananthropotes, true to their name, believe in incorporating stories and holies from all peoples, the church for all mankind. As such, their version of the Saga, the Anthropoiad, contains many more books than the Erdeish or Urworkish Sagas.

Pananthropotes are largely decentralized, a practice they call autocephaly. Churches are regional, tribal, or national, and lead by a patriarch. The ceremonial head of the church is the Supreme Patriarch. Patriarchs are assisted by bishops. Priests are properly referred to as Presbyters. Autocephaly, and the decentralized nature of the Pananthropotes church, was an inspiration for many Urworkish movements.

Reichstag, The

The Reichstag is the closest the HRM has to a legislative assembly. Composed of the words Reich (Realm) and Tag (Congress or Assembly), it is where the Kommandant meets with the lords and rulers of the Realm to settle disputes, discuss law, and lead the Realm. It does not do this well, as the Kommandant himself hardly ever shows up, instead appointing a Tagmeister to lead in his stead, and most of the lands and cities hardly show up either. Only the Casters and the Aufsehers who hold land, or at least their agents, are known for certain to be there. Other agents or ambassadors will come whenever their master feels like spending the gold to send them. It does not help that the Reichstag's decrees are not binding and are only put into law by the lands and lords who choose to do so.

Following the violence of the mid to late 1500s HJ after the death of Ziurin Ludher, it was decided that the Reichstag should be held in a set location for set times of the year from then on. The city of Rüdibrück was chosen as the location of the permanent Reichstag and renamed Reichstadt, as it was now a city of the realm. The population of Rüdibrück was not informed of this change and were furious at the news. To this day, they still refer to their city by the old name and will cross out Reichstadt on any map that enters the city and replace it with Rüdibrück.

Saga

A saga is any grand or epic tale. The Sagas, more properly the Saga of Mankind, is the holy book of Sun-worship. Known by many names and with many translations, it holds one thing at its core: the story of mankind. It details the creation of the world, the rise of the Half-gods, and the struggle of the Long Winter. It also details the lives of the Holies and gives examples of how to live. It is an instruction manual, a book of warning, the greatest collection of songs ever written, and for many in Erebus, it is the only book they may ever own.

The subdivisions, or books of the Sagas, are referred to as "Eddas," even ones not titled as an Edda, such as the Warnings of Holy Heinrich die Langschenkel. Many unhallowed books and writings claim to be lost Eddas, but referring to them as Eddas, rather than unhallowed tales, is considered borderline heresy.

Saught

A saught is a peace agreement made between individuals, neighbors, or lands. The Saught of Bevlaagen ended the Great War.

Schloss

A schloss, in the time of Karalthergroz, was a fortified home with walls and a keep. It has lost this meaning over time and instead is often used to describe an undefended manor home. Schloss can either mean a castle, palace, or country home depending on the context.

Sippe

A sippe, or a clan, is a subdivision within a Stem. A sippe can be everything from an extended family, an entire town, or even a small land. Scholars currently use Sippe to define the different subgroups within a Stem. For example, Zvearrik and Betauven are Sippes within the Teudish Stem.

Skald

Originally, skalds were singers and lore masters who would travel across the known world, teaching about Sun-worship, a role they still possess. However, as the church has evolved, so have the skalds. Now they are any kind of churchgroom with specialized training, such as manuscript writing, history chronicling, and missionary work. The poetic part of their origin remains in the phrase "waxing skaldish."

In Gaulish and Greenmen territories, a skald may also be referred to as an Ollave or an Ollamh. While they are essentially the same, the difference being mostly linguistic, Ollave are considered to be solely historians and poets, rather than any specialized churchgroom. While outsiders can use the terms interchangeably, in Gaulish and Greenmen societies, they are considered two separate ranks.

Soul

All men have a soul. It lives on after the body dies. But after death, a soul does not remain whole. It can fragment, bringing different parts of someone to different afterlives. If a baby is born and given the same name as a deceased family member, it is thought that part of the deceased's soul will join to the soul of the newborn, bringing with it some blessed skill or knowledge. A soul only becomes a soul after it enters a body and is named. Souls cannot be sold, cannot be bargained with, and cannot be lost, at least in this life.

Stead

A stead is also known as a burgh, borough, stadt, or city. When used as a suffix, it denotes a specific kind of location.

A Head-Stead, or Hauptstadt, is the capital of a given region. It is usually the largest city and located along a trade route, major river, or a well-fortified location. The HRM does not have a Head-Stead, as the Kommandant is supposed to be itinerant, but in the current day, Grenzburg serves as the *de facto* Head-Stead. Examples of Head-Steads include:

Lutèce, Gallia
Barkeña, Cataskal
Lúndev, Merkya
Grakgród, Pelanomov
Amtbujshaven, Betauven
Gorunn, Galazee
Vattenstark, Zvearrik

A Free-Stead, or Freistadt, is a designation specific to the HRM. Most were given the designation due to their proximity to an important resource, such as fresh water, salt, or silver. They owe their allegiance directly to the Kommandant and cannot give up land, rights, or anything to their neighbors without the Kommandant's approval.

A Holy-Stead, or Heiligstadt, is any city founded on or nearby ruins built by the Half-gods. *The* Holy-Steads always refers to Midgart, Kölle, and Meinze, the first areas to embrace Sun-worship and the backbone of the church.

A Land-Stead, or Stadtland, is any city which has no overlord and owns a large amount of land. Equivalent to a City-State.

Stem

A stem, also called a tribe or a Stamm in High Rinnish, is the main political unit of mankind. All men belong to a stem, the size of which can vary, The study of stems, Stemken, is a very popular subject, despite its difficulty. This difficulty comes from the fluidity of stems and the fact that they change over time. Not all members of a stem do the same thing or have the same belief, and many will share practices and ideas with neighboring or even rival stems. Despite this, the Stem is still an important unit when organizing, understanding, and discussing mankind.

The major Stems of Erebus are as follows:

The Teudish
The Gauls
The Greenmen
The Wends
The Ibertalla (Also called Southmen)
The Elláasers
The Ambermen
The West-Steppers

Sun-Worship

Sun-worship is one of the largest organized religions on Erde. Mainly concentrated in Erebus, with significant enclaves in Ifrin, Estuwwa, and in the New World. Self-admittedly, Sun-worship is a monotheistic syncretic religion. God, the sun, is the sole deity to be worshipped, the only one to be beseeched. But as Sun-worship spreads, it absorbed the gods and practices of the religions it replaced. These gods became the Holies who are sought after for specific advice and wisdom. The stories, myths, and rites of these gods were also added to the canon of Sun-worship.

While considered the only and original religion, organized Sun-worship in the current age can be traced back to the founding Holy-Steads of Midgart, Meinze, and Kölle. These three were the first cities reinhabited after the Long Winter and where most of the Holies taught. When the Holies were taken to be Einherjar, the three cities formed a confederacy to facilitate trade, rebuilding, and missionary work. As years passed and more and more peoples were turned to Sun-worship, and their heathen ways corrected, a great Churchmeet was held in Midgart to formally organize Sun-worship as a faith. This meeting was overseen by Aufseher Budô of Midgart, who passed away from sickness days before the four-year long meeting concluded. His successor, Gottlieb, was elected Gothi, or High Priest, at the end of the meeting. This began Year One with the calendar now being dated from the end of the meeting. From then on, all years were to be post scripted with HJ or Holy Year.

Until the North-South Schism of 555 HJ, the Church was only known as "The Church" with the appellation of Erdeish, meant to signify the Church was the Church for the entire world, not appearing until sometime around the middle 600s HJ.

Due to its Syncretic nature, the Church has always tried to add additional Holies, Lore, and rites from the different people it encompasses. Though, this has met with criticism. When the first edition of the Sagas (and the first usage of runes as a writing system) was created in 405 HJ by Jost the Runefather, it mainly contained stories and Holies from the Teudish and Gauls. The second edition of the Sagas was created in 718 HJ by Ramiro the Scrivner who refined the Runes and added in Holies and stories from Viteliú, Cataskal, Galazee, and even some from the Lygotian Ecumene and faraway Habaxum. The third and most recent edition of the Sagas was compiled by Snorri the Wordsmith in 1209 HJ. With this came a further refinement of the Runes and more additions from northern and eastern peoples. In 1560, the Churchmeet of Migherri was held to discuss adding to the Sagas stories and Holies from both the New World and the Far East, where due to Cataskal efforts, sizeable portions of Erdeish reside. The meeting ended without reaching a conclusion, and the violence of the following years left the question unanswered.

The religion itself is called Sun-worship. Though some deride this term, it remains the most popular and well-known. Adherents are called Sonnenkind, Sunnish, or rarely, Sunmen. The lands under Sun-worship influence are known as Sonnendom.

Teutonish

Many travelers will frequently remark how odd it is that the Teudish, one of the largest ethno-linguistic groups in Erebus, do not speak Teudish. Instead their language is "Teutonish," which sounds similar but is not the same name. Why is the name of the language different from the people who speak it? Like many traditions and practices of modern-day Erebus, this can be traced back to Karalthergroz.

When Karalthergroz was helmed the first Kommandant in Easter of 801 HJ, he was also given the title of "Marshal of the Church" and told to organize and unify the disparate Teudish tribes in order to strengthen the Church. The Teudish and Wends had fallen into heathen ways, and the church had been backsliding since the schism. Karalthergroz took this mission to heart and set out to do so right away.

One of his first obstacles was that Karalthergroz didn't speak any of the dialects or languages of the Teudish tribes. He only spoke his native language of Frayzen, which while being similar to Teudish, had been heavily influenced by Gaulish languages. However, the very first tribe which allied with Karalthergroz, and who remained steadfast to the Church, was the Teutoner. They did speak the more common Teudish language and dialects, and so their leader became one of Karalthergroz's most loyal and trusted advisors. In official documentation from that time, it is written that all meetings were held "in the tongue of the Teutoners." Due to this, the Teudish language was only known as the Teutoner or Teutonish. Due to the supremacy of Karalthergroz and his successors in early politics of the HRM, Teudish was never recognized or codified as a name for the language. It was only known as Teutonish, a name which has endured to the modern day.

Is Teutonish derived from High Rinnish, the language of the Church? No. But they are cousins. They ultimately come from Ur-Teudish, the progenitor language for both languages, along with many others, which itself comes from Ur-Mannaz, the language spoken by the Half-gods. They are similar and share many words and etymological roots, but Teudish did not come from High Rinnish, despite the Church's claims to the contrary.

Toiler

Also known as peasants, peons, or churls. The lowest social rank in Erebus and the most numerous. Toilers grow the food, cut the timber, dig the ore, and raise the livestock that keep the world moving. Without toilers, the world would collapse. Because of this, wise leaders are keen to make sure their toilers are happy, as history has shown that when toilers group together, violence and horrific bloodshed follow. In Teudish lands, while being free, Toilers are still expected to remain on the lands of their lord, helping him in exchange for protection. The strong guard the weak, and the weak render to the strong is an oft-repeated maxim from the Sagas.

Free Toilers are those who are not tied to the land and are allowed to freely wander and travel, as most are journeymen or craftsmen. Free Toilers should technically be called Wandering Toilers, as all toilers are free.

Toilers occupy a different social structure than serfs, sometimes referred to as bondsmen. Technically, no Teudish, in any land, are serfs, and many see it as a source of pride. While most are tied to the land, toilers are legally allowed to leave the land, though they lose all protections and guarantees from their lord when they do so. Many toilers leave their lands either to seek a new profession, move to more fertile lands, or to become a warrior. Toilers may also choose their leaders, such as Burgermeisters and reeves. And upon the death of their lord, the heir must make a vow before his toilers and receive their assent to become their new lord. None of these rights are afforded to serfs.

Urworkish

Urworkish are those who belong to a church which can trace its origin to the Great Work, a protestation movement against the Erdeish Church. The Urworkish movement believes in returning or bringing back the original, older teachings of ancient Sun-worship. Hence the Ur- in Urworkish. Part of this belief is a rejection of centralized, hierarchal leadership, full-time professional clergy, and Holies not mentioned in the Sagas, with exceptions.

The vast majority of Urworkish in Erebus follow Ludherish-derived teachings, which were originally developed by Ziurin Ludher from 1516 to 1520 and further developed by his followers in the years after. The beliefs of Ludherish-Urworkish were promulgated and definitely pronounced with the Writ of the Free in 1524, which also served as a call to arms for all Urworkish across Erebus.

What do Urworkish believe?

Clergy should be part-time and should be a member of a local community and work outside of Church to support themselves.

The Sagas and Sonntag meetings should be held in the local languages with Ludher himself even beginning a transliteration of the Sagas into Teutonish rather than High Rinnish, even using common turns of phrase in this writing. This would be continued by his successors and even inspired the King Norbert Saga, the *only* version of the Saga authorized in Bythony.

There should be no central authority dictating dogma and wielding authority. Originally Urworkish had no governing body, but following the violence of the 1500s, the Pfarrertagung (Pastor's Conference) was formed to bring together all the disparate Ludherish-based groups. The Pfarrertagung is not binding or a definitive authority but is the best, if only way for Ludherish to solve doctrinal dilemmas and pressing questions. This belief in central authority is not shared by some Urworkish, as the Bythonish, who followed Ludher's example, but vested central authority first in their king and then the High Churchwarden.

Urworkish do not believe in the Götterdämmerung as Erdeish and Pananthropotes do. Rather than a worldwide ending where monsters crawl out of the earth, the Götterdämmerung will instead be a more personalized trial. Each man and woman has their own personal Lightless to battle, and only their knowledge of the Sun and His teachings can help them fight. Because of this, Urworkish are especially quick to fund and support proselytizing missions.

With the previous belief also comes a difference in what the Lightless are. Most Urworkish see them, much like the Pananthropotes, as not physical beings, but as spiritual threats that come about through sin and evil. They tempt mankind into giving them physical form through hatred and evil. They do this through Ermingandz, their king who is an opposite to God. Because of this, Urworkish are more likely to be superstitious and attribute any wrong done to a person as a result of their moral failings.

Many Urworkish will also hold a much greater fear of the supernatural, considering it to be solely evil and capable of corrupting individuals and communities, leading them to sin.

Due to the backsliding which inspired Ziurin Ludher, most Urworkish do not believe in giving any money to a church. A priest must fund himself and work a normal job in order to support his church. Patronage and gifts are allowed, but these should be framed as a gift for the betterment of the community rather than to curry favor.

Urworkish reject the monastic life of Churchgrooms and Churchmaids. During the Hundred Years' Sorrows, many lords who turned to Urworkish beliefs would seize the land and assets of any Vaterhort and Mutterhort within their lands, greatly enriching themselves. These seizures were one of the causes for the violence of the 1500s.

Urworkish especially focus on the Douth of Worksomeness; one of their oft-repeated teachings is that a hard day's work is worth an answering or a beseeching. Idle hands are Ermingandz's playthings.

Due to not having a centralized authority, Urworkish do not hallow additional Holies or add to the Sagas. With exceptions, the only Holies they believe in are the ones in the Sagas. But Urworkish do not seek wisdom from Holies. They are only to learn from their life and deeds.

Urworkish place a greater emphasis on older ideas of leadership, particularly lordly leadership. In Teudish lands especially, a king is to be the warlord, priest, and judge of his lands. This is what made Urworkish teachings so popular and why so many lords turned to it against their traditional faith. This thinking is so prevalent that many leaders, from Herzogs to Bürgermeisters, will lead Sonntag services with some regularity.

Valkyrie

A Valkyrie, or a Walküre, is an angelic-like being who ferries souls to the afterlife. Riding atop swans or eagles, they follow ravens in search of those who have died. Some think that Valkyries only ferry those who have died in battle, referencing their earliest mentions in the sagas, but later Holies have stated Valkyries ferry all dead. Walküre is the proper, High Rinnish name for a Valkyrie, but even priests prefer the more common Valkyrie.

Vé

Across from the door of any proper Erdeish or Pananthropotes church is always a small alcove where sits a statue of God or an image of the sun. In larger churches, the statue will be accompanied by busts of holies and murals depicting scenes from the Sagas. This is a Vé, the focal point of any worship. Urworkish claim that the Vé and the statue are prayed to, but Erdeish teachings state that the Vé is to give a sense of direction when worshipping and that a statue of God will send any beseechings to Him. In Tujue-occupied lands, Vé are illegal, so even in larger Pananthropotes churches, they will construct temporary images of the sun out of tree branches. Urworkish still have a space within their churches for a Vé but instead fill it with an unadorned image of the sun.

Wayfareage

A wayfareage is any travelling done with the intent of visiting a holy site. The Holy-Steads are the most popular wayfareage places, but the city of Altkirche, where Karalthergroz is interred, and Grenzburg, where the Gothi currently resides, are also popular. The various sites and shrines of different Holies are frequent stopping points on any proper wayfarages. While Urworkish do not believe in the necessity of a wayfareage, many affluent Urworkish will take time and visit Wurmkop, where Ludher was branded, and Gruoenberge, where the movement started.

According to the lore, the first wayfareage was undertaken by a young couple roughly two hundred years after the first great Churchmeet. Unable to conceive a child, the couple sought the wisdom of Holy Friia. They decided to journey to the church built on the spot where she delivered the first baby born in the Age of Dawn. This church was located deep in the eastern Weiße Hügel, far from their hometown in northwestern Gallia. Saving what they could, and helped by family and friends, they began the trek eastward, stopping at every holy spot they could find along the way. It took them six months to reach the Church, and upon leaving to return home, the wife discovered she was pregnant. During their travel westward, they detoured and arrived in Midgart, where they met with Gothi Kildebert, who was so moved by their story that he decreed that all good and upstanding Sonnenkind should undergo a wayfareage once in their lives. According to legend, the child born from this wayfareage would go on to found the line that Karalthergroz descended from, though scholars have pointed out this is impossible. (There is considerable evidence, however, that they are progenitors of the Gaulish heroine, Mahaut the Shield-maiden.) To this day, the hometown of Holies Bernaz and Ruvona is one of the most visited wayfareage spots in all of Gallia.

Wild Folk

The term used to denote all the native inhabitants of the New World. Caruser and Vinlander may also be used with some interchangeability. This originates from the idea that those living in the New World are "wild" compared to the "tame" folk of the old war.

It has been suggested by a few explorers that a new term be created, as according to those who have traveled north and south of the Catask holdings in Texihauco, the lands there are settled and have cities that rival even the mightiest in Erebus. Cities in the clouds, cities carved into the sides of mountains, even a green paradise in the midst of a scorching desert have all been made by these so-called "wild" folk. The current suggestion is to use Caruser and Vinlander more often or to simply say New World stems.

Witchcraft

Witchcraft, or dwimmer, is any unnatural powers or abilities used for evil. Also called blackcraft, it is opposed by whitecraft, which are preternatural powers such as healing and the foresight used by seeresses. Witchcraft, according to popular belief, involves bargaining with ruinous powers for otherworldly gain, the killing of innocents, the summoning of lightless from hell, and anything that would harm others to the benefit of the witch or warlock. It should be noted that not all kinds of dwimmer are forbidden or outlawed, and it is not uncommon for a town or hamlet to have a wise woman who can use dousing rods to find water or heal sick animals. However, the line between wise woman and a witch becomes razor-thin during bad harvests.

Witchcraft and witches (and warlocks and wizards) are decried in the Sagas. But, contrary to popular belief, this is more a decry against conmen and charlatans. Repeatedly in the Sagas and Unhallowed Tales, it is written the Lightless have no power, and all power comes from God to do good. So, any who claim to be a witch or warlock are a liar and a cheater and are to be beaten and driven out. Suffer not the witch is often quoted without the rest of the sentence, *suffer not the liar, suffer not the coward, and suffer not the oathbreaker.*

II.

Strixan Ethnicities

Nidus-Strixan

Nidus-Strixans are the most powerful, dominate (in both military and culture), and considered the "original" Strixans, famous for the ancient now lost ability to transform into owls and eagles. While the entirety of the race is now known as Strixans, during the time of the empire, they were known as Nidus-Strixans or Nidunus. Singular Nidunun.

The Nidunus were noted as not having any remarkable features or physical appearances. They possessed every hair and eye color that their brethren had, which most likely resulted from interbreeding.

Striga

The second largest of the group, the Striga were close cousins of the Strixans, sharing similar myths, stories, culture, and even names, though how this came to be was never discovered.

The Strigan were noticeably wider and shorter than the Nidunus, and their skins were always a matte-grey, even for those who did not spend much time in the sun. They were also noted as having a higher prevalence of curly hair than any other ethnicity.

A unique cultural aspect of the Striga was their preferred, if not favorite way, of getting blood. The Striga would kill a creature by breaking its neck, and after skinning it, would present it to be eaten raw, gaining their nutrition from the blood still in the muscles and the fresh bone marrow. They did hunt and drink normally, but the raw feast was a popular social activity.

Lilithans

Though only the third largest of the groups, it is said that none were feared more by the Emperors and Princeps than the Lilithans. They dominated the eastern most regions of the empire, and while loyal to Nidus, were largely a mystery to Strixan culture as a whole. Culturally, they were (in)famous for only revering their versions of Luna and Sol. They never acknowledged nor revered any other deity and were actively hostile to those that did.

Lilithan society was strictly patriarchal in every aspect save one, their priesthood. The Daughters of Lilith, or more accurately the Bat Lilithim, were a secretive and powerful group of priestesses, trained in powerful thaumaturgy, and were advisors and wives to the Melekh of the Lilithans. Both the Lilithan monarchy and the Bat Lilithim were abolished during the Councilorly Era.

Physically, Lilithans were always known for their height. On average, they stood a head taller than a full-grown Strixan tiercel, and this includes Lilithan hens. They were noticeably thinner and lither than their western cousins, though this came with no decrease in strength. Along with their height, their coloring was another noticeable feature. A full-blood Lilithan always had skin that was more of a pale white than grey. It also never became matte in the sun like others.

Leannán

The smallest of the groups, occupying lands north and west of Nidus, the Leannán were both the least and most favorite of all the groups in Nidunus eyes. The Leannán, it was written, were the most beautiful of all the groups with brilliant orange hair and dazzling emerald eyes. Many an emperor and many a princeps took a Leannán as a paramour during their tenure. This was always, sometimes rightfully, suspect, as the Leannán paramour had great influence on the policy and affairs of state, usually pushing for more money and less governance of their home territories.

This, of course, was not the image of every Leannán but the popular one pushed by playwrights and jurists. The group itself was less advanced than any of their eastern neighbors. Many were nomadic with them and their animals following the graze and fruit that seasonally grew. They did accept a sedentary, urban lifestyle following their integration into the empire. Though, history demonstrates this lifestyle was forced on them rather than adopted.

Physically, the Leannán were the most different. All of them possessed a slight point in their ears, which they proudly showed when interacting with the other ethnicities. And according to census data, on average, 78.65% of Leannán only had maxilla fangs, and 87% had red hair. All full-blooded Leannán however did have skin that was closer to blue than grey. In the sun, for a reason known only to the gods, their skin became lighter, rather than matte and darker.

Strixan Biology

In the Councilorly and Imperial eras, efforts to unify the empire and bring all ethnicities together, great focus was placed on the biological similarities the four groups shared. These became rallying cries that transcended culture, custom, and language. Blood was at the forefront, as the need for this sole source of nutrition was above all else, even above Sol and Luna, what truly united the Strixan peoples. But it was more than blood, fangs, and pallid colors that united the empire. How else were the peoples similar?

Diet

From maturity onwards, Strixans need only to consume blood in some form or another. At least a congius (1gal or ~3.8l) is required a week to survive, though it does not need to be consumed all at once. The dominant preference is liquid blood. Sanguinvinum, a thaumaturgical combination of blood and grape-based wine, was and is the main method by which the Strixan populace gets their nutrition. For the Strixans, "blood magic" is synonymous with food preservation. To supplement, and add variety, other aspects of the cardiovascular system can also be consumed. Bone marrow, kidneys, liver, gallbladders, and especially hearts are all regular components of Strixan cuisine. The rawer the organ, the more nutritious. Infamously, during the Imperial era, the more lascivious emperors would spend enormous sums of money on "honeyed veins." These were subsequently banned by the Concilium. While marrow and organs can keep a Strixan alive, they are correctly regarded as merely buying time until fresh liquid blood can be consumed. A maxim regularly shared by legion exploratores is: "marrow will let you see tomorrow, hearts and kidneys the week, but blood will let you see your comrades again."

Strixans can suffer starvation, as one of the only natural causes of nestling mortality is malnutrition. For adults, starvation is a much slower and far more painful process. From accounts of torturers in both the imperial and Councilorly Era, a starving Strixan goes through several steps before dying. The first is that the body ceases to produce *motus* (see below), rending the victim immobile. This occurs three to four days after a week without consuming blood. In days after *motus* ceases to be produced, the victim will begin to digest their own musculature. Two weeks after not consuming blood, the victim will lose all muscle mass. Hair and nails will also fall out. While details on how exactly the victim perishes are unavailable, it is presumed to be unpleasant. Estimates are that a Strixan can survive up to three weeks without blood. However, should a Strixan reach this stage, it is unknown if, but presumed, that consumption of blood can be enough to heal them. Since the cataclysm, starvation has been an ever-present threat, but details of the starvation process are classified and kept from the populace.

As part of their diet, Strixans possess an enzyme within their mouths and saliva that prevents blood from coagulating. This is also an important part of food preservation with the rich hiring personal *sputantor*, or spitter, to flavor their preserved blood with rose water, perfumes, and other luxuries. Strixan fangs lack enamel, leaving them permanently sharp. Non-fang teeth do have enamel coating.

Bloods

One of the starker differences between Strixans and other animals is that Strixans possess two types of blood; the violet-colored blood that circulates in the torso known as *vita*, and the blue-white blood that circulates in the limbs known as *motus*. From birth until maturity, nestlings only have vita, only producing motus after undergoing their New Nights. Strixan physicians, despite millennia of studying anatomy and physiology, have come to an imperfect understanding of why there are two blood types. Both are pumped by the heart, and it is assumed that the two share a similar origin. The current theory, based on dissections, is that at the shoulders and in the legs, there is a natural "filter" that either separates motus from vita or strips vita of many of its components to become motus. When motus passes back through this "filter," it becomes vita. For all Strixans, the dividing line between the two types in the arms is at the shoulder. In the legs, the line is different between the sexes. For hens, vita continues into the thighs and becomes motus at the knees. For tiercels it is at the hips.

Motus, it is understood, aids in movement and allows for quick reactions and nervous response. In studies, those with motus in their arms and legs react, jump, and move far faster than those without. Motus-fueled limbs also heal faster. Curiously, motus does not have any nutritional value for Strixans, leading many to question if it even is blood or should be classified as something else.

Vita, by contrast, functions much more like traditional blood, though physicians are unable to determine if it is similarly made by bone marrow. Strixans can theoretically die of blood loss if enough vita is lost, but their ability to produce vita and to clot wounds is so resilient that the affected Strixan would die of other injuries before severe blood loss became a concern. Consumption of vita is a very rare and often intimate occasion. Aside from combat, the only socially acceptable times vita is consumed are marriages and funerals. During a marriage ceremony, the bride and groom will fill a small ceremonial goblet with their own vita, usually from a cut near the neck or ribs. They will then trade the goblet and drink. During a funeral, once the deceased's heart is stopped, their jugular will be cut, and what vita spills out will be collected in a bowl. The bowl will then be passed amongst family and close friends. Should any remain, it is then sprinkled over the deceased before burial. Astoundingly, these two ceremonies are, with some variation, used by all four ethnicities. Vita can be shared and consumed during other instances, but these often carry a negative and shameful stigma. "Shoulder-biter" is a derogatory euphemism that gained prominence after the cataclysm to shame hens (and a few tiercels) who sell their bodies in exchange for consuming some of their client's vita.

Physicality

Strixans are naturally strong, far stronger than their appearance would have one believe. From the time of maturity, they possess immense physical strength, endurance, agility, and speed. All of this is natural and comes without training. The drawback, at least how philosophers and gymnasts see it, is that they cannot get stronger, faster, or more agile, even with training. Once a Strixan is mature, they are at peak physicality, permanently. A Strixan body is permanent, never increasing or decreasing. It is remarked only hens can gain weight, and that is only from pregnancy, and that weight will disappear. The only way to lose weight is to lose a limb. Though a body cannot be added to, it can be refined. The Striga were famous for their gymnasiums and stadiums, where Strigan tiercels could tone their bodies to have a more defined muscular shape, the same body as seen on statues and in mosaics. As one poet described it, a gymnasium was like a sculptor's studio. The sculptor does not add to a block of marble, but trims it to be a work of art. Physical contests in the Strixan world were not of strength, but of technique.

Regeneration

Another similarity and a source of speculation amongst scientists and philosophers is the Strixans' impressive regenerative abilities. A Strixan body can endure an impressive amount of punishment and still function. Fangs can be lost and regrown in less than a day, as can all other teeth. Any detached limb can be regrown. On average, it takes a week for a finger to return, a month for a hand, half a year for an arm below the elbow, and a whole year for the whole arm. This process can be accelerated by a skilled thaumaturgical physician, for a heavy price. Even complex organs such as the eye and inner year can regenerate to full functionality, though these take decades depending on the damage. Only three organs cannot regenerate: the brain, the heart, and the gonads (testicles and ovaries). Any injury done to those three cannot be healed naturally, and any thaumaturgical healing may not fully heal them. The commentator Corvius once remarked: "A tiercel can be sliced at the waist and lose everything from the hips down. One day again, he will walk, but he shall never again father children. As robust as we are, there are parts of us so precious, the gods have decreed we shall only possess it once."

Allergens

This topic is highly debated amongst philosophers, thaumaturgists, authors, and other prominent intellectuals, though in certain circles, discussing them is seen as taboo. For those who do allow discussion, the nomenclature of this topic varies. Allergens is the most widely-used name with deficiencies, inhibitions, and rarely, weaknesses, also being used. There are three allergens that all Strixan ethnicities share: allium (garlic), Crataegus (hawthorn), and silver. Allium, specifically the cloved bulb, is deadly to all Strixan, whether ingested or touched. Growing it was banned under punishment of death, and any wild growths were sterilized by fire-thaumaturgists.

It is written that ancient Strixans, those who possessed the power of flight in avian form, were immune to allium and silver. As the ability to transform became recessive and eventually lost, so too was the immunity to allium. Crataegus plants were similarly banned and similarly removed with extreme measures. Crataegus causes paralysis in the limbs, and if ingested or introduced into the *vita* bloodstream, can cause complete organ shutdown or severe paralysis depending on the amount. Crataegus can also cause rapid decomposition should a Strixan die with it in their bloodstream. In times when crime was rampant in Nidus and other major cities, it was not uncommon to find a skeleton staked with Crataegus as a warning to rival criminals. Silver is far less toxic than the previous allergens, only causing death if ingested in large doses. This allows silver to be mined for economic purposes, though great care needs to be taken. Signs of silver poisoning include blue discoloring at the corners of and inside the mouth. If held, silver can cause necrosis and can actually prevent regeneration unless the affected limb is amputated. Given silver was far more abundant than allium or Crataegus, it was commonly used as a poison in both fiction and reality. Immunity to silver is rare but families that are immune will frequently take control of silver mines, becoming some of the wealthiest and most influential families in the empire. They frequently intermarry to continue the immunity. Those born with the silver allergen are usually disinherited.

There are other minor allergens as they are known, which are not deadly to Strixans but are annoying. Sunlight, despite being a representation of one of the two major Strixan deities, does cause Strixans to become lethargic and slow. For most ethnicities, exposure to the sun causes a change in skin tone, causing it to become either matte in color, or in some cases, lighter. Running water, mainly in rivers, is also infamous for its odd properties on Strixans. It is noted through many memoirs and travel diaries that should a passenger be asleep while riding in a wagon or cart, and the vehicle cross a bridge or ride a ferry, the passenger will instantly awake, and remain awake, until reaching the other side. Why this occurs is unknown.

The last "allergen" or "annoyance" which is extremely rare, and only occurs in the patrician classes, is curiosity. While often described as a virtue, it has been noted that some upper-class Strixans are so curious that it becomes a detriment. There are many stories, mainly from the Imperial Era, of an upper-class Strixan being so curious, they will take the time to sort and count piles of sand or seeds. It is almost unnatural how they must entirely count and sort the pile, even if they have other duties or obligations. This is the most extreme example, but varying degrees of this curiosity was prevalent enough to warrant discussion.

Sleep

Upon reaching maturity, a Strixan only requires 12 hours of sleep once per week. It is advised to get all hours at once, but sleeping a few hours every few days has the same results. Nestlings require at least 8 hours every other day. After periods of intense physical activity, such as battle, several hours (it varies depending on the activity) of sleep are almost instantly required. Regeneration of limbs and healing of injuries can be sped along with both sleep and regular consumption of blood. Throughout recorded history, it was noted that Strixans sleep best during the day and on land. It was noted in the memoirs of several naval commanders that after a battle, they would need to put into port immediately, so sailors and marines could rest. It was nigh-impossible for a Strixan to sleep while at sea. Failure to receive regular sleep can result in mental degradation and physical weakness. How long a Strixan can survive without sleep is unknown, as any medical records or historical accounts of testing have been lost in the cataclysm.

Pregnancy

The creation of new Strixans has always been held in high regard, though the celebration and veneration of the event has varied from era to era and across cultures. Since the cataclysm however, it has become sacrosanct. Since falling underground, hens have become the most valuable resource in the empire. Creating a new Strixan is, to put it bluntly, a resource-heavy endeavor. From the moment of conception to weaning, the mother requires blood *every* day. Failure to consume blood daily can lead to a miscarriage, and malnourishment can result in a stillbirth. These are the only instances where a nestling can die of natural causes. The minimum amount of daily blood needed is known as the *Mater Potus* or mother's draught. It was roughly a quarter of a congius of blood (8fl. oz., or ~119ml). When the minimum for the Mater Potus was discovered, a master measurement was made and stored in the medical college in Nidus with exact replicas distributed to provincial colleges and civilian medical clinics. Miraculously, when Nidus was sunk, the master measurement was preserved. As the empire recovered and expanded, replica measurements were again distributed. Despite all that has befallen the Strixan empire since the cataclysm, they have never lost a nestling to miscarriage or stillbirth. After a nestling is born, they are nursed until weaning around their first birthday. Either the mother or a Strixan nursemaid must breastfeed the nestling, as non-Strixan milk will lead to malnourishment. Folk remedies believe that consuming the blood of large mammals during pregnancy and nursing, such as bovines, will lead to stronger nestlings, but this has not been corroborated.

Nestlinghood

Nestlinghood is one of the most important, and vulnerable parts, of a Strixan's life. It lasts from birth until 20 years of age with some dividing the period into "nestlinghood" from 0-10 and "fledglinghood" from 11-19. This distinction is entirely cultural and linguistic. Nestlings from all ethnicities were coated in what is known as "youth plumage," a thin, curly, fuzzy layer of feather-like hairs that help insulate nestlings. They are fuzziest when they are weaned with the plumage gradually receding as they age. Youth plumage is normally a light brown or grey color, regardless of future hair colors, though Leannán nestlings have been noted to have a red-orange plumage. Unlike mature Strixans, nestlings are susceptible to the environment and can suffer or perish from extreme high *and* low temperatures, even with their plumage.

After weaning, nestlings begin developing teeth, aside from fangs. While it is still recommended to give them dairy, this is also when they begin to drink undiluted blood. And, unlike mature Strixans, nestlings must also consume meat with raw meat providing the most nutrition. Fangs begin to come in around ages 2 or 3 with hens usually getting fangs first. Some provinces and cultures regard getting the mandible fangs first as a bad omen, but this is an unfounded superstition. Nestlings will lose their milk teeth throughout their nestlinghood but only lose their first fangs after their New Nights. Should a fang be lost before then due to accident, it will not regenerate until maturity. Non-fang permanent teeth can regenerate before maturity.

Around age 4 in nearly all cultures (Lilithans at age 5), nestlings begin to hunt. Under the guidance of their father or a male guardian, they are taught how to listen for, locate, stalk, and then pounce and puncture live prey. A thriving market of animal breeders existed in the pre-cataclysm days who raised and sold docile animals for the first hunt. The animals were small, usually some type of rodent or feline. Even urban Strixans practiced the first hunt with nearly every major city having a dedicated plaza where families could hunt. The first hunt of the Imperator Minor, heir to the throne, was always a cause for empire-wide celebrations.

Nestlinghood was and is regarded as the foundation for a Strixan's future life. Primary education, including social, mundane, and thaumaturgical are all taught during this period. For patricians, etiquette and grace are the predominant focuses of nestlinghood education. For lower classes, they begin to learn their future trade.

New Nights

The New Nights, or the *Novus Noctes*, is the most defining moment in any Strixan's life. It is so universal that the name for the procedure is more or less the same in every language. And yet despite its importance, what actually occurs during a New Nights is largely a mystery.

What is understood is that nearing their 20th birthday, a nestling will fall asleep. They will then stay asleep for several days, anywhere between 7-12. Outliers are extremely rare and largely fictional. It was not uncommon for usurpers to claim the gods had blessed them with a shorter or longer than average New Nights.

Upon falling asleep, the nestling assumes the most naturally comfortable sleeping position for Strixans; completely flat on their back with arms crossed and resting on the chest. The parents and guardians will then move them to a safe room on a bed as close to the ground as possible. The nestling remains motionless in the position for the duration of the New Nights.

While the mechanics of the New Nights is not understood, from observations, one can infer what happens. In a sense, it is a rapid pubescent development; muscles increase in density, hormones begin to pump, breasts develop, testicles descend, and facial hair appears. In a matter of a week, the nestling, all unconsciously, matures into a full-fledged adult. Even the color of hair and skin can observably change during the New Nights.

Upon awakening, the now mature adult Strixan will sit straight up and let out a hiss, their mouth bloody as their adult fangs push out their nestling ones. In urban areas, the parents will be on standby with a congius of undiluted blood for their child to drink. In provincial areas, an animal could also be left tied nearby for the adult to hunt and drink. Either way, it is imperative that fresh blood be given as soon as the adult is awake. Failure to do so can lead to the adult completely losing their senses and attacking any nearby creatures, be they Strixan or animal. It was alleged during the imperial era in patrician households that rogue slaves or wayward servants were "sacrificed" to male members of the household after their New Nights. No definitive proof of this has been recorded, but the rumor persists. Again, these practices were nigh-universal across the breadth of the empire.

Upon consumption of blood, the now-adult nestling is welcomed into the family. In the following days, the tiercels will be taken and added to the roster of citizens, making them eligible for military service and then public office. Hens would be given the palla and join their mother in running the household, or if they show promise and talent, begin to train at an academy or thaumaturgical college. In some extreme cases, hens may be married immediately after undergoing their New Nights, but this practice was repeatedly condemned by writers and magistrates.

Even with the fall of the empire and the cataclysm, New Nights continue to be a cause of celebration, a respite against the cruelties of life underground. Though resources are scarce, many families hold a banquet to welcome their mature child into proper society. It also serves as a fond memory for tiercels before being conscripted and sent to fight the devils.

Strixan life may have changed, but in many aspects, it is still the same. And, it was the same for their cousins to the east and to the west, even if they have now been lost to time.

III.

Strixan Pantheon

There were many gods in the history of the Strixan Empire. Every village, province, region, and ethnicity had their own gods. Only Luna and Sol, or their ethnic variations, were the common denominators. The following were the only ones with dedicated, permanent temples in Nidus, whose priests would answer directly to the reigning monarch, or later, the Pontifex Maximus. The deification of some emperors and empresses was not uncommon in the Imperial Era but was outlawed during the Councilorly Era.

Luna Aeternus and Sol Invictus

The chief deities of the Strixan race and the only two shared amongst every ethnic group. Luna is the moon, and Sol is the sun, watching over their people on Terra, giving them light and guidance to become the mightiest beings to ever walk. They possess unfathomable power and wisdom and are the origins of all life and power in the universe. They are the only two to be properly referred to as a God.

The Deus Loci

These are the children of Luna and Sol, watchers over specific areas of life and civilization. They are referred to as demigods and do not possess the full power of their parents but have considerable influence over their designated area. Each has a sacred day, a temple within Nidus, and a specific libation or sacrifice.

Ductor Ianus (M)

The first-born child of Luna and Sol. The Deus Loci over doorways, arches, gateways, and all entrances. Statues of him were placed over every entrance to Nidus and other major cities. In art, he is popularly depicted as having two faces. Their main celebration is New Years, where they oversee the departure of the old year and the arrival of the new.

Custos Domus (F)

The second born child of Luna and Sol. The Deus Loci of the home, hearth, and garden, protector of the pantry and cellar. Offerings must be made to her before a foundation is laid and on the Ides of the second month. Named for her, the holiday of Domuscalia is held, where every home, street, and city is ritualistically cleaned from midnight to midnight.

Bellator Martius (M)

Third born child of Luna and Sol. The Deus Loci of the legions, weaponsmiths, and individual soldiers. It was believed by some that he fathered a child with an ordinary woman. This child, Selenkles, was a mighty warrior who slew great beasts and whose feats of strength could only be compared to the gods. Martius was a vital aspect of legionary culture, and all victories were credited to him and his parents.

Felix Venos (F)

Fourth born child of Luna and Sol. The Deus Loci of marriage, family, sex, and love. The 12th day of the fourth month, named after her, was celebrated as the marriage of the imperial couple, Aquilius and Noctinna. It was believed Venos presided over the wedding and that all weddings performed in her name and with her guidance were weddings that will be blissful and monogamous. She was a spot of conflict between the Strixans and Striga, as the Striga insisted she and Martius were in an incestuous affair.

Magister Menrva (F)

The fifth born child of Luna and Sol. The Deus Loci of libraries, veterinarians, schools, and most importantly, Thaumaturgy. All state-sanctioned Thaumaturgist wore a lead phalera bearing her image to show they had been properly trained and accredited.

Vigilans Uni (F)

The sixth born child of Luna and Sol. The Deus Loci of dreams, goals, and fate. Despite being the sixth child, Uni is often considered the favorite child of the Gods. She is their messenger, giving direct advice and appearing most often in sacred messages. It is believed she delivered the idea and promise of victory to Aquilius, who then started the empire. She is also the guide to legendary heroes and generals of the Strixan people.

Taberllarius Turms (M)

The seventh born child of Luna and Sol. The Deus Loci of couriers, travelers, and sailors. He is also a psychopomp, escorting departed souls to his parents for final judgment. He is also associated with funerals for this purpose.

The Natura Loci

Not the children of Luna and Sol, but creations of them. They are often considered cousins to the Deus Loci and also considered demi-gods. They are known by many names across the Strixan ethnic groups, but their core character is usually intact. They most frequently are sentinels over specific aspects of the natural world, ensuring it stays in good order. They are also the most temperamental and have a number of rituals and sacrifices associated to appease them.

Hortunlanus Silvestrius (M)

The Natura Loci of forests, trees, and plant life. Offerings must be made to him before trees are cut down. He is the least temperamental of the Natura Loci.

Tersus Diaturna (F)

The Natura Loci of rivers, lakes, and frequently the sea. Her most important job was caring for and watching over the River Raptor, the main source of water and power for Nidus. All aqueducts and baths were built with a statue or image of her included.

Excubitrix Feronia (F)

The Natura Loci of all animal life on land, air, and water. She was the patron of butchers and bloodletters, and a libation of non-blooded wine is to be made before every butchering.

Circumiectus Coelus (M)

The Natura Loci of the heavens and the weather. He is often considered to be the first creation of Luna and Sol and acts as a firmament separating Terra from Space. Many also consider him the first artist, as cloud patterns, light refracting, and even the fabled aurora are credited to his creativity.

Acknowledgments

It would not have been possible to write, edit, and publish *Lost Histories* without a wonderful collection of friends, family, supporters, and well-wishers. It may take a village to raise a child, but it also takes a village to help an amateur author bring their work to light.

First and foremost, my utmost gratitude is to my editor, Victoria. She has the patience of a saint to work with me and re-read my ramblings over and over and over. Without her, this book would never be as polished or clean as it is. She's the best editor a writer could ask for and a good friend.

A huge thank you to my good friend Ben, who was the first to read the roughest of rough drafts years ago when I started. His encouragement really helped me find some solid ground when I didn't know if this could ever have amounted to anything.

Bruce has been a pillar of unwavering support and a true believer in the book. His feedback and opinions have really given me much needed morale boosts and the confidence to go through with publication. Without him, there would be no *Lost Histories.*

To Aspen, for her wonderful artwork on the cover. Her artistic talents blew me out of the water. The cover is so much better than I could ever have dreamed of! She also did the wonderful job of drawing the landscapes and scenic view from many of the locales within the book. She made the world of Lost Histories feel more real.

To Mary, who brought Friedrich and Vytilia to life through her art. She turned words into masterpieces and gave life to the lifeless! I can't wait to see the rest of the cast and creatures of Lost Histories brought to life as the series progresses. I am so fortunate to know so many great artists!

To Kyle, who made the map and helped bring the lands of Erebus and the Holy Realm of Midgart to life. I look forward to seeomg what else we can draw up in the future!

To Amy, for believing in me and helping me find Pacer, who helped on the legal side of things.

To Irene, who helped out with query letters and trying to find an agent. Even though that side never worked out, the help was tremendous and the advice will always stick with me.

And to my Mom, who may never have really understood this whole project but was supportive nonetheless.

To all my friends and family and readers, to Annie, to Spencer, to Cooper, to Shae, to Jake, to Elizabeth, to everyone! There were so many friends, so many supporters, so many who believed in me even when I didn't believe in myself. Thank you all!

And to you, dear reader. This would never be possible without you as well.

Thank you!

Calvin Lionel Edwards

"Historia vitae magistra."

www.ingramcontent.com/pod-product-compliance
Lightning Source LLC
Chambersburg PA
CBHW060542310726
48982CB00009B/1352/J

* 9 7 9 8 9 9 1 7 7 9 3 1 9 *